Torster

The Adversary

The 13th Paladin

Final Volume

Translated by Tim Casey

Copy Editor: Neil McCourt
Proof Reader: James Bryan

For all those who dare to dream

*And remember –
there is nothing more enjoyable than
experiencing a story for the first time*

www.tweitze.de
www.facebook.com/t.weitze
Instagram: torsten_weitze

© Torsten Weitze. Krefeld, 2023

Picture: Petra Rudolf /
www.dracoliche.de

German editor/proof reader:
Janina Klinck / www.lectoreena.de

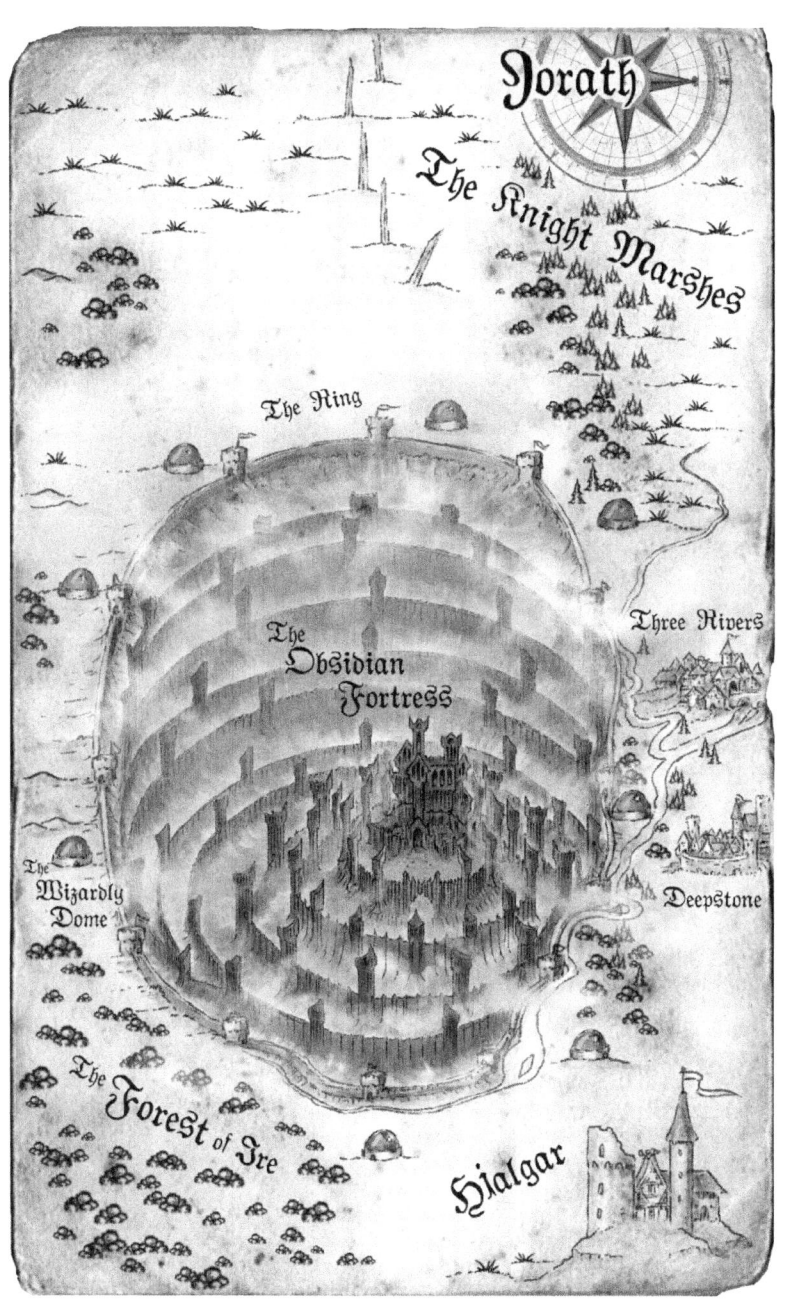

Prologue

The Obsidian Fortress and the Ring surrounding it were so still that it almost seemed as though the final battle had long since been fought, leaving both sides defeated and all the soldiers slain.

A heavy autumn fog enveloped the early morning landscape as Quin-Wa, shivering, pulled her heavy woollen cloak closer to keep herself warm against the cold. The golden-red garment covered her round belly, upon which she had absently rested her hands in a protective gesture.

'Persevere a little longer,' she whispered in the dawning light, as much to herself as to the child within her. 'Your mother must put the world to rights before *you* can greet it.'

She knew that the words were little more than wishful thinking, as insubstantial as the wisps of fog that her breath was creating in the chilly air. Her child could well see the light of the world before she herself would join the other Paladins in their final assault on the relentless Enemy skulking within the Obsidian Fortress. The battle against the Adversary was going to be difficult enough, even without her fearing for the innocent life now growing beneath her beating heart.

Quin-Wa blinked a few unwanted tears away as she thought how much she wished that her child might enjoy a normal, carefree life, far removed from the heavy burden that she, the other Paladins, and their predecessors had been forced to bear for so many millennia.

Her blinking had only caused her eyes to blur, making it momentarily difficult to see the Ring in the distance. Quin-Wa breathed in deeply as she leaned back against the heavy cold wall of Highstone Castle's eastern tower and gazed between two merlons towards the scene ahead of her – a vision both of hope and despair for the peoples of Jorath – and one that had been visible for many moons now. Hope, because for weeks none of the Dark Ones had been able to break through the Ring. Despair, because with every day that passed, the Obsidian Fortress seemed to become more and more impenetrable as an increasing number of armed Low Fangs made their appearance on the walls of the bastion which the Dark god had created for Himself and His armies by means of magic. Magic which had been stolen from the Pall Pillar. Even this early in the morning, the unholy flames from the blacksmiths' forges within the fortress gave the place a supernatural appearance. Every new piece of armour and weaponry that the enemy forged would inevitably increase the number of casualties among the ranks of the free peoples of Jorath. Quin-Wa shivered again, her view of the early morning scene as a place of death becoming visible once more. The Dark god would willingly sacrifice all His servants in His attempt to exterminate the defenders on the walls of the Ring that surrounded Him – even if it meant inheriting a totally dead world at the end of it all. The only thing that mattered to Him was that *He* was the sole ruler.

She turned her head as a shadowy figure moved beside her.

'My Lady – you really shouldn't be outside in this cold. It will do neither of you any good.'

Quin-Wa's smile was as thin as a sheet of papyrus. 'Thank you, Ro-Kani, but I know my limits,' she said, chiding the Night Soldier.

'To serve is my life,' came the predictable reply as the woman dressed in black went down on one knee. 'If my concern for your safety involves irritating you, then I am willing to live with whatever punishment you wish to mete out.'

Quin-Wa sighed and turned to look at the Ring again. 'Just another few moments and I will go in…' she began, attempting to appease her bodyguard, only to break off as her eyes opened wide in astonishment.

There was something moving on the distant walls of the Obsidian Fortress. A shadow that had spent centuries upon centuries stealing into her worst nightmares.

QUIN-WA. ARE YOU STILL PEERING INTO DARK CORNERS WHERE YOU HAVE NO BUSINESS TO BE LOOKING?

The figure raised one of His spindly arms, Quin-Wa sensing the will of the Dark god gathering itself. Immediately, the Eternal Empress covered the eyes of the stunned and gasping Ro-Kani, closing her own eyes tightly as she did so. She sensed something dark and cold gliding above her head, greedily feeling for searching eyes whose light it might swallow for evermore.

'Let us go down!' snapped Quin-Wa, her eyes still tightly closed. 'Quickly – before He hurls another charm.'

Gratefully, she held firmly onto the Night Soldier, who even without looking, nimbly and easily found the entrance to the staircase that led down into the castle. Even as the two women were hurrying down towards the warmth of the fortress, Quin-Wa heard the mocking laughter of the Adversary fading away in her mind.

Now within the protective castle walls, she opened her eyes angrily, using that same willpower with which she had forged an entire nation. With all her force, she created a glimmering ball of light in the palm of her hand. The sorcerous words that she was about to transmit, she would not need to cipher by means of Elven poetry. For they contained no secret that the Dark god did not already know.

'The Adversary – He is back.'

Chapter 1

'Success.'

This one word, little more than a whisper, echoed in Ahren's mind like a raging thunderstorm. Two syllables, breathed out into the balmy evening air of Eathinian, announcing the completion of a dangerous journey which Ahren had begun as a boy, innocent in the ways of the world, a long time ago in sleepy Deepstone.

The thirteen Paladins had been found. And all thirteen were united.

At least I hope so, he thought sardonically as he carefully adjusted his body so that his arm wouldn't go numb under the weight of the sleeping Khara, who was snuggled into him. *We were away from the continent for many moons. Who knows, what the other Paladins got up to during that time.*

A bitter sigh penetrated his thoughts.

Can a hardworking Ice Wolf not have a single night to himself, without having to take care of his wearisome Paladin?

Ahren smiled blissfully. *You have nothing better to be doing anyway, than praising Yoka to high heavens while she sleeps.*

Isn't that a beautiful name? asked Culhen for the umpteenth since Lyssin had given her she-wolf the name. *And isn't she perfect?*

Where is the haughty dignity of an Alpha when it's needed? countered Ahren mischievously. *You are carrying on like a lovestruck godsday schoolboy to me, and yet you haven't exchanged a single word with her since Yoka has been made a companion animal.*

Disquiet bubbled up in Culhen's mind like hot water shooting from a geyser.

You…you think she'll still like me, don't you? Now that she isn't a normal she-wolf anymore.

Ahren silently scolded himself for putting doubts into his wolf's head. *She liked you a lot in the Ice Fields,* he said affectionately. *I don't see any reason for that to have changed.*

I agree, announced Culhen, his reply echoing loudly in the Paladin's mind. *I am perfect. How could anyone not love me? Thank you for reminding me.*

Now that Culhen had been reassured and was basking in his own glory again, Ahren had time to consider his own inner peace. He absorbed the quiet rustling of the gently swaying Eathinian trees and saw how here and there the stars flickered cheekily down through the thick leafy canopy of the Elven forest and onto the softly cushioning moss upon which he and his beloved were spending the hours of darkness. It had only been the night before when they had fought Four Claws in a labyrinth of steam, ice and fire. Now they were lying here, safe and secure.

And united, thought Ahren as he grinned again.

The journey on the wings of the goddess had shaken him and his companions to the core but had also filled them with awe while simultaneously freeing them from all their physical ailments.

Mirilan had continued to carry the remains of that incredible magic within her, which had enabled them to traverse the entire known world from the Ice Fields in the deepest south to the far north, beyond the Elven forest of Eathinian.

Spurred on into flight by Jelninolan's newly created Storm Fiddle, they had kept speaking to a minimum as they had flown within a single day into the embrace of Eathinian's northernmost offshoots.

Ahren turned his head in search of the elf, but she was nowhere to be seen. Jelninolan and Trogadon had walked off into the trees in the early evening, hand in hand. The rest of the companions were still asleep, having surrendered themselves to the intense, cleansing exhaustion that Evergreen offered them in its soft embrace. Deep, and certainly *loud* noises could even be heard coming from the branches above them. Sleeps-in-Treetops was living up to her name, for she had retired into the boughs of an oak, where she was now slumbering on the fork of a large branch, snoring coarsely and destroying the peace of the local squirrels. It was only his euphoria at having not only successfully gathered all the Paladins, but of also uniting them into a single force to take on the Dark god that was enabling Ahren to think clearly despite having been awake for so long already.

All thirteen Paladins are ready. Now there is only one thing left to do – slay the Adversary.

Thinking this thought for even the briefest of moments was like testing out an aching tooth with one's tongue – it sent a shiver down his spine and caused his heart to race as if he had just completed an exhausting run in the forest. Suddenly, the journeying over the past few years seemed like a walk in the park. Now they were preparing to force a self-proclaimed god into submission. A task that no being in Creation had yet managed to complete successfully.

Have no fear. I will be by your side the whole time. Culhen's instinctively uttered words, totally devoid of any self-doubt, smashed through the waves of doubt that were afflicting Ahren.

The Paladin stared up at the sky for a long time, pleading to the THREE as he did so that they would give him some of the wolf's boundless self-confidence, which they, themselves had provided the animal with. But even before they had a chance to hear his prayer, Ahren had fallen back into a deep sleep.

The cacophony of birdsong, the whispering of the leaves in the breeze, and the seductive aromas of countless plants caused Ahren to awaken – as did the small moist nose that was pushing and snuffling into his right ear, and which could only belong to a certain meddlesome fox.

'Rise and shine, Master!' The cheerful voice of his apprentice swept away the last remaining cobwebs of sleep in Ahren's head. 'The sun is in the sky and Uldini wants us to be on our way.'

'Unless you all want us to arrive at the Ring only to discover that the Adversary has long since left His fortress and broken His way through the Ring – and only because we have been dillydallying here,' said the Arch Wizard in his childlike, innocent-sounding voice, which was nonetheless coloured by the speaker's sarcastic impatience. 'The First, Sleeps-in-Treetops and Bergen set off at the crack of dawn to announce our imminent arrival to the elves.'

'We have only had *one* good night's sleep, so we can hardly be accused of dithering,' murmured Khara as Ahren opened his eyes and blinked at the young woman beside him.

His beloved seemed to be well rested, but her unkempt silky black hair suggested that she, too, had only just woken up. She glanced sideways at Ahren, her eyes exhibiting a mixture of warmth and amusement.

'You had better lift your head before Kamaluq bites off a bit of your ear. Your insubordinate apprentice has hidden a piece of sausage meat at the nape of your neck – which the fox is intent on getting his paws on.'

No sooner had Ahren sat up when he heard a joyful whimper followed immediately by a short but loud slurping sound.

'And gone is the treat!' laughed Lanlion, who was sitting on the enormous trunk of a fallen tree, his legs dangling before him. 'I see Culhen has taught the little fellow well.'

Ahren didn't fail to notice the bloodless Paladin's untypical joviality, but when he looked quizzically at his pallid friend, the latter merely shook his head. Any explanation regarding Lanlion's mysterious journey – which had clearly changed him for the better – would still have to wait.

'My wolf has taught Kamaluq everything that is unimportant,' said Ahren, joining in his fellow Paladin's teasing. 'Alas, he forgot to teach him anything important.' Ahren now fixed his eyes on the smirking Hakanu, staring as coldly as he could at the boy. 'And it seems I have failed in the same manner with my so-called *apprentice.*'

Confusion and a considerable degree of discomfiture resulted in Hakanu's face draining of all merriment.

'Master…?' he asked uneasily.

'Don't think I haven't forgotten your little relapse into the depths of futile courage,' growled Ahren. 'Hakanu – the dragon slayer.'

Had the apprentice been subjected to a resounding clip on the ear his reaction would not have been more obvious. He blushed a deep red and he scuffed the soft moss with his foot in embarrassment.

'My spear should have hit the target but…' he began only for Ahren to cut him off with a commanding gesture.

'Because you behaved like a clueless beginner, I have no choice but to treat you accordingly,' he said sharply. 'Here is my bag of herbs,' he added, untying the leather pouch from his belt. 'It is empty. By the time we leave Eathinian, I expect you to have filled both this one and a similar one for yourself containing all the curative plants that we pass by.' His glare bored into the young man's eyes right through to his brain. 'And every evening you will list off to me which plants you have added and in the correct order, following which you will describe their precise healing properties.'

'But…' protested Hakanu.

'No ifs, buts or maybes. I want to hear nothing from you apart from "yes, Master" until I decide that you have learned your lesson,' snarled Ahren. 'Do I make myself clear?'

Hakanu swallowed hard. 'Yes, Master.'

'Good,' grunted Ahren, satisfied. 'I can see eight healing plants in this clearing here. Why don't you collect them while we *adults* discuss matters of importance amongst ourselves?'

Hakanu ground his teeth in silent protest. Then the apprentice withdrew, his master's herb bag in his clenched fist.

'If age hasn't finally caught up with me, I'm pretty sure I can only make out *six* curative herbs around here,' murmured Falk once Hakanu was out of earshot.

Ahren shrugged his shoulders unconcernedly. 'We may as well let my apprentice sweat for a little bit.'

'Aren't you being more than a little unfair?' asked Khara, smiling mischievously. 'The way he threw the spear at Four Claws was masterful. It was simply that the dragon was quicker. His act of bravado could equally have been performed by your younger self.'

Ahren nodded. 'And if I had failed, Falk would have pulled me up on it.'

The old Paladin nodded enthusiastically. 'And how. Ahren would have spent the length of a moon clambering up and down the most devious Ribbon Tree that I could have dreamed up.'

'Have you finished with your idle chatter yet, the lot of you?' snarled Uldini. 'It is high time we were leaving.'

'Trogadon and Jelninolan are nowhere to be seen. Nor are Lyssin, Sleeps-in-Treetops, the First and the two Ice Wolves. Not to mention Muai,' interjected Lanlion from his tree trunk. 'We certainly won't be going anywhere without our companions. What's the rush then?'

Uldini nodded towards *Flamestar*. The crystal ball floating just above his open right palm was flickering – if only barely. 'Quin-Wa contacted me early this morning.' The Arch Wizard fixed his eyes on Ahren. 'The Adversary has been spotted.'

The Paladin's mouth suddenly went dry, while his sudden instinctive attempt at swallowing proved almost impossible. 'You mean…the Dark god has *actually* been seen?'

Uldini nodded grimly. 'No cloud formation in the heavens this time, nor no shadowy outline in the night – the Adversary has shown Himself openly on one of the inner walls of his fortress.'

'When?' asked Falk flatly. The old Paladin's face had turned a deathly pale.

'Yesterday. When we were flying northwards on the wings of the goddess.'

'That was quick,' commented Lanlion as he mulled over the latest news with remarkable equanimity. The composure of the Bloodless was a welcome beacon of calm to Ahren, who was feeling terribly anxious.

'*Too q*uick,' countered Uldini. 'If HE, WHO FORCES can already manifest Himself in bodily form, then He must be back to His former strength – or pretty close to it at any rate.'

'Is it such a bad thing that He possesses His body?' asked Khara, puzzled. 'Would that not make Him more vulnerable in the event of an attack?'

Uldini rolled his eyes impatiently. 'You forget that we are not talking about a mere mortal here. As long as the Dark god was only a fleeting phantom of sheer willpower and magic, He had to spend a considerable amount of his energy trying to…well…to keep Himself together, so to speak. His recreated body, on the other hand, is like a foundation, upon which He can effortlessly manifest his being. And the Adversary has millennia of experience in protecting His shell, in healing it and in recreating it when necessary.'

'This discussion is becoming more depressing with every word that's spoken,' commented Ahren tensely. 'Please tell me that we Paladins are capable of piercing through the Dark god without Him simply being able to resurrect Himself in a newly created body and stroll away while whistling cheerfully.'

'Your gods' Blessings are like water that can extinguish His life,' said Uldini without looking Ahren in the eye. 'At least – for as long as this water is more powerful than his flame.'

Ahren groaned. The doubt in Uldini's voice was impossible to miss, as was the Ancient's clear desire not to waste any more time discussing the matter.

'So, are you afraid that the Adversary will make His escape and play a game of cat and mouse with the Paladins as He used to do in the Dark Days?'

Uldini nodded silently.

'But why didn't He simply let his body…let's say…manifest itself on one of the Isles of the Cutlass Sea?' asked Ahren, stubbornly determined to find out as much information as possible. 'Somewhere far away from the Ring?'

'The Adversary is no *genuine* god,' said Falk, his voice hard. 'No matter what He wants others to believe, the fact is that His body can only manifest itself in the same place where He was forced into submission.'

'At the very point where the Pall Pillar materialised,' added Lanlion. 'Which is now the heart of the Obsidian Fortress.'

'And don't forget – HE, WHO FORCES always was and remains a coward,' said Falk scornfully. 'He prefers to hide behind His armies for as long as He possibly can.'

'Or break through the Ring under their cover,' added Uldini. 'Which is why I would prefer to have all the Paladins in one place sooner rather than later so that we can at last strike out.'

'Why such gloomy prognostications on a glorious morning like this?' Jelninolan's gentle question was audible before she appeared from the surrounding trees in the company of Trogadon. 'This can only mean Uldini has once again firmly taken the reins within our little company.'

A shiver ran down Ahren's spine when he heard those words. An undertone of power had been radiating from the elf's voice ever since their journey on the wings of the goddess – it was as if the breath of HER, WHO FEELS floated with every syllable that the priestess uttered.

'I am merely laying out the facts,' retorted Uldini brittlely. 'And impressing on everyone the need to make haste.'

'Our skirmish with Four Claws is but a day ago,' said the elf in the warm tone that she used when comforting the wounded. 'Let us recover ourselves for a short period. The most difficult battle is still ahead of us. Should we not be in the best possible condition before entering combat?'

Uldini scratched his head. It was clear to Ahren that the Ancient was turning over the measured words of the elf in his mind, looking at them from every angle with his razor-sharp reason.

'Six days,' he muttered finally, nodding curtly. 'It will take me that long to organise the fastest possible means of transport for us to get to the Ring. But then we leave.'

Ahren was surprised at how much he welcomed the breather that Jelninolan had wrested from Uldini – even though the news from the Ring demanded haste. Yet they had experienced a myriad of things in the Ice Fields that he felt he needed to digest and to discuss with the others. It could only be of benefit to order the chaos that he felt within himself before he took on the monumental task of slaying a god.

A self-proclaimed god, said Culhen, correcting his friend, the wolf having entered the clearing along with Lyssin, Yoka and Muai. The mouths of the three animals were dripping with blood, while the young Forest Guardian was breathing heavily, her eyes wide with excitement.

'So many trees!' she gasped. 'Father drew a picture of a tree for me once – when I asked him what a forest was.' She started laughing helplessly. 'I am probably the only Forest Guardian who didn't properly understand the guild to which she belonged.'

'My overconfident apprentice is currently experiencing the delights of a thorough refresher course in what it is to be a Forest Guardian,' said Ahren in a voice sufficiently loud to cause the young warrior to flinch at the caustic commentary. 'You, Lyssin, are heartily welcome to listen to everything I have to tell him about the woodlands.'

Oh, please say yes, begged Culhen, without the young female Forest Guardian being able to hear his thought. The look of the wolf, however, spoke volumes, the animal now looking pleadingly up at her, having lain down at her feet. *Then I can spend a lot of time with Yoka while you lot discuss your human nonsense – and she will notice how wonderful a wolf I really am.*

Muai, meanwhile, growled and shook her head in disgust as she looked at the wolf.

Out of the corner of his eye, Ahren observed how Hakanu, too, was looking yearningly over at Lyssin, the boy's silly expression causing his master to positively fret.

Two lovesick fools at once, he groaned inwardly. *This is going to be fun.*

The pool was deep and clear, and just cool enough to be refreshing in the never-ending early summer climate of Eathinian. Ahren and Khara were alone, the Paladin admiring again his beloved's uncanny ability to sense out areas of water so easily, be they large or small. Following the discussion with Uldini and the others, the companions had split up into smaller groups or gone off alone, and this was the first time in many moons that Ahren and Khara could spend some time in their own company. Time seemed to be flying and the sun was already high in the sky as Ahren floated lazily on the surface of the large pond while Khara lay on a nearby rock, allowing the sun to dry her off.

'What do you think happened to those we left behind on the Ice Fields?' asked the Swordsmistress dreamily.

Ahren played dead as he, too, looked vacantly up at the sky from his floating position on the water. 'When Jelninolan's song started to bring us northwards, I saw the ice around us beginning to melt,' he said. 'I reckon that the army of Dark Ones surrounding us was drowned, thereby presenting no further danger to Yollock and Caldria.'

Khara grunted in agreement – a sound of blissful satisfaction. 'And Four Claws will have finished off the few Dark Ones that survived,' she added confidently. Then a sigh escaped her lips. 'Can you just imagine what would have happened if he had come with us? The mightiest dragon of the lot suddenly fighting on *our* side against the Adversary?' Another sigh. '*That's* something I'd have loved to see.'

Ahren did not answer immediately, enjoying instead the feel of the water that was lapping against his body. That was keeping him afloat. That was keeping him safe and well. 'Four Claws has seen far too much suffering in his life and fought in far too many battles. Yollock knew this. It wasn't for nothing that he sheltered the dragon from the world. I think it is right that he stayed in the Ice Fields.'

'Who?' asked Khara curiously. 'Yollock or Four Claws?'

'Yes.'

'Understood.'

Ahren could sense Khara's broad grin in that one word. 'At least Yollock has not been left behind in his cave completely alone,' said the Forest Guardian as he began to swim towards the bank. 'The thought that Caldria is keeping him company is comforting.'

Khara cocked her head. 'Will she ever talk again, I wonder?'

'Difficult to say,' replied Ahren, pulling himself up out of the water. 'The loss of her magic was a big shock to her.' He smiled wanly. 'But even if she remains mute, it won't bother Yollock. If this man utters ten words in a normal day, it will seem like too many to him.'

'Caldria had to sweat on the Flame Belly ship for moons on end,' said Khara as she smiled at Ahren. 'Hopefully, she will enjoy the cold air of the icy south.'

Ahren lay down beside Khara and stroked a stray hair from her forehead. 'It was certainly bearable in the Fog Fields,' he murmured. 'And I would imagine that our burned-out Fire Wizard will soon use her expertise in controlling heat to find simple ways and means of making some of the simmering pools there useful.'

'Two taciturn individuals enjoying the evening of their lives in seclusion,' said Khara dreamily. 'Sounds heavenly. Why don't *we* give it a go sometime?'

'You have my word,' said Ahren with a smile. Then he winked mischievously at Khara. 'Hakanu will be busy until sundown with collecting herbs. If you can think of any way that we can pass the time until then, I'm all ears.'

The Swordsmistress said nothing, but her smile revealed her intentions.

'…when it's dissolved in water. Then the plant checks bleeding in the stomach.' Ahren could hear the explanation of his apprentice before he saw the boy.

'What a cornucopia,' said Lyssin in amazement as Ahren stepped out from the trees and into the sun-drenched clearing where the companions had set up camp. 'There were only a few mosses and lichens in the Ice Fields that had healing properties – in this place there seem to be plants for every ailment imaginable.'

'If you can find one against cockiness, then let me know immediately,' interjected Ahren, fixing his eyes sternly on Hakanu.

The apprentice lowered his head and concentrated on organising the vast array of prepared creams, infusions, herbs, flowers and stems that he had spread out in front of him on the forest floor.

'Well, *I* found his attack on the dragon downright brave,' said Lyssin, tousling Hakanu's hair energetically as she spoke. 'And his tactic almost paid off.'

'A solitary spear throw is certainly no *tactic*,' countered Ahren through gritted teeth. The besotted young warrior was now gazing so longingly at the female Forest Guardian following her expression of admiration for him that Ahren was sure he wouldn't take in what his master then added. 'And anyway, that solitary word *almost* very often determines the difference between victory and defeat.'

'Don't be so strict with him,' said Lyssin, tousling Hakanu's hair a second time. 'He is still practically only a child.'

If a heavy rock had fallen on his foot, the apprentice's sudden look of horror could hardly have been more pained. Ahren immediately felt sorry for his protégé and quickly pointed down at the lad's collection.

'Now explain to me all the lovely things you have found,' he said in a conciliatory voice. 'If you make a good enough impression on me, we might even discuss a possible spear throwing session for tomorrow.'

Ahren could see how the young warrior suppressed his hurt and disappointment by swallowing hard before beginning to speak.

'This is Fog Root,' the lad began, yet without any of the vivacity that had accompanied his earlier explanations to Lyssin.

Ahren groaned inwardly. Clearly, it was beginning to dawn on his apprentice that there were some battles in life that simply could not be won.

Once Hakanu had obediently listed off his litany of plants, Ahren praised him effusively before sending him off to perform a session of repeatedly scaling and descending a nearby tree.

'Was I too direct?' asked Lyssin as soon as Hakanu was out of earshot.

'When one considers that you have spent so many years in the Ice Fields with no-one but your father, then you were extremely tactful,' said Ahren in a low voice. 'I'm surprised that you even noticed the signs of his... *infatuation*.'

Lyssin's ears turned the same colour as her wild locks of hair. 'Jelninolan and Khara warned me already,' she said before shaking her head. 'No, that's not the right word – I am still unused to using more nuanced expressions. Father was not a very talkative person – as I am sure you already know.'

Ahren nodded. 'It would be better for this particular tooth to be immediately pulled before Hakanu does something really silly.'

Lyssin looked at him in consternation. 'You want to extract one of Hakanu's teeth? Is this some sort of punishment that is carried out on the mainland?'

'No,' laughed Ahren as he placed a hand on the young Forest Guardian's shoulder. 'But I now see that we are going to have to teach you a few things that are not strictly related to Forest Guardianship. Jorath can be a *very* complicated place – especially for a Paladin.'

Lyssin puckered up her nose. 'I can look after myself *very* well, thank you very much,' she said curtly.

'With the bow and arrow, yes – not to mention your short sword,' countered Ahren with a chuckle. 'But what if I tell you there are cities where words are hurled as effectively as weapons?'

Lyssin's eyes lit up with joyful anticipation. 'Tell me more!' she demanded.

Ahren laughed affectionately, waving a warning finger as he did so. 'I will leave that task to others,' he countered with a grin. 'There is a certain dwarf in our midst who likes to do nothing more than relate tales from our adventures – in all their fantastical glory.'

'So, there we were, trapped in the Brazen City, which was on the point of being overrun by thousands of Dark Ones...' proclaimed Trogadon in a terrifyingly gravelly voice as he kicked at a burning branch in the fire, causing sparks to fly off into the darkness.

'Stop that!' snarled Jelninolan. 'The Treetop Runners are nervous enough as it is on account of the flames.'

Ahren smiled to himself as he disappeared into the night's embrace, leaving his companions behind, who were listening with delight to Trogadon's exaggerated anecdotes. He was heading for the solitary figure who was sitting on the fallen tree trunk that he had clearly decided would be his own special retreat.

'Why aren't you sitting with us?' asked the Forest Guardian in a soft voice, having arrived below the bloodless Paladin.

'I like it here,' said Lanlion laconically, shrugging his shoulders – a gesture that Ahren more sensed than saw in the darkness of the forest. 'And you know how fire dazzles me whenever my eyes are peering into the mysteries of the night.'

Ahren sighed. 'Ah, Lanlion. The eternally melancholic poet.'

A self-ironic giggle could be heard from the tree trunk. 'If so – then a poet of the inferior sort.'

'I know quite a few of the bardic songs written in honour of us Paladins,' countered Ahren dryly. 'As long as you keep away from rhyming pain with swain, you will be doing better than many a minstrel scourging this continent.'

Lanlion giggled again – this time, he sounded far more relaxed. 'You seem to be in a particularly affable – if rough and ready – mood today. Why is that?'

Ahren chuckled. In fact, he had been hoping to learn from his friend about the latter's recent pilgrimage, but the shrewd Paladin had cleverly turned the tables on him. 'A part of me wants to do nothing else but bask in the glory of our success in finding all the Paladins,' he said after a short pause. 'While another part of me is whispering urgently into my ear that the hardest part of our enterprise is yet to come.' He pointed towards the campfire, where Jelninolan was humming quietly as she lovingly plaited Trogadon's hair, yanking it from time to time whenever her beloved began to get too carried away by the embellishments that he was adding to the tales he was relating. 'And furthermore, there are those of us who have undergone experiences so extraordinary that I do not know how they have borne them.'

'You mean like Jelninolan,' asked Lanlion teasingly.

'Yes – like Jelninolan – and others not a million miles away.'

The Bloodless shook his head. 'Sometimes you are as subtle as an intoxicated dwarf. Well – what would you like to know?'

'Everything.'

Lanlion snorted mirthfully. 'No creature on the face of the earth can know *everything*. At least I can comfort myself with this thought whenever I reach my own limits.'

'Lanlion,' said Ahren severely. 'It is vital that I know how things are with you.'

'You mean because of my future responsibility as one of the Paladins who will confront the Adversary?'

'Because you are my friend.,' countered the Forest Guardian earnestly.

'Very well then,' agreed the Bloodless. 'But I will keep it short.'

'That will be light relief after an evening of Trogadon's meandering oral epics,' chuckled Ahren as the dwarf began to loudly imitate the Glower Bear which had almost caused the young Forest Guardian's downfall before the gates of the Brazen City all that time ago. 'Why does he *always* insist on highlighting my failures?' muttered Ahren in a low voice.

'Failures and mistakes are what make us human,' murmured Lanlion. 'It is important not to forget them. It is only through them that we really develop.'

'Now we are talking about *you* at last,' said Ahren, looking up at Lanlion with a grin, before clambering up to sit beside his fellow

Paladin, who was perched high above the forest floor on the side of the enormous fallen tree. 'I'm all ears.'

The pale Paladin shrugged his shoulders. 'In fact, my journey was nothing special,' he began thoughtfully. 'It was like a tugging at my chest that led me to crisscross Jorath.'

Ahren frowned. 'That sounds arbitrary and not in the least like a pilgrimage ordained by one of the deities.'

'You keep on forgetting how deep a sleep they are in,' said Lanlion with a trace of sharpness in his voice. 'Much of what they do is confused.' He hesitated for a heartbeat before continuing. 'But after a short time I understood where they were leading me to – whether to old battlefields upon which I had fought and won, or to women and men who I had rescued, or to simple, beautiful memories that had slipped my mind – I became evermore aware of these people and places as the tugging in my chest led me to the descendants of soldiers who had survived, and who still knew that Lanlion the Paladin had saved the lives of their ancestors. I was also led to busy little hamlets, which blossomed now, although in the Dark Days they had been scarred by bloody chaos.' Lanlion sighed audibly. 'The THREE showed me that my deeds had carried weight. That life goes on – even in those places where death had reigned supreme.' By now the voice of the Bloodless had sunk into a whisper. 'And that my manner of existence has nothing to do with my value to Jorath. Does a small child worry in the least whether he or she is saved from a Dark One by a human or by a…'

'Or by a what?' asked Ahren insistently.

'…by an *unusual* Paladin,' murmured Lanlion, concluding his sentence with a crooked grin. 'You thought I was going to say *monster*, didn't you?'

'The old Lanlion would have used such a word.'

'Oh, I am still the same as I ever was,' countered Lanlion. 'Only a little bit wiser and less fixated on a circumstance that I cannot change. Only the gods can do that. Perhaps.'

Ahren laid a comforting hand on the pale Paladin's shoulder. The metal of his armour felt as cold as if it had been lying for years in the depths of a burial crypt. 'If it took a pilgrimage for you to understand what I have known for a long time, then I am glad that you undertook one. As far as I am concerned, you are a Paladin like any other.'

Lanlion grinned. 'Except that it is better if I eat alone.'

Ahren raised a quizzical eyebrow. 'Are you *joking* about your Bloodless condition?'

'I am.'

'Hm. Then I think you should stick to the poetry.'

Ahren was dreaming with fondness about the wet fox's nose that had been borrowing into his ear the previous morning when he was abruptly awakened by a scornful cry. He sat up and blinked several times, while Khara emerged from her blanket and pulled herself up beside him.

The night was already on the retreat, and the first signs of dawn were making themselves apparent in a soft red hue. Uldini and the First were arguing furiously in the middle of the encampment – and it clearly seemed to concern the fact that they had not made a move yet but were still firmly ensconced in this remote part of the Elven forest.

'I have not only ordered a total mobilisation of Eathinian but also announced your imminent arrival – and yet it seems that you lot are doing nothing but sitting around here having one picnic after the other!' fumed the age-old, battle-hardened warrior. 'I was convinced that you were hot on my heels considering that Uldini the Wise, the famed *first* among the Ancients knows full well what a dangerous situation we have been in ever since Lyssin has appeared on the scene. But I am clearly mistaken!'

'I have long since organised our transport to the south!' yelled Uldini angrily. 'An escort with enough Titejunanwas to carry the lot of us will appear in a few days, which means that we will be well able to make up for lost time, you rusty-headed, bloodthirsty old…'

Jelninolan played a single tone on *Mirilan*, and the shouting match could no longer be heard. Ahren could see the two squabblers squaring up to each other, but they were now completely inaudible.

'Let the two of them vent their rage to each other,' said the elf resignedly, 'but I really don't see why the rest of us should suffer for it.'

'You should have started using this little trick on Uldini years ago,' said Falk with a grin. 'And made sure it worked permanently.'

Ahren grinned at his erstwhile master, who was standing there in his Forest Guardian gear, his hand resting on Selsena's neck, the Titejunanwa snorting contentedly. 'Did the two of you ride out?'

Falk nodded. 'An early morning canter alone with my old girl is enough for now,' he said. 'Her joy at seeing me has already been tempered by her glee at criticising everything I say.'

The Titejunanwa snorted, and Ahren sensed the mixture of disapproval and affections that was radiating from the Elven charger. Falk rubbed her nose affectionately.

'At least you are getting *something* from your companion animal,' said Khara sulkily. 'Muai is spending all her time roaming Evergreen in the company of Culhen and Yoka. I bet you anything she is jealous of all the attention that Culhen is showering on the young she-wolf.'

'Yoka likes him a lot,' interjected Lyssin with a distinct lack of tact, Khara immediately frowning in disgust. 'She says she finds him droll.'

'*Droll?* repeated Ahren, rubbing his forehead in puzzlement. 'My vainglorious wolf must never hear that, or his conceitedness will collapse like a house of cards, just as Trogadon's promises to stay sober for an evening do.'

'Hey,' complained the dwarf. 'Keep me out of this.'

By this time both Uldini and the First had realised that no-one apart from themselves could hear a word they were saying, the pair of them now resorting to staring down Jelninolan with looks that could only be described as murderous.

'I think those two want to be relieved of the spell,' said Ahren with a grin.

'Do we *really* need to release them already?' asked Falk, covering his mouth with his hand to hide his laughter.

'I think we should wait until after breakfast,' concluded Jelninolan. 'That way we can be sure that they will have worn themselves out with screaming.'

Chapter 2

By the time Jelninolan dissipated her charm, Uldini and the First had settled down to staring at each other furiously. They insisted on carrying on with their tight-lipped anger even after the elf had gestured to them that they could now be heard by the others again.

'Where are Sleeps-in-Treetops and Bergen, by the way?' asked Lanlion, finally breaking the silence while Ahren, Khara and Hakanu stored away the remains of their cold breakfast in the rucksacks. 'I know that they'd set off with the First to let the elves know that we were back.'

The heads of the companions turned in unison to look at the veteran, who continued to stare icily.

'Are you really going to carry on with your childish silence just because you didn't have a captive audience to witness your explosive rage?' asked Ahren irritably.

'You didn't want to hear what I had to say,' snarled the First through gritted teeth. This was followed by a few heartbeats of silence before he added: 'The pair of them said they wanted to stay with the elves and wait there for you.'

Ahren knew that the First was unused to be being treated in such a manner. Until the conclave in Hjalgar, the age-old Paladin had been treated with a respect, albeit one ruled by fear, that almost bordered on reverence. It had only been thanks to Ahren's resistance that he'd eventually been dethroned from his position at the top of the pile. Now he was merely one of the Thirteen, rather than their undisputed leader. Jelninolan's magic spell had reinforced his new ranking.

And don't forget – he is also ashamed of himself for having lost that self-control he loves so much on the Ice Fields, added Culhen, who was lying close to Yoka. She was chewing on a bone that her fellow wolf had willingly donated to her.

Ahren silently conveyed his agreement to his friend. The First had to be feeling very sensitive at the moment. Many old wounds had been ripped open again during the old man's encounter with Four Claws, while the battle against the dragon had taken a turn that the veteran could never have anticipated. And once again, it had been Ahren who had been the cause of the First not getting his own way. Maybe it was time to heal some of those very same wounds.

'What do *you* think we should do?' asked the Forest Guardian, sitting down opposite the man with the old-fashioned armour and speaking in as inviting a tone as he could manage.

'It is very simple,' said the First after a heartbeat. 'We must proceed to the Ring with all possible speed – before the Adversary breaks through it, making another thousand years of conflict inevitable before we can hem Him in again.'

'Uldini is working on it,' said Khara, settling down beside the age-old Paladin. 'While we others are trying to regain as much strength as we can.' With that she laid a hand on the protective steel of his forearm. 'Much has happened to us all in the icy vastness of the south.'

Ahren half-expected the First to pull back his arm, but to his surprise, the Veteran nodded in agreement. 'I miss *her,*' he said, Ahren immediately recognising that the man was referring to his deceased companion animal. 'There is so much of *her* to be found in Four Claws. *Her* courage. *Her* pride. *Her* stubbornness.'

'Then it is good that a part of her still lives, is it not?' suggested Falk, while Selsena radiated a wave of sympathy and nudged the First's head from behind with her nose.

The age-old Paladin moved his hand up in an awkward gesture, tickling the chin of the Elven charger, who also had millennia of lived experience. '*My* rage...*my* hatred,' he began hesitantly. 'Both of them supported me.' He frowned. 'The loss of one's goal when it involves such emotions...well...it's impossible to put into words.'

'There is, as we *all* know, a certain self-proclaimed god,' said Lanlion from the edge of the clearing, where he was leaning against a tree. 'Focus your rage and hatred on *him*. Then there will be less left over for you to mete out on Uldini here.'

'Good idea,' agreed the Arch Wizard dryly. 'Especially because I really *have* made arrangements that will help us on our journey south. As I already said, an Elven escort will be arriving in a few days to collect us.'

'I think we all need to relax a little,' suggested Trogadon with a twinkle in his eye.

'What plot are you hatching *now*, my dear?' asked Jelninolan suspiciously.

The dwarf grinned and fished a little steel barrel from one of the rucksacks that Lanlion had brought north with the help of Haminul and

Selsena. 'I have some liquid refreshment that will help soothe our anxious minds – well, at least if we are in the company of friends with whom we can laugh and throw dice.'

Jelninolan glared over at Lanlion with a look of both anger and disappointment. 'Does a barrel containing alcohol really count as an *essential* provision?'

The bloodless Paladin pointed at Trogadon. 'Sleeps-in-Treetops said I should bring everything here that strengthens our bodies, our minds and our souls. Which – when it came to our bearded friend here – could only be the barrel.'

'You know me too well,' said the blacksmith, licking his lips in eager anticipation. 'For which I forgive you your overblown manner.'

While Jelninolan sighed in resignation, the rest of the companions gathered around Trogadon's find.

'Don't forget – we must leave some over for Bergen,' advised Ahren. 'If it is drained dry before he arrives, he will never forgive us.'

Conscientious nods were the response, Ahren seeing in the eyes of his friends such a thirst for life that he was sure the barrel would be empty in no time. When Trogadon produced his lovingly polished dice, the Paladin knew that idle pleasure was going to be the order of the day.

'Hakanu – you are relieved from your duties for now!' he called out to the general cheering of the others.

After that his world descended into a maelstrom of merry laughter, good quality schnapps and even better friends.

Humming merrily, Ahren stumbled through Evergreen in search of a place where he could answer the call of nature. The trees kept spinning around him, while the undergrowth deviously rose before him whenever he was about to take another step forward.

'Stupid forest,' he mumbled, holding onto the trunk of a tree with one hand, while trying to loosen his trouser cord with the other.

A tiny part of him knew that he was very drunk – while the rest of his understanding was absolutely delighted with his condition. The threat from the Adversary seemed – thanks to his intoxication – to be at a comfortable distance, and the laughter of his friends along with his own had been good for his soul.

'At least *I* can still stand,' he grunted as he continued to struggle with the knot. 'Not like the First.' He found himself giggling uncontrollably.

The veteran had downed his drinks quickly and with grim determination until he had toppled over like a tree that was being felled, after which he had done nothing more than snore. Jelninolan had said something clever about the age-old Paladin not wanting to reveal more of his vulnerability, but Ahren hadn't really been able to follow the logic of her argument.

'And not because of the alcohol,' he assured himself, finally managing to open his trousers. He stared blankly into the middle distance while a splashing sound added to the forest noises. He looked upwards with a sigh – and was immediately struck dumb.

Above him, a chipmunk with a silver streak down his back was sitting on a low-hanging branch staring at him with the same withering look that Jelninolan and Khara sometimes used when they were particularly disdainful of a person's foolish actions.

'Hello, my little one,' said Ahren, his speech slurred. He held up his hand to the Voice of the Forest. 'Did you want to welcome me personally to Evergreen?'

The chipmunk flinched back from his fingers, leaving Ahren to wonder at the little animal's ability to look so indignant. The tiny part of his mind that was still capable of rational thought whispered to Ahren that he had just been about to stroke the spiritual leader of the elves with his trousers down around his ankles.

'Should…' began Ahren, only to be interrupted by a burp. 'Should we talk tomorrow, maybe?' he asked, smiling broadly in the hope that he was sounding suitably friendly and not like a total idiot.

The Voice of the Forest looked at him for a couple of heartbeats before disappearing into the foliage.

Ahren nodded heavily. 'You did well there, young man,' he mumbled to himself. 'Very diplomo…diplemi…tactful!' He pulled up his trousers again and staggered back towards the clearing. Hardly had he entered the open space with its little fire burning invitingly when he bawled: 'You'll never believe who *I* met just now…!'

The night of raucous merriment was slowly drawing to its inevitable close, providing quite the contrast to the chorus of Low Fangs situated in Ahren's mind, which were now launching into a dwarfish aria while two dozen Glower Bears jumped up and down on an equal number of badly tuned timpani.

'What sort of treacherous brew did Lanlion deliver to us?' groaned the Paladin, dragging himself to his feet and picking his way through his snoring companions towards the only other figure that was also awake.

Jelninolan was sitting at the embers of the campfire, holding Trogadon's head in her lap and stroking the bridge of the snoring dwarf's nose, the latter reacting by twitching his face with a smile but without waking up.

'I had the most abstruse dream,' said Ahren as he sat down beside the priestess. 'I was in the undergrowth and met the Voice of the Forest, but I wasn't wearing my trousers and…' He broke off as soon as Jelninolan turned her head and stared at him, looking for all the world as if she were on the point of an Unleashing. 'Oh, no…' he whispered a heartbeat later.

'The goddess sent forth her most senior servant to congratulate you on your successful search for the remaining Paladins,' said the elf, every syllable falling like a hammer blow and driving Ahren's guilty feelings, which felt like burning nails, deeper and deeper into his already tortured head. 'And you were so drunk that the Voice of the Forest was all but doused in your pi—.'

Ahren raised a hand. 'Ah now, it didn't come to *that,*' he interjected hastily.

'How *comforting* of you to say so. I am so *delighted* to hear that.' Jelninolan's reply dripped with ice – so much so that she could easily have created a glacier on the spot had she so wished.

Ahren groaned again. 'We were all letting our hair down,' he said tortuously. 'I am pretty sure that if a king had wandered into our midst, we wouldn't have suddenly greeted him with pomp and ceremony.'

Jelninolan nodded curtly. 'Alright,' she said after an awkward silence. 'I know that the Voice's visit was a surprise for all of us. But that doesn't make it less embarrassing – either for you *or* for me.'

'Thankfully, there was only one little barrel,' murmured Ahren, hiding his head in his hands. 'A celebration like the one we've just had shouldn't be repeated too often.'

Trogadon's loud snoring seemed to want to contradict Ahren. Jelninolan ran her finger along the bridge of the dwarf's nose again.

'He looks so cute when he twitches his nose like that,' she said with a smile.

Partly because he wanted to distract himself from his pounding head, and partly because he had wanted to ask the question for days now, Ahren turned to the elf and whispered: 'And how are *you?*'

Jelninolan chuckled. 'Good.' The echo in her voice was – even with this single syllable – unmistakable.

Ahren hesitated before asking: 'Have you anything else to add?'

The priestess shrugged her shoulders. 'I am still me,' she said in a low voice. 'If that's what you are asking.'

Ahren wrang his hands nervously. 'What we saw on our journey as we travelled from the Ice Fields to the far north…were they *really* the memories of the goddess?'

Now Jelninolan was looking directly into his eyes, and Ahren was sure that he recognised a barely visible shimmering in the depths of her gaze. 'It was that part of her sense impressions that our understanding could digest,' she said. 'A gift that the goddess had set aside an unimaginably long time ago for the person who would be the first to empathise with her own journey.' She smiled.' Mind you, I doubt that SHE, WHO FEELS had ever expected that the recipients would turn out to be a colourful gang of Paladins, Ancients and companion animals, not to mention a dwarf and a princess. But if there is one thing that I have learned on my long journey in the footsteps of the goddess, it is that although the THREE may have made plans for the living beings of their beloved Creation, they had little idea of the unexpected results that eventually manifested themselves.'

'You mean, the Custodian, for example, who developed into the Adversary,' suggested Ahren earnestly.

Jelninolan sighed. 'Yes. And the elf who became the first of her tribe to visit all the pools of the goddess – but only thousands of years after Jorath came into being.' She frowned. 'I simply cannot shake off the feeling that another elf should have aired the secret a long, long time before me.' She raised her hand before her face and observed it – it was as if she had never seen it before. 'Imagine all the good that the elves of this world could have done if they had undergone the transformation that I went through.'

A shiver ran down Ahren's spine as he listened to the priestess. 'I don't think there are many other elves whom I would trust with the power that has been granted to you,' he said firmly. 'Has it ever struck you that you might have been the first to discover the pools because you were the first to be worthy of their power?'

Jelninolan frowned as she considered what he had said. 'Perhaps – perhaps not,' she responded uncertainly. 'The gods are asleep. Who knows what precisely they have planned for us. Maybe we should recognise that they are all-powerful but not all-knowing.'

Ahren could feel his hairs standing on end. 'What do you mean?'

'I mean that the THREE conceived the *tools* for getting Creation back onto the right course, but that they have left the *method* of bringing this about purely in our hands.' She ran her hands through her hair – as it she had just emerged from the depths of a pool and was brushing away the residual drops of cooling water. 'Maybe it would be better if you didn't listen to me,' she added, smiling tortuously. 'The echo of the goddess is weighing more heavily on my understanding than I would care to admit. Perhaps I think I am seeing a dense jungle filled with convoluted tracks, when in fact there is nothing but a simple, straight path with a clear beginning and an inevitable end – however *that* might appear.'

Ahren was relieved when, three days after his night-time discussion with Jelninolan, more than two dozen elves emerged from the Evergreen undergrowth. They were accompanied by a herd of Titejunanwas elegantly dressed in leather armour, as well as a large number of similarly attired animals of the forest. The unusual sight and the excitement of the companions' imminent departure extinguished at least temporarily the nagging anxiety that Jelninolan's words had awakened in him. Was it possible that the gods were far more disorganised than had been generally assumed? Were they like three adults who had left complicated tools in the parlour for their children, hoping that their offspring would figure out for themselves how to put them to use?

On several occasions Ahren found himself imagining what might have happened if the ancestral elves of the time before the Dark Days had reached the Ice Fields during their journey across the world, airing the secret of the pools of the goddess at the same time. Would *they* have been able to force the Custodian into submission by using the echo of this power? Would they have brought the secrets of that sorcery to Jorath much earlier? And might the emergence of the Paladins never have been necessary at all?

Ahren couldn't stop himself from seeing his brothers and sisters in a new light. Perhaps they were nothing more than a stopgap measure, one of many that the gods had used in their desperate attempts at forcing the Adversary into submission.

Maybe we are not even the last, he thought.

Stuff and nonsense! Culhen's caustic comment crashed into Ahren's mind like a chunk of rock smashing onto a thin layer of ice. *There is no way that I am a stopgap measure – and if I'm not one, then that rules you out as well. And now, will you please help me keep this Elven wolfhound away from Yoka – he's bowing and scraping like the devil knows what.*

As opposed to you? countered Ahren with a grin.

I never bow and scrape, retorted Culhen disdainfully. *I am always polite and attentive. Very different.*

Chuckling to himself, Ahren followed his friend before lending a helping hand as his companions prepared for their new adventure, the doubt within him having been tempered, for the moment at least.

'Is that *really* necessary,' asked Khara, taking Ahren's words out of his mouth.

They had been riding south for four days now, and the First had just announced at supper that the travel party should break up into smaller groups.

'This is purely as a precaution,' explained Uldini in the veteran's stead. 'The Dark god knows that the Thirteen are back and are making their way towards the Ring. As long as we divide the Paladins into the smallest contingents possible, we will prevent him from being tempted to exterminate several at one go.'

'And if he decides to kill one of us precisely *because* we have left the protection of the others?' asked Ahren sceptically.

'Seven Paladins in one group must be considerably easier for the Dark god to locate than two or three together,' interjected Lanlion. 'Our present formation is bound to be like a beacon to him. As soon as we leave Evergreen, we will surely be an open invitation for his armies to break out and attack us.'

'The situation is this – the more Paladins there are together, the greater the likelihood of an assault by the most powerful Dark Ones that the Dark god has to offer,' said the First. 'We are all too familiar with this pattern from the last weeks of the Dark Days.'

'And as soon as we all meet up again,' mused Falk broodingly, 'there will be a new Night of Blood.'

'We can't be certain of that,' interjected Bergen in an almost pleading tone. The Paladin seemed anxious and distracted. Ahren was sure that his friend wanted to get back to his Blue Cohorts and especially to his soul companion, who perhaps had already given birth to their child.

'I have rarely been so sure of anything,' said Uldini harshly. 'The Adversary has already been successful once with His strategy of delaying any final victory on our part by his instigation of the Night of Blood. He will use this ploy a second time – mark my words.'

The First pointed to himself, Bergen and Sleeps-in-Treetops. 'We three, accompanied by an escort of two hundred elves, will approach the Ring from the northwest. Lanlion and Lyssin will move directly towards it from the north, accompanied by the main body of combat elves. Ahren, Hakanu and Falk will travel from the northeast – with Jelninolan and Uldini in your company, they will have enough sorcerous assistance to manage without regular troops. Are we all in agreement?'

'Our group will be small enough to be able to hide effectively from the tentacles of the Adversary,' explained Jelninolan confidently.

Hakanu cleared his throat and suggested haltingly: 'Maybe Master Ahren and I can travel with Lyssin? We could help her find her feet on the continent and…'

'My knowledge concerning Jorath should be sufficient,' interjected Lanlion with a smirk, the face of the First darkening like a thunder cloud. 'I am sure that I will be able to entertain Lyssin over the few weeks of travelling.' He nodded towards her politely, the young woman replying with a friendly smile.

But…but Yoka… began Culhen whimperingly.

Ahren sighed. *You will see her again at the Ring. Please don't behave as childishly as Hakanu.*

The ensuing silent sulk from the wolf was as penetrating as a fanfare of bugles.

'Now that we have *finally* established who is travelling with whom, could we perhaps get going?' asked Uldini in a voice so sweet it was obvious that he was losing his patience.

'We will be taking the route through the Knight Marshes and Hjalgar then?' asked Trogadon, who would of course be accompanying

Jelninolan. He stroked his beard thoughtfully. 'That sounds like a walk in the park.'

'Going by the latest reports that I have only now received, our plaited friend is right for a change,' explained Uldini. 'There have been almost no sightings of Dark Ones in either country on *this* side of the Ring – never mind High- or Low Fangs.'

'That might well change once the Adversary has gotten wise to us,' warned Falk. 'As you have already mentioned, He can in all probability sense seven Champions of the gods in one spot by merely closing His eyes and *thinking* of Paladins. As soon as He notices that we have split up, he will understand that our intention is to sneak up to the Ring from several directions.'

Uldini shrugged his shoulders. 'What do you want me to say?' he whined. 'Everything that we do from now on is going to be a high-wire act. The Adversary seems to be terrified of an ambush by the Paladins. The deities know that we used this tactic successfully on several occasions in the Dark Days. At the same time, we must not make Him nervous to the point that He will attempt to break out through the Ring with his troops. As long as He believes that his scattered servants in the wilderness can waylay us, He won't budge from His current position.'

'Puh! How I have always despised this blind weighing up of options,' commented Bergen, his voice betraying his deep sense of frustration. 'We have gone to all this trouble to encircle the Dark god, only for Him to…' He broke off, Ahren sensing in the ensuing silence the Night of Blood – like an enervating spirit floating amongst them.

'This time it will be different,' said Jelninolan, smiling encouragingly at the others, Ahren noting, however, that her smile hadn't reached as far as her eyes. He could read her deep anxiety all too well, and it only reinforced his own.

'Very well!' said the First authoritatively. 'Everyone knows their route. Good luck. We shall meet up again at the Ring.' Then he whispered something Elfish into the ear of his Titejunanwa, who promptly snorted before trotting away.

'All songs will have been sung ere long, all plans completed, too' said Sleeps-in-Treetop in a singsong voice as she rode after the First. 'What remains will be an ever-decreasing circle of victory and defeat.'

'Now, *that* was helpful,' grumbled Bergen, staring irritably at the departing Ancient. He waved goodbye to the rest of his companions, spurred on his own Titejunanwa and said loudly as he left: 'We had better go too, my good friend. We don't want to fall behind the others.'

Snorting, the animal galloped away as Selsena whinnied loudly, radiating a low wave of sad farewell.

'You must have grown accustomed to having the others around you again, old girl,' said Falk kindly as he gently stroked the bridge of her nose. 'When this is all over you will stay the length of a nice long winter with my family and me in Evergreen. That's a promise.'

Selsena's following wave of emotion was laced with gratitude, but Ahren could still sense a streak of nervousness. Even Falk's unshakeable Titejunanwa was anxiously anticipating what – or rather *who* – would be waiting for them at the Ring.

Although so many elves had ridden away with the First, Sleeps-in-Treetops and Bergen, there were still another two hundred waiting politely in their saddles and looking expectantly at Lanlion and Lyssin.

'Shall we depart forthwith, my dear?' asked the Bloodless in his best, old-fashioned style.

The female Forest Guardian laughed. 'Now you are sounding *exactly* how father had said you would,' she said, clearly charmed.

A fleeting shadow darkened his features. 'Oh, believe me, worthy sister. I am *very* different now to whom I once was.' He gave Ahren a friendly farewell glance before the pair rode off with the remaining elves. Culhen whimpered quietly as Yoka followed the group.

'Chin up,' murmured Ahren before whispering: 'See – she's looking back over her shoulder at you.'

Great, said Culhen dolefully. He paused before asking anxiously: *Lanlion will look after the two of them, won't he?*

If necessary, he will be able to hide them with his magic, Ahren replied, reassuring himself as much as his friend. He, too, had a queasy feeling in the pit of his stomach at this splitting up of the Paladins. It seemed somehow wrong to him that they were going to the front as such a fragmented force – no matter how logical Uldini's reasoning had been in this regard.

'All of a sudden, our group has become so small again,' said Trogadon, scratching his beard. 'This almost reminds me of the good old days.'

'You mean when you were chasing skirts to your heart's content?' laughed Falk.

'Now *that's* unfair,' spluttered the dwarf. He dismounted his pony and stood close to Jelninolan. None of the Elven chargers had seemed willing to tolerate a dwarf on their backs.

'Are you sure that you can shield three Paladins from the Adversary?' asked Uldini with a frown. 'Or should we divide up further? I could travel with Falk, and you could go with Ahren and Hakanu.'

The elf shook her head. 'I have the power of the goddess on my side,' she said. 'As long as our group remains small enough, and I don't need to concentrate on anything else, I can camouflage our presence.'

'I only wish that Jelninolan's magic would also include additional pack- and riding animals,' murmured Trogadon. 'The way is far, and even I wouldn't say no to a comfortable pony.'

'Perhaps *you* would like to hide our group from the prying eyes of the Adversary?' asked Jelninolan sharply. 'Then you are welcome to lay down the rules for the journey.'

The dwarf looked down at the ground. 'Never mind.'

'Then off we go to the east!' announced Ahren, turning in his saddle to look back at his apprentice once everyone was on the move. 'Hakanu?'

'Yes, Master?'

'Your grace period has expired. That tendril ahead of you looks to me like Fare-Ye-Well, or am I mistaken?'

Hakanu sighed. 'Yes, Master.' Then he drew his knife and rode over to the tree from whose branch the thin greenish-yellow plant was dangling.

'Hakanu simply *has* to survive the confrontation with the Adversary,' said Ahren to Khara in a low voice.

She blinked in bemusement. 'Of course, he has to. We *all* do.'

Ahren grinned. 'I meant it completely selfishly. I'm simply having too much fun ordering the boy around the place.'

He and Khara laughed conspiratorially, and Falk's knowing look ensured that Ahren's mischievous pleasure would linger all the longer.

A good week had passed since the Paladins had split up. Ahren and his friends were now in the eastern part of Evergreen and slowly approaching the border to the Knight Marshes. Yet still they had not left the protection of the forest. Through the trees, Ahren could now make out the first signs of an early winter, with fields covered in hoarfrost, and occasional patches of snow in those shaded parts of the countryside that had not yet been kissed by the sun.

'Is this the work of the Adversary?' asked Ahren, pointing towards the Knight Marshes visible in the distance.

'Do you mean the cold?' was Uldini's counter-question, the Forest Guardian nodding in response. 'Quite possibly,' added the Ancient. 'But I doubt that the freezing conditions are a consciously achieved effect. It is more likely that the manifestation of His body has released a sorcerous shock wave, which has temporarily influenced the weather.'

Ahren suppressed the fear rising within him as he remembered the figure, wrapped in black rags, that he had seen during his Naming all those years ago. Even then, he had found himself feeling terribly inferior to the Adversary – and this, although the Dark god had merely presented an *apparition* of His will within Ahren's mind. Without the self-sacrifice of the goblin Tlik, the journey of the Thirteenth Paladin would have ended before it had even begun. Ahren wondered what the sardonic little creature would have to say, now that all the Paladins had been found and the eve of the final battle was drawing ever closer.

'Is there any news from the Ring?' asked Khara, looking at Uldini and rousing Ahren out of his anxious ponderings. The Arch Wizard only received magical messages sporadically now, and they were so cryptic that none of his companions could follow the gibberish that the Ancient alone was able to decipher. Even Jelninolan's knowledge of ancient Elfish poetry was only of limited assistance, the Ancients incorporating ever more passwords and cryptic messages into their reports so that the Adversary would not be able to decode them. Unfortunately, this meant that Uldini required the best part of a day's ride to decode a piece of news that might constitute only a few lines.

'Quin-Wa has advised the Ancients to occupy the Wizardly Domes once more,' muttered Uldini darkly.

'Do you mean she wants to tap into the *Althunol* again?' asked Jelninolan, horrified.

Uldini waved his hand dismissively. 'No,' he said sulkily. 'The mirrors that we installed for the purpose were all rendered unusable once the Obsidian Fortress came into existence and the connection to the pool in the Forest of Ire was broken. Anyway, I ordered Akkad to dissolve my mirror charm on the *Althunol* moons ago.'

'So, why are you so concerned?' pressed Falk.

'Quin-Wa is using the Wizardly Domes as focal points so that the Ancients can cast the Ring and the Obsidian Fortress in a charm net that should dampen the magic of the Adversary.'

'Makes perfect sense,' said Ahren. Why the long face?'

The corners of Uldini's mouth turned even further down. 'Because it wasn't *my* idea,' he admitted. 'I am going to have to suffer Quin-Wa's boasting regarding this matter for centuries.'

The companions burst out laughing, ignoring Uldini's grumbling. Ahren was relieved at this moment of merriment and was intent on enjoying it as much as possible only to suddenly feel his fingers and toes cramping up.

'What the...?' he began, immediately losing all control over his tongue, however, as he fell off Culhen's back, his body now stiff as a board.

AHREN! he heard – it was the horrified voice of his furry friend calling out to him as the others, too, shouted out his name anxiously. *What is wrong with you?*

Every muscle in my body seems to have seized up, explained the Paladin laboriously, using his mental connection to the wolf. *I can't...breathe!*

Strangely, he felt absolutely no pain. If anything, it seemed as if all the fibres in his body had turned into ice, penetrating his understanding and numbing him with an overpowering frigidity.

'*Do* something, Jelninolan!' he heard his beloved Khara cry out. He, himself, could see nothing, his pupils having rolled upwards.

With all the willpower he could muster, the Paladin finally managed to slip into Culhen's mind, where the numbness and rigidity of his body no longer paralysed his thoughts. Now he was looking through Culhen's eyes, observing how the elf was kneeling over him and closing a laceration that he had suffered on falling to the ground. Then she pulled up one of his eyelids, felt several places on his neck and tentatively pressed a finger in the soft spot below his earlobe.

'What's going on here?' asked Khara urgently, her blades drawn as she scanned the forest.

'Are we being attacked?' growled Trogadon. He had raised his hammer and was turning on his own axis, searching out the surrounding undergrowth. Hakanu, meanwhile, had positioned himself so that he was standing over the prostate Paladin, his eyes blazing and his spear at the ready. 'Have no fear, Master! I will protect you,' he promised grimly.

Ahren's curiosity won out for a moment – even over his own rising panic – as he observed Jelninolan shaking her head and exchanging a knowing look with both Falk and Uldini.

'Is it the Stasis?' asked the old Paladin, Jelninolan nodding in response.

'Not the best omen given our imminent battle against the Adversary,' opined Uldini.

'What's happening to him? Talk to me!' interjected Khara cuttingly. 'Now!'

Jelninolan signalled to the Swordsmistress as well as to Hakanu and Trogadon that they should put away their weapons. Then she placed a hand on Ahren's chest while seeming to listen out for something. 'It is already receding,' she said, looking at Falk and Uldini. Then she turned her head towards Culhen. 'And you, my friend, had better lie down on your side. Soon you are going to experience the same thing as Ahren has.'

Uneasiness rose in Culhen like noxious fumes in a swamp as he followed the elf's instructions. *This doesn't sound good at all.*

Jelninolan, Falk and Uldini don't seem unnecessarily worried, said Ahren reassuringly, while trying to control his own anxiety. *Although I think it's high time they came up with an explanation!*

Hardly was Culhen lying on his side when Jelninolan visibly relaxed and began looking alternatively between the wolf and his master. 'You are currently experiencing that which we call the Stasis.'

'You have arrived at the point in your lives when you cease ageing,' murmured Falk, his eyes glittering with tears. 'The moment in which the gods prepare you for an eternity of fighting.'

Uldini rolled his eyes. 'Let's not over-mystify the situation,' he grunted. 'Akkad and I are of the opinion that this point in time simply marks the moment of complete union between the god's Blessing and the soul of the Paladin, within which it has secretly made itself at home.'

Falk threw the Arch Wizard a withering look. 'That must be nice for the pair of you,' he said sarcastically. 'I have *experienced* the Stasis and let me tell you that it is far more than the mere by-product of a magical process. Afterwards one feels…well…different. More *abstracted* from the world, one could say.'

Hakanu looked wide-eyed at the old Paladin, and Ahren couldn't tell whether his apprentice was aghast at or inspired by the prospect of an eternity of fighting.

Oh, oh, said Culhen, Ahren sensing that the wolf, too, was beginning to cramp. *It's starting. I didn't feel at all good when it happened to you.*

No need to panic, advised Ahren reassuringly. *I made that mistake. It feels as though you cannot breathe, but that will wear off after a few heartbeats. As long as you breathe calmly in your current position, you will soon feel as though you have done nothing but spend a night under a covering of snow.*

Providing nothing worse happens, came the sarcastic riposte.

Ahren concentrated on steering the focus of his understanding back to his own body, which now merely felt numb, but nothing worse than that. The tips of his fingers and toes were tingly, and even trembling ever so slightly. Apart from that, he had regained control of his eyes.

'It won't take long,' said Jelninolan, comforting not only Khara, but also Ahren and Culhen.

The Swordsmistress looked down on the immobile figure of the Forest Guardian, her eyes so filled with sorrow that Ahren felt his very soul seizing up. 'In other words, I will continue to grow old while he remains trapped in the prime of his life?' she asked in a low voice.

'Unless we slay the Adversary, of course,' countered Falk reassuringly. 'Then the reason for the agelessness of the Paladins will be null and void.'

'Let us hope so at any rate,' added Uldini.

'Supposedly so wise, yet still has no idea of when to keep his trap shut,' growled Trogadon, glaring at the Arch Wizard.

Ahren wanted to stand up and embrace Khara or at the very least whisper to her that all would be well, but his cool, numb body prevented him from doing so. He therefore concentrated on sending her all his love and compassion by means of a look. The thought of watching her age until she would finally leave him alone on this earth was almost unbearable, and he pushed the awful concept down into the depths of his being.

We will exterminate the Adversary, he swore to himself. *Not only for Jorath and the THREE – but also for Khara and me.*

The Swordsmistress knelt behind Ahren and placed his head on her lap. Then she gently stroked his hair as she gazed into his eyes. The young couple silently promised each other that they would overcome this obstacle, too, and suddenly the numbness gripping the Forest Guardian seemed markedly less terrifying. Two dozen heartbeats later and he was already able to hold her hand and shortly after that, he managed to sit up and look around. Culhen was still lying on his side, suffering the process of agelessness stoically. Muai had sat down beside the wolf and was cleaning his ear with her coarse tongue.

She knows that I don't like it when she does that, he complained. *And that I can't defend myself.*

Well now, the way I see it, her green eyes suggest that she is feeling compassion for you, countered Ahren. *And one rarely sees her looking like this.*

It's all part of the disguise of this over-sized cat.

Feeling a hand on his shoulder, the Forest Guardian turned his head. Falk was kneeling beside him. 'How are you feeling?' the old man asked gently.

'Still a little stiff,' Ahren replied, gingerly getting to his feet. 'And everything feels as it's half a finger's width away from me if you know what I mean.'

Falk nodded grimly. 'When you wake up early tomorrow morning, you will no longer notice this little divide. One grows accustomed to it surprisingly easily.'

Ahren nodded and gave Khara a fleeting kiss to reassure both himself and her that everything was still the same between them despite the Stasis. To his relief, his feelings for her effortlessly overcame the tiny cleft that he felt, which otherwise separated him from his surroundings.

'Just another common-or-garden day in the life of a Paladin,' he whispered to her, managing a trembling grin in the process.

'At least, now I know who will take over the woodcutting duties in later life,' countered Khara, but her smile was little short of tortured.

Ahren squeezed her hand lovingly before looking at the others. 'What a decidedly unpleasant experience.'

'And extremely dangerous too,' said Falk with a frown. 'Thrice in the Dark Days it came to pass that the Stasis afflicted the chosen Paladin in the middle of the battlefield. Dozens of lives were sacrificed in rescuing them. On one occasion, a fatally wounded Paladin was saved with just sufficient time for him to pass his Blessing on to his daughter.'

Ahren pursed his lips. 'The gods really could have put some more thought into their plans,' he grumbled.

'Why don't *you* try putting together a complex mosaic consisting of thousands of moving parts – right in the middle of a deep sleep,' retorted Jelninolan sharply. '*Then* you may criticise the THREE to your heart's content.' The echo in her voice reminded him of how close she was to *her* goddess, and it was this realisation which caused Ahren to fall silent rather than the import of what she had said. Clearly, she had over the course of time overcome any doubts she may have had regarding the Stasis.

'Criticising the gods won't get us anywhere,' said Trogadon, slapping Ahren cheerfully on the back. 'As the well-known Dwarfish proverb puts it: "You cannot take more from a mine than the mountain has to offer". In other words, one should not change that which cannot be changed.'

Uldini snorted. 'No wonder that Jorath has never boasted an outstanding Dwarfish philosopher.'

How are you, big lad? asked Ahren, having noticed that Culhen's paws were beginning to twitch.

Actually, not too bad at all, was the surprisingly jocular response. *If Yoka and I are not going to age any more – well that certainly does have its advantages.* A sudden brief stab of shame overcame the wolf, which Ahren felt clearly, thanks to their connection. *Apologies – that was a little crass of me.*

Ahren squeezed Khara's hand again and looked up at the low clouds scudding over Eathinian's canopy of leaves. 'The Stasis only reverses once one has found a successor, right?' he asked grimly.

'That's right,' said Falk in a low voice. 'And one never knows when the Stasis is liable to strike. In my case, I had reached forty winters. Only when I chose my daughter, did my body again follow the sands of time – only to stop anew during…'

During the Night of Blood. Those unspoken words weighed heavily on the companions – even when Culhen managed to get to his feet again.

'Let us ride on then,' announced Uldini, breaking the silence. No-one in the little group objected.

The following days were weighed down by an oppressive mood that not even Evergreen could lift. One frosty evening, it simply became too much for Ahren.

'We have to talk,' he said as he and his companions were setting up camp in a little cluster of trees that provided some shelter from the whistling wind, and where a pot of stew was now bubbling over a small fire.

'What do you mean?' asked Falk gruffly.

Ahren frowned. 'We need to talk about the things that we haven't discussed although they are of vital importance. How exactly are we going to stop the Adversary? Do we have a plan? Will it be enough for all the Paladins to simply stab Him to death for the thing to be settled? And how are we going to prevent the onset of a second Night of Blood once the thirteen of us are together?'

Falk's face froze in a grimace of pain, while Selsena whinnied shrilly into the dusk.

Slow down there, advised Culhen anxiously, Khara placing her hand on Ahren's arm and shaking her head gently.

'Don't ask all the questions at once,' she murmured. 'Especially as most of them are opening up old wounds.'

The young man nodded and gave Falk an apologetic look. 'We *must* discuss these matters,' he pleaded. 'This constant silence isn't doing any of us any good.'

Falk nodded hesitantly but said nothing.

Uldini glanced over at Jelninolan, the elf responding with a shrug of her shoulders before speaking. 'This evening is as good a time as any other,' she said. 'It might not be a bad idea at all for us in our little group to figure out how thing should proceed.'

The Arch Wizard made a face as if he had bitten into a lemon before registering his agreement with a curt nod. 'In fact, Jelninolan, Falk and I had wanted to wait until the Ring before conversing over the points that Ahren has just now listed. Doubtless, the First and the other Paladins, not to mention the Ancients, will want to throw their ideas into the mix too.' He looked deep into Ahren's eyes, the childlike figure's gaze revealing something that the Forest Guardian could only interpret as a profound uncertainty. Ahren shivered and instinctively placed one hand on Khara's, while with the other he stroked Culhen absently. Hakanu picked up Kamaluq and hugged him, the animal whimpering nervously, while Trogadon filled his pipe in expectation.

'There are two principal problems in fact,' said Jelninolan. 'How *precisely* can the thirteen force the Adversary into submission? And how do we prevent the Dark god in His rising panic from launching a destructive counterattack, with the aim of destroying the soul companions and their offspring?'

Falk groaned. 'We have been so stupid and selfish,' he said, his self-hatred evident in his voice. 'First, we abjured those soul companions who had survived the Night of Blood and who then succumbed to old age. Then we waited for centuries on the arrival of the Thirteenth Paladin only to weaken on the eve of the decisive battle, the gods having tempted us with the siren call of love.'

'I *could* say that I warned you beforehand,' began Uldini haughtily, only to hesitate on seeing Ahren's glowering stare. 'But I shall magnanimously refrain from doing so,' he added through gritted teeth.

'The main thing is, we are in a similar strategic situation as we found ourselves in during the Night of Blood,' murmured Jelninolan sadly.

'Look at it from the deities' point of view. They want to make sure that there will be a new generation of Paladins if the assault on the Obsidian Fortress fails or if several Champions of the gods fall in battle,' mused Trogadon, puffing on his pipe. 'Hence the abundance of soul companions.'

'If *that* is their plan then it is as full of holes as so many of their other ones,' countered Ahren. 'Hakanu, Lyssin and I, for example, will arrive at the Ring *without* any offspring. If we should die there, well...' He said no more as Khara squeezed his hand with some force.

Uldini hadn't failed to spot the gesture. 'It was *your* Paladin who instigated this discussion,' he said to the Swordsmistress. 'Now we need to talk about possible unpleasant eventualities.'

'The tradition among us Paladins has been – ever since soul companions have come into existence – as follows,' began Falk in a calm voice as he looked directly at Ahren. 'Those who have already chosen a successor protect the others who do not yet possess one. In other words, we who have children can, if we are mortally wounded, pass on our Blessing by means of an Ancient, thereby keeping our life spark alive for as long as is necessary. Therefore, we are...more expendable than you others.'

'But such a procedure is nothing short of immoral!' protested Hakanu, squeezing Kamaluq tight. 'No Paladin can be more valuable than another.'

At last, Ahren recognised a hint of responsibility in the bearing of his protégé, which he had missed ever since Hakanu had lost his Fox Guards. It seemed that it was only the lad's concern for others that managed to quench the burning desire for heroic action, which seemed so often to flare up in the heart of the young warrior.

'This strategy has been forged through bitter experience,' commented Uldini darkly. 'Should we fail at the Ring, those Paladins who cannot pass on their Blessings must be kept alive at all costs.'

'Jelninolan?' asked Ahren weakly, already knowing the answer, however. Rationally, there was no other solution apart from the one that Falk had just described.

The elf swallowed hard. 'We are discussing the worst-case scenario,' she said. 'If even only one Paladin falls, our entire assault on the Adversary collapses immediately – for there will be no Thirteen again to take him on.'

Ahren rubbed his forehead. 'Right,' he said with a sigh. 'All thirteen must confront the Adversary together or we call the whole thing off. Those with offspring protect the others who are still childless.' He massaged his temples with the tips of his fingers. 'Imagine the thirteen of us *do* make it as far as the Dark god. What happens then?'

'You swing your swords at Him for as long as it takes for Him to die,' suggested Trogadon, wiggling his bushy eyebrows knowingly. 'Experience tells me that this tactic can be very effective.'

Ahren smiled indulgently at the dwarf before looking expectantly at Uldini and Jelninolan. 'Is that right?' he asked. 'Is it really as simple as that?'

'You *know* the answer,' countered Uldini, snorting irritably when Ahren didn't react. 'We simply have no idea.'

'WHAT?' asked Hakanu, aghast.

'Previously we twelve were able to wound the Adversary with our weapons, but He rose up again and again,' said Falk. 'Over a dozen times we forced Him to the ground, but He refused to die. It was only after the Ancients had erected the Pall Pillar, and we hemmed Him in with our weapons that his body finally dispersed before being absorbed by the blackness of the pillar.

'His incorporeality is history now, too, by the way,' snarled Uldini through gritted teeth. 'Ever since our arrival back from the Ice fields, HE, WHO FORCES is bestriding Jorath again.'

'It is, to put it bluntly, only hope – albeit considerable – on our part that the thirteen Paladins possess enough power to prevent the Adversary from rising again after suffering a mortal wound,' explained Jelninolan in little more than a whisper.

'But this isn't enough!' exclaimed Ahren. 'We must have *some* sort of clue, *some* sort of idea regarding how we can use our gods' Blessings against the Dark god! What do we do if our weapons against Him prove *ineffective*? If, in fact, we need to have performed a ritual or something beforehand? Or if there is a prayer that we need to intone, or…'

'Then the gods would have revealed these to us a long, long time ago,' murmured Jelninolan, 'during the time when they sent out the first Paladins – or, at the very latest, in the centuries that immediately followed.'

'This is why we are assuming that our weapons and our combined gods' Blessings will be sufficient,' said Falk. 'You have not yet experienced it, Ahren. When all thirteen Paladins are united, the feeling of exhilaration is indescribable. I am firmly convinced that the Adversary will not be able to defeat us if we stand united before Him.'

'And this is where we come to our second question – how do we prevent the Adversary from instigating a second Night of Blood?' asked Khara anxiously.

'We cannot do that,' said Uldini, Ahren noticing how Falk flinched on hearing those words. 'To claim otherwise would be a bare-faced lie. We can only do all in our power to prepare for the inevitable counterattack and to delay him sufficiently until all our energies are bundled together in the one spot.'

'Which will inevitably cause a Night of Blood,' added Trogadon, tapping the remains of his tobacco into the fire.

'As has been said, we will not be able to prevent it,' said Jelninolan, confirming Uldini's statement.

'However, our opening position is far better this time,' explained the Arch Wizard, now staring at Falk, who was nervously clenching his fists. 'Ahren's friend Likis has transformed Deepstone into a fortress – with a castle included. The Blue Cohorts, the Night Soldiers and several Ancients are already holding fort there – not to mention at least three Paladins.'

Muai snarled.

'*And* their companion animals,' chuckled Khara, translating for the big cat. 'Many of them blame themselves for the death of the Thirteenth and are intent on not making the same mistake twice.'

This news surprised Ahren. Never before had he considered the fact that the old Paladins' animals had endured the Night of Blood too – with all the dreadful consequences that had unfolded following the death of his predecessor.

Poor Muai, said Culhen. At first Ahren thought that he had misheard, but then the wolf got to his feet, went over to the cat and began cleaning behind her ears, which the feline acknowledged by means of a low growl.

'Now Kamaluq wants to be spoiled as well,' said Hakanu with a chuckle, before placing the struggling fox on the ground. In no time at all the three companion animals were a wet, squirming coil of fur, paws and tongues.

'That one night resulted in so many scars,' whispered Ahren with a shudder.

'And scars can prevent one from moving with the necessary agility – both physically and mentally,' murmured Khara, looking anxiously at Falk, who was gazing into the fire.

Jelninolan shook her head sadly. 'We Ancients are also not entirely innocent of the Thirteenth's death. We assured the Paladins that they were secure under the protection of our charms – that the Adversary would not be able to sense them.'

'And we were wrong,' added Uldini bitterly.

Falk pursed his lips but said nothing.

Ahren remembered what had happened next from the previous stories that he'd heard. There had been a final, fatalistic uprising by the remaining Paladins against the Adversary. In this they were assisted by the Ancients, who created the Pall Pillar, the Dark god finally being well and truly buried beneath their wizardly sorcery.

And that was followed by the great falling-out, he thought. *The Paladins scattered to all corners of Jorath, while the Ancients licked their wounds in their towers, in exotic palaces or in the depths of the forests.*

Our task is complex, said Culhen, ceasing his grooming of Muai and fixing his golden eyes on Ahren. *First, we must prevent a massacre like the Night of Blood, or the unity of Paladins and gods will be shattered –*

probably for ever. No rational living being could survive such horrors a second time. It has taken eight hundred years, not to mention you, to gather the Paladins again. In the event of such a catastrophe, they would shatter like brittle glass.

Ahren nodded. He gazed first at Falk, whose wrinkled yet stoical features seemed to match the faint grey of his eyes. Then the young man turned his attention to Uldini, who was kneading his hands nervously, before his gaze settled on Jelninolan, who couldn't hide the deep scepticism that she was feeling. The Forest Guardian then exchanged looks with Trogadon, the dwarf nodding knowingly at him as he skilfully refilled his pipe with fresh tobacco. Finally, Ahren looked at Khara, the Swordsmistress smiling confidently back at him.

We three, who are free of memories pertaining to the bloodbath of that distant night, are going to have to protect the others, said Ahren in silence, summarising this realisation both for himself and for his wolf. *We are going to have to be the bulwark against which the Adversary's rabble will smash to pieces.*

Culhen's doughty determination allied itself to his own, and Ahren suddenly believed that he could move mountains by dint sheer willpower alone.

And after that, announced the wolf with all the dignity of an Alpha, *after that, we will free Jorath from the evil of the Dark god, so that no living being will ever feel fear again, and all will be able to forge plans for their future lives, unhindered.*

Chapter 3

Ahren had hoped that the open discussion of their most urgent problems would have improved the mood among the group, but the opposite was the case. Almost all his companions had been brooding silently for days now, while Ahren hadn't failed to notice Uldini and Jelninolan conjuring up and rejecting plans again and again without ever discussing them.

It almost seems to me as if the Adversary has already won – even though all the Paladins have been tracked down and are now united, muttered Culhen in frustration before shaking himself violently, almost throwing Ahren from his saddle in the process.

They spent the whole time searching for the missing Champions of the gods, and now all the worries that they had suppressed are rising to the surface, explained Ahren. *Think of how often Uldini and Falk have lectured us on the importance of taking one step at a time on our long journey. Now that we have almost arrived at our destination, they are finding it hard not to worry about the chasm at the end of the route that we will somehow have to traverse.*

Let's have a rest, suggested Culhen. *A full tummy will do us all good.*

Ahren chuckled. *Especially, you.*

I am only thinking of our friends, countered the wolf snippily.

'Let us pause for a while and have something to eat,' Ahren called out to the others.

'The idea of a small fire and a little stew doesn't sound half bad,' said Trogadon, winking knowingly at the Forest Guardian. 'Especially, considering that Evergreen's warm embrace will soon be behind us.' The blacksmith pointed south to where the Knight Marshes began, hardly a hundred paces further on, its coldness almost tangible in the wan moonlight. They had travelled as far east in Eathinian as was possible, and now they would have to continue their journey outside the charmed forest.

'Good idea,' said Uldini. 'Let us postpone the inevitable for a little longer.'

Ahren ignored the ambiguity of the Arch Wizard's words as with practised hands he built a small fire, using the fallen branches of a nearby tree. 'Which of you would like a portion of —?' only to jump backwards with a curse as a flame suddenly flared up.

'Damn it, Uldini – where *are* you all hiding?' It was Quin-Wa's furious voice intoning from the burning wood. On hearing her mistress, Muai raised her head and purred delightedly. 'The Adversary is constantly badgering the Ring with His treacherous little curses, and the Ancients have their hands full trying to counter his magic from the Wizardly Domes.'

'It *is* clear to you, is it not, that HE, WHO FORCES can hear us?' asked Uldini angrily. 'And that he will be able to locate us through *your* magic?'

Quin-Wa's snort was magnified by the crackling of the fire. 'I am no beginner,' she retorted. 'It's taken me four days to prepare this spell – and to adapt it with regard to the danger you have mentioned. As soon as the first branch has turned to ashes, you *must* extinguish the flames. But your every word is secure until then.'

Silently, Ahren picked up a waterskin and uncorked it. Khara, Hakanu, Falk and Trogadon did the same, the little group forming a circle of nervous guards, their eyes fixed on the fire before them. Ahren noticed that the wood was being consumed with unnatural speed thanks to the heat.

'You had better hurry,' he said to the still hesitant Uldini.

'We are still in Eathinian,' the Arch Wizard finally replied. 'Our route will take us through the Knight Marshes and the eastern part of Hjalgar before we reach Deepstone at the Ring.'

'Delightful,' said Quin-Wa cuttingly. 'Perhaps you would like to make a little detour via King's Island while you're at it. They say that the Silver Cliff is always worth a visit at this time of year, too.'

'We had to split up,' retorted Uldini. 'I sent a message on the matter already.'

'Had the Paladins merely maintained a distance of five furlongs from each other, that would undoubtedly have sufficed,' snarled Quin-Wa.

Out of the corner of his eye, Ahren could see how Uldini was clenching his fists. 'I couldn't take the risk. Or would *you* like to be responsible for a cunning ambush on the part of the Adversary destroying the laborious efforts of centuries so close to our goal?'

The loud crack of a burning branch caused Ahren to flinch. Trogadon already had his waterskin at the ready as he prepared to empty its contents onto the fire, but the Paladin stopped him.

'Not yet,' he whispered, pointing down at the scorched branches that had not yet fully disintegrated. 'We still have a few heartbeats.'

'How is everyone?' asked Falk urgently.

'Fine.'

It was all too easy for Ahren to imagine Quin-Wa irritably rolling her eyes as she responded to the question.

'There is no reason for you *not* to believe me. After all, I am spending my time surrounded by pregnant or breastfeeding soul companions and Paladins. I can hardly hear myself think with all the idle chatter assaulting my ears.'

Falk breathed a sigh of relief.

'Faster,' Ahren murmured to Uldini, pointing down at a burning branch that was glowing a reddish-white as it began to disintegrate. It was as if an alien force were trying to suck all the life out of its flame. Ahren understood all too well, whose power it was that was tugging at the tongues of fire.

'We are certainly going to need another six weeks before we get to Highstone,' said Uldini firmly. 'Unless you are about to tell me that the Ancients in the Wizardly Domes will be unable to withstand the enemy sorcery for that long.'

'Six weeks!' Quin-Wa's voice echoed with a mixture of frustration and resignation. 'That will be tight, but I will make sure that the Ancients somehow hold out. Please beware of—.'

Whatever it was that the Eternal Empress had intended to say, it was swallowed up by the hissing sounds of a fire being extinguished as the branch that Ahren had indicated to turned into ash while Ahren and his friends used their waterskins to put out the flames of the fire. The darkness of the night seemed deeper than before, indeed almost tangible, Ahren sensing that invisible claws were reaching out for him.

Jelninolan whispered some words which still carried a trace of the power that had so recently possessed her, and the impenetrable blackness gave way to a cheerfully glittering starlit sky. 'What Quin-Wa did there was risky,' said the priestess solemnly. 'She must be greatly concerned about the Ancients.'

Uldini caused *Flamestar* to light up and illuminate their encampment as he chewed thoughtfully on his lower lip. 'Each of our decisions can bring us closer to victory – or to defeat,' he groaned in frustration.

'Just to reassure you – I think it was right that our group split up,' said Jelninolan gently. 'The fact that the Dark god is concentrating on our defenders at the Ring is a good sign. It seems that He is planning on holding out behind His high walls until His magic exhausts the Ancients and decimates the soldiers at the Ring – at which point He will break forth with His army.'

Khara cocked her head thoughtfully. 'Might He fear an ambush?' she asked. 'If He really *is* unable to locate the travelling Paladins on their various routes, perhaps He suspects that you are only waiting for Him to leave the Obsidian Fortress so that you can trap Him as soon as He finds himself in a vulnerable position.'

'Possibly,' said Falk, smiling wanly. 'The thought that the Adversary is just as afraid of us as we are of Him appeals to me. And that He, like us, is trying to second-guess our plan.'

Ahren sighed. 'This stumbling around in the dark isn't getting us anywhere. The greatest service we can do for the women and men at the Ring is to get there as quickly as we can – and in one piece.'

The night was drawing to a close and Ahren was standing at the edge of Evergreen, looking pensively out onto the frost-covered Knight Marshes. The contoured landscape glistened in the moonlight – it was as though the broad fields, distant castles and modest farmsteads were under the influence of a mighty spell.

'So, this is where you've been hiding,' whispered Khara from behind him. Ahren turned his head. His beloved had approached from the encampment, a woollen blanket draped over her shoulders and wrapped closely around her. 'Evergreen is finding it difficult to resist the coldness of the Knight Marshes,' she quipped as she stopped beside the Forest Guardian and leaned into him. When Ahren didn't respond, she squeezed his hand. 'What is troubling you?'

Ahren nodded towards the Knight Marshes. 'I asked Culhen to have a look around. All that talk about ambushes has made me nervous – but he was unable to sense any Dark Ones in our immediate surroundings.'

'But that's good, isn't it?'

Ahren frowned. 'But he found hardly any signs of life either. Whole villages seem to be deserted.' He looked towards a lonely watchtower on the border to Evergreen, which seemed to rise in the distance like a warning finger. 'Even the fortifications seem to be bereft of occupants.'

Khara gently turned his head with the fingertips of her free hand. 'Because you have created an alliance worthy of its name,' she reminded him. 'Why should the Knight Marshes station valuable soldiers on the towers that are guarding the borders to her allies?'

'And the empty villages?' Ahren hated the doubt that he could hear in his own voice. He felt the weight of the world on his shoulders, and he feared that one false move on his part could bring about disaster.

'It's the war,' Khara replied simply. 'According to Uldini, once the harvest was complete, everyone capable of bearing a weapon was ordered to the Ring. The rest of the adult population are hiding out with the children in the large towns and most spacious castles. The riders of the Green Sea are the only ones entrusted with protecting travellers in the hinterlands of the realms bordering the Ring from any Dark Ones not louring in the Obsidian Fortress.'

Ahren nodded. 'Of course. Both sides are gathering for the one final shuddering clash.'

Khara shifted her weight impatiently from one foot to the other. 'It does not come down to who *begins* the attack in a battle – but rather, which attack *ends* the confrontation.'

Ahren gazed out into the bleak wintery night of the Knight Marshes, which lay before them as if bereft of all life. 'You know as well as I do that sometimes it only takes the first blow to ensure victory.' He hugged Khara close to him. 'And I fear that if we are not quick enough, then it will not be *us* who strike it.'

Their ride out of Evergreen proved as dismal as Ahren had feared it would be. Jelninolan played a quiet, endlessly repeating melody, which she had promised would shield them from any dangers caused by malignant sorcerous senses that were trying to track them down. And so, they rode south, past deserted farms that lay empty and silent under the morning frost – like corpses on a vast battlefield. The occasional soaring castles that they encountered were, on the other hand, packed with old people, children, and those unfortunate wounded who had returned to their homeland in the hope of offering whatever help they were still capable of giving.

'We had better stick to ourselves,' advised Uldini as Ahren began to lead the travel party towards one of the grey strongholds. 'Jelninolan's spell is protecting us from the prying eyes of the Adversary, and I do not want to run the risk of rumours reaching Him regarding our present location – whether it be through one of His spies or by virtue of local gossips only too eager to tell the world that they have had the privilege of meeting three Paladins.'

'Aren't you being a little extreme?' suggested Trogadon, who was stretching his back as he sat on his little pony.

Ahren could tell from the patient animal that it would love to have been able to do the same.

'Indeed, a less far-sighted individual might consider our entire travel itinerary exaggerated,' countered the Arch Wizard forcefully. 'One security precaution more is hardly going to change things much.'

They took their break, therefore, in one of the abandoned farmhouses, eating their cold midday meal in gloomy silence.

I'm already missing Eathinian, complained Culhen, who was chewing on a bone that he had discovered in one of the otherwise bare storerooms.

Things will look up for you soon, said Ahren reassuringly, tousling the fur between the wolf's ears. *I am certain that Likis will have reserved an entire herd of cattle for you in Deepstone.*

Culhen licked his drooling chops. *Oh, yes – that sounds like him alright! Hopefully, we'll be there soon.*

Ahren enjoyed the moments of banter with Culhen. They distracted him from his worries, and not for the first time he wondered if the wolf was deliberately trying to divert his attention to other, more trivial matters.

His other companions, too, seemed to concentrate on innocuous topics of conversation – it was as if no-one had the *courage* to articulate that which was lying ahead of them before finally reaching Deepstone and with that the Ring.

Day after day they rode further south, and with every league that they journeyed, the momentousness of the war became more evident. The entire Knight Marshes seemed to be holding its breath, waiting with nervous anticipation for the battle against the Adversary to begin. Travelling merchants were few and far between, the little group making sure to steer well clear of any that they noticed, while the only other signs of life consisted of scattered bands of highway robbers, who chose to stay well away from the clearly well-armed travel party. A quick exchange of glances was enough to ensure a rapid retreat into the undergrowth on the part of the ne'er-do-wells.

'How I would so much like to teach them a lesson,' grunted Ahren as once again a handful of scrawny figures with cudgels and primitive bows sought refuge behind a hill, having noticed that Ahren and his companions were no easy pickings.

'You would only be treating a symptom, but not the disease itself,' scolded Falk. 'The Ring is swallowing up enormous amounts of provisions and drawing all the knights of the realm. Once the war has been won, both will be returning from the front, and the highwaymen and -women will vanish, just like the starvation and the defencelessness of the populace.'

Ahren nodded silently and rode grimly onwards towards the Ring.

He was standing on a desolate field. All around him were nothing but ruined buildings and scattered skeletons dressed in rusty armour, their lifeless fingers still holding their long since broken weapons, which they had desperately wielded before falling dead to the ground. There was no sun and no sky – only an all-encompassing mass of seething clouds that overshadowed the never-ending war between the Paladins and the Adversary, which had started so many thousands of years before – or had it been *tens* of thousands? Ahren had been fighting for so long that he had lost all sense of time.

Beside him, the First was fighting a Glower Bear, the veteran's movements mechanically repeating themselves as he sent the monster crashing to the ground, only for it to rise again every time, the old man muttering again and again under his breath: 'Our mission is not yet complete. Our mission is not yet complete.'

A shiver running down his spine, Ahren turned around and saw an aged man who seemed completely insane in his Deep Steel Armour and holding a glittering spear while engaged in a morbid circular dance of death with a long-dead Sicklehopper, feinting and stabbing in an endless cycle.

'Eternally enduring is the lot of the Champions of the gods,' croaked the fellow, Ahren realising to his horror that it was none other than Hakanu who was speaking.

Ahren, now panic-stricken, spun around on his axis in an attempt to look away from the dreadful sight, only to spot Falk kneeling before a line of graves, his head bowed. One of the headstones bore Onja's name, while another had Khara written on it, with a phrase carved underneath: *Farewell, my love – only the Paladins remain alive, fighting forever.*

Ahren tore at his hair with both hands and screamed with all the power he could summon – he screamed until a distant, yet instantly recognisable voice called out to him.

'Wake up!'

Ahren was shaken into consciousness by the sheer terror caused by his nightmare. He sat up, his heart hammering violently in his chest.

He and his companions were lying in the barn of a half-ruined estate, which was now being run only by a blind, amicable manager with the assistance of a lame kitchen maid. Apart from the Forest Guardian only Culhen was awake, the wolf standing at the entrance door and peering through the cracks between the warped wooden timbers, observing the snow-covered landscape with its white fields and scattered leafless coppices, everything cast in the weak light of the moon.

It is she, said the wolf solemnly, filling Ahren's mind with a vision of a woman standing patiently beside a black-furred Hanta on a frost-covered field. She was looking up to the heavens while the snow fell silently all around her.

Ahren's racing heart calmed a little as anxiety and hope struggled with equal force within his breast. The Woman in Black was waiting for him. Whenever she turned up, weal and woe were closely intertwined.

Go to her, he advised Culhen. *Greet Camentumar. He will be delighted to see a familiar face.*

Culhen pushed his nose against the barndoor, opened it as gently as possible and slipped outside, while Ahren got to his feet and put on his cloak. Neither Uldini nor Falk trusted the Woman in Black, who had only as yet spoken to Khara or him. For a heartbeat he wondered if he should wake up the Swordsmistress, but then decided against it. If her dreams had remained undisturbed, then this night-time visitation must have been meant for him alone. He, too, slipped out, closing the door carefully behind him.

His hide is as black as the woman's dress, said Culhen in surprise before exchanging worthy looks with the Hanta.

It seemed to Ahren that the two companion animals were trying to calculate if they could defeat the other in the event of a skirmish. Finally,

Camentumar snorted and bowed his head for a moment, as if he were nodding politely. A heartbeat later and Culhen had done the same.

He seems wilder somehow, murmured the wolf anxiously. *More dangerous.*

Ahren sensed the aversion that his friend was feeling.

More like a Dark One.

Ahren froze momentarily, his eyes scanning the Woman in Black and her companion more keenly. The stranger's back had stiffened, and her shoulders seemed cramped. She had her arms crossed in front of her, and even from ten paces, Ahren could see in the wan moonlight that she was tense. Having decided that Culhen presented no danger, Camentumar was looking instead from left to right and from right to left. Wherever his now coal-black fur was not protected by plates of armour, it seemed to be full of dried blood.

The two of them are afraid, thought Ahren, this realisation causing his own anxiety to increase with a force that he had never experienced before. This was the same woman who had, without batting an eyelid, thrown herself and the hunter over the bridge in Thousand Halls. If the stranger was truly afraid – then Ahren could do nothing but share her feeling.

'Why is it only now that you are standing before me again?' he asked in greeting. 'There were moments on the Ice Fields when I could really have done with both your help and your advice.'

The stranger shook her head, a movement as gentle as a spider's web swaying easily in a warm summer breeze. 'I had to gather my strength,' she said. 'My assistance the last time – well, let us say that it did not go unnoticed.' A shiver ran down her spine, powerful enough for Ahren to clearly observe it. 'As soon as…' she was struggling to speak now, and her fear was almost tangible. 'As soon as I *involve* myself the next time, my role will become clear.'

'You mean that then the Adversary will know on *whose* side you are?' murmured Ahren. He had his own suspicions regarding the Woman in Black, but until now he had said nothing about them. But the time for secrecy was slowly coming to an end, like everything else that concerned the war against the Dark god.

'You are correct.'

Ahren was dumbfounded. He had expected almost anything – a furious denial, a long-winded explanation, even an angry stomping away.

But the fact that she had simply confirmed his suspicion that she was in league with the Adversary stunned him. 'Are you a High Fang?' he asked.

A slight hesitation. 'No.'

Only a half-truth then, thought Ahren. *She is still keeping her big secret to herself.*

Her presence is a danger, warned Culhen. *If the Adversary is able to track her down, then He can perhaps do the same with us – through her.*

Ahren glanced back at the barn. Uldini had been most insistent with his warnings. Just as Jelninolan had hidden the group during the day with her sorcerous melody, so too did the Arch Wizard protect them from discovery at night by means of a charm circle. The spell was limited to the outhouse, and two Paladins were never to leave the building together for fear of being located. If the same applied to one Paladin in the presence of a servant to the Adversary, then…

'He *cannot* sense me,' said the stranger, correctly reading his anxious look. 'I have made sure of that.' She glanced towards the east. 'I am safe until the sun rises.'

Ahren pursed his lips. 'Does the Adversary control you?' he asked.

'Sometimes.'

Ahren's cold look was sufficient encouragement for her to continue.

'I try to stretch out for as long as possible any minor task He gives me – so that He employs other servants for His darker schemes. In this way, I win for myself some limited…freedom, during which times He forgets about me.' She laughed. It was a dark, joyless sound. 'Which He does quite often, in fact.'

Ahren, she has just admitted to being an active servant to the Adversary, said Culhen in alarm. *Who can say how many soldiers she already has on her conscience?*

I know. But I will only condemn her when I have some more details. She deserves that much at least, having already saved our lives so often.

Uldini will be enraged if he finds out about this, warned Culhen. *And Falk is hardly likely to heap praise on you either.*

Ahren reached for the wolf's ears and began tickling them reassuringly, the action calming down the animal significantly and causing him to growl with enjoyment.

Camentumar shook his head, the Woman in Black then looking at the Hanta.

'Now?' she asked. 'Are you serious?' Then she sighed and hugged the animal by placing her arms around his neck.

This gesture softened Ahren's antipathy like a ray of sunshine melts the frost on a snowbound meadow in winter. 'Why are you here?' he asked, the compassion in his voice surprising even himself. Despite Camentumar's gloomy appearance and the feeling of wildness that he radiated, the Hanta seemed less driven than in the immediate aftermath of Blazing Eyes' death. For this alone, the Woman in Black had earned – despite her admission – a little leeway at least.

The stranger kept her eyes fixed on Camentumar, who was pushing hard against her. 'You must not travel to the Ring,' she said. 'Not yet.'

Ahren looked at her in astonishment. 'And why that exactly?'

'There is some news that you must hear.'

Ahren crossed his arms. 'I'm listening.'

She shook her head. 'Not from me. From a ghost.'

His inner resistance began to increase despite the good will he was feeling towards her. 'Are you a necromancer perhaps, who can communicate with the dead?'

She threw him a tortured look, which pierced through her veil and held his eyes like prisoners. 'Does the name *Belsarius* mean anything to you?'

Ahren blinked in utter astonishment. 'An Ancient, long since deceased,' he said after a pause as he tried to recall what little he had learned about the man whom Uldini had admired beyond all measure. 'They say he was a genius among the Ancients.'

'Indeed, he was,' said the woman sadly. 'I have never heard anyone say a bad word about him. No small achievement in itself.'

'You *knew* him?' asked Ahren.

'Alas, no. But I would have loved to have met him. Some things would perhaps have developed...differently.'

Ahren ground his teeth as his patience began to wear thin. 'I am trying to respect your penchant for ambiguity as much as I can, but unless your words will soon begin to make sense, my group and I will continue on our journey to Deepstone when day breaks.'

The Woman in Black continued to stroke Camentumar, and Ahren was not sure which of the pair was finding the gesture more soothing.

'How are the Paladins planning on subjugating the Adversary?' she asked. 'Are you going to stab Him until He breathes his last?'

Ahren flinched. There it was again, the open wound that he had been carrying with him for some time now. 'According to what knowledge we have, that *should* work,' he replied cautiously.

Beware, warned Culhen. *Maybe the Adversary can pluck information from her mind at will.*

If He could do that, she would be long since dead, countered the Paladin. *She helped us out of hopeless situations so often, don't forget.*

'Belsarius worked on this question,' said the Woman in Black. 'Long before the Night of Blood – when the world still harboured hope for a seamless end to this never-ending war.' The bitterness in her voice was unmistakable.

Ahren's scepticism was growing. 'How is it that you, of all people, know of his investigations, but none of the other Ancients do? Especially as according to yourself you never met Belsarius.'

The Woman in Black's hands suddenly stopped their stroking movement, but still she kept her eyes fixed on Camentumar – it was as if she did not want Ahren to notice any stirring of emotion from beneath her veil. 'It took me centuries to discover that Belsarius was trying to find an answer to the mystery of how the Paladins could use their gods' Blessings to extinguish the Adversary. And several more centuries to locate the place where he was doing his research.' She stroked the Hanta again, her body language clearly suggesting that she had gotten herself under control again. 'My interests did not lie in Belsarius himself. But he was posing the same questions as I was, and so his hunt became mine, too.'

'And what did he find out?' asked Ahren.

Now the woman's hands fell limply beside her, as if they had been suddenly afflicted by a terrible world-weariness. 'I do not know,' she whispered. 'His knowledge is contained within his Sanctum. Beyond my reach.'

Ahren narrowed his eyes. 'He secured his knowledge with a charm, did he not? One that the servants of the Dark god could not penetrate.'

The Woman in Black nodded. 'This magic circle does not distinguish between intent and allegiance,' she admitted dolefully. 'It judges as severely as does the rest of the world.'

It all sounds too wishy-washy to me, interjected Culhen. *And have you noticed that her story of a so-called Sanctum will tempt us away from the Ring – and with promises of knowledge and power to boot?* The wolf pressed his nose against Ahren's cheek. *This is exactly what a servant of the Adversary would do to distract us or even to lure us into a trap. What if, at this moment, she is not herself at all? Would we even notice if that were the case?*

Ahren found it impossible to sweep away his friend's doubts. Could he afford to trust the words of the Woman in Black? Indeed, could he afford *not* to?

'Where is this Sanctum to be found?' he asked abruptly.

The sense of relief on the part of the stranger was impossible to miss. 'In Kelkor,' she said. 'In a little, secluded valley, hidden in the side of a mountain, forty leagues north of the Silver Cliff.'

Kelkor, thought Ahren. *The land of monsters and giants.*

And goblins and fays, added Culhen. *Don't forget – that's where we picked up Tlik.*

Ahren's heart was sore as he remembered the ugly goblin and the ultimate sacrifice that the little fellow had made. *A land teeming with friends and enemies,* thought the Forest Guardian. *No other part of Jorath has so many Dark Ones – apart from the Southern Jungles and the Obsidian Fortress.*

The perfect spot for an ambush, added Culhen.

'I cannot decide this alone,' said Ahren after a pause. 'Come in with us and make your request before the others.'

The Woman in Black shook her head forcefully. 'On no account,' she said. 'I know how many of your companions feel about me. Uldini could…well…he could react *impulsively*'.

Ahren shrugged his shoulders. 'Then I will forget that this conversation ever took place, and we will travel on to the Ring.'

'So stubborn,' said the stranger, shaking her head. Then she swung onto Camentumar's back and looked down at Ahren. 'I have said what I have wanted to say,' she announced coldly. 'Indeed, I had hoped to the end that Uldini would eventually try to find answers beyond the confines of his own head. You can do what you think best as far as I am concerned.'

Ahren couldn't miss the annoyance in her voice.

'If truth be told, I am responsible neither for the obstinacy of the Paladins nor for the pig-headedness of the Ancients.' With that, she spun Camentumar around, the Hanta then trotting away before she looked back over her shoulder one last time. 'If you *do* suddenly decide to go to

Kelkor in search of Belsarius' secret, then make sure that Uldini believes it was *his* idea. He loves to have his brilliance confirmed.' With that, she rode off into the fading night before finally disappearing in the murky fog of the approaching dawn.

Camentumar left no tracks behind, muttered Culhen crankily as he sniffed at the untouched hoarfrost on the barren field. *Why didn't the weird woman let you know how she pulled off a trick like that? At least we would then have gotten some information that was really worth knowing.*

Ahren looked thoughtfully to where the stranger had disappeared. *We will decide for ourselves if that which she said is useful or not.*

Culhen's head shot up and he fixed his golden eyes on those of his Paladin. *You are not seriously thinking of going on a wild goose chase in search of some mysterious information belonging to a long dead Ancient, are you?*

Ahren did not reply, trudging back to the barn instead. Culhen uttered a low growl, but then concentrated on listening in on the Forest Guardian's thoughts, the young man making no effort to block him. The simple truth silenced the wolf faster than any argument. A conflict was raging inside his friend's head – between a desperate hope for answers and a terrible fear of some dreadful subterfuge that would lead to catastrophe. The simple fact was this – Ahren had no idea of how to answer Culhen's question.

'A penny for your thoughts.'

Khara's voice and smiling face roused Ahren out of his reverie. Uldini had used *Flamestar* to ensure that the barn was comfortably warm, while Falk had employed his culinary skills to create a hearty stew of peas and bacon from their rapidly dwindling supplies, the smell of which was making the younger Forest Guardian's mouth water.

'I…' he began, before suddenly breaking off as he found himself unable to utter the white lie that had just now come into his head. 'I have to talk to you,' he murmured. 'Alone.'

The Swordsmistress's eyes widened in surprise. She then nodded. 'After breakfast,' she said. 'We can search the farmhouse for provisions, and while we are doing so, you can tell me what is bothering you.'

Ahren squeezed her hand surreptitiously, then noticed Culhen's penetrating stare.

Khara has a clever head on her shoulders, said the Paladin defensively. *I want to hear her opinion. After all, she trusts the Woman in Black more than either Uldini or Falk.*

Now I'm really curious, said Culhen sarcastically. *Especially as you will also be getting Muai's verdict simultaneously – and for free.*

The snarling from the tigress left no room for misinterpretation as Ahren described the Woman in Black's night-time visitation, while the four of them supposedly searched the main farmhouse for food.

'Muai is convinced that we will fall right into a trap if we go to Kelkor,' said Khara with a grin as she pointed to the big cat, who had narrowed her eyes, and whose tail was swinging wildly from one side to the other and back as if she had seen a Dark One.

'I'd never have guessed if you hadn't told me,' Ahren chuckled. 'And in fact, she and Culhen are of one mind for a change.'

Hold on a heartbeat, protested the wolf. *I only said that the words of the Woman in Black might be leading us into an ambush. But of course, I am not the least surprised that this flea-ridden, prejudiced pussy cat immediately suspects a trap.*

Ignoring Culhen's snootiness, Ahren concentrated on Khara's reaction. 'Well? What do you think?'

'The Woman in Black saved me from a condition of utter despair in the Green Sea,' she said after thinking for a few heartbeats, 'and our entire group from perdition on several occasions. Without her, we would never have saved Onja from the Hunger Cadavers.' Khara crossed her arms in a determined gesture. 'I see her as a friend – even if a decidedly eccentric one.'

'She revealed herself to be an enemy of the THREE,' countered Ahren anxiously, 'and admitted that she was a servant of the Adversary.'

Khara shrugged her shoulders. 'Some of our allies in the war against the Obsidian Fortress are pirates and cutthroats. Even Gol-Konar is on the list of places, whose help you would not turn down in our conflict with the Dark god. If the Woman in Black has a reputation as a servant of the Adversary but seems to be repeatedly on *our* side, then that is good enough for me.'

'She *is* right, you know,' said a gravelly, good-natured voice, which caused Ahren to flinch. A heartbeat later and Trogadon was standing in the doorway, an unlit pipe hanging from the corner of his mouth. 'I had no intention of eavesdropping,' he added, his eyes twinkling, 'I only wanted to help "look" for something to eat.' He took the pipe out of his mouth and pointed its stem towards Ahren. 'But your story was much more exciting than that wooden crate of wrinkled white cabbage over there.'

Ahren sighed. 'You believe, too, do you, that we should come up with some vague excuse for veering away from the battlefield?'

Much to Ahren's surprise, the dwarf shook his head. 'We must first separate your newly acquired knowledge from the woman who delivered it,' he said cryptically.

'What do you mean?' asked Khara, leaning against an old stove.

Trogadon proceeded to light his pipe with great deliberation, and Ahren was convinced that his look of concentration didn't concern the activity he was performing with his hands, but rather the words that he now began to utter. 'The Woman in Black ordered you to trick Uldini into pondering over Belsarius and his investigations, isn't that so?'

Ahren nodded.

'Good,' added the dwarf. 'Then this is precisely what we will do.'

'But…' countered Ahren, only for the dwarf to wave a finger in warning.

'We will test the stranger's idea,' said Trogadon. 'Without the identity of the messenger casting a shadow on the actual information.'

Ahren understood and laughed in relief. 'If Uldini, Falk, Hakanu and Jelninolan like the idea of searching for Belsarius' Sanctum, then we will know that the Woman in Black's proposal makes sense. And as soon as they have come to such a conclusion, we can still reveal the risk of an ambush to them.'

'Precisely,' said the dwarf grandiloquently. 'You see how simple life can be when one allows others to take some of the load that weighs heavily on one's shoulders.' His eyes, twinkling anew, spoke volumes.

While Ahren mentally sought for and found Culhen's agreement, he looked over at Khara. When she nodded, his heart skipped with joy. The quartet were united in their belief.

'Then let us figure out how we can steer Uldini's thoughts in the right direction.'

It took another two days of riding through the deserted Knight Marshes before the first opportunity arose for them to subtly begin implementing their plan. It was late evening, and they were all sitting at a simple fireplace in the dining room of a modest hostelry. The taciturn, one-armed landlord and his wife had already retired for the night, and the companions were conversing in hushed tones as they gazed into the flames. The mood was calm and pensive, and Ahren reckoned that now was the ideal time to make his first move.

'Have you come up with any ideas yet on how we can implement our gods' Blessings against the Adversary?' he asked Uldini in a whisper as he leaned in towards the Arch Wizard. 'After all, we *are* getting nearer to the Ring all the time now.' By now, Ahren had concluded that the reason for the Arch Wizard's circuitous eastward route could only be because the childlike figure was trying to win more time for thinking.

'Nothing concrete,' grunted Uldini impatiently. 'But I am considering several options.' He glared sideways at Ahren. 'At least, as long as I am not being disturbed by idiotic questioning the whole time.'

Ahren kept as neutral a face as possible before continuing to speak. 'On the *Queen of the Waves* you told me that Belsarius, too, had concerned himself with this theme. Did he never reveal to you his conclusions on the matter?'

Uldini's eyes welled up with tears as he gazed into the flames. 'We had little opportunity to discuss it. He was killed during a skirmish on the border between Hjalgar and Kelkor.' The Arch Wizard swallowed hard. 'The ambush consisted of three High fangs, a horde of Low Fangs and several giants that had been corrupted by the Adversary.'

Ahren's heart was beating fast now. *Take it nice and easy,* he warned himself. 'And what was he *up* to in Kelkor?'

Uldini shrugged his shoulders. 'He was probably testing out one of his inventions,' he muttered irritably. 'Half his experiments ended in disaster. This was why he always sought out an uninhabited valley whenever he was testing out a new spell or one of his peculiar apparatuses – so that he wouldn't endanger anyone, you understand.'

'Did he not leave behind any drawings?' asked Ahren.

Culhen, who was lying directly in front of the fire, raised his head and gazed at his Paladin. *Very subtle,* he commented with a chuckle.

Uldini isn't exactly making it easy for me, countered the Forest Guardian defensively.

'Of course, he did,' grunted Uldini, his voice becoming yet more irritable. 'He had a chamber on King's Island full to the brim with notes.

After his death, I retrieved them for study purposes.' He sighed gloomily. 'Belsarius' mind was incredibly sharp. It took me years to figure out half of his documents. Indeed, in the end I was left with no choice but to ask Akkad to help me decipher the mechanical aspects.'

Filled with a sudden ray of hope, and unable to stop himself, Ahren blurted out: 'Akkad always tried to emulate Belsarius, too, and he would have known him *longer* than you did. Isn't it possible that the two of *them* discussed the Adversary and how our gods' Blessings might be used against him?'

Uldini's face suddenly resembled a thunder cloud. '*Most* unlikely,' he snarled. 'And now let me *think!*'

Ahren nodded and leaned away again. *That was a bit awkward. Uldini worships Belsarius,* said Culhen, giving Ahren an accusatory look. *Implying that Akkad was perhaps closer to the deceased Ancient wasn't exactly a wise move.*

The Forest Guardian surreptitiously glanced at Uldini, who was pensively rubbing his chin and staring into the fire, as if the flames would provide him with all the answers that he was looking for.

Let's wait and see, said Ahren. *Maybe my little prod was enough to get the ball rolling, so that we will soon have more clarity regarding the Woman in Black's information.*

'Our plan is proving more difficult to implement than I expected,' said Trogadon a few days later as he, Khara and Ahren were once again 'searching for food' in the storeroom of a deserted farmhouse. 'I tried to find out if Jelninolan and Belsarius ever discussed the final battle with the Adversary, but it seems that they did not know each other well enough. Also, my beloved elf wasn't particularly drawn to him as a person, so engrossed was he with the creation of inanimate objects.'

'And Uldini's pride is proving an obstacle,' explained Ahren, waving his arms in frustration. 'He simply *refuses* to accept the possibility that Belsarius might have placed his trust in someone else as well.'

'And if we simply wait until Deepstone before trying to shed light on Belsarius' secrets?' suggested Khara, who was at that moment retrieving two wizened carrots from a brittle wicker basket. 'Just as well that we're soon going to be in Hjalgar,' she said with a shake of her head.

'Hopefully, we will have more chance there of replenishing our stocks. It almost seems as if all foodstuffs in the Knight Marshes have been swept away.'

Ahren drummed his fingers on the dusty table that dominated the cottage kitchen. 'If we first travel to the Ring and then head for Kelkor again, we may well waste moons. The Ancients in their Wizardly Domes will weaken more and more with every extra day that we delay the inevitable showdown in the Obsidian Fortress.'

Trogadon grunted in agreement, and for a while they were all silent, each caught up in their own private thoughts. Then, much to Ahren's puzzlement, a wicked smile appeared on the dwarf's face.

'Time for our secret weapon,' said the blacksmith, rubbing his hands gleefully.

'Master?' asked Hakanu with his usual enthusiasm two days later, while he and Ahren trained in the yard of a deserted farmhouse. 'Is it not *possible* that this *Belsarius* fellow *hid* his drawings regarding the Adversary somewhere? I mean, if they were *really* that important, he would hardly have run the risk of a spy on King's Island getting his hands on them, right?'

Trogadon, who was enjoying the feel of the winter sunshine on his face as he stood in the doorway of the main house, was struggling to stop himself from shaking with laughter as he casually glanced over at Uldini, who was at the west end of the building, drawing his protective overnight charm in the snow. A powerful smell of food being cooked wafted across the yard. Falk and Jelninolan were preparing the meal together, having decided to use the rest of their provisions and, if the aroma was anything to go by, they had added plenty of herbs and spices. Muai, Culhen and Kamaluq had set off to a little wood in the immediate vicinity, where they would hunt for their own food, while Ahren's apprentice had chosen this very moment, in his own impetuous and innocent manner, to draw the Arch Wizard out of his shell.

'Uldini says that he went through all the notes that Belsarius had completed,' Ahren replied as matter-of-factly as possible, launching a succession of downward blows on his apprentice as he spoke, the boy either skilfully batting them away or nimbly evading them. Even when the master tried provoking his young apprentice by presenting what seemed like a possible opening towards a swift victory, Hakanu used the opportunity instead to gain for himself a more advantageous long-term position by moving nimbly to the space between Ahren and the wall of the house. Ahren hoped that Hakanu's failure against the dragon was precisely the mistake that the boy had needed for him to finally understand the difference between bravery and bravado.

'Then he must have looked for his mentor's possible hiding place, right?' asked Hakanu. 'That was *very* clever of him.'

Trogadon, still at the doorway, scowled on hearing the apprentice's clumsy attempt at intrigue. Ahren, Khara and the dwarf had known full well that Hakanu's lack of diplomatic skills, not to mention his generally awkward manner in society, meant that the boy could only be of limited use in their subterfuge, and they were well aware of the risk they were taking in having let him in on their plan. Having gestured to the lad to say no more, Ahren glanced over at the Arch Wizard. If Uldini had overheard their dialogue at all, he certainly wasn't showing any reaction.

'It was worth a try,' the Forest Guardian whispered to his apprentice. 'But let's wait a while before casting another bait.'

Hakanu nodded, then launched an attack, using his spear with some skill, and with an impressive awareness of his surroundings and of how to shift his own body. Ahren saw Khara nodding approvingly, her gesture giving him a sense of relief. She was observing the boy's progress and had confirmed the Forest Guardian's belief that in this regard at least, he had one less thing to worry about when it came to the assault on the Obsidian fortress.

When Ahren, Hakanu and Khara entered the parlour of the farmhouse that evening after their exhausting training sessions, they were greeted by an unexpected sight. Uldini was sitting cross-legged in the middle of a complex charm circle that took up half the floorspace. He was mumbling to himself and staring into *Flamestar,* which was hovering in front of his eyes.

'What's going on here?' asked Ahren, deliberately playing dumb.

'You know full well what,' said Jelninolan, grinning. 'After all, you and your apprentice have been abusing Uldini for days now with your non-stop references to Belsarius and his supposed bolthole.' She stared hard at the Forest Guardian. 'Wherever *that* idea came from.'

'Does it matter as long as it is a good one?' asked Trogadon, the picture of innocence as he placed his arm around the elf's waist. 'It *is* a good idea, isn't it?' he added quietly.

Jelninolan gave the stew another stir, making sure it wouldn't stick to the pot before passing on the wooden spoon to Ahren so that he could continue. 'As long as it isn't merely a flight of fancy – then, yes, it is. The idea that Belsarius had more insight into the Adversary than is generally known is certainly attractive.'

'Let us just let Uldini at it,' said Falk, throwing Ahren a look of disappointment. 'Then this little farce here won't have been a complete waste of time. Either he will confirm that this hideaway really *does* exist, or we can *all* forget what a certain woman has whispered into your ear.'

Ahren thrust out his chin belligerently. 'I only want to make sure that we don't make a major mistake just before our assault on the Obsidian Fortress. And if that means coping with Uldini's pride in a devious manner, then so be it.'

Falk pursed his lips and raised his eyebrows. 'You may thank the THREE that Selsena is on your side this time. 'Because she unexpectedly fell asleep on the day in question, it was some time afterwards that she sensed what the night-time visit was all about. Lucky for you, she has only now let me in on what happened.'

An almost apologetic snorting could be heard coming from outside.

'Our little charade has been somewhat of a disaster,' murmured Khara to her beloved. 'The only one who still seems to be in the dark is Uldini.'

Ahren pulled over a chair for himself and dutifully continued to stir the stew. Trying to keep a secret in this group for any length of time seemed an impossibility, yet strangely enough, Ahren found this thought rather reassuring. 'Well, are we all agreed?' he asked the others in a low voice. 'If a certain someone can ascertain the existence of Belsarius' Sanctum, will we pay it a visit on our way to the Ring?'

Falk crossed his arms firmly in front of his chest. 'And where exactly is it – *supposedly?*'

'In Kelkor,' said Khara, replying before Ahren had a chance to.

'Just near enough for it to be worth a try, while also being far enough for us to waste precious time,' interjected Jelninolan anxiously.

Ahren shrugged his shoulders apologetically. 'Hence our attempt to get information from…well…you-know-who…in a somewhat irregular manner.'

'You would do better to concentrate on the stew,' growled Falk. 'Jelninolan and I have created a veritable masterpiece out of the bits and pieces we had available.'

'We are going to have to stock up on provisions in the next larger settlement or castle that we reach,' said Trogadon. 'Only a few of us should go – in disguise, too – so that we can allay Uldini's concern that we might be recognised.'

'If we are really going to end up travelling to Kelkor, then we may as well venture into a town or city,' countered Falk. 'The Adversary is never going to expect us to be running *away* rather than *towards* Him.'

'Are you certain?' asked Uldini at that moment, barking loudly into the depths of *Flamestar*. 'Then fetch him forthwith!' he snarled to the unfortunate person in the distance that was at the receiving end of his magic.

Ahren listened to the Arch Wizard, while he was happy to observe, out of the corner of his eye, that all his friends had also focused their attention on Uldini. Only the furry faction of their little group lay in a ball of hair and paws, sleeping the sleep of the righteous, while – not for the first time – Ahren was thankful that Selsena was with the travel party again, her empathetic senses being capable of alerting the companions to approaching danger.

'Shut your trap and listen to me,' growled Uldini suddenly as he gesticulated at *Flamestar*. 'Akkad says that Belsarius frequently used to retire to a particular valley in Kelkor. Do you know *why?*' Whatever the answer was, the veins on Uldini's temples began to pulsate dangerously. 'Of *course,* it's my business!' he snarled at his opposite number. 'It is *everyone's* business here! Did it ever occur to you that Belsarius may have stored things in this Sanctum that might be *useful* to…' Uldini fell silent, presumably interrupted by his counterpart. 'I understand,' he said curtly. 'Yes – we shall see one another soon. Farewell.' Then he waved his hand and *Flamestar* sank to the floor, the flame within it having gone out.

'The last part didn't sound good,' said Hakanu unnecessarily, his comment being met with a frosty stare from his master.

Uldini, meanwhile, got to his feet and turned to his companions only to stop dead in surprise. 'What is going on here? Since when have my communications via crystal ball been a matter of general interest?'

'Well, it's impossible not to be curious, given the complex charm circle,' said Khara calmly as she nodded down towards the drawing on the floor.

'Security precautions,' muttered Uldini defensively. 'I wanted to conduct a similarly open discussion as Quin-Wa did some days ago but without resorting to her criminally reckless fire charm.'

Muai growled half-heartedly. Had she not been lying half asleep on her back and penned in between the fox and the wolf, her verbal complaint would undoubtedly have been more terrifying.

Ahren cleared his throat. 'What did you ask about?'

'What about indeed?' snarled Uldini. 'What is it that you have been assaulting my ears with for days now?'

'And?' asked Jelninolan in a gentle, soothing voice.

The Arch Wizard breathed out wearily – it was as if he had just been defeated in a skirmish. 'Belsarius often spent time in a place that he referred to as his Sanctum. Apparently, he made some fleeting references to the refuge when speaking to Akkad – indeed, he talked more frequently on the subject to the First.'

But not to Uldini, thought Ahren. That had to be very hurtful to the Arch Wizard.

I wonder why Belsarius didn't let our friend in on the secret, mused Culhen languorously in his half-sleep.

Ahren could see in the eyes of the Arch Wizard that the childlike figure had been asking himself the self-same question. 'Do you think we might find answers there?' he asked Uldini.

To his horror, the Arch Wizard shook his head. 'Following the death of Belsarius, the First made his way to Kelkor with the intention of searching the Sanctum. He says that it was covered over by a landslide.'

Ahren's eyebrows shot up. This was an important piece of information that the Woman in Black had *not* shared with him. What else was she hiding? 'And was he *certain* that nothing of value could have survived this landslide?'

Uldini rubbed the top of his bald pate as he pondered. Finally, he spoke. 'The First is quick to declare things lost that are not immediately decisive for the outcome of the war. And he looked down on Belsarius' experiments and magic – he considered it far too *peripheral*. I was always of the opinion that my mentor only worked so closely with the First in the hope that the age-old soldier would tolerate him as the being the first among the Ancients.'

'Have you any idea why Belsarius never mentioned his Sanctum to *you?*' asked Trogadon with all the subtlety of a blacksmith's hammer.

'Our time together was much shorter than you might imagine,' snarled Uldini. 'After my stay with *Auntie* Jelninolan,' he glanced gratefully at the elf, who was smiling at the form of address that he now so rarely used, 'and thanks to Belsarius' leadership, my meteoric rise through the ranks of the Ancients began.' Uldini turned away, trying to blink away his tears. 'We were sure that many happy shared years were yet to come. Perhaps he would have told me of the Sanctum once he had found the answers that he was looking for. At that point in my life, I was only interested in results, and did not appreciate the slow and laborious ways of turgid research.'

'As opposed to Akkad,' suggested Jelninolan. 'Doubtless, the tendency of the two Ancients to perform meticulous experiments *together* led to Akkad being informed of the Sanctum during the course of their many conversations.'

'Are we not clutching at straws here?' asked Falk. 'After all, we are talking here of a place of rack and ruin. A place that had fallen into its decrepit state long before the Night of Blood, it seems. A place that no-one who knew of it considered important. A place whose wreckage didn't even seem to be worth searching through. And now, suddenly, this self-same location is supposed to contain the answer to all our prayers?'

Ahren closed his eyes for a heartbeat and screwed up his courage. 'The Woman in Black says that an important secret is being preserved there. And now that we *know* that the place exists, *I* believe her.'

Uldini's eyes narrowed as he glared coldly at Ahren and the others. 'So *that* was your game,' he snarled. 'You wanted to manipulate me into examining the information of this mysterious woman – as if I were nothing more than an unwitting puppet on a string.'

'Not really *unwitting* as such,' said Khara ruefully. 'More…*unbiased*, I would say.'

'Bah, humbug!' The force of the Arch Wizard's two words could have smashed a stone to smithereens.

Ahren waved his hands apologetically. 'The important thing is that we now know that this Sanctum exists. And there is every likelihood that Belsarius has hidden important answers there.'

'The question is this – can we afford to ignore this information?' added Jelninolan, throwing the question out into the room.

Uldini let out a barrage of curses while Falk nodded stoically before responding.

'Off to Kelkor, then.'

Chapter 4

The sullen silence that accompanied the travellers during their weeks of journeying through the Knight Marshes had – thanks to the decision to search for Belsarius' Sanctum – yielded to a kind of nervous euphoria. Ahren's own emotions fluctuated between a giddy hopefulness that they would find something of critical importance in the ruin, and a dreadful fear that they were on a wild goose chase in search of documentation that had long since lost any relevance.

The weather grew colder with every day that passed, and by the time the first jagged Kelkorian peaks appeared on the horizon, the companions had already, at short notice, purchased in an anonymous border town six pack horses, some essential equipment, as well as provisions to keep them going. The dilapidated bourg, located at the meeting point of the Knight Marshes, Hjalgar and Kelkor, seemed to depend on its survival through chevaliers of fortune in search of easy wealth as either gold-diggers or the hunters of exotic beasts. However, now that the war had absorbed the majority of daredevil swashbucklers, the local trades people were only too delighted to offer their wares at a 'knockdown price' to Trogadon, who tried and failed to lower the outlandish fees being demanded.

'For this amount of gold coins, I could have bought the entire town,' complained the dwarf, and not for the first time, as he glared at Falk. 'Why did you stop me from forcing their prices down to a reasonable payment?'

'You saw the rundown state of their houses, didn't you? Not to mention the merchants' hollow cheeks?' countered the old man firmly. 'Consider our gold to be a donation to a municipality from which war has taken everything – without a single sword being struck in anger against the town.'

Ahren squinted as he saw in the distance a shadow with leathern wings gliding through the heavens. The imminent sunset with its vaporous veil made it difficult to identify the creature, and the young man could not make out any further details.

'Was that a *dragon?*' asked Hakanu with considerable excitement.

'And if it was?' asked Ahren, staring coldly at his pupil.

The latter swallowed hard. 'Then I would…uh…observe it from a distance with the requisite caution and…uh…only approach it if it was *absolutely* necessary.'

Ahren grunted but said no more.

'That was an Ogre Bat,' explained Falk. 'Unbelievably stupid, damn big and completely harmless. The giants who live here claim that the creatures are tasty.' The old man scowled. 'An assertion that I am not in a position to confirm.'

'At last, you are sharing with us your vast experience as a trophy hunter who was fond of the bottle' said Uldini caustically.

Ever since they had changed direction for Kelkor, the Arch Wizard's mood had been decidedly cantankerous. Whether it was because the existence of the Sanctum was no longer a secret or because he was fearful of the emotions that a visit to his deceased mentor's bolthole would inevitably stir up, Ahren could not tell.

'Concentrate on using your crystal ball and keeping us warm,' retorted Falk angrily.

Uldini shook his head vehemently. 'Oh, no. I am not going to fall into *that* trap a second time – I learned my lesson in the Ice Fields. As long as no-one here is freezing to death, you will not get me to waste my precious magic on such trivial creature comforts.'

'*Creature comforts,* says he,' growled Trogadon in his gravelly voice. 'It won't be long until the temperatures here will resemble what is considered a warm day on the Ice Fields.'

'Based on what Akkad, the First and the Woman in Black said about the location of the Sanctum, I suspect it must be in a valley near one of those peaks there,' said Falk, pointing at a group of five snow-covered mountains, which were huddled together as if protecting one another from the horrors of the rest of the world.

'What do you think?' asked Khara in a low voice as she turned to look at Ahren. 'Two or three weeks travelling through snow and ice until we reach it?'

He nodded. 'After our experiences on the Ice Fields, this will be nothing,' he said with a smile, nodding towards the pack horses. 'Especially as this time we have the right equipment.'

They had already been travelling for over a week along the snowy foothills of Kelkor when one day, Ahren spotted, instead of the regular sightings of exotic beasts and the occasional appearance of solitary Dark Ones, five towering figures. The creatures seemed to be tottering towards the travel party through the sleet, which had covered the landscape in a sheet of whitish grey, blurring the contours of the approaching spectres and limiting visibility to a couple of dozen paces. Ahren peered strenuously at the slowly emerging figures and hurriedly placed his hand on Hakanu's arm, his terrified protégé having made a move to grasp his spear.

'These are friends,' he explained in a low voice as he raised his hand in greeting. The giants, all of them wrapped in a multitude of furs and resting massive two-handers athwart their incredibly broad shoulders, waved back awkwardly, broad smiles breaking out on their chiselled faces.

'Speak to them slowly and politely,' murmured Trogadon to the others. 'Fast talk is considered an insult among the tribe of the big folk.'

'It would be best if *you* made the introductions,' suggested Jelninolan. 'After all, you know the giants of Kelkor better than the rest of us.'

Trogadon wiped some snow from his beard before looking over irritably at Falk, who responded, however, by waving dismissively.

'The thing is,' said the old Forest Guardian, 'my…uh…memories of my time in Kelkor are somewhat hazy.' He cleared his throat apologetically. 'And my encounters with the giants were not always of a harmonious nature.'

'Isn't it odd how this seems to have happened to you in so *many* places?' asked Khara oh so sweetly.

Falk mumbled incomprehensibly under his breath while Selsena whinnied with mirth, sharing her amusement with the others.

The giants approaching them stopped in their tracks and slapped their thighs with delight, their laughter echoing back from the mountain slopes.

'Giants are *very* sensitive to magic that influences their emotions,' murmured Jelninolan. 'It would be best if Selsena toned it down a little.'

Culhen squirmed anxiously beneath Ahren as the five figures drew ever closer. *Even a fully grown, undoubtedly glorious wolf like me could be envious of them,* said the companion animal uncertainly. *What do they feed their giant children? Entire cows? Dragons?*

Ahren thought immediately of the Ogre Bat that he had seen, whereupon Culhen shook himself in disgust.

Thanks a lot – but I think I'll remain only as large as a horse, concluded the animal.

'The glorious Champions of the gods and their everlasting wizard friends from the expanse of Jorath greet the valorous and imperious warriors of the Kelkorian heights!' shouted Trogadon as loudly and as slowly as he could to the giants who had now come to a halt.

Ahren had to tilt his head back as far as possible so that he could see up into the eyes of the giants who, much to his surprise, glittered like finely cut quartz crystals. Decorative scars ran along their cheeks, each one as thick as the Forest Guardian's finger and the length of his forearm.

'Before you, stands a child of the Silver Cliff, named after the great *Trogadon* himself, who oft wandered in awe among the big folk and who valued nothing more than to admire their songs and enjoy their famed hospitality,' added Trogadon, ending his greeting with considerable pomposity.

'The Blue Moss-Stone Warriors welcome the polite dwarf and his esteemed companions,' rumbled the foremost figure, whose hollow, reverberating voice revealed the speaker to be a giantess – a fact which Ahren, somehow, had simply not anticipated. She spread out her arms and nodded to her four companions. 'We five are the tribute that the Blue Moss-Stone Warriors will offer to this eternal war which has so balefully dispersed the Pall Pillar, causing its cloud to spread throughout the middle-land. We shall *tear* down the black walls, behind which the *spawn* of the Adversary are lurking, and our swords shall slay *multitudes* of them and silence them *forever*.'

'And *I'm* supposed to be a show-off?' murmured Hakanu.

Ahren gave his apprentice a surreptitious dig in the ribs before turning his attention once more to this most peculiar parley.

'A great task of incalculable importance awaits us in those mountains that stand together like conspirators guarding a secret!' called out Trogadon as he looked up at the giantess and pointed at the nearby massif. 'Any story that you can relate to us concerning these peaks will echo forever in our memories as evidence of the Blue Moss-Stone Warriors' unbounded generosity.'

'Suddenly, the dwarfs don't seem like the most complicated creatures I've encountered,' whispered Khara with a chuckle into Ahren's ear.

The Forest Guardian grinned but waved a warning finger.

'Shh!' hissed Falk, covering his mouth with his hand. 'The hearing of giants is very poor. They consider whispering in their presence to be a hostile act.'

Now that's something I well understand, interjected Culhen. *I don't like it either when others whisper to each other about me.*

'Great are the dangers to be found on these mountains, and great is the number of those who have been lost,' announced the giantess sadly, her words immediately dampening Ahren's previously cheerful mood. 'Since the moon has twice been absent from the heavens, a greyness has settled on the slopes of those mountains, causing so many giants to come to grief. All those who considered these peaks to be their homeland rest now forever, uncomplaining and unmoving, on cold rock or in sheltered clefts.' Having said that, the four giants behind the speaker raised their hands to hide their eyes and paused for several heartbeats, as if performing a silent mourning gesture. Then they lowered their hands again, allowing the giantess, who was as high as a tall tree, to add: 'We wish you the fortune of the deities as you make your ascent, but we cannot accompany you on the paths you must take – for they offer nothing but *death* to us giants.'

Trogadon played nervously with his beard. 'They will go any heartbeat now,' he mumbled without moving his lips. Then he said in a loud voice: 'Tell us then, what dreadful monster has caused such misfortune to so valiant a tribe of giants – so that we may prepare for the horror that we shall be approaching.'

Uldini rolled his eyes. 'It is as if one were listening to the hammiest travelling players in the world performing at their most bombastic.'

Jelninolan reached over to the Arch Wizard and covered his mouth with her hand. He looked daggers at her, which didn't bother the priestess a whit.

'Be ye afraid, for there be only one manifestation of horror mighty enough to banish the big folk from the mountain slopes – and they be the Wrath Demons.'

All colour drained from Trogadon's face, while Falk cursed under his breath.

'Yet ye will find not merely one of these nightmares incarnate in the heights, but *three*.' The giantess looked down at Trogadon, her eyes laced with sadness. Then she turned away and stamped southward with her four companions. 'Truly dark hath the world become,' she murmured with all the loudness of a tree being felled. 'Long be the nights and short be the summer. It be well past time that the gods brought an end to this aeon of pain.'

'Of course – it *had* to be Wrath Demons,' scolded Uldini angrily once the giants had disappeared. 'It *couldn't* be anything as simple for us to deal with as a slope filled with Low Fangs.'

Hakanu turned to Ahren. 'Master, what are Wrath Demons?'

'Certainly not Dark Ones,' the Forest Guardian replied. 'Otherwise, I would have heard of them. He looked at Falk, who was still muttering curses.

'Wrath Demons are exceedingly rare,' the old man replied, interrupting his own steady stream of maledictions. 'They arise when a Fury Wind nests in a giant.'

'What do you mean by *nests*?' asked Ahren, confused.

'Do you remember the time in Kelkor when Trogadon swallowed the Grief Wind so that he could hold it prisoner for a while?' asked Jelninolan.

'Of course. His act of bravery saved our lives.'

'Something similar happens in the creation of Wrath Demons. Giants are susceptible to emotional magic, and a Fury Wind, one of the Original Beings, consists purely of magical emotions. Because the big folk cannot resist the berserk frenzy that the so-called *Fury Winds* whip up, it ultimately means that the visitation of just such a gale results in nothing short of the tribe's destruction, the giants having been gripped by a bloodthirsty incandescent rage.'

The ominous look on Falk's face resembled an imminent storm front. '*Unless* one of the giants sacrifices themselves by *swallowing* the Fury Wind, just as Trogadon did with the Grief Wind that time.'

Ahren was still nonplussed. 'But if the giant has nothing to counter the sorcery with…' he began.

'The tribe kills him or her,' countered Uldini brusquely. 'The possessed giant is repeatedly hit until they die – along with the Fury Wind.'

'How gruesome,' said Khara, aghast.

A member of the pack will always sacrifice themselves to protect the others. Culhen's words, filled with dignity and respect, reverberated in Ahren's mind. *I can understand it only too well.*

The Forest Guardian leaned forward in his saddle and patted his friend beneath his helmet, which Culhen had been wearing again ever since their arrival in Kelkor.

'It is the only way for the giants to defend themselves against this sort of sorcery,' said Trogadon sadly, continuing his explanation. 'We dwarfs believe that the reason for this dreadful situation is because HE, WHO FORMS made the big folk *too* big. Hence, there is an imbalance between HIS essence and the Blessing of the goddess, which beats too weakly in their hearts.'

'And why are *those* three Wrath Demons still living?' asked Khara after some moments of silence.

'Because the tribe was unable to defeat them,' muttered Falk darkly. 'This happens occasionally – when the Wrath Demon is particularly strong and the tribe unusually small.'

'Or when two or more Fury Winds sweep through the mountains simultaneously,' added Jelninolan, exchanging a knowing look with Uldini. 'Which happens maybe once every five hundred years.'

Ahren nodded. 'And you believe that these Wrath Demons were *deliberately* created?'

Uldini's brooding face left no doubt but that he completely agreed with the elf's opinion. 'It can hardly be a coincidence that three Wrath Demons are wreaking havoc precisely where we suspect Belsarius' Sanctum to be. I would bet anything that the Adversary is up to His neck in these shenanigans.'

'And he didn't even need to use Dark Ones in creating an effective defence,' added Khara. 'He simply steered three Wrath Winds in the right direction.'

'Can the Dark god really command Original Beings?' asked Hakanu, wide-eyed.

'Perhaps. Now that the Adversary has awakened, I would on no account underestimate His power,' muttered Uldini.

'Especially as he only has to *entice* the Wrath Winds,' said Falk. 'They have no genuine consciousness of their own, so all it takes is the slightest of steering. A gentle sorcerous impulse would have drawn them to these mountains.'

'We must alert the Ring,' muttered Ahren with a frown. 'If the Adversary suddenly entices all the Grief- and Wrath Winds towards the Obsidian Fortress, they will wreak havoc as they sweep over our armies enroute.'

'Let *me* deal with that,' said Jelninolan, immediately creating a *Rillan*. Then she recited a few lines of Old Elven poetry before sending the magical message soaring into the sky. 'I hope I wasn't *too* cryptic,' she murmured.

'So, can we take it that the Adversary knows about the Sanctum?' asked Trogadon. 'Is it possible that it was *He* who was behind the landslide that initially buried it?'

'*Or* He got information about the location from our black-clad lady friend,' muttered Uldini grimly. 'This little detour of ours is stinking more and more to high heaven.'

Ahren rubbed his neck. 'The Woman in Black said that servants of the Adversary could not enter the Sanctum. Perhaps HE, WHO FORCES decided to resort to the Wrath Demons for that reason – so that in their fury, they would slowly but surely destroy whatever was left of the hideaway.'

'The good news is that the Dark god must be really terrified of what we might find out if He has gone to the trouble of transforming these giants into Wrath Demons,' interjected Hakanu. 'Which must surely mean that we are on the right track, right?'

'The Wrath Demons presumably want to keep curious eyes well away from the Sanctum. Hakanu has hit the nail on the head,' said Uldini before suddenly frowning and adding: 'Why does my last sentence sound so completely *wrong?*'

Nervous laughter rose from the little group as knowing looks were exchanged.

'Well, shall we confront these Wrath Demons?' asked Falk after a pause, his voice sounding decidedly resigned.

'We have come this far,' said Trogadon, weighing the hammer in his hands, 'One more skirmish is hardly going to matter.'

Four more days passed by before they reached the mountains, where they suspected Belsarius' Sanctum to be. And although winter already held

Kelkor in its icy grip, Ahren couldn't help feeling that their journey through the craggy region of Jorath was quite *comfortable* – if one compared it to the merciless Ice Fields from where they so recently escaped.

The snow-covered, coniferous forests were filled with an abundance of game, there were sufficient caves within which the group could find refuge whenever night set in and the beasts that resided here provided a welcome challenge to Ahren, Falk and especially Hakanu, who listened eagerly to the teachings of his master.

The apprentice used every opportunity to broaden his knowledge of Forest Guardianship, particularly regarding those creatures, which although being a part of Creation, could still prove a danger to the peoples of Jorath. Ahren watched as, day by day, the young warrior developed into a young lad that he could truly be proud of – his pupil was now a far cry from the boy who had experienced such a humiliating failure on the Ice Fields.

'Stay nice and quiet now,' whispered Falk as the three Forest Guardians, down on their hunkers and hiding under an expansive bush, observed an over-sized brown bear that was fishing in an icy river for a rare type of yellow-bellied trout. The creature was larger than a Glower Bear, and its size and powerful presence were awe-inspiring. 'Kelkor-Pelts are very good-natured – provided one doesn't disturb them when they are either fishing or sleeping,' added the old man in a low voice.

'Sounds like a certain dwarf acquaintance of mine,' whispered Ahren with a chuckle, his quip earning him two grins in response.

'Do we wait until it goes or try to make our way around the bear?' asked Hakanu in a low voice, Ahren having to stop himself from hugging his apprentice. The old Hakanu would have picked a quarrel with the creature or even thrown his spear in a futile heroic gesture.

Falk scratched his beard and pondered before responding. 'Kelkor-Pelts are very persistent when it comes to hunting, and this one here looks like he has interrupted his hibernation because he is so hungry. It is very early in the day yet, so I reckon he'll be catching trout for a while yet.' The old man looked up at the low-hanging clouds, which seemed to promise a fresh fall of snow. 'I wouldn't like to get a nasty surprise from the weather either while we wait for this big fellow to have his fill.'

A loud splash was audible as the animal dropped his enormous paw into the river and retrieved a squirming fish, which quickly disappeared down the bear's impressive gullet.

'This creature seems *very* hungry,' murmured Ahren. 'I don't think he'd give it a second thought if he decided that *we'd* make a tasty morsel.'

'Many animals in Kelkor have been touched by HIM, WHO IS, and are therefore tougher than their conspecifics,' replied Falk. 'Otherwise, they would hardly have survived here, given the sheer number of Original Beings that are running riot in these climes.'

'Let us return to the others,' suggested Ahren. 'We will tell them that this ford across the river is already occupied.'

The three Forest Guardians withdrew, reaching Trogadon, Jelninolan and Uldini after a short march towards the east. There was no sign of Culhen, Muai and Kamaluq – which was hardly a surprise. Ahren knew that the trio would turn up, satisfied and full once they had finished their frequent hunting forays. Initially, he had been worried that they might get into difficulties, but his anxiety concerning the animals' welfare had evaporated once Culhen had enthusiastically reported to him how the Shimmer Fox had frightened away with a lightning flash an enormous, fanged creature with long, shaggy hair.

'A bear is fishing ahead of us,' said Ahren, giving Khara a quick peck on the cheek. 'We had better look for a different place to cross the river.'

Uldini scanned the gurgling watercourse, which was a good six paces across and dissected the sweeping valley as it ran from east to west, cutting them off from their destination hidden among the closely packed mountains to the north. Forested slopes graced the landscape as far as the eye could see, giving the surroundings a desolate, yet also sublime appearance.

'Then it would be best if Jelninolan and I transported you across,' said Uldini after some heartbeats of pondering. 'Better to sacrifice a little magic than yet more time.'

'Any sign of Wrath Demons nearby?' asked Falk, looking towards Jelninolan and Selsena.

The elf and the Titejunanwa used their supernatural gifts to check for the giants that were dominated by the Wrath Winds. Finally, the Elven charger gave a low whinny and shook her mane, Jelninolan, too, answering in the negative with a dismissive wave.

'If they don't happen to be sleeping because of exhaustion, we would certainly *hear* them *long* before Selsena or I would *sense* them. Wrath Demons are anything but quiet.'

'It is better to err on the side of caution rather than find ourselves stumbling across these giants,' insisted Uldini, emphasising his standpoint. 'And now, let us get across this river and—'

A distant scream, filled with scorn and hatred, uttered by a throat that was certainly much bigger than that of a human, elf or dwarf thundered down the slope causing Ahren to stagger with sudden fear. Everyone apart from Trogadon stumbled under the sheer force of expressed rage as if they had suddenly been caught by a violent gust of wind.

'Kamaluq is in a terrible panic. I can sense it clearly despite the distance between us.'

Ahren, meanwhile, had picked up on Culhen's unease. 'It seems that our companion animals have been the first to find the giants – or perhaps the giants have found *them*.'

Falk cursed angrily. 'I told them until I was blue in the face that they should go hunting in the area that is *behind* us so that precisely something like this would *not* happen.'

'We will scold them later,' said Khara, nervously playing with the handles of her blades. 'Muai is terrified and running away from the Wrath Demons. And, what's making me nervous is the fact that she is coming directly *towards* us with giant leaps.'

'*Giant* leaps?' echoed Trogadon, winking at the Swordsmistress. 'Nice choice of words there.'

'How best does one fight these Wrath Demons?' asked Ahren, unshouldering *Fisiniell* and turning to Falk.

'Uh...' Falk shrugged his shoulders. 'I've never had the pleasure of doing so.'

'Unbelievable!' snarled Uldini. 'You could have informed us earlier, you know.'

'I assumed Trogadon would explain what to do.'

'*Me?*' asked the dwarf, taken aback. 'Just because I lived in the Silver Cliff does *not* mean that I know everything about Kelkor. Have you any idea how *rare* Wrath Demons are? I for one have *never* encountered one.'

We are bringing three guests with us. Ahren could now hear Culhen's voice, the wolf being sufficiently close for communication to be possible between them. *I do hope that you have prepared an appropriate welcoming committee.*

We'll see, countered Ahren dryly. 'Does *anyone* here know how we can effectively fight Wrath Demons?' he asked, looking at the others.

'If we ever get out of this alive and word gets round that a motley crew of Paladins and Ancients behaved on encountering three Wrath Demons like a gaggle of gods' day pupils at their first Autumn Festival, then…' scolded Ahren before fixing his fury on Hakanu. 'And *you* – stop laughing *now!*'

'Yes, Ma…mas…ter,' stammered the apprentice, almost doubled over with a combination of mirth and terror.

Suddenly, there was a flash of blinding light among some trees in the distant, which was immediately followed by a multi-voiced cry of fury. Terror now took full control within the boy.

'Kamaluq has made them *really* angry,' he reported fearfully.

These giants don't need any excuse to be angry, announced Culhen. *So, come up with something quickly!*

Ahren watched in disbelief as the Kelkorian trees on the slope half a league or so to the north of them began to move as though they were dry branches among some inconsequential shrubbery. The treetops swayed violently from side to side, and there was a loud cracking and crunching as the Forest Guardian observed fir-, spruce- and pine trees being easily knocked over like skittles on the gentle incline ahead of him.

'Oh, no!' exclaimed Khara as one of the fallen trees was suddenly hurled like an improvised spear between the tops of its fellows, whizzing along before hitting the ground with a crash. Even from this distance, Ahren could feel the power of the impact.

They are throwing entire trees at us! complained Culhen, aghast. *Trees!*

Ahren ignored his friend's fear so that he could think clearly. 'Any ideas?' he asked the others.

'Killing them would be extraordinarily difficult, not to mention a damn shame,' muttered Falk, scratching his beard. 'There are only a couple of hundred giants left in Jorath. Losing three would be a considerable loss.'

'Jelninolan, do you think *you* might be able to lure the Wrath Winds out of those three unfortunates?' asked Khara, only reluctantly drawing her blades.

Ahren understood her hesitation all too well. Given the size of the giants, she might as well have been armed with needles.

'I can *try,*' said the elf sceptically. 'But even if I succeed, the charm will need some time to become effective.'

'Then you'd better start straight away,' urged Ahren nervously.

Jelninolan carefully, and almost as if performing a ritual, took *Mirilan* out of its bag, placed it on her shoulder and began to play a low, extraordinarily complex melody which immediately created images of clear, still mountain lakes, of fallen snow and of white-capped trees in the minds of the listeners. 'I will try to remind them of who they once were – dignified beings, filled with inner peace and serenity. She glanced over at Uldini. 'But I am also going to need a charm circle to amplify my song once it has reached its maximum power.'

'I'll get cracking,' muttered Uldini, picking up a nearby branch and beginning to draw the first, mystical runes on the muddy riverbank.

Ahren nodded. 'We will distract the Wrath Demons in the meantime.'

'*Great* idea,' growled Trogadon sarcastically. 'And *how* do you propose to do that? My hammer will hardly be effective, let alone your blades.'

Ahren nodded towards *Fisiniell* and Hakanu. 'A few well-placed Deep Steel arrows and an accurately thrown spear should give even a giant something to think about,' he replied confidently. 'And I suggest that you use your crossbow.'

The blacksmith slapped his forehead in annoyance at his own forgetfulness before taking the heavy weapon from his rucksack.

Ahren pointed first at Hakanu and then at Uldini, who seemed to be in a trancelike state as he continued drawing. 'Give him cover, boy, and do *not* leave his side,' he commanded his apprentice. 'If a giant attacks, the two of you must make a run for it. Carry the Arch Wizard if necessary.'

The young warrior nodded hesitantly as he adjusted the spear in his hand.

Selsena whinnied as Falk sat back into the saddle. 'My old girl will hopefully distract the giants with a few well-aimed waves of emotion,' he said, attaching his shield to his forearm.

Another tree flew through the forest, splintering as it slammed into a mighty fir not one hundred paces away. The onrushing companion animals were like three hurtling shadows in the snow-covered forest.

'No time for my armour,' muttered Falk. 'It seems I will have to confront these Wrath Demons as half a knight and half a Forest Guardian.'

Ready or not – here we come! announced Culhen, who was already leaping across the river. His landing sent water spraying everywhere. *Brrr*, he said, shaking himself violently as soon as he reached Ahren.

'Thank you *very* much,' growled Trogadon, who was standing beside the Thirteenth, as he wiped the icy water from his face. Meanwhile, Muai crossed over the watercourse in a far more elegant manner, holding Kamaluq by the scruff of his neck in her mouth.

The giants roared their scorn up to the heavens as they made their merciless advance. Ahren's first, fleeting impressions of the Wrath Demons was of a depraved version of those giants whom the companions had already encountered on their journey here, these ones having wild and unkempt hair, filthy clothing and insanely distorted facial features.

'Should we perhaps withdraw to the forest on the southern slope?' he asked.

Falk shook his head. 'We must remain by the riverbank. This is the only place where we have the freedom of movement to outmanoeuvre the giants. In the forest, they would use the trees as weapons against us.'

Ahren ducked instinctively as a slim spruce whooshed over his head like a crude arrow before uprooting two more trees behind them and coming to a shuddering halt. 'Makes sense,' he muttered to Falk.

'Diversion is the order of the day!' barked Falk to his companions. 'Selsena can run away from them, but if any of the rest of you find yourselves in their path, think of the following – giants are good sprinters but hopeless when it comes to turning in tight situations. Let's hope that the same applies to Wrath Demons. Think of the Moss Giant that we encountered at the *Althunol* – that will give you a good idea of what giants are capable of.'

Ahren swallowed hard on hearing those words. He remembered with sadness that violent confrontation which had been such a terrible experience. But then, the first of the Wrath Demons burst out of the trees, with an insane look on its wide-eyed face, and threads of spittle hanging from the corners of its mouth. The time for action was well and truly upon them.

On my back! commanded Culhen, the Forest Guardian swinging into the saddle without a second thought.

'Come here, you roaring mass of muscle!' yelled Falk ferociously, Selsena sending such a powerful wave of sarcasm that even Ahren found himself gritting his teeth.

The insane, crystalline eyes of the giant fixed themselves on the Paladin riding away on his Elven charger. Within a heartbeat, the monster had flung a tree after the pair. Then he began the chase.

Falk had already spurred Selsena from a tempting canter into a gallop, and now they hurtled along the riverbank in a westerly direction so that the incredibly heavy missile landed harmlessly behind them. The Wrath Demon, having swallowed Falk's bait, hook, line and sinker, was now bearing down on Falk and the Titejunanwa with a furious cry and with his arms greedily outstretched as the old Forest Guardian continued to yell derisively.

'No-one move,' murmured Uldini absently, the Arch Wizard continuing to draw runes and squirls in the mud. 'Perhaps the other two Wrath Demons will follow their angry friend…'

The edge of the forest before them exploded as the two remaining possessed giants stormed out of the trees, their furiously flailing fists transforming the trees into kindling before the pair leaped over the river and landed in the middle of the companions, their eyes fixed solely on the musicking elf.

'Grab Jelninolan!' gasped Khara in Ahren's direction as she elegantly jumped to safety and away from the heavy tread of a giant foot. 'Her music seems to be drawing the Wrath Demons towards her.'

'Of course it is,' grunted the Forest Guardian irritably, picking up the fiddle-bearing elf nonetheless and setting her down before him in the saddle. 'Anything else would have been far too *easy*.'

My poor back, complained Culhen as he stormed eastward, the two Wrath Demons focusing solely on the wolf with his pleasing sounding load. *Hold on tight!*

Trogadon won a little precious time for Ahren, Culhen and Jelninolan by hoisting with a grunt of fury the crossbow onto his knee before aiming it at the two giants and dispatching a bolt. The immediate dreadful sound that followed as the projectile – as thick as a strong man's forearm – sank into a giant leg, resembled two heavy rocks rubbing against each other during a landslide. The hulk's limb buckled, causing him to stumble against his companion, who was greedily reaching forward for the elf. The outstretched hand changed direction as the giant wreaked revenge on the pesky dwarf for his interference by landing a backhanded slap on Trogadon, who was thrown into the air and flew in a wide arc towards the line of trees to the south, where he landed with a cry before performing an involuntary somersault.

'Trogadon!' gasped Jelninolan, who was still weaving her musical magic, while Ahren's heart sank at the thought of what had befallen his squat friend. But there was nothing he could do about it there and then, except to use the extra few heartbeats that the dwarf had gained for them to concentrate on the far from easy task of keeping himself and the fiddling elf safely on Culhen's back, the wolf now making a sharp turn along the watercourse and hurtling further east. A sudden blast of wind and a shadow passing over them confirmed to Ahren that they had narrowly avoided being hit by a tree that the Wrath Demon had hurled after them.

That was close, thought Ahren as Culhen leaped over a boulder, the Paladin suddenly recognising the part of the bank that they were racing towards. 'Back!' he roared, as the terrible truth dawned on him. 'We are heading straight for a...'

The enormous, shaggy creature that only now had been blissfully fishing in the river, stood up on his hind legs and bellowed his annoyance at the onrushing Culhen.

'...Kelkor-Pelt,' muttered Ahren, ending his sentence lamely.

You could have thought of that earlier, groaned Culhen. *Hold Jelninolan firmly – this is going to get very uncomfortable.*

The wolf raced straight towards the upright and threatening bear, while from behind could be heard the heavy steps of the uninjured Wrath Demon getting closer and closer, having left his limping companion in his wake.

'Culhen...' began Ahren, the wolf now a mere five paces from the looming Kelkor-Pelt in front of them.

Ahren's friend reacted curtly. *I know what I'm doing,* he snapped.

'Culhen!' This time Ahren shouted as the Kelkor-Pelt, his claws ready to strike, fixed his eyes on the onrushing wolf.

Trust me. The canine's message was astoundingly confident, even as the bear lunged at the three.

'CULHEN!' yelled Ahren, now panic-stricken, condemned as he was to somehow keeping both his own swaying body and that of the priestess on the back of the wolf, who seemed to have suddenly adopted the worst habits of Hakanu. Already the paws of the enormous Kelkor-Pelt were sweeping forcefully down towards Ahren and Jelninolan, the creature looming before them like a shaggy wall, which Culhen was clearly hell-bent on crashing into at full force.

Duck! said the wolf, clearly delighted with himself as he immediately followed his own orders. Gritting his teeth, Ahren leaned forward over his friend as low as he could, pressing Jelninolan down simultaneously, but in such a manner that she was still able to continue her fiddle-playing.

Half a heartbeat later and Ahren's world had become totally chaotic.

One of the bear's paws hit him on the right shoulder just as he heard the rapidly approaching whoosh of a flying conifer. The Forest Guardian was swept from the saddle the instant the six paces-long fir tree flung by the limping Wrath Demon flew low over Culhen, hitting the massive bear in the middle of his chest.

While Ahren was helplessly flying through the air, thanking the gods for the durability of his Deep Steel armour, he saw how Culhen took advantage of the Kelkor-Pelt's moment of disorientation by slipping past him, leaving the hairy beast standing in the way of the uninjured Wrath Demon. The two rivals were overcome with fury as they attacked each other, the bear antagonised beyond belief by the tree that had hit him, the giant by the Wrath Wind that was raging within him.

Ahren would undoubtedly have given the violent spectacle of the two hulks more attention if he hadn't had more important things to be concentrating on at that moment. Branches snapped under the force of his flight while sharp needles pierced through every weak point of Ahren's armour as the Thirteenth Paladin did his best to curl up into as compact a ball as possible, trying as best he could to protect his arms, legs and face from damage.

If I'm lucky, the branches will prevent me from crashing—

Ahren's head banged against a small spruce, causing him to groan and ricochet like a badly aimed arrow through the undergrowth, branches and thorns tearing at him from all angles until he finally came to rest, with a myriad of scratches.

'Armour that is made up of nothing but moveable plates *does* have its drawbacks,' he grunted as, thoroughly dazed, he struggled to his feet. Needles were stuck into him wherever there were gaps in his protective gear. There was a terrible din in his ears – it was if the combined bugles of Thousand Halls were sounding simultaneously, while a low voice within him seemed to be saying that he was urgently needed, but to whom the voice belonged, or where the speaker was, he simply did not know.

He looked down and saw the blood seeping out from under his armour. 'I must have fallen from my horse,' he murmured as he blinked. Somehow, the world refused to stop dancing in front of his eyes.

Thrown off a wolf, more like, said Culhen, forcefully getting through to Ahren's befogged mind and laboriously pulling him back out of his trance by using their connection to enable the young man to observe the dramatic race between the the armoured animal with Jelninolan on his back and the two bruised Wrath Demons, who were a dozen paces behind the wolf and the elf. *Jelninolan wants me to tell you that her song will soon reach its climax, at which point she needs to be standing in Uldini's charm circle with these giants also in attendance – otherwise, the song will be unable to free the poor creatures from the Wrath Winds. And then we will have to fight them to the death.*

Ahren gritted his teeth in an effort to concentrate. *You must turn west,* he said to Culhen as he stumbled towards the edge of the trees, trying to ignore the pain of dozens of pine needles stuck into his skin beneath his armour. *For the moment, you are fleeing downstream, while Falk and Selsena are heading upstream! You are luring the giants away from the charm circle.*

By now, the river had come into Ahren's view. He stared at the lifeless body of the Kelkor-Pelt and swallowed hard. Suddenly, the needles and his countless cuts and bruises didn't seem half so bad. At least, when one considered all the things that a Wrath Demon *could* do to an enemy.

He saw the two giants moving away before him – one of them with a bolt stuck in his leg, the other with deep gashes to his back. Ahren shivered at the thought of the latter being able to survive a Kelkor-Pelt's bear hug.

I'm running out of energy, complained Culhen, and Ahren sensed the increasing weariness of the wolf. *Any form of distraction would be gratefully accepted.*

Ahren felt for *Fisiniell* – but his hand clutched fresh air. Grunting irritably, the Paladin looked over his shoulder only to see that his bow was precisely where it belonged. This time, he consciously felt for the weapon, yet his fingers grasped a good hand's width away from what he was seeking. Clearly, his brain had been more violently shaken than he thought it had been.

It took four attempts for his befogged mind to register the exact position of the weapon and for him to implement the hand-eye coordination necessary to secure the bow in his fingers. The fact that his right soldier was hurting terribly was a further blow to his confidence.

I'm out of commission, big lad, groaned Ahren, finding it an enormous effort to even get this message across to the wolf. He gritted his teeth again, this time in frustration. *I'd better make my way back to the others. There is something seriously wrong with my head.*

I always have to do everything myself, said Culhen, nevertheless finding it impossible to hide the concern behind his truculent words, while Ahren cursed himself for his injuries. *I will try to find an opportunity to make a detour around the two giants, but for the moment, I will have to keep running east!*

Still holding *Fisiniell*, Ahren struggled up along the river, all the while following – in so far as his dazed mind permitted – Culhen's attempts at evading the giants by engaging in daring manoeuvres just beyond the reach of the Wrath Demons, who were nonetheless gaining on him. The wolf leaped from one bank of the river to the other as often as he could, thereby forcing his clumsy opponents into changing their direction. Through Culhen's ears, Ahren could also hear the never-ending, accelerando of the elf's increasingly complex fiddle-playing, the priestess swinging wildly this way and that like a rag doll as she clung onto the wolf's saddle for dear life.

'We really *are* stuck between a rock and a hard place,' mumbled Ahren to himself as he desperately tried to hold onto his reason. Every movement that he made was sending darts of pain to dozens of places on his body, while in the distance, his companions were only recognisable as shadowy spectres. He was finding it increasingly difficult even to *think* in complete phrases. Ahren staggered on to his friends, meeting Khara and Hakanu, who had raced towards him.

'What happened?' asked the Swordsmistress breathlessly. 'Where are Culhen and Jelninolan?'

'They're playing catch-me-if-you-can with two furious giants,' giggled Ahren. The strange looks that his beloved and his apprentice gave him caused him to immediately try to grasp hold of his fleeting concentration. 'A Kelkor-Pelt swiped at me, and I slammed against a tree,' he explained, managing to point at his head. 'With this,' he added, suddenly feeling incredibly proud of his undoubted quick-wittedness.

'He must be concussed – and badly,' said Khara in alarm. 'Help me get him over to Uldini.'

Ahren looked at Hakanu, and from the depths of his mind, a fragile thought managed to bubble to the surface of his rapidly failing understanding. 'Uldini. Protect,' he mumbled, pointing at his apprentice.

'There is no Wrath Demon far and wide,' said Hakanu slowly and deliberately, Ahren responding with an equally slow nod.

'There is blood coming out of his ears.' The Thirteenth Paladin found the strange woman's voice strangely attractive, and she smelled wonderful, too. 'A bad sign if ever there was one.'

'Uldini!' yelled the young man from beside the injured Forest Guardian, but the addressee shook his head irritably at the noise. 'Ahren has hurt his head – and it doesn't look good!'

A small, strangely self-important looking boy with far too serious a face for a child of his age observed Ahren keenly as the Forest Guardian was led by the woman to a very complicated looking circle full of flourishes and angles, which covered the mucky riverbank over several paces and upon which the grumpy young fellow was standing.

'Ni…ice,' said Ahren in a slurred voice and reached down to touch the patterns only for the boy to slap his fingers hard and glare at him.

'Ow!' exclaimed the Forest Guardian as he jutted his chin belligerently. 'Bold boy!'

'The THREE have really blessed me this time,' sighed the little figure in a voice that Ahren somehow felt suggested that what was *said* was the direct opposite to what was *meant*. 'On the very last stage of our journey, would you believe it, the head of the Thirteenth Paladin has turned to mush.' The boy grunted irritably before stepping out of the nice-looking patterns, which were giving Ahren a headache, however, so elaborate were they. Suddenly, the crystal ball in the boy's hands flared to life, whereupon he held it right in front of Ahren's face.

'Look – in – there,' said the boy slowly, over-emphasising every syllable.

Ahren fixed his eyes on a maelstrom of wild colours and patterns that raged within the flickering flame in the core of the orb. 'What a neat trick!' he laughed, clapping his hands and sensing that his mind was being seduced more and more by the interplay of colours and tongues of burning light. Humming to himself and perfectly content, he allowed this to happen, luxuriating in the feeling of security that the colourful display was releasing within him.

Now hands were touching him all over. 'He is badly bruised and has little cuts everywhere,' he heard the boy say. 'I had better patch up his body while *Flamestar* takes care of his mind.'

Ahren then heard a barrage of funny and colourful curses from the little fellow, which caused the Forest Guardian to repeatedly chuckle.

'Stop using bad language and heal him,' said the woman.

Then a bugle sounded.

Falk! The thought hit him immediately, his mind slowly beginning to clear.

'The signal for retreat,' said Hakanu. 'Falk undoubtedly wants us to prepare for his luring the Wrath Demon towards us.'

'Then let us hope that Jelninolan will get here in time, too, with her two giants in tow,' murmured Khara anxiously. 'I really don't want us to have to keep Falk's Wrath Demon in check for any length of time until all the giants have gathered by the charm circle. Especially as Ahren here isn't even capable of peeling an apple at the moment.'

'Not…true…at all,' replied the Paladin flatly as he continued to gaze into *Flamestar*. The patterns in the orb were making more and more sense to him. Ahren intuitively understood that as soon as had a complete grasp of the forms and colours, the spell for curing his mind would have completed its work. The fact that Uldini was simultaneously treating his physical wounds with traditional magic was only vaguely apparent to the Forest Guardian through the gradual disappearance of pain. 'One gets a simple bang to the head and already one's beloved has stabbed one in the back,' he added in an almost normal voice as he attempted a smile.

'That almost sounds like my master again,' he heard Hakanu ascertaining with relief.

A furious scream from relatively close by was followed immediately by Khara's voice. 'Uldini, how much longer do you need to put Ahren back together again? This giant to the west, hot on the heels of Falk and Selsena, looks *incredibly* angry – even for a Wrath Demon.'

'Don't rush me,' snarled Uldini. 'I'm sure you would like your Paladin back to his old self again. I don't want to make a mistake that might lead him to using his legs when it is his arms that he intends to manoeuvre.'

Keep looking at the colours, thought Ahren, mentally scolding himself as he tried even harder to ignore his surroundings and follow the patterns within *Flamestar. The merry colours and forms are your friends.*

Uldini's magic, blazing in the core of *Flamestar,* penetrated further and further into Ahren's mind, ordering, connecting and smoothing things in the Paladin's skull – even things for which the young man had no name.

'Hey! Why are you lot standing around like idiots?' roared Falk, the old man's voice cutting as easily through his protégé's efforts to concentrate as the dorsal fin of a shark slices through the surface of a calm, blue sea. 'You *do* see the giant thundering towards you, right?'

'Ahren hurt his head!' shouted Khara. 'Uldini is putting his mind to rights!'

The ensuing grunt from Falk and the snorting of Selsena confirmed to Ahren that the old man and his Titejunanwa were very close now.

'Hakanu! Khara! Come to *me!*' commanded Falk, Ahren then hearing the familiar scraping sound of the Swordsmistress unsheathing her weapons. 'Let's ensure that Uldini and Ahren have the time that they need.'

The urge to escape from Uldini's charm was almost irresistible as both his anxiety regarding the imminent skirmish and his fears for his friends' safety rose – alongside his returning reason.

'I feel like myself again!' shouted Ahren above the quickly approaching roars and the loud stamping sounds of the Wrath Demon. 'Can I…'

'*No!*' snarled Uldini, cutting him off. 'As long as *Flamestar* is still showing you images, you *must* keep looking at them. It would be a shame if, during the storming of the Obsidian Fortress, you could only experience it with all the intellect of an indoor plant.'

Ahren gulped and said no more. Condemned to idleness while leaving his friends to their own devices in a life-or-death situation was almost impossible to suffer.

'*Good* Thirteenth,' said Uldini in a sickly-sweet voice.

Immediately, Ahren's self-control was put to the hardest test imaginable as a war cry from the giant sounded ferociously from the

Forest Guardian's immediate vicinity, followed immediately by a splintering cracking sound right beside the wounded Paladin.

'Get away!' cried out Khara to someone, and then Ahren heard Falk groan.

'That was close,' gasped the old man. 'Let's try confusing the big fella so that he continues to concentrate on us.'

Ahren's entire body was tingling with anxiety – it was as if all his nerves had caught fire. Khara, Falk and Hakanu were risking their lives not five paces away from him, and all he could do was watch *Flamestar* slowly burning out…he gasped and concentrated anew on the play of colours before him. what he was looking at really *was* becoming simpler and slowly getting darker. The charm was ebbing away!

'To your left!' yelled Hakanu, and once again the ground trembled thanks to the stomp of a giant foot.

'Thank you!' came the relieved response from Khara. 'By the THREE, my blades are hardly scraping his skin at all.'

'Finished,' said Uldini in a dreamy voice to Ahren's right, the Thirteenth Paladin feeling the briefest touch of a child-sized hand on his forearm. 'Good as new.' The Arch Wizard's voice seemed far away, for having now performed his traditional healing magic, it sounded as if the childlike figure's head was in the clouds. At that very moment, the last flickers in *Flamestar's* core went out, and Ahren blinked as he looked away from the crystal ball.

At last – he could now support his friends!

Chapter 5

Suddenly, he was master of all his senses again.

Dammit, Ahren, answer me! Culhen's voice reverberated in the Forest Guardian's head as the young man tried to assess what was unfolding around him.

Sorry, I was completely gone there for a moment, said the Paladin, nocking an arrow to *Fisiniell's* bowstring as a precaution. *I suffered a nasty blow to my head.* The Wrath Demon that Falk and Selsena had lured away was looming directly in front of him and was performing a kind of deadly dance with Khara, Hakanu, Falk and Muai, his four companions running around and between the legs of the giant and goading him with quick yet ineffective attacks. The bellowing creature kicked, stamped and hit wildly around him, without managing to injure them. Even in the few heartbeats it took for Ahren to get his bearings, he saw how a foot of the Wrath Demon failed to connect with Khara by no more than a hair's breadth, while a punch of his hand only missed Muai because the tigress saved herself by leaping quickly into the icy river.

Jelninolan's song is becoming ever more frantic. I think it will soon be finished, announced Culhen. *The two giants are still hot on my heels, and I have used up all my energy making a detour around them through the trees. I hope you have the welcoming committee ready because we are coming towards you again.*

Ahren looked the furious colossus up and down as he tried to locate a suitable target for the arrow. The Wrath Demon seemed to be completely ignoring both the Forest Guardian and the Arch Wizard, but whether this was down to the fact that neither of them had launched an attack on him or because he was so preoccupied with his four assailants, Ahren couldn't say. The most important thing, however, was that they all kept the giant occupied until Jelninolan could speak her magic.

The Paladin's eyes then focused on the artful circle of magical runes which was waiting for Jelninolan's arrival not three paces away from the furiously stamping Wrath Demon. If the giant made one false move...

Without giving it a second thought, Ahren aimed at the giant's left knee and dispatched the arrow. This was immediately followed by a gruesome crunching sound as the Deep Steel drove into the joint, causing the Wrath Demon to buckle to his left and away from the charm circle.

'Hakanu!' yelled Ahren in a commanding voice, whereupon his apprentice reacted immediately. The boy drew back his spear and hurled it at the giant's injured knee. When Hakanu called back his weapon, the crunching sound was repeated, the Wrath Demon's knee giving way completely under the weight, at which point the massive creature collapsed onto the ground with a shuddering impact.

'Keep him occupied!' shouted Ahren as he glanced over at Falk and Khara. 'He mustn't get to his feet again.'

'Easier said than done, considering that we don't want to kill the poor fellow,' gasped Falk as he began to wave his sword around in front of the giant's face, so that the harassed Wrath Demon would try grasping at the old man and his weapon, rather than consider standing up.

Khara and Muai, the latter now dripping wet, sprang into action beside Falk, imitating his tactic so that the giant could do nothing but hit clumsily out at them like an inveterate drunkard after a hard day's drinking in his local tavern.

'Hakanu – come over to me!' shouted Ahren, the young warrior immediately hurrying to be by his master's side. Ahren pointed upstream, squinted his eyes and peered searchingly. 'We will have to hold up the Wrath Demons that are following Culhen and Jelninolan,' he said through gritted teeth, his anxiety clearly audible.

Hakanu glanced over his shoulder at the wounded giant ten paces behind them, whose attention was still focused on the tireless efforts of Muai, Falk and Khara. Selsena's efforts were clearly tiring her out now, however, as the Titejunanwa struggled to emit waves of mockery, which were becoming ever more irregular. Nonetheless, they still enraged the Wrath Demon sufficiently whenever he managed to coordinate his movements to some degree. 'How are the two of us ever going to manage to tame the other pair of Wrath Demons?'

Ahren inhaled sharply as the outline of Culhen came into view on the riverbank. The wolf was still little more than a shadow in the distance, but the Paladin knew that it would only be a couple of dozen heartbeats before Culhen and his priceless mount would reach them – along with the two Wrath Demons, who had now broken out of the forest behind the wolf, and at whom they were furiously hurling uprooted trees.

'It will suffice if we manage to slow down the Wrath Demons,' said Ahren, extending *Fisiniell* until he could feel his arm muscles burning with the effort. The Forest Guardian scanned the falling leaves at the forest edge so that he could determine the strength and direction of the wind. Then he slipped into Pelneng and raised the bow so that the arrow would fly in a flat parabola. He exhaled, adjusted his aim one last time, and shot.

The Deep Steel missile glittered in an aura of shimmering light as it covered the immense distance in no time at all before passing over Culhen and Jelninolan. Then it began to sink on its low arc until it finally slammed into the hip of one of the Wrath Demons.

You're welcome to aim a bit higher, complained Culhen. *I am too exhausted to evade any low flying arrows.*

'That was…that was *incredible!*' gasped Hakanu, looking at Ahren wide-eyed. 'That shot must have travelled five furlongs!'

Ahren shook his head. 'A practice shot – nothing more than that,' he said. 'From this distance the arrow simply didn't have enough force to cause the giant any significant damage. Anyway, it's hardly a spectacular feat to hit a target that is a good ten paces tall and four wide.' He frowned. 'But now at least I know that the Wrath Demons are easily distracted. Can you see how the head of the fellow that I hit keeps turning this way and that as he looks from Jelninolan to me and back again. If we can vex those two Wrath Demons for long enough, we will hopefully buy Jelninolan the time she needs to bring her song to a conclusion in Uldini's charm circle.' He nocked another arrow and aimed carefully. 'And then let us pray to the THREE that the spell will work.' He let go and the projectile whizzed on its way. 'Or else we will have to kill these three unfortunates to save our own skins.'

The second arrow hit the Wrath Demon, provoking nothing more than an annoyed grunt as it lodged in the giant's upper arm – its relative ineffectiveness seeming to underline how dangerous such a fight to the death would be for Ahren and his companions.

'I will pepper the giant on the left with arrows, you aim for the one on the right.'

Ahren had already fully extended *Fisiniell* when he saw out of the corner of his eye that Hakanu hadn't made a move. Surprised, and about to utter an admonishment, he turned to look at his apprentice only to hesitate as he recognised something he had never previously observed in the eyes of the seemingly paralysed young warrior – *doubt*.

'What…' began Hakanu, only to stop and swallow hard before continuing, 'what if I hit Culhen?'

'You have managed more difficult throws in your time,' countered Ahren harshly. 'Four Claws was at least as far away when you hurled your spear at him – and you were only aiming at his eye, not at his entire body.'

Hakanu nodded, chewing hard on his lower lip. Ahren immediately wished he could have given himself a clip across the ear. Of course, his apprentice was now remembering the fateful throw that had cost the lad so much. His attempt to finish the fight against the dragon with a final act of heroism had failed miserably when the beast had tossed him violently away. And now, his master had once again undermined his confidence by treating him – as he had so often done before – as a raw beginner. Ahren had been so intent on hammering home the need for caution that he was now also eroding the self-confidence of his protégé.

Then hurry up and help Hakanu find his courage again, complained Culhen sharply. *I really could do with those fellows on my heels being distracted.*

Culhen's exhaustion was more than apparent through the connection between man and wolf, while Ahren could clearly see how the distance between his friends and their pursuers was reducing. Time was of the essence!

The Forest Guardian quickly dispatched another arrow, this time aiming it higher and at the face of the giant on the left, who slowed down a little and raised his hand to catch the projectile, which, however, bored into his forearm.

'Hakanu!' yelled Ahren, drawing another arrow from his quiver as he fixed his eyes on his apprentice. 'I am firmly convinced that your throw will be successful. You have proven yourself so often already. Do not allow one miscalculation in the Ice Fields to undermine all that you have achieved.'

'But you have made it abundantly clear to me that I must learn everything from the start again,' the young warrior replied, looking at his master in confusion. For once, words failed Ahren. Had he been too hard on Hakanu after the lad's failure with the dragon? Had his anxiety over the imminent confrontation between the Paladins and the Adversary distracted him to the point where he had not bothered to take care of his apprentice's spiritual development?

Culhen's howling roused Ahren out of his misgivings, the giant on the right having almost made contact with the wolf by means of a punch and only failing because the animal had stumbled sideways in his energy-sapping run.

AHREN! screamed Culhen.

The Thirteenth Paladin shot an arrow at the giant who had just launched the attack, thereby slowing him down a little – only for his furious companion to pick up speed, gaining ground on the flagging wolf.

'Listen to me, Hakanu,' said Ahren, now shooting at the two giants alternately with as much speed as he could manage. 'It is right and proper that I was disappointed in your attitude during our fight with Four Claws – but that does not mean that you must cast aside all the things that you have been taught. This feeling of doubt that you feel inside you – this is something that we *all* experience, and it is a feeling that assails us again and again. The trick is to find the necessary balance between caution and courage and to recognise when the one or the other should have the upper hand. Here and now – and let there be no doubt about it – Culhen needs your *courage* above all else.'

The exhausted wolf was now no more than two and a half furlongs away from his friends, but it was clear to Ahren that his four-legged friend was doomed to lose this unequal race without the dual intervention of master and apprentice. A quick sideways glance revealed to the Forest Guardian that Hakanu was still going through an internal struggle, the boy now looking doubtfully down at his spear.

'Hakanu,' implored Ahren, I *trust* you. *Culhen* trusts you. Prove yourself to be the Paladin that you always dreamed of. Help me to save Culhen and Jelninolan.' He looked deep into Hakanu's eyes. 'Be a *hero.*'

Hakanu trembled momentarily, his eyes suddenly blazing with ambition as they had so often done before. 'Yes, Master!' the young warrior exclaimed before spinning around to face the giants. In one supple movement, he pulled his throwing arm back, his face the picture of concentration. The glove, which channelled the apprentice's innate magic, glimmered for under a heartbeat, and then Hakanu hurled his spear so that it flew at the speed of light in a low arc towards the possessed giants.

Ahren shot off his own arrow and watched as the missile of his apprentice whizzed no more than half a hand above the head of the enraptured Jelninolan only to land with a crunch that could be heard even from such a considerable distance as it smashed into and through the kneecap of the giant on the right.

The hulk collapsed, the mindless fury of his companion momentarily pausing to look down in disbelief at his fellow Wrath Demon. This allowed Culhen to gain some precious ground, Ahren immediately peppering the gobsmacked giant with arrows as soon as he had gotten over his initial shock.

'Very well done, Hakanu,' said Ahren, his voice shaking with emotion as he continued to shoot, focusing solely now on the knees of the left giant, *Fisiniell's* force proving evermore effective, the shorter the distance became.

As Culhen, with Jelninolan on his back, finally reached Ahren and Hakanu, the other two wounded Wrath Demons were stumbling and limping after them with looks of wide-eyed insanity on their faces. Although they had slowed down and were clearly suffering, Ahren knew only too well that their inflamed bloodlust would only make them all the more dangerous when it came to close combat fighting.

'Help…me!' gasped Jelninolan through gritted teeth. Her bow and fingers were moving so swiftly on the strings that it was almost impossible for Ahren to follow them, while the melody that *Mirilan* was furiously expressing convinced the Forest Guardian of the imminent magical climax that Jelninolan's charm was about to reach. Quickly, he and Hakanu lifted the elf off the now kneeling wolf.

'To the circle!' muttered Ahren, he and his apprentice then carrying the musicking elf to the edge of the magically decorated area, where they gently set her down. The priestess moved slowly, step by step, into its centre, her music growing all the while louder and more dominating as it assaulted Ahren's ears and mind, causing him to sink to his knees with a gasp.

Ahren saw how Khara only managed to evade the grasp of one of the giants by leaping out of his reach before collapsing. Hakanu, like his master, was now kneeling and struggling for air on the ground.

At some point in the skirmish, Muai had landed in the river again, where the tiger was still lying half submerged in the water, her powerful flanks rising and falling with some effort. Selsena was prancing protectively over Falk, who was lying unconscious having suffered a blow to his head.

Jelninolan's magic seems to be having more of an effect on us than on the giants, thought Ahren anxiously as he did his best to ignore the overwhelming force of the music. *We are all on the point of exhaustion. Who are you telling?* retorted Culhen, who was panting heavily as he cowered beside him.

Meanwhile, the two wounded giants were tottering ever closer, their hands stretched out like greedy claws. Ahren tried to lift *Fisiniell*, but Jelninolan's urgent music thwarted any effort at coordinating his movements. He shuddered to think of what her charm might have done to his mind had Uldini not succeeded in righting his damaged head in the nick of time. Having thought of the Arch Wizard, he managed to turn his head sufficiently, so that he could see the childlike figure, placing a few pebbles into a neat pattern on the riverbank as he hummed absently to himself. Clearly, he was so absorbed in implementing his traditional magic that not even the elf's music was affecting him.

'Jelninolan!' exclaimed Ahren. 'The two other Wrath Demons are almost upon us!' Already, the ground was vibrating thanks to their irregular steps. 'And the third one is slowly getting to his feet again.'

'Only another…couple of…heartbeats,' gasped the elf.

Ahren looked at the distance that the giants still had to travel. 'We don't have that much time!'

Beside him, the exhausted and trembling Hakanu was stretching out his hand towards the advancing giants and groaning with an effort that suggested he was trying by dint of pure willpower alone to move a mountain. When the hulk to the right screamed in pain, Ahren understood what it was that his apprentice was attempting – the spear that had lodged deep in the hulk's knee was now responding to its master's command by twisting and pulling with all its might in an effort to return to Hakanu's grasp.

The tortured creature stumbled, held onto his companion and straightened up again, everything happening under the noses of the Paladins, who were battling with Jelninolan's magic.

Then Ahren heard from behind him a single word being uttered. 'Finally!' gasped Jelninolan, before an extended, extraordinarily clear sounding note brought her song to its conclusion. The ensuing silence tortured his ears and his mind even more than the complex melody he had only now been subjected to. It was as if his mind was now trying to digest the no longer audible echoes in an effort to make sense of what he had heard. The whole world suddenly seemed under water, while all its colours and contours appeared blurred in the absolute silence that surrounded him. Ahren blinked only once, and that one movement seemed weirdly to last the length of an entire season – if not longer.

Can...not...think, murmured Culhen, his voice sounding distorted within the Paladin's mind.

Then the effect was over. It was as if a cord had snapped that had been stretched too far. Ahren, suddenly free to move, yanked *Fisiniell* up to defend himself against the Wrath Demons. But they stood there as if turned to stone, blinking in the sunshine and taking no notice of either their wounds or the flickering winds that were breaking forth from their noses and mouths.

'Are those the Wrath Winds?' murmured Hakanu from beside Ahren.

'I think so,' replied the Thirteenth Paladin. 'But it seems they have been...tamed?'

'Cleansed would be a better word,' said Jelninolan, her voice hoarse with exhaustion and betraying no hint of an echo. 'For the moment, these Wrath Winds are experiencing that peace that they experienced immediately following their creation.' Her voice sounded sorrowful as she continued: 'Very soon they will become saturated with negative emotions again and their eternal hunt will resume.' She pointed at the giants. 'Simply driving the Wrath Winds out of their bodies would only have ensured that the magical beings would have lodged within some of us. Hence, I needed to come up with a solution that would bring the Wrath Winds temporarily under control.'

'What will happen to the giants now?' asked Hakanu, while the translucent shadows that had controlled the hulks were carried gently away by the wind.

Jelninolan drew her bow across *Mirilan's* strings, creating one extended note, whereupon the two standing giants immediately collapsed. This was followed by the sound of thunderous snores coming from three enormous throats. The elf looked wearily up at the heavens. 'There are enough clouds present,' she mused. 'My strength should suffice for one final spell – as long as I remain within Uldini's circle. Then I will need to rest like him.' With that she nodded towards the Arch Wizard, who was still humming happily away to himself as he sorted out pebbles by the river. 'He must have really exerted himself.'

Ahren finally pulled himself together, an effort that cost him a considerable amount of willpower. His friends, too, slowly straightened up – at least, those of them who were capable of doing so. Jelninolan's magic had caused them to expend some of that elemental driving force inherent in all living creatures. The Paladin had experienced enough charms by no to know that they were all suffering a reaction to the magical song that they had endured.

'Everyone alright?' he asked, his gaze finally resting on his old master. 'How is Falk?'

Selsena whinnied, sending out a wave of reassurance, which contained within it no more than a hint of anxiety.

'He was grazed by a massive fist,' explained Khara, who was swaying a little from side to side, her face drawn 'And Muai put in such an effort that she can barely stand anymore. She confused one of the giants with a succession of wild leaps and acrobatic attacks.' The shadow of a smile appeared on her lips. 'In fact, she almost resembled a playful kitten having great fun with an enormous ball of wool.'

A growl of protest could be heard coming from the riverbank as the tigress began staggering towards her companions. She came to a halt beside Culhen, then pushing the wolf's flank with her nose until he gave in and lay down. She immediately settled down beside him, curling herself up and resting against his fluffy stomach. Within three heartbeats, she was fast asleep.

I wasn't expecting that, said Culhen, looking at the resting feline with consternation. *Although – when she's right, she's right. Good night.* Then he rested his head on Muai's furry neck and closed his eyes.

'You mentioned a magic spell?' asked Khara, looking over at Jelninolan.

The elf nodded. 'I will charm snow to fall from the heavens as soon as everyone is together…' She stopped suddenly, frowned and asked: 'But where is Trogadon?' Each syllable she uttered sounded more anxious than its predecessor. 'I know he was caught by one of the giants' first blows.'

Ahren flinched guiltily, then scanned the scene. 'He was flung towards the southern slope of the mountain,' he said regretfully. 'We had better go and look for him.'

Khara, too, suddenly looked thoroughly miserable. 'I'm sure nothing bad has happened to him,' she murmured, trying to reassure the priestess.

'You mean, not *one* of you dunderheads thought about my Trogadon?' snarled Jelninolan, the echo in her voice re-emerging and increasing threateningly.

Hakanu raised his hand. '*I* did,' he said, his face beaming. 'I sent off Kamaluq to look for Trogadon. It seems, our blacksmith is lying asleep somewhere in the forest. I told Kamaluq to stand guard over him. He was to warn me if there was any danger and use his lightning flash as a distraction should the dwarf need help.'

'At least *one* of you had a bit of common sense,' growled Jelninolan. 'Well – what are you all waiting for. Go find my dwarf while I prepare the snow spell.'

Ahren and Khara flinched in unison. 'Bring us to him,' said the Paladin, looking at his apprentice.

'This way,' said Hakanu hurriedly as he ran off to a small swathe in the forest that had only recently been formed – as though something *very* hard and *very* compact had hurtled between the trees – more than likely a Pure Dwarf.

'What are the chances that Jelninolan won't tell Trogadon of our somewhat neglectful attitude?' asked Khara in a low voice.

Ahren merely shook his head in resignation.

'Kamaluq's over *there!*' exclaimed Hakanu, who was well ahead of them. By now they had raced a good twenty paces into the forest, and the swathe of destruction that the dwarf's unplanned flight had caused was truly impressive. Ahren was in no doubt that if a normal dwarf had suffered the blacksmith's fate – never mind a human – they wouldn't have survived the journey, given the number of splintered and broken branches that lined their stocky friend's flight path.

Ahren knew that it had been nothing short of a miracle that his own skull had remained intact after the enormous fist had swept him off Culhen's back. And had Uldini's magic not been there to keep his mind in some sort of order…

'Good fox!' exclaimed Hakanu, his voice echoing through the forest as Ahren caught sight of Kamaluq, who was whimpering joyfully and clearly enjoying the affection of his Paladin. While undoubtedly a very smart animal, the fox often behaved like a harmless, innocent and even clumsy whelp. When Hakanu picked up his little friend to hold in his arms it suddenly struck Ahren that Kamaluq behaved in such a puppylike manner precisely because he *was* so smart. In this way, he had his young Paladin wrapped around his little finger – or rather, his front paw.

'I'm delighted that we have Kamaluq again, but…where *is* Trogadon?' asked Khara, looking from left to right and back again. Ahren, too, scanned the nearby undergrowth, but his friend was nowhere to be seen.

'There!' Hakanu grinned as he pointed upwards.

Ahren followed the direction of his apprentice's finger and was surprised to see the dwarf lying on the forked top of an old fir tree that was so weighed down by its unexpected guest that it was leaning against its neighbour tree. Although Trogadon's face was splattered with blood, the calm, rhythmical rising and falling of his substantial chest suggested that the stocky blacksmith had survived his aerial adventure relatively unscathed.

Khara squinted as she stared up at the sight in silence. 'He's well and truly wedged up there,' she murmured. 'The crown of the fir tree is under enough pressure as it is and looks as though it will snap completely if any additional weight is added by us trying to rescue him.' She looked at Ahren in consternation. 'How are we going to get him down from there?'

The Forest Guardian took his time as he deliberated over the options that were open to them. Then he shook his head. 'I'll be right back,' he muttered and stomped off.

'Where are you going?' asked Khara, non-plussed.

'Seeing as we have annoyed Jelninolan enough as it is, I may as well locate one or two axes among our supplies that we can put to good use…'

'You did *what?!*' shouted Jelninolan with such force that Ahren feared the snow-covered slopes might drop their heavy load with fright.

'They *felled* me,' chuckled Trogadon.

The dwarf had woken up when Ahren and Khara were working on the tree, whose crown had been holding the blacksmith captive.

'The tree*,*' said Ahren with a groan. 'We felled the *tree* in which you were stuck – there *is* a difference.'

'I would be only too delighted to make it abundantly clear to you what I think of this *difference*. If I wasn't trapped in this circle…'

'The fall from the treetop wasn't too bad at all,' said Trogadon, trying to reassure the fuming elf. 'Compared to connecting with a giant's fist, the experience of being *felled* was no worse than stumbling over an uneven cobble on a badly paved street.'

'We *didn't* fell you,' countered Ahren, wringing his hands as he glanced over at Jelninolan, whose fury wasn't showing any signs of abating. 'So, can you *please* stop saying that!'

'Oh, no!' snapped the elf coldly. '*First,* you forgot him. *Then* you felled him.'

Trogadon looked at Ahren, Khara and Hakanu in disbelief. 'You mean – you *forgot* me?' he echoed, aghast.

'*I* didn't,' countered the apprentice hurriedly before pointing at his master and the princess. 'But *they* did.'

Trogadon's good mood vanished like the sun behind a rapidly gathering thunderstorm.

'Why doesn't Jelninolan allow the healing snow to fall while I explain to you in the utmost detail what exactly happened after your little flight through the treetops? Then you might understand why we temporarily lost our overview of the situation.'

Khara nodded in agreement and Trogadon crossed his arms belligerently.

'Well then – get on with it,' growled the blacksmith as the first snowflakes began falling from the sky, their healing charm already soothing the aching wounds of not only the companions but also those of the sleeping giants.

The day was already drawing to a close by the time the little group had, at least to some extent, regained some of their strength. Falk's body had been rubbed with the healing snow, a process that he had welcomed with a barrage of curses and considerable shivering until he had recovered sufficiently to administer the necessary torture himself.

Trogadon, on the other hand, had danced about in the snow gleefully, proving once again how indomitable Pure Dwarfs were. Much to Ahren's relief, the blacksmith seemed to have already forgiven the Paladin's and Khara's momentary carelessness.

Jelninolan, totally exhausted, was fast asleep on her mattress near the riverbank, but the Forest Guardian was certain that the disdainful look on the elf's face reflected her continuing anger at him and his beloved.

Uldini was slumbering by her side, while the weary companion animals lay in a circle around the two Ancients and rested. Ahren and

Khara made up for their previous carelessness by keeping guard, thereby allowing Falk and Trogadon to play dice a few paces away from the others, the two almost dozing off on several occasions, they were that weary.

In marked contrast to the two old warhorses, Hakanu was fizzing with all the energy of a growing boy in the nearby trees as he practised his spear throwing and the art of calling the weapon back to him. The young warrior was like a different person since his masterful throw at the distant Wrath Demon, which had worked so well and resulted in him saving both Culhen and Jelninolan. The apprentice's self-confidence had returned, and Ahren had to stop himself from worrying that Hakanu might be tempted into an act of reckless derring-do the next time they found themselves in a dangerous situation. It was high time that he placed his faith in his protégé – even if the young warrior sometimes behaved in a manner that Ahren did not necessarily approve of. The truth was beginning to dawn on the Forest Guardian that this was perhaps the most difficult lesson for any good master to learn – and that he needed to truly be there for his apprentice.

'What are you thinking about?' asked Khara from the other side of the campfire, her head cocked as she gazed at him quizzically.

Ahren looked back at her and shrugged his shoulders. 'The fact that I will never quite manage to tame Hakanu's boundless courage,' he replied with a sigh.

The Swordsmistress nodded. 'Perhaps you don't need to. Teach him what you know, and he can learn the rest for himself. Remember how he began to control his previous daredevilry as soon as he became responsible for the Fox Guards.' She glanced over at the apprentice and smiled as he whooped with joy and called back his spear, with which he had just successfully hit the top of a fir tree a good two and a half furlongs away. 'I know that you have had to constantly check him during his training – but you need to believe that he will find his *own* way. All you can do is pass on the torch to him so that he can see where he is going.'

Ahren grinned. 'How philosophical,' he teased. 'And what happened to those never-ending drills with which *you t*ortured him – not to mention *me* in former times – so that we would become better at close-combat fighting?'

Khara's eyes glided knowingly over to her Paladin. Her calm demeanour suggested that she hadn't fallen for his trap but was remaining serious. 'I think that we *all* need to let go of our cherished habits now that the end of the war is nigh. A few press-ups or a couple of ascents of a ribbon tree will hardly change Hakanu now. But perhaps a sense of *freedom*, and a *genuine* self-confidence regarding his own abilities will blossom within him if *we* place *our* trust in him.'

Ahren watched his apprentice for a considerable time in silence before finally waving the lad over. The Forest Guardian didn't fail to spot how Hakanu's shoulders immediately tensed up as the lad trotted over to his master.

'Sit down,' said Ahren, his face betraying no emotion whatsoever. His apprentice immediately did as he was told, his shoulders sagging in the process. Clearly, he was awaiting a lecture, which only made Ahren purse his lips, so angry was he with himself. At this, Hakanu bowed his head, misunderstanding his master's gesture completely.

What a disaster, thought the Forest Guardian bitterly. He exchanged looks with Khara, who smiled at him encouragingly. He cleared his throat.

'Hakanu,' he began, noticing immediately how raw his voice sounded. He cleared his throat. 'Hakanu,' he repeated, this time making sure to make the word sound warmer and more genuine. 'You saved the lives of both Culhen and Jelninolan – you know that, don't you?'

His apprentice looked at him uncertainly. 'Yes?' he replied tentatively. Clearly, the apprentice felt that there was something fishy going on.

I would have reacted precisely the same way with Falk, thought the Forest Guardian, unable to prevent himself from chuckling. Somehow, this source of his sudden merriment – which sprang from his own days as an apprentice – was precisely the impulse that he needed to continue talking.

'Your throw was *excellent*. And your idea of calling back the spear from the giant's leg at that precise moment undoubtedly saved all our skins. Had the Wrath Demons reached the magic circle before Jelninolan had finished her song, the skirmish would surely have ended badly for us.'

Hakanu looked at Ahren in wide-eyed wonder, the latter then continuing to speak in a friendly voice.

'The fact that you thought of Trogadon's welfare, even in the heat of battle, is proof of your developing sense of responsibility.' The Forest Guardian took a deep breath before adding: 'Which is why I have decided to erase your mistaken attack on Four Claws from my memory.'

Hakanu's face broke into a grin, and his eyes took on that infamous look which Ahren recognised all too well – his protégé had now stopped listening to him, so caught up was he now in imaging his heroic feats of the future.

'Thank you, Master!' exclaimed the young warrior, beside himself with joy. On an impulse, he hugged Ahren before leaping up and running over to the sleeping Kamaluq. 'Wake up! Wake up! You'll never guess what just happened!'

'And suddenly, he behaves so childishly again,' murmured Ahren, shaking his head as he watched the laughing Hakanu pick up the sleepy fox and run off with him along the riverbank.

'You have done the right thing,' said Khara. 'Hakanu makes it all too easy for others to underestimate him. But just because he displays his emotions so openly, doesn't mean that his heart isn't in the right place.'

Ahren stared into the fire and mulled over what his beloved had said. It had never been his protégé's heart or his emotions that had concerned the Forest Guardian – but rather, the lad's *understanding,* which yielded far too often to his undoubted courage.

'We must get away from here!'

The words had slipped out of Uldini's mouth even before the Arch Wizard opened his eyes following his exhausted slumber.

Ahren flinched and shook himself in an effort to rid himself of the numbness that had inevitably overcome him during his night watch. The campfire was no more than a pile of glimmering ashes now, and dawn was fast approaching, but clouds filled the sky, depriving the landscape of any moonlight as it lay there, dark and silent.

'What do you mean?' asked Ahren in a low voice, trying not to disturb his sleeping companions. He, Hakanu and Khara had taken it in turns to keep watch, and now the Forest Guardian and the Arch Wizard were the only ones awake in their makeshift encampment.

'The Adversary!' exclaimed Uldini breathlessly as he struggled to his feet. 'I suspect that He knows *precisely* where we are…we must get away from here!'

But how…?' began Ahren, only to break off as the realisation dawned on him. 'The *magic*,' he said, looking knowingly at the Arch Wizard. 'You and Jelninolan used far too much magic for us to remain undiscovered.'

Uldini nodded. 'Our grand plan concerning the Wrath Demons demanded far more of an effort than expected. The disguise charm was not sufficient to hide all the spells,' the childlike figure added as he proceeded to shake Jelninolan awake. 'Healing your head with *Flamestar*, protecting the charm circle, not to mention patching up your battered body were in themselves three extremely powerful spells. We are talking here about a veritable beacon of sorcery.'

'Oh, so that was why you were playing with pebbles on the riverbank,' said Trogadon as he scratched his tummy, sat up and smacked his lips before letting out a deafening yawn. 'Being *felled* really does make one tired.'

Ahren looked at the dwarf, a tortured look on his face. 'Please stop saying that. We felled a *tree* in which you were well and truly stuck.'

'This is what happens – one falls asleep and misses all the best stories,' grunted Falk from the far end of the encampment. 'I want to hear *every* detail now.'

Ahren rubbed his face wearily. 'And it had been such a *peaceful* night,' he muttered. Then he proceeded to wake up the rest of his friends so that they could quickly make their escape – before the Adversary would subject them to another surprise, and doubtless one on a similar scale as three furious Wrath Demons – if not worse.

***

As had so often been the case over the previous weeks, Quin-Wa couldn't sleep. If her thoughts weren't with the Ancients, who were relentlessly casting spells in an effort to resist the Adversary, then she worried about her beloved Sun Emperor, who was currently traversing his empire. Or she would fret over the Paladins now waiting with nervous anticipation in Highstone and at the Ring for the arrival of Ahren and the other Champions of the gods. Or she fretted over the Soul Companions who had converged on Ahren's hometown because it contained a castle that was supposedly impregnable to the Adversary. Or…

She snorted. The list of her worries was long enough already and growing by the day. The very *fear* of a repetition of the Night of Blood seemed to be creating the circumstances that once before had brought death and unbearable sorrow to the families of the Paladins, who seemed to be on the horns of an intractable dilemma. Either the Soul Companions scattered and were thereby more difficult to track down but far more vulnerable should they fall into the hands of the Dark god, or they gathered on one spot behind protective walls and hoped that they would be able to survive the inevitable onslaught of the Adversary.

The Eternal Empress paced the chemin de ronde atop the eastern tower of Highstone, her silent refuge ever since word had gone around that it was better not to disturb her whenever she was up here.

'This waiting is well-nigh unbearable,' she murmured to herself as, heavy with child, she absently caressed her stomach. 'Then we had no idea that the Night of Blood was bearing down on us, but *now*...' She didn't dare to utter her thoughts. Now the Paladins carried with them terrible memories of the Dark Days – memories that enflamed their fears and shattered in ways that they did not understand whatever self-confidence they possessed. She could see it in the eyes of the Night of Blood veterans – the almost primeval fear that seemed to be taking hold of them and was even affecting those who only knew of that terrible time through the stories that had been handed down to them.

There was a simple truth buried deep below the analytical reasoning of the Eternal Empress – a truth that she had never dared to express even when she was on her own. If the Adversary had understood human nature that little bit better, He would, as soon as the very *first* Soul Companions had appeared on the scene, have hunted them down unmercifully. The will of each and every Paladin would have shattered like glass – with the exception of the First's perhaps – Quin-Wa was not sure if anything could shake *that* ice-cold man.

She looked over towards the Obsidian Fortress, barely visible in the darkness of the night. 'But this was always your problem, was it not?' she whispered to her archenemy as if He were standing directly opposite her. 'You do not understand us. And that was the cause of the troubles that have afflicted us ever since – a Custodian who had no concept of whom He had to protect.'

The whistling of the cool wind between the merlons and the resultant smoking of the burning torches at the entrance to the tower were the only responses that she received.

Quin-Wa shook her head. The time for philosophising was long past. Soon, weapons and magic would once again determine the fate of Jorath.

She began walking slowly towards the stairwell that led down to the interior of the castle when she felt her mind being gently tugged, an action which instinctively caused her to turn again. A ball, sheer black at its core but with a purple corona was rising from the Obsidian Fortress and soaring into the night sky. Moving in a high arc, it easily passed the multi-coloured charms that were beaming up from the Wizardly Domes that circled the Ring with the sole intention of neutralising any enemy objects. Now it was flying directly towards Quin-Wa.

Behind her, she heard the Night Soldier preparing to pull her ward back into the safety of the castle, but the Eternal Empress stopped her with a firm hand gesture.

Initially, Quin-Wa had feared an attack – a premature attempt by the Adversary to destroy Highstone Castle and all those within it. Yet she had soon realised that the unholy object's flight path suggested a different route. The Adversary's magic ball hurtled a good ten leagues northward, past Deepstone before beginning to slow a little as it then continued its journey to the east. Quin-Wa frowned.

There was nothing *there* that justified such an effort on the part of the Dark god. Why, by the THREE, would it fly towards that godsforsaken place that went by the name of Kelkor?

***

The sun had risen some time earlier, but one star had not disappeared from the clear, winter sky – a black dot with a purple corona, which seemed to be heading directly towards Ahren and companions. They had spotted it shortly after they had set off, and it had quickly become apparent to both Jelninolan and Uldini that it was a powerful charm of the Adversary hurtling in their direction. Consequently, the companions had picked up speed and already travelled a considerable distance from where they had fought the Wrath Demons. Now they were deep in the valley that the possessed giants had haunted, and hoping earnestly that they would find the Sanctum of Belsarius.

'And you *really* believe that we will find refuge from this flying object in the tower or whatever it was in which this Belsarius fellow did his research?' asked Trogadon for at least the eighth time already, yet admittedly expressing what was troubling both Ahren and Culhen.

'Yes,' grunted Uldini.

'His assurance would be much more comforting if his responses weren't so monosyllabic since this curse has been hot on our heels,' murmured Khara, Ahren nodding in reply.

'You should really leave him in peace,' said Jelninolan flatly. 'You know Uldini well enough by now to understand that he only flees enemy magic when it's absolutely necessary.'

Ahren looked at the elf with a mixture of concern and anxiety. 'The same could be said about you, could it not?'

She stroked her hair, her fingers visibly trembling. 'Yesterday was a more than exhausting day for both of us. The more time that we can buy before this black Bane Curse of the Adversary reaches us, the better.'

'And did not your veiled girlfriend in black say something about protective barriers that prevented *her* from gaining entry into Belsarius' hideaway?' growled Uldini. 'My hope is that they will save *us* from *that* there,' he added, waving vaguely skywards.

'Very clever,' said Falk, nodding approvingly. 'We will use magic that was put in place centuries ago to save ourselves.'

'Assuming we get to Belsarius' Sanctum in time,' muttered the Arch Wizard.

Can you ask the Ancients what sort of sorcery that is, which is hunting us down like a bloodhound? asked Culhen as he looked back over his shoulder and up towards the heavens. Then the big animal shivered fearfully, causing Ahren's teeth to chatter. *On second thoughts,* added the wolf, *I'd rather not know.*

'Why *now* of all times?' asked Hakanu, expressing the very question that was troubling Ahren. 'Why didn't the Adversary send such a curse after us much *earlier?*'

Uldini snorted. 'A piece of magic so ugly as the one you see up there in the heavens would rob even the Dark god of considerable power. Jelninolan successfully hid our whereabouts until the desperate skirmish with the Wrath Demons. Anyway, the Adversary was busying Himself with a succession of attacks on the Ring…' The Arch Wizard trailed off and for a few heartbeats he cocked his head. 'Indeed, perhaps this black magic might even be a *good* portent. It seems that our presence in Kelkor is making the Adversary nervous. So nervous, indeed, that He has abruptly changed His plans and is expending His energy on this magic, from which he will need days if not weeks to recover.'

Falk scratched his beard. 'If you are right, then we have won for the Ancients in the Wizardly Domes some desperately needed respite.'

'Let us hope that the price we have to pay for this diversion won't be *too* high,' murmured Khara as she looked over her shoulder and up at the Bane Curse.

No-one responded to the words of the Swordsmistress, Ahren and his friends increased their tempo in silence, however.

Chapter 6

The midday sun shone almost perpendicularly down onto the deep valley surrounded by the three steep mountain slopes. The companions had already crossed through the solitary hidden pass, whose narrow, natural path Ahren had only noticed when he had spotted for a heartbeat a black Hanta, who had seemed then to vanish into the sheer rockface behind it. Clearly, his mysterious, black-veiled ally was waiting somewhere in the vicinity of the Sanctum and had sent forth Camentumar to alert the travellers to the right route. The Thirteenth Paladin had decided, however, not to mention the presence of either the beast or the Woman in Black for the moment, Uldini's mood being irritable, to say the least.

The Adversary's sorcerous ball was coming ever closer and had begun its gradual, inevitable descent from the heavens like a slow-moving, foreboding falling star, heading directly for the companions.

Ahren scanned long and hard for the Sanctum once they had fully traversed the pass that had led them into the valley from the south. 'There!' he exclaimed. 'That must be it!'

'I see it too,' agreed Falk, pointing at the same shadow among the jagged rocks that his erstwhile apprentice had spotted. 'That might once have been an archway.'

Hakanu craned his neck and looked in vain. 'Well, all I can see is an endless number of stones.'

Ahren shook his head. 'Take a closer look,' he murmured encouragingly. 'I, too, only saw rock, moss and jagged shadows initially.' He pointed at the expanse of rubble. It seemed as if the entire flank of the northernmost of the three mountains had one day simply slipped down, showering the little valley with rocks that, taken together, would have been sufficient to build a palace. The result was a labyrinth of large, grey stones and wildly growing plants which dazzled the eye and would undoubtedly slow down their progress through the valley. 'Do you see behind those two rocks there that are wedged together? You can just about make out the shape of an archway in their shadow.'

Hakanu squinted and frowned. 'Are you *sure* that's an entrance?' he asked.

'It would certainly be better if Ahren *wasn't* mistaken,' snarled Uldini, waving his arms vaguely up at the sky. 'Because while we fight our way through this valley at a snail's pace, the Adversary's charm is getting dangerously close. If there is *no* Sanctum waiting for us over there, we will be hopelessly exposed to this blasted Bane Curse.'

'What alternative do we have?' asked Khara, turning to the two Ancients. 'Would it be possible to dissolve the approaching Bane Curse if we rest here for a while and give you two the chance to recover?'

'I would prefer if we took our chance in this valley,' said Jelninolan nervously. 'I can already sense the dark power trying to grasp at us from the heavens. Without the support of complex defensive runes, a skirmish with this magic would be…well…*challenging.*'

Uldini nodded in agreement but said nothing.

'Would Muai be able to confirm or dismiss what I believe I am seeing?' asked Ahren, pointing at the distant shadow. 'After all, she has the best eyes of all of us.'

I really wish you'd stop harping on about the feline's talents. It's getting me down, complained Culhen.

Really? And I thought it was me that got you down by sitting on you all the time, chuckled the Forest Guardian.

Culhen snorted. *You'd be far better off sticking to killing Dark Ones than trying to crack jokes. Your attempts at humour leave a lot to be desired.*

Meanwhile, Muai had performed some elegant leaps and was now sitting on top of an impressively jutting rock, her green eyes looking northward. Then she uttered a low growl, whereupon Khara gave a sigh of relief.

'She says that she really *can* see an archway.' When the Swordsmistress looked over at Ahren, however, he could see the doubt in her eyes. 'But it has been badly damaged by the avalanche. No wonder that the First thought the Sanctum was lost when he searched the area.'

Trogadon pointed at the slope of the northern mountain. 'I wager one of the plaits on my beard that this rockfall was *not* caused by Mother Nature. I am certain that it took sorcerous folderol to loosen an entire mountainside. The mountains here are simply far too big.'

'*Folderol?*' repeated Jelninolan, her eyebrows raised in mock surprise.

'You know what I mean, my heart,' grunted Trogadon.

'No, I *don't*, my dear,' countered the elf tartly. 'But never mind – I could just as easily introduce you as the *metal basher* should we encounter strangers – I'm sure that they would *know* what *I* mean.'

Trogadon raised his hands defensively. 'Alright, alright. I apologise for my flowery language.'

'May I remind everyone of the deadly charm that is getting closer with every passing heartbeat?' interjected Falk caustically, Selsena underlining his concern by sending a wave of anxiety so powerful that it shook Ahren and the others to the very core. 'Perhaps we should leave such trivial debates until we are safe.'

'The undergrowth in this valley is terribly dense for the most part, while half of the rocks are taller than a man and almost impossible to scale. Culhen and I will ride on ahead to figure out the best route. You can then follow us,' said Ahren immediately, patting his furry friend's neck affectionately. 'He can jump better than Selsena, which means that the two of us will be best able to negotiate the confusion of stone and brush.'

This suggestion was immediately countered by a low growl from Muai, who was still sitting on her rock, her tail whipping slowly from side to side.

'I have been told to report to you that my tigress will also look for a route that we can follow.'

Well then, it will be interesting to see which of us is faster, grumbled Culhen, immediately leaping into the waist-high undergrowth of knotty tendrils and thorny bushes. The Paladin could only manage an apologetic look over his shoulders as his wolf hurtled off with his master, a bumpy and unequal race then ensuing between Culhen and Muai, wolf and rider making their zigzag way through the valley with a mixture of brute force and long strides, while the tigress proceeded by combining daredevil leaps from one jagged boulder to the next with quick ascents up the sheer rockfaces, all the while trying to be the first to make out the best route towards the archway for Ahren, his wolf and the travel party behind.

Ahren briefly considered bringing the nonsense to an end, but the competitive spirit between the two companion animals spurred both of them on to such an extent that he thought it better to allow Culhen his fun. Soon, they had left their companions so far behind that the Paladin resorted to creating markings for his friends by using *Sun* to score the rocks on either side of the path that Muai and Culhen had located. The wolf's stomach fur was already full of burrs, while tufts of his white hair now decorated many of the thick and prickly blackberry bushes that they had passed. Nevertheless, Culhen stormed onwards relentlessly, focusing both on the way ahead and on the big cat leaping the same direction but over their heads.

'If a crazed mind had created this labyrinth, it could hardly have been more complicated,' muttered Ahren, he and Culhen having progressed across half the valley, although having covered twice the distance thanks to the multitude of detours involved.

At least we're not cheating on our journey through this lunatic maze, sulked Culhen as he glared at Muai, who had leapt long and gracefully from one rocky ledge to the next, while the wolf fought his way through a sprawling, snow-covered climber. *And what sorts of plants are these that can survive such harsh winters?*

Kelkor is a land of primeval wonder, Ahren reminded his friend. *Be happy that no deadly tendrils have made themselves at home here. If Trogadon is right about the avalanche not having been a natural event, then you can be sure that the Adversary or some of His powerful servants were behind it. And if you add the three Wrath Demons as unwitting protectors of the valley, then we can certainly count ourselves lucky that the local plants have not fallen under the control of the Dark god.*

Culhen didn't reply – he was too busy growling as he disentangled himself from yet another thornbush that had seemed to be lying in wait for him, hidden under the hard snow only to wrap itself around the wolf's front paw. This unplanned hold-up meant that Muai was now no more to be seen, having left Ahren and his friend in her wake.

'You are late.'

Ahren turned his head quickly to see where the voice had come from. Although he had expected the presence of the Woman in Black, he was still surprised by her sudden appearance on a rock directly ahead of him where only a dozen heartbeats earlier, Muai had been standing and staring down challengingly at the entangled wolf. Now the features of the tigress had been replaced by those of the lurking stranger, who with shoulders tensed up seemed to be peering through her veil at the Thirteenth Paladin, casting some sort of mysterious judgement upon him.

'We were held up by three giants,' replied Ahren with a frown. 'Wrath Demons that you hadn't forewarned us about.'

'They were the latest attempt by the Adversary to hide the valley from inquisitive eyes,' countered the black-robed figure.

'Are you going to *finally* talk to my companions?' asked the Forest Guardian irritably. 'Or why have you made an appearance now of all times?'

The Woman in Black shook her head firmly. 'I will continue to stay in the shadows for the moment – until Belsarius' secret has been revealed.' She paused before continuing: 'And after that…it will be time for a council of war and the beating of drums when all veils will have to be removed.'

From behind Ahren, came the faint echo of Trogadon's laughter, the stranger's shoulders then appearing to tense up even more. 'Belsarius protected his Sanctum with more than simply magic,' she said urgently. 'Beware of traps, too. This is all I have to say for now.' Then she retreated from the rock ledge and vanished. Not ten heartbeats later, Muai reappeared at the same place, the big cat appearing unusually confused as her nose sniffed the air.

'We had a visitor!' shouted Ahren to the tigress. 'But the Woman in Black is gone again.'

Muai responded with a low, dissatisfied growl as she paced around the top of the boulder.

It is not only the Woman in Black that is confusing her, explained Culhen, within whom a feeling of unease had manifested itself, which very quickly affected Ahren. *Something else is making the big cat nervous. Otherwise, she would never have come back to us but would have been basking in the glory of having won our little competition.*

Ahren scanned the labyrinth of jagged rocks, unruly shrubbery and all-blanketing snow. Suddenly, he was all too aware of how distant they now were from the rest of their companions.

Can you smell anything? he asked Culhen, sinking simultaneously into the wolf's senses.

The companion animal pointed his nose upwards. *Nothing out of the ordinary,* the wolf replied, sounding less than convincing.

Ahren raised his hand, indicating to Muai that she should stay where she was. 'Kelkor is the land of monsters and Dark Ones,' he whispered just loudly enough for the tigress's keen ears to pick up the information. 'Best if we stay here and wait for the others.'

Muai cocked her head, then gave a warning growl so insistent that Ahren immediately turned his head and looked back in alarm.

Rising incredibly slowly over the edge of the southern mountain peak like a second sun was the spinning Bane Curse. The tendrils of its purple corona licked the surface of the slope as the orb travelled, extinguishing with every touch the trees, the shrubbery, the snow and even the bluish lichen that covered most of the rocks, leaving nothing but a naked and dead wasteland in its wake.

Ahren nervously chewed on his lower lip before speaking. 'On second thoughts, let's get a move on and keep an eye out, insofar as it's possible, for those traps the Woman in Black talked about.'

Muai growled again, then leapt onto a nearby rock. From there she looked down at Culhen, changing the tone of her voice almost imperceptibly. The wolf barked and proceeded to fight his way through the undergrowth, which cracked beneath his weight, until he arrived at the base of the boulder upon which Muai was temporarily enthroned. Then the tigress leapt to the next rock, repeating her command.

'Am I mistaken, or are we making quicker progress now,' asked Ahren, who was busy hacking away with *Sun* at the particularly thick sections of undergrowth in an effort to make the route easier for their friends behind them.

Muai and I are now working as a team, admitted Culhen bashfully. *She figures out from above the least dense route through the valley, and I smash a way through the tendrils and thorns.*

Despite the dangers that they were presently facing, Ahren couldn't suppress a smile. Even after all this time that the wolf and the big cat had spent in each other's company, their friendship was still very much based on instinct. He was about to praise Culhen for his spirit of cooperation when the wolf suddenly flinched, almost unseating the Forest Guardian and throwing him into the undergrowth.

'What happened?' asked the Paladin aloud, so surprised was he.

Something bit me, complained Culhen, lifting his front right paw. Two tiny red points glistened on the animal's white fur. *It hurts – like as if a dozen ants are running through my veins.*

A snakebite! The thought took Ahren by surprise. *Here – in the snow?*

Culhen, meanwhile, was limping onward to Muai's latest stopping place, only to flinch again. *Now it's bitten me in the tummy.*

Ahren stared down at the snow-covered shrub that Culhen was now passing but could make nothing out other than thin, flexible branches and several creepers until…

'There! A snake!' he exclaimed as one of the pallid tendrils suddenly moved, a surprisingly narrow head with two tiny blue-shimmering eyes revealing itself. With lightning speed, the creature bit at Ahren's leg, its two fangs, however, sliding harmlessly along his Deep Steel armour.

Now that the Forest Guardian had caught a glimpse of the danger, he identified the animal immediately.

'Those are Frost Adders. One of the rare snake species that the THREE created which can survive the cold. They remain immobile for moons on end in a sort of paralysis only to spring to life when prey comes within their grasp or if they feel that they are in imminent danger.'

Ow, exclaimed Culhen, Ahren sensing through their spiritual connection that the wolf had been bitten a third time – this time in his back right leg.

'A single bite is painful for a human but by no means fatal,' muttered Ahren, remembering what he had learnt. 'But several bites in a row undoubtedly are, because more and more poison pumps through the veins.'

Culhen redoubled his efforts at catching up with Muai, the growling feline now sitting on a rock, below which was one of the few clearings within the valley. Before the wolf reached the space, two more snakes had sunk their fangs into his unprotected extremities.

Animal Blessings or no Animal Blessings, this is really beginning to hurt, complained the wolf with a whimper as he sprang onto a smooth surface of snow, which was free of rocks and shrubbery.

Filled with compassion for his furry friend, Ahren jumped down from the saddle and proceeded to draw his Wind Blade through the crusted snow. Frost Adders generally stayed in the undergrowth, from where they could attack passing hares or other such prey, but occasionally they would hide under a blanket of snow like this one.

'Got you!' grunted the Paladin, rather pleased with himself, as his blade found and swept away a lurking snake.

Feel free to cut the nasty creatures in two, complained Culhen.

These aren't Dark Ones, remember, countered Ahren, reminding his friend. 'And if one chases them away, Frost Adders won't attack again,' he added aloud so that Muai would understand that it wasn't in fact necessary to kill the animals. The look from the tigress spoke volumes, however. If one of the slim creatures dared to approach Muai, she would finish them off forthwith. 'Please warn the others,' added Ahren, earning another withering glare from the big cat. Clearly, she had long since informed Khara of the snake's presence in the area.

The Paladin poked a little longer in the snow to protect Culhen from any further attacks only for the wolf to nudge him from behind with his nose.

The sorcery is getting closer, warned his four-legged friend, Ahren immediately jumping into the saddle with a curse. By now, the awesome curse had shoved its way completely over the top of the mountain and was now rolling inch by inch down the slope like a slowly setting sun, leaving in its wake a desert of lifelessness. His concern for Culhen's welfare had again distracted the Paladin from the silent threat that was incessantly approaching.

'How are you feeling?' asked Ahren, the wolf now leaving the snake-free area of rifled snow.

My whole body is tickling, Culhen replied. *But the bites aren't hurting anymore.*

It seems, then, that your Animal Blessing is a good antidote, thought Ahren, relieved. *As long as you aren't bitten too often and in too short a time, the magic should be able to protect you.*

The Paladin felt Culhen flinching twice in quick succession. *That's all very well for you to say. It seems to me that the population of Frost Adders is increasing, the closer we get to the Sanctum. What are all these critters doing here anyway?*

Perhaps they are a safety measure introduced by Belsarius, suggested Ahren. As he communicated, he sliced in two a Frost Adder that was about to bite the wolf. His love of animals didn't extend to any that endangered Culhen's life. *It would certainly suit the nature of the peace-loving Ancient, from what I have heard about him. These snakes are not immediately mortally dangerous, but they would undoubtedly deter any unwelcome visitors from this valley.*

Great, grumbled Culhen. *No wonder we're encountering one danger after another if not only that genius Belsarius, but also the Adversary is trying to keep everyone away from the Sanctum.* Again, the wolf was bitten, but this time the ensuing cramp was so painful that the wolf almost threw Ahren from his saddle a second time, he was shuddering so much.

'Culhen,' began Ahren, only for a gentle, sleep-inducing melody to fill the valley, which immediately created images of a soft bed and a warm blanket in the Paladin's mind.

Jelninolan, you lovely elf! exclaimed Culhen with delight. *Look, Ahren – the snakes are all curling up and closing their eyes!*

Ahren turned in the faint hope of seeing his friends somewhere in the labyrinthine rock landscape – only to gasp in amazement.

Resembling a monster with a multitude of arms, the sheer-black Bane Curse was now rolling down the distant slope towards the valley – but this time with all the speed of an avalanche! 'Jelninolan's song must be *attracting* the sorcery,' groaned the Forest Guardian. 'Muai, Culhen! Now it's up to you! We must get to the Sanctum as quickly as we can!'

The two companion animals wasted no time but feverishly began to figure out the quickest route to the shaded archway. The two monolithic rocks leaning against each other as their eternal duty demanded and sheltering the now clearly visible entrance in their shade, resembled two frozen sentries guarding the Sanctum. Ahren reckoned the distance to the archway at no more than two and a half furlongs, but thanks to the maze of stubborn plants and sharp rocks, it would probably take several dozen paces more than a sprint of five furlongs along a flat surface.

Ahren slashed feverishly at the undergrowth that Culhen was smashing through with brute force, trying to make the route easier for Khara and the others. Time and again, the young man looked back over his shoulder in search of his friends, but all he could see was the black monstrosity of a Bane Curse with its unholy purple tentacles greedily licking the landscape, destroying every living thing they touched. Ahren knew that his companions, lacking the speed and leaping ability of the wolf, would make considerably slower progress, and the fact that there was still no sign of them, worried him greatly.

They were no more than three dozen paces from the weathered doorway when Muai, directly ahead of them, began to growl in a tone that could best be described as deeply frustrated. Once Ahren had crashed his way through some particularly stubborn shrubbery and reached the tigress, he summarised the situation that lay before them in what to Ahren's ears sounded like the perfect reaction: *Ugh!*

Ahren clenched his fists and ground his teeth as he dismounted the wolf and looked down the cleft that stretched a good thirty paces across from the base of one of the monoliths to the base of the other, thereby creating a kind of natural moat, cutting them off from the archway. The Paladin tried to imagine the sheer force of the avalanche that must have rolled down the slope to have caused such an almighty gash in the earth.

'We would have to leap at least eight paces. Not even Muai could manage that, no matter how long a run-up she had,' groaned the Paladin as he turned to look back. The ever-approaching Bane Curse was an all-destroying monstrous ball, which had already traversed half the valley, and still Ahren's friends were nowhere to be seen. He quickly deliberated if he should turn and go back to search for them, especially as neither he nor Culhen could do anything about this crevice. Given the short time left before the Bane Curse would reach them, only sorcery could help them cross the gorge that separated them from the Sanctum of Belsarius.

At the very moment when Ahren had finally forced himself into making a decision – namely to look for the others – he caught sight of Khara in the distance between some jagged rocks, her black hair resembling an ebony fan as she raced towards him, with no sign of the Warrior Pin that normally kept the strands in place.

'Watch out! Crevice ahead!' he roared at the top of his voice.

'We know that already!' yelled Khara back at him. 'You're not the only one able to see through the eyes of your companion animal, remember!'

Muai purred with self-satisfaction before jumping from her rock down to Ahren and Culhen. The Paladin now fixed his eyes on the Bane Curse, which was spinning closer and closer to the approaching group, including the fiddle-playing elf as she hurried along.

'Better if you *stop* playing!' screamed Ahren. 'Maybe the sorcerous ball will slow down!'

'*Not* a good idea!' bellowed Trogadon in his gravelly voice, the dwarf hurtling towards the Forest Guardian as fast as his short legs would carry him, holding the violently twitching Hakanu in his powerful arms. 'I don't think that your apprentice will survive another snakebite.'

'What by all that is holy…?!' began Ahren as his friends became fully visible among the rocks, their battered states presenting a truly sorry sight.

Falk was limping as if he had a very poorly made wooden leg, Uldini was holding the unconscious Kamaluq in his arms as he floated forward, Khara's hands were clearly badly swollen, while Jelninolan looked as white as a sheet. Only Selsena appeared to be unhurt, but *why* she wasn't carrying her limping Paladin on her back was a mystery to Ahren.

I will get Falk, said Culhen, already bounding forward to the old Forest Guardian. Ahren, too, ran towards his companions, and no sooner had he reached them when he took the unconscious fox from Uldini, the little animal's chest heaving up and down as if he, like the others, had been sprinting for his life, while his companions appeared thoroughly distressed. The many little bites that decorated the furry fellow were silent witness to the torture that the young fox had suffered.

'A nest of adders!' spluttered Khara. 'Muai's warning came too late, alas. It seems that *you* must have disturbed the snakes, and *we* ran right into them.'

'Later,' snarled Uldini. 'Or we will end up sharing the same fate as these slippery creatures.'

Ahren now raced back north, towards the cleft a good two hundred paces further on, and it seemed as if all the Dark Ones of the Obsidian Fortress were hunting him down. He glanced over his shoulder, immediately cursing himself for his folly. The snake-like purple tendrils of the pitch-black sorcerous ball were clearly visible as they greedily licked at the bushes, quenching all life forms in the blink of an eye, turning everything to a fine dust, which the gentle breeze day then carried away. The deathly silence, which immediately ensued seemed all the more terrible on this chilly winter's day, for it signalled the sudden, heartless expiration of those life forms which had defied all odds and managed to flourish over the centuries in Kelkor, even in the harsh conditions of the terrain.

'Faster, faster, *faster!*' yelled Ahren, foolishly trying to shove the floating Uldini with his free hand.

'Leave it,' snarled the Arch Wizard. 'I am trying to concoct a little trick that will get us across the crevice in one piece so that we won't end up slaking the ravenous hunger of this damn Bane Curse. Your interfering is only distracting me.'

Ahren stopped himself from protesting angrily, moving over to Trogadon instead, who was struggling to keep up thanks to his shorter legs. 'Can I help?' gasped the Paladin.

'Take the lad's accursedly awkward spear from me,' muttered the dwarf, the sweat pouring down his face as he stomped onward in energy-sapping staccato movements, eating up the distance to the crevice, step by painful step.

Ahren placed Kamaluq in the crook of his right hand, using his left one to grab his apprentice's weapon, which Trogadon had been holding across his heaving chest.

The blacksmith let out an audible sigh of relief before slinging Hakanu over his shoulder like a sack of flour. 'I've been wanting to do this the whole time.'

'Damn and blast it, how can you manage to stay on this swinging hobby horse for any more than ten paces?' cursed Falk, who was now astride Culhen, holding on for dear life and swaying madly from side to side like a reed on a riverbank in the midst of a gale.

You can tell the old geezer that he's more than welcome to get off and walk if... began the wolf only to trail off as a low whispering sound came from the rear. Ahren could now feel the fine dust tickling his nose, the incinerated remains of bushes, shrubs and everything else that had been living immediately behind them only a heartbeat earlier.

'Rock crevice ahead!' yelled Falk, Culhen coming to a sudden halt at the edge of the cleft which halted any progress to the Sanctum. Ahren calculated that he and the others had no more than two dozen more paces before they would reach the obstacle.

'Uldini, it's high time for a miracle!' gasped Jelninolan, now ceasing her fiddle-playing.

Ahren silently doubted that there were any living Frost Adders left that would have been charmed by the elf's song anyway. This time, he withstood the temptation to glance back over his shoulder, looking instead at the childlike figure beside him, who was mumbling quietly to himself as he floated along. Three more paces to the abyss, but Ahren and his friends did not dare to reduce the speed of their run. Culhen was preparing to leap, Muai and Selsena on either side of the wolf.

Ahren... pleaded the wolf fearfully. *The sorcery is right behind you all!*

Two more paces to the crevice.

'Uldini!' yelled Khara furiously. *'Do* something!'

One pace.

Ahren stumbled as he suddenly no longer felt the weight of the rucksack on his back, burnt to a cinder by a licking tongue of the Bane Curse.

'ULDINI!' roared a chorus of terrified voices as the companions leapt forward towards certain death in a final act of desperation…their feet then magically touching a shimmering, almost invisible surface that took the form of a bridge, arching from one side of the crevice to the other.

'Faster, dammit!' groaned Uldini. 'I can only maintain this kind of improvised spell for a few heartbeats at most!'

In order to free himself of the weapon, which was only getting in his way, Ahren hurled it full force with his left hand so that it flew through the entrance that awaited them five paces beyond the archway, while he pressed the suffering Kamaluq close to his chest with his right arm, gathering all his reserves of energy to pump his legs, which seemed almost to be burning with fire. He ran faster than he had ever run before, surrounded by his similarly panic-stricken friends, straight towards the stone archway, in whose frame he could now make out complex magical runes.

Let us hope that the Woman in Black spoke the truth, thought the Forest Guardian, the little group of adventurers already storming into the passageway – four paces across and a good four paces high – and into the darkness of an unlit tunnel.

Suddenly, there was an almighty atonal screeching sound that resembled no living being, nor no lifeless material either – it simply sounded *false* somehow, as if all the laws of Creation were screaming out in pain.

'The Bane Curse is forcing its way into the tunnel! The protective charms are failing!' gasped Uldini, horrified. 'Jelninolan, we must immediately reinforce them!'

The two Ancients spun around within the gloom of the passageway, Jelninolan's aura of True Form and Uldini's blazing *Flamestar* lighting up the hewn rock around them.

Threads of liquid white and blazing yellow shot forth from the Ancients, both of whom had sunk groaning to their knees, while the purple tendrils of the black ball snaked their way forward along the stone towards the companions. The world beyond the tunnel was a wall of such sheer blackness that Ahren could only have described it as the very essence of an existence lacking the completeness of life.

'Too...*strong,*' groaned Uldini. 'Run for your lives!'

Ahren looked in horror at the Arch Wizard. A sorcery that was too powerful for Uldini *and* Jelninolan was impossible to accept – let alone imagine!

'We will unleash ourselves,' groaned Jelninolan through gritted teeth. 'Get yourselves to safety!'

With every heartbeat, the Bane Curse of the Adversary was now driving the Ancients further and further back. Only five paces separated the two from the deadly charm.

'They are both going to sacrifice themselves,' whispered Khara in astonishment. 'We must *do* something, Ahren!'

'Only...the...Paladins are important!' gasped Uldini. 'You *must*...survive. Now RUN!'

It was only a minimal adjustment of his weight that Ahren made as he prepared to take his first step into Belsarius' Sanctum, but he hated himself for it.

'NO!' sounded a voice with all the solidity of a rock and with such grim determination that the very mountain would have flinched had it been able to. Trogadon stepped beside Jelninolan and placed a calloused hand on the elf's shoulder. 'This world will either greet us as a *united* band of brothers and sisters or we will *all together* be turned to ash and scattered by the wind.'

'What...what is your plan?' asked Uldini as the dwarf took a step towards the duelling energies.

'Trogadon,' whispered Jelninolan. 'Please...save *yourself.*'

The dwarf did not look at the two Ancients but instead took a step forward and inspected the tunnel with the darting flames of the Adversary's sorcery, now less than a hand's span away. The first tendrils licked at the stocky fellow, but now Jelninolan, with an almost animalistic growl, restrained the flaming tentacles, bathing them in a white fire that radiated her True Form like a cold sun. Then the blacksmith raised his hammer – gripping it so tightly with both hands that his knuckles were a blinding white – and prepared to strike.

'This is *magic!*' shouted Uldini in a strangled voice. 'You cannot strike it, you *oaf!*'

'True – I can't do *that,*' countered Trogadon, sounding remarkable calm. 'But I can do something *better* – namely, use my *head.*' With that, he slammed the hammer with all his might against the roof of the tunnel before immediately leaping backwards as with an almighty noise, the rock ceiling began to crumble and collapse. The Bane Curse ceased its embrace of the two Ancients, reverting to darting futilely against them before being completely stopped by the mass of rocks that, with an incredible primeval force, finally sealed the tunnel into which the companions had fled.

Ahren, almost choking because of the dust that the collapse had caused, coughed and spluttered as he and his friends rushed to safety, fleeing deeper and deeper into the Sanctum of Belsarius.

Once the sound of falling rocks had faded away, and their flight had come to an end, Ahren and his friends looked in disbelief at Trogadon, who was whistling to himself contentedly.

'What?' asked the blacksmith, the picture of innocence, but with an undeniable sparkle in his eye. 'Surely you *all* saw how this Bane Curse was so greedy that it never gave a second thought to the pure, mountain rock.' He pointed at the collapsed section of tunnel behind them. 'Now that nasty spell is buried underneath the debris and will no longer snake its way forward.'

'But that was…that was…' stammered Uldini.

'That was *wonderful!*' exclaimed Jelninolan, tugging the dwarf by the plaits on his beard and kissing him hard. 'My clever, stubborn, *amazing* Trogadon!'

'Does that mean, then, that our *dwarf d*efeated a deadly charm that you two *Ancients* could not vanquish – and he did so by means of a *tunnel collapse?*' asked Falk, blinking in disbelief.

Ahren looked over at Uldini in anticipation. The Paladin's head was spinning after all that had happened – a moment earlier he had feared losing two of his closest friends, and now…

'It is a little more complicated than that,' countered Uldini tartly, wiping the blood that was dripping from his nose. 'Indeed, it is true that the charm will starve now, not being able to get any nutrition from beneath the rocks that might reinvigorate it, and because of this, the…uh…well…'

'So, Trogadon *did* kill the magic,' interjected Falk, cutting off the Arch Wizard.

'That's *not* what I said…' retorted Uldini furiously.

'Just wait until Hakanu hears that one can *kill* charms,' chuckled Khara. 'He will insist on skewering the next spell that comes along with his spear.'

'Oh, please, *no!* groaned Ahren. 'Can't we simply tell him that it was the curse itself that caused the tunnel to collapse and thereby caused its own destruction? Just to give me *some* peace at least.'

The companions laughed just a little too hysterically for Ahren to feel any genuine relief, the Forest Guardian now feeling a lump in his throat. Death had been inches away! Had it not been for Trogadon's moment of inspiration, Jelninolan and Uldini would no longer be with them.

He exchanged a look with the blacksmith, who merely nodded almost imperceptibly before returning to enjoying the attention of Jelninolan, who was whispering sweet nothings into his ear. Ahren could see that the elf's hands were trembling – there was no doubt that both she and Uldini, who was still trying to stanch his nosebleed, were completely shattered out by their recent exertions.

'May I point out in the midst of the general relief we are feeling that our way back is now *blocked* to us?!' blurted out Falk. 'Without willing to diminish Trogadon's inspiration, there is no doubt that dying of thirst and hunger is no less unpleasant than suffering the same fate by means of a Bane Curse.'

Selsena whinnied in annoyance and butted the old Forest Guardian in the back with her head. The wave of scolding that emanated from her left no-one in any doubt as to what she thought of her Paladin's tactlessness.

Jelninolan threw Falk a withering look. 'I am sure that *my* Trogadon has thought of *all* eventualities…' she began, only for the dwarf to cough politely, causing her to trail off.

'Well, to be perfectly honest, Falk *does* have a point,' muttered the blacksmith, clearly embarrassed. 'We don't have the tools necessary to get ourselves out the way we came in, and if Belsarius' Sanctum doesn't…uh…have a rear exit, then…well…we're stuck between a rock and a hard place if you…uh… pardon the pun.'

'This day is getting better and better by the heartbeat,' sighed Khara, stroking the now growling Muai.

Ahren? whined Culhen. *Are we really trapped in here?* The rumbling of the wolf's stomach was impossible to miss in the confined space. *I can't imagine anything worse than not having anything to eat. You know how much I love food!*

The Forest Guardian wearily rubbed his eyes and pointed down the passageway. 'As there is only one direction in which we can move, I suggest we follow the tunnel. I am sure that Belsarius neither dwelled nor carried out experiments in a dark and gloomy passage. Let us find his living quarters and hope that we can rest there. Then we can discuss matters further.' He picked Hakanu up off the ground and threw him over his shoulder before taking Kamaluq in his free hand. 'And please keep an eye out for my apprentice's spear,' he added with a sigh. 'Bad enough having Culhen tormenting me over his missing meal. I could really do without my protégé blaming *me* for the loss of his weapon.'

His overwhelming sense of relief at his companions having all successfully emerged alive following their death-defying flight from the Bane Curse had temporarily distracted him from truly appreciating the lamentable condition of some of his friends. The rag-tag group of gasping, coughing, and limping travellers that were now dragging themselves painfully along the tunnel, carrying those members who were unconscious, in no way resembled the healthy troop that had crossed over the border into Kelkor only a few weeks before.

The exertions of the two Ancients had truly caught up with them. Uldini floated silently in front, while *Flamestar,* which the Arch Wizard was employing to illuminate the broad passageway, led deeper and deeper into the gloom, its erratically flickering light bearing eloquent testimony to the childlike figure's indisputable need for a recovery sleep.

Jelninolan trotted along behind Uldini with a blank look on her face, gently guided by Trogadon, who had placed his right hand around the elf's waist, holding her left hand in his own.

Selsena's nervousness on account of the mass of rock that surrounded her was being painfully felt by the others, while Hakanu was a sleeping bundle, lying athwart Culhen's back, with Falk snorting as he limped alongside the wolf. Ahren was still carrying Kamaluq in one arm, the slumbering fox occasionally whimpering whenever his paws twitched wildly. At least, the animal's breathing had calmed and become regular once the Forest Guardian had placed under the creature's tongue some of the herbs which Hakanu had placed in his master's belt pouch during their stay in Eathinian. Ahren took this to be a positive portent of what might happen next.

Khara, who had suffered considerable scratches, walked with Muai alongside the Forest Guardian, which gave him the opportunity to give her a peck on the cheek.

'What *happened* out there?' asked Ahren in a low voice. 'It looks as if you all had an unpleasant encounter with a Horde Bull.'

Khara scowled. 'These damn snakes happened,' she said. 'Muai's warning only reached us *after* we stumbled upon the creatures.' She pointed her chin towards the sleeping Kamaluq. 'This little fellow came out the worst of us. He trotted right into the nest as they were waking from their paralysis. The fox must have been bitten at least a dozen times before we had a chance to react.'

Falk grunted irritably. 'Your apprentice threw himself at the beasts immediately, of course, in an effort to help Kamaluq, while the rest of us, too, did our bit, hacking at the snakes. But the spear, as you can imagine, proved itself to be a most inadequate weapon against the tiny, squirming creatures, so he was left with no alternative other than to pick up the fox and remove him from the immediate danger.'

'And the whole time, he himself was being bitten by the Frost Adders,' added Khara. 'He had hardly run five paces when he collapsed, unconscious.'

Ahren felt a sudden wave of understanding for his protégé. Of course the lad had acted on the spur of the moment – after all, his companion animal had been in mortal danger. 'It's clear to me why Uldini and Jelninolan are completely exhausted,' he said. 'But why is Falk limping? And surely, Selsena should let him ride on her back?'

The emotions that the Titejunanwa had been projecting immediately changed. Her latent anxiety was replaced by a mixture of embarrassment and tetchiness.

'Don't you worry, old girl,' said Falk, patting her gently on her nose. 'It wasn't your fault.' Then he turned to Ahren. 'We had to break through some particularly thick scrub, which was teeming with snakes. Some of them crept under Selsena's armour and bit her there. My poor Titejunanwa had no other choice but to throw me off and roll on her back until the Frost Adders were squashed to death. She is riddled with bites beneath her saddle. I sprained my right ankle during my fall.' He laughed self-ironically and shook his head. 'A lame knight and his charger, who cannot be ridden. We really *are* a noble pair!'

The Titejunanwa responded by radiating a feeling of affection and mild amusement as she snorted, gently rubbing her cheek against that of the old Paladin.

'Once the snakes had launched such a relentless attack on us, Jelninolan decided to conjure up her sleep magic even though she feared that the charm might speed up the approach of the Bane Curse.' The Swordsmistress wearily ran her fingers through her unkempt hair. 'And as it turned out, her concern was justified.'

Ahren turned to look at his beloved beside him. 'There is still a major gap in your story. Can you tell me what's happened to your Warrior Pin?'

Khara glared at Falk. '*Someone* decided in his panic to use it for digging out dead snakes from under Selsena's plate armour.'

Ahren had rarely seen Falk look as embarrassed as he clearly now was. 'I have already *told* you that I'm sorry,' muttered the old man through gritted teeth. 'And anyway, I wanted to make totally sure that the Frost Adders were all dead, and the needle was the only implement I could think of that could get under Selsena's armour.'

From under her tunic, Khara pulled out the symbol of her status as Swordsmistress, the pin now caked with dried blood from the snakes. 'I am *not* going to stick this into my hair in its current condition,' she muttered through pursed lips.

'I think we're getting somewhere!' exclaimed Uldini from the head of the group, everyone else immediately focusing their attention on the Arch Wizard. 'It seems that the tunnel ends at a spiral staircase, which leads *downwards*.'

Ahren scratched his head thoughtfully. 'Clearly, Belsarius was careful to avoid taking any unnecessary risks. We have already proceeded deep into the mountain, and yet we are about to go downwards, too. Whatever it was he was tinkering at, he hid it deep in the bowels of Jorath.'

The companions began their silent descent of the generously broad spiral staircase that had been hewn into the mighty rock, and to Ahren it seemed as if they were journeying into a time long since past – to an age when Belsarius had still been very much alive and the Dark Days had raged furiously above them.

Chapter 7

They descended the spiral staircase for a good one hundred steps, all the while making sure that Culhen and Selsena had enough room to manoeuvre their way downwards. Ahren suspected that the stairwell had been designed with such generous dimensions so as to enable the transportation of whatever bulky materials that Belsarius had undoubtedly needed to perform his many experiments. As the Forest Guardian ran his fingers along the smooth walls, an idea struck him.

'Although Belsarius was an Ancient, his time must have been precious to him. He can hardly have constructed the Sanctum all on his own. I wonder did he employ help from the Silver Cliff?'

Trogadon grunted in agreement as he carefully assisted his disoriented beloved, step by step down the stairs. 'It's possible. Either he came upon a competent group of Dwarfish mercenaries, or he signed a contract with a Clan. Whoever helped him, the Ancient must have forked out a considerable amount of gold to ensure that his accomplices kept their mouths shut regarding the location of this place.'

Khara frowned. 'Perhaps he didn't pay enough, and his master builder revealed its existence. We have enough evidence to suggest that the Adversary found out about Belsarius' side project, and, the Woman in Black knows of the Sanctum too, of course.'

Trogadon glared at Khara and jutted out his chin belligerently. 'Dwarfs are no *traitors!*'

Falk chuckled. 'But they are famed for their notoriously loose tongues. Otherwise, how would I know what Jelninolan calls you when you are alone together, my good *Sweet Pea...*'

'Button it!' snapped the blacksmith, his face turning a deep red. 'I only let that slip after an inordinate amount of Elven wine, and you *swore* never to tell anyone!'

Falk raised his hands in a gesture of innocence as he grinned broadly.

'The winding stairs will reach its conclusion any heartbeat now,' muttered Uldini flatly.

The fact that the Arch Wizard was still bleeding from his nose and ears troubled Ahren, who reached into his belt bag for some styptic ointment, which the Ancient accepted gratefully before applying it to the affected openings.

'Oh,' murmured Uldini a heartbeat later, having now come to a stop. He waved a hand weakly in the direction of whatever it was that he had seen. The monosyllable suggested considerable disappointment. 'What a *terrible* waste,' he then added.

Ahren pushed his way forward until he was standing beside the floating, childlike figure. It didn't take long for him to understand why Uldini was so deflated, the flickering light of *Flamestar* illuminating the large chamber in front of them, which had undoubtedly been the hub of the Sanctum but was now ankle-deep in water. An extended working area occupied the centre of the cavern, where an insatiably curious mind had once spent his time tinkering with apparatuses or carrying out experiments. The surrounding walls still held numerous wooden shelves filled with scrolls – or rather, what was left of them. Mould covered every inch of the wood and papyrus contained within the large room, which now resembled nothing less than a graveyard of lost knowledge.

Ahren's heart sank as he came to the only possible logical conclusion. 'We will not find a single clue to the secrets that Belsarius brought to light here.' He hadn't wanted to sound so defeated, but it was clear that his entire mission to Kelkor had been nothing less than a complete waste of time – which had almost cost them their lives, to boot.

And we are also going to have to try to find a way out of this place before it becomes our final, sodden resting place, he added mentally.

A hunt only ends in failure once the scent is lost, recited Culhen, repeating an old saw of Falk's that Ahren had always found particularly annoying during his apprenticeship. *Let's have a good look around before writing this enterprise off.*

'It's best if we fan out,' said Ahren, forcing his voice to sound more encouraging. 'All who are conscious and in full command of their faculties should look through the shelves and see if any of the scrolls have been spared of mould.'

By now, Falk had plucked Hakanu from Culhen's saddle and placed him gently on the uninjured part of the Titejunanwa's back. 'Selsena and I will try to find a dry spot for those who need rest,' he said, nodding towards the opposite end of the chamber. 'If my eyes aren't deceiving me, I can see another archway over there. Hopefully, *some* of the Sanctum is not under water.'

'Jelninolan and I will come with you,' said Trogadon. 'Then you can orientate yourselves a little by using the light of my beloved's magic.' He turned to the elf. 'What do you think, my heart? Shall we seek out a nice, soft bed for your weary head?' Ahren looked at the weak glimmer that surrounded the priestess, undoubtedly the visible remnant of her True Form's aura. Then he glanced at Uldini. The light from *Flamestar* was no more powerful now than that of a candle flickering in the wind.

'The two Ancients must have been within a hair's breadth of an Unleashing...' he murmured with a shudder.

Stop moping over what might have been, muttered Culhen, who was wading unhappily through the stagnant water. *You'd be better off concentrating on making sure that all the effort we've gone to won't have been a fool's errand. Oh...and please ensure that we get out of here, too. I'm starving.*

You are a fount of wisdom and a beacon of hope, countered Ahren tartly.

I know, said the wolf conceitedly. *This is down to the fact that I was sent to you by the gods so that I could support you in all that you do.* He trotted back to the entrance and lay down on a dry step of the spiral staircase.

Ahren was about to counter with a sarcastic remark but then held back. For one thing, he sensed the wolf's hunger pangs caused by their wild chase through the undergrowth. Then there was Culhen's anxiety at being condemned to inaction in their present situation. Finally, the Paladin knew all too well his companion animal's strategy. The wolf's little barbs were designed to distract Ahren and prevent him from falling into too morose a state. Looked at like that, Culhen was not inactive at all, but a great help.

You're welcome. The animal's comment had come so quickly that there was no doubt that he had been listening in on Ahren's thoughts. *If you need any more reassurance, you will find me guarding the stairwell.*

'There is *nothing* here!' snapped Uldini, angrily tossing a mouldy scroll into the water and creating a considerable splash. 'Not a single letter is legible!'

'I would appreciate it if you didn't make waves,' countered Khara coolly. 'Unlike you, the rest of us are unable to float above the water, which, by the way, is up to the top of my boots.'

'We are standing – or floating – in the middle of a mountain of lost knowledge, and all *you* care about are your wet feet!' snarled the Arch Wizard.

Ahren waded purposefully towards the childlike figure before the latter had a chance to continue scolding. 'You need a rest and are disappointed. Perhaps we should stop for now and lie down for a bit. It has been a difficult day.'

Uldini opened his mouth to protest but said nothing once he realised that Ahren was not to be persuaded.

'We're going,' called Ahren aloud, looking over at his wolf, who had settled down comfortably on a half landing with Muai and Kamaluq, both wolf and cat now protecting the recovering fox in the warm, furry nest they had created for him.

'I wonder if Hakanu sometimes asks himself *whose* companion animal the fox *really* is,' murmured Khara, who hadn't missed where Ahren had been looking.

The Paladin grinned. 'I know what the answer would be if you asked Muai or Culhen.'

'Are you coming, or would you prefer to stay in the dark with your livestock?' muttered Uldini from the archway. 'If a mouldy library full of soakage appeals to your tastes, then I am sure you can find a couple of shelves to sleep on.'

'I think I preferred him when he was exhausted,' grumbled Khara.

Ahren rubbed his beard. 'Uldini was an ardent admirer of Belsarius. Finding his idol's work completely destroyed must have shaken him to the core.'

The Swordsmistress turned to look at him. 'You are remarkably calm considering that all Belsarius' research into the Adversary seem to be destroyed.'

Ahren shrugged his shoulders in a gesture of resignation. 'I am simply relieved that we are all still alive. That Bane Curse was nothing short of terrifying.'

'It was merely a *taste* of what we can expect when we confront the Dark god!' snarled Uldini, who had lost his patience and was floating ahead under the arch. Ahren and Khara quickly followed, the Arch Wizard and his illuminating orb having already disappeared.

Beyond the exit was a corridor, narrower and lower than the one that had led to the spiral staircase.

'The really unwieldy objects mustn't have made it into this part of the Sanctum,' murmured Khara.

Ahren nodded. With the help of the flickering light, he was now examining with interest their surroundings.

'Are these…*runes?*' he asked, pointing at the irregularities in the walls, which at first sight had seemed nothing but the normal texture of rock that had been worked into a tunnel formation.

Uldini froze as soon as heard the Forest Guardian's words, then looked at the walls, wide-eyed. 'I must be more exhausted than I thought,' he muttered. 'What we can see here are artfully disguised charm circles. Any servant of the Adversary who dared to walk along here would have collapsed and died within a heartbeat.'

'Why wait until here?' wondered Ahren. 'Why did he not create this form of defence at the entrance to the Sanctum?'

Uldini frowned. 'Yes – why didn't he?' With that, he floated on without saying more.

'Come to think of it, the exhausted Uldini is as hard to bear as the irritable Uldini or the cheerful Uldini,' muttered Khara.

Ahren smiled wanly. 'You mean, you can see a difference?'

The pair laughed, forgetting for a heartbeat all their problems – but only until they found themselves without light again, the Arch Wizard once again disappearing ahead of them.

Cursing, they hurried through the ankle-deep water along the gently ascending corridor, hoping that they wouldn't be swallowed up by the darkness.

'Well, this really *is* comfortable,' commented Trogadon on spotting Ahren, Khara and Uldini, who had finally come to the end of the extended corridor, which curved into a room that the Paladin could see was a surprisingly generous sleeping cavern.

The square chamber was a good eight paces broad and wide, its smoothly worked ceiling displaying in the half-light a complex Charm Circle, the same pattern being replicated on the floor. The sight of both produced in Ahren a strangely uneasy feeling.

He was reassured, however, by the attitude of his friends, who had already made themselves and their slumbering companions as comfortable as possible. The half-rotten furniture had found a new use thanks to the pragmatism of both Trogadon and Falk, for it now provided the fuel for a little campfire that the pair had lit in the middle of the room, the glow producing only a modicum of light but sufficient heat to warm the weary travellers. The shallow angle of the passageway that they had only now negotiated ensured that any water running down the walls drained away, leaving the room considerably drier than the one they had left, with only a couple of tiny glistening rivulets.

The companions had spread their blankets and bed rolls around the campfire and were either sitting or sleeping on them while Selsena was dozing in a corner of the room. Ahren was about to add his own bundle when he remembered that his rucksack had fallen victim to the Bane Curse. He would have to make do with one of the extra blankets that Trogadon always carried with him, while a new razor was also required – that could wait, thought the Forest Guardian, for their first task was to get out of the Sanctum in one piece.

'This looks *perfect,*' snarled Uldini once he had reached Falk and Trogadon. Hovering between them with his arms akimbo and looking at the improvised campfire he added: 'Incinerate *everything* that has withstood the sands of time, why *don't* you!'

'It was only a couple of chairs and a table,' murmured Falk in a surprisingly conciliatory voice. 'I sincerely doubt that Belsarius carved his precious secrets into the furniture like a daydreaming godsday pupil, carving letters into his desk out of sheer boredom. And I really cannot imagine that these bits of wood were of any sentimental value to him. Therefore, there is no doubt that they are performing a last service to *his* guests by warming us all up.'

'And there is a flue here too,' added Trogadon, lighting his pipe and then pointing the stem at a corner of the ceiling, beneath which lay several rusty pots and pans. 'The old boy built a cooking area for himself. For an absentminded wizard, he made sure that his Sanctum was *very* well equipped.'

'Belsarius loved creating things with his own hands when at all possible.' Uldini's words were almost impossible to understand, for he was now mumbling in a low voice. 'He always used to say: "If we ever want to improve the lot of those humans who have no magical powers, then we must understand the effort they expend in their daily lives".'

Trogadon puffed away at his pipe. 'He sounds as if he had a lifetime of experience with a lot of spare time that he spent as he pleased. Speaking for myself, I never fail to be grateful to both you and Jelninolan whenever you make our journey easier.'

Falk guffawed. 'Which means that you must be the one dwarf in all Jorath who takes a sympathetic view of magic.'

'Uldini, do you feel strong enough to at least take a look at the injured amongst us?' asked Ahren as he and Khara settled down by the fire. 'If we are going to find a way out of here, then it would be best if each of us had enough strength to move of our own volition.'

The Arch Wizard frowned, the flickering light in *Flamestar* immediately extinguishing as the childlike figure lowered himself gently onto the floor before going first to Hakanu, then to Kamaluq and finally to Jelninolan, placing his hand momentarily on their foreheads and closing his eyes as he did so.

'These three are already sleeping themselves back to health,' he muttered, trying – and failing – to suppress a yawn. 'Something that I myself should do.'

Khara looked at him sceptically. 'Can't you do *anything* for them?'

Uldini shook his head. 'Not if I am going to heal Falk's ankle.'

The old Paladin looked away in embarrassment, the Arch Wizard shrugging his shoulders apologetically as he turned to Khara.

'Even a sprain is a challenge for me at the moment.'

'Then you'd be better off helping Selsena,' grunted Falk. 'The old girl's back has been bitten through and through.'

The Titejunanwa shook her head and snorted. Her disdain for the proposal was evident even without her communicating this through her usual waves of emotion.

'As usual, your companion animal is making much more sense than you are,' grumbled Uldini. 'The bites are tiny and will heal of their own accord. And regarding the poison, her Animal Blessing will take care of that. The same can be said for Kamaluq. Hakanu's god's Blessing will have the same effect, of course, while all Jelninolan needs is a good sleep. Which leaves only a curmudgeonly old knight who somehow managed to injure himself in such a way that magical intervention is called for.'

Falk nodded hesitantly when Uldini gestured to him that he should lie down. Then the childlike figure placed his hand on the Paladin's forehead and mumbled something under his breath, whereupon the old man immediately dropped off to sleep.

'Peace at last,' grunted Uldini, settling down on his own mattress and looking over at Ahren, Khara and Trogadon. 'I take it that I can rely on the three companion animals at the entrance to keep guard?' he asked with a yawn. 'It would be a pity if I woke up to discover that this cave, too, had collapsed.'

Trogadon glared at the Arch Wizard. 'My help didn't bother you when you were struggling against the Bane Curse. It's high time you were quiet and closed your eyes.'

Uldini nodded wearily. 'Do not wake us,' he said to Ahren. Then from his lying position and with his eyes closed, he reached for *Flamestar*. Tiny sparks of light issued forth from the core of the crystal ball and danced momentarily like artificial stars above the improvised campfire before raining down on the injured and exhausted companions. Immediately, the bodies of the recipients relaxed as the magic sank through their skin with a soft glimmer.

Ahren turned to Khara and was about to speak to her when she suddenly fell into a deep sleep, one of the sparks having landed on her, too.

'Begone!' growled Trogadon, waving his hand to shoo away three sparks that were attempting to land on him, and even as Ahren saw the dwarf's eyes closing, he felt a feathery touch on the back of his neck. Immediately, he was overcome by an irresistible weariness as he fell onto his mattress like a stone.

Ahren was sitting at a round table. The lights of distant candles were dancing on its engravings, revealing patterns and lines that were strangely familiar to him.

'But this is the council of war table on King's Island,' he murmured, disorientated.

The characteristic snort of the First penetrated his consciousness. 'Of course it is, you greenhorn! Where else are we going to plan our assault on the Obsidian Fortress?'

In a daze, Ahren looked around, suddenly realising that all the Paladins were assembled around the table and were staring at him expectantly. Horrified, he saw that each of them had suffered one dreadful injury or other. Sunju was holding her right side, the blood dripping down between her fingers. Fisker was wearing a patch over where his right eye had once been. The Father of the Mountain was missing an ear…

Quickly, Ahren looked down at the map of Jorath again, unable to comprehend the suffering that had revealed itself to him.

A dream, he said to himself. *This must be a dream! I am trapped in the Sanctum of Belsarius, am I not?*

His deep-seated fear of the cold, hard reality – namely, that he was hemmed into the middle of a mountain – was nothing compared to the dreadful vision that his inner thoughts were presently torturing him with.

'What *is* your plan?' asked the First urgently, having turned to look at the Forest Guardian. 'All attempts at vanquishing the Dark god have ended in failure. Tens of thousands of soldiers have been slaughtered while protecting us during our retreat to King's Island.'

Falk leaned forward, the bloody stump of his right arm glittering in the candlelight. 'The enemy is on the march. We *need* a plan!'

'We have tried everything,' interjected Sunju. 'Please think of *something,* Ahren.'

'Save us!'

'Save Jorath!'

'Save Creation!'

The desperate, chaotic pleas of his fellow Paladins rained in on the Thirteenth, who could only sit there helplessly, not knowing what to say. Paralysed, he watched as the map of Jorath began to turn black, like an ever-extending blob of ink, starting from the point that indicated the Obsidian Fortress, the darkness then expanding, creeping closer and closer to the little drawing which represented Kings' Island. There was *nothing* that Ahren could do but watch the blackness swallowing up every last contour on the table, spreading out more and more until it touched the Paladins before overwhelming them with a tidal wave of nothingness.

Ahren awoke from his nightmare with a start and looked around, panic-stricken.

He made out the sleeping outlines of his friends lying on their mattresses – here and there, came the sounds of loud snoring or low whimpering. The fire in the chamber had burned down, with only a few glimmering pieces of timber casting the cave in as surreal a glow as the war table in Ahren's dream.

'A restless night?' asked Trogadon in a gravelly murmur from his sleeping area a few paces away. The Paladin saw that the dwarf's eyes were open, the blacksmith peering curiously over at him.

'Don't ask,' grunted Ahren, tapping his forehead. 'Too many worries in here.'

The low, rumbling laugh of the dwarf seemed in the dimly lit chamber to vanquish the Paladin's glumness. 'The day when you stop worrying will be the day of the world's downfall – or perhaps the day when we finally save Jorath from the Adversary for once and for all.'

Ahren scowled. 'It seems to me that our journey to Kelkor has done more harm than good. Being trapped within a mountain with half of us unable to keep our eyes open through sheer exhaustion is a high price to pay for a few mildewed scrolls.'

The dwarf now propped himself up on his elbows. 'Damned sleep charm,' he growled. 'My eyes keep closing although I don't want them to.'

Ahren had to smile. 'It seems that Uldini is forcing us to rest.' He stretched demonstratively. 'And for once it would appear that I am *not* the person who has had to physically suffer the most.'

Trogadon chuckled. 'Enjoy the moment while you can. I'm sure it won't be long before *I* will have to pull your battered body out of some battlefield or other.'

The smile immediately vanished from Ahren's face, the dwarf now realising that he had put his foot in it.

'I cannot sleep anymore,' whispered the Paladin. 'But you should try to get some more rest. After all, you are our best hope of getting out of this mountain in one piece.'

'It's always the dwarf who has to come to the rescue,' said his friend, making a final attempt to lighten the mood again. Then he closed his eyes, and within a few heartbeats the blacksmith was fast asleep.

Ahren soon gave in to his inner restlessness, getting to his feet in the silence so that he could explore in more detail the chamber that had been Belsarius' sleeping quarters whenever he had pursued his experiments within the peace and quiet of the Sanctum. Because of the dilapidated nature of the furniture and the fact that a lot of it had been used as fuel for the fire, Ahren found it difficult to get a grasp of the Ancient's chamber, which Uldini placed so much faith in.

Lost in thought, he moved around in silence before finally stopping in a corner of the cavern, where an alcove had caught his eye. It was too narrow for a human to fit into, but big enough for Ahren's arm, which the Paladin put in, stretching it until his hand touched the stone wall to the rear. He looked up to see if he could see an air shaft, or some other clue that might reveal to him the purpose of the peculiar niche.

'Did you find anything interesting?'

Ahren spun around with such speed that he banged his head off the edge of the recess. 'Please don't creep up on me like that,' he muttered, giving Khara a strained smile. 'I'm nervous enough as it is in this underground prison.'

Khara looked at him apologetically. 'I didn't want to wake the others.'

Ahren looked over at their sleeping friends. Even Selsena was snoring quietly – a sound that he had rarely heard the Titejunanwa make. 'I think Uldini's magic is going to allow us to sleep until we are well healed and re-energised. Which is why *we* two are awake already, having gotten off relatively lightly in this latest skirmish.'

The Swordsmistress nodded. 'And what *exactly* are you doing here?'

Ahren shrugged his shoulders. 'I don't really know. This whole journey seems so pointless to me now – even though the Woman in Black was convinced that we would find some invaluable information here.'

Khara placed an arm around his waist and gently drew him towards her. 'No-one could have known that water would have seeped into the Sanctum over the years.'

Ahren grunted impatiently. 'What I simply don't understand is that Belsarius, too, hadn't calculated on it – and yet he is supposed to have been unbelievably *clever*.'

'We can ask Trogadon about the seepage when he wakes up – although *I* think it's simply a result of the landslide.' Khara waved vaguely up at the ceiling. 'Some sort of fissure must have formed as the slope of the mountain tumbled towards the valley.'

Ahren's shoulders drooped. 'You're probably right. It seems that I'm simply too stubborn to accept defeat.'

Khara grinned. 'Have you come up with any idea yet of how we can get out of here again?'

The Paladin looked at her thoughtfully before speaking. 'Our best bet is to make use of Trogadon's knowledge.'

'You mean – "he who traps us in the mountain must get us out of it again?"'

Ahren found himself grinning. 'I wouldn't say *that* to him. But his know-how regarding mountain rocks is second to none. Just think of the damage he caused to the tunnel entrance with a single blow of his hammer.'

'But now we have masses of rock blocking our escape. I think we are going to need the sorcerous skills of Jelninolan and Uldini to help free us.'

Ahren glanced over at the two Ancients. 'They are so exhausted that I really don't think they're going to wake up for a considerable while. And when they do, will they have regained sufficient strength to be able to clear the tunnel by magically moving all those tons of rubble?' The Paladin and the Swordsmistress said nothing for a while, enjoying their silent companionship, which proved comfort enough as they pondered their predicament.

'Why don't we check our supplies?' suggested Khara finally. 'So that we have a rough idea of how long we can last down here without starving to death.'

Ahren pointed at the water that was seeping out of the rock in this chamber, too. 'We have enough to drink anyway – if you think of how much dripped from the walls in the research room as well.'

Khara frowned. 'Where does the seepage actually disappear to?' she asked before kneeling and examining one of the inch-wide rivulets which flowed from the sleeping chamber towards the larger cavern. 'It disappears down the passageway towards the research room – and then?'

Ahren scratched his beard and mused. 'If you think about it, the relentless dripping should have flooded the entire Sanctum after all this time. Which means, there *must* be a drain.'

Khara's eyes narrowed. 'And where there is a drain, an exit point cannot be far away.'

'I'm not so sure.' Ahren hated being the bearer of bad news, for the last thing he wanted to do was to dash the hopes of his beloved. 'We are talking about an outflow that needs to be no more than the width of my little finger.' Then he pointed at Selsena. 'And remember that we are going to need an aperture wide enough for a Titejunanwa and a huge wolf to squeeze through.'

The Swordsmistress jutted her chin belligerently. 'It's worth investigating, surely? Or do you have something better to do?'

Ahren nodded hesitantly. 'First, we'll check the supplies, then we'll look for the drain. We might as well find out how critical our situation is.'

'That was so disappointing.' Khara wiped the slime from her right arm and grunted in disgust.

Better if you don't point out to her that you were right all along, chuckled Culhen, quite unnecessarily.

If his sense of time was accurate, then a good portion of the night had now passed, and the day would soon be breaking. Once he and Khara had ascertained that the provisions would last the group for no more than three days, the pair had set about trying to follow the water current. Meanwhile, the three companion animals on the winding stairs had woken up and observed the two with considerable amusement. Ahren had decided to ignore Culhen's witticisms, realising all too well that the wolf's mood would soon take a turn for the worse once the food supplies ran low.

'What were you able to feel?' asked Ahren as tactfully as possible.

Khara shook her head. 'A little gap in the floor – perhaps a pace long but no more than half the width of a finger across. The water can flow through it, but it's completely useless to us.'

'It would have been too good to be true if our freedom was so easily attainable.'

Khara rinsed out her arm in that part of the cave where the seepage hadn't been contaminated by the slimy remains of wood and rotten paper. 'Let us return to the others,' she said. 'Maybe one of them has woken up and has come up with another idea.'

Muai, Kamaluq and I will stay here, announced Culhen. *We refuse to dirty our paws in slime unless absolutely necessary.*

There's food in the other cave, Ahren replied casually.

On my way.

The Paladin watched in amusement as Culhen jumped into the water without further ado before turning and gently picking up Kamaluq by the scruff of his neck with his fangs. Muai quickly got to her feet with a growl and followed the pair with a concerned look.

Khara giggled. 'She is complaining that the good-for-nothing wolf will drop her little darling into the mire.'

I heard that! came the prompt retort, causing Ahren to sigh.

'I will spare you the response of my wolf before he and Muai get used to making fur fly through *our* heads and by means of *our* voices.'

Oh, said Culhen, suddenly enthused. *What a wonderful idea! Can you tell Muai that I...*

No, Culhen!

But...

I said no!

This was followed by an offended silence, Ahren then giving a satisfied grunt.

'Your one, too, right?' asked Khara.

'And how!'

Holding and hands and chuckling at the idiosyncrasies of their companion animals, the couple returned to their companions, the fears and dangers that surrounded them temporarily pushed to the back of their minds for a moment of innocent happiness.

'This wouldn't fill up *anyone*,' complained Trogadon, looking down at the little chunk of cheese and the tiny piece of bread that Jelninolan had pressed into his calloused hand. 'I got more than that for breakfast as a babe in arms.'

The elf looked coolly into his eyes. 'Get us out of here and I will personally prepare a celebratory feast for you. Until that happens, we will have to make do with rationing.' The faint trembling in her echoing voice betrayed the elf's current weakness despite her doing her best to sound as normal as possible.

'I am still sad that I missed Trogadon's heroic hammer blow,' said Hakanu.

Much to Ahren's and Khara's delight, all their friends were already awake by the time the couple had reached them – even if none of the wounded had yet fully regained their strength. Falk kept rubbing at this ankle, Hakanu's fingers were trembling as he lifted the cheese to his lips while Uldini was ashen faced and completely exhausted. Clearly, Ahren had overestimated the power of the Ancient's sorcery or perhaps the healing sleep hadn't been so effective on account of Uldini's own present weakness.

Trogadon cleared his throat, but then proceeded to nibble at his bread before clearing his throat a second time.

'What are you trying to say, love?' asked Jelninolan, gently encouraging the dwarf.

'My hammer blow really wasn't *that* heroic,' admitted the blacksmith. 'There was a weak point in the ceiling that I made use of. Dwarfs like to include them in the building process if the tunnel is to be permanently sealed up at some future date.'

Uldini's head spun around. The Arch Wizard, who a heartbeat earlier had been lacking in all energy, was now glaring at the dwarf intently. 'And you are only telling us this *now?!*'

Trogadon nodded. 'The lack of supporting beams, and the fact that the tunnel was deliberately built beneath a pre-determined breaking point only reinforces my point. It was built so that it could be collapsed in an emergency.'

Uldini slapped his thigh in delight as he guffawed, only stopping when he noticed that Ahren and the others were looking at him in bewilderment.

'Don't you *understand?!'* he exclaimed, the delight in his voice unmissable. 'Belsarius planned to bury the entrance if his Sanctum was discovered by the enemy.'

Falk drummed his fingers impatiently on one of his greaves. 'And?'

'Belsarius would never have *deliberately* buried himself,' concluded Uldini, his eyes fixed on Trogadon again. 'If you dwarfs build such tunnel traps, it is hardly with the intention of creating rocky graves for yourselves, right?'

Trogadon shook his head. 'There is always…' He stopped in his tracks, groaned and slapped his forehead, '…an escape route!' he shouted. 'But of course! There must be a secret exit here somewhere.'

It seemed as if Uldini had suddenly rediscovered his zest for life as he looked triumphantly at his companions, the expression on his face suggesting that he – and *only* he – had already vanquished the Adversary. 'I always knew that Belsarius wasn't idiotic enough to retreat into an oversized, rocky *dead end* for his experiments.'

'I don't want to spoil the party,' murmured Ahren. 'But we cannot assume that the escape route wasn't buried by the landslide.'

This was greeted by a stunned silence.

Sometimes you really do put your foot in it, complained Culhen. *And I was already making plans for an enormous dinner as soon as we got out of this godsforsaken mountain!*

'Let us first look for this exit,' said Falk eventually, trying to improve the mood a little. 'Then we will know if it is intact or not.'

Uldini pointed up at the crystal ball, which was hovering and glimmering just below the ceiling. 'We should go room by room. Much as I don't want to admit it, this tiny light charm is draining my energy no end.'

'Perhaps we won't *need* to search *all* the caverns. Remember the deadly protective charms that we saw on the ceilings as we made our way from the research room to here,' interjected Ahren, filled with renewed hope. 'Weren't we wondering why they were positioned so deep within the Sanctum?'

Falk pointed at the ceiling and the floor. 'And there are more of them here.'

'Bulwarks against the enemy,' growled Trogadon in his gravelly voice. 'First, hard rock, and then deadly sorcery.'

Khara looked over at the tunnel and then up at the Charm Circle in the ceiling. 'If I were Belsarius and feared a rear-guard action...' she began as she strode over to the corridor before turning her back to it, '...then I would make sure to have positioned enough sorcery between myself and the attacking Dark Ones to give me the chance to open a secret door.'

Ahren looked at what his beloved was now studying. The protective charms ran almost the entire length of the walls within the chamber. There was only one narrow section free from the convoluted lines and symbols, and that was on the wall *directly* opposite the corridor.

'I know where we must look!' he exclaimed, walking over to the very same alcove that he had noticed earlier. 'The exit must be *here!*'

'Uh...' countered Trogadon in a voice that took the wind right out of the Paladin's sails. 'To be perfectly honest, this is a classical niche for...' The dwarf's voice had now become an incomprehensible mumble.

'Spit it out!' barked Falk. 'Selsena is in urgent need of daylight again.'

The Titejunanwa whinnied her agreement.

'Uh...for a Dwarfish privy,' muttered Trogadon, looking apologetically at Ahren before demonstratively sticking out his rear end into the alcove and going down on his hunkers. 'Only the bucket is missing.'

'Ahren, the treasure seeker,' mocked Falk with a grin.

'I could have sworn that the exit would be situated here,' murmured the Paladin with a mixture of embarrassment and defiance as he ran his fingers along the back wall of what had once been the privy.

'Considering how careful Belsarius was – if you think of all the safety precautions he put in place here – then he must surely have chosen a more subtle form of flight rather than a jakes,' commented Trogadon with a grin before raising his hammer.

'Oh, no,' said Jelninolan, trying to grasp the handle. 'You are *not* going to whack anything without informing us precisely what *exactly* your purpose is.'

'But, my heart,' said the blacksmith, gazing in wide-eyed innocence at his beloved and pouting his mouth in a manner that would befit any lady at court, 'do you *really* trust me so little?'

Jelninolan could only giggle as she withdrew her hand. 'Just be careful,' she warned him gently.

Trogadon nodded. 'Everyone, listen closely,' he said, then gently tapping his weapon against the back wall. A solid, dull sound could be heard. 'Anyone who can – knock gently on the stone. As soon as you hear a hollow sound, you will have found the way out.'

Immediately, an array of blades, long and short, were drawn as was a spear, each of them being used to tap against the rock, the companions having each taken a section of the cavern's back wall.

If the motivation behind your activity wasn't so deadly serious, I would mock once again the eccentricities of you bipeds, commented Culhen conceitedly.

And if I didn't know that a certain worthy Alpha was above such smugness, I would say to you – get your nose out of our provisions. Now, Culhen!

I only wanted to make sure that everything was still there. After all, Muai is a devious thief, and Kamaluq can even camouflage himself.

If we are short of anything, a similar amount will be deducted from your next portion, scolded Ahren without bothering to turn around.

Behind him, he heard the pitter-patter of paws quickly retreating from the food supplies.

What a nerve, sulked the wolf. *You keep tapping away at your privy and see if it doesn't lead to freedom after all.*

Ahren stopped himself from snapping back, not least because it had now become painfully clear to him that the others had, indeed, left him to examine that part of the wall where the no-longer-mysterious alcove was.

'I *have* something!' exclaimed Hakanu, the rest of the group immediately gathering around the apprentice. The lad tapped the blunt end of his spear against the wall in front of him again, Ahren recognising, indeed, a minimal difference in the sound of the weapon against the rock.

'To be honest, it doesn't sound *particularly* hollow,' muttered Falk.

'*You* should know,' teased Uldini. 'You hear that noise every time you hit your head.'

'*Very* funny.'

Trogadon, meanwhile, had moved Hakanu out of the way and was now tapping away with his hammer at the area around the spot that the apprentice had discovered, all the while using a piece of coal from their campfire to mark the points where the noise changed from bright to dull. After some heartbeats, the dwarf had marked out a black square on the wall, a good two paces wide and high. He stepped back from his work of art and gave a satisfied grunt.

'These here are the dimensions of the door. What a piece of work! But even though I now know *where* to look, I can't make out any crack at all. All we need to do now is to prise it open somehow. From the sound of the echoes, I suspect that the rock must be at least a pace thick.' His eyes were sparkling impishly. 'This Belsarius fellow's grounds for thwarting his enemies were really *solid.*' With that he looked at the others, wiggling his eyebrows while his companions groaned at his appalling punning.

'Your sense of humour is rocky, to say the least,' countered Falk dryly, 'and it certainly hasn't unlocked any *doors* for you if you want to rise to the rank of court jester.'

'Not you, too,' groaned Uldini, glaring at the old Paladin. 'I am at least as relieved as you lot at the fact that we may have found our possible escape route, but I *strongly* suggest that all witticisms be left until we have seen the light of day again.'

By now, Trogadon was pushing against the door of rock so hard that his face had turned a deep red. 'You're all welcome to help me if you like,' he groaned through gritted teeth.

Ahren, Falk and Culhen immediately put their bodies – and more particularly their muscles – to use, but the door simply refused to budge.

The dwarf wiped the sweat from his brow once the quartet of gasping volunteers had abandoned their efforts. 'Either there is some sort of mechanism for revealing the passageway or Belsarius used magic to put the mass of rock in place.'

'I would wager it was the latter,' said Uldini, looking critically at the seemingly unmoveable obstacle.

Falk gave the Arch Wizard a pleading look.

The childlike figure waved his hands dismissively. 'There is more of a chance of me in my weakened state inadvertently causing an Unleashing than of my revealing the passageway.'

'Jelninolan?' asked Khara, but the elf shook her head.

'It is taking all my strength of will to stay upright. Uldini and I need to spend at least two weeks in bed before even thinking of performing sorcery on the scale you are proposing.'

'Then make yourselves comfortable,' growled Trogadon with a sigh as he raised his hammer. 'I will deal with the door in the traditional manner and get it open that way. One hammer blow after another.' Then he slammed the implement against the rock, the heavy stone immediately beginning to groan and ache like a wounded animal as dust and splinters flew across the cavern.

The ceiling and walls creaked and scrunched, the meagre trickle of water swelling into a rivulet as the floor beneath the companions' feet bucked like a recalcitrant Ice Wolf, who had been deprived of a decent meal for too long.

No-one dared to move until, a few heartbeats later, the tremors abated.

'What was *that?*' asked Hakanu, breaking the anxious silence that had ensued with his trembling voice.

'Magic,' snarled Uldini darkly, then pointing at the secret door. 'Subtle magic was always a typical hallmark of Belsarius. If Dark Ones wanted to use this escape route, which method would they use to open it, do you think?'

'Brute force,' replied Khara.

Uldini nodded. 'Precisely. I wager *Flamestar* that there is a charm circle just beneath this secret doorway, positioned there to significantly magnify any use of force and throw it back into the cavern.'

'In their attempts to open the door, the Dark Ones would bury *themselves,*' whispered Hakanu in awe. 'Ingenious.'

'Alas, this effect also applies to us,' interjected Ahren. 'Unless we wait for our Ancients to recover enough so that they can open the stone door for us or freeze the spell below.'

Which might take weeks,' warned Jelninolan.

Trogadon shook his head. 'We don't have that much time. Culhen is so hungry that he will gobble us all up within a week.'

The wolf whimpered. *Now that's below the belt...*

This was followed by a low growl, which, surprisingly enough, came from Muai. Khara chuckled. 'My tigress would like it to be known that the wolf will not be the only one attending the feast.'

'It's nice to be thought of so highly,' commented Falk dryly. 'Even if only for the quality of one's flesh. Why do I suddenly find it strangely reassuring that Titejunanwas are herbivorous by nature?'

Selsena whinnied and emitted a wave of merriment that momentarily dissolved the tension affecting everyone's mood.

'What are our options?' the young Forest Guardian asked, looking at his companions.

'The only thing I can think of is my hammer,' said Trogadon with a shrug of his shoulders. 'And it will take me dozens of strokes before the door even begins to smash.'

'Maybe my spear can help,' suggested Hakanu. 'If I throw it with enough force, my magic, channelled through the weapon, might cause the rock to crack.'

Trogadon shook his head as he looked towards the secret door. 'This type of rock does not split easily. It tends to crumble rather than break in two.'

'Belsarius really did think of everything,' murmured Uldini, chewing on his lower lip.

Ahren racked his brains as he tried to think of how he could be useful, but neither his bow nor his Wind Blade were of any benefit in the current dilemma. 'And what if we tried to *dig* our way through the buried entrance instead?' he asked, looking at Trogadon.

The dwarf shook his head apologetically. 'That would take at least as long as waiting for our two Ancients to regain their full strength.'

Time is a luxury that we cannot afford, announced Culhen. *You in your fancy boots may not have noticed, but thanks to the quake caused by Trogadon's strike the cracks in the ceiling have widened. There is so much water flowing out of them now that the seepage on the cavern floor is rising.*

Ahren looked down in surprise, groaning when he saw that an inch of water was already covering the entire surface area.

'Dammit,' he said.

His friends, seeing where he was looking, immediately understood what was troubling him.

'Should I not give my spear a try, after all?' asked Hakanu.

'Magic or no magic, your weapon would do no more than dent the wall,' muttered Falk. 'And we have no guarantee that the Bane Charm won't cause the entire cavern to collapse through the impact.'

'Hold on a heartbeat,' interjected Jelninolan, gesturing to the others for silence. 'Hakanu has just given me an idea.' With that she took *Mirilan* out of the bag.

'You must not cast a spell, auntie,' pleaded Uldini. 'I can sense how dangerously close you are to an Unleashing…'

Jelninolan pointed at the ceiling and the stone door. 'Sometimes in life, you have to take a risk.' She placed her Storm Fiddle on her shoulder. 'I will be very careful,' she murmured as she closed her eyes.

Watching the elf concentrate so hard was causing Ahren's heart to beat more rapidly. Uldini's urgent warning seemed almost too mild as Jelninolan placed her bow on *Mirilan's* strings, this simple gesture alone bringing forth the full force of the priestess's True Form. A burning light blinded Ahren, forcing him to look away.

'My heart…' began Trogadon anxiously. 'This is no gentle glimmer that you are radiating. It is a furiously raging forest fire.'

'I know,' groaned Jelninolan, her voice echoing with such force that it seemed as if she had only now stepped out of *all* the sacred pools of the goddess simultaneously. 'Only *one* tone,' she murmured pleadingly. 'I need only *one* tone…' Then she drew her bow incredibly slowly across the strings of the Storm Fiddle, a deep, vibrato issuing from the heart of the instrument. The elf's corona lit up, tentacles of sheer white light whipped across the cavern, Ahren flinching violently as the magic even penetrated his Deep Steel armour and seemed to burn his skin.

Jelninolan was standing on the verge of an Unleashing. One false move and it would overwhelm her completely – along with all her companions!

'Perhaps you should stop now,' croaked Ahren, his mouth dry.

To his surprise, Jelninolan gave a tortured smile. 'But I *have* already stopped.'

As the Paladin looked at her in bemusement, she winked back at him, then turned to Trogadon.

'Hakanu's magic and spear may not be the correct combination for seizing control of this stone door, but perhaps *your* hammer and *my* tone will suffice.' Then she lowered *Mirilan* down to the dwarf's weapon, the low, vibrating sound pouring like water into the head of the mighty Dwarfish hammer, the fiddle itself then falling completely silent. Jelninolan gave a sigh of relief, and her aura dissolved, while Trogadon's arms began to tremble in time with the vibrato.

'It's like riding an unbroken horse!' exclaimed the dwarf, his teeth chattering. 'And as you all know how much I *hate* horse-riding!'

'Whatever strength you can put into it, the magic now present within the hammer will transform *your* power into more vibrations,' explained Jelninolan, looking deep into the dwarf's eyes. 'But you have only one strike – then the charm will dissolve.'

'He only has one attempt anyway,' warned Uldini. 'Belsarius' Bane Charm will ricochet the magically strengthened power back into the cavern. Either our enterprise will work, or we will be crushed by the mountain.'

'I have put all *my* energy into the charm,' said Jelninolan, who by now was shaking so much that Ahren was holding her up and keeping her from collapsing. 'Now it is up to *Trogadon.*'

'And once again it's left to the dwarf to sort everything out.'

Ahren was convinced that the trembling in the blacksmith's voice wasn't only down to the magical vibrato in his weapon.

'Then I had better put my hammer to good use.' Trogadon began to swing his weapon around his head, the hammer moving in ever faster circles as the dwarf strove to create as much force as possible for the decisive strike.

'Be at the ready, everyone!' shouted Falk, waving the others towards him until they formed a tight semi-circle around Trogadon. 'Once the hammer hits home, we will more than likely have no more than a few blinks of an eye to get out of the cave.'

A whimper was heard as Culhen brusquely picked up Kamaluq by the scruff of the neck.

'Good idea,' said Ahren aloud, taking the listless Jelninolan in his arms. 'Are we all set?' he asked, observing then the nods from his nervous yet grimly determined companions. '*Go!*' he commanded, his eyes now fixed on Trogadon, the Forest Guardian tensing up every muscle in his body, ready to sprint the moment the hammer smashed into the rock.

Trogadon's muscles were now straining so much that it seemed as if thick ropes were bulging from beneath the skin on his arms and neck. Then he yelled long and hard – the sound growing in volume the longer he roared – at the same time swinging his weapon twice more in an arc around his head before smashing it with incredible violence against the grey rock, his scream having reached its ultimate crescendo.

For a heartbeat, Ahren was convinced that the world was coming to an end.

In front of him, solid rock was transformed into the finest of dust, the same thing happening at lightning speed to the walls around him and the ceiling above. He was aware of nothing but the pouring of suddenly released water, the rumbling of instantly exploding rock and the lightning-fast manifestation of a grey veil filling the space, a veil so dense that not even the light of *Flamestar* could penetrate it.

'Out, out, *OUT!*' bellowed Falk, but the Thirteenth had already sprinted away, clasping the coughing Jelninolan close to his chest as he passed under Trogadon's still raised hammer, racing into the gloom, which revealed itself to be a tunnel, two paces broad and two paces high.

'Careful!' screamed Hakanu.

The rumbling sound of the rocks behind Ahren increased in volume until it was as ear-splitting cascade, announcing to all who cared to hear that the cave behind was collapsing.

'Khara!' yelled Falk.

Every fibre of Ahren's body screamed at him to look back, but he knew that he had to run as fast as his legs would carry him. His friends were depending on him to get out of the way as quickly as possible so that they, too, could get clear of the tumbling, deadly rocks.

Trogadon cursed. 'I *have* her!' he yelled.

Faster, Ahren, faster! urged Culhen, the Paladin storming through the passageway so dark that he wouldn't have been able to see his hand before his face had he placed it there. He prayed to the THREE that the tunnel wouldn't bend sharply and cause him to run headlong into a mass of rock.

'IS EVERYONE IN THE TUNNEL NOW?!' screamed Uldini, as the rumbling of crashing and splintering rocks became a thunderclap, creating a compression wave so forceful that even Ahren, at the head of the group, was thrown violently forward along the passageway. Jelninolan flew out of his arms in the process while he, himself tumbled along the uneven surface before finally coming to a stop in a heap on the ground, spluttering and coughing into a cloud of dust. Thoroughly dazed, he blinked up at the gentle light that had suddenly appeared diffusely before him.

'Jelninolan?' he gasped, coughing some more as he felt for the elf, terrified that the friends who were following might trample her to death in the general chaos. Before him, he saw two feet belonging to someone who was upright. *Jelninolan!* Gasping, he crawled towards her. 'The THREE be praised,' he wheezed. 'I was terrified that…'

Then it struck him that he was looking at the feet of a *man* wearing the sandals so beloved of people in the south of Jorath. Blinking, he peered up through the thinning veil of dust at the smiling stranger standing above him.

'Welcome, Paladin. I have been expecting you for some time now.'

Chapter 8

'Oh, *really!*' exclaimed Trogadon angrily, the dwarf right behind Ahren. 'Why is Jelninolan lying here on the floor like a log that has been tossed aside…'

But the Paladin was not listening. He struggled to his feet and peered in surprise at the figure standing before him grinning amicably. Long, curly brown hair framing a plump face and styled in a manner that suggested that the fringe was carelessly hacked at with a knife whenever the strands began to bother the bearer during his daily tasks. Intelligent, greenish-brown eyes, a slightly crooked, narrow nose and a large head completed the young man's first impressions of the stranger. His thumbs were hooked under his leather belt which struggled to contain his corpulent belly, and although the man stood there perfectly still, he radiated an impatience born out of an enforced period of idleness.

'Who are *you?*' asked Ahren, who was still struggling to gather his thoughts. His mind was dimly aware of the voices of his friends calling out to one another that they were fine before shouting out his own name.

'Welcome, Paladin,' said the man again, Ahren finding the repetition strange to say the least. 'I am…Belsarius – or at least, one could *put* it like that.'

Ahren blinked slowly and coughed, his lungs ridding themselves of any remaining dust. Then he blinked again. The Paladin wondered if he had perhaps hit his head when he had been thrown forward. Maybe he was only imagining the man.

No! interjected Culhen sharply. *That peculiar old codger really is standing in front of you.* The wolf sniffed in the man's direction. *Either the rock dust is playing tricks with me, or this fellow doesn't smell of anything at all. Be careful, Ahren.*

The left hand of the Thirteenth moved slowly down to the grip of his Wind Blade. 'As far as the world is concerned, Belsarius died a long, *long* time ago,' he said sharply.

'Really?' asked the stranger without batting an eyelid. 'How regrettable.'

Khara appeared to Ahren's right, like a ghost clad in white breaking forth from a veil of fog.

'So this is where you've been hidi—' She broke off. 'Oh,' she added. She looked first at the stranger, then at Ahren's hand resting on his weapon. Immediately, her own two blades slid out of their scabbards.

'This fellow claims to be Belsarius,' said Ahren slowly, keeping his eyes firmly on the motionless man.

'Uldini!' called Khara over her shoulder into the slowly settling dust. 'We need you here.'

'If that good-for-nothing Paladin has broken his skull yet again, I swear I'll…' grumbled the Arch Wizard, scurrying forward. Then he fell silent too, Ahren observing out of the corner of his eye how suddenly ashen-faced the childlike figure had become. *'Belsarius!'* gasped the Ancient.

The Forest Guardian puffed up his cheeks as he tried to take in what he had heard. Either this person really *was* Belsarius – or he was someone who looked exactly like him. 'Culhen says that he has no individual scent. Might we be looking at a Doppler?' His fingers closed around the handle of his weapon, ready to draw it the instant the Arch Wizard nodded.

'Hello, Uldini Getobo, sixth among the Ancients,' said the stranger matter-of-factly to the childlike figure. '*You* haven't changed.'

'And never will,' grunted Uldini in the mechanical tone of voice that suggested he had uttered a tired old cliché for the thousandth time at least. 'This is how we always greeted one another when we were alone,' murmured the Arch Wizard in a pained voice. 'Whoever this man is, he is no Doppler. Only Belsarius knew our introductory formulae.'

By now the dust had settled sufficiently for Ahren to have a quick glance around him. They were standing in a bare room, whose floor, walls and ceiling, however, were decorated with a multitude of magical runes that had been carved into the stone and which were also the source of the diffuse light that illuminated the chamber. The sheer complexity and abundance of patterns reminded Ahren of the Flame Chamber on *Alina's Rage,* except that the artistic nature of these decorations here were of a far higher quality – as if their creator had spent days on end working on each individual carving.

'Is that…?' began Falk as the rest of the companions gathered in a circle around the stranger.

Belsarius looked at the old Forest Guardian. 'Welcome, Paladin. I have been expecting you for some time now.'

'Yes. It is he,' muttered Uldini flatly.

'But...'

'I know.'

Belsarius greeted Hakanu with the same words as he had used previously with Falk and Ahren. However, he did not acknowledge the others at all. He seemed only interested in Uldini and the Paladins, smiling at them with a nonchalance that belied the tension in the air.

'This entire room is dripping with magic,' said Jelninolan, who was leaning heavily against Trogadon's shoulder. 'I can taste it effortlessly.'

Uldini blinked, held *Flamestar* up in front of his face and observed the room through his crystal orb. 'All the magic lines are directed at...*him*,' he murmured in surprise, pointing at the figure who claimed to be Belsarius.

'This is indeed so, Uldini, sixth among the Ancients.'

'Why does he call you that the whole time?' asked Hakanu curiously.

'Because I was not always the first among the Ancients,' muttered Uldini. He directed his next words at the stranger. 'If you really *are* Belsarius – how did you survive the ambush of the Dark Ones on the Hjalgarian border? And who was the dead man wearing the clothes of Belsarius, whose body was retrieved after the skirmish with those servants of the Adversary?'

The plump-faced Ancient continued to smile. 'That is a question I cannot answer.'

Ahren frowned. 'There is something fishy going on here.'

'You don't say!' Falk's voice dripped with sarcasm.

'I mean that he is behaving in a most peculiar manner,' countered Ahren, pointing at the figure directly before him. 'Have you not noticed that he is moving his head and *nothing* else? The rest of his body is perfectly still. And his face never changes its features.'

'What *are* you?' asked Khara bluntly, but the stranger completely ignored the Swordsmistress.

'It seems as though he is only acknowledging Uldini and us Paladins,' commented Hakanu. 'I hardly *ever* say this – but I'm getting goosepimples.'

'What *are* you?' asked Ahren, repeating the question his beloved had posed.

Belsarius, still smiling, looked at the Forest Guardian. 'I am the *Echo* of Belsarius.'

Uldini gasped in horror. '*Impossible!*'

'How perverse!' snapped Jelninolan, disgusted.

'Any chance of an explanation here?' asked Falk impatiently.

'The Echo of a person is like a splinter of their personality – trapped and kept alive by means of magic,' muttered Uldini. 'I know of only two occasions when such an experiment was attempted. Both times, the wizards involved lost their minds during the process, the ritual failing miserably.'

A cold shiver ran down Ahren's back. 'Why that?' he asked in a low voice.

'Because an Echo always anchors a part of the person's soul within it,' replied Jelninolan tartly. 'It is like if one splits off part of one's personality and keeps it contained within a Charm Circle.'

'Why would one want to do such a thing?' asked Khara, bemused.

Uldini shrugged his shoulders. 'Because one is curious to know if it is even possible. Or one is tempted by the fame one will earn if one pulls it off. Or perhaps because one believes that two incomplete versions of oneself are better than a complete one.'

Jelninolan snorted. 'There *was* a theory that one could export all one's negative qualities and continue to exist as the *perfect* individual.'

'Well, judging by this fellow, the original Belsarius simply got rid of his most non-committal smile,' said Trogadon, poking the Echo in the ribs. His finger disappeared through the outline of the man as tiny sparks danced their way up the dwarf. 'That's tickly,' he chuckled.

'If you have finished sticking your sausage finger into one of the greatest masterpieces of arcane art, then I would like to find out what Belsarius had in mind with this Echo,' snarled Uldini, glaring at the blacksmith.

'And quickly, too, would be good – before this chamber fills up with water,' interjected Hakanu, pointing at the stream that was pouring in from the collapsed tunnel.

'Not *again*,' groaned Falk. 'Is there an exit here anywhere?'

Ahren glanced around the circular room with its perfectly smooth wall. 'I don't believe it,' he growled. 'It's as if we are caught in a mousetrap – or stuck in an ever-repeating nightmare.'

Falk shook his head. 'Right, then. Uldini and Ahren can talk to this Echo. Belsarius must have left it here for good reason. Meanwhile, the rest of us will see if we can find a way out of this chamber. If Belsarius had no intention of getting trapped in here himself, then it is only logical that there must be another exit.'

Without saying a word, the friends divided themselves up and began tapping the wall.

Ahren gave Uldini a questioning look, the Arch Wizard replying with a shrug of his shoulders. Taking a deep breath, the Paladin asked the first question that had come into his mind. 'Why did Belsarius create you?'

The Echo looked at him with the same, impenetrable smile that Ahren had gotten to know so well in such a short time. 'To store information for the Paladins, while at the same time hiding it from the Adversary.'

Ahren flinched, the import of the words taking the young man by surprise. The others had broken off their work as soon as they had heard the explanation, everyone now staring at the Echo in disbelief.

'Well, the *wily* tinkerer,' murmured Uldini admiringly. 'He didn't rely on scrolls that might be destroyed or fall into enemy hands. Instead, he created an Echo that the Dark Ones couldn't sound out, because it reacts only to Paladins and other specially chosen people.'

'What *sort* of information?' asked Falk impatiently, having renewed his tapping of the wall with the hilt of his sword. Ahren noticed his erstwhile master glancing nervously at the stream of water flowing out from the ruined tunnel and dispersing through the room.

Belsarius shrugged his shoulder. 'That is a question I cannot answer.'

'What's *that* supposed to mean?' Trogadon's voice mirrored the same confusion that Ahren was sensing in his own mind.

Culhen snorted scornfully. *Considering how clever Belsarius is supposed to be, his Echo is remarkably stupid.*

'Uldini?' Ahren asked in a low voice. 'Do you know what he means by that answer?'

The Arch Wizard kneaded his hands as he considered how to respond. 'This Echo is…well…*limited*, if my first impressions aren't deceiving me,' he said, cocking his head and peering at the silent, immobile Belsarius. 'It seems that his creator did not splinter off *entire* parts of himself. This is why the Echo does not move and always has the same expression on its face. It is merely a vessel containing certain information – but completely without individuality.'

'That's all well and good,' growled Falk. 'But why won't he reveal the information that he has? He has already said that he is storing it on our behalf.'

'This phantasm is a simpleton,' interjected Jelninolan from the wall that she was inspecting. 'Too dull to react as a human would. We need to be more focused with our questions.'

'Its obtuseness might also be another defence,' suggested Hakanu, Ahren nodding approvingly at his protégé's insightful comment. The young warrior, however, pointed apologetically down at Kamaluq, who was staring intently at the Echo of Belsarius. 'It was *his* idea, not mine,' explained the lad. 'He suspects that this is a way of repelling a Doppler disguised as a Paladin who intends to fool the Echo. Although any potential Doppler would have to ask the right questions, too, to get the desired answers.'

'Was this Belsarius fellow paranoid by any chance?' asked Trogadon cuttingly. 'I mean, one can go too far when it comes to firewalls.'

'Says the dwarf whose fellows built massive labyrinths in the mountains whose entrances are guarded with enormous crossbows to discourage any unwanted visitors,' interjected Falk with a guffaw.

Trogadon pursed his lips. 'This here is *completely* different.'

Ahren waved a hand in front of the Echo's face in an effort to get its attention. 'My name is Ahren, and I am the Thirteenth Paladin,' he said, introducing himself politely. 'I am here of my own free will – neither the Adversary nor His servants have forced me to come, and there are neither High Fangs nor Dopplers present in this chamber.'

The eyes of the Echo glowed yellow for a heartbeat – as though a candle had briefly flamed inside its skull. 'I recognise the righteousness in your words,' said Belsarius.

Uldini whistled through his teeth. 'That was a Truth Charm, which must be embedded within the Echo. You mentioning the Doppler clearly activated it.'

'*I* mentioned it first,' complained Hakanu in a low voice, hitting his spear off the wall half-heartedly. By now, every inch of the chamber wall had been thoroughly checked, and Ahren's companions were now returning morosely to the Forest Guardian and Uldini.

'It seems that the Echo must be addressed directly before it responds,' said Khara. She tapped the water with her boot, creating a ripple which ran out in all directions, the floor now being completely submerged. 'I suggest that you pick up the pace of your questioning.'

Uldini snapped his fingers so that the Echo would look at him. 'Do you possess information which would be useful in the war against the Adversary?'

'Yes.'

The Arch Wizard rolled his eyes. 'Would you share it with us?'

'Yes.'

Uldini clenched his fists in frustration, his knuckles turning white. 'This Echo is a complete moron. Belsarius should be ashamed of himself.'

'Did your creator find out how one can defeat the Adversary?' interjected Falk angrily.

The Echo looked at him. 'No.'

Ahren's heart sank, but he posed the next question, nonetheless. 'Did he figure out a way of *helping* the Paladins to defeat the Adversary?'

'Yes.'

Jelninolan, arms akimbo, shook her head. 'Well, this really *is* overly fastidious, even for Belsarius – the fact that one has to pose a question so *precisely* for one to have any hope of getting the desired answer.'

'What can he possibly have discovered that made him so afraid?' wondered Uldini, speaking more to himself than the others.

Ahren looked over at the Echo in the hope that the magical construction would reply, but it remained mute, of course.

Culhen transmitted an image to his friend of a wild bull being encircled by a pack of wolves. *Try gradually getting the truth out of him by showering him with questions.*

Ahren tickled his companion animal under the chin. 'Can you share with us your master's knowledge?' he asked, trying his luck.

'Yes.'

'We knew that much already,' sighed Falk.

'This guessing game would be much more fun if it weren't for the fact that the water level is continuing to rise,' complained Trogadon. 'I would like to remind you all at this point that dwarfs *can't swim.*'

The gurgling of the slowly but steadily increasing pool was a grim warning that time was running out and that they had better redouble their efforts. The anxiety that the young Paladin was now feeling was reflected in the eyes of his friends, who kept looking to see if there was any sign of an escape route.

'He knows, then, of a way of helping the Paladins force the Adversary to his knees,' summarised Falk hastily. 'But what *form* does this help take?' He looked at the Echo. 'Is it a weapon?'

'No.'

'Of course, it was *you* who had to be the first to think of a blade,' snarled Uldini.

Falk shrugged his shoulders. 'A lance would have appealed to me.'

'You're so unimaginative.'

'Falk's idea wasn't bad,' interjected Khara. 'Now we know that it isn't a weapon. What else could help us against the Adversary?'

Uldini's face now lit up. 'Did Belsarius discover a spell that could be used against the enemy?'

'That is a question I cannot answer.'

'Ye gods,' growled Uldini. 'Did Belsarius discover a spell that can help the Paladins in their struggle with the Adversary?'

'No.'

'This is so cryptic,' groaned Trogadon, the dwarf then exaggeratedly waving his arms in circles. 'I have watched you all. This is what you do when you're swimming, right?'

'I really hope not, my love,' replied Jelninolan with a chuckle.

Ahren noticed how his protégé was kneeling in front of Kamaluq, looking deep into the fox's eyes.

'Are you sure?' whispered Hakanu. Then he looked up at Belsarius and recited in a somewhat wooden manner, as if reading from a scroll: 'We now know that Belsarius has discovered something that should help the Paladins defeat the Adversary. Please take note.'

The eyes of the Echo lit up. 'I understand,' it said, its voice even betraying the tiniest hint of satisfaction.

'Very good,' said Falk, looking at Kamaluq. 'Clever fox.'

Selsena glared at her Paladin, even Ahren sensing her clear annoyance. '*You* want praise?' countered the old man as he turned to look at the Titejunanwa. 'Then *help*.'

The charger shifted her hoofs in the water uneasily before sending out a wave of reassurance and mental clarity that simultaneously refreshed Ahren and focused his attention.'

'Much better,' said Falk, stroking her neck. 'That's my girl.'

'Right – not magic and not a weapon,' said Khara, summarising what she knew. 'What else could help us?'

Ahren remembered the Woman in Black? 'Is it a person?'

'No.'

'Nice try,' murmured Uldini appreciatively. 'Is it a particular place?'

'No.'

'I'm beginning to develop a certain aversion to the word "no", no matter how much Selsena is trying to calm us down,' muttered Khara. 'And the fact that this Echo is ignoring me altogether is neither improving my mood nor helping my creative juices.'

'No weapon, no magic, no person, no place,' murmured Falk. 'What's left?'

'Is it a prayer?' blurted Hakanu, suddenly wide-eyed.

'No.'

'Darn it. I was sure I'd solved the riddle.'

'A prayer is, in fact, merely a sort of *magic* that the gods employ us to recite…' explained Uldini patronisingly, only stopping when Falk glared at him.

'Maybe we're becoming a little too specific in our approach,' suggested Ahren, turning to the Echo.

'Is it an object?'

'No.'

Ahren groaned in frustration. 'Is it a particular *circumstance?*'

'Yes.'

Falk clapped his hands in delight. 'Progress at last!'

Ahren nodded. 'Please take note that we now know that it is a particular circumstance that will help the Paladins fight the Adversary.'

Again, the Echo's eyes lit up. 'I understand.'

'A circumstance, a *circumstance*,' grumbled Uldini as he mused.

'The fact that the Thirteen Paladins must be united is a *circumstance,*' interjected Jelninolan. 'Perhaps there is another one that we are not yet aware of.'

Ahren suddenly felt dreadfully uneasy as a thought struck him. 'Do all the gods have to have *reawakened?*'

Jelninolan stared at him in horror. 'Oh, please – no!' she exclaimed.

'No,' said the Echo.

Everyone in the chamber breathed a sigh of relief. 'That would have been a *very* long war,' muttered Trogadon, and Ahren was certain that he was expressing what everyone else had been thinking.

'We should only ask questions whose answers we *want* to know!' joked Khara. Immediately, she flinched, however, as cold water began to run down the inside of her boots.

Hakanu picked up Kamaluq, the wolf already having begun to swim in the pool. The little animal gratefully rubbed his head against the young Paladin's face and whimpered. 'Has it to do with a particular *time?*' asked Ahren's protégé, expressing the question his companion animal had communicated.

'Yes.'

A deathly silence descended on the chamber. Ahren hardly dared to breathe as his mind tried to come to terms with this latest revelation.

'Let us not jump to conclusions,' muttered Uldini after several heartbeats, the anxiety clearly evident in his voice. 'What *time* can Belsarius have been referring to?'

Ahren raised his hand in warning. 'Please take note that we know that the assistance to be given to the Paladins in our struggle against the Adversary consists of a particular time period,' he recited.

'I understand.'

Falk rubbed his face with his hand. 'Right, then,' he muttered. 'Must the Adversary be killed during daylight?'

'No?'

'Then when the moon is out?' asked Hakanu.

'No.'

'A *season?*' suggested Ahren hopefully.

Please don't let him say autumn, growled Culhen.

'No.'

Falk's face lit up as came up with an idea. 'A harvest moon?'

'No.'

'Damn it!'

'A phase of the moon?' interjected Uldini.

'No.'

Trogadon splashed the ever-rising water angrily, which now reached up to his thighs. 'The *real* Belsarius can count himself lucky that he's already dead – for I would surely have drowned him in this miserable lake by now for this nasty guessing game he came up with.'

Ahren could hardly bring himself to articulate the next question. 'Does it have to be a *particular* day?'

His companions stared almost pleadingly at the Echo. The Paladin, too, was certain that they were praying earnestly for a *no.*'

'Yes.'

'But of course!' fumed Trogadon. 'I mean – why would the THREE make our task easy for us if they could chain us hand and foot and make us wade through a swampland of obstacles.'

'Do *not* blame the deities!' countered Jelninolan angrily. 'They are all too aware of the mistake they made when they created the Custodian. Ever since then they have helped as much as they could.'

'Alas, it doesn't always feel like that,' murmured Falk.

Uldini turned to the Echo. 'Please take note that we know that the assistance that will be given to the Paladins in their war against the Adversary consists of a particular *day.*'

The eyes of the Echo were glowing. 'I understand.'

Ahren flinched. 'Am I imagining things or is the gleam in its eyes getting more intense?'

Jelninolan nodded. 'Perhaps that suggests we are getting closer to the right answer.

Oh, yes – please, announced Culhen. *This water is freezing, and there is nothing as inelegant as a wolf with a head cold.* Then he sneezed theatrically.

Ahren ignored both his friend and the coldness in his legs caused by the ever-rising water level. The submerged magical runes glowed, their diffuse light giving a mysterious sheen to the clear liquid. Ahren's fear that they all might drown in this hidden chamber was growing all the while – and it was exacerbated by the fact that they were so close to their goal.

'Are we really going to have to list off all the days of the year now?' asked Falk urgently.

Uldini shook his head. 'Let us begin with the more obvious candidates. 'Is it an equinox?'

'No.'

Uldini frowned in bemusement. 'One of the solstices?'

'No.'

'Is it a certain day of the year?' asked Hakanu.

'No.'

'Great question,' said Khara, impressed. 'Even if I don't like the answer.'

'Well, the Echo's penchant for secrecy is working splendidly,' snarled Uldini. 'I am seriously considering melting the runes on the walls myself, and I'm sure that the servants of the Adversary would have put an end to this *dumb* Echo long ago had they been able to.'

'You're not helping,' scolded Jelninolan.

'I *am,*' countered the Ancient angrily. 'Myself, at least.'

Ahren was now feeling at a complete loss and sick to the stomach. With every question it was becoming increasingly obvious how difficult it was going to be to unlock the secret that Belsarius had hidden so deviously in his Echo.

'Well, I simply don't know what to ask anymore,' he announced, deflated.

'If it isn't a particular day in the year, then it must be a time that doesn't repeat itself annually,' mused Uldini.

Jelninolan pointed upwards. 'There are other powerful moments in time. So far, we have all been concentrating on the moon. Perhaps it has something to do with a constellation of the stars.'

Uldini suddenly beamed at the priestess. 'But of course! You are the *best,* auntie! Belsarius, is the day in question connected to a point in time when the stars in the heavens are aligned in a particular pattern?'

'Yes.'

Oh, great,' commented Trogadon dryly. 'Now we just have to go through *all* the constellations.' Then he went down on his knees so that his head was barely above water. 'Blub, blub, blub.'

'You'll be surprised!' countered Uldini combatively before listing off zodiacal signs at an amazing speed. With each one he asked if it was of significance to the day in question, and if so, was it to be seen in the northern sky or not. Much to Ahren's surprise, the Ancient was not satisfied with the very first *yes* but kept probing and probing until he finally fell silent.

'I *am* impressed,' said Falk in spite of himself, the old man seemingly untroubled by the relentlessly rising water, whose coldness was now causing Ahren to shiver. 'There were constellations in there that even *I* have never heard of.'

Uldini didn't react, closing his eyes instead. 'The Archer rides atop the Great Gelding one winter in every five hundred,' he murmured. 'But it is only with every second simultaneous appearance of these zodiacal signs that the Maelstrom is also visible, and the phenomenon of the latter *enclosing* the two aforementioned signs in a constellatory manner is even rarer. If we then add the sign of the THREE, which must also be apparent in the heavens, then we are talking about a day that repeats itself once every…let me think…yes…if my calculations are correct…once every thirteen hundred years.'

'Well, isn't that just *great!*' spluttered Falk. 'I think I would have preferred the variation where we would have to wait for the reawakening of the gods. That's sure to happen earlier.'

'Can you tell us when this constellation will next take place?' asked Ahren nervously, barely managing to prevent his teeth from chattering. Uldini shook his head.

'I would need maps of the stars, which I do not possess, alas. I will have to consult Akkad or Quin-Wa on the matter as soon as we arrive in Highstone.'

Ahren nodded nervously as he pulled his hands out of the water. 'Another good reason for getting there as quickly as we can. Belsarius, please take note that we know that the assistance for the Paladins in combating the Adversary involves waiting for the day when the Archer, the Great Gelding and the Maelstrom are simultaneously aligned with the sign of the THREE, all being then visible in the northern sky.'

The eyes of the Echo glowed with such force this time that Ahren was momentarily blinded and forced to look away.

'And about time,' it said, its voice sounding quite different – almost *authentic*. 'Now only one question remains,' it added. 'The most precious one of all.'

Ahren, still dazzled, could just about make out that Uldini was peering dreamily at the features of the long gone Ancient.

'*Why?*' croaked the childlike figure hoarsely, the Echo laughing in reply.

'Very good,' announced Belsarius warmly. 'The queen of all questions. The word which solves all the mysteries of Creation if one utters it often enough.'

'I am delighted that you two sorcerers are enjoying your little *tête-à-tête*,' growled Trogadon in his gravelly voice as he held onto the pommel of Culhen's saddle for dear life. 'But I *would* appreciate it if you brought it to a close – preferably in a manner that would reveal an escape route to the rest of us.'

Although the Echo's voice now suddenly possessed a considerable portion of *life*, it still showed absolutely no reaction to the dwarf's words. Instead, it looked at Uldini as a master would his favourite student. 'Everything in Creation follows a pattern' it began. Spring follows winter, autumn follows summer. Day follows night and night follows day. First, we have the ebb, then the flow.'

'Oh, great,' growled Trogadon. 'And I was afraid that it was going to be a *rambling* explanation.'

I really don't know how I'm supposed to swim with Trogadon on my back, whined Culhen nervously.

'Can you do anything about the rising waters?' asked Ahren urgently.

'Alas, no,' countered Belsarius with an expression of genuine regret, only his head and chest above the surface, the liquid simply flowing through him. 'I know nothing of any water.'

'It remains a magical construct,' interjected Uldini. 'It has absolutely no comprehension of any information that has not already been put into it.'

'Then please ensure that this Echo delivers the intended message to us,' urged Falk, looking imploringly at the Arch Wizard. 'Perhaps then it can be *really* useful to us.'

Ahren watched Hakanu carefully place Kamaluq on Muai's back, the big cat treading water and looking precisely as enthusiastic as one would expect any wet feline to feel.

'Everything follows a pattern,' murmured Ahren, prompting the Echo, the latter picking up on those words with relish.

'Precisely. And this pattern is also recognisable when applied to the Adversary.' The apparition raised a hand, and suddenly a blanket of magical lights decorated the ceiling. 'Here is the constellation of the stars as it appeared the very night that the THREE created the Custodian.'

Uldini was staring so fascinated at the magical illusion above that he temporarily forgot to swim and immediately began to sink. Ahren grabbed his friend's robe and pulled him to the surface.

'And the Custodian can be slain when this constellation is in the sky,' whispered Uldini, grinning broadly.

'Incorrect,' replied Belsarius, his voice gentle. 'When the stars are thus aligned, he can most *easily* be slain. There is a time for sowing and a time for reaping. If one breaks the harmony of the circle that permeates all things, then one must fight against not only one's enemy but also against the *power* of the circle itself.'

Falk groaned as he began to perform his first swimming strokes with his arms. 'Does that mean that the Paladins have had misfortune while trying to confront the Adversary over the millennia because they kept attacking at the wrong *time?'*

Belsarius nodded. 'Every action has its right time. Better to dive down to the lakebed in the middle of summer than in the depths of winter when the surface is frozen over and deadly.'

'How?' asked Uldini, flabbergasted. '*How* did you discover the correct stellar arrangement?'

'Of course!' complained Trogadon. 'This question is *much* more important than how to save our damn lives.'

Belsarius looked very pleased with himself as he pointed up to the ceiling again. 'I found paintings in caves – they were from the age when the first humans, dwarfs and elves were released by the gods into the wide expanses of Jorath. These primitive drawings first depicted three over-sized beings – and then, at some point a fourth appeared. And every tribe had their own versions of these drawings, all depicting the same constellations.'

'The creation of the Custodian must have been displayed all over Jorath then,' said Jelninolan, who was, like Uldini, awestruck by the sight above her, which she watched dreamily as she swam on the spot. 'In those days, the young tribes must have believed that a fourth god had been born – one who would from then on keep watch over them.'

'That was, in some respects, the plan,' gasped Khara, who was helping Trogadon to keep above water. 'Until the Adversary betrayed us and the gods because of His lust for power and his vanity.'

'Please, let the friendly Echo finish saying what he has to say so that we just *might* get out of here alive,' pleaded Trogadon in a sickly-sweet voice, the dwarf now sitting, thanks to Khara's assistance, on Culhen's back. The wolf had to tilt his head back to avoid swallowing water, while Ahren's anxiety was increasing all the time.

'But I still have so many *questions!'* exclaimed Uldini plaintively, the agony in his voice feeling like a stab to Ahren's heart.

Ahren! urged Culhen, madly doing a doggy paddle to keep himself and the dwarf above water. *We have run out of time!*

'Please take note that we now know that the Adversary can best be challenged when the alignment of the stars in the sky are the same as the very day He was created!' called out the Paladin, his fingertips now able to touch the ceiling of the chamber.

'*No!*' groaned Uldini, but already the eyes of the Echo had lit up again.

'Oh,' it said, its features suddenly appearing kindly, somewhat confused and so down-to-earth that suddenly, Ahren felt a deep sympathy for the construct. The Echo waved a hand. 'My, but it *is* damp here – this must be most uncomfortable for you.' It looked at Uldini. 'Our little chat will have to wait a while longer – if the gods are merciful.'

Uldini nodded sadly. 'Farewell, old friend.'

Belsarius smiled. 'Farewell. And lead the Ancients well and wisely.' Then the Echo dissolved and with it the play of lights on the ceiling. A moment later and the runes on the walls were gone too, their light no longer illuminating the chamber.

In the blink of an eye, it was pitch black, with only the sounds of splashing water and the heavy breathing of the companions audible as the little group sought to keep their heads above water.

'You mean, that was *it?*' gasped Falk furiously. 'He gives us a load of instructions and then leaves us here to *drown?*'

Ahren's head banged off the ceiling. He flinched in surprise and breathed in metallic-tasting water which made his lungs burn. As he coughed, he heard a flurry of colourful curses coming from Trogadon.

'This cannot be,' whispered Uldini. 'Belsarius would never…' His voice faded away as *Flamestar* blazed into life, revealing a cavern filled with water to within a few inches of the ceiling.

Khara reached out her hand until she touched Ahren's the Paladin's panic increasing as Culhen whimpered, water beginning to run down his up-turned nose.

Ahren…

Before Culhen could say more, a rumbling sound echoed through the chamber, seeming to come from all directions at once. The runes blazed to life again, but this time they were swathed in a fiery corona – even burning under the very water itself. Then the light was extinguished, and at that precise heartbeat one half of the chamber wall disappeared too – so abruptly that it seemed as though it had never existed.

Ahren and his friends were unceremoniously swept from the flooded cavern into a passage at whose end was a spiral staircase like the one that they had used to enter the Sanctum. This one led upwards and seemed to be inviting them to safety.

Tossed like a bucketful of fish that one empties on a dock after a successful day's trawling, the companions were thrown against the steps. Coughing and spluttering, they sorted out their limbs before struggling to their unsteady feet. The looks that Ahren and his friends shared with each other betrayed the terror they had all been feeling – the terror that they might have drowned miserably here in this secret vault at the end of the world, thereby condemning Jorath itself to extinction.

Suddenly, Uldini, who was still standing in the passageway, began like an angry four-year old to splash the water around him, which was still up to his waist. 'We had enough time for a few more questions!' he wailed. 'What we saw at the very end *was* Belsarius in his *completeness* and not only the part that was storing the information for us.' His voice faded away to a whisper. 'That was the *real* Belsarius.'

'Or that is how *you* felt him to be, at least,' murmured Jelninolan gently. 'But Belsarius died a long time ago. And we all know why.'

'The Adversary had him killed so that his knowledge would die with him,' added Ahren, the elf nodding in agreement. 'But Belsarius had already preserved the knowledge in his Echo.'

'He predicted it,' sobbed Uldini, tears pouring down his cheeks. 'He predicted that the Adversary would kill him, so he created the charm.'

'He must have noticed that the servants of the Adversary were hot on his heels,' mused Falk sadly. 'That must have been why he formed the Echo and lured them away, so as to prevent them from finding his Sanctum.'

'But they found it anyway,' countered Uldini harshly, spitting out his words as if they were poison.

'They never found his Echo,' said Khara in a soothing voice. 'His knowledge survived and was finally revealed to us.'

'Is there any chance that we might climb this spiral staircase?' asked Trogadon plaintively. 'This passageway is filling with water, and I've had enough of fearing death by drowning.'

The shivering group silently began to move. Ahren's head was still spinning with what they had learned so recently. *Every action has its right time,* Belsarius had said. Could it really be that the millennia-old task of the Paladins had failed until now because they had somehow missed the information that Belsarius had finally discovered? But if what the Echo had confided to them really *was* true, why had none of the other *Ancients* ever seen a connection between creating and destroying the Custodian, who had come to be known and feared as HE, WHO FORCES.

Don't forget that according to Uldini this Belsarius possessed a particularly remarkable mind, interjected Culhen, who was pulling himself up the spiral staircase with difficulty. *It wasn't only magic that was very important to him but also the temporal world and the history of Jorath. Do you know of any other Ancient with such a wide range of interests and talents?*

'We've arrived!' announced Trogadon triumphantly. 'The end of the spiral staircase has…' His shoulders sagged. '…*not* been reached. Of course, the exit is blocked.'

You can't be serious,' groaned Falk, staring up at the dwarf.

Muai growled.

She smells fresh air,' said Khara, relieved. 'The rockfall mustn't be *too* deep.'

'Some good news at last,' sighed Hakanu. Then he craned his neck to see up around the turn in the stairs, where Trogadon was. 'Would you like me to come up to you and throw my spear?'

The companions groaned in unison as Ahren placed his hand heavily on the shoulder of his protégé.

'I think we need to have a little chat about how it isn't necessary to solve *every* problem by using your spear…'

Finally, the cathartic crashing sound of rolling rocks echoed down the confines of the spiral staircase, accompanied by a refreshing gust of cold wind and a shimmer of indirect sunlight that reached as far down as where Ahren was standing. He could hear the gurgling of water coming from below him – it was as if the rising seepage was expressing its disappointment that the Paladin and his companions would not, in the end, meet their end in its wet embrace.

'Let's get out of here,' murmured Khara, summarising his own wish, although it took a bit of squeezing on his part before he finally stumbled out of Belsarius' Sanctum. Pulling himself upright behind Culhen and beside Khara, he breathed the fresh mountain air deep into his lungs, smiled, and looked around him in wide-eyed admiration.

'Well, isn't that a *fantastic* view!' exclaimed Falk, spreading his arms and turning on his own axis.

They were standing on a mountain saddle that had been spared the landslide which had destroyed much of the valley below them. The sun was already low in the sky, illuminating the crusty snow around them, making it seem as if the companions were standing on a sparkling carpet of diamonds. The air was cold but not cutting, the upward slope beside them protecting the little group for the most part from the wind. There was no sign of life anywhere, which was reassuring, considering that they were in Kelkor, the land of monsters and Dark Ones.

'It would be nicer without snow,' murmured Hakanu with a crooked grin. 'Ever since the Ice Fields I've been yearning for the burning heat of summer.'

'We are alive and a great deal more knowledgeable than we were even a day ago,' countered Ahren with a shrug of his shoulders. 'This is a victory in itself.'

Hakanu's grin became broader. 'Indeed, you are right, Master.'

Falk affectionately patted Selsena, who was beginning to prance. 'Would you listen to that young buck – always wanting what he does not have.' Then he cocked his head and frowned. 'What do you mean, *I* was just like that for the first hundred years?'

'Much as it pains me to spoil the party yet again,' interjected Uldini cuttingly,' but I must remind you that our supplies are wet through, thanks to the icy water – and that includes our bedrolls. It is too cold to spend the night out here in the open – but before anyone asks, I am completely *unwilling* to risk an Unleashing only for the sake of drying off a few woolly blankets.'

'At least Trogadon was so slow with clearing the passage that our clothes are halfway dry now,' chuckled Falk as he scanned the area and wrapped his arms around himself. 'But Uldini is right – we must urgently find shelter.'

'What about going back into the tunnel and spending the night there?' suggested Hakanu, only for Khara to grab him by the chin and turn his face towards the opening through which they had just come. The first trickles of water were springing up and turning into little frozen puddles in the cold mountain air. 'Oh,' whispered the lad meekly.

'By dawn, the Sanctum will be completely under water,' murmured Uldini sadly. 'It has fulfilled its mission – and now it is no more than mounds of rubble and a few water-filled caverns in a forlorn mountain.'

Jelninolan placed a comforting hand on the Arch Wizard's shoulder, while he, most untypically, snuggled into her.

'Ahren, Trogadon and I will try to find a way down this mountain saddle,' announced Falk, taking his bow from Selsena's back. 'With a bit of luck, we might find an unoccupied cave where we can stay overnight while our things dry off. Tomorrow morning, we will continue our descent. Along the way, we Forest Guardians can hunt for food to keep us going until we finally arrive in a more civilised milieu. From then on, the journey to Deepstone will surely be less eventful than it has been, at which po—. I'm sorry, but is *no-one* listening to me?' The Paladin frowned angrily.

Ahren grinned and pointed south to a point in the sky that was growing bigger by the heartbeat. 'If you hadn't been so wrapped up in your own thoughts, Selsena would surely have let you in on the secret,' he chuckled. Then he ruffled Culhen's fur, the wolf howling with delight.

Sun Shimmer is coming! Sun Shimmer will save us all!

Chapter 9

As always, the descent of the Roc was a sight to behold, but it was only when Sun Shimmer prepared to land that Ahren realised how much the enormous bird had grown in the few years since she had been hatched. The chain mail stretching across her chest had expanded hugely, its outer edges glittering in the giveaway sheen of Dwarfish Steel, while its centre, directly over her heart and lungs was still composed of Deep Steel.

Yet, even more impressive than the stature of the companion animal, from whose nape Sunju was waving down to them, was the wooden box, resembling an oversized wheelless cart, which was strapped to the Roc's torso with leather straps, each as broad as a man. Ahren was pretty sure what the purpose of the construction was, and he was even more certain that a few heated discussions with the companion animals were about to commence. Then a dark, wrinkled face, framed by white hair appeared over the top of the wooden frame.

'Lost without trace, yet nonetheless found – a place where a true friend to second death was bound,' intoned Sleeps-in-Treetop, looking at Uldini with a mixture of scorn and pity. 'If your heart was not bleeding at this moment, then I would have to tell you how wearying it is having to pick you up repeatedly, as if you were a childlike lazy-bones, too silly to make their way home on their own.'

'Oh, go drool over a Pallid Frog!' snapped the Arch Wizard.

Sleeps-in-Treetops licked her skinny lips and chuckled. 'Tempting – but not now.'

'Quin-Wa sent us,' announced Sunju as Sun Shimmer folded in her wings and settled down on the snow. 'We were to follow the sorcerous scent of the Adversary's Bane Curse. She reckoned – or rather, *feared* – that it was intended for you once you hadn't appeared in Deepstone as arranged.'

Ahren cocked his head quizzically. 'Why didn't *you* pick us up weeks ago in Eathinian?'

Sunju shook her head apologetically. 'Undertaking long journeys by air has become dangerous,' explained the pale woman. 'Servants of the Adversary combined with His devious spells are a constant danger to Sun Shimmer when she's in flight. Had the Dark god not exhausted Himself by hurling forth His Bane Curse after you, I would never have dared to seek you out here – not even with the invaluable help of Sleeps-in-Treetops.'

'Pinions beyond number, some black, some white,' chanted the Ancient, shaking her head mournfully, 'their beaks tormenting Sun Shimmer when she's in flight.'

'You will see what we mean on our return journey,' said Sunju, glancing back at the old woman. 'At least, we now have Jelninolan and Uldini with us, both of whom can help keep the Dark Ones at bay that will be harrying us in the skies.'

Uldini cleared his throat. 'Ah…well, regarding *that*…'

'…don't count on us,' murmured Jelninolan, ending the Arch Wizard's sentence.

'It would be better, Sleeps-in-Treetop, if you *listen* to what they say,' grunted Falk, his eyes fixed on the shamanic Ancient. 'You do *not* want Jelninolan and Uldini unleashing themselves with all of us sitting here in this nutshell on the back of a Roc, do you?'

That's enough, whined Culhen. *I'm walking back.*

Ahren, like his furry friend, wasn't taken at all by the idea of trusting his life to a few wooden planks. But the wolf's refusal was annoying him.

Get in – now! he commanded.

Absolutely not. Remember the gondolas in Thousand Halls? We crash-landed in one of them! But at least, that one was made from metal! And we were enclosed! This structure here is nothing but a few bits of wood hammered together and isn't even as high as my chin. I am not a complete idiot!

'Climb in via the tail feathers,' said Sunju, nodding towards the ramp that Sun Shimmer had created with her rear plumage. 'Take care, though – they are as hard as oakwood by now, but they are by no means indestructible.' With that, she glared at Trogadon, who had been stamping all over the feathering in his desire to get onto the Roc's back.

The dwarf gave the pale woman an embarrassed look, but his joyful anticipation was still evident in the sparkling of his eyes.

'Khara, would you be so good as to urge Muai on board?' asked Ahren before emphasising his next words: 'So that my *cowardly* wolf can see how safe it is up there.'

The tigress growled, whipped her tail from side to side and glared at the Forest Guardian through her half-closed eyes.

'Uh...I'm afraid there's a problem,' whispered Khara. 'She, too, is refusing to enter this...*death trap* as she calls it.'

Ahren rolled his eyes. 'You *can't* be serious!'

See! crowed Culhen triumphantly. *Even a stupid pussy cat knows when it's a bad idea to climb into a flying wheelbarrow.*

By now everyone had clambered onto the Roc's back except for Ahren, Khara and their two companion animals. Even Selsena was standing rigidly with her head held high in the oversized wooden cart. Falk was standing beside her, looking no less petrified. Uldini and Jelninolan, on the other hand, seemed remarkably relaxed – although this was probably down to their complete exhaustion, which dampened most of their emotions – an effect that Ahren had noticed again and again whenever the pair had finished performing challenging sorcery.

Hakanu was sitting at the very front of the cart with the broad grin on his face that he normally reserved for when he was daydreaming about performing heroic deeds. He was absently stroking the shivering Kamaluq. Doubtless, the clever animal remembered that there wasn't a single ballad or legend about flying foxes, but many concerning foolish beings of all kinds who fell to their deaths from the heavens.

'Is there a problem?' asked Sunju. 'Sun Shimmer is anxious to get going. The snow under her tummy is beginning to make her cold.'

'Our valiant companion animals are *afraid!*' shouted Ahren before adding with a mischievous grin: 'It seems that they do not believe Sun Shimmer is capable of carrying us all safely to Deepstone.'

The head of the Roc immediately turned towards the two hesitant animals, the eyes of the massive creature then focusing angrily on Culhen and Muai.

Now that was mean, complained the wolf, who immediately scampered up the feathers and leapt into the wooden box with all the energy of a whelp, looking for all the world as if he was entering the comfiest little box in all Jorath. Not three heartbeats later, Muai was in the cart, growling in annoyance.

Khara laughed and gave Ahren a peck on the cheek before she curtseyed affectedly and gestured towards the tail feathers. 'Shall we, my good Paladin?' she asked in a courtly manner. 'Our air carriage awaits us.'

'But of course, Your Ladyship,' he replied with an air of pomposity, the young couple than proceeding to flounce their way on board.

Khara watched him with her eyes sparkling, and the Forest Guardian was quite proud of the fact that his hands and legs only minimally trembled as they climbed into the wooden box.

Although the wind whistling past the enormous Roc was icy and causing all the travellers to shiver, the night-time flight over Jorath was one of the most memorable journeys that the Paladin had ever experienced.

The short flights between the mountains of Thousand Halls were nothing compared to the distance covered by Sunju's companion animal during the long hours of darkness. Beating her wings surprisingly slowly, the Roc soared upon the currents, eating up league after league as Ahren looked down in astonishment onto the snowy landscape below. First there were the snow-covered, jagged mountains of Kelkor, which were replaced when the night was half over by the cultivated fields and rich Hjalgarian forests. The Paladin saw whole towns and villages from the back of the Roc, all of them looking peaceful as smoke wafted up from the chimneys of the houses, each one resembling a skilfully crafted toy that a nobleman might buy for the entertainment of his children during the Autumn Festival.

'Breath-taking, isn't it?' murmured Khara for at least the eighth time as she snuggled in closer under Ahren's cloak.

The Forest Guardian chuckled. 'This flight would be more enjoyable if it weren't for the complaining of my wolf.'

Oh, what a dreadful fate it is to be bound to someone who allows his most loyal friend to plunge to his death from on high, complained Culhen.

He and Muai were cowering beside each other in the middle of the box, lying as snug to the timbers below them as they could manage, their noses pressing hard on the floor. Narrow wooden benches equipped with leather safety belts ran along the insides of the walls for the two-legged occupants.

You realise that Sun Shimmer can hear you? teased Ahren with a shake of his head.

Culhen had thrown himself headlong against legions of Dark Ones in his time, but the thought of depending on the Roc's flying ability terrified the wolf.

I don't care, he retorted sulkily. *I will happily apologise if we ever get out of this nightmare alive!*

'This wolf is such a moan,' muttered Ahren.

Khara snorted. 'Tell me about it. Muai has announced more than once that she will not spend another day by my side unless I force Sun Shimmer to land forthwith.'

The tigress responded with a low growl which finally turned into a plaintive miaow.

Khara looked up at the firmament, suddenly totally engrossed by the stars which now seemed so close. 'Tell me something – do those constellations ahead resemble what we saw in the Sanctum or am I imagining things?' she murmured.

Ahren was immediately alert. Was it possible that *now* was the very moment that they should be grabbing the Adversary by the scruff of the neck?

A quick look was enough to ease his anxiety, and he breathed a sigh of relief. 'They are not in the correct position,' he said, pointing at a group of five stars forming a simple pattern. 'There is the Archer. One always sees it over Hjalgar at this time of year.' His finger moved rightward to a group of six stars positioned almost in a line. 'That is the Great Gelding, racing across the heavens at a terrific gallop. You can actually *see* it moving as its stars streak across the night sky. They say that of all the signs of the zodiac, the Great Gelding is the least predictable – every evening, it follows a different track. At the moment, it is far too far away from the Archer to be a part of the constellation that we observed.'

Khara frowned. 'But the eight stars *surrounding* the Great Gelding and the Archer constitute the Maelstrom, don't they?'

Ahren nodded. 'Yes – but if I understood Uldini correctly, the *distances* between them all must be exactly as we saw them. The Archer is clearly not riding the Great Gelding yet.' He smiled wanly. 'In fact, it looks as if he is running after the unfortunate animal.'

Khara giggled, the relief evident in her voice when she spoke. 'For a heartbeat I was worried that…' She couldn't bring herself to finish the sentence.

'I know.' Ahren peered at the stars again. 'The sign of the THREE is missing as well – the equilateral triangle of stars has already set for the night.'

Khara shivered, pressing herself closer to her beloved. 'It still makes me feel queasy to see most of the groupings that Belsarius talked of in the firmament above us.'

Ahren nodded and stared up at the twinkling lights which had suddenly taken on such a portentous role for the future of Jorath. 'I am no astrologer, which is why I cannot say *when* the constellations we saw will be in the correct position. And when it comes to the perfect alignment of four constellations, it must involve a considerable amount of work to ascertain *precisely* the instant when this will manifest itself for the second time.' Hugging Khara, he reassured her – and himself – by adding: 'Luckily, we are flying to a location full of wise Ancients, one of whom will hopefully provide us with the necessary answer.'

Khara nodded, averting her eyes from the stars.

'At least Trogadon is happy,' whispered Ahren conspiratorially, hoping to distract the Swordsmistress from her worries as he pointed with his chin towards the blacksmith. The dwarf and Jelninolan had slung their arms over each other's shoulders, the pair appearing to be perfectly content, both with themselves and the world. While the elf was enjoying the moment with her eyes half-closed, the dwarf was grinning so broadly and looking so wide-eyed that Ahren couldn't help thinking of the three crazed faces of the Wrath Demons, those unfortunate giants who were hopefully still enjoying their healing sleep. Ahren earnestly wished that the giants would awaken again sometime soon, healed in both body and mind.

'Your apprentice is lapping it all up, too,' murmured Khara with a grin, turning to her beloved and giving him a knowing look.

Ahren cursed. 'Hakanu! Your arms must stay *within* the cart!' he hissed.

His protégé pulled in his hands, with which he had been trying to touch the clouds, and obediently sat back down on the bench. 'But Master! We are securely strapped!'

'That doesn't interest me,' countered Ahren firmly as he checked his own strap for the umpteenth time. 'What if something tries to attack us from the clouds, forcing Sun Shimmer to take evasive action?' he continued. 'Be *aware* and *always* be ready to hold on tight.'

You are so gruesome, complained Culhen. *How can I survive up here any longer if you insist on filling my mind with visions of horror? AND WHAT AM I SUPPOSED TO HOLD ONTO?*

'Thank you *very* much for terrifying my Titejunanwa,' commented Falk bitterly from the rear of the cart. 'She had just gotten used to her *unfamiliar* situation.'

'Have no fear!' shouted Sunju from the nape of the mighty bird's neck. 'Sun Shimmer is flying in a northerly arc around Kelkor. She is determined to avoid all the creatures that live in the mountains and that might possibly attack us up here. I certainly have no intention of encountering the three Wrath Winds that you expelled from the giants. Sleeps-in-Treetop is giving us additional protection, insofar as she can, by means of her magic. In other words, we will be safe enough until we reach the area surrounding Deepstone.'

Ahren frowned at the female Paladin's choice of words. 'And what will happen when we *approach* the city?' he shouted back.

Sunju glanced over her shoulder, shooting him a warning look and shaking her head almost imperceptibly. The Paladin swallowed hard.

'It seems this flight will be more turbulent than I thought it would be,' whispered Khara, having seen Sunju's reaction to Ahren's question.

'It's good that Culhen is so occupied with his own concerns,' murmured the Forest Guardian. 'If he had noticed, he would be in a total panic now.'

Are you talking about me? asked the wolf nervously.

Yes – but we're only saying good things, said Ahren, reassuring the animal with a white lie.

For the rest of the night, the Forest Guardian regaled Culhen with stories and images of their previous triumphs, distracting himself, too, from thinking about the potential aerial dangers that might be lurking ahead of them.

The slowly rising sun on the eastern horizon was now casting its golden rays on the landscape below wherever it managed to shine between the peaks which stubbornly continued to cast their own gloomy shadows, providing a shifting interplay of light and dark on the land in the valleys below.

Ahren had been sleeping for quite a while, and Culhen, exhausted, had finally nodded off just before dawn.

A cry rang out: 'We've been thwarted!'

Alerted by Sunju's warning, the Paladin sat up with a start, his efforts at standing only failing because of the leather strap tied around his waist.

Disorientated, he looked around for a heartbeat. His companions, too, were awake and agitated, and as soon as Culhen opened his eyes in alarm, the wolf's terror flowed straight into Ahren's mind.

What happened?

The animal was so panic-stricken that the Paladin immediately slipped into the Void, hoping to pull Culhen into the emotionless trance. But within a couple of heartbeats, the Void was no more than a mass of mental rubble, torn apart by the increasingly restless wolf.

What happened? What happened? he repeated again and again.

'We are getting company!' shouted Sunju.

'That's an understatement if ever there was one!' bellowed Trogadon, Ahren recognising a flicker of genuine disquiet in the dwarf's eyes. The squat figure pointed down beyond their starboard side.

'Damn it, but I've never seen so many Swarm Claws,' grunted the blacksmith.

Ahren craned his neck, but it was only when Sun Shimmer's wing had completed its downward trajectory that he was able to see the very thing that Sunju and Trogadon had alerted them to. An enormous cloud of Swarm Claws was rising from the giant, black ramparts of the Obsidian Fortress, that stone-built symbol of the Dark god's power which lay to their right only a few furlongs away. It almost seemed to Ahren as if the very blocks of the pitch-black fortification had broken away as each and every Storm Claw that had previously been lying in wait on the extensive walls, on the crenels, the merlons and towers now soared as a unified horde, the Dark Ones beating their wings as they rose to greet the Roc, with the sole intention of preventing the mighty bird from continuing her flight towards Deepstone.

'It won't be long before we are under attack!' Sunju called out through gritted teeth. 'I had feared that our sudden take off yesterday might not go unnoticed. Clearly, the enemy was expecting us to return!'

'But what can we *do?*' asked Khara anxiously, her hands on her Wind Blades, which, in view of the overwhelming force rising ever upwards, she instinctively understood would be no more effective than Ahren's bow, Trogadon's axe, or Falk's broadsword.

Ahren looked over pleadingly at Jelninolan, but her eyes were half-closed – the elf seemed to be in dreamland, while Uldini, stretched out on one of the benches and securely tied with two belts, was snoring loudly. There would be no help coming from these two Ancients – that much was clear, Ahren then turning his attention to Sleeps-in-Treetop, who was already pointing a bony finger at the sky.

'Feather light, ye weighty powers, Forget ye not the heavy showers.'

'Those are fleecy clouds,' murmured Khara, taken aback. 'What could Sleeps-in-Treetop possibly be chanting about?'

Ahren shrugged his shoulders in bemusement as he watched how the individual misty wisps began gathering around them to create a large, fluffy cloud.

'Sweep up to safety,' intoned the Ancient cryptically, Sunju hesitating, however.

'That will bring us right *over* the Obsidian Fortress – to precisely the place we *don't* want to be.'

Ahren heard the scepticism in her voice.

'I could veer south and try to escape from them that way,' added the pale-faced Paladin. She paused before adding: 'Although the longer flight *would* tire Sun Shimmer, enabling the Swarm Claws to catch us…'

'Courageous duplicity or blood-soaked fleeing,' countered Sleeps-in-Treetop, unimpressed. 'Which would *you* like Sun Shimmer to experience?'

Sunju cursed. A heartbeat later, Sun Shimmer began her furious ascent, the bird banking violently to get above what was now the *only* thick cloud, spreading across the sky. Both Culhen and Muai scraped the wooden floor with their claws, nevertheless losing their grip and sliding along the timbers in the flying cart. Selsena found her own unique solution to the problem by lying on her stomach and boring her spiral horn deep into the outer wall, where it became well and truly stuck.

Ahren! yelled Culhen, panic-stricken, his claws finding far less of a grip in the wood than Muai's sharper ones, the big cat lying flat on the floor with her ears pulled as far back as they could go.

As the wolf's sliding speed suddenly increased, Ahren tried to cut himself loose to help his friend, only for Trogadon to beat him to it. the dwarf dug his calloused hands deep into Culhen's fur, then held on with all his might, groaning with the effort until Sun Shimmer came out of her banking and floated straight through the air again.

Ugh, muttered Culhen, looking at Ahren with his big wolf eyes. *Please tell him not to let go until we've landed.*

The Paladin nodded gratefully over at Trogadon, the dwarf replying simply with a wink. Then the blacksmith dragged the petrified wolf closer to him before tickling him affectionately.

'Uncle Trogadon won't let you fall – don't you worry,' he growled in his gravelly voice.

The fact that Culhen did not respond in any way was more than enough proof to Ahren that his friend was terrified out of his wits. This flight would definitely *not* be the subject of boasting by the wolf at some later date – *if* they made it to Deepstone alive.

Meanwhile, Sunshine glided over the Ring far below them and then passed the outer walls of the Obsidian Fortress. The dark palace loomed like a fat spider stuck in the middle of enemy territory, surrounded by dozens of elliptical obsidian ramparts with heavy gates to the north, east, south and west.

'Master, look!' exclaimed Hakanu gleefully, as if he was looking in awe at an avalanche without noticing that it was, in fact, heading directly for him.

Ahren craned his neck again and saw that the cloud beneath them was shrinking into a thick, black mass.

'Very good, very good,' croaked Sleeps-in-Treetops in a self-satisfied tone – as though she were praising an obedient guard dog. 'And now – *release!*'

Hardly had she finished speaking when the cloud below them burst. There was an enormous, continuous roar, which Ahren recognised as the sound of raindrops hammering. He risked another glance down over Sun Shimmer's flank and was stunned to see what seemed like a wall of water slamming down towards the ground – right into the middle of the soaring swarm of Dark Ones. The screeching of the beasts was deafening, the beating of their wings slowing considerably on account of the drops raining down on them with breath-taking speed.

'Now!' Sunju commanded.

In an instant, Sun Shimmer folded her wings and began a daring nosedive. It felt to Ahren as if not only his stomach, but *all* his innards had shot up into his gullet. Even Trogadon began to curse, the dwarf still managing to hold the wolf within his grasp, while Muai had now dug her claws into an empty bench, as if she were a kitten grasping its favourite ball of wool.

Ahren gritted his teeth as the icy airstream forced tears out of his eyes. The Forest Guardian's magic cloak flapped behind him helplessly like a flag in the midst of a violent storm.

Falk's hands were clasping Selsena's back, but Ahren was not sure if the old Paladin was holding *her* secure or if she was his erstwhile master's precious source of comfort. The two Ancients were still fast asleep, and it was only Hakanu, holding the petrified Kamaluq close to his chest, who seemed to be having the time of his life as he yelled his excitement at their downward plummet.

'Madness!' gasped Falk in the chaos as the Roc slammed through the cloud of dazed and lurching Swarm Claws. 'We must be completely mad, trying to break through them like this!'

Those disorientated Dark Ones not quick enough to perform evasive manoeuvres were smashed to pieces as the heavy armour of the enormous bird smashed into them. Suddenly, the air was full of splattering blood and screeching bodies, but it took no more than a few heartbeats before they were through the living – and dying – wall of claws and beaks.

As they approached the fortress with speed, Ahren's fear grew even more. Already, he could make out the outlines of countless, High- and Low Fangs, Sickle Hoppers, Glower Bears and Horde Bulls, all of them scampering wildly between the walls and on the ramparts and towers of the monstrous defensive facility.

Had this abrupt nosedive really been planned? Or had Sun Shimmer perhaps been surreptitiously struck by a spell and was now hurtling down with her charges right into the heart of enemy territory? Yet, neither Sunju nor Sleeps-in-Treetop seemed at all panic-stricken, the Forest Guardian immediately deciding to place his trust in the Roc's inexplicable action – in the hope that it was part of some mysterious plan that would clarify itself at some later point.

'Veer a little to port side!' screamed Sleeps-in-Treetop, who was staring intently at a point on the horizon which Ahren could not quite make out.

Sun Shimmer banked accordingly, this time more gently so that the companion animals were able to maintain their position without too much difficulty.

'The Swarm Claws!' exclaimed Khara, horrified. 'They have regrouped!'

A glance over his shoulder confirmed to Ahren that the winged Dark Ones had sufficiently shaken off the effects of the downpour to enable them to re-form behind and above the Roc, the living cloud of leathern wings, sharp beaks and deadly talons preparing to launch their final, deadly aerial assault.

'Faster, my beauty, faster!' cried Sunju, Sun Shimmer immediately picking up speed as the bird uttered an extended, piercing, raw-sounding caw. The pinions of the enormous bird were two incredible forces of nature left and right of the wooden cart, beating with unimaginable power. The force of the air stream was almost as strong as that during their nosedive, and Ahren once again had to wipe the tears from his eyes.

'I don't want to spoil the party!' shouted Falk, who was looking over his shoulder with concern and staring back at the Swarm Claws,' but the fiends are slowly catching up!'

'Confident is the mouse when the ravenous cat sees not the approaching dog!' screeched Sleeps-in-Treetop with an insane grin. Then she turned to Sunju. 'Veer a little more to portside. Then five furlongs forward!'

Sun Shimmer immediately followed the Ancient's instruction, and just as Ahren was wondering where exactly the Roc was heading for, he saw it – the castle, standing proudly in the centre of what had once been nothing more than a sleepy village – Deepstone!

As fast as he could manage it, Ahren tried to take in as many details of the modern conurbation and its fortress as they basked in the early morning light, and he quickly concluded that there was not much remaining of the original Deepstone from his childhood. The old village square had almost completely disappeared, although the tree that had always been its central point spread its leaves in the courtyard of the impressively tall castle. The old forge, which had already expanded considerably when he had last visited the town was now almost as expansive as a manor, while the houses in the old town compared favourably in height and grandeur with those that could be found in Three Rivers.

He caught sight of the outer reaches of the city, beyond the new wall that had been built by the calloused hands of dwarfs, but Ahren had no more time to continue his aerial inspection of his hometown in any kind of peace and quiet, for Sleeps-in-Treetop was now laughing maniacally, waving a bony hand at the Swarm Claws, their dark bodies getting ever closer. Suddenly, the air was filled with a humming sound which caused Sun Shimmer to tumble, while Ahren completely lost his bearings. Khara gasped in pain beside him, Culhen howled his fear, while Selsena whinnied shrilly and Muai snarled, her ears flattened.

'Is this an assault?' groaned Ahren.

'Yes!' exclaimed Sunju triumphantly. 'But on *those* there!' She pointed in the direction of the Swarm Claws at the very moment when the humming sound ceased and the pain in Ahren's ears abated.

The first of the Dark Ones had now flown into the area where the phenomenon had manifested itself, the creatures suddenly screeching in agony. Ahren had to blink twice, for he could not believe what he was seeing.

'What the…?!' he exclaimed as Swarm Claw after Swarm Claw began to plummet, the Dark Ones beating their wings forlornly as if the air could no longer hold them up no matter how hard they worked.

'Is it not lovely to have friends?' shouted Sunju with a chuckle, pointing down to her right and left.

Ahren quickly glanced to where she had indicated, the rising sun casting its rays on two Wizardly Domes, one south and one north of the Roc. Sunju had plotted her course through the invisible line that bound the two buildings together.

'We call these zones Arcane Walls,' explained Sleeps-in-Treetop with unusual clarity before adding, 'two spirits in two places make a new united rampart.'

Ahren groaned inwardly. So much for clarity.

'Powerful spells can be cast along the lines between two Wizardly Domes if both wizards on guard simultaneously recite the same charm while they connect their magic,' explained Sunju. 'The spells work on the ground as well as aerially. The enemy is not alone in being capable of forging ambushes.'

'What sort of a spell *was* that?' asked Hakanu inquisitively, taking the words right out of Ahren's mouth.

'A charm that Quin-Wa invented,' said the pale-faced woman. 'I don't understand *all* the details, but it somehow blocks the birds' sense of orientation.' She patted Sun Shimmer's neck affectionately. 'Luckily, my Roc is so big that she can resist the spell.'

Khara frowned. 'And why didn't the Ancients wait until we had passed through the Arcane Wall? My ears are still ringing.'

'Stretching magic over such a distance is a difficult, often imprecise art,' interjected Sleeps-in-Treetop. 'Like throwing a pebble into a little pond barely visible in the distance. Doable but you can count yourself lucky if you are successful.' She looked sullenly at Khara. 'And what you are demanding, Your Highness, is that one throws the pebble onto a precise *point* in that pond.'

'I never demanded *anything,*' protested the Swordsmistress. 'I was merely asking a perfectly innocent question.'

Sleeps-in-Treetop snorted.

'The Ancients are very proud of their Arcane Walls,' explained Sunju hastily. 'The process of synchronising the magic in the towers was only developed a moon ago, and it has already been of considerable assistance in deflecting the Adversary's Bane Curses, which would otherwise have swallowed many of our defenders by now – *literally* on some occasions.'

The Roc squawked and turned her head so that she could see Sunju.

'And now Sun Shimmer can only traverse the Ring or fly in its immediate vicinity with the help of the Arcane Wall. You have seen for yourselves what usually happens when we approach the Ring from the air.' The pale woman shivered. 'The first time – when the Swarm Claws had formed into the shape of an enormous, grasping hand with the intention of tearing us to shreds, it was only an audacious plummet directly onto the courtyard of Deepstone Castle plus a considerable portion of luck that saved us from certain death.' She swallowed hard. 'The skirmish that ensued between the defenders and the screeching Dark Ones was a bloody sight I would not like to behold again.'

'The deed is done, the friends are won,' croaked Sleeps-in-Treetop as she pointed a bony finger at the other occupants of the flying cart. 'Past is the time of flight, the parley is now in sight,' she added in a sing-song voice.

'That means, I suppose, that there will be a council of war in Deepstone?' asked Falk as he looked over at Sunju, who nodded.

'Are…' Ahren hesitated before pulling himself together and asking the fateful question, '…are all the other Paladins already present?'

Sunju smiled wanly. 'Yes and no.'

Ahren's mouth suddenly felt dry. 'What do you mean?' he asked. In his mind's eye, he could see Lanlion and Lyssin with a line of Dark Ones preventing their progress, while Bergen and the First were somewhere else, hacking their way through an army of Low Fangs. Had the

Adversary used His cunning to scatter all the Paladins to the four corners of Jorath again?

Sunju seemed to have read his mind, for she looked at him reassuringly. 'The rest of the Paladins are in the vicinity of the Ring,' she said. 'But only eight of them are actually *in* Highstone. Too many of us in one place could lead to disaster within days.'

Ahren nodded. None of them had any desire to inadvertently cause a second Night of Blood. But at some stage, *all* the Champions of the gods would have to meet up.

But who can say when? The mortifying thought flashed through Ahren's mind. *Considering what we found out in Belsarius' Sanctum, the right moment to attack the Adversary may only manifest itself in hundreds of years' time.* His head was suddenly flooded with images of him surviving battle after battle at the Ring while those of his friends who were neither Paladins nor Ancients were either killed in the skirmishes or died of old age. It didn't bear thinking about! He was now so horrified that he could hardly breathe.

Calm down now – there's no need to worry, said Culhen reassuringly, the wolf's mental voice washing away Ahren's panic like a refreshing, mountain stream. *It won't be long before Uldini and Jelninolan wake up. Then they and Sleeps-in-Treetop, together with Akkad – who is bound to be waiting for us – will have a discussion. They are four of the cleverest heads in all Jorath, not to mention Quin-Wa. They will certainly know when this constellation is going to make a reappearance. And even if Uldini has to force the stars into position – a way will be found.*

Ahren looked over gratefully at his wolf, who still lying flat against the floorboards. *Thank you,* said the Forest Guardian.

Don't mention it, replied Culhen solemnly. *And in return for my incredible wisdom, you will get me off Sun Shimmer's back the heartbeat we land, won't you?*

Ahren couldn't stop himself. He burst out laughing, his friends then turning to look at him with considerable concern.

Sun Shimmer banked lazily one last time, performing an elegant curve over the city below them. Deepstone's outer wall glittered in the sunlight, so newly hewn were the bricks that reinforced the already impressive defences.

'Not even King's Island can boast such walls!' shouted Falk admiringly over the whistling wind.

'Dwarfs, humans and Ancients have done incredible work,' explained Sunju, pointing down at the city's heart, which had taken the place of what had once been Ahren's home village. 'What Deepstone has endured since the outbreak of war, other settlements would only experience over dozens of winters.'

'It is as if the old Deepstone is dead and buried,' murmured Ahren. Khara responded by squeezing his hand. The Forest Guardian then pushed away his emotions and forced himself to analytically observe what lay beneath – a castle with high, thick walls, an easily defendable donjon, and four tall towers with a Dragon Bow mounted on each – the parallels with the palace on King's Island were unmistakable. Then there was the densely built-up city with its own defences consisting of two thick stone walls which, like the circles on a cut tree-trunk, told of the city's rapid expansion over the past several years. Beyond the conurbation was an open plain of half a league or so, stretching as far as the Ring, two leagues of which seemed to be particularly heavily manned.

Ahren made out the Eastern River, now crossed by several bridges. He saw wooden platforms for crossbowmen and -women beyond the Ring proper, as well as two trenches with a multitude of spears pointing out of them in the hinterland in case the circular defence should break, and which could only be crossed by means of some easily removable planks. There were the two Wizardly Domes, one far to the north and one an equal distance south, their occupants capable of creating an Arcane Wall capable of passing right though the gloomy gate of the Obsidian Fortress to the west of the Ring – indeed, it almost appeared as if the mysterious fortress of the Dark god belonged to a friendly neighbour who lived nearby and who would happily come by for a slice of Godsday cake.

Sleeps-in-Treetop turned and understood what Ahren was looking at. 'Yes,' she said. 'The Adversary has His eyes fixed on Highstone Castle and all who reside there. Both sides know full well that the fighting will begin here.' She paused, and for the briefest of moments, Ahren recognised an emotion in the haggard woman's features that he would never have expected – fear. 'The only question is – whose blood will be the first to spill in the final battle.'

Sun Shimmer beat her wings strongly before descending to a broader part of the eastern castle wall, whose stone surface was scored with scratches – evidence that the Roc had been making frequent use of the area.

Hardly had the enormous bird landed when Culhen leapt out of the cart with a howl of relief, closely followed by Muai and Selsena, who had successfully extricated her horn from the timbers, the Titejunanwa then giving a whinny.

'She says that she will never complain about a stable again,' chuckled Falk as he stretched, several of his bones cracking audibly. 'We'll see how long she keeps *that* promise.'

Trogadon smiled dreamily and bowed towards Sun Shimmer. 'I thank you for this exquisite gift, good Roc,' he said formally. 'You have made a modest dwarf more than happy.'

An enormous bird's eye looked towards him, Sun Shimmer then squawking in a manner that suggested – to Ahren's ears at least – that she was *laughing*.

'She has asked me to tell you that you undoubtedly possess many attributes,' said Sunju with a chuckle, 'but that modesty is definitely *not* one of them.'

Placing his hands defiantly on his hips, Trogadon stared belligerently at Ahren. 'What *has* your wolf been saying about me?'

'Leave me out of it,' laughed Ahren, joining in the silliness which was typical of his friends after episodes of great tension. 'You are perfectly capable of destroying your reputation on your own.'

'Much as I have enjoyed the flight,' interjected Khara as she loosened the leather strap, 'I am now looking forward to a cosy fireside, a hot cup of tea – and perhaps even a bath.' She yawned. 'I wouldn't say no to a soft feather bed either.'

The words of the Swordsmistress reminded Ahren of his own physical condition. He pulled his magic cloak around him and shivered as he began to feel the waves of weariness overcoming him.

'We could probably all do with some peace and quiet,' he murmured. Yawning, he unstrapped himself, stood up and walked unsteadily towards Sun Shimmer's tail feathers which pointed invitingly down to the stone surface. He paused to look seriously at Sunju, Sleeps-in-Treetop and the head of the Roc. 'I would just like to say a big "thank you" to the three of you. Without your assistance it would have been a long, cold journey home.'

'*Home?*' asked Khara in a low voice and with her eyebrows raised quizzically from where she was waiting on the solid, inviting stone of the castle wall.

Ahren walked down to her with a shrug of his shoulders. 'I was born in Deepstone, and here is where I grew up – whether or not I recognise the place.' Then he pulled her towards him with a smile, held her lovingly, breathed in the scent of her dark hair and whispered: 'But I can hardly wait until we are released from our duty, and we can create our *own* home.'

Khara smiled, too, then kissed him.

For a brief moment, all was well.

It was a hesitant, almost timid knocking that woke Ahren. The tower room with its large but plain bed where he and Khara had yielded to their exhaustion was dimly lit. The Forest Guardian could not tell if it was still the day of their arrival or if the sun was on its westward journey a second time.

It's afternoon, mumbled Culhen sleepily.

Looking through the eyes of the wolf, the Paladin understood that his friend was lying on the castle chemin de ronde, snuggled into Sun Shimmer's plumage. Before him lay Muai and Kamaluq, and Ahren thought that he could make out several more companion animals, all of them happy to be in the Roc's company. Sun Shimmer's influence must have become even stronger, perhaps on account of her increasing size.

No need to be jealous, added Culhen. *We have been discussing everything all day and are very tired.*

Ahren was no stranger to the companion animals' councils of war, and he knew that there was no need for him to ask what the subject of their conversations had been – although a part of him suspected that they might have done a lot of gossiping about the Paladins, too.

'Are you awake,' mumbled Khara beside him, the Swordsmistress seemingly having lost a protracted battle against her heavy woolly blanket, the result of which was that she was sticking out from under and looking distinctly uncomfortable.

Ahren sat up. 'Don't know yet,' he replied truthfully. 'I was so worn out after our flight on Sun Shimmer that I hardly remember how we ended up in here.'

Khara glanced at him teasingly. 'With remarkably little pomp and ceremony, anyway.'

Ahren chuckled. 'That's not really what I meant – but, yes, you're right. 'We had a Night Soldier with local knowledge accompanying us, didn't we?'

'Mm,' murmured Khara as her eyes began to close again. Within three heartbeats she was fast asleep.

Ahren gently tugged at the blanket until it was lying properly on his beloved so that she was in a more comfortable resting position. Then he stood up and grabbed his clothes. He would come back later to keep the slumbering Khara company again, but for now he was determined to explore Castle Highstone and perhaps step outside into the surrounding city. The thought that some of his old friends from days gone by might be in the vicinity piqued his curiosity.

He slipped into his trousers and then out through the door – only to stop dead in his tracks.

Directly facing him stood a Night Soldier, so close that, if she was an assailant, she would have already dispatched him with ease.

Ahren swallowed hard, and as the woman eyed him coolly, he suddenly realised that he was unarmed. She said nothing – she didn't need to – as she continued to stand there motionless, her hand resting easily on the handle of her sword, ready to spring into action.

'I…uh…I'll fetch my armour,' muttered Ahren, suddenly feeling once again like an awkward apprentice whose master had spotted his carelessly tied knot or badly shot arrow.

The Night Soldier remained stock still. Ahren withdrew into the chamber, cursed silently as he put on his armour and picked up his weapons before returning to the passageway. The woman still hadn't moved. Her eyes scanned Ahren's figure, examining the Deep Steel over his clothing and the scabbard of his sword – then she stepped aside and gave a slight bow.

The Paladin pulled back his shoulders, suddenly strangely proud of himself – it was as if he had passed a particularly difficult exam. The time that he had spent as Meng-Un among the ranks of the Night Soldiers would, it seemed, remain with him to the end of his days.

'Lead me to the other Paladins!' he commanded brusquely, trying to remind himself that he was more than a mere lackey in the service of the Eternal Empress.

The cloaked woman moved noiselessly down the stairwell, Ahren following, full of joyful anticipation at the prospect of meeting his old friends and enjoying some cheerful conversation.

'Sit down!' said Quin-Wa irritably, Ahren immediately doing as he was told.

He should have known that his mysterious bodyguard would take him first to her mistress, who was both Ancient and Paladin.

The room in which Quin-Wa received him was little more than a bare cell with a narrow bed made from rough wood and a simple table with a couple of stools. The fireplace with its three burning logs was competing against the cold wind whipping in through the solitary barred window, which more than likely had previously been a loophole. If Ahren hadn't known better, then he would certainly have believed Quin-Wa to be a *prisoner* of the castle.

'Nice to see you,' continued the Eternal Empress.

'That is not what your tone of voice is telling me,' Ahren countered lightly in a vain attempt at lightening the icy atmosphere that permeated the room. 'I fear that you might transform me into a frog at any moment.'

Quin-Wa rubbed her round belly. 'This waiting is torture,' she muttered.

Ahren nodded. He didn't ask the Eternal Empress if she was referring to the gathering of all the Paladins, to giving birth or to the new Night of Blood. He decided not to ask. After all, the answer would be *yes* one way or another. Instead, he nodded politely at her bump.

'When is the baby due?'

The Ancient snorted. 'She is over a week late. It seems that I am carrying a decidedly single-minded heiress under my heart.'

Ahren raised an eyebrow quizzically. *'She?'*

'I am an Ancient,' countered Quin-Wa with a dry laugh. 'If I cannot even sense the sex of my own child, then I had better hurry up and hand over my jade throne to someone more capable.'

The corners of Ahren's mouth twitched as he tried not to laugh. 'You're already working on it.'

Now Quin-Wa was chuckling. 'Yes – you have a point. Perhaps you *are* referring to the woman who will one day ascend to the Eternal Empire throne – we shall see.' Her face became serious, almost distressed. 'But for her to have a chance of becoming my successor, there are still a few tasks that need to be carried out – if I am not mistaken.'

Ahren tried to keep his response light-hearted in an effort to give Quin-Wa courage. 'In fact,' he countered, 'there is only *one* task – to wipe HIM, WHO FORCES off the face of Jorath for once and for all.'

The Eternal Empress nodded. 'And yet there are still a couple of obstacles before this goal can be achieved. A fortress, for example, that takes up a considerable portion of the Borderlands – one that is teeming with Low- and High Fangs – all of them armed and ready.'

'Not to mention an army of Dark Ones,' added Ahren casually.

'And the last child of the Dark god,' Quin-Wa reminded him with a nod.

'And whatever will await us once the Thirteen are all gathered in the one place,' whispered the Forest Guardian, completing the list.

'Yes.' The single word uttered by the Eternal Empress was as brittle as poorly forged iron in the depths of winter.

For a while, the two were silent. Then Ahren nodded towards the walls of the bare, narrow room. 'Isn't this...cell...a little too *basic?* I mean...considering your condition?'

Quin-Wa shook her head. 'It's perfect precisely *because* of my condition.' Then she performed a tiny hand movement, Ahren immediately gasping and screwing up his eyes. For a heartbeat, he believed the room to be ablaze, but then it became clear to him that every inch of the floor, the ceiling and the walls was decorated with tiny, glittering, fiery-red runes. Quin-Wa performed another gesture and the Bane Charm faded away as quickly as it had manifested itself.

'I like to look after my own security despite the countless precautions that the other Ancients insist on implementing,' explained the Eternal Empress, her tight smile failing to hide the tension evident in the corners of her eyes.

Ahren cleared his throat. 'Is there a reason why we are having this conversation in private? Surely, we should be talking about these obstacles within the context of a council of war, shouldn't we?'

Quin-Wa leaned in. 'What took you all to Kelkor? she asked through half-closed eyes. 'What was so damn important that shortly before the imminent battle against the Adversary you went off and did a detour of forty odd leagues and caused the most powerful Bane Curse in centuries to hurtle after you?'

Ahren chewed on his lower lip. 'It would be best if Uldini explained it all to you...'

'He's *asleep!*' snapped Quin-Wa. 'As is *Jelninolan!* And having examined their eyes, I would calculate that they are going to remain in that state for the next few days without sorcerous intervention. Meanwhile, Muai has been too busy yapping with Sun Shimmer and the rest of them. The only thing *she s*aid to me was that your little adventure was *very* wet and that she would like to have done nothing better than to tear Belsarius limb from limb had he been living, which made absolutely *no* sense to me!' She stared deep into Ahren's eyes. 'Which is why I am asking *you.*'

The Paladin groaned, sat down on one of the stools and leaned back against the stone wall. 'You'd better make yourself comfortable, for this story is neither particularly short nor is it exactly laden with good news. It all started with a visit from the Woman in Black...'

'Unbelievable!' gasped Akkad, whose face had drained of all colour once Ahren had explained to him of what had happened during their diversion to Kelkor. 'What you are telling me...why, it...it *pulverises* most of our current theories regarding the Adversary!'

Ahren waved his hands helplessly. Night had fallen by now, and he was relating the same story for the third time. As soon as Quin-Wa was more or less in the picture, she had dragged him hot footed to Sleeps-in-Treetop, who had then sent for Akkad. Now the four of them were sitting in the castle's eastern tower – in a high-ceilinged room that was clearly furnished out as a council chamber, large enough to hold thirty people comfortably.

'Now listen to me – I am *not* going to tell the story yet again,' said Ahren, whose weariness was making him stubborn and uncooperative. All he had wanted to do was to meet up with old friends, yet here he was, being questioned non-stop in a manner that was beginning to resemble a cross-examination. He pointed at the large, circular council table on whose surface had been carved a detailed representation of the Obsidian Fortress, the Ring and the surrounding area. Deepstone and its castle were particularly prominent. 'Why don't we simply drum up all the decision makers and start our council of war?'

'*Because*, my dear Ahren,' explained Akkad wearily, 'what you have told us might mean that we will have to delay this battle against the Adversary until – and I am speaking literally – the stars are *favourable*.'

'Can you imagine how the rulers of the Jorathian realms would react to such news?' asked Quin-Wa. 'Many of my fellow sovereigns – and I, too – have already committed everything that our countries have been able to provide – be it soldiers, materials, or provisions. Last autumn, many of the most fruitful fields were already laid bare, and now supplies for the army at the Ring are slowly but surely running out.'

Ahren nodded. 'Even a delay of a couple of years would completely drain the realms' supplies,' he whispered. 'Not to mention the damage that would be undoubtedly done to the morale of the troops if the Thirteen Paladins suddenly announced that the time for the final battle had not yet come.'

Akkad went to one of the small, thick-glass windows and stared out into the darkness, his eyes fixing on the green points of light that could be seen here and there in the distance, the blazing fires of the Obsidian Fortress presenting a constant reminder of the enemy's war preparations. 'I *could* draw up some star charts, but it would be a time-consuming task – and it would not only be embarrassing, but also potentially deadly should I end up making an error in predicting the *precise* reappearance of this special constellation. I have long wondered *why* the Adversary has insisted on pulling back behind black protective wall after black protective wall instead of simply weakening us with the captured magic of the Pall Pillar and slipping out from the noose that we have put around His neck.' The portly Ancient rubbed his neck as he pondered. Then he concluded: 'In light of the latest information, I cannot think of any solution that doesn't cast a decidedly gloomy light on the future of *all* of us here.'

Chapter 10

Culhen's fur was soft and warm against Ahren's back, a welcome contrast to the cold stone of the castle wall.

Are you going to tell me what's bothering you, or should I simply sniff around in your memories?

The wolf's question caused the Paladin to flinch. He stared up at the stormy night sky and tried to make out the order of the stars above him, only to be defeated in his efforts by the clouds scudding across the firmament at speed – as if they were intent on getting as far away from the Obsidian Fortress and as fast as the wind would carry them.

'The Ancients are, to put it bluntly, at a loss as to how they should proceed,' he said, speaking aloud as he tried to make sense of his disorganised thoughts. He sighed. 'And we are condemned to waiting until Akkad works out *when* the constellation will appear.'

'That sounds exciting.'

Ahren quickly turned his head, spotting Lyssin, who with her she-wolf Yoka was approaching the group of companion animals to whose company he himself had fled. Culhen leapt to his feet, dumping Ahren unceremoniously onto the hard stone.

'Ow!' exclaimed the Forest Guardian. 'At least now I know where your priorities lie!'

Ignoring his friend, Culhen whimpered and danced around Yoka, who stood there in silence, ignoring the wolf completely. Ahren realised that this was not down to arrogance or coldness, but because the eyes of the she-wolf were fixed on those of the Roc.

Give her a few heartbeats, the Paladin advised. *This is the first time that Sun Shimmer has welcomed her.*

Culhen froze. *Oh. Of course.*

Then, with his tongue lolling, he lay down beside the she-wolf, his spirit vanishing from Ahren's mind. It seemed that the companion animals were now having their own private discussion.

Lyssin snapped her fingers before Ahren's eyes. 'I'm talking to you,' she said before frowning. 'Why can't I hear Yoka anymore? She always yaps from one end of the day to the other. It's almost too much to bear.'

Ahren's grin was as spontaneous as it was genuine. 'You mean, she's reached that stage so quickly? Believe me – once she has completed her vocabulary learning, she *will* quieten a little.'

Lyssin rubbed her temples and sat down beside Ahren. 'Am I mad or what?' she asked, perplexed. 'First, I wanted nothing more in life but for Yoka to give me some peace, but now I'm already missing hearing her voice in my head!'

Ahren looked at her knowingly. 'Believe me, I understand you all too well.'

The young woman snorted. 'Oh,' she began, imitating her companion animal in an artificially high voice, '*isn't* that a lovely butterfly. I wonder does she want to be my friend? I wonder what her name is and…and…and what she *tastes* like, her parents *must* be somewhere around here, surely, I wonder how butterflies are able to fly at all, and why aren't they blown away by the wind? They must have some sort of sixth sense when it comes to predicting storms and why…?' She broke off, her voice having been drowned out by Ahren's laughter.

'Now *that* was impressive,' he said, wiping the tears from his eyes. 'You said all that without drawing breath once!'

Lyssin grunted and pointed at Lyssin, who was sitting silently. 'Well, she doesn't either.'

'Alright, I'll admit that you seem to have ended up with a chatterbox. But it could have been worse. Fisker has been blessed with a smart-aleck monkey. It's still too dark for you to see him, but Cassobo must be lurking about somewhere.' Ahren observed the young woman beside him keenly. She seemed just as unflappable here as she had been in the Ice Fields – where she had grown up – and in Eathinian before they had all divided up for their journey here. 'How *are* you?' he asked.

Lyssin shrugged her shoulders. 'I'm doing fine.' Then she cocked her head. 'Although – I *do* miss the ice. And father.'

Ahren nodded. Yollock's stoical manner had, when it came to bringing up his daughter, ensured that she was almost unshakeable, and for a heartbeat he wished that all the other Paladins had been raised by the monosyllabic old man. Then his mind was filled with an image of thirteen silent Paladins, all of them scattered to remote parts of Jorath, where they did their own thing, completely ignoring the fates of their fellows. He shook his head. 'How was the journey with Lanlion?'

'Pleasant.'

Ahren sighed. 'You remind me of your father.'

'That may be so,' chuckled Lyssin. 'I have learned that too many words over too many days tire me out. For a start, there was Yoka's endless chatter, and then there was Lanlion, who simply would not stop talking.'

Ahren looked sideways at his fellow Forest Guardian with a sceptical look. 'Now *that* I find hard to believe. Lanlion is far more taciturn than I am.'

Now it was Lyssin's turn to look at him critically. 'Based on everything *he* told me, that particular adjective would be better applied to *you*.'

'Ah, now...'

'Or what *exactly* are you doing out here with all the companion animals instead of snuggling up beside your slumbering Swordsmistress?'

Ahren rolled his eyes, knowing when he was beaten. 'You've caught me there.'

'Do I *want* to know what you are brooding over?'

'That depends. Do you want to have a peaceful sleep tonight?'

'I'd have nothing against it.'

'Then it would be better to wait until the council of war before I tell you.'

The young woman nodded. 'Agreed.'

At that moment, Ahren wished that he could be more open with the Forest Guardian.

She pointed at Yoka. 'How much longer is she going to sit there saying nothing?'

'It depends. During the conclave on King's Island, the discussions under Sun Shimmer's watchful eye lasted for days – they only had breaks for feeding and sleeping.'

Lyssin snapped her fingers again. 'Wasn't that when Falk got to know Onja? And *you* had an encounter with a necromancer?'

'I see that Lanlion has explained to you every detail of our journeying. Even those parts in which he, himself, didn't feature. In another life I could easily imagine him as an extremely conscientious archivist.'

'Should we go in?' asked Lyssin. 'Lanlion is in the great hall of the castle at the moment, talking to Fisker and Bergen.'

Ahren had already gotten up but shook his head regretfully. 'No more than four Paladins may gather at any one time if no Charm Circles have been created,' he said. 'Quin-Wa told me that in no uncertain terms.' He nodded towards the silent, shadowy figure standing before the stairwell that led down into the castle interior. 'The Night Soldiers are under strict instructions to ensure that we do not meet up in large groups.' Then he looked towards the west at the Obsidian Fortress looming threateningly in the distance. 'We don't want to wake up any sleeping dogs – not yet, at any rate.'

On one of the towers that flanked the eastern gate of the Obsidian Fortress, he could make out the indistinct form of an enormous figure. Pyres to its right and one to its left, accentuated the silhouette of this over-sized being, visible even from this distance as an ominous black stain.

It was Hate, the last remaining child of the Adversary. According to the residents of Deepstone, this transformed Doppler of the Dark god was often to be seen on the walls or towers of the Obsidian Fortress, sometimes alone and at other times with captured soldiers, whom he would slay in full view of the Ring's soldiers before hurling them down from the high walls – doubtless with the sole purpose of intensifying for the Jorathian defenders that emotion which gave the monster both his name and his power.

'Should I stay here?' asked Lyssin. 'I promise you that I will be suitably moody and silent in your presence.'

Ahren smiled. His fellow Forest Guardian's sense of humour was blossoming outside the Ice Fields. 'Off you go,' he said. 'Get to know your brothers and sisters as well as you can. I will stay here and look forward to meeting them tomorrow.'

His weariness was like a hesitant beloved, calling to him only when the night had already run half its course. Ahren had once again been digesting the many discussions he had been a part of since his arrival in Highstone, and it struck him that he was like a young puppy chasing after its tail, his efforts amounting to nothing more than futilely going around in circles. The companion animals sitting there in silence, mentally debating in their own private world seemed to him like a metaphor of the council of war that he himself would soon be participating in.

Ahren had just nodded to the Night Soldier, signalling that he would now be descending the stairs into the castle when he suddenly felt a draught of wind that even penetrated his magic cloak, causing him to shiver. Immediately, the Night Soldier collapsed soundlessly onto the stone floor – as if he had suddenly fallen asleep, while a shimmering wall of black created a barrier between the Thirteenth and the group of deliberating companion animals.

'What's going on…' began Ahren, only for the answer to peel out of the darkness of the night.

'Ahren,' said the Woman in Black. 'You have survived.'

The Paladin turned slowly to face her. 'I *would* express my gratitude to you, but that would be gilding the lily somewhat. After all, Belsarius' Sanctum was very well protected.'

The stranger was a vision of darkness on the parapet, an impenetrable silhouette in front of the stormy night sky, across whose vastness the clouds were now racing with ever more urgency.

All of Creation seems in a state of upheaval, thought Ahren darkly.

'Alas, I cannot tell the future even if sometimes I give the impression of being a prophetess,' explained the Woman in Black soothingly. 'I *did* tell you that I could not pass the protective charms of the Ancient. The best I could do was to make an educated guess regarding what was waiting for you *in* the Sanctum.'

Ahren saw the hunger glittering in the woman's eyes when for the merest of moments, the pale moon shone cast its whiteness through a break in the clouds, lighting up the black veil before her face.

'Did you find anything?' Her voice betrayed merely the slightest sliver of hope, but there was something else as well – was it *greed*?

Ahren made certain to keep his features perfectly impassive. 'Yes.'

The Woman in Black swayed back and forth like a reed in the wind before leaning in towards him. 'And?' she whispered.

'Belsarius discovered something.' Ahren was delaying the moment when he would have to decide whether to give this woman – who, after all, remained under the control of the Adversary – the information that the Ancient had gone to such lengths to hide. 'Something that is both a blessing and a curse.' *It all depends, really, on whether the constellation will reappear in the distant future or very soon,* he added mentally.

The Woman in Black stiffened. 'You are not going to tell me, are you?' she asked wearily.

Ahren raised his hands apologetically. 'Should I?'

The mysterious woman glanced west to the fortress of her master. 'Perhaps, it is best if you don't – yet,' she conceded. Then she reached under her robe and pulled something out. She threw the object at Ahren's feet, the Forest Guardian sensing it becoming evermore solid and tangible as it came towards him even as the Woman in Black faded away to nothingness.

Ahren bent down and picked up a charred piece of wood. He looked up in bemusement, but the mysterious woman had disappeared.

'Throw the log into the fire,' murmured a voice in the wind, fading away like the last sigh of a vanishing ghost. 'I will come. And then you will have all the answers that I undoubtedly owe you.'

Ahren swallowed hard on hearing those last words. And later, as he lay safe and sound in his bed beside his peacefully slumbering beloved, he couldn't answer the question that was tormenting him – had the Woman in Black uttered a pledge to him, or had it been, in fact, a threat?

The door to the chamber was swung open with such exuberance that the Forest Guardian was out of the bed with his Wind Blade drawn even before he was fully awake.

'Surprised?' asked Likis tentatively, a tray in his hands laden down with bread, honey and other delicious morsels to eat. Behind him stood Lina, holding a bundle which she was swinging gently this way and that. The Keeper, unlike Likis, amused rather than embarrassed.

'I told you from the word go that barging in like this was a bad idea. I mean, poor Ahren is as tensed up as a Dragon Bow during a siege.' She smiled at the Paladin. 'Nice to see you again – even if it's high time you learned that when meeting up with friends after a long period, it's always advisable to wear trousers.'

Ahren grunted and threw his blade onto the bed. Only then did he notice that Khara wasn't lying in it anymore. He discovered his beloved cowering in the shadow of a large oak wardrobe. She was holding both her weapons and was as skimpily dressed as he was. At least, he wasn't the only one who looked as awkward as Falk did whenever the old man was forced to take part in a parade of honour.

'The whole castle – no – the whole *city* is strewn with magical and temporal protective measures for fear of an attack on the Paladins, their soul companions *and* their children, *all* of whom are under the care of

Highstone,' he said to Likis. 'Do you *really* believe that a morning ambush is an appropriate greeting?'

'This castle is my home,' countered Likis defensively as he looked for somewhere to set down the tray. 'I hardly notice all these Protective Charms and guards anymore. For me, Deepstone is the safest place in all Jorath.' Finally, he spotted Khara, who quickly used the blanket to cover herself, her face turning bright red. 'Oh...*ah*,' spluttered the young man.

Lina grinned. 'What my oh-so-clever husband *wants* to say is that he is sorry, and that we shall both retire gracefully and wait outside,' she chuckled.

Likis could only manage a nod, the young couple quickly leaving the chamber, closing the door gently behind them.

'What sort of a mad idea was that?' asked Khara, looking over at Ahren.

The Forest Guardian shrugged his shoulders. 'Gleeful anticipation mixed with good intentions and a dollop of cockiness?' he suggested. 'That sums up Likis' character.' He shook his head. 'Things could have been far worse.'

'What do you mean?'

'In the old days, Likis and I would play tricks on each other all the time. Imagine if he had leapt out of our wardrobe? We would have cut him to pieces in a heartbeat.'

There was general surprise as Ahren and Khara – who had in the meantime hurriedly dressed – entered the dining hall of Highstone, accompanied by Lina and Likis. The tall ceiling, the narrow, barred windows, as well as the long tables and the solid but simple wooden benches were exactly what Ahren had expected – Highstone's furnishings were utilitarian, and the dining hall was no exception. The elaborate Charm Circles on the floor and ceiling provided not only a marked contrast to the general simplicity, however, but were also grim reminders of the dangers that lurked beyond the castle walls. Nonetheless, Ahren could only smile when he saw so many familiar faces.

'Fisker, Hakanu, Bergen, Lanlion, Quin-Wa, Falk, Sunju, Lyssin…' Ahren listed off the Paladins who waved back at him one by one. He paused. 'So many of us in the one room?'

Likis grinned at him. 'A decision was reached that we should call together the council of war today already, by which time you will all have met up anyway. In the meantime, we can figure out if these Charm Circles work effectively,' he explained as he toyed with his chain of office. 'By the way, I am supposed to attend, too, on behalf of the Jorathian rulers, who are looking after business in their own countries during this hard winter.'

Ahren looked solemnly at his brothers and sisters. The time for playing cat and mouse was over at last. 'Is Highstone ready?' he asked Likis.

His friend nodded eagerly. 'The best troops that Jorath has to offer are guarding this city and her castle, we have enough defensive magic to turn a horde of Dark Ones to dust in the blink of an eye, and let us not forget the fighting strength of you Paladins, which will surely tilt the scales in our favour. Oh, and of course there is also the Hearts Hall…'

'Hearts Hall?' asked Khara.

Lina nodded. 'Yes – borrowed from the *Hall of Hearts*. Dwarfs built it, you see. They insisted on the name.'

Ahren whistled through his teeth in admiration. Likis hadn't exaggerated. The Jorathian tribes had been hard at work ensuring the protection of the Paladins, their soul companions and offspring.

'Are you just going to keep standing there or shall we start eating?' snarled Uldini as he floated past the Forest Guardian. The dark rings around the Arch Wizard's eyes suggested that he still hadn't fully regained his energy following his days and nights of deep sleeping. Yet the childlike figure, like all the others, would have no further opportunity to rest.

'Stay where you are – then there will be all the more for me!' Ahren immediately recognised the unmistakable, gravelly voice of Trogadon, and a heartbeat later, he saw the chuckling blacksmith entering the hall, supporting Jelninolan and sitting her down at the nearest available bench. The elf looked even more exhausted than Uldini, but even before Ahren had the chance to admonish Trogadon for not making her stay in bed a little longer, the dwarf peered at the Paladin, shook his head and whispered: 'Don't think I haven't tried.'

Akkad and Sleeps-in-Treetop were the next to whoosh past Ahren, the four Ancients immediately huddling together to discuss their plans.

'If we don't sit down soon, there won't be any room for us,' murmured Khara, tugging Ahren's sleeve. 'Come on – let's say hello to our old friends.'

The Forest Guardian nodded. He was torn between worrying about the dangers lurking outside the four walls of the castle and rejoicing at the heart-warming, convivial atmosphere within, which provided some very welcome relief and a chance to make merry with his friends.

Finally, he pulled himself together and threw himself into the open arms and hearty welcomes of his friends – who, of course, peppered him with light-hearted barbs, as was their wont.

The rays of sunlight beamed through the narrow windows, and Ahren was in stitches laughing at Fisker's hilarious yarn of how Cassobo had taken it upon himself to court a sweet little chimpanzee. The Forest Guardian was convinced that his friend was exaggerating wildly in his storytelling, but that did nothing to dampen his enjoyment.

More and more familiar faces had gathered in the chamber, and those present spent a considerable portion of the time greeting one friend after another. Yantilla had arrived, accompanied by Chief Marshall Falagarda, while Kamkanzakur, the ruler of Thousand Halls, had sat down beside Trogadon, the pair of them immediately getting down to the very serious business of carousing. Soon another figure entered the room, frowning as he looked around him while holding a *very* familiar helmet under his arm.

'The First!' exclaimed Ahren, waving the age-old Paladin towards him, the veteran's boots immediately stomping loudly on the floor as he approached the Forest Guardian.

'How is it that *every* time I arrive during a crisis, I find myself interrupting a feast rather than a meeting on strategy?' growled the First instead of saying hello.

'And a very good day to you, *too,*' countered Ahren with a disarming smile. Then he pointed at Fisker. 'It was our wayward brother's idea that we should first eat, drink and be merry and *then* begin our council of war. Many of us have not seen each other for a long time, and we all agreed that it was the perfect opportunity to have a laugh and a chat so that we will be completely focused when it comes down to the serious business in hand.'

The First stared at Ahren, then at Fisker. The ex-pirate beamed back at the old man and fluttered his eyelids in a gesture of feigned coquettishness.

'That was…that was…. *not* the worst idea in the world,' muttered the First, finally.

'Hear ye! Hear ye!' bellowed Bergen from the other side of the table. 'The world really *must* be on the edge of the abyss for the First to praise Fisker!'

'That was *not* praise,' growled the veteran brusquely.

'Yes, it was,' countered Bergen dryly. 'By your standards, undoubtedly.'

Ahren laughed even though Bergen's words had keenly raised his awareness of what those in the room were *really* thinking. All the Paladins, except for the First, Lyssin, Hakanu and himself were celebrating a little *too* intensely. They reminded him of the nobility on King's Island or in Cape Verstaad, who tried to compensate for their latent fear of the dangerous world beyond their four walls by wearing an over-abundance of jewellery. Friendship and camaraderie could dance together all they liked in this room, but everyone felt the fear that was lurking under the table with its dagger drawn, ready to strike at the first sign of weakness.

The First continued to stand there uncertainly, but as no-one else stood up to make room for him, he sighed and sat down beside Ahren, grabbing a piece of bread and a spicy chunk of cured sausage from Thousand Halls, the smell of which had caused Ahren's eyes to water.

The First ate his fill in silence, Ahren glancing sideways at him from time to time. There was something about the man in his archaic armour that gave the Forest Guardian goosebumps, and he felt a sudden urge to storm out of the room with his Wind Blade in his hand while yelling the Paladin mantra.

'You can sense it *too,* can't you?' murmured the First, having washed down his food with a goblet of diluted wine. 'The Blessing that is tugging at us.'

Ahren nodded. So *that* was what was moving within him. The gods' Blessing that lodged in each and every Paladin seemed to be innately aware that there were nine more of its kind in the room. That was why it was surging within Ahren like a tidal wave, ready, willing and able to play its part in overwhelming the Adversary. 'I have never experienced it as being so…*single-minded*,' admitted the Forest Guardian in a whisper.

The First stared at him intently. 'Then wait until the other Paladins are with us and there are no Charm Circles present to dampen the Blessing.' He pursed his lips. 'If the Adversary allows us that opportunity. Our present gathering must already be raging like a tornado in his head.'

Suddenly feeling dizzy, Ahren took a deep breath. Everything was moving so fast now. Only a short time ago, the Paladins had been keeping their distance from each other as they tiptoed around various locations in different parts of the world, but not now the vast majority of them were gathered together in the one room.

'Where are the other three?' he asked anxiously.

The First pointed down to the floor. 'Aluna is in the Heart Hall. She was grazed by a Bane Curse on the way over here, which caused a complication to her pregnancy. She needs plenty of rest.' The First glanced over at Sleeps-in-Treetop. 'Our riddling Ancient claims that Aluna will recover – all she needs is time.'

Ahren flinched. Time was a sensitive topic – as he knew only too well. It was possible that they might have considerably more of it than any of them would want. 'And Trimm?'

'He is keeping his mercenaries in check.' The First sounded impressed despite himself. 'Our cowardly brother recruited anyone and everyone capable of holding a weapon who was willing to fight for gold. Soon, the Ring will be twice as well fortified as it was a moon ago – and will remain so at least until Cape Verstaad runs out of funds to pay the mercenaries.'

Ahren nodded. Trimm had, after all, kept his word and arrived. That he had also brought with him an army of hirelings who would beat a way clear for the cowardly Paladin until he was finally forced to face the Dark god was, on the other hand, not in the least surprising. 'What about the Father of the Mountain?' pressed Ahren, wanting to learn more about the final Paladin, whose whereabouts he was in ignorance of.

'He's motivating the troops at the Ring,' muttered the First, unable – or unwilling – to hide his disdain for their absent comrade. 'If he could, he would gently hold the hand of each person currently on duty at the front.'

Ahren frowned. 'You would prefer it if his old, bloodthirsty self was back, would you?'

The First guffawed. It was a harsh, barking sound. 'Of *course,* I would prefer to have *Darkan* present. The time of mild and friendly banter is almost over. And he was one of the best when it came to shedding the blood of others.'

'I am glad that I only got to know the Father of the Mountain, then,' countered Ahren energetically. Then he placed a hand on the First's shoulder. The veteran's metal armour felt cold to the touch. 'Be careful that *you* don't revert to your old ways,' he said in a low voice. 'The Eternal Ice should have taught you what suffering ensues when taking a fanatical, narrow-minded approach.'

The First and Ahren stared at one another for an extended period before the old man said: 'The gods have created us very differently. You fulfil your role – I will fulfil mine in *my* way – as I have *always* done.' With that, he got to his feet and strode to the door where he paused to glance back at the laughing Paladins before shouting in a hard voice: 'The council of war will start forthwith. Get yourselves ready!' Then he marched out of the dining hall, leaving a wave of disenchantment in his wake.

'Well, I certainly won't miss that old spoilsport once we've slain the Adversary,' announced Fisker, trying to sound humorous.

'What you've said sounds so *weird*,' interjected Bergen as he looked at the others. 'I mean, talking about the time *afterwards*.' A heavy silence descended on the room.

'I'm off, then,' grunted Falk, getting to his feet. 'The First has managed to put us all in a foul humour again. Anyone else in the mood for a council of war?' Then he stomped out of the room without waiting for an answer, the others following in dribs and drabs until only Ahren, Hakanu and Khara were left.

'Master?' asked the apprentice, looking repeatedly at the doorway. 'Why aren't we going as well?'

'Stubbornness,' muttered Ahren, Khara shaking her head and laughing in disbelief. 'I refuse to simply dance to the First's tune.' He picked up a piece of bread from the table and chewed on it grumpily. 'The approaching battle is clearly bringing out the worst in the First. I had better remind him that he no longer commands the Paladins.' He swallowed both the food and, metaphorically, the anger that had been rising within him. '*Now* we can go,' he said, Hakanu breathing a sigh of relief.

As the Thirteenth followed his protégé under Khara's critical eye, the boy trying hard not to rush forward enthusiastically, Ahren pondered over the possibility that the imminent discussion might well be the last such that he would ever be involved in.

The war would soon reach its conclusion.

One way or the other.

The council chamber was a veritable hive of activity when Ahren entered the round room of the castle's eastern tower. It seemed considerably more impressive and livelier in daylight now that it was full of attendees. The other nine Paladins from the dining hall were present as were the four Ancients, Kamkanzakur, Falagarda, Likis, Yantilla, Ahren's other companions and quite a few adjutants, who were busily sharpening their quill pens and straightening their piles of parchments which they would use to write dispatches and to record any decisions that the council of war was going to reach.

'At least there are no bards present to mangle whatever is discussed here into heroic lays for the troops,' muttered Ahren grimly.

'Here you are at last,' growled the First, beckoning the Thirteenth to sit. The Forest Guardian picked a chair directly opposite the veteran, the latter acknowledging his younger counterpart's decision with a curt nod.

'Are the two of you involved in *another* private battle?' asked Falk in a low voice, as he and Khara sat down beside Ahren.

'I don't know yet,' muttered his former apprentice. 'But I am ready to call a halt to his gallop if he starts suggesting sacrificing entire kingdoms in pursuit of his aims.'

'The First is so close to his goal,' interjected Khara, 'which he *has* been pursuing since time immemorial. It will hardly be a surprise if he falls into his old habits.'

'Perhaps you are right,' countered Ahren coolly. 'But it *will* be regrettable and highly dangerous.'

By now, all the participants had taken their places, the First then nodding towards the heavy double doors, which were then slammed shut from the outside by the sentries – a combination of Fox Guards and Night Soldiers.

Sleeps-in-Treetop leaned in over the council table and placed one hand on the dark wooden surface, whereupon hundreds of runes were suddenly illuminated, decorating the entire room for a glorious heartbeat before fading away as quickly as they had appeared. 'The council chamber is secure,' she announced in a scratchy voice before firmly closing her eyes. Clearly, the Ancient would use her sorcerous powers to guard over the room while crucial strategy was being discussed.

Quin-Wa got to her feet. 'Before we begin, I would like to announce that I shall be speaking not only on my own behalf but also on behalf of my husband, the Sun Emperor.' Immediately, four of the adjutants set about recording the information on their parchments.

Quin-Wa having sat down, Likis immediately stood up. 'And it is *my* honour to represent King Blueground, the Green Sea *and* Cape Verstaad.'

The First nodded. 'Most of the Jorathian rulers are hereby represented in one form or another. Please take note of the following as well – ten Champions of the gods are present in their function as generals of the army, as is Chief Marshall Falagarda, who at the start of winter was unanimously entrusted with overall military authority of the Ring.'

Ahren smiled appreciatively at the tall woman, who made a striking impression in her navy-blue uniform, and with her chest decorated with medals. She stood up with a determined look on her face.

'Enough of the formalities,' she began, the others in the room nodding their approval. 'If we prove victorious, no-one will give a fiddler's curse as to how many titles were assembled in this chamber on this day.'

Fisker laughed loudly, while Ahren bit his lips in an effort to contain his amusement.

'I think it would be best if I give you all a quick overview of the situation regarding the Ring and our troops.' Not meeting with any objections, she began to go into details while the adjutants picked up wooden toothpicks with coloured pennants, which they placed in the little holes that had already been bored into the representation of the Ring, which was situated on the council table. The woman listed off dozens of units as well as the strength of each one, pointing confidently at different locations without ever hesitating for a heartbeat to gather her thoughts. Ahren was impressed not only by the number of soldiers now guarding the Ring, but even more by the way in which Falagarda was exhibiting her competence.

Once all the pennants were in position, Falagarda looked confidently at her audience before coming to the core of her report. 'As can clearly be seen, the Ring is controlled by a large variety of troops from all the allied countries. Dwarfish siege experts are busily constructing catapults and battering rams under the shelter of the Ring, close to the gates of the Obsidian Fortress, while cavalry from the Green Sea *and* the armoured cavalry of the Knight Marshes are controlling the hinterland of the Ring and guarding our supply lines. Elves, dwarfs and humans are watching every inch of the Ring, with even several *giants* having only now joined our forces. I took the liberty of assigning them special duties as they have had difficulty adapting to the local military doctrine.'

Bergen raised a hand. 'In other words – we are as ready as we can possibly be?'

The Chief Marshall nodded.

'That's enough of the good news and the self-congratulatory tone,' snarled Uldini. 'What about the enemy?'

Falagarda signalled to the adjutants, other pennants being then placed at various points within the Obsidian Fortress. This time, the woman waited until the last marking had been positioned.

'Please take a close look at the structure of the Obsidian Fortress, which we have been able to recreate thanks to Sun Shimmer's overflights during the last few moons.' She pointed at the middle of the table, Ahren then examining the model in detail, but the sheer number of towers, walls and bulwarks rising up from the wood made for a confusing sight.

'An analysis would be helpful,' suggested Bergen, breaking the silence that had fallen over the room, Falagarda nodding in response – as if she had expected just such a proposal.

'I, too, was confused initially. Let us begin in the centre – or rather, in the heart of the stronghold.' She pointed at a shape resembling a palace, not in the middle of the Obsidian Fortress but rising in its eastern third. 'If you look closely, you will see that the core of the citadel is surrounded by twenty walls that are elliptical rather than circular. In the east they are closest together, while the distances between them vary, seemingly indiscriminately, in the north, south and west.'

'*Why?*' exclaimed Hakanu, Ahren nodding at his protégé approvingly. 'Who would build a fortress so asymmetrically?'

The First leaned forward. 'It is a mistaken belief that all strongholds are built in a uniform manner. Every military fortification is designed according to the lay of the land on which it stands. A mountain fortress is completely different to a castle in a valley, for example.'

'But we are talking about level ground here,' muttered Khara, toying with her Warrior Pin before straightening it again with an impatient grunt. 'Why did the Adversary pick the eastern part of the former Borderlands to situate his…palace?'

'Magic,' said Akkad quickly. 'Creating the Obsidian Fortress took an enormous effort. I suspect that He needed all the hidden force lines that are present in the land to…well…to *anchor* the fortress, so to speak.'

Ahren chewed his lower lip for a heartbeat before speaking. 'In other words, when He built the fortress, He followed the mystical Power Lines are only visible to those with sorcerous abilities?'

Akkad nodded. 'And he would have tapped into every source of magical power that can be found in the Borderlands.' The portly sorcerer pointed at several bulwarks to the east, north and south. 'Hence the structures that you see here. They are situated directly above those focal points of concentrated magic.'

'The palace, too?' asked Fisker, all ears.

Akkad shrugged his shoulders. 'I suspect that is the case. But the Adversary is shielding His centre of power from enemy sorcery quite successfully – so, I cannot confirm it.'

The First pointed at the boundaries of the Obsidian Fortress. 'The Adversary not only has those magical resources at His disposal, but He has also taken care of his military strategy. It seems that He particularly fears possible attacks from the Knight Marshes, the Green Sea, the Forest of Ire, the Eternal Empire and the Sunplains.'

'Or to put it more simply – the only country He does not fear is Hjalgar,' added Likis, smiling self-deprecatingly.

Falagarda shook her head. 'It is true that the smallest distances between the defensive walls are to the east, but that is where the most dangerous Dark Ones are stationed. Age-old Blood Wolves for example, enormous Glower Bears, Horde Bulls – and let us not forget *Hate*, the last remaining child of the Dark god.' She tapped on the grooves representing the twenty ramparts. 'Furthermore, the eastern walls are the tallest and thickest. In other words, approaching from Deepstone would be short but onerous.'

The First had been studying the map thoughtfully. 'An attack from the north-east – from the Knight Marshes – would probably be our best option. The journey to the centre of the fortress would not take too long. There is no river directly beyond the Ring to hinder us. *And* we could put more soldiers in position there than here in Hjalgar.'

Falagarda nodded. 'I agree. But let us now come to the strength of the enemy troops. According to our calculations, there are over forty thousand Low Fangs, one thousand High Fangs and ten thousand other Dark Ones within the Obsidian Fortress. Furthermore, there is an unknown number of Swarm Claws, but I think we can safely assume that there is a ratio of five of the deadly birds to each of the Adversary's foot soldiers.'

The mood in the room darkened as the heavens would before a gathering storm.

'But this is *good* news, isn't it?!' exclaimed Hakanu, taken aback by the general reaction of the others. 'If I was calculating correctly, then we possess more troops than the enemy.'

'Only just,' countered Falk. 'And you aren't taking the fortress walls into account. Should we need to scale them, we will only successfully do so if we have thrice the number behind us for us to have any chance of achieving our goal.'

'*And* you can hardly say that one foot soldier carries the same strength as a Glower Bear,' interjected Quin-Wa curtly.

'Never mind the fact that the Low- and High Fangs are equipped with both armour *and* weaponry,' added Trogadon, 'even if no self-respecting blacksmith would stand over the shoddy workmanship involved.'

Sunju got to her feet and walked around the table, her eyes fixed on the many grooves. 'The good news is this – if the Adversary wants to break through the Ring, then He will have the same problem as us – namely, an insufficient number of troops.'

'Which means that the stalemate continues,' said Lanlion glumly, summarising the situation accurately.

'How are things on the sorcery front?' asked the First, looking at Quin-Wa, who promptly nodded towards Akkad.

'I have been somewhat distracted over the past few weeks,' said the Empress, touching her belly. 'Our tinkerer has a better overview than I do.'

The much-beloved Ancient waved his hand, an irregular grille of glowing lines suddenly connecting the carved symbols of the Wizardly Domes. 'The Arcane Walls are helping to deflect the Bane Curses being hurled over from the heart of the Obsidian Fortress,' he said. 'Losses among our soldiers has fallen within the last moon from one hundred and fifty per day to less than ten.'

Ahren gasped. He had already heard how the Ring had been suffering under the attacks from the Adversary, but the sheer number of those slain caused him to shake his head in disbelief. 'So much senseless death,' he murmured.

Khara squeezed his hand in silent commiseration.

Akkad waved his hand a second time, whereupon some of the Arcane Walls immediately dimmed, the other ones shining more powerfully. 'Experience has shown that some of the Ancients work better in pairs than others. Then there are their varying levels of skill when it comes to using the charms, *and* their individual reservoirs of inner strength. What you are looking at here are the most powerful and effective Arcane Walls that are currently operating.'

Hakanu craned his neck, the corners of his mouth immediately turning down. 'But now there are only *five!*'

'Your apprentice is making great progress!' announced Fisker, winking at Ahren. 'He has already learned how to count.'

'Only as far as ten,' replied Ahren with a grin. 'And it took me the whole winter to teach him that.'

Hakanu crossed his arms belligerently. 'Like master, like pupil,' he muttered.

The Forest Guardian guffawed, and for a moment the council of war was given over to the sounds of laughter and cheers of mock derision. It took an icy look from the First to restore order and to make Ahren suddenly feel once more as if he was a pupil being chastised in the godsday school.

'Can we reposition *these* Arcane Walls to more advantageous locations if necessary?' asked the First sharply as he glared at Akkad.

The sorcerer nodded. 'Tuning them in correctly, however, is a laborious process – *and* one must consider the journey time when moving from one dome to another. Every repositioning of the Ancients would mean gaping holes in our defences lasting for days at a time – this is why I have been wary of implementing such a policy.'

'Can we weaken the enemy through focused sorcery?' asked Sunju. 'For example, by having a fire run along an Arcane Wall, which would burn any Dark Ones nearby?'

Akkad nodded. 'This would be possible alright – but until now, the Adversary has successfully used Bane Curses to repel every attempt at a sorcerous attack. Furthermore, the burning Arcane Wall could not be used as a magical defence during the incineration.'

'Which means, when it comes to sorcery, the Ring and the Fortress are of equal strength, too?' probed Khara. Akkad shrugged his shoulders apologetically and said nothing.

'In other words, the war might drag on like this forever,' grunted Falk as he glanced over at Ahren. 'Alas, this reminds me of the gloomy scenes from the Dark Days.'

Images of villages razed to the ground and fields of scorched earth flashed through the mind of the young Forest Guardian. The longer the troops were massed at the Ring, the more Jorath was slowly but surely being bled dry. The scales were tipping more and more in the Adversary's favour with every day that passed.

The First stirred again by pointing at Uldini and Jelninolan. 'Now that we have an overview of where we stand, we need to talk about some information that has been delivered from the dim and distant past. The deceased Belsarius left behind a message which Ahren and his companions discovered during their journey to Deepstone – and from what *I* have heard, it is of critical importance.' The angry tone in the First's voice suggested that the veteran had already strenuously tried, and failed, to uncover exactly what it was that Ahren and the others had found out in Kelkor. The Forest Guardian quickly suppressed the selfish sense of satisfaction that he couldn't help feeling – after all, this was *not* the time for petty victories or malice.

Uldini floated uncertainly up from his seat before positioning himself above the centre of the map, giving him the appearance of a robed deity watching over his miniature world.

'I only wish our news was more hopeful…' he began before explaining in short, sharp sentences what they had learned about the Adversary in the Sanctum of Belsarius.

As the Arch Wizard spoke, Ahren could see the colour draining from the faces of all those present as they heard for the first time, Belsarius' theory.

By the time Uldini had finished his report, Ahren could sense that the fighting spirit which had previously been so tangible in the council chamber had completely evaporated. Almost pleadingly, he looked at the others – his fellow Paladins, the Ancients and the dignitaries – for any flicker of confidence. However, he was greeted with nothing other than empty eyes, behind which each and every individual was doubtless trying to digest what they had only now heard.

'When?' asked the First, his question mirroring the one that had been tormenting Ahren ever since leaving the Sanctum. 'When, according to what Belsarius predicted, will we confront the Adversary face to face?'

Uldini opened his mouth, then closed it again. He looked over at Akkad, who could only spread out his arms in a gesture of helplessness.

'I am working on it. But the calculations are wearisome, and I am awaiting news from some of the Ancients in the Wizardly Domes who are more learned in astrology than I am, and without whose help I cannot make progress,' admitted the eldest of the immortal sorcerers. 'For the moment, we haven't the faintest idea of when the Adversary will be vulnerable.'

Ahren looked down at his hands and said nothing. Akkad had given the worst answer possible.

They were caught up in a terrible war against a self-proclaimed god. And yet they were paralysed because they were missing one piece of the puzzle. A piece that could lead to glorious victory – or ignominious defeat.

Chapter 11

The First's fist crashed onto the wooden tabletop, creating an almighty creak.

'This is *unacceptable!*' he thundered. 'We cannot allow ourselves to be paralysed by an unproven theory! We are so close to our goal!' With that he uttered a groan so pained that stones would weep.

'I agree with the First,' said Falagarda in a calm voice. 'The supplies in the storerooms along the Ring are running low. Besieging the Obsidian Fortress unnecessarily for an extended period only because of a suspicion enunciated centuries ago by a long-dead Ancient will surely cost us too many lives and quite possibly end in our defeat.'

'But can we afford to ignore the warning that Belsarius so carefully hid for us?' asked Jelninolan cautiously.

'I cannot and *will* not believe that a stellar magical moment is the key to our victory,' interjected Bergen in a tone of deep frustration. 'One would have thought that the gods would have given us a *hint* during all this time since the creation of the Paladins, so that we wouldn't have been wasting our energy attacking the enemy like idiots and constantly risking our own destruction because *His* moments of weakness only occur once in a very, very, *very* blue moon – if you pardon the somewhat clumsy metaphor given the astronomical nature of what we are talking about!'

'The gods are *sleeping,*' snarled Uldini. 'They have never exactly distinguished themselves when it came to clarity regarding signs or concrete clues.'

'Belsarius was mistaken!' exclaimed Fisker. 'He simply *must* have erred!

Ahren knew precisely what was going to happen next but simply couldn't prevent it. Slowly but surely, the council chamber was transformed into a seething cauldron of argument and counterargument, as the attendees attached themselves to one side or the other. Those who supported Uldini and Jelninolan were convinced that Belsarius had been right in his theory, while those who sided with the militarily accomplished Falagarda and the First insisted on concentrating on the cold, hard facts of the present situation at the Ring.

During the course of the day, the mood became increasingly fraught and despairing, but Ahren was simply too weary to intervene – not least, because he himself was torn between the two sides and could not decide where he should lend his support. He exchanged a look with the First, and for one, precious heartbeat, a spark of mutual understanding seemed to fly between them – something that had rarely before occurred.

'Silence!' bellowed the First, successfully attracting everyone's attention.

Ahren gave the age-old Paladin an appreciative nod before seamlessly taking on the role of the friendly chairman. 'I suggest that we continue our discussion tomorrow,' he said in a mild-mannered voice. 'This was a lot of information to take in at one time. If we all mull over the challenges overnight, when we gather again tomorrow, we may find ourselves agreeing on a plan of how to move things forward. The break will also give Akkad a little more time to work on his calculations.'

Nods of support and a few sceptical mutters greeted Ahren's suggestion, while Khara placed a hand gently on Sleeps-in-Treetop's shoulder.

'Release us,' murmured the Swordsmistress. 'Your work is done for the day.'

The Ancient didn't open her eyes, her fingers slipping from the tabletop, as the magical runes that helped to disguise the gathering of so many Paladins in one place glimmered for a heartbeat once more in the council chamber. Concerned, Ahren made to move towards her only to hear the first loud snores coming from the Ancient.

'You had better leave her in peace,' croaked Uldini hoarsely in a trembling voice, the Arch Wizard sounding equally as exhausted. 'She will find her way to bed once she has rested here for a little.'

'Open up!' yelled the First, the heavy double doors immediately being swung back by the sentries.

Trogadon leapt to his feet. 'The THREE be praised!' he groaned in relief as he scampered off down the passageway. 'I drank far too much,' his voice echoed back into the chamber, fading away as the scolding blacksmith continued from afar: 'Which idiot came up with the idea of cooping us up for half the day without access to a privy?'

'We had better arrange a few toilet-breaks tomorrow,' commented Falk dryly as he got up with a groan. 'Otherwise, there will surely be an unfortunate accident – and we don't want either the bards or the adjutants to be recording *that.*'

This was greeted with some scattered laughter as the room continued to empty. Even Sleeps-in-Treetop stumbled out with a yawn, leaving only Ahren, Khara and Akkad, the former two looking expectantly at the latter.

'Did you find our council of war so refreshing that you cannot get enough of it?' asked the Ancient with a knowing wink. 'Or is there something on your minds?'

Ahren sighed. 'We are going to need a solid basis for any decision that we make regarding when and how we go for the Adversary's jugular.'

Akkad smiled understandingly. 'I take it that apart from wanting to know the *exact* moment of the constellatory alignment, you wish to be certain that Belsarius' theory really holds water.'

'Absolutely. Do you think you can do even more research? According to Uldini, no-one has a better understanding than you of how the Dark Days unfolded – thanks to your advanced years.'

The much-loved Ancient crossed his arms on his portly stomach. 'Although remarking upon my age is not exactly polite, I will admit that I do have quite a few summers under my belt. More than I care to remember, in fact.'

Khara cocked her head and peered at Akkad. 'And? Do *you* believe that Belsarius was right?'

The Ancient frowned and looked at the Swordsmistress sceptically. '*My* answer would come from the heart, but what we need now is a rational calculation.' He looked from Ahren to Khara and back again, his face suddenly appearing strangely distracted. 'You must understand – when one has experienced as many things in one's life as I have, the details of long-past events that followed similar patterns tend to merge into each other – and regarding the *written* history of the Dark Days – well, all I can say is that what has been handed down to the present generation is not without considerable gaps. We do not know, for example, exactly *when* they began. It was always the largest collections of manuscripts that tended to be destroyed during times of greatest conflict, and with them the most precious drawings…' The Ancient's voice had quietened gradually throughout his speech until now it was only an incomprehensible mumble, Akkad looking absently into the middle distance. Finally, his lips were moving in complete silence, as if he were performing an inner monologue.

'Akkad?' murmured Ahren anxiously.

The Ancient simply shook his head in silence before leaving the council chamber, totally lost in thought.

'This means, I suppose, that we won't see him again until he has solved whatever problem it is that is bothering him,' chuckled Khara.

Ahren looked out the window towards the clouds of Swarm Claws performing complicated aerial manoeuvres in the western sky. 'And even if he does come up with answers, the question is, will we *like* what we hear?'

Khara pulled her beloved to his feet in silence, the young couple leaving the empty council chamber behind them as they walked out into the passageway.

Oh, what a wonderful day it was, swooned Culhen, snuggled up in a corner of the room the four of them were sharing. The wolf had settled down beside the fireplace, he and the slumbering Muai having created their usual ball of fur.

'Well, I'm delighted that *you* enjoyed yourself,' murmured the irritated Forest Guardian aloud from the bed, where he and his beloved were lying. They had filled in their companion animals on the events in the council chamber, the tigress then yawning disinterestedly before curling up and falling asleep, leaving Khara alone with her worries, while Culhen, who had completely ignored the import of Ahren's report, concentrated instead on relating endless anecdotes about Yoka, which annoyed the Forest Guardian considerably.

...and then she actually called Cassobo a trumped-up simian, added Culhen with a chuckle.

Tell me – did anything useful come out of your discussions? asked Ahren irritably. *Something that might actually help us defeat the Adversary.*

How incredibly rude! exclaimed the wolf. *Did I interrupt you when you told me about your day?*

Ahren gritted his teeth, transmitting his impatience wordlessly through the mental connection that they shared.

Today was important, I'll have you know, announced Culhen solemnly. *Sun Shimmer introduced Kamaluq – and more importantly,*

Yoka – to the other companion animals, which led to them sniffing us – and then we sniffed them in return.

And? Ahren was all too aware of his tactlessness, but there were simply too many unanswered questions for him to be listening to endless tales of the companion animals and their rituals.

In this way, our connections to each other were reinforced. This is important, for it means that Sun Shimmer will be able to communicate with all the companion animals in the upcoming battle – even if they are many furlongs away.

'WHAT?!' exclaimed Ahren, inadvertently rousing Khara out of her slumber.

The wolf gazed at him smugly with his golden-yellow eyes. *You mean you don't know?* he asked accusingly. *It is not only Sun Shimmer's body that is expanding all the time – but also her ability to communicate with us companion animals. Her plan is that all the Paladins present in the Ring will be able to exchange information with one another through us.*

You mean that if I say something to you, and you pass it on to Sun Shimmer than she will be able to forward the message to…let's say Hanulf?

I am so lucky that I was landed with one of the brighter Paladins!

Ahren was torn between strangling his arrogant wolf or kissing him. Instead, he decided to try something out. *Right. Please tell Hanulf that he and the Father of the Mountain should make their way to Highstone with all possible speed. And ask Eken to pass on the following message to Trimm – I command him to wait in the vicinity of Deepstone and be ready to come to the castle when instructed.*

Ahren's connection to his friend broke off – a sure sign to the Forest Guardian that Culhen was now in contact with Sun Shimmer.

'Would you mind telling me what's going on?' asked Khara impatiently. 'You wake me up and look for all the world as if Culhen has just delivered a message from the THREE to you announcing that all will be well.'

Ahren nodded towards his wolf. 'He claims that Sun Shimmer is capable of contacting all the companion animals who are at the Ring.'

Done, announced Culhen smugly. *The Father of the Mountain asked me to tell you that he will be arriving tomorrow. Trimm says that he has already taken up lodgings in a very comfortable tavern four leagues east of Deepstone, where he will wait until the moment that the Thirteen are finally summoned.*

'And it seems that Culhen was not exaggerating,' added Ahren with a sheepish smile. 'I have, within a couple of heartbeats, communicated with *both* the Father of the Mountain *and* Trimm!'

Khara clapped her hands – twice. Once with joy, and the second time angrily, Muai's ears immediately flattening.

'Bold cat!' she scolded. 'How could you have kept such important information from me?!'

Muai gazed at her through her half-closed eyes before turning away languidly and settling down to resume her slumber. The corners of Khara's mouth twitched irritably.

Ahren breathed a sigh of relief, allowing himself a little smile of satisfaction. 'At least *one* piece of good news after such a frustrating afternoon.' Then he looked at Muai and Khara. 'Is everything alright between you two?' he asked in a murmur. 'I thought that Muai's wish to sleep near you rather than in Quin-Wa's room was a sure sign that your bond was growing even stronger?'

Khara scowled and bit her lower lip. 'If only,' she muttered. 'The simple truth is, however, that Her Royal Majesty Muai the First is jealous of the daughter, whom *Cochan* is now carrying. Hence, she is staying with me so that she can torment me with her sulkiness.'

The tigress growled in a low voice, the expression on Khara's face suggesting in no uncertain terms that the silent conversation that was now taking place between the Swordsmistress and the big cat was far from amicable.

Do you see how lucky you are having me? asked Culhen cockily.

Rubbing his eyes and shaking his head, Ahren decided that the best thing to do would be to try to get some sleep rather than involve himself in any more verbal sparring with his wolf.

After all – their worries and needs could multiply at any time now, day *or* night.

'Wakey-wakey,' whispered Khara into his ear before giving him a peck on the cheek. 'You don't want anyone barging in with breakfast again now, do you?'

'That's why I locked the door last night,' muttered Ahren, who wanted to do nothing more than keep his eyes firmly closed. The sweet forgetfulness that sleep had bestowed upon him had been a welcome balm, and as the countless unanswered questions now latched onto his mind again like enervating leeches, he abandoned himself momentarily to the fantasy of simply staying where he was, slumbering until the Adversary was finally vanquished.

You heard the good lady, young man, interjected Culhen with a mixture of good humour and feigned severity. *Out of bed with you so that we can make you into a worthwhile member of the human race!*

Culhen?

Yes, Ahren?

I hate you.

The Paladin still hadn't opened his eyes, but even from beneath the top sheet with which he had covered his head he could hear the panting laughter of the wolf.

Sensing the beam of light that suddenly streamed through the narrow window once Khara had pulled back the curtain, the young man poked his head out and opened his eyes, much as he was loath to do so.

Culhen and Muai were already standing by the door, waiting to be let out, looking for all the world like two domestic pets.

Sun Shimmer is calling us, explained Culhen with a note of urgency. *And the door is locked – thanks to you.*

Ahren got up, turned the key and let the two animals out. He gave the Night Soldier who had been standing guard outside a nod, the impassive, black-clad woman reciprocating the gesture. Then he closed the door again.

'Our two furry monsters are good practice for later,' said Khara, looking at him mischievously.

'Later?' asked Ahren, nonplussed.

'When we have children. The little ones will doubtless be just as much of a handful as Culhen and Muai. Well – if they take after *you* at any rate.'

Ahren raised a quizzical eyebrow. 'Or after *you.*'

'Or after *both* of us,' added Khara with a chuckle.

Suddenly, the imminent battle against the Adversary didn't seem like the biggest challenge that he would get to face in his life.

'Hmm,' murmured Khara, looking him up and down. 'Just the two of us at last. And we still have a little time until breakfast.' She walked towards him.

He grinned. 'What *are* you thinking of?'

She shrugged her shoulders in a gesture of innocence. 'This day is going to be difficult enough. We might as well begin it with a little pleasure.'

Ahren tried to think of a quick riposte, but already she was kissing him, and he willingly submitted. For a few precious heartbeats, all their problems and fears were forgotten.

If the previous day's breakfast had been conducted in an atmosphere of reckless merriment, this morning's meal was sombre and muted, the burden of responsibility weighing heavily on the Paladins, the Ancients, the rulers of Jorath and the rest of Ahren's companions. From time to time, anxious murmurs could be heard coming from the various tables.

Ahren was all too aware of the tension in the air that was afflicting everyone in the dining hall. Those who the previous day had been pleading for a quick assault on the Adversary were constantly glancing critically at the others, who had emphasised the need for caution and consideration. Ahren hated the fact that a squabble was threatening to shatter the unity of the council of war, and he kept craning his neck to see if Akkad was coming through the door of the dining hall with some information that might improve the mood. Then, much to his surprise, he saw that both Uldini and Jelninolan were looking remarkably well-rested. He stood up and wandered over to the two Ancients.

'Although I am delighted to see the pair of you looking so hale and hearty, I have to ask myself how this is possible,' he murmured to his two friends in greeting.

'I asked exactly the same question earlier,' announced Trogadon, his voice betraying his scepticism. 'And I didn't find their answer particularly comforting.'

Jelninolan gently stroked the plaits on her beloved's beard before looking up at Ahren. Her eyes were sparkling just a little too artificially. 'Do you remember the reinvigorating effect of the Althunol?' she asked.

'Yes...I do,' replied Ahren hesitantly. 'It enabled us to forget our pain and exhaustion.'

'And yet they were still present,' grunted Trogadon.

Uldini waved his hands dismissively. 'We have drunk a mixture of water from *all* the pools of the goddess. The effect is considerably more potent.'

Ahren looked at the Arch Wizard in surprise. 'From *all* the pools?'

Jelninolan shook her head. 'From the three that are not covered over by ice,' she murmured. 'My fellow elves took small amounts from the sacred pools in the Forest of Ire, in the Nameless Desert, and in Eathinian. They then stored each supply in specially woven magic receptacles in case we would need the sacred waters for a particularly complex spell. Early this morning I mixed a handful from each vessel together in the hope that the three spring waters would strengthen each other while at the same time overriding their individual flaws.' She smiled. 'And it turns out that I was right in my hunch.'

'Although there *are* still side-effects,' admitted Uldini, yielding to the highly critical stare that was coming from Trogadon. 'I feel the magic within me…well…bubbling erratically. It almost feels as if one has filled a water container too quickly, and there is now a danger of the liquid overflowing. I don't think we should take this kind of shortcut again for a while.'

Jelninolan nodded. 'Still, it has saved us days or even weeks of sleeping. A truly precious gift from the goddess.'

Feeling a heavy hand on his shoulder, Ahren turned to find the First staring at him expectantly.

'Shall we begin?'

Much to the Forest Guardian's surprise, the question sounded not in the least rhetorical but absolutely genuine. Clearly, the First was relying on both himself and Ahren to sing from the same hymn sheet during the council of war, thereby lessening the tensions among the other participants. This realisation confirmed to the Forest Guardian how critical the age-old warrior considered their situation to be, a shiver immediately running down the young man's spine. If the council of war descended into a squabble about how to proceed, then the Adversary would already have landed a considerable blow to the midriff of the Paladins – and that without resorting to Bane Curses or losing a single Dark One.

Not for the first time, Ahren was suddenly beset by the misgivings that had been torturing him for some time. Indeed, were Uldini not so certain regarding the veracity of what they had learned in the Sanctum, Ahren would have been convinced that the whole episode in Kelkor had been nothing more than a cunning ruse on the Adversary's part.

Inevitably, the image of the Woman in Black came into his mind – she who had pointed him towards the hiding place of the deceased Ancient. And again, he began to doubt her intentions. There could be no better trap than to reveal an uncomfortable truth at precisely the *wrong* time, thereby encouraging the natural tendency towards scepticism that was the lot of all thinking beings, and which so often proved corrosive.

Nervously, he felt the charred piece of wood in his pocket, and he wondered if he should burn it *before* the attack on the Obsidian Fortress. The First cleared his throat, rousing the young man from his brooding reverie.

'Let's get this over with,' said the Forest Guardian, his voice almost cracking with anxiety.

'I can only reiterate what I have already said – namely, that with every moon that passes our logistical problems will increase,' said Falagarda icily. 'Our entire strategy was based on the Thirteenth and Yollock returning from the Ice Fields and finding a heavily armed ring of soldiers who would *immediately* be led into battle.' She pointed at the table map with all its pennants. 'If we end up having to carry on with this siege because the stars are unfavourable or whatever it was that Belsarius was trying to tell us, then at least half our forces will be forced to return to their farms so that they can grow crops for the other half – if that doesn't happen, then Jorath will be subjected to its worst ever famine. The only ones then filling their bellies will be those Dark Ones picking whatever is left of our emaciated corpses!'

'Very vivid,' commented Uldini caustically. 'Thank you *so* much.' Clicking his fingers, a small cloud of sheer black suddenly appeared above the model Obsidian Fortress in the centre of the council table. 'Let me summarise briefly – once again – *my* position for the esteemed Chief Marshall. If we storm haphazardly into enemy territory and discover that the Adversary's force is too strong, we will have initiated – in the best-case scenario – a new era of Dark Days, involving one bloody attempt after another at hemming in HIM, WHO FORCES a *second* time.'

Ahren was silently grateful to the Arch Wizard for not having openly stated the *worst-case* scenario – Jorath would not have the centuries necessary to wait for another Thirteenth Paladin, the Adversary now knowing how to avoid being trapped in a new Pall Pillar.

'We are going around in circles again – just like yesterday,' murmured Falk as he glanced anxiously at his protégé. 'Except this time, the tone is much rawer.'

Ahren drummed his fingers on the tabletop as he pondered. He knew that he himself was partly responsible for the intractable situation in the room, the advocates of the two sides appealing to him directly on several occasion for his support. Whether the Forest Guardian liked it or not, there was no doubt that *his* word held more weight than that of the others, and indeed he could almost single-handedly make the decision regarding if and when the assault on the Obsidian Fortress should be launched. This meant, however, that he felt an almost unbearably heavy weight on his shoulders – and, for the moment at least, he simply did not know which option was the right one. Even amongst his friends, there was disagreement – which only made Ahren's dilemma worse.

Hakanu was, of course, in favour of an immediate assault, his position being shared by the First, Bergen and Falk, all of whom were particularly familiar with the needs of the armies. Quin-Wa, Jelninolan, Uldini, Lanlion and Fisker, on the other hand, believed in Belsarius' theory and did not want to take any further action without more information. The rest of Ahren's friends seemed as lost and undecided as he himself was feeling.

'Perhaps we should take a break…' he began, only for the council chamber doors to suddenly swing open as Akkad burst in, carrying an armful of parchments.

'Let me *in*,' he muttered to Sleeps-in-Treetop, his fellow Ancient briefly suspending the Bane Charm so that the portly fellow could get to the council table.

As the double doors closed again, and Akkad sorted out his many drawings and scribblings, Ahren took a closer look at the Ancient. The man's robe was terribly creased, and his eyes were so hollow that the Forest Guardian was certain that Akkad had not slept a wink since the previous day. The feverish look on his face, however, was triumphant – even if his features suggested that the information he was about to disseminate was far from good.

'You were successful, weren't you?' asked Ahren, Akkad nodding solemnly.

'Sit back and listen,' said the Ancient. 'For what I have to tell you all is going to be the most important thing you will have ever heard…'

Despite his pompous announcement, it took a while for Akkad to actually begin relating what he had discovered. Only after fastidiously arranging his parchments on the table and rearranging them several times did he finally glance around him at the members of the council of war and clear his throat.

'The first thing I would like to say is that I am now firmly of the belief that Belsarius' theory holds water, and that the power of the Adversary is influenced by a particular constellation of stars.'

This remark was greeted with murmurs of disbelief and low curses by those who had been focussing their attention primarily on the logistical problems facing the army.

'What exactly do you mean?' asked Falk sharply. 'Are you saying that at a certain point in time He will be unable to conjure up a few Bane Curses or that his resistance will completely collapse?'

'A good question. Alas, I cannot yet answer it,' replied Akkad, nodding down at the parchments in front of him. 'It is just that something struck me. A...*pattern* one might call it. Let me go through what I have found with you all, and then we can decide on how to react.'

'Well, the wily old fox,' murmured Khara, her hand over her mouth. 'He is leading us exactly the way that he wants us to go, using a softly, softly approach.'

Akkad waved his left hand, a pattern of sparkling lights immediately appearing above the table, Ahren recognising them immediately – four zodiacal signs forming a harmonious constellation.

'We can safely assume that the paintings of the early Jorathians closely represent the order of the stars in the sky when the Custodian was created.'

He pointed down at a parchment filled with columns of complex numbers, beside which were a series of phrases. Was it, Ahren wondered, a list of the many constellations that appeared above Jorath?

'This particular constellation appears every...' with that, the clever man's eyes ran down the numbers and names, while everyone present – Paladins, Ancients, humans, dwarfs and adjutants – held their breath, '...thirteen hundred and forty-two winters.'

Falagarda looked at him stony-faced. 'And why should these particular zodiacal signs influence the Adversary in any way? And even if they do, how is it that this didn't strike anyone during the considerable period *before* Belsarius was born?'

Akkad raised a warning finger. 'One question at a time,' he countered forcefully. 'I am doing my best to explain my investigation as clearly as possible and would prefer to present what I have discovered in the most logical order.'

Hearing a low sigh to his right, Ahren turned to look. Trogadon was reaching for a full tankard of wine, which he picked up before tilting back in his chair and staring irritably up at the ceiling. For the blacksmith's deeds *always* carried more weight than words.

'Right, then – every thirteen hundred and forty-two summers,' snarled Uldini, repeating Belsarius' calculation. '*And?* Go *on!*'

Akkad nodded gratefully at the Arch Wizard before clearing his throat a second time. 'I concentrated my research on what Belsarius had said – that every action has its right time and so forth. I feel that he was referring to the phases of activity and rest, which we can find in periods, long and short, ever since the creation of Jorath. Summer and winter. Day and night. The waking and sleeping patterns of all life forms. Or – if we consider the *longest* cycle that I can think of – the creation of Jorath and the continuing sleep of the gods.'

'Interesting,' murmured Quin-Wa, her eyes flashing. 'If your theory is right, the gods will enter a new phase of creation when they awaken.'

The First raised a hand in frustration. 'Please – no endless discussion about the essence of the THREE or the meaning of life,' he barked. 'We have enough things to be discussing without being distracted by issues that are completely irrelevant.'

'Uh...yes,' said Akkad, looking apologetically at Quin-Wa. 'Although I *do* find the Eternal Empress's line of thought fascinating, I agree with the First on this occasion.' He pointed at the points of light above the map. 'I proceeded on the assumption that the Adversary, too, follows a rhythm that influences His power, and that it is somehow connected to His moment of creation. The stars themselves, of course, have no *effect* on the waxing and waning of His strength – they *do*, however, make it apparent. They are like a sort of sundial if you will. I began on this basis to search for evidence of Belsarius' theory, and I believe that I have discovered something.'

'In only one night?' asked Bergen sceptically.

Akkad nodded. 'Imagine an enormous forest in which you must find a particular tree. A thoroughly onerous task – unless you have points of reference that will assist you. If you know that it is located at the northern edge, and that it must be an oak, for example. With every clue, your search becomes easier.' He pointed again at the glowing constellation floating over the map. 'This here was a *very* helpful clue. All I had to do was to recapitulate the course of the Dark Days insofar as my own memory would permit, while I also sent sorcerous messages to those of my fellow Ancients who have a similar love for history.'

Jelninolan gasped. 'But the Adversary would have *heard* your questions,' she countered, aghast. 'You have endangered the very secret that Belsarius went to such lengths to keep *hidden!*'

Akkad looked at the priestess reassuringly. 'I couldn't have been more careful with my formulations. I can assure you that no damage was done in this respect.'

'What was the result of your little excursion into the history of the Dark Days?' asked Fisker nervously.

Akkad's face reflecting the seriousness of the situation, he looked at everyone in the room before speaking again. 'I have discovered that the Adversary is all too aware of His weakness and is doing all in His power to *disguise* it.'

'Could you be a little more *precise?*' muttered the First, his arms crossed belligerently.

Akkad nodded. 'I tried to compare our greatest victories and most humiliating defeats in our war against the Adversary to those years when this constellation was visible in the firmament.' He raised a hand and used his fingers to list off the events. 'The case of Enthulia, initiated by the Adversary, which through His cunning intrigue distracted the realms, playing them off, one against the other. The extended era of peace when the Dark god was almost vanquished after the northern battles. Then the heyday of necromancy when we were constantly kept in check by the sorcerous servants of the Adversary. All these phases of the Dark Days took place shortly *before* the conjunction of the stars we see here.'

Lanlion leaned forward. 'You mean, they were all proxy wars and intrigues designed to keep us *distracted!*'

'And times like the Extended Peace were more frequent,' added Jelninolan.

Akkad nodded. 'Alas, I couldn't precisely pin down these unusually long dormant phases during the war. I *do* believe, however, that the damage done to the *records* of the Jorathian realms during the Dark Days was *not* down to chance.'

'The Adversary ensured, therefore, that the concealment of His weakness lasted for as long as possible,' said Bergen before cursing colourfully.

'This is precisely what struck me, too,' agreed Akkad. The Ancient pursed his lips, Ahren noticing how the scholar was struggling with himself.

'You discovered something else as well, didn't you?' suggested the Forest Guardian, gently cajoling the corpulent man.

'Indeed, I did. We suffered our greatest defeats in the centuries *following* the constellatory manifestation.' Akkad swallowed hard. 'The betrayal of the Lost Tribe, for example, or the devastation heaped upon the Sunplains, the results of which are still evident in its landscape.' The Ancient sighed. 'And then there was the death of the Thirteenth when we believed that we had finally encircled the Adversary.'

Ahren instinctively held his breath. The sudden silence in the room convinced him that everyone else was doing the same.

'Are you…are you telling us that the Adversary lured us into a trap during that dreadful time?' asked Falk through gritted teeth.

Akkad nodded, his features displaying both sadness and pity. 'Absolutely. The previous conjunction of the stars we see here had appeared only a few centuries before the Night of Blood, at which point the Adversary's power was still only beginning to wane. It was the perfect opportunity for Him to *feign* weakness before the Champions of the gods.'

The First slammed his fist on the table with such ferocity that Ahren saw splinters flying in all directions. 'He made bloody *fools* out of us!' The words the age-old Paladin spat out were positively dripping with bloodthirsty vengeance.

'And if the Ancients had not come up with the Pall Pillar idea, He would in all probability have destroyed us in the time thereafter!' gasped Uldini, distraught. 'We believed that we had conquered Him but in fact we were on the edge of the precipice.'

'Who says that it wasn't simply a succession of coincidences?' countered Yantilla, glancing at the others in the room before fixing her eyes on the Thirteenth. 'We must make absolutely certain that we are not simply on some wild goose chase.'

Ahren looked at Akkad and the older Paladins. Their faces spoke volumes. 'It *is* true, isn't it?'

Quin-Wa nodded. 'Suddenly, so many things are making sense,' she said. 'Why the Adversary strode forth into battle on some occasions, while hesitating on others, even resorting to employing his servants to fight on his behalf.'

'It also explains why He didn't constantly repeat his most successful tactics,' snarled Uldini. 'He had to keep an eye on the state of His energy, preserving Himself when necessary, while at the same time *not* revealing His temporary vulnerability.'

Lanlion pointed at the miniature version of the Obsidian Fortress. 'May I take it that my interpretation of the enemy's defensive tactic is correct? Does He currently find Himself in a weakened phase?'

Ahren immediately turned to look at Akkad, the young man silently praying that the Ancient would nod in agreement.

'In principle, yes,' murmured Akkad, a jubilant roar immediately breaking out among the listeners. 'BUT!' he shouted over the noise, 'the situation is more complicated than you might think.'

The cheering subsided immediately.

'Oh, spit it out!' bellowed the First angrily.

Akkad pointed at his parchments. 'As we already know, our best chance of vanquishing the Adversary lies with attacking shortly before or at the precise moment when the stars are aligned in the constellatory form we have spoken about. And I have discovered the following – that this point in time is imminent.'

Ahren's chest tightened. 'And when *exactly* will that be?' he asked in a low voice.

Akkad took a deep breath before speaking. 'The day after tomorrow.'

'But that's *fantastic!*' exclaimed Hakanu, clearly overjoyed, before he looked around at the others, quickly concluding that no-one shared his enthusiasm. 'Or isn't it?'

Falagarda, who had been cursing under her breath, waved her arm angrily at the map. 'Do you see all these soldiers? Putting them into positions for a coordinated attack alone will take two days. Never mind organising the siege weaponry.'

'Nor will we have sufficient time to adjust the Arcane Walls to our plans,' groaned Uldini. 'Then there are the wearisome rituals that might help us in battle.'

'And if we simply take the time that we need – however number of days?' asked Bergen. 'After all, we are taking about the Dark god depending on His cycles of strength, which stretch over centuries. In other words – ebb and flow. How important can a single day after His moment of greatest weakness possibly be?'

Akkad cleared his throat yet again, Ahren realising how he was beginning to hate the sound. 'Let us use your own metaphor. Imagine the emergence of the constellation as a tidal wave racing towards the shore. During the period when it is gathering strength, it pulls right back and the water level sinks.' He pointed at the twinkling stars. 'Until the exact moment when it races forward, overwhelming the shoreline before flooding the entire countryside. This means, we must conquer the Adversary before the constellation disappears again.'

'Are you saying that we had our best opportunity for victory over the past few years, and that we won't have enough time in the next couple of days?' grunted Trogadon in his gravelly voice. 'Damn unfortunate if you ask me.'

'It has nothing to do with misfortune,' countered Akkad. '*Ahren* is responsible.'

The Forest Guardian looked up with a start before pointing at his own chest. 'Why are you blaming this disaster on *me?* he asked, flabbergasted. His mind was racing now. Had he done something seriously wrong during his search for his fellow Paladins?

Akkad beamed at him. 'I didn't mean it like that. During my research, I kept asking myself why the gods hadn't over the course of so many centuries ever given the slightest hint as to when was the best possible moment for attacking the Adversary.'

'I was wondering the same thing myself,' murmured Sunju, nodding in agreement.

'But this is exactly what they *did* do. At least three times,' continued Akkad. 'The first time was when they gave the peoples of Jorath the gift of magic. Sending out the first Paladins was the second occasion. And as for the third,' he pointed at Ahren, 'well, *that* coincided with their creation of the Thirteenth. Each of these lesser gifts manifested themselves several decades *before* the appearance of the constellation.'

Quin-Wa rubbed the bridge of her nose as she pondered. 'And you believe that they did this to force the peoples of Jorath into action at a particular time, thereby turning the course of the war in their favour?'

Akkad shrugged his shoulders. 'It's certainly a possibility.'

'But why such complicated, circuitous methods?' asked Ahren sceptically. 'Why didn't the THREE speak directly to one of their servants about this aspect of the war? I mean, the goddess alone, contacted us through Khara and Jelninolan on quite a few occasions.'

'Are *you* able to direct your dreams so easily?' interjected Jelninolan. 'You surely remember how *vague* the visitations always were. Perhaps the gods have been adopting this approach since the beginning of the Dark Days but have failed because *we* have been lacking the imagination to interpret the messages correctly. Hence, they decided to introduce upheavals – which would make a confrontation with the Adversary at the right time more likely.'

'It's a bit like shooting at pigeons with Dragon Bows,' chuckled Trogadon.

Ahren's thoughts, meanwhile, were entirely taken up with his own place within this never-ending roundelay of cause and effect. 'So, did I take too long?' he asked in a low voice. 'Had *I* only managed to gather all the Paladins a few moons earlier would the Adversary not now be able to point *His* loaded crossbow at *our* heads?'

'Think about it rationally,' murmured Falk in gentle voice. 'Ever since the beginning of our journey, we have had the feeling that the Dark god was delaying the moment of confrontation. Now we know that apart from the aftereffects of the Pall Pillar and His fear of the Paladins, He had another motive.'

'Delaying us for long enough until his power returns,' added the First gravely. 'The Obsidian Fortress is bulwark and trap at the same time. It is intended to keep us away from Him for as long as the constellation is in the sky. If we reach Him *after* that, we will be too late.'

'But it was always stated that the Thirteen Paladins could destroy the Adversary!' interjected Yantilla angrily. 'Now we have them all, let us simply ignore those stupid stars.'

'You're not *listening!*' snorted Quin-Wa. 'For many, *many* centuries there were thirteen Paladins and yet they – *we* – never succeeded at getting to the Dark god.' She pointed at the canopy of stars above the table. 'And now, at last, we know why.'

'It is like a contest between two wrestlers in the Arena,' murmured Khara, breaking the silence that had momentarily set in. 'Each must wait for the decisive moment if they wish to emerge victorious – otherwise, their attacks will fail, and they risk defeat and death at the hands of their opponent.'

'Accursed Obsidian Fortress,' muttered Lanlion. 'Despite the good service that the Pall Pillar did for us before Ahren's appearance, it may now be – having fallen into the enemy's hand – the cause of our defeat. The Adversary has built His citadel cunningly. If we cannot break into it in time, He will begin his invasion of Jorath.'

'What can we do?' asked Falagarda helplessly. 'Attack although our troops are insufficiently prepared? The enemy territory is teeming with Dark Ones that have hidden behind their high walls. Our armies will be wiped out before even half of the fortress is in our hands.'

Again, a heavy silence descended upon the council of war. Ahren was tempted to suggest that they all take a break, but the cold, hard fact was that they were running out of precious time.

Suddenly, Khara stirred beside him. 'If we keep the idea of the two wrestlers in our minds, each eyeing the other while awaiting their opportunity, then there *is* something we could try,' she murmured pensively. 'Something that the opponent cannot resist – if one of the combatants – in this case, *us* – presents an opening.'

'You are talking about a ruse,' said Fisker. 'You want us to trick the Dark god, then.'

'Impossible,' countered the First. 'It has been tried so many times already and it has always failed.'

'But this time we know *all* the rules of this tortuous game!' protested Fisker. 'An essential advantage when cheating successfully.'

'Well, then,' snapped Uldini. 'Tell us about this plan of yours for putting the Adversary on the rack.'

'Uh.'

'Just as I thought.'

Already, Falagarda was in her element as she pointed at Khara and Fisker in turn. 'If – and I mean *if* – we implement your crazy idea of attacking the stronghold of the enemy with our troops not properly positioned, insufficient siege weapons and badly situated Arcane Walls then we are going to need a subterfuge so extraordinary that the bards will sing of it for aeons to come.'

'Not forgetting that this subterfuge – as you call it – must be implemented in next to no time,' added Falk.

'Or we can simply try our luck against a reinvigorated enemy force that we have been unable to conquer for millennia, and which has slaughtered countless unfortunates,' suggested Trogadon, taking another draught of wine for good measure.

Again, the council chamber was silent as baffled looks were exchanged. Every now and then, a someone would open their mouth, only to close it again without actually having made a suggestion.

Finally, Uldini floated upwards and over the table, waving his hand dismissively, thereby forcing Akkad's constellation up to just below the high ceiling. 'Let us summarise what we know. The Adversary will be vulnerable for another two days. He knows His own weakness, which He has successfully hidden from the world thus far.' He paused for a heartbeat before continuing. 'But does He know that we have discovered His secret?'

'At the very least He realises that we travelled to Kelkor, His Bane Curse having followed us there,' murmured Jelninolan. 'I very much doubt that He is exhausted to the point of *not* being able to think rationally.'

Uldini nodded, grinning deviously, nonetheless. 'But He *cannot* know that we reached the Sanctum. After all, it was only shortly thereafter that we were flown here, battered and bruised, by Sun Shimmer. Therefore, He will surely not risk giving up His considerable advantage by reacting too hastily.'

'What *are* you thinking, you old intriguer' asked Quin-Wa.

Uldini floated around in a circle, his hands clasped behind his back as he stared up at the twinkling lights. 'If the Adversary believes us to be ignorant, then that gives us a *massive* advantage we can work with.'

'Except we have no idea of what the Dark god knows or doesn't know,' said the First coldly.

Ahren could tell from the veteran's tone of voice that the old man had reverted to his old way of thinking – for him, this battle was already lost, and he was already planning the next one.

'I suggest,' continued the First, 'that we keep the Adversary imprisoned within the Ring for as long as possible before allowing Him to break out at a location of *our* choosing. We will decide on a country that we are prepared to sacrifice. Then we will surround Him and His followers in that place – but this time, there will be no Obsidian Fortress to protect Him.'

Ahren stared at the age-old Paladin in disbelief. 'You *cannot* be serious!' he spluttered. 'Why do you *always* want to sacrifice someone or something as soon as the going gets tough?'

'Because this is how the world works, Ahren.'

The Thirteenth got to his feet and walked over to the fireplace. 'Not *my* world,' he countered decisively as he took the charred timber from his pocket. Then he threw it onto the blazing fire, asking himself silently if he had made the correct decision.

'What *are* you doing?' asked Fisker, craning his neck so that he could see the flames. For a few heartbeats, they took on a green hue before returning to their normal colours.

'We want to get an insight into the mind of the Adversary,' said Ahren, without turning to look back at the others. 'I am now making sure that we gain access to His knowledge.'

Chapter 12

Ahren waited for several heartbeats in eager anticipation of the Woman in Black making an appearance, but nothing happened. Now he stood there by the fireplace, completely at a loss as the other council members observed him sceptically.

'What *have* you done. Thirteenth?' demanded Falagarda.

'You *do* realise that this piece of wood contains a mysterious magic that you have released by igniting it, don't you?' added Quin-Wa indignantly. 'Magic, which thanks to its slumbering state, you managed to carry straight through our Bane Spell.'

'Uh...I...' stammered Ahren, flummoxed by what he was hearing.

'The wood came from *her*, did it not?' sighed Uldini. 'The Woman in Black?'

'From *whom?*' asked Lyssin, perplexed.

'She is Ahren's sinister protectress,' explained Lanlion. 'She comes and goes as she chooses, is in league with the Adversary, and her assistance almost cost Khara her life in the Green Sea.'

Ahren shook his head indignantly. 'Oh, come on now! Describing her like that, you're making her sound far more devious than she really is. After all, she saved Culhen's life – and mine – from certain death when we were being chased by the Hunter.'

'And she led us to Onja on King's Island,' added Falk flatly. 'Without her, the Hunger Cadavers would have caused my soul companion to join their haunted ranks.'

'Did I hear correctly?' asked Falagarda incredulously. 'This mysterious woman is a follower of the *Dark god?!*'

'It isn't as simple as that,' countered Khara, trying to support Ahren. 'At least – that's how *I* see it.'

Ahren shook his head again. 'She said I could call her by burning the piece of wood. She has information that only a servant of the Adversary could possibly possess. If anyone can tell us if her Lord and Master suspects that we have unmasked his secret, then it is she.'

'And since *when* do we trust the word of the enemy?' asked Falagarda angrily, throwing her arms in the air.

'My master only learned of the Sanctum *from* the Woman in Black!' exclaimed Hakanu, coming to his teacher's defence. Ahren groaned, covering his face with his hands.

'In other words, this whole theory of the so-called Echo of Belsarius is based on clues provided by a servant of the Adversary,' muttered Kamkanzakur. 'If you ask me, this calls into question *everything* that we have discussed thus far.'

'I smell a trap,' grunted the First. 'You lot have been hoodwinked by this woman and her Dark god.'

Jelninolan stood up, her arms on her hips. 'Surely such an elaborate ambush would be far too circuitous for the Adversary. Why would He allow one of His servants to save the Thirteenth's life on more than one occasion instead of simply having him killed?'

Falagarda shook her head. 'Please make your decision – either the Adversary is sly enough to lead all the free nations of Jorath *and* the Paladins a merry dance by allowing Himself to become beleaguered during the Dark Days only to – by means of a perfect plot, no less – weaken the Champions of the gods dramatically during the Night of Blood *or* He is incapable of such guileful subterfuge – in which case, you have proven the theory so recently postulated to be redundant.'

'She's right,' muttered Quin-Wa. 'If the Adversary really *did* lure us into a trap that time, then He might do so again at any moment.'

The First clenched his armoured fists. 'I say we arrest this woman as soon as she appears. Then we can get the truth out of her – by force if necessary!'

Ahren took a step forward, raising his hands commandingly. 'No-one will touch a hair of her head,' he said firmly. 'It was *I* who called her here, and if she comes, she will do so of her own free will. Whether or not we like what she has to tell us is neither here nor there. She may leave again whenever she chooses.'

Uldini rubbed his temples wearily, his eyes flashing like two trapped stars. But the Arch Wizard said nothing.

The entranced Sleeps-in-Treetop shifted in her seat, the runes in the chamber lighting up and extinguishing again. 'Mind and heart must be *ad idem* when the black one appears. Eat, drink and be merry, but be not afraid to weep. Then return here when you have all found yourselves again. Once all words have been spoken, the fate of the world will depend on our decision.' She pointed at the double doors of the chamber, which flew open with a crash – much to the surprise of the Night Soldiers standing guard in the passageway.

'I believe that we are all being expelled from the council chamber,' murmured Falk dryly as he got to his feet, Ahren and the others still staring at the cryptically gifted Ancient. 'And I *do* think that she has a point – a break would do us all good.'

Ahren followed his former master's example by standing up and accompanying the old man. Behind him, he heard the scraping of chairs, and it wasn't long before the room was empty – except for Sleeps-in-Treetop, who raised her hand in a commanding gesture, the double doors slamming shut again instantly.

'What does the old crow have up her sleeve, I wonder?' asked Uldini curiously, as he began to float back towards the closed council chamber.

Jelninolan grabbed his robe and gently pulled him towards her. 'You'd best leave it,' she advised. 'Sleeps-in-Treetop usually has very good reasons for doing what she does, and her insights are quite remarkable when she is committed to a cause.'

The disdainful snort of the Arch Wizard was more suited to the response of a spoilt child, suiting, in fact, his own appearance.

'How *civilised,*' commented Quin-Wa dryly. 'I think that I shall pay the Heart Hall a visit during this enforced break in proceedings.' She placed a hand on her stomach. 'Aluna deserves to be put in the picture.'

'May I come with you?' asked Khara, her eyes lighting up. 'I would so much like to see what the future of the Paladins looks like.'

On hearing these words, Ahren shivered. The future of the Paladins. As far as the Forest Guardian was concerned, the glut of soul companions and the offspring to the Champions of the gods was nothing more than the THREE making certain that the war against the Adversary could go on should the present batch of Paladins fail in their mission.

'I'll go too,' he heard himself say. It would do him good to remind himself for whom he was fighting. And if he and his brothers and sisters were successful, then no child of Jorath would ever again have to bear the burden of fighting the Adversary.

Quin-Wa nodded. 'The way to the Heart Hall leads into the depths. The dwarfs who constructed it had only the safety of its inhabitants in mind, and because there is no mountain as such…well, you will see for yourselves.'

'Are you coming too?' asked Ahren, turning to Falk, the latter shaking his head, much to the surprise of the younger Forest Guardian.

'I already paid Onja and our daughter a visit this morning, and as we still haven't agreed on a name, there is a certain amount of tension between my wife and I.'

Bergen laughed, slapping the old Paladin on the back. 'In other words, my stubborn brother here is too *proud* to abandon whatever name it is that he considers most suitable and is refusing to yield to his good wife.'

Falk stuck out his chin belligerently. 'Branhilma is a name with a long tradition in the Knight Marshes.'

'Ah,' murmured the Thirteenth, doing his best to suppress a grin. 'I understand.' Then he headed off through the castle in the company of Quin-Wa. Khara and Bergen.

They continued their descent until they reached the ground floor of Highstone, making their way to a large door made of pure Dwarfish Steel, located in the middle of a huge room surrounded by thick, windowless walls. Fifty dwarfs wearing heavy armour and carrying broad shields and weighty axes stood in an impenetrable circle around a set of steel double-doors. In the four corners of the room, Ahren could see smaller-sized Dragon Bows situated on pivoting stands by means of which the quartets of dwarfs responsible for each could easily swing the long-range weapons, pointing them in any direction, as required.

'The Shield Chamber. Guarded by elite soldiers from Thousand Halls,' explained Quin-Wa. 'Hand-picked by Kamkanzakur and sworn to protect the Heart Hall.'

'Even an army of Dark Ones would have considerable difficulty getting past *these* guards,' murmured Ahren, impressed.

'Which is exactly the plan,' added Bergen as he looked around nervously.

As Quin-Wa neared the doorway, four of the dwarfs beat their breastplates with their fists before allowing the Eternal Empress and her companions to pass. Then Ahren watched the woman pointing at two inconspicuous stones that were situated at waist height in the masonry on either side, magically depressing them ever so slightly. This was followed by a scraping sound as the handle-less double doors slowly swung outwards.

'Even if a Dark One *did* manage to break in here, it would still have to find this mechanism first and then figure out how it worked. By which time, it would hopefully have been overpowered,' explained Quin-Wa as she stepped into a mausoleum-like staircase illuminated by hurricane lamps.

Curious, Ahren craned his neck, seeing at the end of the narrow descent another plain set of Dwarfish Steel double-doors. Once he and the others arrived in front of it, Quin-Wa knocked on the metal in a complicated rhythm.

'What is the password?' said a bright voice from within which sounded human rather than dwarfish.

'The burden of the heart is hard to bear.'

Hardly had the empress uttered the words when the heavy bolt was pulled back with a scraping sound, the doors then slowly swinging open. Ahren and Khara exchanged surprised looks as they saw how thick the metal was. Beyond was another square-shaped room of a similar size to the one that the dwarfs above them were guarding – except that *this* one revealed dozens of familiar faces, all of them grinning at him.

'My Ice Wolves!' he exclaimed, excitedly greeting his bodyguards by placing his hand on his chest and looking from one to the next. The last time he had laid eyes on most of them had been shortly before the Thirteenth Fleet had been attacked by the leviathan. It warmed his heart to see that so many of them had survived. He suddenly felt a stab of guilt as he silently acknowledged that he hadn't given Yantilla and her troop a second thought since his arrival in Highstone. 'Hakanu is, in this respect, a far better commander than I am,' he murmured regretfully.

'*What* was that?' asked Bergen in surprise.

Ahren quickly shook his head. 'Oh, nothing,' he replied, doing his best to ignore Khara beside him, who was grinning knowingly.

The Ice Wolves were standing in a semi-circle, guarding another door at the opposite end of the room, and running along the floor between the men and women dressed in their characteristic tabards was a multitude of runes, barely visible as they pulsed a glimmering red.

'This is the Rune Chamber. Do *not* step on the lines,' said Quin-Wa firmly. 'The sorcery cannot distinguish between friend and foe. The Protective Charms associated with them should on no account be unintentionally released.'

'Aren't these safety measures a little *too* extreme?' asked Khara.

'How would *you* answer this question if *your* new-born baby was lying in the Heart Chamber, your other children already having been *slaughtered* by servants of the Adversary?' asked Bergen, his voice raw with emotion.

Mortified, Khara said nothing.

Ahren shook as many hands as he could, all the while following Quin-Wa's advice by glancing down to make sure that he didn't touch the runes as he moved through the room. He wondered what it was that had driven Yantilla to post the bodyguards of the Thirteenth here of all places, but then it struck him that he would have acted in precisely the same manner had he been in her place. There were no soldiers that he trusted more than his Ice Wolves when it came to carrying out such a vital task. The gaunt woman clearly knew him inside out by now.

Quin-Wa pointed at the next set of Dwarfish Steel double-doors. 'Would you be so kind?' she asked the two guards on either side, whereupon they each pulled open their wing. The metal lit up with runes that glimmered for a couple of heartbeats before fading away again.

'Let me guess,' said Khara. 'If enemy hands touch this steel, they don't live long enough to regret their mistake – am I right?'

'They and all other Dark Ones within the room,' explained the Eternal Empress. Again, they descended a staircase, at whose end, however, a set of double doors was already open, beyond which was an impenetrable darkness.

'Why have the lanterns down here been extinguished?' asked Ahren uneasily, once they had reached the bottom of the stairs. His hand moved instinctively to the handle of his Wind Blade.

Bergen rested his fingers lightly on the Forest Guardian's sword arm. 'The darkness in the Blades Chamber serves a function,' said the blonde Paladin. 'You shall find out for yourselves.' Then he walked purposefully forward, immediately being swallowed up by the gloom. Quin-Wa followed, Ahren and Khara then doing the same – but with considerably more caution.

'What does this mean?' murmured the Thirteenth as he felt his way through the sheer blackness. 'How am I supposed to know where to go?'

'Allow yourself to be led,' said Quin-Wa, the enjoyment she felt at Ahren's discomfiture evident in her voice, which caused the young man to grunt irritably.

Suddenly, hands were grasping him gently by the shoulders from behind, turning him slowly but surely towards the left. His ears pricked up at the unmistakable rustle of a Night Soldier's clothing. Then he heard the same sound coming from another of these ruthless warriors and then a third time. They were surrounding him, tugging every now and again at his cloak or pushing him gently in the back, causing him to sway in a particular direction.

'Do not resist,' warned Bergen. 'The floor, the walls and the ceiling are full of jutting metal barbs and sharp blades – ready to sever the limbs of those who do not know their way through the Blind Labyrinth. The Night Soldiers will lead us safely through.'

Closing his eyes, Ahren's mind was filled with long forgotten memories of the lessons he himself had attended during his training to become a member of the fearsome troop. Slowly but surely, as he took one careful step after another, the darkness around him changed from being hostile territory to becoming merely an obstacle that his active senses could overcome. He felt the coldness of metal to his left and right as well as the warmth radiating from the guiding Night Soldiers.

Ahren sensed that the ruthless fighters leading him through the labyrinth were beginning to give him more and more room, now that they realised that he was able to glide through the darkness like one of *them*. The sense of unspoken camaraderie combined with the comfortable peace of unconditional surrender calmed and distressed him equally.

Following numerous turns and dozens of heartbeats, he sensed a wall of coldness looming ahead of him – the next set of Dwarfish Steel doors.

'We have arrived,' he said, surprised at the coolness of his own voice.

'Impressive,' murmured Quin-Wa.

'Unsettling is the word *I* would have chosen,' grunted Bergen.

Ahren felt how Khara clasped his hand in hers. The skin of his beloved seemed almost to be burning.

'Are you alright?' she asked in a low voice.

Ahren cleared his throat. 'Yes,' he said, relieved that he could hear emotion in his voice again.

'I do apologise. I should have warned you,' murmured Quin-Wa in the darkness. 'This room that we have passed through is permeated with a fine mist of Dream Leaf. It is excellent for heightening the sensibilities of the Night Soldiers.'

'Not to mention raising memories in me that I had long believed to be rid of,' whispered Ahren with a shiver. 'A bit of forewarning would certainly have been welcome.'

Instead of replying, Quin-Wa hit the tip of her staff against the steel – three hard knocks followed by a final soft one.

A chink of light appeared immediately in front of Ahren, causing him to squint before he found himself staring directly at the metal tips of crossbow bolts. The four she-dwarfs who then lowered their weapons in the little antechamber were familiar to him.

'Thirteenth!' exclaimed Taninil's companions in a confusion of delight, Ahren suddenly feeling himself transported back to the Hall of Hearts when Khara, Uldini and himself had illicitly gained access to the sanctuary of the dwarfs with the intention of giving the Thousand Halls she-dwarfs a renewed voice. Taninil's redheaded companion was clearly heavily pregnant, which didn't prevent her from joining her friends in the last line of defence before the Heart Chamber.

'We must stop meeting you with our crossbows cocked,' she said coquettishly.

Ahren pointed at the woman's round stomach and grinned. 'I see you *did* manage to wrap the Father of the Mountain around your finger as you had hoped to do.'

Her smile was answer enough. It seemed that the gods had decided to make that particular Paladin with his dwarf-like attributes even closer to the squat folk by allowing him to become the father of one.

'If you ladies wouldn't mind, we would like to pay Aluna and the others a brief visit,' said Quin-Wa in a friendly yet firm voice.

Behind her the doors were closed on the outside by the Night Soldiers, the four she-dwarfs giving way to Ahren and his friends. Before them was a large hall, which looked like a smaller version of the best protected cave in the Dwarfish kingdom. It, too, had its separate bathing chamber and a balcony high above which ran around in a circle, enclosing a considerable area with a comfortable looking resting place at its centre containing a fireplace. The air was filled with aromas wafting up from little pots filled with herbs and spices, and the chamber was dotted with elegantly carved wooden cradles and comfortable beds. The women within the room were chatting to each other in pairs or small groups, many of them pregnant, while those of them who were already young mothers looked happy but weary.

Quin-Wa pointed at a small room off the central chamber. 'If my fellow sufferers are willing to bide their time down here until the Adversary is slain, then they should at least be allowed to chat, bathe and sleep without being bothered by foolish Paladins.'

'But you are a Paladin, too!' protested Bergen, immediately raising an apologetic hand, however, on seeing Quin-Wa's icy look. 'Alright, alright,' he murmured, tugging at Ahren, the two of them retreating into the little chamber with its benches, skilfully carved out of the rock, and abundantly cushioned.

'The she-dwarfs have clearly brought their idea of a traditional Hall of Hearts with them,' chuckled Ahren, 'even if I would have liked to have met their soul companions and children.'

Bergen pursed his lips. 'They are enduring so much hardship as it is, so I cannot bring myself to complain,' he said. 'As long as they are safe, I will endure their strange rules with patience.'

'That *is* good to hear.'

Ahren turned to see who it was that had spoken from the doorway to the waiting room and beheld a small, wiry woman with a chiselled face, whose brown eyes radiated such strength that he thought she could easily be an officer leading her troops into battle. With her white toga in the Sunplains style, she didn't fit in here. Indeed, Ahren could easily imagine her wearing toughened leather, chainmail or even a full suit of armour.

'Carlai,' said Bergen with a smile, immediately standing up and embracing the woman gently.

Ahren looked away discreetly as the couple kissed each other romantically. After a dozen or so heartbeats, he loudly cleared his throat, Bergen and his soul companion chuckling in response.

'It seems that this chamber offers some visitors *more* than merely a place to wait,' said Ahren mischievously.

'He really *is* as clever as you claim him to be,' commented Carlai.

'Sometimes,' said Bergen dryly.

The soul companion stared at the blonde Paladin. 'Something is bothering you.' It was a statement, not a question, and somehow it was a relief to Ahren that Khara wasn't the only one who had the gift of *always* correctly reading the face of her beloved.

Bergen frowned. 'Can't a Paladin simply have a pleasant time with his beloved without having to…' he began, only to receive a painful clip on the ear. 'Ouch!'

'Even when you were my commander, I could tell when you were fibbing,' she scolded.

The woman's words reminded Ahren that he was looking at a member of the Blue Cohorts.

'Come on then – spit it out!'

Bergen rubbed the side of his head. 'We must decide between two courses of action, either of which might push Jorath over the edge of the abyss. And the council of war is split. Furthermore, we are running out of time.'

Carlai looked at Ahren. 'Isn't it *your* job to bring unity?' she asked angrily. 'Bergen told me that you could even talk a bear into coming out of its cave if necessary.' Her tone of voice was rough – typical, thought Ahren, of mercenaries all over Jorath.

The Forest Guardian sighed, while Bergen looked at him, shrugging his shoulders apologetically. 'I would gladly lead the council to a decision if I only knew which the right one *was,*' he muttered, his inner turmoil leading him to slam his fist on the stone bench. The resultant pain in his fingers left him in no doubt as to the foolishness of his gesture.

'Oh dear,' said Carlai. 'And yet Bergen tells me that you *always* know what is right.'

'Tell me – do you two talk about anything else apart from me?' asked Ahren irritably.

'Do *not* take out your foul mood on my beloved,' growled Bergen, suddenly resembling the bear that Ahren was supposedly going to talk out of its cave.

'If you cannot keep the peace, then be off with the pair of you!' The warning voice had sounded so breathless and shaky that Ahren did not recognise it, but when Quin-Wa and Khara led the pale and terribly emaciated looking Aluna into the little room, Ahren leapt to his feet to help her sit down. The heavily pregnant woman's stomach was so swollen that it seemed to the Forest Guardian it was about to split open.

'How…how are you?' he asked anxiously.

'I will feel considerably better once I have been told what it is that is being discussed in the council chamber,' snorted Aluna. 'So many centuries of being alive and now I am quite possibly missing the most important council of war ever held in Jorath because I gambolled right into the middle of a Bane Curse like a skittish young foal and am now down here, protecting two lives beneath my heart thanks to a rather attractive pirate.'

'*Twins?*' Ahren couldn't hide his delight, grinning broadly, the smile only vanishing when Aluna gave him an icy look.

'And it seems that both of them are fighting for my god's Blessing,' she joked, her eyes feverish. 'At least, that's what it feels like.' She bent over for a heartbeat and groaned. 'I frankly admit that I am afraid of giving birth. Jelninolan assures me that the Bane Curse has vanished, but I nevertheless feel that the two rays of sunshine inside me are going to drain me of all my strength in their efforts to see the light of day.' She groaned again. 'Why, oh why, weren't the THREE as merciful to me as they were to Sunju? She has been spared a soul companion until now.'

'I'm afraid you are under an illusion,' countered Quin-Wa cheerfully. 'Sun Shimmer told Muai that Sunju has regularly been sneaking off to meet a handsome falconer residing in Highstone.'

Aluna shook her head. 'The poor thing.' She found it impossible to resist a smile, however.

Khara nodded towards the Eternal Empress and the one-time pirate. 'Am I correct in my assumption that you two would both prefer to postpone the assault on the Obsidian Fortress?'

Ahren looked up suddenly. 'But of course,' he muttered. 'We can hardly allow you to confront the Adversary in your present condition.'

Aluna's mood having changed in an instant, she looked at the young couple calmly – indeed, she seemed almost business-like. 'What are you talking about?'

Ahren first took a deep breath, then he quickly filled Aluna and Carlai in on the latest developments.

'What a bloody mess,' remarked the mercenary.

'What do you think we should do?' asked Aluna, fixing her eyes on the Thirteenth.

Ahren threw his hands up in a gesture of frustration. 'Why does *everyone* keep asking me that?'

'Because you normally *always* have an opinion and are never afraid to express it,' countered Quin-Wa, raising an eyebrow.

'Not this time,' grumbled Ahren. 'I hope…'

A loud commotion from the door to the Heart Hall stopped him in his tracks.

'What is going on?' asked Bergen, wide-eyed, his hands reaching for his weapon.

'News from the castle gates,' announced the redhaired she-dwarf, her crossbow slung casually on her shoulder. 'A black-robed lady is asking to be admitted. She wishes to be brought to the Thirteenth.'

A shiver ran down Ahren's spine. 'I am coming,' he said quickly. 'It's best if I meet her at the gates and personally lead her through the castle.'

'And who might this visitor be?' asked Aluna cagily.

'The Woman in Black,' grunted Bergen.

The eyes of the blonde Champion of the gods nearly popped out of her head, so taken aback was she. 'Are you *serious?* Did not the last report state categorically that she is a *High Fang?*'

Quin-Wa nodded.

'But she isn't a *normal* High Fang,' countered Ahren firmly.

The Eternal Empress fixed her eyes on him. 'Let us hope so,' she muttered.

'We had better hurry,' murmured Khara, gently embracing Aluna. 'I agree with Ahren that we should get to the castle gates before all the others. I can easily imagine the First taking matters into his own hand and putting her in chains.'

Ahren flinched. It wouldn't surprise him if half the members of the council of war applauded such an act. Interesting as it might be to see how the Woman in Black would react to being taken into custody, Ahren really didn't want to know the outcome of such a move. He waved at Carlai and Aluna, then turned on his heels.

'You are leaving us already?' asked the redheaded she-dwarf.

Ahren replied with a nod, pulling one of the double doors open enough so that he could squeeze through, Khara, Quin-Wa and Bergen following him out. Getting to the castle gates seemed an eternity to the Forest Guardian, first being led through the darkness by the Night Soldiers, then carefully stepping his way between the magical runes under the curious eyes of his Ice Wolves in the second guarded room, before finally passing through the ring of Dwarfish warriors.

'Hopefully, we won't be too late,' murmured Khara, expressing precisely what her beloved was thinking.

They went out into the bailey through a side door, the Forest Guardian breathing a sigh of relief when he saw the black-robed figure standing unharmed between two of the Blue Cohorts, waiting patiently.

'You won't allow your people to do anything stupid, will you?' asked Ahren, turning to Bergen.

The blonde Paladin shook his head. 'The Blue Cohorts are under instruction to support the defence of the castle by keeping watch on the ramparts and at the entrance. *I* certainly did not tell them to hold up our visitor if that is what you are asking.'

It was clear to Ahren that Bergen had not really answered his question as he increased his pace. Out of the corner of his eye, he saw another postern in the main castle building fly open, the First together with Falagarda and Yantilla hurrying towards the main gate.

'Quin-Wa?' pleaded Ahren, glancing sideways at the Eternal Empress.

'I hope you know what you're doing,' she murmured before changing direction and confronting the new arrivals, a heated argument involving colourful invective immediately ensuing, which would have done a pair of squabbling merchants proud whose ox and carts had collided with each other.

'Let her pass!' exclaimed Ahren as soon as he was within earshot of the sentries.

The two Blue Cohorts hesitated before looking at Bergen for help.

'Do what he says, damn it!' he fumed before turning to Ahren and muttering: 'You owe me one.'

The Woman in Black paused for a heartbeat before walking under the raised portcullis. Ahren noticed that the shadow of the archway seemed to, quite literally, stick to her figure – a phenomenon that he had often seen occur to Lanlion, thereby shielding him from the sun. Was it possible that the stranger was a Bloodless? Shivering, he suppressed the thought to concentrate fully on the here and now.

'You have arrived,' he said, his voice sounding more formal than he had intended.

She bowed her head a little. 'As promised.' Then she nodded towards the furiously arguing Paladins. 'Where does my journey lead me now, Thirteenth? To the tower or the dungeon?'

Bergen narrowed his eyes. 'As if we could ever imprison you against your will.'

'Oh, but that you most certainly can,' replied the mysterious woman, Ahren trying to hide his surprise. 'I need every bit of strength that I have to prevent myself from being seen by the Adversary.' She pointed at Bergen's axe. 'One blow and my life is over.'

Ahren frowned. Was this a test? Why was the woman almost goading Bergen into attacking her?

'If you are hoping for a quick release,' said Khara from beside her beloved, 'then you are in for a disappointment. First, you must answer our questions. After that we will see.'

The Woman in Black almost imperceptibly bowed again. 'Spoken like a princess.'

Khara pointed at Quin-Wa's extended stomach. 'If the THREE are merciful, then soon I will no longer be Cochan's heir,' she said.

Ahren carefully observed the Woman in Black as she looked over at the heavily pregnant Ancient. Her sudden flinch was impossible to miss, and he even thought that he saw a tear falling behind her veil.

'Let us go to the council chamber,' said the Woman in Black, her voice little more than a whisper. 'The many charms that I can sense even in front of the castle will hide me sufficiently without my having to drain myself of my remaining energy.'

Ahren nodded curtly, then led the little group straight towards the First, Quin-Wa, Falagarda and Yantilla, all of whom were still arguing heatedly.

'What are you planning?' asked Khara in a low voice. 'I mean, we can easily avoid them.' She pointed at the postern from where they had entered the bailey.

'I am certainly *not* going to move around like a thief in the night – especially through a fortress that has been erected as a symbol of unity,' countered Ahren forcefully. 'The only thing that concerns me is that the First doesn't arbitrarily draw conclusions on his own. I would rather confront him here than before the assembled council.'

'Divide and conquer,' murmured Bergen, Ahren nodding in agreement.

'You *do* realise how stubbornly you are behaving, don't you?' thundered the First once the two groups had come together. 'Inviting the enemy into our midst.'

'Today I am not your enemy,' said the Woman in Black calmly. 'Unless you force me to be.'

Ahren rolled his eyes. 'Can we at least agree to *talk* first?' he asked.

Yantilla was clearly struggling to contain her anger, only nodding half-heartedly and turning away once Ahren had given her a stern look, leaving her in no doubt that disobeying him was out of the question.

Falagarda, however, seemed far less willing to compromise. 'Do not allow her lies to lead us into dire misfortune, Ahren,' she pleaded. 'We are not yet ready for an assault.'

'Silence!' snarled the First. 'Every word that this woman hears will eventually get back to the Adversary!'

To Ahren's horror, the Woman in Black nodded. 'A keen observation.' She pulled her robe in tighter. 'If I do not soon come into the protection of the Bane Runes, my Master will inevitably pick up on what I see and hear.'

The First made a move to reach for the weapon on his back, but Ahren placed a hand on the old man's forearm.

'We will *talk*,' said the Thirteenth firmly. 'Must I remind you of Four Claws? Engaging in a dialogue with him instead of fighting him for centuries would have saved you, him and many in Jorath from so much suffering.'

Ahren hated pouring salt into the still fresh wounds of the First, but his words had the desired effect. The veteran's face was suddenly filled with doubt as he stood there in silence. This was sufficient for the Forest Guardian to lead his group past the age-old Paladin.

When they were halfway to the council chamber, they were met by Likis, who had been hurrying towards them. He glared at the Woman in Black as if she were a Glower Bear.

'Is this *her?*' he murmured.

'It is indeed,' replied the woman, highly amused.

'Be so good as to call the council together,' said Ahren to his friend. 'The sooner we get the answers that we need, the faster we can reach a decision that hopefully won't lead to rack and ruin.'

'How dramatic,' commented the Woman in Black dryly as Likis shouted out instructions to his servants while the others continued on their way.

Ahren turned sideways to look at her.

'You do not agree with my decision, then.'

'Oh, but I do,' she replied. 'One false move and Jorath has a new god – a *single* god. And he will by no means be merciful – nor will he *ever again* lie down and go to sleep.'

A shiver ran down Ahren's spine on hearing the woman's words, but what bothered him the most was the sobriety with which she spoke – as if she didn't expect to be alive whenever the outcome of the war was decided.

'I think I heard a tone of resignation in her voice,' whispered Khara into his ear, thereby confirming his own suspicions. They would, thought the young man, have to judge everything that the mysterious woman had to say in the light of the low value she seemed to be placing on her own life.

Before Ahren had time to brood any more, they had reached the council chamber, whose doors were wide open. Only Sleeps-in-Treetop was in the room, and once Ahren had led the group in, the gaunt woman pointed at the fireplace, in which the Forest Guardian had burned the piece of wood.

'One to one,' muttered the Ancient cryptically. 'My diligence is your shield *and* your cage.'

The Woman in Black, however, seemed to understand what the shaman meant, walking straight over to the fireplace. Immediately, two complicated circles began to glimmer, one on the floor around her, the other on the ceiling, each of them containing dozens of sorcerous runes and with a diameter of a good three paces.

'Impressive,' said the Woman in Black. 'She has investigated the magic in the burnt log to discover how best to supress my power.'

'Your strength is like water from a poisoned well,' countered Sleeps-in-Treetop sharply. 'You would be a better person without it.'

The Woman in Black snorted but showed no other reaction.

Ahren sat down near the new Charm Circle so that he could lend the stranger some support if the mood in the council chamber were to become hostile. Khara, clearly understanding his motivation, sat down beside him.

Slowly but surely, all the council members came into the room, Ahren's closest friends following his example by placing themselves in the vicinity of the Woman in Black, who was standing there in silence. The more the room filled, the greater the atmosphere of mistrust seemed to grow. Hardly had the last person – Likis – entered the room when the double doors were slammed shut and Sleeps-in-Treetop fell, once more, into a trance, thereby magically sealing the large chamber. Ahren immediately got to his feet, thereby seizing the initiative.

'This woman has come here of her own free will and just as willingly placed herself in a ring of Spells. She is ready to answer our questions. In view of the fact that *I* deliberately invited her and am grateful to her for saving *my* life on more than one occasion, I expect everyone here to show her, at the very least, a modicum of respect.'

'Let's get this over with,' growled the First. 'As soon as she has spewed out her "truths", we can have her removed from the chamber again.'

Ahren glared at the veteran. 'Let us *please* listen to what she has to say first before making any judgements – *understood!?*' he barked. He was just on the point of asking his first question of the stranger when the chamber doors opened again, and Culhen trotted haughtily in.

I have been selected to be the eyes and ears of the companion animals, announced the wolf as he sauntered in an exaggeratedly serene manner towards Ahren. The wolf's voice sounded strangely hollow in the young man's head. *As we are all connected to Sun Shimmer, the others are unable to hear their Paladins.*

Ahren affectionately tickled Culhen under his chin. He suddenly realised how much he had missed his friend. *And how is it then that we can talk to each other?*

Because both Sun Shimmer and I are concentrating really hard. Imagine that you are standing in a doorway between two rooms. Sun Shimmer is in one chamber, and your mind is in another.

'Camentumar sends greetings,' said the Woman in Black to the wolf in a low voice. 'He had no desire to yield to the authority of a city, never mind a castle, and is wandering around in the hinterland.'

Culhen lowered his head respectfully to the stranger before sitting down on the floor, close to Ahren. *The way I see it, you have once again provoked the majority of your allies to turn against you,* said the wolf, his tongue lolling. *This is what happens when I let you out of my sight for even one day.*

Can we just leave it, please? muttered the young man miserably. *This situation is going to be difficult enough to manage without your sarcastic comments.*

'Why is Culhen here?' asked Falk, his question earning murmurs of approval. 'And where are *our* animals?'

'They are attending a meeting with Sun Shimmer,' explained Ahren. 'Culhen is their representative, so to speak.' He was half expecting objections, but the other Paladins proved mature enough to accept the situation.

The First got to his feet, and Ahren cursed inwardly. Culhen's appearance having distracted him momentarily, he had now lost the initiative and would no longer be able to steer the council of war from the beginning.

'Given that the Thirteenth has summoned this servant of the Adversary without consultation, I propose that we vote on whether she has the right to speak here or not.'

The veteran had spoken through gritted teeth, his features unyielding. Ahren was convinced that he was now paying the price for having wounded the age-old Paladin by having referred to Four Claws.

'I vote that she answer our questions and gives us as much information as she can,' said Ahren, raising a hand. Those beside him quickly followed his example, as did nearly all the Paladins – only the First voting the other way. He was joined by Kamkanzakur, Falagarda and Yantilla, the age-old Paladin clearly having all the military decision-makers on his side.

'Aluna being unable to attend, I shall speak on her behalf,' announced Quin-Wa. She peered long and hard at Ahren before adding: 'We both support the proposal of the Thirteenth.'

The First waved his hand dismissively before pointing angrily at the Woman in Black, who was still standing quietly in the Charm Circle. 'Then speak!'

'What do you want to know?'

Ahren looked at the stranger. 'You drew my attention to Belsarius' Sanctum,' he said. 'Is the Adversary aware of what the Ancient discovered through his research and does he know of his theory?'

The Woman in Black shrugged her shoulders. 'Perhaps. What *is* his theory?'

'A trick!' snarled the First. 'She is *spying* on us – no more than that!'

Ahren sighed. They would make no progress if this continued. Trust needed to be developed in some way. 'Why don't we begin by you telling us who you *really* are?'

'You mean, *what* she is!' interjected Falagarda witheringly.

'Alas,' murmured the Woman in Black, her eyes fixed on Ahren, her voice taking on a tone of earnest confidentiality. 'Perhaps you *are* right. From the moment I looked away from the Adversary, there has been no more going back for me anyway. Once He has enough time, He will be able to read my mind and discover where I have been today and with whom I have spoken. And, His suspicions having been thereby aroused, He will take apart my mind – bit by bit – and discover in the recesses of my memory how I have helped you all.'

The fatalism in the woman's voice was so unmistakeable that Ahren had no choice but to believe her. It was no wonder that the stranger seemed so disconnected from existential concerns. By stepping into Highstone, and more particularly, by appearing at the council of war, she most definitely had signed her own death warrant.

'Why don't you take off your veil – as a simple gesture of trust,' murmured Ahren gently.

The Woman in Black chuckled joylessly. 'If that is *all* you want,' she said in a voice that suggested that Ahren had requested that she strangle the Adversary with her bare hands.

She turned away from him and the assembled council of war, so that she was now facing the crackling fire.

'I am no High Fang,' she said.

Then she raised her arms, so slowly and shakily that it seemed as though there were millstones weighing them down.

'Nor am I a Doppler.'

Inch by inch, her fingers neared the material in front of her face,

'I am merely a soul who strayed into the machinations of the Adversary…'

Suddenly, she grasped the material, and it seemed to Ahren as if she had not only grasped her veil but her entire *self*.

'…a soul who found nowhere to shelter but in the company of her torturer.'

Another tug, which caused the Woman in Black to flinch as she ripped off the flimsy cloth that had hidden her identity for countless years.

'I am no more than a human who loved.'

Weak fingers propelled the torn veil into the fire. A short crackling sound, a feeble burst of flame and then nothing was left of the filigree protection that had covered the face of the Woman in Black for so long. She turned around.

Ahren saw pale skin, sunken eyes, a narrow nose, and thin lips tightly pressed together. This woman had certainly once been beautiful yet seemed to have long since forgotten that this had been the case.

'*You!*' snarled Falk.

'*Traitress!*' hissed Sunju.

'*Seize her!*' screamed Fisker.

'*Kill her!*' commanded the First, his voice hard as naked steel.

The sudden growling from behind Ahren's back as well as Khara's cry of warning alerted the Forest Guardian.

'*AHREN!*'

The Thirteenth spun around, his reflexes alone compelling him to draw his Wind Blade and drive it against Falk's sword, which the older Paladin, now racing past his protégé, was attempting to swing wildly at the head of the Woman in Black.

The sharp sound of steel on steel echoed through the chamber, Ahren's arm aching agonisingly from the impact. Falk had aimed his stroke with all his strength, his crazed eyes showing not a trace of mercy or rational understanding. The features on his mentor's face resembled that of a Wrath Demon lost in a surging sea of furious emotions which seemed to have overwhelmed every part of what distinguished Falk's personality.

'Culhen!' yelled Ahren in desperation, rousing the wolf out of his shocked paralysis.

The animal leapt up and barged, growling into the other Paladins that were trying to join Falk in his madness.

Beside Ahren, Khara's blades slipped out of their scabbards, the Swordsmistress then beginning an elaborate circular blade dance, using her weapons to create a defensive cocoon of steel around the Woman in Black, who still stood there in silence.

'*Cochan!*' she called out to Quin-Wa. '*Cochan* – what in the name of the THREE is *happening* here?'

The Eternal Empress, no less paralysed than Lanlion, had not joined in the assault of the Paladins on the stranger, but her eyes resembled crystals of ice as they bored relentlessly into those of the Woman in Black.

'You have no ordinary servant of the Adversary standing before you,' she said in a loud voice that could just about be heard above the skirmish involving Culhen, the First and Bergen, not to mention the snorting and gasping of Ahren and Falk, both of whom were trying to push the other out of the way with the hilts of their weapons. Even Uldini and Jelninolan were arguing with each other in a heated exchange, the eyes of the Arch Wizard glaring with rage, while those of the elf reflected the sorrow that she was feeling. Akkad reacted to Ahren's pleading look with a slow shake of his head while Kamkanzakur, Falagarda and Yantilla observed the unfolding chaos before them in bewilderment. Lyssin and Hakanu, on the other hand, followed Ahren's example, shielding the Woman in Black from the furious Paladins with defensive swings of their weapons.

'Out of the way!' growled Falk furiously. 'You have no idea who she *really* is!'

'Then *tell* me!' roared Ahren, rage fermenting inside him like a volcano about to erupt after centuries of dormancy. Falk's eyes glanced over at the stranger that Ahren was protecting with all his might. 'This…*woman! She* is the cause of all the woes that have assailed us Paladins for centuries on end! *She* is the one who thrust the dagger of the Thirteenth into his own chest!'

Ahren blinked in surprise at Falk. Then he lowered his weapon, stunned.

The old Paladin, another wave of fury taking hold of him, snarled through gritted teeth: 'Don't you *understand?* The Woman in Black – her name is *Lirana!*'

Chapter 13

Lirana.

The name that had been erased from the Jorathian vocabulary centuries previously. The name that like no other stood for treachery and weakness of character. The name whose utterance had ever since been strictly forbidden.

Until now.

Taking advantage of Ahren's momentary paralysis, Falk shoved him aside as the old man raised his blade. Immediately, the younger Forest Guardian threw himself at his erstwhile master, the two of them crashing to the floor in a confusion of arms and legs.

'Let...go...of...me!' groaned Falk, trying to free himself from his former protégé.

'Hakanu! Lyssin!' grunted Ahren through gritted teeth. 'Help me stop this *madness!*'

The two young Paladins, who, like him, were untouched by the centuries of resentment that afflicted their fellow Champions of the gods, leapt to Culhen's assistance, immediately doing their level best to stop their brothers and sisters in their furious attack, the skirmish ebbing and flowing in what amounted to a temporary stalemate before the stoically standing Woman in Black.

Lirana, thought Ahren, flabbergasted. *This woman is really the legendary Lirana.*

I have an idea, interjected Culhen, knocking over the knife wielding Fisker before the blonde Paladin had the chance to drive his weapon forward.

A heartbeat later, those Paladins possessed with fury suddenly staggered violently, with only the First remaining unperturbed and unbowed.

'Selsena...' groaned Falk, cocking his head, while Sunju, Fisker and Bergen, too, murmured the names of their companion animals.

Sun Shimmer has broken off her connection to us, explained Culhen smugly. *At this very moment, the unruly Paladins here are being castigated in no uncertain terms.*

Quickly getting to his feet, Ahren positioned himself before Lirana, his Wind Blade pointing forward in a low, defensive position.

'Stop this *madness!*' he shouted, glaring at the First, who was intent on fighting his way past Culhen.

'*Never!*' snarled the age-old Paladin, spitting out the word. 'She got away from us during the Night of Blood and was never seen again. We all took a vow that we would make her pay for her heinous crime!'

Ahren heard a snort of bitterness from behind. 'As if I have not paid a hundred times over for what the Dark god made me do.'

The First was about to make another effort at shoving his way past Culhen when Ahren exploded with rage, abandoning any inhibitions he might have felt.

'THAT'S ENOUGH!' he yelled, the ferocity in his voice causing his own ears to ring, and the guards outside to push the doors open in horror.

Ahren pointed at the unfortunate sentries before screaming: 'CLOSE THOSE DOORS!' In the blink of an eye, the council members were left alone again.

'WE ARE PALADINS!' he bellowed furiously. 'NOT *MURDERERS!*'

Falk retreated a step from his erstwhile apprentice and sheathed his weapon. 'You are right – *we* are not murderers. But *she* is.'

'I see,' murmured the Woman in Black – *Lirana*. 'So, all those rumours that I heard were untrue – that Aluna and Fisker spent years as pirates on the Cutlass Sea, creating bloody havoc? Or that the Blue Cohorts hired themselves out to bored nobility, involving themselves in conflicts which led to countless deaths on either side for the sake of a quick profit? Or that the Father of the Mountain was at one time a bloodthirsty lunatic, whose allies were more terrified of him than his enemies?'

'Those are all false comparisons,' muttered the First.

Ahren could see how the old man's heavy sword was slowly sinking to the floor.

'Dead is dead,' countered Lirana, her heartless reply echoing around the chamber. 'I suspect that the friends and families of those countless victims would see things *exactly* as I do.' She pointed at Ahren and the First. 'Indeed, Hjalgar would have been razed to the ground were it not for the intervention of a certain *greenhorn* – or am I mistaken?' She was almost whispering now. 'Who knows – maybe I, too, could have resisted the promises made if someone like Ahren had been around in those days.'

'No, you wouldn't have,' said Jelninolan in a low voice. 'Not if what we were told really happened.'

Lirana laughed. Ahren had never in his life heard such a despairing sound.

'And how could you *possibly* know what happened at that time? After all, you all wanted to kill me without giving me a chance of uttering a single sensible sentence.'

'You were spewing nonsense,' countered Lanlion. 'You were raving something about having to save your child. That the death of the Thirteenth had been your only option.'

Ahren beckoned Culhen over to him, the two along with Khara, Hakanu, Lyssin and finally Trogadon, forming a protective wall around the Woman in Black. The Forest Guardian positioned himself so that he could see everyone, silently vowing not to attack for as long as the parleying continued – no matter how poisonous the atmosphere on both sides was. He did not want to experience a second time the chaos that had taken hold of the room.

'Do you even *know* what it is like to have the Dark god take possession of your mind? To sense Him *bending* your thoughts until the merest whisper on His part is all that is necessary for you to hear and believe.' She shook her head slowly. 'No, you *can't* know. Because you are all protected by your precious gods' Blessing.'

Ahren raised his hand. 'I know full well what it feels like,' he countered. 'Before my Naming, the Adversary formed a special relationship with me, my gods' Blessing not yet having become a part of me.'

A flicker of compassion sparkled in Lirana's eyes. 'And?' she murmured., 'Were *you* able to resist Him?'

Ahren remembered his dreamy walk along the top beam of the *Queen of the Waves'* mainsail and his subsequent plummet into the cold, foamy waters. He shook his head. 'Her words – they make so much *sense*. He promised me that I would save all Jorath, that a truce between Himself and the Paladins would spare countless lives...' His eyes were filled with pity as he looked at Lirana. 'Was it...like that...for *you?*'

She nodded, and for a precious heartbeat his world was reduced only to the wife of the deceased Thirteenth and himself. 'He told me that...if I...if I stabbed, then our child would live...that the Blessing of the dead Thirteenth would pass over to...to our Valhan,' she stammered, Ahren seeing clearly that she was doing her best to hold back her tears. 'He said He only wanted to buy time…the time it would take for a growing boy to become a Paladin himself…He wanted to *flee*…He wanted to *live*…' her voice had cracked now, '…He wanted to get the Paladins to call a halt to this endless war.'

'The perpetrator paints herself as the victim,' snorted the First scornfully. 'And *you* believe her!'

Ahren felt overwhelming pity for this woman who had lost not only her beloved and her child in the Night of Blood but also her home, her identity and her *humanity*. He couldn't imagine how long it must have taken her to force herself from being a broken servant of the Adversary to becoming this woman standing courageously before him despite knowing full well that she was an outcast from all society, while at the same time being completely under the thumb of Him who had been the cause of all the horrors that had befallen her.

'*I* understand you,' he said in a firm voice as he looked deep into her eyes. 'And I cannot apportion blame to you for your actions. The Adversary alone is responsible for the Night of Blood. Not you.'

Covering her mouth with her hand in an expression of disbelief, it seemed for a heartbeat as if all life had seeped away from her – as though the judgement that Ahren had passed had released the curse that had kept her alive for all those years. She collapsed onto the floor and wept, and Ahren turned to face the scornful looks of his brothers and sisters.

'You have no right to declare her innocent,' fumed Bergen. 'You weren't *there.*'

'But I experienced something similar to what happened to her,' countered the Forest Guardian, jutting out his chin. 'And, like her, I failed to prevent the Adversary from entering *my* mind. Am I His servant too? Must *my* name also be erased from the Jorathian annals as Lirana's has been?'

'You never murdered a Paladin,' muttered the First.

Ahren waved his arm angrily. 'But I *almost* did,' he snarled. 'I leaped into the churning seas. I *almost* killed a Paladin – namely, the Thirteenth – *me!*'

'But all the sorrow that her deed unleashed…' murmured Sunju.

Again, Ahren raised a hand, stopping the words that already knew without hearing them. 'Lirana did not slay *your* children.'

The Paladins flinched at his uncompromising words.

'Her weakness caused the death of only *one* person – if I can believe the scanty enough details that you all relayed to me concerning that terrible night. It was the henchmen and assassins of the Dark god that performed the bloody deeds that broke *your* will.' He pointed down at Lirana, who was now sobbing uncontrollably and indisputably racked with grief. 'She only took the Thirteenth from you – rendering you all incapable of instant revenge.'

'It was *peace* that she took away,' countered Lanlion. 'She took from us any chance of lasting peace. And of our being able to carry out our task.'

'That she did *not*,' said Jelninolan, moving in beside Ahren and before Lirana.

Ahren wished that he could give her an appreciative hug.

'If what we all believe is true, then the failure of the Paladins was a foregone conclusion – thanks to the cunning of the Dark god, who made us all believe that we were on the point of achieving the goal that we had been striving for – namely, to bring about an enduring peace throughout Jorath.'

Lirana looked up at the elf in surprise, her shimmering eyes refracting her spiritual brokenness. 'What do you mean, Jelninolan?'

'As if you didn't *know*,' snarled the First. 'It was *you* who made Ahren aware of this *so-called* secret, which has led to this climax in your second-rate, *hammy* performance.'

The Woman in Black slowly got to her feet. Then she gazed at the First for several heartbeats, seeming to think carefully about what she would say. 'I do not know of this secret that you speak of,' she murmured. 'Even if I spent a long, long time trying to discover it, my…master…having ordered me to destroy it.'

Ahren was all ears now. So, the Woman in Black had neither accidentally nor of her own free will stumbled across Belsarius' Sanctum? Why, then, had she lied to him?

'I am only a simple warrior,' said Kamkanzakur, 'and my stomach is turning at the fact that this woman refers to the Adversary as her master.' He pointed at Lirana. 'But may the THREE strike me dead on the spot if she isn't telling the absolute truth at the moment.'

'I agree,' added Likis. 'Think about what we know concerning the latest deeds that this woman you all call Lirana has carried out. She may well have murdered the Thirteenth, but *this* Thirteenth here…' he pointed at Ahren, '…she has saved *his* life on more than one occasion.'

'One good deed does not wipe out a bad one,' fumed the First.

'Please don't say that!' interjected Fisker, turning to look at the others. 'Aluna and I have done enough questionable deeds in our lives to earnestly pray for atonement.'

'The same applies to many of us,' said Falk in a low voice. Maybe we *did* condemn Lirana somewhat too hastily. Over the past centuries, we have all learned through our own actions how easy it to is to cause suffering to others when one's heart has been broken and one's judgement has become impaired.'

Ahren sensed the first cracks in the wall of hatred surrounding the Woman in Black, the young man throwing himself at this chink of hope like a certain greedy wolf would upon being presented with a juicy leg of lamb. Culhen immediately began to drool at his friend's analogy.

'Tell us about your life,' he said to Lirana. 'What happened to you *after* the Night of Blood?' He knew he was taking a considerable risk, but if the woman's tale of woe affected the Paladins positively, then he could at last steer the council of war back to becoming a productive meeting.

'I fled,' said the Woman in Black, her voice now devoid of all emotion. 'Fled from my deed, fled from the Paladins who wanted my head on a pike, fled from the images flooding my mind.' She struggled to clear her throat and pointed at a chair, Ahren pushed it into the Charm Circle that still surrounded Lirana, the woman then sitting gratefully on the well-upholstered seat. 'What I did *not* understand in my despair and madness was that I was not only running *away* from things – I was also running *towards* something.'

'The Adversary,' said Quin-Wa without hesitation.

Lirana nodded. 'Even before the sun began to rise, I was standing before Him. He mocked me for my sorrow, and He sneered at me for His having found it so easy to dispatch one of the Champions of the gods through my intercession.' She was clenching her fist so hard now that Ahren could see blood seeping out from between her fingers, her nails digging into her palms. 'In an effort to kill Him, I threw myself at Him, so great was my pain and despair. He laughed, picked me up off the ground as a child might pluck a daisy on a meadow, and said to me: "JUST AS IT IS IMPOSSIBLE FOR ME TO DIE AT YOUR HAND,

SO YOU SHALL NOT FIND DEATH THROUGH ANY OTHER HAND BUT MINE." Then He tossed me aside – as if I were an apple that He had bitten into – only to have found a worm within it.'

'Sounds like a Bane Curse,' murmured Uldini, who seemed to have recovered enough to make a meaningful contribution.

Lirana nodded. 'I soon learned that neither hunger nor thirst nor even wild animals could harm me. My body…survived…no matter how maltreated it was. For the first few years, I sought an escape from my torture. Poison, blades – there were few means that I did not try.'

'You should have come to *us*,' growled the First, raising his sword. 'Using our gods' Blessings, we would surely have cut through your Bane Curse.'

Lirana ignored his provocation. 'The Adversary would never have allowed it. Time and again, I would seek Him out in the Pall Pillar. I would plead with Him, curse Him, do *anything* in the hope that He would use His power against me. Instead, He bound me with every visit closer to His sleeping will.' She frowned. 'In the first years after His defeat, His resting mind seemed strangely…contented – despite His imprisonment. This mood gradually changed – He became like a chained dog that was never fed. Over the centuries, His vengeful streak and fundamentally evil nature grew evermore powerful – as did His fear of a possible reappearance of the Thirteenth Paladin.'

Ahren exchanged a knowing look with Khara, his beloved nodding almost imperceptibly. Lirana had given the first hint that the Adversary's trap really existed – the trap which had finally culminated in the Night of Blood and the death of the Thirteenth.

'He began giving me tasks to perform, and it didn't take me long to realise that I *had* to carry out His wishes. It was as if I was on an invisible leash, being dragged from one job to the next.' She wrang her bloody hands. 'I did what He commanded. Slowly, I began to put up less and less resistance.'

The First snorted angrily, but she kept on talking – as if her words were an avalanche, which having started to roll, was now unstoppable.

'I noticed that my submissive behaviour bought me a certain amount of freedom – it was as if the Adversary lost interest in me because I didn't fight back. Finally, I had years to myself during which time He didn't even bother looking for me mentally. It was then that I began to build a second life for myself.' She fixed her eyes on Ahren. 'A life in which I did my level best to regain some sort of personal power.'

The Forest Guardian nodded understandingly. 'The Woman in Black was born.'

'But how did you acquire all the magical skills that Ahren saw you perform?' asked Uldini, perplexed. 'After all, you didn't have any sorcerous gifts when you fled during the Night of Blood.'

'There is no doubt but that those powers are the dark gifts of her master,' grunted the First. The age-old Paladin's disdain for the others' interest in her story was clearly audible.

Lirana shook her head. 'Dark Ones do not touch me, and my body neither ages nor will die. Those are the gifts that the Adversary gave me. In His eyes I am a gruesome trophy and a useful but otherwise average spy, who was His eyes and ears during His imprisonment within the Pall Pillar. Most of my power comes from other, *no less dark* sources.'

'Oh, Lirana,' murmured Jelninolan. 'Whatever *have* you done?'

The woman raised her head proudly. 'I did what was *necessary* – that which was necessary for me to able to save Ahren, Culhen and Onja.'

A shiver ran down Falk's spine on hearing his beloved's name mentioned. The old man was unable to look at Lirana.

'Could you be a *little* more precise, please?' snarled Uldini. 'How could you have become powerful enough to successfully take on the Hunter on the bridge in Thousand Halls?'

Lirana tugged the collar of her black robe, revealing a little of her pale skin upon which tiny, spidery scars could be seen, which were instantly recognised by Ahren.

'*Blood Magic*,' he murmured, his eyes narrowing.

The Woman in Black nodded. 'There are rituals that come from the beginning of the very time when magic began to seep into the world. Crude, brutal forms of Blood Magic, whose sorcery only one out of a hundred casters would survive.'

'But survival was not a problem for *you,*' murmured Lanlion.

Again, Lirana nodded. 'Nine times I successfully cast a Blood Circle on my skin. Nine times I should have perished but didn't. And each time, a little of the magic that had streamed through me during the primitive ritual *remained.*'

Jelninolan looked thoroughly miserable, her face a mixture of horror and disgust. 'You are like a metamorphic wound in the flesh of Creation.'

'I have been called worse,' said the Woman in black, smiling wanly and shrugging her shoulders. 'And, anyway, I had already *been* cursed – from the very moment that the Adversary dug His claws into my reason. Everything that I did from then on was an attempt to regain control of a part of my life.' Again, she raised her head proudly. 'And it *worked.* I learned how to hide miniscule parts of my mind from my Master whenever He didn't pay complete attention to me. I made sure not to attract His attention, serving Him so loyally that He no longer considered me His prisoner but rather a true follower – a child's toy that He had smashed into pieces only to put me back together again in the shape that He wanted.'

'Which is nearer the truth then you are willing to admit,' said Lanlion in a low voice. 'You dance with the night to escape from the darkness.'

Lirana deliberately ignored the Bloodless. 'My power grew – as did my freedom. Finally, the Adversary sensed the appearance of the new Thirteenth, and my plan began to unfold. He sent me forth to destroy Belsarius' Sanctum.' She gave Ahren an apologetic look. 'I did all in my power to delay carrying out my task, thankfully failing when it came to the defensive spells of the deceased Ancient.' She cleared her throat. 'In the past few years, I alternated between seeking out Ahren on the one hand and helping him to the best of my abilities, while on the other hand, I would tinker about in the valley where the Sanctum was, setting up defensive strategies that seemed plausible to Him who was commanding me.

'The Wrath Demons,' muttered Falk through gritted teeth. 'They were *your* work, weren't they?'

Lirana nodded. 'Among other things.'

'The landslide?'

'The Adversary was responsible for the first, considerably older one, but yes – I *was* behind the second one, many moons ago,' she admitted. 'It was vital I ensured that the entrance to the Sanctum remained hidden.'

Ahren narrowed his eyes. 'The Wrath Demons almost *killed* us.'

Lirana nodded towards Jelninolan. 'Why do you think I decided on giants possessed by Wrath Winds? I was certain that a certain Storm Weaver would be able to charm the Original Beings.'

The First sighed loudly. 'She even *admits* to putting you into danger,' he grunted. 'Why are we even listening to her?'

The Woman in Black remained unaffected by the old man's barb. 'The Adversary loves grand gestures. Giants that are possessed, collapsing mountains – such things give Him great pleasure. They distracted Him, which gave me the room that I needed.'

Ahren asked himself how many of the things she had related to him were true and how many were cunning lies, enabling her to carry out her double-cross.

Does it matter? asked Culhen, glancing sideways at Ahren. His yellow eyes looked remarkably relaxed. *She did what she had to so that she could help us now. The clever Alpha doesn't care why the snowstorm gives him cover. All that interests him is making use of it.*

Where is your pragmatic approach whenever you're hungry or want to be groomed?

Culhen yawned expansively. *There are limits, Ahren.*

The Forest Guardian looked at the black-robed woman expectantly, but she shrugged her shoulders. 'There is no more to be told. I made my choice and now I am here – to help you for the last time.' She turned her face to the assembled council of war. 'If you let me.'

'No easy decision,' growled Kamkanzakur. 'And if Belsarius was right, then it is one that we must take quickly.'

On hearing those words, Lirana's eyes flickered momentarily. Ahren could see that she was unused to uncertainty. As a first-class spy, gaining information was the very foundation of her own survival.

As is her ability to deceive, the young man's conscience added.

Suppressing his own doubt, he turned to Sleeps-in-Treetop. 'How long can you maintain the Charm Circle around Lirana?'

'For more days than we have at our disposal.'

Ahren shuddered.

'What are you thinking?' whispered Khara.

'Do you promise to remain within this sorcerous circle until we release you?' he asked Lirana instead of answering his beloved.

'If the council so wishes,' she said, smiling wanly. 'But please bring me a bed and a chamber pot at least or no-one will want to hold a meeting *here* tomorrow.'

Trogadon chuckled. 'I *like* her.'

Jelninolan's icy stare stopped him in his tracks, however.

Smiling at the blacksmith, Ahren then addressed the council of war. 'Now is the time for you to ask Lirana whatever questions you may have – even if it means us having to let her in on the secret of Belsarius.'

'Do we *really* have to do that?' asked Akkad. 'I, for my part, already understand – from having listened to her story – that the Adversary also believes what Belsarius was so certain of.'

Ahren nodded. 'But does He know that *we* know?'

'I'm getting a headache,' complained Hakanu. 'Who knows what and why?'

'I *have* a headache already,' added Lyssin. 'So much talk! I really *do* miss the silence of the Eternal Ice.'

The two young Paladins grinned at each other.

The heavy silence that ensued was finally broken by Khara. 'Palnah can help,' she said. 'I know that she is already staying in Highstone – on account of her being with child. Her power should be able to recognise Lirana's true nature.'

The Woman in Black suddenly spun around within the Charm Circle, Ahren fearing for a heartbeat that she was about to flee. Then she stiffened and stood still.

'Do what you must,' she said coolly.

The First dispatched a servant, and it wasn't long before the double doors of the council chamber opened again, the woman entering who for so long had used her long hair as a veil between herself and the world. Now her features seemed quietly determined as she clasped her hands below her extended stomach, her face radiating the calmness and nobility of an expectant mother.

As she approached, nothing could be heard but the sound of her footsteps, her eyes fixed firmly on the Woman in Black. She stopped directly outside the Charm Circle and looked the other woman up and down.

It almost seemed to Ahren as if he was observing two sisters, who had found each other after a long, long time, both fearful of saying anything in greeting. Palnah and Lirana *recognised* one another – but in a manner that the Forest Guardian simply could not comprehend. The fingers of the women touched fleetingly. Then they both dropped their arms by their sides.

'You *must* believe her,' said the Brajah, breaking the silence.

Ahren breathed a sigh of relief. 'We *can* trust her, then?'

Palnah looked at him, slowly shaking her head. 'That is not what I said.'

'Well, *this* is helpful,' grunted the First sarcastically.

'I recognise the true core of a person,' countered Palnah sternly. 'This does not make me into a clairvoyant.' She turned to the assembled council. 'This woman is made up purely of pain and willpower. Both have led her here. But one of the two may weaken through you. *You* decide which half will survive. Believe her – or break her in two with your scepticism.' Then she walked out of the chamber, her shoulders slumped, and her long hair hiding her bowed head.

Khara, her arms folded and her chin pointing determinedly, looked at the others. 'You all heard Palnah. We must believe Lirana.'

'That is *not* how she put it,' growled the First.

'This is all getting ridiculous,' muttered Fisker, turning to Lirana. 'Does the Adversary know that we have found out —'

'Fisker, *NO!*' yelled the First.

'— that His power peters out every thirteen hundred years or so only to return full-force with one blow?'

Falagarda, Kamkanzakur and Yantilla all groaned simultaneously, the First glaring at Fisker as if he wanted to strangle him there and then.

'What did you say?' whispered the black-robed woman. 'His power…*wanes?*'

'A little more with every day that passes,' declared Trogadon loudly, winking at Fisker as he spoke. 'And you're *right* – this verbal game of cat-and-mouse has been going on for far too long.'

'Foolhardy dwarf!' scolded Uldini.

Trogadon pointed at Lirana, who seemed to be murmuring quietly to herself as she recovered from the shock. It was clear to Ahren that this mistress of machinating was now drawing her own conclusions regarding the events of the previous centuries.

'Do you *see* her hopping out of the Charm Circle and scampering away to tell her Lord and Master?' countered the blacksmith sharply. 'We've been looking that damned gift-horse too long in the mouth!'

'But…' stammered Lirana, '…the Night of Blood…the encirclement of the Adversary?' She looked pleadingly at Ahren in the hope of his offering her some words of comfort, at least.

Seldom had the Forest Guardian taken on a task with such willingness. 'We believe that it was a trap for the Paladins. the Dark god made all Jorath believe that His back was against the wall.' Ahren swallowed hard before continuing. 'Then He attacked with all the power He could muster – and slammed full force into your unprotected spirit.'

Again, Lirana sank to the floor, but this time, instead of sobbing quietly, she keened, so loudly and penetratingly that Ahren believed the very stones of the council chamber would weep. A tidal wave of grief and inexpressible loss assailed the ears of all those present, Ahren feeling the tears rolling down his own cheeks in pity.

Lirana wept for her Paladin.

She wept for her murdered child.

She wept for her life before the Adversary which she remembered so clearly in her mind's eye.

She wept at the fact that her own fate had led her inexorably into darkness.

Ahren looked at the faces of his friends, of his companions and of the other council members. Nowhere did he see mistrust in their tear-filled eyes, only overwhelming compassion and understanding for the lament, which Lirana was wailing into the world after so many years of silent pain. Even the First was gazing into the fire, a melancholy look on his face as he slowly turned the handle of his sword. It was as if Lirana was representing all those who suffered from having lost their loved ones in this senseless strife.

The members of the Jorathian council of war stood there for a long time – only when the setting sun kissed the horizon did the sobbing and wailing of Lirana give way to a silence that was nothing short of deafening.

The cold, winter wind whistled past Ahren's ears, blowing away the last echoes of the wailing sorrow that he had been witness to.

The council chamber lay almost deserted below, only the exhausted Lirana – now fast asleep on the bed that had hurriedly been placed in the Charm Circle – and Sleeps-in-Treetop remaining, the Ancient ensuring the continued functioning of the protective charm that surrounded the sorrowful woman, the remaining council members having long since streamed out of the room to go in search of their own private sphere. Ahren had chosen to go up the spiral staircase, and he was now standing on the battlements of the eastern tower, one hand on the nape of Culhen's neck, the other resting on one of the cold, stone crenels. A Night Soldier stood guard in the shadow of the stairwell, Ahren feeling the sentry's eyes piercing into the back of his head like two pinpricks. The Thirteenth looked up at the starry sky. Broken cloud scurried across the firmament, reminding him of the Woman in Black's shredded veil that had hidden the terrible sorrow for so long.

'I do not think anyone in the castle was reckoning on this turn of events.'

Ahren could only smile at the almost stilted voice. 'Did Khara send you up to keep an eye on me?'

Lanlion stepped beside the Forest Guardian. His pale fingers looked like alien beings as he laid them on the dark stone. 'She has descended to the Heart Hall with Quin-Wa. Aluna and the soul companions have a right to be informed of everything that was discussed and revealed today.'

Ahren nodded. 'I wonder what Lirana thinks of the fact that deep below the ground, a new generation of Paladins are lying in cradles or soon to be born? And how does she *feel* about it?'

'These are difficult times for us all,' murmured Lanlion, staring into the night. 'What a wonderful view.'

'For your eyes, perhaps,' chuckled Ahren. 'I can see only a tenth of what you can in this darkness.'

Lanlion reached for the Forest Guardian's face, the latter waving his arm dismissively, however. 'Leave it be. I don't need that sort of vision for now. You'd be better off preserving your strength.' He hesitated, staring silently at the Bloodless for several heartbeats as he pondered over the question that he had wanted to put to his fellow Paladin for some time now.

'Spit it out,' said Lanlion, who hadn't failed to notice his friend's puzzlement. The smile of the Bloodless was, even with the presence of his long canines, nothing short of disarming.

'What happened to you during your…pilgrimage?' He paused, Lanlion giving him an encouraging look. 'What *exactly* occurred on your travels? What *changed* inside you?'

The Bloodless shrugged his shoulders. 'I have already told you – I was reminded that I am more than an accursed being.' He pointed downwards. 'Just as Lirana is more than a servant of the Adversary. The gods revealed to me that I am not to equate my *condition* with my *deeds*.' He moved his hand moved back and forth between himself and the

Forest Guardian. 'A bowman is responsible for using his weapon responsibly. Just because my powers are more...*exotic*, does not mean that I am exempt from the code of conduct applicable to all beings who have the power to take or *protect* lives.'

Ahren smiled at Lanlion. 'It almost sounds as if you have achieved a sense of inner peace.'

The Bloodless reciprocated the friendly gesture. 'What is it that Falk always says? It's a start.'

The two chuckled, Ahren sensing his melancholia, which had been weighing him down since he had ascended to the top of the tower, lifting ever so slightly.

I have been instructed to report that the council of war is resuming, muttered Culhen with a snort. *I'm really not so sure if I like the fact that we companion animals have suddenly been lumbered with the responsibility of being messenger boys and girls.*

Lanlion sighed. 'Haminul says that our pause for breath is at an end. And he is complaining unmercifully about his new responsibilities.'

Ahren pointed at Culhen and rolled his eyes.

I saw that, grumbled the wolf.

Leaving the cold night air behind them, the trio descended the staircase, Ahren realising with a shudder that he would, all in all, much rather keep watch on the battlements than take part again in their discussions on how to approach the battle with the Adversary.

The crackling from the fire was the dominant sound in the chamber even though the entire council of war and the scribes were in attendance. Also audible was the sound of Lirana's slow, steady breathing, signifying that the former soul companion was still asleep and that no-one was willing yet to awaken the woman, who had sobbed herself into exhaustion.

Finally, Uldini cleared his throat. 'Hear ye! Hear ye! Having all listened to the words of Palnah and Lirana, as well as the statements regarding Akkad's beliefs, the time is now upon us for the council of war to reach a decision regarding how we are to continue the endless battle against the Adversary.'

Already, the scratching of the quill nibs on the parchments could be heard as the Arch Wizard's statement was recorded for posterity.

'Damn it all, Uldini,' grumbled Trogadon impatiently. 'I know you want your stilted blather to be recorded for all eternity, but can't we simply talk like normal beings in here?'

The scratching of the nibs continued. Ahren bit his lip in an effort not to laugh, but the giggling from Khara, Hakanu and Lyssin suggested that others were maintaining their dignity with considerably less success.

'Uh…well…I…' muttered the Arch Wizard, glaring at Trogadon. 'Are all in agreement that we take Belsarius' theory to be true?'

'I don't see how we have a choice.' Kamkanzakur's voice rumbled like falling rocks. 'And this truth forces us to make a crucial decision.'

'Do we organise an orderly campaign against the Adversary or hurl ourselves forward pell-mell and hope for the best that the Paladins somehow manage to get to Him?' interjected Falagarda, forcefully stating what the dwarf had been thinking.

'An accurate if not entirely *neutral* sounding assessment, my dear,' commented Quin-Wa dryly.

'We have already experienced what happens if we don't confront the Adversary at the right time,' muttered Bergen. 'So, it's true – we really *don't* have a choice.'

'I agree.'

This was met by a stunned silence, Ahren staring – as did everyone else – in disbelief at the First.

'*What* did you say?' asked the Forest Guardian sceptically, wondering if the words of the age-old Paladin were nothing but a rhetorical ploy.

'I *agree*,' repeated the First. 'If…' he hesitated. 'If Lirana and Belsarius are right, then the outcome of the many battles that I have fought in my long life suddenly make sense. The pattern behind the Adversary's belligerent actions suddenly makes sense, and therefore, I now agree with Akkad. I am all too aware of the victories that were almost gifted to us, of defeats that should never have occurred…' His voice began to quake, and he cleared his throat. 'My companion animal would now be alive had I recognised the cyclical nature of events much earlier.'

Sunju placed a comforting hand on his forearm. 'We were *all* blinded. All *Jorath* was. The Dark god made sure of that. Even now, we cannot rule out that we are not walking into a particularly cunning trap laid by the Adversary.'

'So, do we attack with all possible speed, then?' asked Falk, looking at the other council members.

'When *precisely* does this constellation appear again?' asked Fisker, fixing his eyes on Akkad.

'The day after tomorrow – in the evening. It will fully manifest itself shortly after sundown.'

'Which means we have only two days to prepare?'

'That's what it looks like,' murmured Fisker, reaching for a carafe of wine. 'Anyone else need a drink?'

'Don't overdo it,' growled Falk. 'Even if your monkey is smarter than you are, we might need your brains at some point.'

Fisker bowed mockingly. 'Your faith in me is almost as encouraging as your words of motivation.'

'*Enough!*' The First spoke in little more than a whisper, but it was enough for Fisker to immediately close his mouth. 'We need a *plan,*' added the age-old Paladin.

Trogadon, having taken the jug from Fisker, now filled his goblet to the brim with one hand while he pointed at Khara with the other. 'What about the suggestion that our princess made earlier – of fooling Him with a trick.'

Jelninolan nodded. 'Now that we all believe the Adversary to be unaware of our new knowledge, we can use it to our advantage.'

'But how?' asked Sunju.

'We must lure Him into taking the first step,' intoned Uldini. 'He must believe that the start of the battle is *His* idea.'

Falk shook his head. 'Why should He risk coming out of his fortress if He only has to wait another two days for his full strength to return?'

'If HE, WHO FORCES were a disciplined or patient being, He would still be the Custodian of Creation,' interjected Jelninolan.

Ahren nodded to the priestess before rubbing his neck and staring up at the ceiling of the council chamber, where the shadows of the night were playing cat and mouse with the flickering light from the fire. 'We have to attack Him at the point where He is most vulnerable.'

'His *addiction to power*,' said the First.

Ahren continued to stare upwards. 'And His *fear,*' he murmured.

'And His *pride,*' added Khara. 'Think of all those crippled species of Dark Ones, like the Sicklehoppers, for example. Although the Adversary mutilated so many of His servants in frankly ridiculous ways, He refused point-blank to correct his errors.'

'His *arrogance* is boundless…' murmured Uldini contemplatively.

Closing his eyes, Ahren sought out Culhen's mind, which once again was connected to Sun Shimmer's. *Do you lot have any ideas?* he asked.

But of course. Overweening pride dripped from the wolf's response, as the animal sent him an image of a fat rabbit scampering across an open field. A black-feathered hawk was circling overhead. *I hope you understand what we mean.*

Ahren opened his eyes and chuckled. 'Our companion animals have an excellent idea. And I think I know how we can go about implementing it…'

He began to talk, placing all his faith in his own instinct, which had so often led him to the right solution if usually by means of unusual paths. The longer he spoke, the more the faces of the listeners became filled with horror. Only Hakanu's grin became broader with every sentence that his master uttered.

The conclusion of Ahren's briefing was met with an unmistakable, collective groan, which, however, was drowned out by Hakanu's hoop of joy.

The night was dark, and the moonlight was Ahren's only companion as he walked through the deserted streets of Deepstone. The final words of the council of war were still ringing in his ears – words of a daring plan that had now been concocted.

The last ever plan of this war – *if* it succeeded.

Ahren ran his fingers along the stone wall of what had once been the mayoral residence. Even this building, which had once been the crown jewel of Deepstone, was now no more important than the other stone houses that formed what was now the old town. Ahren found it difficult to recognise anything here from his childhood days – when he had wanted to be nothing more than an apprentice – under the watchful eye of a kindly master.

Wandering through the streets and across the broad avenues, Ahren's mind was a jumble of thoughts – ranging from those events local to here in his early years to the looming threat that was so imminent.

Tomorrow would mark the turning point and determine the fate of Jorath. This simple fact made him dizzy. The years of searching for all the Paladins had been accompanied by a recognisable goal, but the journey's end was nigh. All the words had been spoken, all the plans had been forged, all the trump cards had been carefully placed in position.

Ahren came to a sudden halt as he suddenly realised where he had arrived.

Low, simple gravestones surrounded by well-tended grass. Many things in Deepstone may have been moved, but the old graveyard still lay within view of the chapel, now considerably more imposing than in the days when Ahren had been an innocent godsday pupil, learning under the kindly tuition of Keeper Jegral. Slowly, he walked among the graves, coming to a halt before one in particular, his tears making it impossible to properly read the inscription that he was already familiar with.

'Holken…' he whispered with a lump in his throat. 'We have managed it, Holken. All the Paladins are united.' The breath of a whisper would have been louder than the words that Ahren was barely uttering.

The young man wiped away his tears and looked up at the night sky. The stars were staring coldly down, including those which in no time at all would be dancing their deadly roundelay – announcing either the end of the Adversary or the destruction of Creation as Ahren knew it.

'If you could only see Deepstone now,' he continued, looking down again at the final resting place of his deceased friend. 'It even has a castle. You would be so proud…'

He swallowed hard. He clenched his fists so tightly that it hurt.

'No-one…' the Paladin's voice was growing stronger, '*no-one* who died in this war will have died in vain. I promise you that.'

Ahren paused for a heartbeat – it was as if he was hoping that his friend would give him some sort of signal – some sort of *blessing* for the fateful day that still lay ahead. But instead, only a cloud pushed itself before the moon, casting the graves around the Paladin in a deep darkness.

Ahren nodded mutely. He could not wait for the light. It was time for him and the other Paladins to drive the darkness away – for once and for all.

Chapter 14

A heavy morning mist resembling an expansive burial shroud covered the flat land between Deepstone and the towering fortifications of the Ring – it was as though Mother Nature could hardly wait to prepare the field of death for the imminent battle.

Ahren repeatedly clenched and unclenched his fists as he paced back and forth like a caged animal behind the parapet on top of the western tower. His eyes kept glancing from the Obsidian Fortress to the hilly, snow-covered terrain north of Deepstone as he scanned the landscape nervously.

Didn't there use to be wheatfields there? he asked himself. *Long before a certain greenhorn touched a gods' stone, starting all this madness?* Try as he might, Ahren was unable to reconcile this countryside, now blanketed in fog, with his memories of childhood. The city of Deepstone had swallowed up what the boy Ahren had once considered his whole world and hidden it behind the new defensive walls.

The river of Time carries everything away, mused Culhen philosophically, the wolf lying in his full armour in a corner of the fortified tower top, beaming with joy because Yoka, wanting to warm herself, had decided to cuddle up to him. *It seems only yesterday that I was everyone's favourite whelp, whose every whim was acceded to – and now look at me – here I am, a stately Alpha who will soon have a litter of whelps to take after me.*

Ahren chuckled. *Sun Shimmer is circling up there above the blanket of cloud. Are you sure that she isn't listening in on you? And passing on your foolish words to Yoka?*

Culhen suddenly raised his head and whimpered. *She would never do that, would she?* The wolf looked at Yoka, who merely gazed back at him before cuddling in closer. *Phew,* said the wolf. *That was close.*

'According to Yoka, your animal has a *very* high opinion of himself,' murmured Lyssin to Ahren, who was still anxiously pacing.

Culhen whimpered again. *Oh, no! What a dastardly crow Sun Shimmer is!*

A loud, angry caw split the sky. 'You'd better stop talking,' said the young man aloud to his furry friend, 'before you alienate *all* the companion animals.'

Not receiving a reply, Ahren understood that his message really *had* gotten through to his generally obdurate wolf.

'Not Yoka,' said Lyssin, shaking her head. 'For some reason, she finds Culhen's boasting cute.'

Another whimper, but no prompt retort. Ahren was beginning to believe that his wolf might indeed be capable of learning manners.

His fellow Forest Guardian, who didn't seem in the least bothered by the cold, and who was sitting in her united cloak on a crenel between two merlons, frowned and pointed at Yoka. 'She simply won't stop babbling. And it's *always* some nonsense that inevitably makes me laugh.'

Ahren peered at the stoical looking Champion of the gods. 'Hm,' he murmured, 'You don't look that amused to me.'

'I'm laughing *inside*.'

'Ah, I *see*,' said Ahren in a lightly mocking tone. He was now leaning against the parapet and staring out onto the mist. 'What's keeping him?'

'He was supposed to set off at daybreak,' said Lyssin, calmly reminding the anxious Paladin. 'Which entails a march of four leagues while incorporating all the peculiarities of your plan. So, he cannot possibly be here yet.'

'I know,' grumbled Ahren.

'Ah, I *see*,' she murmured, imitating what he had said with a grin.

The Thirteenth looked sideways at Lyssin with a self-deprecating smile. 'Should you not – as the newest member of our select little group of Champions – be a little…I don't know…less *forward*…perhaps?'

'No idea,' said Lyssin matter-of-factly. 'Father never brought me up like that. What were *you* like as a freshly baked Paladin?'

Ahren groaned at the memory. 'Stay the way you are,' he muttered.

Lyssin laughed – and it wasn't *inside* this time. She glanced affectionately over at Yoka and chuckled. 'Why can't my she-wolf stop blathering nonsense all the time?'

Ahren looked over at the she-wolf. 'Companion animals understand instinctively what their Paladins need in moments of crisis. I see it like this – they are the anchors that keep us connected to Jorath.'

'Hm – I wonder is *that* why the First always seems as though he exchanged his heart for a lump of ice? Because he has been without his companion animal for such a long time.'

Ahren cocked his head and mused for a moment. 'I often wondered the same thing. I have come to the conclusion that his mood is mainly down to his having been the first of the Paladins to be formed. He has never handed on the sceptre of his monumental task, and now it seems as if he cannot separate himself from it.'

'You know – I think that it would do him good to hear that,' said a voice from within the tower, which Ahren immediately recognised as Khara's. His beloved emerged through the archway of the heavy oak door, now open, but which normally barred access to the staircase within the castle. 'I have been instructed to report to you that all the Paladins are in position – including the Father of the Mountain.'

Ahren nodded gratefully to her. 'So, we are now only waiting for Trimm.'

'Isn't that always the case?' countered Khara with a smile.

'How is Palnah?' asked the Thirteenth. 'After her having to use all her powers yesterday…'

'She is resting safe and sound in the Heart Hall,' the Swordsmistress replied.

Ahren breathed a sigh of relief. This meant that the new-born babies, the pregnant Paladins and the soul companions were all secure deep below the castle. This plan with all its hair-raising risks was surely going to prove bloody enough without endangering the most vulnerable among them.

Khara took from her belt bag two small, buff-coloured, wax discs, handing one each to Ahren and Lyssin. 'Akkad says you should press them onto your armour – preferably directly over your hearts.'

Ahren looked down at the object in his hand and recognised the sign of the THREE, which had been painted on it with a substance unknown to him. 'What *is* this?' he asked.

'An experiment of our much-beloved Ancient,' said Khara. 'All the Paladins should wear the signet, which – if it works correctly – will dampen the gods' Blessing call between you so that more of you can gather in one place without the Adversary being able to pick up your scent.'

Lyssin stared down at her disc. 'And what happens if these things *don't* do what they're supposed to?'

'Well, I'm not really sure,' murmured Khara, shrugging her shoulders. 'There was something said about you all then growing a second head, I think.' She began to grin. 'To be honest, I wasn't really listening to Akkad.'

'*Very* funny,' muttered Lyssin, pressing the signet onto her chest. 'You are more than welcome to keep my *hilarious* she-wolf company. Then you can both make each other laugh.'

Khara smiled knowingly. 'You'll get used to her.'

Lyssin nodded towards the Obsidian Fortress in the distance. 'Then I had better get a move on. If I understood everything that was said in the council of war correctly, then we will all be up to our necks in skirmishing until tomorrow evening – however it ends.'

Ahren fixed his eyes on the young woman and stared at her for several heartbeats before speaking. 'Your father would be very proud of you.'

Lyssin shrugged her shoulders. 'I know.'

The sound of a bugle echoed from the north, causing Ahren to spin around and peer between the merlons. Although he could make out nothing, a shiver ran down his spine. The first part of their plan was about to unfold. The first signal had sounded, ushering in – if all went well – the beginning of the end of the Adversary.

'It has begun,' whispered Khara from beside him. Then she gave him a peck on the cheek. 'I'd better get into position. Wish me luck.' Then she was gone, Ahren peering pensively through the doorway, his beloved already having been swallowed up by the darkness of the stairwell that led down into the castle.

'We are *all* going to need luck,' he murmured before pulling himself together and turning to Lyssin. 'I do apologise that you are going to have to put up with me, but I need someone to whom I can relate our strategy for one last time. The first thing we will do is await Trimm's arrival, so that…'

The longer Ahren talked, the better he felt, especially as the stoical Lyssin was listening patiently. Having finally finished his monologue, it was only another couple of heartbeats before the bugle sounded a second time, now not half a league from Deepstone. Ahren breathed a sigh of relief. Everyone was in position. If the Paladins were to win this first round against the Adversary, then they would at least be in with a chance of achieving victory.

The relentless fog continued to blanket the plain – as though the Adversary had personally cast the area with an evil spell. To Ahren's chagrin, this meant that he could not make out the spectacle unfolding to the west.

Thousands of soldiers wearing all sorts of armour and moving in various formations were marching to the front of the Deepstone walls. In their midst was an unmistakable figure – even in the fog – dressed in barbed, Deep Steel armour and standing in an open military carriage drawn by four powerful horses.

'Make way there!' bellowed Trimm, Ahren able to make out his fellow Paladin's voice thanks to Culhen's fine hearing. 'Make way for the Grandee of the THREE and his armed forces!' Then the army of mercenaries, which the grandee had brought all the way from Cape Verstaad in the far south of the Sunplains, began to move towards the Ring. Ahren cursed quietly as the fog swallowed up the boisterous troops, forcing him to rely solely on Culhen's ears.

Eken says that everything apart from the fog is running to plan, said his wolf reassuringly.

At this moment, Ahren would have liked to have hugged Sun Shimmer for her ability to act as a conduit between the companion animals.

Did I mention to you that I really like that ball of fur? Maybe because he can't stand Muai. And he has a wonderfully dry sense of humour, added Culhen cheerfully.

Suddenly, the wolf became anxious. *Uh-oh.*

Ahren's heart skipped a beat. *What do you mean 'uh-oh'?* It was enough that the Paladin was struggling with the burden of what they were all trying to achieve here, without falling victim to demoralising self-doubt. After all, their plan depended so much on the Thirteenth not losing courage!

Eken wants to improvise because of the fog. He says, he has an idea.

'By the THREE, please, *no!*' groaned Ahren aloud.

Their plan was as fragile as a brittle layer of ice on a pool in the first cold day of winter. They were already having to fight with one hand tied behind their back. No Uldini, no Jelninolan, no Blessing Band, no…

Ahren stopped listing off the self-imposed restrictions that they had imposed upon themselves in coming up with their plan. They were absolutely necessary if the daringly complex nature of their deeds was to have any chance of resulting in the death of the Adversary the following day. The fact that Trimm's indolent tomcat, whom Ahren found impossible to take seriously, was already considering *improvisation* at the beginning of this damned tortuous process made the young Paladin break into a cold sweat.

'Tell Eken that a thousand lives are at stake – no, that all Jorath might be lost!'

Through Culhen's ears, the Paladin could hear the sound of angry voices and the clanking metal of soldiers marching in full armour.

'Take advantage of the fog,' pronounced Trimm in a pompous voice. 'The enemy cannot see us.'

Ahren licked his lips anxiously. The corpulent Paladin had already deviated from what he was supposed to have said.

The noise of thousands of moving bodies, as well as the sounds of loud cursing and heated arguments became evermore audible. Ahren craned his neck in frustration, unable, however, to see anything but the accursed fog.

'That's enough,' he muttered. 'Culhen – we are going to ride there now. Who knows what other nonsense Trimm will get up to.'

'We must remain in our positions,' countered Lyssin in a calm voice. 'You told me so yourself earlier – and in no uncertain terms.'

Ahren stopped himself from uttering a smart retort and remained where he was. Suddenly, he was glad that Hakanu wasn't with him – otherwise, he and his protégé would undoubtedly have stormed over to Trimm, each wildly waving a flag, and thereby ruining their plan completely.

The sounds of chaotic jockeying and tussling from within the blanket of fog that were now reaching him through Culhen's ears suggested that a full-scale battle was beginning. It seemed that Trimm was perfectly capable of ruining everything without Ahren's assistance.

I'm slowly beginning to worry, too, announced Culhen. *This damnable miasma might well destroy our plan.*

Ahren stared down at the billowing whiteness that simply wouldn't thin out. The morning was proceeding apace, the first rays of light now shining through the gaps in the clouds.

'If the sunshine doesn't start doing its work, I am going to have to ask Jelninolan to intervene,' he thought out loud. 'And yet, our trap is supposed to seem as *natural* as possible.'

'Be patient,' said Lyssin calmly. 'If there is anything I am an expert in, then it is winter weather.' She flashed her teeth in a fleeting, toothy grin. 'The fog is going to lift soon.'

Ahren paused for a heartbeat before nodding. Not trusting Lyssin's assessment would be as foolish as ignoring any advice Sunju might have regarding the raising of Rocs.

The noise from the soldiers at the Ring was easing, Ahren realising that the sound of bedlam would remain ineffective for as long as the blanket of fog remained in place.

Ahren – look! The sun is breaking through at last!

Seldom had the Forest Guardian so welcomed the golden orb as he did at this moment. The fog covering the entire plain to the west of Deepstone was gleaming white, the clouds of mist beginning to evaporate under the energy of the sun's rays. Either Lady Fortune was smiling on them, or the Storm Weaver had decided to give the weather a little nudge. Ahren fervently prayed it was the former, for the Adversary would surely sense Jelninolan's sorcerous intervention, no matter how exhausted He was by the Bane Curse.

The sun nibbled away at the fog like water devouring a pile of salt. Already, the Ring was clearly visible, with figures darting chaotically this way and that on top of it as soldiers changed places with reckless abandon. From this distance, it was impossible to make out the details, but Ahren knew that the enemy would be observing the scene with considerable interest from the walls and towers of the Obsidian Fortress – a seemingly thoroughly amateurish changing of the guard on an entire section of the Ring, commanded and overseen by the very Paladin whose reputation as being both not only thoroughly incapable but also cowardly had preceded him – Trimm, the self-proclaimed Grandee of the THREE.

The established veterans of the Ring, now being driven from their positions by devil-may-care mercenaries, put up considerable resistance, shouting angrily at their replacements and even, from time to time, resorting to fisticuffs as they attempted to counter the foolish, contradictory orders of the Paladin who was now in command. Ahren imagined the self-congratulatory smile on the pompously armoured man, who was basking in his own glory while plunging the Ring into a state of pure chaos along two leagues of its wall.

An experienced warrior might perhaps have wondered what Trimm was doing so near the front and why he wasn't content to remain where he felt most comfortable, namely at the very rear of this enormous army. But this trap had been organised, not for a cool head, but rather for someone of a completely different ilk. For some*thing* quite different.

'Come on! Get on with it,' murmured Ahren, his body shaking with anticipation as his fingers drummed on the crenel in front of him. 'Swallow the bait, you beast.'

For a while, there was no reaction from the Obsidian Fortress apart from the scornful shouts of the High Fangs and the animalistic grunts of their low brothers and sisters – but just as Ahren was about to give up any hope of the chaos at the Ring achieving its goal, he heard a chorus of bugles, blaring out their command to the heavens.

The two enormous wings that made up the massive eastern gates of the Obsidian Fortress were suddenly shoved unmercifully open by a pair of charging Horde Bulls, creating a route for a veritable flood of Dark Ones to stream out of the citadel and hurtle towards the weakened section of the Ring. With rising fear, Ahren observed *Hate*, dressed in his roughly hewn, clunky suit of armour, leading the rabble, a two-hander in each fist, and – as expected – riding on a fiercely bellowing Glower Bear, whose own armour had been cobbled together from the breastplates of many a fallen soldier. The army of raging Dark Ones was already halfway to the Ring by the time Ahren had recovered from his shock.

'This *isn't* how we planned it, is it?' gasped Lyssin beside him.

Shaking his head, Ahren spun around to face the steps. 'The enemy *was* supposed to emerge, alright, but it was supposed to take far longer for them to open the gates.' Ahren bounded down the stairwell, three steps at a time, crashing repeatedly against the smooth stone walls without slowing down. After all, what were a few bruises when the fate of the Ring was in the balance?

On reaching the ground floor of the castle's main building, he and Lyssin ran into Falk and the First, who had been watching from the northern tower. The Paladins rushed into the bailey, from where they could see Fisker, Bergen and Hakanu racing from the other end of the castle towards the stables.

'I told you from the start that this would go wrong,' growled the First as they continued to run.

'*Hate* has come out and the entrance into the Obsidian Fortress is open,' countered Ahren, trying to lend his voice more confidence than he was feeling. He swung himself up onto Culhen's back. 'Now all we need to do is to defeat him and secure the eastern gate – then we will have cut off the Adversary's right hand and taken control of a bridgehead to the interior of enemy territory.'

'*If* the Ring can withstand the assault for long enough,' barked the First, glaring at the young man.

The wax signet that Akkad had made for the Paladins were – now that so many Champions of the gods had gathered in one place – had melted and were little more than large spots of dirt on their armour. Ahren suppressed the thought that the state of the wax was nothing but a symbol of the disintegrating plan that they had so painstakingly plotted.

The Forest Guardian leaned as far forward as he could, so that Culhen could gain the necessary momentum for an assault without the wolf tiring too much.

'Run, big lad,' he whispered into his friend's ear, the animal immediately taking off at full speed.

'We'll see you at the Ring!' yelled Khara from behind, but before Ahren had a chance to reply, the wolf was carrying him pell-mell out the castle gates and through the streets of Deepstone, where Ice Wolves and the sentries normally on duty were keeping the road from the castle to the outer, western city-gate free of pedestrians. Ahren was greeted with yells of encouragement and whoops of joy from windows and footpaths as the residents – both recent and long-established – of his home place cheered on the Thirteenth as his wolf galloped furiously along.

Sun Shimmer says that the Dark Ones have reached the Ring, reported Culhen, the Roc's silhouette visible high in the sky, from where the enormous bird had the perfect view of the battlefield. Already, the first waves of Swarm Claws had been dispatched from the battlements of the Obsidian Fortress with the intention of driving Sun Shimmer away.

'Faster, Culhen!' cried Ahren, urging on his wolf while simultaneously trying to suppress the panic that was threatening to overwhelm him.

Once they had passed through the outer gates of Deepstone, leaving the last cheering residents behind them, the Forest Guardian was able to see the Ring clearly. Immediately, he slipped into Pelneng, bypassing his sense of panic and concentrating instead on comparing the actual state of play before the enormous, fortified wall with his original plan in case there were any final adjustments that he might make.

In fact, he and his fellow Paladins had hoped to have enough time to approach *Hate* stealthily from different points, being protected by the wax signets as they tightened the noose around him. The idea had been that the news of their gathering around the Adversary's only surviving offspring would not reach Him too soon – in which case, they would be able to trap *Hate* before he had a chance to retreat to the Obsidian Fortress.

In the meantime, the chaos on the Ring would have been transformed into an organised defensive formation, enabling them to force the army of Dark Ones back. However, there was not enough time for one or other of their plans to materialise, thanks to the unexpected appearance of the two forward-storming Horde Bulls.

Suddenly, the trap that they had set for *Hate* had turned into a genuine threat to the Ring!

At least all our hectic efforts look authentic, thought Ahren. *The Paladins are swarming out of Castle Highstone to save their brother who is in difficulties, while we suffer losses at the Ring that cannot so quickly be replaced by reinforcements.*

One helper has arrived already, at least, said Culhen comfortingly. *The Father of the Mountain will give Trimm some back-up until we get there.*

Ahren fixed his eyes on the Ring, soaring in the distance ahead of him and upon whose walls skirmishing was already taking place. Blood Wolves, Sickle Hoppers and Low Fangs fought their way ferociously through the screaming men and women who were desperately trying to hold the line. Lines of archers stood at the ready between the onrushing Culhen and the Ring. Should the commander of this section of the defensive wall see no hope of maintaining control of the huge barrier, then there would be only one solution – to dispatch wave after wave of arrows, thereby sweeping the top of the Ring clear of both friend and foe, the projectiles peppering all and sundry. At that point, reinforcements would be able to move towards the wall in the hope of securing the bulwark before the enemy could. It would all come down to a game of chance, costing the lives of hundreds – if not thousands.

A game of chance initiated by none other than the Paladins themselves.

Culhen's sprint brought Ahren to the rear of the waiting archers, and because the wolf could read his friend's mind, the animal headed straight for the commander, a glowering dwarf from Silver Cliff with a broad helmet and an even broader shield, who was standing on one of the countless bridges that spanned the sparkling river, which flowed no more than three hundred paces from the wall of the Ring.

'Thirteenth!' bellowed the officer, slamming his hand against his heavy breastplate in greeting. 'It doesn't look good. As soon as I get the signal that the two Paladins are safe on the Ring, I will issue the order to wipe the wall clean!'

Ahren instinctively wanted to protest, but a glance at the battlements was enough to persuade him that the commander had no other choice. There were only a few scattered defenders still standing amongst an overwhelming force of Dark Ones.

Suddenly, red smoke began to rise from one of the three towers that soared up from the overrun section of wall, the dwarf beside Ahren then nodding.

'That is the sign. The Paladins are in safety.' His voice became a thundering roar: 'Archers, nock your arrows! Crossbowmen and - women, be at the ready!' Then he took a bugle from his belt and sounded two long notes to ensure that his command was audible to everyone on the battlefield. The first of the Low Fangs were already hurrying clumsily down the stairways of the Ring, their eyes lusting after blood and fixed on the serried ranks of the soldiery.

Without hesitating, Ahren pointed at the Dark Ones. Immediately, Culhen stormed forward, past the disciplined lines of marksmen and - women. 'Where are the spear throwers that are supposed to secure the vanguard of the formation?' the Forest Guardian muttered before cursing under his breath.

Look at the wall, replied Culhen. *There you will see their corpses.*

Ahren understood immediately. The chaos had led to improvisation, whereby every close-combat fighter capable of defending the Ring had raced up onto the wall, leaving their long-range comrades defenceless unless they had successfully retreated behind the ditches with the protruding spears five furlongs away, which had rendered them unable to offer any support at the Ring, however. Now some of the surviving spear throwers were so panic-stricken that they were shooting their precious missiles at the onrushing Dark Ones, instead of waiting to perform the intended task of clearing the overrun wall.

'Shoot!' roared the commander with more power than any human or elf could attain even before Culhen had passed the foremost row of long-range combatants. This was immediately followed by an extended blow of the bugle, both of which initiated extraordinary whistling and twanging sound as thousands of bowstrings vibrated and an equal number of arrows whizzed through the air only to fall as a deadly surge on top of the wall.

Thank goodness they all seem to know what they're doing, muttered Culhen, Ahren immediately sensing the anxiety of his friend. *I counted at least eight arrows whizzing past us only a hair's breadth away.*

Ahren drew his Wind Blade. By now they had reached the front of the archers' formation, and so too had the Dark Ones. 'We are the only reinforcements at the moment,' he whispered into Culhen's ear. 'Let us try to hold up as many of our opponents as we can, so that the bowmen and -women can do their work. And tell Sun Shimmer that we have suffered many more casualties than anticipated. Falagarda must be informed so that she can call in reinforcements from the north and south of the Ring.'

Culhen raced towards the foremost Dark Ones now only a few paces from the ranged attackers and the snarling Ice Wolf with his weapon-swinging rider.

Another command rang out, the next wave of arrows whizzing over Ahren's head and towards the wall, which was filling with more Dark Ones than the young man believed possible. The time for watching was over, he thought, as he leapt off Culhen's back, landing on two Low Fangs, which had been intent on attacking the flinching archers in the first line. Howling furiously, the wolf lunged at three more of the deformed creatures. A merciless skirmish ensued.

As he was falling, Ahren stabbed one of the Low Fangs directly in the chest, a grotesque looking creature with an overlarge head protected by a clunky helmet, before landing clumsily on the other, a fiend with overlong arms, whose jagged axe scratched along the Forest Guardian's shoulder without, thankfully, finding an opening in the Paladin's ribbon armour. Collapsing onto the ground with his two opponents, Ahren took advantage of the fact that he was now lying on the living Low Fang by pulling his blade out of the dead Dark One and in the same movement drawing the weapon along the face of his slavering opponent before the creature had managed to squirm out from under Ahren's body. The Paladin then rolled sideways, got to his feet and quickly wiped the blood of the slain Low Fangs from his face.

Already, the next attackers were rushing towards him as a third salvo of arrows swept all remaining living creatures from the wall, upon which piles of bodies were now to be seen, the protruding arrows making them appear like grotesque porcupines. The war was already showing its darkest side and it was still morning.

Ahren hurtled towards three more Low Fangs, immediately seeing that one of them was an extraordinarily ugly-looking creature with eyes on its cheeks and holding short swords in each of its three arms. Another of the monsters was clutching a spear three paces long, which was attached to an arm of similar length.

They are adapting their weaponry to suit their deformations, concluded the Forest Guardian.

Already he was in a deadly dance of thrusting and feinting as the trio of Low Fangs began to encircle him. Cursing loudly, Ahren got to temporary safety by performing a diving roll which brought him out between the legs of one of the creatures, drawing the side of his blade along the inside of its right thigh before he came out the other side. The Paladin then lightly got to his feet – something that could not be said of the injured Low Fang.

They are devious, commented Culhen, who was making bloody hay amongst the creatures. *Can you believe it? They've been trying to skewer me with half a dozen roasting spits.*

Ahren sensed that three of the weapons had snapped, one half of each now sticking out of the wolf. It was only the battle frenzy that was keeping the animal's pain at bay.

There must be High Fangs around here, thought Ahren, taking advantage of a brief moment's respite between two parries to scan the shadow of the wall. Yes! He saw them – four figures, snarling instructions to the Low Fangs.

He smashed the spear of the long-armed Low Fang which had miscalculated by lunging too far forward, before running under the forward thrusting shaft and slaying his opponent with a single stab. His reward was two short swords thrusting down on him which would have found a gap in his ribbon armour were it not for the fact that the Paladin was by now so experienced in battle that he instinctively turned his body, the moveable metal plates then giving him optimal protection.

Alas, he was unfamiliar with dealing with a *three*-armed opponent, the latter's final blade finding its way deep into Ahren's left upper thigh before he, for his part, managed to stab his own sword into the Low Fang's stomach, immediately wiping the triumphant leer off its face.

Culhen, I need you here, said Ahren, who had already used his uninjured leg to get to his feet but was now facing six more Low Fangs charging towards him. The Dark Ones had recognised him, abandoning their attack on the ranged fighters in their lust to acquire considerably more valuable booty.

Quickly preparing, insofar as his injured leg would allow him, for the inevitable onslaught of the six Dark Ones, Ahren suddenly heard a familiar voice from behind.

'*Ahren! Culhen!*' bellowed Falk. '*Duck!*'

Immediately, the Forest Guardian fell flat on the ground. *Play dead, wolf!* he commanded his friend, who collapsed unceremoniously, before rolling convincingly onto his side.

Ouch! muttered Culhen, having accidently driven the tip of one of the broken spears deeper into his flesh. *I don't even need to play dead – I feel as if I already am.*

Another blast of the bugle split the sky.

'Crossbowmen and -women! *Shoot!*' bellowed the commander.

Bolts whizzed past over Ahren's head before mowing down the onrushing Dark Ones and slamming the skulking High Fangs against the wall.

That was close, commented Culhen. *Would anyone object if I lie here for a while and slowly bleed to death?*

'Get up, you lazy good-for-nothings,' roared Falk, sitting in Selsena's saddle as the Titejunanwa came thundering into Ahren's field of vision. 'We have a wall to defend!' Then Paladin after Paladin rode past the young man, heading directly for the broad steps that led up to the chemin de ronde on top of the Ring as they yelled out the age-old battle cry.

'PALADINIM THEOS DURALAS!'

The Blessing within Ahren made his ears ring, his entire body tingling, from his heart to his fingers and even to the tips of his toes, an overwhelming sense of euphoria sweeping away his exhaustion. His blood rushed wildly through his veins, and before he knew it, he was back on his feet, any pain that he had felt seeming to have vanished as he raised his Wind Blade towards the heavens while echoing the Paladins' battle cry at the top of his voice. He ran over to Culhen, who had also – if not with quite the same enthusiasm – stood back up, the young man swinging up and into the saddle before urging the wolf towards and up the broad staircase.

This part of the Ring had a chemin de ronde on top, a good five paces across, as well as high merlons on the side facing the Obsidian Fortress, which provided considerable protection from flying arrows or bolts. Any other time and Ahren would have spent longer admiring the bulwark, but now the chemin de ronde around him was littered with the corpses of both friend and foe, all the bodies having been peppered with arrows. Hence, there was room for two things and two things only – determination and courage. They simply *had* to hold this wall!

The Paladins divided themselves up as well as they could before making their way to the towers nearest to them. Between the merlons, Ahren saw an extraordinary number of Dark Ones gathering before the open double doors of the Obsidian Fortress. There was no doubt but that they were preparing a second assault.

'Trimm!' yelled Falk. 'Where *are* you?'

'According to Eken, he and the Father of the Mountain are in that tower over there,' replied Lanlion, pointing at one of the turrets. 'At least, that is what Haminul said to him. This indirect communication through Sun Shimmer is anything but perfect.'

'You mean this tower here?' asked Fisker anxiously. 'The one with the broken door?'

Ahren wanted to dismount Culhen to make it easier for the wolf to progress between the piles of bodies, but suddenly the pain in his injured leg caused him to flinch and pause – it seemed, that the initial effect of the Paladins' war cry had already worn off.

'Hakanu, look after your master,' said Falk, glancing over his shoulder at Ahren. 'And think about what fate awaits those foolish enough to race away from their brothers and sisters on an over-weening Ice Wolf.'

Hakanu, a broad grin on his face, approached Ahren with the flask in his hand that Jelninolan filled every morning with a few mouthfuls of the sacred water, whose magical power was kept fresh thanks to the latent magic of the apprentice.

'Culhen first,' grunted Ahren, pointing at the wolf's wounds. 'And don't you dare elaborate on Falk's little lecture with some opinions of your own.'

'No, Master.'

The young warrior seemed so cheerful that one could easily imagine him on his way to an Autumn festival rather than being surrounded by piles of slaughtered men and women. Hakanu's irrepressibility never failed to surprise Ahren. In fact, now it was more than welcome as far as the Forest Guardian was concerned. The young warrior pulled the spear-tips out of Culhen's side before pouring some of the healing water onto the wounds.

'Falk, your shield is needed!' shouted the First. 'You and Hakanu with his spear must secure the tower! Anyone who has nothing better to do, throw the corpses off the wall – Dark Ones on one side, our own women and men on the other! We need room here to fight – or we will end up dead as well!'

The apprentice pressed the flask into Ahren's hands, before hurrying away in silence. It seemed that since arriving in Highstone, the boy had somehow become *everyone's* property.

At last, they consider him a fully-fledged – if still rather green – member of the group, interjected Culhen, whose wounds were already healing. *I seem to remember you being ordered to do this, that and the other too, when you were a lad.*

Ahren glanced over at Lyssin, who was searching among the corpses, pulling out any arrows that might be used a second time and creating the impression that she had been a member of the Paladin group for centuries already.

A salvo of arrows flew over Ahren before slamming into many of the Dark Ones that had been shoving their way between the corpses of their predecessors on the other side of the wall – all preparing themselves for a renewed onslaught on the Ring. Among the attackers, Ahren could make out Glower Bears and Agony Boars, not to mention countless armed Low Fangs which were being organised with almost military precision by a selection of High Fangs.

'Lyssin!' yelled Ahren, pointing at the dastardly commanders.

The young woman nodded, already beginning to shoot as her fellow Paladin poured the last of the sacred water onto his leg wound. 'By the THREE, we have already used up all this water, and the battle has hardly begun!'

You can blame Hakanu, countered the wolf loftily. *Can I help it if the boy loves me so much that he gave me the lion's share of the sacred water?* Meanwhile, the animal was twisting and turning before Yoka, making sure that she would see just how many spear-tips Ahren's apprentice had extracted him.

Lyssin burst out laughing as she shot another High Fang, sending it tumbling to the ground. 'Yoka is saying that she would be considerably more impressed if he *hadn't* been hit so many times despite wearing such impressive armour.'

Ahren's friend immediately abandoned his showing-off.

The older Forest Guardian's leg was healing slowly but surely, so he took advantage of the time to help Lyssin out by using *Fisiniell* to thin out the rows of High Fangs, causing the Low Fangs to return to their natural condition of relative stupidity.

'They are preparing for another assault!' shouted Khara from the end of their section of wall. 'And there are still too many of them for us to repel them all.' She pointed at the rows of ranged fighters behind her. 'Our arrows and bolts are still keeping them at bay, but I can see that we are quickly running out of projectiles!'

Ahren ceased shooting for a heartbeat to get a better picture of the strategic situation to his rear. Khara was correct in her assessment. Already, baskets of replacement arrows were being distributed amongst the marksmen and -women, and it was clear to the Paladin that it would take them a couple of dozen heartbeats to refill the quivers sufficiently – enough time for the Dark Ones to storm the wall again and force the Paladins into deadly close combat.

'Where are our reinforcements!' yelled Bergen, Ahren pricking up his ears.

'Selsena says that according to Sun Shimmer, foot soldiers from the north and south are streaming towards this vulnerable section of the wall!' shouted Falk. 'But they still have at least half a league's march ahead of them *and* they must also fill in any gaps in the Ring as they approach if we want to maintain control of the rest of the fortification. Unfortunately, us lot are stuck in the middle!'

Ahren's hope of immediate reinforcements burst like a soap bubble in the wind.

'We should have known,' muttered Bergen. 'But of course, *we* have to hold out the longest.'

'Lyssin!' shouted Ahren. 'We still have a good hundred heartbeats before we will have to shoulder our bows and continue with our blades.'

His fellow Forest Guardian nodded, grimly redoubling her efforts. High Fang after High Fang fell to the ground amongst the mass of Dark Ones. It was clear to Ahren that the cowardly creatures were trying in vain to take shelter behind the bulkiest of the Low Fangs. The precise aim of both the Forest Guardians meant, however, that they were still hitting their targets.

Ahren? asked Culhen.

What?

You're humming. This is conduct most unbecoming in such a situation.

Embarrassed, the Forest Guardian cleared his throat before falling silent, not without noticing Lyssin winking cheerfully at him.

'Father always says that it is no shame to be happy when one is working.'

'Tell me, have any of you seen *Hate?*' asked Fisker, craning his neck over a crenel to get a better look at the approaching army of Dark Ones, which was still streaming out of the open gates of the Obsidian Fortress in what seemed like a never-ending stream. 'After all, we are here because of *him*.'

'Perhaps he has retreated back into the citadel,' suggested Bergen.

'I see his Glower Bear,' growled the First, pointing at an enormous figure lying close to the wall and riddled with arrows and bolts. The animal was so huge that Ahren could easily imagine *Hate* simply springing from its back onto the rampart...

A loud scream sounded from the tower into which Falk and Hakanu had disappeared, which was immediately followed by an extended yell: *'Maaake Rooom!'* Ahren couldn't believe his eyes when Trimm suddenly appeared on the *roof* of the tower before leaping, arms and legs akimbo and falling all the way down to the ground.

'Trimm!' he exclaimed in horror.

'There's nothing wrong with him,' muttered the First irritably. 'The two aspects of war that Trimm mastered early on in his career were running away and falling. He's probably broken a couple of bones, but that's about it.'

Ahren was about to reply when one end of a rope from a grappling hook came flying over the parapet at the top of the tower, closely followed by the Father of the Mountain, who quickly began lowering himself onto the chemin de ronde. The squat Paladin was bleeding from a cut to his forehead but seemed otherwise unharmed.

'What a villainous fellow this *Hate* is,' he grunted as he continued his descent. 'Oh, and hello all, by the way.'

This was followed by a furious cry from near the top of the tower, the Father of the Mountain then tumbling, still holding his end of the rope, which had clearly been cut.

'Damn and blast it,' muttered the Paladin as he struggled to his feet. 'The body of this Blood Wolf would have made my fall so much more comfortable if it hadn't had so many arrows sticking into it.'

'You're soon going to wish that this was your only problem,' muttered the First as he pointed to the bowmen and -women to his rear. 'One more salvo and then there will be no more help from *them* until their quivers have been refilled.'

'A few sharpened sticks are hardly going to delay the big fellow on the tower anyway,' growled the dwarf-like Paladin. 'He fought Trimm and me *all* the way up, tearing apart twenty guards in the process while at the same time keeping Falk and a young lad unknown to me – who can only be Hakanu – at bay.'

As if to underline his point, *Hate* suddenly appeared between the merlons above, holding a dead soldier in his hands. Leering at her corpse, he used his extraordinary strength to then rip her apart. The ranks of the marksmen and -women shuddered as one, a hail of missiles then flying towards the last remaining child of the Adversary.

'There goes our remaining cover,' commented the First dryly. '*Hate* knows full well how to provoke our troops.'

'Dark Ones before us, *Hate* above us,' murmured Bergen dryly, perfectly summarising the situation. 'A normal day in the life of a Paladin.'

Falk and Hakanu stumbled out of the tower – the old man's shield was hanging from his arm, now bereft of strength, while Hakanu was missing his weapon.

'Where is your spear?' asked Ahren, staring at his apprentice in disbelief.

The lad pointed up at the *Hate*. 'Stuck in his back – so deeply that I cannot call it back.'

'Did you lose something, little Paladin?' sneered the child of the Adversary from above, the darkness in his voice causing a shiver to run down Ahren's spine. 'Yes – I thought I felt an itch in the small of my back.' He reached behind and pulled out what now seemed nothing more than a puny twig from beneath his right shoulder blade before tossing it down, the spear landing with a clatter before the frustrated-looking apprentice. 'If you throw that miserable shard of steel at me again, I will skewer a couple of squirming soldiers with your precious toy before ramming it into your puny stomach, *boy.*'

'I *hate* this monster.'

'Which is precisely what he wants. It is what gives him his power,' scolded Ahren. The sounds of shouting and the angry shuddering and clanging of weaponry were echoing up to the Paladins on the wall. It was only a matter of several heartbeats before the Dark Ones would launch their assault. The Thirteenth roared at the top of his voice: 'We *must* lure *Hate* away from our soldiers. He gains his nourishment from *their* desire for *his* death.'

'Well, I would have nothing against putting his head on a pike,' muttered Trogadon as he ascended the steps, gasping for air. 'Did I miss anything. My pony isn't the fastest...'

Then the first of the Blood Wolves leapt up the side of the wall and the time for mock-cheerful jokes and death-defying bravura was over.

To Ahren, it felt like an eternity of striking, stabbing, feinting, parrying, and shouting out warnings.

The wall was filling with more and more Dark Ones of all shapes and sizes, making manoeuvrability increasingly an issue. All the while, *Hate* was screaming his commands out over the battlefield, peppering them with dreadful threats to the defenders of what he intended doing to them and their families, thereby provoking both friend and foe equally.

Ahren could see how the power of the creature was growing and it took him little time to figure out the fiend's plan. The Paladins would grow increasingly weary as evermore injuries were inflicted on them, while the room on the wall for fighting became increasingly restricted.

Hate, meanwhile, was feeding on the disgust that thousands of soldiers felt towards him.

'But why isn't he fighting?' asked Lyssin, hacking at the head of one of the few Sickle Hoppers that was assaulting the Ring. 'What is the monster waiting for?'

'The right moment,' replied Ahren grimly. 'It seems he has learnt a lot since his last encounter with us Paladins.' The Forest Guardian tried his best not to let his voice betray his increasing concern at this realisation.

Don't forget, he now possesses the essence of his dead siblings – and this is strengthening him, too, said Culhen. *He is smarter and stronger than the last time.*

Ahren smiled grimly as he skewered an Agony Boar that had used a pile of dead Dark Ones in an effort to storm the wall. *At least, Hate does not possess the power of Revenge,* he countered. When Four Claws had burned the child of the Dark god out of his consciousness, he had destroyed it for ever. At least, the Paladin *hoped* so, for he had not seen any billowing cloud of smoke rise – which *had* been the case when the other children of the Adversary had perished.

Culhen sank his teeth into a Low Fang before shaking his head violently and flinging the creature over the wall. Gravity took care of the rest. *Let us hope that you are right,* muttered the wolf. *I wouldn't mind if* Hate *didn't hold the power of all the children within him.*

A growling Blood Wolf leapt onto the battlements, slamming into the yelping Culhen. Ahren was about to come to his friend's aid only to feel the swipe of a powerful paw against his back, which threw him head over heels off the Ring. The snow-covered ground raced up towards him with such speed that the Thirteenth hardly had time to turn himself in the air so that he would land feet first. Stabs of pain shot through his torso and legs even though the Forest Guardian had tried to lessen the force of impact by transforming the excessive momentum into a series of violent forward rolls, which converted, with the assistance of his armour and the carpet of snow, the expected breaking of bones into a collection of bruises and strains.

'Ouch!' was all the benumbed Paladin managed to say once he had come to a stop.

'Good tumble!' gasped Trimm, who was sitting on the ground, leaning against the wall, with blood coming out of his mouth and ears, looking in his barbed armour like a hedgehog that had been run over by the wheel of a carriage. 'Now, if you had thrown yourself forward with just a little more speed, your knee wouldn't hurt so much now.'

'Thanks for the advice,' growled the still dazed Forest Guardian.

The fog in his head had lifted sufficiently, however, for his concern regarding Culhen to increase. He slipped into his friend's mind, hoping as well to ameliorate his own pain, but to his horror the only thing that he could see through the animal's eyes was blackness.

CULHEN! he mentally roared as loudly as he could.

Oh, you are still alive, muttered the wolf in greeting. *And I had thought that we'd both bitten the dust simultaneously.*

Ahren tried to feel his friend's pain, but nothing registered. *How bad is it? Can you...can you feel anything?*

The dead Blood Wolf is weighing heavily on my nose, muttered Culhen grumpily. *And the Glower Bear that turned you into a flying Paladin decided, of course, to collapse on top of my back. I am lying under a mountain of corpses, and no-one has lifted a finger to help me. So, I soon won't be feeling anything at all anymore unless someone pulls me out of here.*

Ahren felt such a wave of relief that he decided to pass no comment on his wolf's churlish attitude. *What happened exactly?* he asked as he gingerly tried to get up, his movements proving to be slow, shaky and sore.

The other Paladins happened, muttered Culhen, still sounding thoroughly annoyed at his present situation. *Lyssin shot two arrows directly into the Blood Wolf's eyes while Hakanu's spear flew through the head of the Glower Bear like a silver thunderbolt. That young lad has a pretty decent aim now.*

Ahren shuffled to the steps, Trimm smiling encouragingly at him but without making an effort to move. The corpulent Paladin had clearly decided that he had performed enough heroic deeds for one day. The Forest Guardian would have loved to settle down beside Trimm and the sleeping Eken. Instead, he struggled up the stairs, intent on getting a better picture of what was unfolding.

The archers were readying themselves for another phase of sustained shooting while the welcome reinforcements were slowly but surely moving in from either side of the vulnerable section of the wall, which the Paladin and his friends had been defending so valiantly. How Ahren wished that Uldini and Jelninolan could support them, but their magic would be needed at a later point – assuming, of course, that the Thirteenth and the other Champions of the gods would somehow complete the first part of their plan.

Hate continued to command and mock those on the battlefield at will from the very top of the tower. Ahren had no idea how they were going to attack him, this child of the Adversary, who had the crenellations to protect him. Ascending the narrow spiral staircase while *Hate* launched attacks from above was out of the question. There were plenty of heroic epics about solitary soldiers valiantly resisting entire armies by defying them from their position at the tops of towers. The child of the Adversary would undoubtedly hold all the trump cards from up high.

Out of the corner of his eye, Ahren saw the commander waving up at him. Clearly, the archers were ready to shoot again.

'Get clear of the chemin de ronde!' shouted Ahren to his friends. 'Into the towers! But by the THREE, do *not* take on *Hate* in combat!'

'Spoilsport!' yelled Bergen.

'You all heard Ahren! Let us make room for the archers!' commanded the First.

'So, your little Paladins don't *want* to fight,' sneered *Hate* gleefully down to the waiting bowmen and -women from his position at the top of the tower. 'They hide behind walls – as they always do – while you lot are *killed* – and that, even though I am standing here waiting for them!'

He wants them to shoot at him again, murmured Ahren. *And force us into doing something stupid.*

'No-one may climb on top of this tower!' he screamed. 'And that applies to you, too, Hakanu!' he added, without needing to turn his head to his apprentice.

'Yes, Master,' replied the boy through gritted teeth.

Isn't there something that you might be forgetting? asked Culhen tartly. *An enormous Ice Wolf still lying buried on the chemin de ronde?*

Buried is right, said Ahren as he moved back to the set of stairs as one Dark One after another took advantage of the Paladins' retreat to storm the wall. *You will be safe from the arrows if you stay under the corpses.* He raised his arm as he looked at the commander.

Ahren, don't you dare!

The bugle sounded as soon as Ahren brought his hand down. Then, still on the steps, he immediately ducked as a sheer wall of crossbow bolts swept the enemy on the chemin de ronde clean away while a hail of arrows flew in an arc above the parapet, landing on the slavering masses below on the far side of the Ring.

No, no, no! whimpered Culhen. *I can feel the bolts slamming into the Glower Bear – and believe me, it is not a pleasant experience!*

Ahren prayed to the THREE that none of the projectiles would inadvertently hit his wolf. Partly, because he wanted to see Culhen hale and hearty again, but mainly because if his furry friend *were* hit, it would be a bone of contention between them for evermore.

Oh, woe is me! wailed the animal as bolts flew all around him and arrows darkened the skies. *The most loyal companion to a Paladin, abandoned by his so-called friend and used as target practice by a horde of blind marksmen and -women.*

Ahren used the silence that followed his companion animal's outburst to slip into Pelneng and free himself from the pain of his fall. He felt for the Wind Blade, which had slipped out of his grasp when he'd tumbled, sheathing it once his hand had found it. Then he took advantage of his spiritual calmness to unshoulder *Fisiniell* and nock a Deep Steel arrow to his bowstring of twisted unicorn hair.

Again, he glanced at the commander, pointing then at the bellowing colossus on top of the tower, who was standing on the merlons, goading the archers into seeing him as a target. Another shouted command followed by a short, sharp bugle blast and a mass of arrows resembling a swarm of hornets descended on the hysterically laughing *Hate*, who rained down, for his part, a hail of insults onto the soldiers below. The child of the Adversary had deliberately placed himself into what seemed a vulnerable position, so that the projectiles would harmlessly hit him, thereby unwittingly enabling Ahren to fix his aim on the cackling diabolical monstrosity from the steps below.

The Forest Guardian took a deep breath, extended his bow, aimed and then shot. The arrow flew precisely along the course he had intended, grazing the back of the enormous creature before disappearing from Ahren's view.

For a heartbeat, Ahren feared that he hadn't hit the target, but then the crudely forged armour protecting *Hate*, slipped off his massive body, Ahren's perfectly aimed missile having cleanly cut through the straps that had held the metal sections in place. The breastplate was so battered by the missiles dispatched by the regular ranged fighters that it could no longer withstand the barrage.

The Paladin quickly shouldered his bow and crawled behind the corpse of a Glower Bear to avoid being seen by the now rabid creature. Hopefully, the proud child of the Adversary would draw only one possible conclusion from Ahren's spontaneous act of deceptions...

'You *maggots* will pay for this!' bellowed *Hate* furiously at the archers. 'I will grind you all to dust even without my armour!'

Then with a furious cry, he flung himself off the tower, and not three heartbeats later, he had struggled to his feet in the snow and was already hurtling after the fleeing marksmen and -women.

'Why were you tempting him down to *me?*' whimpered Trimm, glancing at Ahren before pulling himself up with a groan from where he was lying at the foot of the wall. 'I thought we were friends.'

Ahren, however, was already sprinting down the steps, unshouldering *Fisiniell.* Shooting an arrow at *Hate,* he simultaneously delivered Culhen an urgent message. *Tell Sun Shimmer that we have Hate outside the Ring at last. All Paladins must get into position.*

Ahren pulled arrow after arrow out of his quiver, aiming them at the gleaming, glasslike black skin of the monster, causing the child of the Dark god to finally turn around, no longer focusing on the terrified archers. It said something for the courage of those men and women, for they immediately began shooting their arrows and bolts at the Dark Ones on the far side of the Ring, giving the Paladins the opportunity to begin fanning out on the wall.

Good cat, groaned Culhen, Ahren smiling grimly as he heard his four-legged friend. *At least Muai is trying to free me.*

Ahren had no time to turn and see what was happening behind him, for now *Hate* was giving him his undivided attention. He shouldered *Fisiniell* beside his now empty quiver and drew his Wind Blade, which seemed, when compared to the two-handers that the obsidian-coloured colossus was holding in each hand, to be nothing more than a wooden plaything that a young boy might use when playing soldiers with his friends in the back yard. The eyes of the Adversary's offspring, glowing red like two burning coals, were searing into those of the Thirteenth.

'This time there will be *no* getting away from me!' snarled the monster before lunging forward.

Ahren knew from their last encounter – shortly before the Adversary had created the Obsidian Fortress with the magic He had stolen – that his weapon would leave no marks on the skin of this colossus, the young man deciding that for the moment he would not even attempt to approach *Hate* too closely. It was sufficient for the young man to stay alive for as long as he was confronted by the onrushing attacker.

Hence, he ducked, leapt and parried as well as he could, so that the two enemy weapons with their serrated blades would not tear him brutally to shreds. The last time, *Hate* had used two-handers that had been seized from his enemies, but now it appeared as if he was using weapons that had been forged especially for him in the heart of the Obsidian Fortress, and which were the perfect length for the monstrous being's long arms.

It wasn't long before Ahren began gasping, his acrobatic feinting actions bringing him closer and closer to complete exhaustion, while his battered body was being tested almost to beyond breaking point thanks to the effectiveness of the trance that he was in.

I won't be able to keep this up for much longer, thought Ahren. *It's high time —*

'Take *that*, you deformed *monstrosity!*' bellowed Trogadon, a bolt a forearm thick and made from gleaming Deep Steel whizzing past Ahren.

The young man felt an overwhelming sense of relief as the dwarf's projectile slammed into the middle of *Hate's* chest. He began lowering his Wind Blade in anticipation of having a welcome breather – only to witness how the bolt simply ricocheted off the skin of the creature before clattering to the ground.

'What the…? was all the Thirteenth Paladin managed to say before an almost casual swing of a two-hander sent him flying high into the air.

Clearly, the teeth of the monstrous child's blade were capable not only of inflicting gruesome injuries but also of getting snagged in an opponent's armour, flinging the unfortunate away with extraordinary power.

Nothing is going well today, thought Ahren.

Then he slammed into the snow.

Chapter 15

The impact was so severe that Ahren's tortured muscles were unable to steady him, the Forest Guardian rolling violently along the snowy surface and looking for all the world like the heavy leather ball which Falk had made him practise with when they were master and apprentice in the Eastern Forest.

Strange, what one thinks of when was being flailed no end, mused Ahren numbly.

Keep thinking rationally, warned Culhen, the presence of the wolf in his mind clarifying the Paladin's thoughts just in time for him to evade *Hate's* stomping foot by twisting sideways.

'PALADINIM THEOS DURALAS!'

Roaring the Paladins' war cry, Falk threw himself between Ahren and the cockily grinning colossus.

'If you want *him,* you will first have to get past *me!'* The old man's shield glittered in the sunshine as he held it protectively over Ahren, who was now struggling to his feet.

'The measly shield of a measly man,' laughed *Hate* scornfully, simultaneously performing a downward stroke on Falk with both swords. The clash of steel on steel was deafening, Ahren's erstwhile master buckling considerably under the force. 'Three attacks and you will be kissing the snow,' promised *Hate* with a dark smile. 'After which you can watch how I divide this weakling here into tasty little morsels.' With that, he pointed his blades at Ahren.

'I haven't been described like that in a *long* time,' murmured the younger Forest Guardian, positioning himself beside Falk. He had to tilt his head back to look *Hate* in the eye. 'But you are entitled to your own opinion.'

Laughing mockingly, *Hate* raised his weapons, the two Paladins immediately springing left and right, forcing the creature to divide his attention, their tactic, however, coming to naught. Completely ignoring Ahren, *Hate* again hammered his blades into Falk's shield. The old man groaned as he sank onto his knees.

'Two,' counted the monster with a leer.

Ahren sensed his own rage seething within him and even breaking through his Pelneng. Remembering their original plan for evading *Hate's* special powers, he sank deeper into his trance – past Pelneng and down into the Void. His head became clear, all his emotions vanishing into a sacred nothingness. There was only him and his opponent.

'Falk,' he said calmly. 'Think of your role in this combat.'

The old man struggled back to his feet, retreated a pace and took a deep breath. Then his face became expressionless – a reflection of the smooth features that Ahren, too, displayed. 'Ready,' said Falk in a cool voice.

Perplexed, the child of the Adversary looked from one Paladin to the other. 'Where is your hate?' he asked cagily. 'I can sense it – buried deep in your hearts.' Then he guffawed. 'You are not going to defeat me this way.'

'We do not want to defeat you,' said Ahren, stabbing his Wind Blade towards one of the beast's glowing eyes.

A grunt and an irritated parry was the response.

'We only want to keep you in check.'

Again, *Hate* laughed – this time Falk aimed his blade at their opponent's eye. 'You cannot stop *me!*' exclaimed *Hate* fervently. 'I shall *sweep* the pair of you away!'

As if to prove his point, he drove his blades towards Falk, the latter quickly raising his shield. But this time, the colossus did not aim directly at the old man, jamming his swords on the two sides of the Paladin's metal sheet instead. With a loud grunt, he lifted Falk into the air before hurling him backwards, causing him to fly off like a leaf in the midst of an autumn storm.

'This is your *plan?!*' guffawed *Hate*. 'You want me to *laugh* myself to death at your pathetic efforts?'

Khara slipped into the gap created by Falk's unwished-for retreat. 'His language is becoming more complex.' The voice of the Swordsmistress was quiet and calm. She, too, was, in the Void's firm grasp. 'Before he could only grunt words like "kill" or "hate".' Then Khara spun out of Ahren's field of vision, ducked beneath the raging monster's assault and allowed her blades to perform a teasing dance before his face.

The child of the Adversary, holding a protective weapon before his face, staggered away from Khara. As she in turn began to retreat a little, the colossus managed to kick the Swordsmistress hard in the back, throwing her into the air, her white robe fluttering in the wind before she hit the snow, several paces away.

On seeing what had happened to his beloved, Ahren found himself struggling, albeit successfully, to remain in the Void. Next, Culhen leapt forward, biting at the child of the Dark god, thereby preventing him from breaking free from the current melee. Slowly but surely, they were running out of warriors who had mastered either Pelneng or the Void and who could therefore get close to *Hate* in relative safety.

'You won't be able to deny your hate forever!' rejoiced the child. 'I can feel it bucking against the chains you have placed around it!'

'These three are not alone,' said another voice, Ahren once again struggling to maintain his position in the Void, a feeling of hope having flared wildly within him on the arrival of Lanlion. Finally, after all the setbacks during this first step in their battle against the Adversary, they had arrived at the point where Ahren's daring plan might yet come to fruition.

'Now you have to deal with us, too,' added the Father of the Mountain, the unequal pair joining those who were already tackling *Hate*.

'Two more pathetic individuals with repressed emotions.' *Hate* yawned in a clearly exaggerated manner. 'How *boring*. I think it best if I kill one of you five here and now – then we will see for how much longer you can keep your hate under control.'

Ahren beckoned to his friends to fully encircle the child of the Adversary before pausing for a moment to glance around. The rest of the Paladins were defending the Ring, the archers had retreated a hundred paces from *Hate,* while the reinforcements from the north and south were under strict orders not to come any closer until the child of the Dark god had been subjugated.

'Now,' he whispered to his friends, immediately throwing himself at the giant, swinging his Wind Blade at the two-hander to the left, Falk aiming at the one to the right with his own two-hander. Khara was suddenly a whirlwind, her glittering blades dancing fiendishly close to the enemy's body while Lanlion slipped into position behind the back of the colossus, who now found himself fighting on five fronts. The Bloodless stood there, his arms outspread as he wove a cloak of blackness and threw it over the shoulders of the surprised *Hate,* seeming to pin the giant to the ground.

'You misunderstand my true nature,' said the Father of the Mountain sadly, who with both hands was spinning the Deep Steel ball that was braided onto the end of his long plait. 'I hate *nothing* in the world.'

Then, while Falk, Ahren and Khara distracted *Hate* sufficiently so that he could neither block nor evade the attack from the Father of the Mountain, the dwarf-like figure let the steel ball fly with such force that it smashed into *Hate's* chest, causing the child of the Dark god to stumble backwards, his red glowing eyes opened wide in shock as he spat out a fountain of blood.

'But you are standing in the way of permanent peace in Jorath,' added the Father of the Mountain, swinging the ball forward a second time. When it hit the right shoulder of the colossus, it made a loud cracking sound.

At last, something is working, commented Culhen, while he, Muai and Kamaluq helped the other Paladins maintain their positions on the wall. *After the failure of Trogadon's bolts, I was really beginning to worry about our plan.*

Although Ahren silently agreed with his friend, he continued to focus his attention on *Hate*, either stabbing repeatedly at the monster's eyes or driving his blade against the sword in his enemy's left hand.

This fight was revealing a simple truth that even *Hate* was beginning to understand – Khara, Falk, Ahren and Lanlion were only a side-show, a simple diversionary tactic, enabling the Father of the Mountain into combat, without a hint of anger in his body, the child of the Adversary. The supporting quartet possessed the ability to push their own dark emotions out of the way, so that *Hate* could not nourish himself upon them. The Father of the Mountain, on the other hand, had long since rid himself of hate and bloodlust – hence, he was probably the only being in all Jorath capable of stopping the raging giant.

Again, the Deep Steel ball spun through the air, hitting the stomach of the obsidian-coloured creature. Ahren could see *Hate's* eyes turning to peer at the Ring.

'Your pride has caused you to become separated from your army,' said Ahren, the coldness of the Void clearly audible in his voice.

Again, the ball smashed into the giant. Again, *Hate* winced in pain.

'And you never imagined that anyone existed who might be a danger to you in combat – someone who extinguished the fire of hate within him a long, long time ago.'

Another blow.

Hate tried to break out of the circle of warriors, but Lanlion's coat made the colossus' movements cumbersome, while Ahren, Falk and Khara were all now aiming their attacks on his eyes, realising that this was clearly his weak point.

'Father will tear you all to pieces,' snarled *Hate* malevolently. 'And then He will put you all back together again – according to *His* will.'

'This is what happened to *you*, then,' said the Father of the Mountain gently. 'No wonder that you despise the world so much.' Again, he spun the steel ball, and just as *Hate* stepped out from beneath Lanlion's magic cloak, the dwarf-like Paladin's weapon slammed into the giant's temple.

Hate stumbled, then crashed to the ground.

Ahren and Khara glided over him. They glanced at each other for the blink of an eye, then raised their blades.

'May you find peace in the embrace of the THREE,' murmured the Father of the Mountain. Then the Wind Blades did their business, plunging into the abyss of the fiery-red glimmering eyes of pure evil, which in their last heartbeat of life promised them all the most painful death imaginable.

Hate screamed scornfully one final time before being transformed into a cloud of smoke.

The last child of the Adversary had been vanquished.

'That was much easier than anticipated,' commented Trogadon cheerfully, as he approached with his crossbow on his shoulder. 'By the way, the wall is free of the enemy for the moment,' he added casually, pointing back over his shoulder at three dozen or so foot soldiers who with their broad shields and long spears were clearing away the many corpses on the bitterly contested section of the Ring.

'Well, I found this skirmish anything *but* easy,' groaned Falk as he shuffled wearily over to the others before dragging himself up onto Selsena's back, the Titejunanwa letting out a low whinny, thereby expressing to everyone else her concern for the old man's welfare.

'The beginning of our subterfuge could have run more smoothly,' admitted Ahren. 'But the only thing that counts is the result.' He pointed in front of him – an empty space but for two gruesomely serrated two-handers. '*Hate* is gone – for evermore.'

'Which brings us to the next stage of our plan,' said Khara as she fixed her eyes on Trogadon. 'Do you have the powder?'

The dwarf nodded solemnly.

'Then you should put it to use before the Dark Ones realise what has happened to their army leader,' murmured Lanlion. The Bloodless looked as white as chalk. Clearly, his creation of the dark cloak which he had draped around the child of the Adversary had drained him of all energy.

'Are you alright?' asked Ahren anxiously. 'Do you require...?'

'Blood,' said Lanlion soberly as he nodded. His features remained calm and relaxed. 'The days in which I could only dare whisper of my needs are over now.'

'I thought you didn't need it anymore,' said Trogadon, who was now rummaging around in his rucksack.

'I'm fine without it – as long as I don't have to perform sorcery.' Lanlion looked around for a heartbeat before the hint of a smile appeared. 'I will be back in time,' he added, then mounting Haminul and riding off.

Ahren watched the Bloodless for a couple of heartbeats before recognising a figure standing by a half-built catapult – whoever it was seemed to have been waiting for his pale friend. The Forest Guardian could hardly believe his eyes. It was Yantilla – and as soon as he dismounted the Black Bodach, she embraced the Bloodless.

'What's going on?' he murmured.

'War is like a clarion call for some people,' said Falk, steering Selsena to his former apprentice. Lanlion and Yantilla, meanwhile, had been enveloped by a deep blackness that didn't look in the least natural. 'They realise how much time they have been squandering by not following the impulse of their hearts.'

'Is she his *soul* companion?' asked Khara.

Falk shook his head. 'Lanlion's Blessing is as warped and knotted as the roots of an old tree. He will never be able to pass it on. The THREE can do no more for our friend. He must find his own happiness.' Then he winked at both Khara and Ahren. 'But in *your* case, everything seems to be going swimmingly.'

Are you all enjoying yourselves? asked Culhen sharply. *And are you all nice and relaxed as you exchange idle gossip? Would you like me to get the First to bring you some hot tea?*

Ahren guiltily turned his thoughts to his wolf's senses as he simultaneously turned to face the wall of the Ring. Clouds of arrows were flying over the Paladins and their companion animals, slowing down the progress of the attacking Dark Ones. Meanwhile, some of the Paladins were helping the spear carriers to clear the chemin de ronde of enemy corpses, Culhen having just spat out a piece of Sickle Hopper.

'Right. Finished,' grunted Trogadon cheerfully, Ahren glancing over at the dwarf. His squat friend was standing beside a small brazier on which he had neatly spread a greenish powder. The blacksmith was holding a flint and a piece of steel in his hands as he looked expectantly at Ahren.

The Forest Guardian nodded. 'The quicker Akkad is here, the better.'

Trogadon struck a few sparks over the brazier, the green powder then hissing, igniting and burning, rising into the sky in the form of a single green cloud. Satisfied, the blacksmith tested the temperature of the brazier with a quick touch before packing it back into his rucksack. 'That was precisely the right amount of signal powder. Perhaps the mixture of Dwarfish metals and Elven herbs will lead to less resistance between our two folk once victory is ours.'

Falk shook his head. 'Don't bet on it.'

'I wish we had more than *one* Ancient available for the next stage of our plan,' murmured Khara as she tapped her fingers on the handles of her weapons.

'Sleeps-in-Treetop is guarding Lirana in the Charm Circle, Uldini and Jelninolan are preparing for tomorrow, while Quin-Wa is coordinating the Wizardly Domes, where the remaining Ancients are situated, ready to resist any Bane Curses cast by the Adversary,' said the Father of the Mountain. 'All we can do is trust that Akkad soon gets here from Deepstone.'

'I know,' countered Khara with a pained smile. 'But that doesn't stop me wishing that we had more sorcerous support.'

'We *all* do,' commented Trogadon. 'Even if I will swear blind to any dwarf that I never admitted such a thing.'

The grin on the face of the blacksmith was infectious enough for all the companions to forget their troubles for a few brief heartbeats.

Ahren tickled Culhen behind the ears before putting the wolf's helmet back in place.

Better? he asked gently.

Thank you, said his friend politely. *I always start sweating there whenever the fighting starts.*

Ahren patted the wolf's flank. *I know, big lad.*

The hordes of Dark Ones were gathering before the Obsidian Fortress for their third assault. A brittle, temporary peace hung over the battlefield, the land having turned into an unappetising mush of snow and blood. Ahren wondered whether the reinforcements for the Ring would get to the Paladins in time or if the Champions of the gods would be forced to try and hold the wall on their own yet again.

'Here he comes,' said the First. 'And about time.'

Ahren and his companions on the wall turned expectantly to look towards Highstone. The Forest Guardian quickly caught sight of a solitary rider, whose stature was unmistakable.

'Fat but without spiked armour,' growled Trogadon with a broad grin. 'That has to be Akkad.'

'You *do* know that I can hear you?' asked Trimm irritably, who was sitting on a wooden stool that he had managed with considerable effort to retrieve from the northern tower of their section of wall. Eken was sitting beside the corpulent Paladin, his flattened ears suggesting to Ahren that he was even less happy to be here than his Champion of the gods.

'If you weren't present, then we wouldn't have half as much fun teasing,' countered the dwarf with a chuckle.

'Silence!' snapped the First. 'We have only one opportunity and must ascertain if the troops are in position. The heavy losses this morning were far greater than we had even feared.'

'For *Hate* we also supposedly only had one chance, and yet it took us *three* goes,' admitted Trogadon ruefully. 'I'm still annoyed that my bolt was completely ineffective this time.'

'And how much more good fortune and time are we going to waste?' snorted the First, pointing up at the sun now high in the sky. 'The way to the Adversary is long and tomorrow evening is drawing nigh.'

'Steady on there,' interjected Ahren. 'Our nerves are on edge…'

'And our ribs are broken,' complained Trimm.

Ahren threw his chubby brother a poisonous look. 'And yet, we have still managed to gain a partial victory that no-one can take away from us – all the children of the Dark god are dead.'

'And with them, the last Dopplers of Jorath,' added the Father of the Mountain gloomily. 'It would have been nice to have been able to save at least some of these Original Beings. They might have returned to serving the THREE once the Adversary was gone forever.'

'They made their choice a long time ago,' snarled the First. 'And now – enough with the sentimentality! The unexpectedly sudden assault of the Dark Ones has cost us hundreds of men and women whose fighting ability will be sorely missed in the upcoming battles.'

The matter-of-fact way the age-old Paladin referred to the lost lives – as if their deaths was merely an inconvenient obstacle on the way to victory – annoyed Ahren greatly, yet his own experience of war caused him to secretly admit that the veteran had a point.

'Falk and Lanlion are gathering mounted reinforcements,' he said. 'With the warriors of the Green Sea and the armoured fighters of the Knight Marshes our plan will surely bear fruit.'

The Father of the Mountain shook his head. 'We do not know that.' He pointed at the slowly increasing number of horses and riders approaching. 'The soldiers will bring us to the place that we wish to travel to – but only Akkad can ensure our next triumph.'

'May the THREE protect us,' muttered the First harshly. '*His* war magic was never that impressive.'

'Remember that *we*, too, must take responsibility for the outcome of the battle,' countered Ahren impatiently. 'I know that you and some of the others were very sceptical of our previous plan, which, admittedly, did not run at all smoothly, but I would appreciate it if you stopped complaining all the time.' The Forest Guardian knew in his heart that the upcoming night would bring with it even greater challenges, but the only thing he could do now was to push all fear right out of his mind.

'Our archers are running out of arrows again,' said Khara before pointing down at the Dwarfish commander, who was shouting out orders to the marksmen and -women. 'It's soon going to get *very* uncomfortable on this wall again.'

Ahren pondered the situation for a couple of heartbeats while he looked down at the battlefield on the other side of the wall. Low Fangs and High Fangs were bustling about beyond Lyssin's shooting range, while a multitude of Dark Ones were roaming through the flat land between the high walls of the Obsidian Fortress and the Ring, waiting for the hail of arrows from the defenders to cease. 'They are gathering for another assault. Clearly, none of the High Fangs has realised that *Hate* has fallen.'

'The servants of the Adversary have never been known for their humility,' mused the Father of the Mountain.

'But HE, WHO FORCES must have noticed *Hate* expiring,' interjected Khara. 'Why hasn't the Adversary warned His troops?'

The First frowned. 'The Bane Curse with which He tried to eliminate Ahren and the others in Kelkor was made up of powerful magic that had never existed before – created with a sense of desperate urgency and gnawing existential fear, and with the intention of us never uncovering His secret. If He truly is close to the nadir of His power now, then it is quite possible that He has not yet awoken – thanks mainly to sheer exhaustion.'

Ahren gave the First a warning look. Large parts of their plan were based on the Adversary reacting in particular ways. They had all agreed not to speak of their hopes and fears for the upcoming battles in case the Dark god might have sent out either Moon Runners as scouts or troublesome Swarm Claws to spy on them.

The First acknowledged Ahren's stare with a nod. It was better not to tempt fate with too many words.

Now that you are considering all our fates, interjected Culhen, *have you decided how you are to proceed without the necessary foot soldiers?*

Quickly and cleverly.

Can you be a little more precise, please?

The Forest Guardian hesitated. *I'm still working out the details.*

I feared as much, muttered the wolf.

'Let's hope for the best,' murmured Khara, pointing her chin to the stairs leading up to the battlement from below. 'Akkad has arrived.'

The well-rounded Ancient quickly climbed the steps, his waddling looking less than dignified. 'I rode as quickly as my horse could carry me.'

'The poor thing should be awarded with a medal for its efforts.'

'Trogadon!' scolded Ahren.

'Alright, alright – I'll be quiet. The cheeky grin on the dwarf's face suggested that he wouldn't be keeping his promise for long.

'*Hate* is dead, and the Ring is once more under our control,' reported Bergen, pointing at the gathering mass of Dark Ones and the Obsidian Fortress soaring behind it. 'The enemy gates are still open, but with the next assault, one or two of the High Fangs might suspect that their commanding officer has spent a little *too* much time on this side of the Ring. That will surely put paid to our opportunity.'

During the Paladin's speech, Akkad had removed from a bundle on his back a small, opaque-looking pane of glass, secured in a frame of hammered iron. The Ancient whispered a few words on its dull surface before it suddenly glittered as if it was lying in the morning hoarfrost on a bitterly cold winter's day.

'Let me see,' he murmured, holding the glass so that he could look through it at the Obsidian Fortress.

'Hm,' he said.

This was followed by ten heartbeats of silence, during which time another hail of arrows kept the Dark Ones at bay.

'Hm.'

'Get on with it!' growled the First.

'We are both fortunate *and* unfortunate.'

'Well, this is the best news I've heard all day,' commented Bergen dryly.

Akkad beckoned Ahren and the others to stand behind him so that they could all see through the pane. The opaque glass swallowed up all the details beyond it, the Obsidian Fortress appearing like a dark shadow beneath a clouded sky. Yet, Ahren could see something else through the charmed object. Something that they would be depending on for the next step in their plan. A glittering, golden ribbon stretched from north to south through the landscape. A dozen paces high, the phenomenon seemed like a second, aethereal wall of light hitting against a gate of the Obsidian Fortress – alas, not the outer one.

Fisker muttered a curse, Cassobo's chattering, too, certainly wasn't reminiscent of an Elven poetry recitation. 'The Arcane Wall is colliding with the *second* gate of the fortress.'

Squinting his eyes, the First stared past the glass. 'Eight hundred more paces of enemy territory at a minimum from the open gates to the second wall that we will have to negotiate,' he growled. 'You said that the Arcane Wall would cut right through the outermost gate.'

Akkad shook his head. 'I stated most clearly at our meeting yesterday that the Arcane Wall would be subject to distortion if we were to ask the Ancients in their domes to tap into the natural lines of magic that exist in this area. Which is why this Arcane Wall is slightly arched and leading through the second rather than the first eastern gate.'

Now Bergen was uttering expletives too.

'But it is all the stronger because of this,' added Akkad in an almost apologetic tone. 'Otherwise, the local magic would not be able to warp the Arcane Wall in this way.'

'Strong enough to hinder the Dark Ones between the first and second wall of the fortress?' asked the Father of the Mountain, who was genuinely curious. 'For, alas, if we are to push forward to this Arcane Wall, we will be deep within enemy territory.'

Akkad said nothing but shook his head hesitantly.

Ahren chewed on his lower lip to stop himself from cursing along with the others. The two Horde Bulls that had previously burst open the gates of the Obsidian Fortress and been snorting loudly as they waited outside the citadel were now being commanded loudly into position by High Fangs from the ranks of the assembling Dark Ones. Ahren understood where the powerful horns were going to aim for – the postern situated directly under the Paladins. It seemed that the Champions of the gods gathered here on this section of the battlements were too tempting a bait not to be swallowed – hook, line and sinker.

'We must decide,' said the Thirteenth. 'Are we going to try – as planned already – to push our way through to the Arcane Wall and thereby provide a bridgehead for our armies or are we not?'

All eyes turned to the First. 'Will it be possible to hold the position until early tomorrow?' asked Bergen in a low voice.

No-one else asked why this length of time was so important. They all knew the plan already and therefore the terrifying answer.

'From a strictly military point of view – no,' growled the age-old Paladin. 'But with sorcerous assistance – perhaps.'

Akkad put away his glass pane and pointed towards the inside of the two gates. 'Get me over there, and I will support you with every sinew in my body.'

The First looked deep into Ahren's eyes. The Horde Bulls snorted and scraped their hoofs on the snowy ground.

'Our plan might be an all-out attack with no return,' warned the veteran.

Ahren swallowed hard. There was no time for further debate. Out of the corner of his eye, he could make out Khara nodding her agreement –

her features displaying her full trust in her beloved. The Father of the Mountain smiled – he had made his peace with himself and the world. Then he, too, nodded. As did Trogadon, Bergen, Akkad, Fisker... Within a few heartbeats everyone had indicated their silent support. The Forest Guardian looked towards Deepstone, across the flatland directly behind the wall to where the defenders were marching towards him and his friends. Falk and Lanlion, too, were already visible on the horizon – and with them their allies from the Knight Marshes and the Green Sea. He straightened up.

This is the beginning of the end – one way or the other.

'We will attack.'

'Are you *sure* that you four will manage it?' asked Bergen for the third time already.

Ahren fixed his eyes on his broad-shouldered brother.

'Do *you* think you can manipulate your axe correctly? Or would you rather *practise* a little before the skirmishes begin?'

'Never mind.'

'My, but you were *very* caustic there,' whispered Khara into the Forest Guardian's ear.

'I'm nervous too, you know,' admitted Ahren equally quietly, turning his head to look once more at the Obsidian Fortress. Lyssin and Trogadon were standing to the right of a merlon, while he and Hakanu stood to its left. Beneath them was the eastern postern of the Ring while ahead of them the Horde Bulls began their cumbersome-looking assault, which would increase in speed in no time at all.

'Don't forget,' warned the First harshly. 'Wait until the very last moment!'

Ahren suppressed a snort. As if he could possibly forget such an important detail as *when* precisely to shoot! 'I'll aim left, you to the right,' whispered the Forest Guardian to his apprentice.

'As soon as you shoot, I will let my spear fly, Master!' The joy, so apparent in Hakanu's voice caused Ahren to groan. The lad's fiery enthusiasm was still burning brightly. Still, he wouldn't chastise his protégé. They were going to need as much inspiration as they could get in combatting the Dark god.

Ahren took a deep breath. The archers' artillery had long since ceased. It almost seemed as if both sides of the conflict were waiting for the two enormous, ox-like creatures with their lowered heads to begin hurtling towards the double-gates, heavily barricaded with metal supports.

I cannot believe that we are really doing this, said Culhen nervously.

An old lesson that Falk taught me once, explained Ahren. *If possible, let the enemy do your work for you.*

'They are attacking on a broad front!' yelled Bergen, the main mass of Dark Ones suddenly bellowing and moving forward, the Horde Bulls now galloping in front of them. 'Prepare yourselves!'

A good third of the enemy horde was heading straight towards under Ahren's feet – in the hope of spilling through the gates that were about to be smashed, while the rest of them raced towards the piles of corpses that were blocking their way, providing makeshift, macabre steps up to the crenellations.

Ahren concentrated fully on the Horde Bulls, hurtling towards him, their hooves thundering. The monsters were so huge that they could almost see over the wall if they were to lift their heads. Ahren could feel the stone under his feet shaking – as if the very wall itself feared the imminent impact.

'Not yet,' murmured Ahren, more to himself than to his waiting companions.

A flood of Low Fangs, Blood Wolves, Glower Bears and Agony Boars filled the slipstream of the two Horde Bulls aiming unerringly for the two gates.

'Not yet,' said Ahren a second time, noticing Hakanu's restlessness beside him.

The Horde Bulls with their pulverising hooves barged their way through the first piles of corpses that had formed in front of the Ring gates during the battle.

'Ready!' commanded the Forest Guardian as he fully extended *Fisiniell*. Hakanu hefted his spear in preparation. The sheer weight of the Horde Bulls compressed whatever bodies were left before the gates while the two beasts continued to maintain their speed.

Their horns were less than a dozen paces from the heavy doors.

'NOW!' bellowed Ahren, letting his arrow fly. Hakanu's spear was dispatched an instant later, the sharp bang of the baffle plate on Trogadon's crossbow piercing Ahren's eardrums.

Even as the Forest Guardian was reaching for a second arrow, the Horde Bulls smashed into the doors.

Wood splintered.

Steel squeaked and warped.

The chemin de ronde shook so violently that Ahren was knocked off his feet.

The Horde Bulls had broken through!

The only question that remained was – had Ahren and the three other ranged attackers done their work well. On all fours, the Forest Guardian crawled to the opposite side of the battlement, holding his breath as he pulled himself up to his feet at the balustrade.

'Ha!' exclaimed Trogadon, who had done precisely the same thing. 'Clean shots all round!'

Both Horde Bulls, mortally wounded, were staggering forward over what remained of the doors, but could only drag themselves a few paces further before collapsing in two heaps on the snow. Two arrows, a bolt and a spear had penetrated the eyes of the beasts before boring into the head of the two creatures, which were now breathing their last.

A thick cordon of both archers, crossbowmen and -women was arranged in lines only a few paces beyond the now dead monsters, and Ahren could see how many of the defenders were trembling like leaves. The soldiers had literally placed their lives in the hands of the four marksmen. If only one of the Horde Bulls had possessed sufficient strength to continue the assault, the result would undoubtedly have been a massacre. But the compact formation of the ranged fighters was essential, for now the next critical step was to follow – one in which the Paladins had to reciprocate by placing all *their* faith in the soldiers' abilities.

'Their assault has begun!' screamed Bergen, Ahren instantaneously spinning around. *Fisiniell* fell with a clatter on the chemin de ronde as *Sun* almost flew into his hand.

Already, those Dark Ones that had seen the congestion and decided against forcing their way through the shattered doors were clambering up the wall.

An Agony Bear fought its way up a pile of corpses on the opposite side of the chemin de ronde to where Ahren was standing before snorting and lunging at the Forest Guardian. Even before Ahren had a chance to react, Khara was dancing alongside the creature, bloody cuts immediately decorating its throat as it collapsed in front of the Paladin. Although Ahren wanted to thank his beloved, he already found himself springing forward, skewering a Low Fang that was intent on attacking Khara from behind.

Trogadon swung his hammer at a Glower Bear intent on killing Ahren while Culhen forced back a Blood Wolf that was preparing to bite the dwarf in the head.

So, it continued – the deadly cycle of attack, mutual support and defence, all along the entire section of wall between the two towers, Ahren and his friends trying to gain the upper hand over the stream of enemies.

Behind him, Ahren could hear the noise of crossbows dispatching their bolts followed by a chorus of Dark Ones screaming in agony. He allowed himself a grim smile. It had truly begun.

He thrust and stabbed, parried and swerved, and whenever he failed, his armour protected him from serious injury. Nonetheless, the ferocious battle took its toll, the blood splattering the defenders no longer merely that of their opponents. Ahren wished that more of his brothers and sisters were here, so that the power of their gods' Blessings would benefit them more.

'Are we almost done here?' gasped Bergen. 'My aching bones are wearying, and I don't know for how much longer…'

Loud cheering from the ranks of the defenders interrupted the Paladin, Ahren quickly finishing off a Low Fang with a thrust of his weapon before turning his head to look. The lethal semi-circle of crossbowmen and -women, supported by the arrows still being shot from the lines of archers had achieved the desired effect, the Dark Ones' assault having come to a halt, the enemy force now beating a hasty retreat – the High Fangs issuing the new commands, which the servants of the Adversary were obeying.

Ahren raised his arm three times in rapid succession, whereupon three short blasts from the bugle sounded. The army of ranged attackers created a gap in their midst, creating room for the reinforcements which included Falk and Lanlion.

'Wonderful,' murmured Bergen beside Ahren, the latter nodding in agreement.

Convoys of cavalry from the Knight Marshes and the Green Sea, led by Falk on Selsena and Lanlion on Haminul, stormed over the glittering snow and through the destroyed gates of the Ring, scything their way through the fleeing Dark Ones, hooves pounding and steel blades slashing this way and that.

The section of wall that Ahren and his companions had been defending emptied itself as the enemy army retreated towards the Obsidian Fortress – whose gates were slowly beginning to *close!*

'Advance!' bellowed the First, racing towards the steps. 'Time to get a foot in the door!'

'Do we *never* get a heartbeat's peace?' asked Fisker, blood pumping from a nasty cut to his right cheek.

'You should know better than to ask a question like that,' countered Bergen with a laugh. 'And – to be honest with you – it's nice to be the attacker once in a while.'

'We have only just about managed to successfully defend ourselves from a multitude of Dark Ones and now we are immediately expected to storm the walls of a citadel,' murmured Khara. 'Perhaps you should temper your optimism just a little bit?'

Bergen, accompanied by Ahren, was racing down the steps to where horses were already waiting for them. 'But we have a pair of open doors through which we can gain access,' he replied.

Ignoring both his own cuts and bruises and those of his friend, Ahren swung himself into Culhen's saddle. He pointed at the scattered corpses of Dark Ones riddled with bolts. 'These, here, were tempted by what they assumed was a viable opening.'

Bergen's face darkened. 'You *really* know how to cheer a person up!' Then he rode on ahead, following the First and Fisker who had already reached the remnants of the Ring's doors.

The Horde Bulls did their job – amazing! commented Culhen, racing through the gap between the two enormous corpses, Khara and Akkad on either side of him on their mounts. *First, they pushed the dead Dark Ones out of the way. Then they broke through our reinforced doors – it would have taken us way too long to unbolt them. And finally, they provoked the foolhardy victory frenzy on the part of the Dark Ones that turned into a fatal assault – for them!*

Ahren couldn't help smiling a little in satisfaction. They had turned the supposed strength of the enemy to their own advantage.

Having emerged from the shadow of the Ring to observe the Obsidian Fortress ahead of him, as well as the battlefield strewn with corpses with the snow glittering white and red, a thought suddenly struck him that he simply couldn't ignore – what if the Dark god had regained His power already and was merely waiting to turn the tables on Ahren and his companions by using precisely the same tactic?

We will find out soon enough, murmured Culhen in the Paladin's mind. *The Obsidian Fortress awaits us.*

Although Ahren had been certain since they had come up with their plan in the council of war that a deadly skirmish awaited them once they left the protection of the Ring, the reality was transpiring to be quite different.

Falk's and Lanlion's troops drove fleeing Dark Ones before them, while simply mowing down those other servants of the Adversary, which, with their hooves and flashing steel, had succumbed to their bloodlust and were foolishly trying to stand their ground against the well-armed riders.

Of course, the onrushing cavalry did not proceed unscathed, Ahren noticing the occasional corpse of an ally, lying in the snow beside their dead horse – most of them victims of Glower Bears, which had then met a similar fate – but there was not a single living member of the enemy army there to resist by the time the Paladin and his friends were thundering through the blood-speckled snow. The cavalry was the broom and the Dark Ones, the leaves being swept clean away.

'This is too easy,' shouted Fisker anxiously, the gloomy walls of the Obsidian Fortress looming ever larger ahead of them, its very blackness seeming to swallow all the light of the sun.

Ahren shivered as he silently acknowledged a certain grudging respect towards the enemy bulwark that they would soon be attempting to storm.

'Does anyone else get the feeling that we are riding right into a trap?' continued the blonde, curly-headed Paladin.

'Shut up,' growled Bergen. 'Before you provoke any more misfortune.'

The first arrows shot from the top of the high walls of the Obsidian Fortress rained steeply down towards them, slamming into the earth around the attackers.

Culhen stumbled when a projectile ricocheted off his helmet, while Ahren flinched as an arrow glanced off the ribbon armour on his left shoulder with a bright clanging noise.

'Thank you *very* much,' barked Bergen, glaring at the Paladin with the golden locks as he took a shield – which a forward-thinking squire had provided him with – from his horse's saddlebags. The other companions followed his example – with the exception of Ahren, who was sitting on Culhen and therefore had no shield.

Why is it always me? complained the wolf, picking up speed. An arrow grazed the tip of his tail, causing him to howl.

What would Yoka have to say about that? commented Ahren. *After all, she has to hurtle along without any protection whatsoever.* He immediately regretted his words, Culhen having immediately veered sideways to provide as much cover to the Ice Wolf with his body as he could manage at full speed.

'At least, Muai is with Quin-Wa!' shouted Khara. 'There is no way that Culhen can take care of *two* unarmoured companion animals!'

Ahren thought for a heartbeat about the Eternal Empress. She would also play her role in the last stages of today's plan. Then a shudder ran through him, his left arm suddenly hanging numbly by his side.

What the...? he thought in a daze, a rock the size of his head having landed with a dull thud in the snow. The enemy fighters were hurling down chunks of stone at the Paladins from the crenels high above! And one of them had hit his limb!

'Faster! Faster! *Faster!!*' he yelled, quite unnecessarily, Culhen and the others knowing full well what to do.

'They let the cavalry through safely!' bellowed the First, glancing back over his shoulder. 'They want to split us up and —'

With a nauseating crunching sound, a rock hit the head of the age-old Paladin's horse, both veteran and animal collapsing on the snow in a tangle of arms, legs and hooves.

Culhen! commanded Ahren as he forced himself to think straight, the wolf reacting immediately by fixing his fangs around the unconscious First's right arm and dragging him away from the slain mount.

It was only a few paces to the life-saving archway in the Obsidian Fortress which would offer them protection from the deadly missiles, but Culhen was hit several times – and the First once more – before they finally reached the shadow of the broad vaulted archway, where they stopped to draw breath.

I think I will have to thank Trogadon yet again, said the wolf, licking his bleeding front paw. *The armour that he forged for me has saved my life at least three times during our advance from the Ring to here.*

Ahren remembered all the hits he himself had suffered today but which had resulted in nothing more than plenty of cuts and bruises. When this war was finally won, Ahren was going to make sure that all Jorath knew how much they owed the dwarf for the ensuing peace.

The blacksmith in question finally arrived under the archway, holding a large shield protectively over his pony, the Father of the Mountain in their slipstream. The dwarf-like Paladin had run all the way, spinning the ball at the end of his plait above his head at a stunning speed, thereby deflecting every missile that had been hurled down at him. The face of the normally calm and centred Paladin was red and gleaming with sweat.

'We are caught in a trap,' grunted Bergen, pointing ahead. Now and again, a rock would fall on the western side of the entrance, a clear sign that the Low Fangs were only waiting on the battlements for the companions to stick their noses beyond the protection of the gleaming, black archway.

By now, the cavalry under Falk's and Lanlion's command had lost both their panache and their advantage. With worried glances at the Paladins under the archway and Akkad crouching next to them, the mounted soldiery circled in the area between the first and second walls of the Obsidian Fortress, waiting for a signal from the Paladins to tell them that the assault was to continue. The Dark Ones lurking in this section of the citadel were slowly regaining control as they began to increasingly hem the cavalry in.

'We have to push through to our allies,' muttered Fisker, stating the obvious. 'If the cavalry are forced into turning back to help *us*, they will be assaulted with rocks from above the arch and also by Dark Ones to their rear, forcing them against the wall and into further danger.'

'The First isn't moving at all,' said Khara, who was tending to the unconscious man. 'And this swelling is like a second head.'

'That's not good,' commented Fisker glibly. 'Then he will be able to bark commands at us on the double when he wakes up.'

Ahren rubbed the back of his neck. He looked over to Khara for help, for he was completely at a loss. Had they taken one chance too many? Had they pushed their luck too far?

'Whatever we do, we had better do it soon,' said Hakanu, pointing over his shoulder. 'The Dark Ones who were positioned on the outer wall are slowly coming down the steps and moving in our direction.'

For the briefest of moments, Ahren peered out from under the archway, immediately understanding what his apprentice meant. Countless Low- and High Fangs were descending, antlike, down narrow sets of stairs that seemed to have been designed by a penny-pinching master builder. It would not be long now until the companions were completely surrounded.

'Akkad simply *must* break through,' murmured Ahren. 'As soon as he reaches the Arcane Wall, he can release his magic once again and then save us all.' He looked earnestly at the Ancient. 'You *can* do this, can't you?'

'Em…' The man's hesitant response caused a shiver to run down the Forest Guardian's spine.

'Does anyone else have an idea of how we can reach our goal? Otherwise, retreat will be our only option.' Ahren's mouth was dry as he spoke.

His question was followed by several heartbeats of tense silence, broken eventually by a low snarl that alerted the young man. Eken was staring at Trimm, his glittering eyes narrowed, the tail of the tomcat whipping slowly from side to side. The injured Paladin had tried to stay out of the way of the main battle, only participating when his life was truly in danger as he had no wish to suffer further physical pain.

'I absolutely will *not* do so,' said the grandee sternly, picking up his companion animal and glaring at him. 'That *you* of all companion animals would even suggest such a thing!'

Eken snarled again, but this time he sounded more urgent, and even fearful.

'Yes, I *know* that we are all trapped here.'

'Is there any way that we can *help* you?' Bergen's voice dripped with sarcasm. 'I mean, it's not as though we have any other worries apart from watching the pair of you argue with one another.'

Squirming out of Trimm's grasp, Eken jumped down and began demonstratively licking that part of his fur that the Paladin had been holding.

Clearly, their private discussion continued, until eventually Trimm murmured meekly: 'It's easy for *you* to say. It's not *you* who will be risking their skin.'

The tomcat simply stared calmly at his friend before slowly blinking once.

'Alright,' sighed the corpulent Paladin. 'But don't start caterwauling if I'm killed because of you.' He turned to face Ahren and the others, his bald head bobbing as he swallowed hard several times.

'Would...would it...would it help if *Akkad* got *my* armour?' asked Trimm, his voice trembling.

'Absolutely,' replied Bergen instantly. 'Out of your barbed shell with you.'

Trimm bit on his lower lip. Ahren knew his cowardly brother well enough to understand what an effort this heroic act of self-sacrifice was for Trimm.

'You might well be saving *all* of us,' said Ahren encouragingly. The other companions nodded in agreement. The Forest Guardian then turned to Eken. 'We will look after him well – and that's a promise,' he said, looking down at the cat. 'And we are grateful to you for having persuaded him.'

Eken rubbed against Ahren's leg, leaping quickly away to his own Paladin once he noticed Culhen's jealous stare.

Trimm gulped, nodded, then reached for the gorget of his barbed Deep Steel armour. The corpulent man seemed to pull at something for several heartbeats before first the breastplate and then the other parts of the armour fell away, revealing a kind of chest harness of leather plates to which barbs had been attached.

'Ah, I understand,' muttered Trogadon with an appreciative nod. 'The pieces of metal are simply hung onto the harness, their weight causing them to slide into each other.'

'Let's get on with dressing Akkad,' said Khara, pointing both at the approaching Dark Ones to the east of the archway as well as the cavalry west of their improvised temporary accommodation, the horses and their riders becoming increasingly encircled.

Trimm peeled himself out of his leather underclothes, Ahren noticing that although his brother hadn't lost any weight, he *was* looking somewhat more muscular. Trimm acknowledged his look.

'There wasn't enough time to slim myself down, so I tried to make sure that I would be able to move in my armour with at least a modicum of grace.' While he was speaking, he helped Akkad put on the armour by skilfully hooking the sections into place on the Ancient.

'It's a little tight,' said Akkad with a tortured grin. 'Maybe I shouldn't have eaten breakfast.'

'What is the plan?' asked Khara, looking at her companions.

Ahren pointed at Culhen. 'He will carry Akkad over to Falk and Lanlion. Then the cavalry will make a charge for the gates, and our armoured Ancient will activate the Arcane Wall.' The Forest Guardian refrained from explaining what would happen if Akkad *failed* to ignite the sorcery of the Wizardly Domes in the manner intended. 'Meanwhile, we will engage the Dark Ones behind us.'

'Yet another tug-of-war?' groaned Fisker.

Ahren looked down at his aching left arm. Since they had arrived under the archway, the feeling had returned in his hand, but his fingers simply refused to stop trembling.

'I know what you mean,' he murmured to the ex-pirate. The Forest Guardian sensed that his own battered body wasn't able to take much more.

'None of us is in good shape,' said Bergen, who was standing awkwardly, having received a blow to his right knee.

'Ready,' said Trimm squeakily. 'Akkad has his armour on – and I am standing here, battered and bruised, dressed only in my trousers while a horde of Dark Ones is advancing on us...' The corpulent Paladin's voice faded into terrified murmuring, Ahren pressing him gently down onto the ground beside the unconscious First.

'We will take care of you,' he murmured.

Trimm nodded nervously before holding on for dear life to the age-old Paladin, as if the First, even in his sleep, could come to his rescue.

'Oops! This is trickier than I thought it would be,' said Akkad, who was trying to find a comfortable position in Culhen's unique saddle.

Akkad is really heavy, commented the wolf as the Ancient continued to adjust himself.

'No more time,' murmured Bergen. 'I got Karkas to convey our plans to Selsena via Sun Shimmer. The Titejunanwa was able to tell Falk. The message from him is that the cavalry has almost no room to manoeuvre.

If they are pushed any nearer to us, they will be greeted by a hail of rocks.'

'Akkad?' asked Ahren.

'Yes?'

'Hold on tight.'

'What do you —'

Go! commanded the Forest Guardian, the wolf immediately sprinting away as though someone had told him that a roast joint of meat was waiting for him at the gleaming black gates of the second wall of the fortress. At least a dozen rocks ricocheted off Akkad's and Culhen's armour, the wolf using all his power in his attempt to reach Falk and Lanlion. Then Ahren turned to face the first of the Dark Ones – an onrushing Blood Wolf.

Ahren was about to evade the animal, but then a Glower Bear came to assist the creature. Despite his best efforts, the Thirteenth could not avoid being pushed back by the sheer weight of the two Dark Ones.

'Fall Back!' he roared, 'or we will be *overrun!'*

Whimpering, Trimm did as he was told, dragging the still unconscious First by the arm until Trogadon took over from the fearful Paladin, pulling the age-old warrior out of the danger zone with more success.

'They are driving us out into the open!' yelled Bergen, whose right foot was already illuminated by the bright midday sunshine. Not three heartbeats later, a rock landed on the trampled snow within an inch of him. The Paladin cursed colourfully.

Ahren and his friends did their level best to gain the upper hand over the Blood Wolf and the Glower Bear in what was now a very confined area, but they had run out of time, for the monstrous creatures, clearly under the control of a High Fang, were pushing them ever more out into the open.

A rock plummeted down a hair's breadth away from Ahren, the Paladin groaning with frustration before yelling at the top of his voice: *'RUN!'* He nearly tripped over himself as he began to carry out his own instruction: *'To the second gateway!'*

It was a hopeless undertaking, for already dozens of Dark Ones were approaching them from the west – but Ahren simply had no idea of what else he could do.

The cavalry around Falk and Akkad began to gallop towards the gate, a good eight hundred paces away, the gap between Ahren's little group and the men and women on horseback now growing by the heartbeat. The Forest Guardian took a step towards the rescuing cavalry. He was about to spur his friends on with an encouraging roar when something hit him violently in the back, catapulting him forward before he found himself inadvertently ploughing his way, head over heels, through the snow. He heard Lyssin screaming, the Father of the Mountain cursing furiously, Fisker gasping and Trogadon shouting furiously.

When his vision had sufficiently cleared to be able to see properly again, he caught sight of the Agony Boar that must have rammed into him. The sharp-tusked creature was now charging at him again, its head bowed, Ahren quickly calculating that there was simply no way that he could get out of the way in time. To the young man's horror, he also caught sight of Khara being shaken this way and that by a Blood Wolf that had her clamped between its gleaming teeth, while two Low Fangs were stabbing at the bloodstained Fisker. Bergen was trying in vain to pull his axe out of a collapsed Glower Bear. Then he saw a High Fang jumping straight at him.

I'm done for, thought Ahren, his mind suddenly strangely calm. *In fact, we are all done for – well and truly.*

Chapter 16

The eyes of the Agony Boar narrowed, its squeals hurting Ahren's ears with their dissonance. The Forest Guardian barely had time to mentally prepare for the impact of the Dark One's tusks before his opponent was already on top of him, casually sweeping aside the Paladin's already malfunctioning sword arm, which now snapped like a blade of grass beneath a horse's hoof.

Culhen cried out to Ahren, but the wolf's words were washed away in a wave of pain as the pig-like creature repeatedly rammed against the Paladin's chest, a rib breaking with each violent thrust.

'Khara...' he murmured, his fading vision catching a brief sight of the Swordsmistress being slung through the air by a salivating Blood Wolf, the upper right side of her robe drenched with blood.

The Agony Boar squeaked as it aimed straight for Ahren's face, the Forest Guardian's world turning to blackness...

...only to become, after a single despairing heartbeat, blindingly white as an unbearably powerful light enveloped him and tossed him about as if it were the surging wave of a stormy sea, playfully seizing hold of a careless swimmer. Ahren felt both weightless and extraordinarily heavy at the same time. Suddenly, he was lying on his stomach, his mouth filled with snow. His broken arm sent hot needles of pain shooting up to his mind, while every tortured breath gave his broken ribs another opportunity to voice their agonised protest.

He lay there gasping, and it was only after many heartbeats that it suddenly occurred to him that there was one thing missing from his little world of pain – the sound of combat all around him. He wanted to get to his feet, or at the very least, turn his head, but all strength had deserted him. The sheer number of injuries inflicted on him during the course of the day, which he had managed to suppress in his fighting frenzy, now demanded their tribute, having turned him into a helpless lump of flesh encased in armour that simply refused to budge.

Suddenly, he felt Culhen's rasping tongue licking the snow from his face. The wolf's nose pushed, prodded and snuffled close to his own, the soft fur of his friend rubbing against the young man's cheek.

Ahren? asked Culhen cautiously, as if from a great distance.

I am still alive, countered the Forest Guardian. *At least, I think so.*

Then you are in the best of company, reported the wolf, clearly relieved. *The Father of the Mountain is bandaging Khara's bleeding arm, the First is still fast asleep and Trimm lost consciousness when a Low Fang caught his upper thigh with a swing of its club.*

Ahren suddenly felt a pain that was not his own.

The rest of us are in a similarly sorry state.

Summoning all his strength, the Forest Guardian grasped Culhen's fur with his functioning arm and dragged himself onto his knees. With that, he caught sight of the wolf's face and flinched in horror. His friend's helmet was nowhere to be seen, and the left eye of the animal was caked in blood and swollen shut. Culhen was holding his left front paw in a hanging position in front of him, while blood was dripping from the tip of his tail.

'Oh, big lad,' murmured Ahren compassionately. 'You *look* how I *feel.*'

I hope you don't mind if I return the dubious compliment. The wolf nudged him gently with his nose before licking his face once again, this time concentrating particularly on a cut to Ahren's right cheek.

'Is...' Ahren began, only to break off momentarily and cough painfully. 'Is everyone still...*alive?*' With that, he looked around for the first time, instinctively squinting. More damage must have been done to his head than he had first thought. The world was cast in a yellowish white glow, which seemed to literally stick to his friends. There was no sign whatsoever of the Dark Ones that had been attacking them.

'Yes – so far,' said the Father of the Mountain solemnly, the dwarf-like figure approaching him. 'Although the First and Khara are definitely in need of sorcerous intervention.'

Ahren grunted painfully as he pulled himself fully upright so that he could get a better picture of his immediate environment. He knew that he should be concerned about his beloved and the age-old Paladin, but his mind seemed strangely numbed – it was almost as though the Void had him in its grip. The second gateway of the Obsidian Fortress existed no more. Fragments of the two heavy doors lay scattered on the ground, the two towers on either side of the archway having collapsed on top of themselves. Akkad was kneeling a few paces in front of the ruins, his head bowed, his hands pressed together as though he were praying urgently to the THREE. Trimm's armour, now in pieces was strewn around the area – whether deliberately cast off or flung away by the

Ancient's sorcery, Ahren could not tell. The yellowish glow seemed to be pulsating from him, its light being cast dozens of paces in all directions, and at whose perimeter hordes of Dark Ones were standing, running and snorting chaotically, many of the creatures marked with fresh battle scars.

'Is this a Shield Charm?' asked Ahren, confused.

'Yes,' the Father of the Mountain replied. 'The light is driving them away. Akkad muttered something about wanting to imitate the special lanterns of the Wrath Elves with the help of the Arcane Wall.'

'This charm here is different,' said Lanlion, the pale, blood-spattered figure in his black armour doing justice to any terrifying ghost story that might be told while sitting around a lonely campfire. 'The power of the Bane Lanterns would not have been sufficient to protect us this close to the Adversary. Furthermore, he is not using any Blood Magic – but only sheer sorcerous power.'

Ahren heard a deep scepticism in the voice of the Bloodless. 'Is this a bad thing?' asked the Forest Guardian.

Lanlion raised his arms defensively. 'I have no wish to complain. Akkad has saved all our lives. But the fact is – he is expending enormous amounts of magic with every passing heartbeat – not only his own, but also that of the two Ancients in the domes at either end of the Arcane Wall, not to mention the magic of the Energy Line to which the Arcane Wall is tuned. It is like diverting a whole river in an attempt to keep a bucket that has no bottom filled to the brim.'

'How long will he be able to keep this up?' croaked Bergen, whose throat looked terribly red – as though some fearsome creature had almost strangled him to death.

'It depends on how powerful the land is upon which he is kneeling,' said Lanlion, nodding towards Akkad. 'He could tell us if he only had the time to.'

'We must get our most seriously wounded back to the Ring,' muttered Ahren as he struggled over to Khara. The Swordsmistress was unconscious. Using her golden sash, the Father of the Mountain had applied a pressure bandage under her right shoulder, tying off her badly injured arm. The fingers of Ahren's beloved looked incredibly pale in contrast to the bloodstains that speckled them.

'There is still time,' said the Father of the Mountain. 'Falk has already broken through to the east with Selsena and the surviving cavalry and will demand assistance for us. He hopes that Jelninolan will be able to donate one of her bottles of Healing Water as well.'

Ahren looked down at Khara and then over to the First, whose swelling looked as though some creature was trying to break through the man's skull from within. Now the young man regretted having been so wasteful with Hakanu's water at the beginning of the battle.

We were wounded, Ahren, was Culhen's gentle reminder. *Without the Healing Water you wouldn't have stood any chance against* Hate, *and I would have been torn to shreds on the wall.*

Ahren scanned the area with concern. 'Where is Hakanu?'

The Father of the Mountain pointed at the destroyed gateway. 'Youthful curiosity,' he murmured.

Ahren dragged himself over to Akkad but resisted the temptation to tap the Ancient on the shoulder for fear of disturbing his concentration. The man's lips moved constantly, the Forest Guardian suspecting that Akkad was channelling the magic with his prayer.

So, we have reached the point where all we can do is pray, he thought morosely.

'...and when your spear hit the target, I thought my heart would stop beating,' Ahren heard Lyssin croon, and she seemed genuinely taken by his protégé's achievement.

'One of my better ideas,' Hakanu replied. The apprentice sounded exhausted but content.

Ahren picked his way through the remains of the gateway, noticing as he did so that the light of Akkad's charm ended a little way beyond the shattered arch. The Ancient was like a lantern, protecting only those who enjoyed the benefit of his light.

Ahren found the two young Paladins not two paces beyond where most of the rubble lay, both of them sitting on two large, smooth, blocks of obsidian situated just within the circle of magical light. A little to their right stood Trogadon, directly on the edge of the spell. The dwarf was swinging his hammer at any Dark Ones foolish enough to come too close to him. There was already an impressive pile of bodies lying at his feet. Four arrow shafts protruded from the warrior's body, but they didn't seem to deter him from continuing his unequal battle.

'Ahren,' he said cheerfully on seeing the Paladin. 'Come over here and give me a hand at releasing these damned creatures from their existence while they still can't attack us. After a day of skirmishes, it is really relaxing to exact revenge without fear of suffering more damage.'

Ahren nodded towards his own left arm, which was hanging uselessly like a dead thing. The throbbing caused by the break was almost like a tried and trusted travelling companion, so familiar was he by now with such injuries. 'I'd better not,' he said, glancing past the remains of the destroyed second gateway.

Almost five furlongs beyond was the third gateway. Black, tall, smooth, flanked by two towers. And as yet undamaged.

Although Ahren knew that there were many more of these walls until the heart of the citadel, it seemed to him as though they were trapped in one of those never-ending nightmares where one ran and ran yet made no progress. 'Two walls have been breached,' he murmured.

'There are still eighteen to go,' said Lyssin in a low voice. Ahren looked at her and nodded. 'This fortification seems endless to me,' she added before pointing at the low clouds above them. 'Sun Shimmer did as she had promised – she played an endless game of cat-and-mouse with the Swarm Claws of the fortress so that they would not swoop down on us here. Those creatures hate our Roc from the bottom of their evil hearts.'

'And the way they were trying to hunt down Sun Shimmer when we were landing!' said Hakanu with a broad grin. 'It seems the Dark god has given them the impulse to prevent Sunju and her enormous bird from hovering unhindered over the fortress.'

Lyssin said nothing, simply placing a hand on the boy's shoulder and shaking it gently. It seemed to Ahren as if he were observing two war veterans enjoying a brief moment's respite in the heat of battle.

No, he corrected himself. *More like brother and sister taking care of one another.* The thought gave him courage.

'What was that I heard about your spear?' he asked, fixing his eyes on his apprentice.

The lad nodded towards the rubble around them. 'As soon as I thought we were all going to die here, I became so angry that I focused all my magic into a single throw and flung the spear against this entrance.' He shrugged his shoulders. 'The only thing I could think of was that we *had* to break through to the Arcane Wall.'

'At the very same moment, Akkad released his Light Charm,' muttered Trogadon, slamming his hammer into a pouncing Fog Cat. 'I am no magician, but it seems that the spell gave Hakanu's throw a little extra...force.'

The apprentice nodded at the spear beside him, stuck into the ground between two rocks. 'The shaft is still red-hot. I don't think I should try the same trick again any time soon.'

Ahren remembered Khara and the other wounded companions. 'Let us hope that the rest of the day runs more smoothly. It would be a welcome relief,' he said. Then he pointed towards the east. 'I'm going back to Khara. And the three of you might think twice about continuing to dance on the edge of the volcano – if you understand my meaning. Firstly, we don't know if Akkad's charm will suddenly weaken, and secondly, I can see Low Fangs with bows and spears gathering back there.'

Hakanu and Lyssin looked over at the third gateway, in front of which six High Fangs were barking out orders and literally whipping their troops into what – with a little imagination – could be described as a crude military formation. A shiver ran down Ahren's spine. Dressed in armour, equipped with weapons and organised into an army, these Dark Ones of the Adversary would – once free of the shackling Ring – fall over Jorath like a plague.

'Let us return to the others,' said Hakanu, helping Lyssin to her feet, the latter playfully wiping the dirt off her knees as if they had just enjoyed a very agreeable picnic. Suddenly, a heap of rubble – the remains of one of the towers – began to rumble, causing Ahren to spin around in horror, his arms and ribs protesting painfully in response. First, Yoka's head, then the rest of her body emerged from the pile of rocks, until the Ice Wolf was standing beside him, shaking the dust from her fur.

'What's going on here?'

This was followed by the sound of a protesting whimper and a flash of light, Kamaluq manifesting himself not four paces away from the Ice Wolf.

'Stop complaining,' laughed Hakanu. 'She won fair and square.'

The fox, still uttering offended tones, slunk off towards Akkad.

'I never knew that he was such a sore loser,' said Hakanu apologetically as he glanced at Lyssin, the latter merely shrugging her shoulders in response.

Ahren looked quizzically at the two young Paladins, only for Trogadon to clarify the situation. 'The animals were playing hide-and-seek. Yoka was the winner.'

Ahren shook his head in disbelief. 'It seems that a *lot* of us suffered blows to the head today.' Then he made his way to his other friends, his eyes gazing towards the east, from where hopefully reinforcements would soon be coming. Despite the silly pranks that were being played, the bitter truth was that if help didn't arrive soon, they would be left completely to their own resources if they were to have any chance of successfully fighting their way back to the Ring.

The afternoon had passed at a leisurely pace without any sign of the longed-for troops. From time to time, Ahren had checked on his beloved's state of health, but as there was nothing that he could do for her anyway, he had slowly but surely drifted off into a state of semiconsciousness.

He was rudely awakened by the flapping of a pair of enormous wings and the screeching of hundreds of malformed birds. He looked up and recognised Sun Shimmer who was almost plummeting downwards, directly towards Akkad's charm. Behind her, like a living thunderbolt, were the Swarm Claws hunting her down.

'Out of the way! Out of the *way!*' screamed Sunju, waving her arms wildly.

Paladins scattered in all directions, Ahren throwing himself with a groan on the unconscious Khara as Sun Shimmer hit the ground, creating a veritable inferno of wildly tossing snow and enormous, dancing feathers, the enormous bird screaming in pain. Here and there, blood was seeping from her plumage – testament to what she had suffered at the beaks and claws of her pursuers during this exhaustingly long day.

Oh, how I hate these so-called birds, growled Culhen, baring his fangs as Yoka howled in anger, Cassobo chattered wildly, and Kamaluq whimpered as loudly as the little fox could manage, while Haminul whinnied urgently. Sun Shimmer was *their* queen, and she was injured. The companion animals were screaming for vengeance.

'Just as well my good bear is guarding the soul companions in Highstone,' murmured the Father of the Mountain. 'It isn't easy to provoke Hanulf, but if he saw Sun Shimmer in her present condition, he would challenge all the Dark Ones of the Obsidian Fortress single-handedly.'

Ahren narrowed his eyes and peered up at the Swarm Claws. There were so many of the birds above them that they darkened the sky – although they, too, were avoiding the light being cast by Akkad's charm.

'I am pleased that you have come,' he said, turning to Sunju, 'but the way things are looking, you and Sun Shimmer are now stuck here along with us.'

The pale woman swung herself off the Roc's back and rubbed the bird's beak. 'We heard of your critical situation through Eken, and Trimm's fat tomcat can be *very* persuasive when he wishes to be.' The purring animal quickly trotted over from his resting Paladin and rubbed himself against Sun Shimmer's claws.

'I wonder where he gets it from?' murmured Ahren with a crooked grin.

Sunju looked around at the others, raising her eyebrows with a look of concern. 'And for a change, Eken *wasn't* exaggerating. You really *do* look like a sorry lot.'

'You don't need to tell us,' Fisker countered caustically. 'We were here for the whole thing, you know.'

Sunju nodded towards the wooden construction on Sun Shimmer's back. 'You'd better load the injured up here and then get on yourselves.'

Although he was sorely tempted, Ahren refrained from immediately handing Khara over to the protection of the Roc. 'We would love to accept your offer, but as more or less all of us are wounded, we would have to leave Akkad here on his own. Something we cannot do,' he said.

'Yes – we can, and we *must*,' countered Bergen hoarsely. The blonde Paladin was shaking with pain, while his neck had now turned a purple colour. 'The fact that he is holding our position here and creating a marching zone for our troops tomorrow was always part of the plan, in case you've forgotten – which also stated, if I'm not mistaken, that we were to return to the castle with *all possible speed.*'

Ahren pointed at the lurking Dark Ones, now assembling outside the third, as yet undamaged gateway of the Obsidian Fortress – just beyond where the Light Charm reached its limit. 'Our *plan* envisaged us taking control of the *first* gateway and establishing a bridgehead there by reinforcing it with soldiers and weaponry. Then we were going to check the ring structure of the fortress for signs of weakness that we could take advantage of at dawn tomorrow.'

'Nothing has changed in this respect,' muttered Bergen defiantly. 'Except that we have advanced to the gateway *beyond.*'

Ahren shook his head. 'And the Dark Ones have cut us off from our supplies. If we fly away on Sun Shimmer, then Akkad will be left totally on his own. Should his magic run out…'

'If such a thing is to happen, then four hundred extra soldiers won't make a blind bit of difference,' said Lanlion. 'The Dark Ones will overrun them all, anyway.'

Ahren muttered a curse. 'We should have broken off once *Hate* had been slain,' he grunted. 'What *was* I thinking, trying to drive forward with this godsforsaken idea despite so many things having already gone wrong?'

Sunju placed a hand on his shoulder. 'Have faith in those who remained behind,' she said with a smile. 'Sun Shimmer informed Muai, and Quin-Wa is already busily adapting our plan to the new circumstances.'

Ahren muttered gruffly: 'She is powerful but completely on her own, unless she tears Uldini and Jelninolan away from their preparations —'

A succession of loud whizzing sounds caused the Forest Guardian to break off. They seemed to be coming from the east, sailing high through the late afternoon sky.

'She *isn't* alone,' announced Sunju, the ground under Ahren's feet suddenly trembling. 'All the armies of Jorath are by her side.'

The whizzing and shaking faded away, and it was only when one of the towers of the first obsidian gateway collapsed in on itself that Ahren understood what he had experienced. 'The catapults!' he grinned.

'Human *and* Dwarfish,' Sunju confirmed. 'You have forgotten that your presence here has tempted the guards away from the outer walls of the fortress. Which meant that every horse and giant was employed in bringing the catapults from their safe positions behind the Ring to where they are now positioned – in no-man's land. At last, the siege weaponry can be put to use.'

With an ear-splitting bang, the second tower of the outermost wall collapsed in on itself, and with it, the remains of the first obsidian gateway. Low Fangs rushed along the shaking ramparts, driven on by furiously crying High Fangs. The more monstrous of the Dark Ones were searching for a way eastward through the rubble of the gateway so that they could stop any further progress on the part of the siege weapons now positioned before the main gateway to the Obsidian Fortress.

'Hopefully, there are troops out there that can protect the catapults,' murmured Fisker sceptically.

'Humans, elves *and* dwarfs,' said Sunju. 'United in their determination to wipe this fortress and its owner off the face of Jorath.'

'You sound like Uldini when he thinks the bards are listening,' teased Trogadon, slinging Trimm onto his shoulder to carry him to Sun Shimmer.

'Or like Lanlion on a cheerful summer's day,' added Bergen.

'Oh, mock all you like,' said the Bloodless, smiling wanly, glancing up at the circling Swarm Claws before beginning to attach Trimm's armour to the unconscious fellow. 'You are only jealous because your vocabulary consists of little more than a couple of dozen grunting noises.'

'Will I *ever* get used to this pointless blather?' asked Lyssin as she carefully helped Ahren carry Khara onto the back of the Roc.

'It's a bit like the noise of battle,' said Ahren before his voice was drowned out by another salvo of catapult rocks, which were methodically beginning to pound the outermost wall of the Obsidian Fortress. 'At some point, you simply don't hear the ruckus anymore.'

For a heartbeat, she looked at him in confusion. Then she giggled.

'See? he murmured gently. 'You understand already.'

The sun hung low above the walls of the Obsidian Fortress as Ahren and his companions carefully strapped themselves and all the injured to the flying wooden coach. Ahren glanced one last time at the kneeing Akkad.

'We will return,' he promised. 'And by that time, help will have already reached you.'

'Why don't we simply wait here until the army has arrived?' asked Fisker nervously. 'The Swarm Claws above us are already whetting their beaks in anticipation of Sun Shimmer ascending and serving them their supper.'

'It will take too long for the soldiers to get here,' countered Bergen. 'We still have other work to do this night, and we must all be healed for us to be successful, remember.'

Ahren understood the scepticism of his shrewd brother all too well. Flying on Sun Shimmer's back through a cloud of bloodthirsty birds was going to be anything but a pleasure.

Where have those days disappeared to when a single Swarm Claw was my greatest challenge? he asked himself, remembering his tree-climbing in Eathinian when he had unwittingly rescued the Voice of the Forest from one of these fiendish raptors.

Culhen snorted beside him. *And even then, you needed the assistance of your loyal wolf.*

The wolf's mood was at its nadir. It had taken all of Ahren's energy to persuade his friend not to take the chance of storming his way through the enemy ranks instead of climbing one more time on top of the Roc.

'Hold on tight!' shouted Sunju. 'It's going to get uncomfortable!'

Ahren rested his right hand momentarily on the handle of his weapon. Then he caught sight of the leather straps holding him and his friends secure within the coach.

I'd best not risk a dodgy thrust, he thought, leaning protectively instead over Khara's limp body. He and his friends would now be nothing more than living shields for those who were too wounded to look after themselves. Even Eken seemed intent on protecting his Paladin from all misfortune, for he had curled up directly beside the unconscious Trimm, the feline's eyes alert to danger. All around the Forest Guardian, those who were still conscious followed Ahren's example, drawing the injured close to their own bodies.

Sun Shimmer's enormous frame shuddered, the enormous bird ascending into the sky with an almighty beating of wings and a furious cry. Ahren could do no more than gasp and laboriously raise his injured arm so that he could cover his eyes with his hand before they were already above Akkad's protective light, the world around the Thirteenth immediately consisting of screeching throats, hacking beaks and tearing claws. The leathern pinions of the Swarm Claws slammed against his armour, so close were the Dark Ones to him, searching for a bloodthirsty way through the gaps in his armour. Stinging pains to his arms, legs, stomach and ribs increased as more and more sharp beaks met with success. Ahren didn't dare take his hand from his face, knowing full well that his eyeballs would be plucked from him in a heartbeat. He prayed to the THREE that he was sufficient protection for Khara so that she could survive the relentless raptorial attacks but already he was beginning to feel cold and weary on account of the blood that he was losing.

So many, groaned Culhen, who had pressed himself flat on top of Yoka, ensuring that his armour was protecting them both. Ahren sensed that considerable damage had been done to his friend's front paws, however.

Don't give up! said Ahren for the umpteenth time on this day that never seemed to end. The Forest Guardian seemed to be drifting evermore into a darkness that promised relief from his pain. *It…won't…be…long…*

Ahren? asked Culhen urgently from far, far away. *Ahren!*

Then he felt the hacking and cutting of the Dark Ones no more.

'What a bloodbath,' said a rumbling voice as he gradually returned to his senses. 'And I'm speaking literally.'

The Paladin opened his eyes and looked up at the ceiling of a cave illuminated by candles. Pleasant aromas tickled his nose. He was lying in water, his armour trying to drag him down, but someone was supporting him from behind so that he wouldn't sink.

'Khara…' he whispered.

'She is floating beside you in the water – if that's the right word for this brew,' added Trogadon.

Ahren turned his head slightly, recognising the dwarf behind him, standing up to his chest in water and holding him afloat.

The Paladin frowned. '*Is it…blood?*' he asked, noticing the dark hue of the liquid.

'A damn lot of blood,' muttered Trogadon. 'Ours, to be precise. Those raptors tried to rip us to shreds up there.'

'How…?' Ahren was finding it difficult to speak.

The dwarf shrugged his shoulders. 'As Sunju said, it wasn't far to our allies. Quin-Was was waiting for us at the front. She conjured up a sudden storm that swept the Swarm Claws from our backs – it was like the first winds of winter ridding the trees of their most stubborn autumn leaves.'

Ahren tried turning his head a little further to the right – and then he saw Khara. Her face was pale but not deathly. He breathed a sigh of relief, tensed up his neck muscles and looked around.

'The Heart Hall,' he murmured, the candlelight, the smells and the walls of the cave gradually appearing as a whole before him.

'Precisely,' grunted the First, who was standing on the edge of the pool. The boil on the veteran's head had completely disappeared, and his archaic armour was clean and gleaming. 'I can only say that I was lucky to have been hit by that rock,' he said with a smile that seemed joyless and empty.

Ahren shivered. The eyes of the age-old Paladin were filled with compassion. Something was *very* wrong here.

'Who...?' he asked flatly, immediately aware that there was no sign of Culhen in his mind.

Any strength left within him drained from his body, and if it weren't for Trogadon's support, he would have sunk into despair and beneath the surface of the bloody water.

'Culhen...?' he whispered.

'...is with the other companion animals. They are mourning with Sun Shimmer and wish to be left alone,' explained the First quickly.

'Who?' asked Ahren, repeating his question and stricken with guilt that he was relieved that it hadn't been his beloved wolf who had closed his eyes for ever.

'Eken,' murmured Trogadon, who seemed to be looking at something or someone in the distance.

The Thirteenth straightened up in the water, his body little more than a puppet whose strings were being violently manipulated by his mind, now thoroughly distraught. Everywhere in the large pool within the square-shaped chamber – an imitation of the bathing chamber in the genuine Hall of Hearts – there were floating, unconscious Paladins and their companions, all of whom were pale but none of them exhibiting any outward signs of injury. The sight of the red water, from which the faces protruded, had something terrifying about it, something *final*.

Trimm was floating in the water at the far end of the pool. His face seemed calm, his eyes were closed.

'He...he doesn't know yet, does he?' Every word tore at Ahren's heart.

'No,' said the First tonelessly. 'He still hasn't awakened.'

The young man's mind was racing. The loss of a companion animal...

His mind refused to co-operate. It almost felt like there was a wall of ice – like the one behind which Four Claws had endured his exile in the cold south. The dreadful consequences that awaited Trimm having lost his beloved Eken seemed somehow visible but *blurred* to Ahren – unreachable and securely locked away.

'Should we wake him up?' he asked. Without thinking, his eyes had focused on the First. If there was anyone who could understand what Trimm was about to endure, then it was the man who had lost his dragon in battle so long ago.

'It would be good if you and Trogadon could get the others out of the sacred water and bring them to their rooms,' said the veteran. 'I will take care of Trimm.'

For a moment, there was a deep understanding between Ahren and the otherwise coldly calculating old man.

The Forest Guardian struggled out of the water, lifting Khara into his arms, her pale, smooth skin peeking out from beneath her robe. Hardly had he stepped out of the pool when he saw the soul companions standing at a respectful distance in the front section of the Heart Hall. Palnah's face was grief-stricken. Ahren, carrying Khara in his arms, stepped towards her.

'Is Trimm already awake?' she whispered.

'We…would hear it if he was,' said Ahren hoarsely. 'Please instruct some of the Night Soldiers to remove the sleepers from the pool.' He paused. 'Except for Trimm. The First will talk to him as soon as he wakes up.'

Palnah bit her lower lip. 'Shouldn't I be there with him?'

Ahren swallowed hard before replying. A tear ran down his cheek. 'Better wait until the First has broken the news to him. Your Paladin will need you then.'

Then he walked past Palnah and made his way up the long ascent from the Heart Hall to the surface of Jorath. Behind him, he heard the Night Soldiers following at a respectful distance, each carrying the limp bodies of one of his friends. A shiver ran down his spine. Ahren couldn't escape the feeling that he was the leader of a funeral procession, bearing the Champions of the gods to their final resting place, while at the same time he was fleeing a terrible responsibility that the First alone would have to shoulder.

On reaching the final turn before the Shield Chamber came into view, Ahren thought he heard from behind an extended, agonising cry of despair, so powerful that its very anguish would have caused the Obsidian Fortress to collapse if the THREE had only known the true meaning of the word *justice*.

But the deities were sleeping, and whatever rightful justice awaited the Adversary for His dreadful deeds, it would be up to the Champions to mete it out.

Ahren couldn't stop tapping his armoured hands repeatedly on the stone crenel before him on the western tower of Highstone.

Clank. Clank. Clank.

There was something calming about the sound of steel on stone. It gave him the illusion that he was doing something, *anything*, while Trimm negotiated the abyss of despair that every Paladin feared in the depths of their hearts.

'Are you preparing to tear apart the fortress of our enemy with your bare hands in the early morning?' The deep, calm voice came from the stairwell leading down into the castle.

'I will do so, if necessary,' murmured Ahren, without turning to look at the Father of the Mountain.

'It has been a bad day.'

Ahren laughed coldly. 'Which will be followed by a bad night.'

'One step at a time.' The squat, dwarf-like figure stepped beside him. 'Today, we have been shown how fragile the plans of mortals can be.'

'I am beginning to think that the plans of the gods are no less fragile.'

'Perhaps.'

The single word jolted Ahren out of his gloomy mood. He peered in amazement down at his fellow Paladin.

'What?' asked the Father of the Mountain, a faint smile on his lips. 'Were you expecting me to make a passionate defence of the THREE? I didn't know Eken well, but there is, nevertheless a fury raging within me such as I have not experienced in centuries.'

Ahren's eyebrows shot up in concern, but the Father of the Mountain waved a hand dismissively.

'Don't worry – I'm not going to revert to my former bloodlust,' he said. 'But it will be easy for me to give the Adversary a piece of my Deep Steel ball tomorrow, I can tell you that much.'

Ahren closed his eyes – as if through this gesture he could lock out the world with all its cares. 'I am plagued by doubts,' he admitted.

'Aren't we all?'

The Forest Guardian opened his eyes again and nodded towards the distant beam of Akkad's spell, rising out of the encroaching night. The armies of the free Jorathian nations were still skirmishing with those Dark Ones stranded outside the third wall of the fortress, which meant that they still hadn't reached him, so that it almost seemed as though a solitary traveller had strayed off his route and lit his campfire before the second destroyed gateway of the Obsidian Fortress.

'Eken is dead, and on the eve of the decisive battle, Trimm is nothing more than a broken man, drowning in sorrow. And all for the sake of a few hundred paces of land that we succeeded in winning.'

'Do not forget *Hate*. We slew him.'

Ahren nodded joylessly. 'There are still more than enough Dark Ones for everyone,' he said bitterly.

The Father of the Mountain placed a hand on his shoulder. 'Long ago, in the ancient past, the dwarfs of Thousand Halls didn't succeed in conquering their highest peaks in one day either.' With his other hand, he pointed towards Akkad's light. 'They needed camps, from where they could make progress the following day.'

Ahren grunted. 'Our special mountain must be scaled by the time the next sun sets. And I wager that the welcome we receive at the end of our ascent will be far from friendly.'

'Nevertheless,' murmured the Father of the Mountain approvingly. 'I already hear a hint of humour in your voice again. Do not allow gloomy thoughts to smother that for which we are fighting. A weapon guided by vindictiveness possesses a blade capable of stabbing into one's own flesh.'

Ahren sighed. 'How I long to be sitting beside you on the Ice Pate, listening to your words of wisdom.'

'As if you would have been able to stand it for long,' snorted the dwarf-like Paladin. Then he turned. 'I hear steps. It seems I am not the only one who wishes to check up on you.' With a faint smile and a final wave, the Father of the Mountain tactfully withdrew to the opposite end of the tower top as Hakanu appeared in the shimmering light of the storm lantern, which was swaying gently in the breeze.

'Master?' he asked shyly, Ahren beckoning to the lad welcomingly.

'How are you?' he asked his protégé.

'Good.' The word was uttered with a speed which suggested that Hakanu wanted it to pass his lips before his mind had the chance to replace it with a more honest one.

'Yes,' murmured Ahren. 'Me, too.'

The silence that ensued was like an oppressive wall between the two Paladins.

'I miss Kamaluq,' admitted Hakanu, finally. 'I know it is self-centred of me, but there is nothing I would prefer to do than press him to me, sob into his fur and not let him go until I have mourned for Eken with the dignity that the poor tomcat deserves.'

Ahren nodded, his heart filled with compassion. 'I wish I could tell you that we have enough time tonight for you to do such a thing, but…' He didn't need to finish his sentence. Their plan had still not been fully implemented and it was not going to pause during the hours of darkness.

Hakanu shifted from one foot to the other, his anxiety beginning to gain the upper hand over his grief. 'Do you think the Adversary will…?'

'We will see,' said Ahren. 'We will see *very* soon.' Then, to distract his apprentice, he added: 'You did very well today. I think that I can let you go off on your Long Week as soon as the sun rises the day after tomorrow.'

Hakanu beamed. 'Really?' he asked, only for his mood to dampen a heartbeat later. 'But does the Long Week have to start so *soon?* I mean, I would *really* like to take part in the festivities once we have wiped the Adversary off the face of Jorath…'

Whatever it was that Hakanu had planned on saying next, it was lost in Ahren's violent hug. He tousled his protégé's hair and forced his own heart to become infected by the young warrior's enthusiasm. They simply *had* to be victorious the following day or Eken's sacrifice, and the sacrifice of all those other lives on the Adversary's conscience – if He even had such a thing – would have been in vain.

'Ahren – come quickly!'

On hearing Likis' cry, the Forest Guardian, who had been about to enter his room to see how his beloved was, spun around. His friend from childhood days was looking at him wide-eyed, a look of sheer terror on his face.

'Come over to the window!' With that, he beckoned to the Paladin and ran into a nearby dining room.

Ahren felt a lump in his throat as he quickly followed Likis. A dull rumbling noise rolled through the stone of the castle, and for a heartbeat, the Paladin thought that the catapults must have started shooting at the Obsidian Fortress again. But the vibrations in his bones continued unabated now, Ahren suddenly imagining a herd of Horde Bulls galloping towards Deepstone.

Arriving beside Likis, he looked out the window. It didn't take him long to wish it *had* been rampaging Horde Bulls.

The Obsidian Fortress seemed to be smelting. Its walls were buckling and falling in on themselves, immediately transforming into a dark, oily, shimmering veil of deepest crimson, which then rose and spun around in the air directly above the heart of the citadel.

'It seems as though the Dark god has finally reawakened,' whispered Likis.

'And it seems as though He doesn't like what He has discovered,' muttered Ahren with an undertone of grim satisfaction.

'Is He really dissolving His fortress?' asked the lank ruler of Hjalgar.

'Only the section that has already fallen,' said Ahren, nodding towards the spectacle beyond the thick, crown glass windows. 'Look – the destruction only extends as far as the third wall of the fortification.' The rumbling quietened, the vibrations in his own bones and in the stone walls around them dying away, too. Only the swirling cloud of darkest crimson remained, suggesting a shining darkness – if such a thing were even possible.

'What sort of a cloud *is* that?' asked Likis, expressing the very same question that was troubling Ahren.

'Let us find out,' murmured the Paladin as he turned to make his way to the council chamber.

Lirana was still in the large room, well protected within the Charm Circle from the prying eyes of her Dark Lord. Sleeps-in-Treetop, looking more cadaverous than ever, sat with drooping eyes in her chair at the council table, from where she kept the protective charm active. Quin-Wa, Lanlion, Falk and Fisker were also sitting at the round table, their bloodshot eyes staring vacantly, their mouths tightly closed. The flames were blazing and sparking in the fireplace, Ahren finding the heat most welcome.

'Are the others still sleeping?' he asked instead of a greeting.

'Or are hoping that they will not be woken up,' muttered Quin-Wa darkly. 'Poor Trimm.'

'I saw what happened by peeking between my fingers,' whispered Fisker as he shivered. 'The Swarm Claws simply plucked Eken from Sun Shimmer's back and —'

'Enough!' snapped Ahren. 'Let us hear the horror of this special story on a more suitable occasion.' He nodded towards the narrow window. 'First, we need to discuss the centre of all evil over there.'

'What you are looking at is pure magic,' said Quin-Wa. 'You must all remember how the Adversary seized the power of the Bane Cloud and that of the charmed mirrors to create His Obsidian Fortress.' She pointed her chin towards the west. 'Now He is releasing some of this magical power, but why exactly, I cannot say.'

'To strengthen Himself,' said Lirana immediately.

'What makes you say that?' asked Falk, peering at her sceptically with narrowed eyes. Ahren could see that his erstwhile master had recently been weeping. They were all suffering with their grief-stricken brother.

Lirana turned her face towards the thick windowpanes. 'Do you see how the interior of the cloud is slowly sinking – like a tornado?' That is the Dark god sucking up the raw power into Himself.'

'So much for our hope that He would not recover himself in time before our assault tomorrow,' muttered Fisker grimly.

Falk cursed. 'He has sacrificed the two walls of the Obsidian Fortress that are of no more use to Him and gaining power in the process.'

Ahren looked over at Lirana. 'Can He do so repeatedly?'

The Woman in Black nodded. 'Every wall that you break through will, sooner or later, serve as nourishment once He has no more tactical use for them.'

'The closer we get to Him, the more sorcery He will have at His disposal,' said Quin-Wa. 'It is as though He is counteracting His weaknesses.'

'Still, at least He is still lurking *behind* his walls like a fat spider in its web,' said Ahren with a confident tone that belied the fear that had gripped him. 'It seems that He wishes to survive tomorrow at all costs before He will even think of completely surrendering the Obsidian Fortress. Which means that He is still vulnerable.'

'Perhaps we have frightened Him enough for us to be able to avoid the night-time part of your plan…' began Fisker, only to be interrupted by Lanlion stumbling into the chamber.

Blood was running from the cursed one's nose, ears and eyes. Before Ahren could get to his friend, his fellow Paladin grabbed onto the back of a chair, sending both himself and the piece of furniture crashing to the floor.

'Another curse is rolling in,' he wheezed. 'The Adversary is strangling the night! I can feel it no longer!'

Ahren rested the head of his friend on his lap and looked helplessly at his companions. Their features displayed their own dismay, but when the Paladin turned to look at Lirana, the Woman in Black pointed at the windowpanes in the chamber.

'The sky,' she murmured calmly, as though resigned to her fate. 'It is gone.'

Ahren frowned, then looked through the window towards the Obsidian Fortress – but could recognise nothing. Then it hit him like a bolt from the blue. He recognised *absolutely* nothing. No distant light from Akkad. No cloud swirling above the Obsidian Fortress. No stars in the firmament. Only an all-devouring *emptiness*, which seemed to begin directly beyond the window. It was as if all Jorath had been swallowed whole by the Dark god.

'I must see to the guards immediately,' gasped Likis, rushing out of the chamber.

A scratching began, as if a thousand sharp claws were scraping along the thick castle walls in search of any unsecured entrances.

DEATH ALREADY WALKS AMONGST YOU, echoed the voice of the Adversary. AND HE HUNGERS FOR MUCH MORE THAN A SOLITARY, SCABBY TOMCAT!

Ahren and the other Paladins exchanged nervous looks. The next stage of their plan had already begun to unfold, albeit in a completely different manner to how they had hoped it would. Humiliated, robbed of His only surviving child, and having woken up with the enemy within the walls of His citadel, the Adversary had reacted with a mixture of injured pride and fear, in the manner that He had *always* done – by ruthlessly launching a sudden assault on the assembled Paladins, who had brazenly and openly gathered as a united force.

To weaken the Dark god on the eve of the decisive battle, the Champions of the gods had been ad idem during the previous day's council of war – they would take the most extreme risk imaginable. And thus, it had come to pass – they had challenged HIM, WHO FORCES to a second Night of Blood!

Chapter 17

'All soldiers – down off the battlements!' yelled Ahren, the guards of the council chamber immediately rushing off to relay the command – as though furious Agony Boars were hot on their heels.

I'd be only too delighted to have to deal with a couple of Agony Boars compared to this sorcery, announced Culhen.

Ahren immediately imagined a scene of horror – with his wolf engaged in a struggle against the odds with a horde of Dark Ones in the unnatural blackness. *Where are you?*

In a safe place, murmured his furry friend, reassuringly. *All of us companion animals saw the Bane Spell hurtling towards us, and we fled inside – with the exception of Karkas and Sun Shimmer. Two heartbeats later and the cloud had already sunk down over the castle.*

Cloud?

A floating piece of nothingness, added Culhen hesitantly. *At least, that's what it looked like – as if it were a cloud of sheer darkness.*

Lanlion shook his head numbly before straightening himself in his chair. 'This sorcery...it feels like the Pall Cloud - except significantly denser.'

Quin-Wa narrowed her eyes. She seemed to be sensing something specific. 'He has shrouded us in a section of the old Pall Pillar – or in a perverse version of it, at any rate.'

'How can that be?' asked Fisker in disbelief.

The heavily pregnant woman shrugged her shoulders. 'The Pall Pillar was never really gone, don't forget. With the help of Sven's treachery, the Adversary turned it into the Pall Cloud – and then, with another sorcerous robbery, into the Obsidian Fortress. Now, He has released a piece of the original spell to create this black prison around Highstone.'

Ahren shivered. 'Can He keep us imprisoned here until the following dusk?'

'No, He cannot,' said Lirana with such certainty that Ahren breathed a sigh of relief. 'I can feel the essence of His spell weakening with every heartbeat. The morning sun will have burned away the darkness surrounding us – by the very latest.'

'Plausible.' Quin-Wa nodded. 'This section of the Pall Pillar possesses no anchor, unlike the one we used. Hence, it cannot endure for an extended length of time.'

'I'm delighted that you, who are knowledgeable in the ways of magic, are *ad idem*,' muttered Fisker, looking anxiously at the walls and ceiling. 'The only question that remains is – what do we do against these Dark Ones that seem intent on scraping their way through these stones.'

'Use your brain!' snapped Quin-Wa. 'Muai has reported to me that the companion animals didn't see any Dark Ones at all before the Bane Spell descended, and I sincerely doubt that the Adversary is capable of commanding an army to float through the air in the middle of this cloud or He would have destroyed the Ring by means of such a tactic a long time ago.'

Falk grunted, Ahren observing how the shoulders of the old man seemed to relax. 'You believe these noises to be nothing but phantasmagoria?' asked the old Forest Guardian.

Quin-Wa nodded. 'The scratching is supposed to put us on edge.'

Ahren rubbed the back of his neck. 'And through this deception, we will not be able to tell when the genuine Dark Ones have reached the castle.'

'Cassobo says that according to what Sun Shimmer and Karkas can see as they circle above Highstone, only the castle has been enveloped. Which means the henchmen of the Dark god will first have to break through the front and overrun Deepstone before they get to us at all.'

Ahren heard the fearful trembling in Fisker's voice, while Falk nodded in understanding at the uncertain Paladin.

'That time, too, we believed ourselves to be secure.'

Despite Ahren's best efforts, none of his brothers and sisters who had survived the Night of Blood had every spoken in detail about their life-changing experience. Not even the First had broken their unwritten vow of silence.

'What happens next?' he asked Falk in a low voice.

'Bloodshed and death.'

'Falk...'

The old Paladin raised his hand in a defensive gesture. 'High Fangs,' he muttered hoarsely. 'High Fangs will arrive, the likes of which you have never seen before.'

Fisker looked over to Falk as if in search of permission. Then he whispered: 'They resemble humans in every way – unless one can see beneath their habits…'

'Good, then, that the castle is sealed off already,' murmured Ahren anxiously. 'But by the THREE, being informed of this earlier would have helped us with our preparations.'

Falk shook his head. 'It is a blessing that the battlements have been emptied on account of the Bane Spell. It means that at daybreak, there will be fewer corpses for the sun to cast its rays on.'

Ahren sensed the fatalistic mood that had gripped the room. 'Right, then – everyone down to the ground floor. We will all assemble in the Shield Chamber as arranged and wait there for the assault.'

'What happens to us?' asked Lirana, pointing towards Sleeps-in-Treetop, whose head was nodding, as she sat half-asleep in her chair.

Ahren chewed on his lower lip uncertainly. The council of war had taken no further notice of the Woman in Black, and the Paladin was certain that she had deliberately waited, only posing her question when the pressure of time would force Ahren into giving her an answer.

'Lock the doors,' he said, finally, looking at both Lirana and Sleeps-in-Treetop. 'Seal them with spells if necessary. Neither of you will fall victim to the assassins that will be hunting us down as long as you do not present yourselves to them. In all probability, they will not even bother entering this part of the castle.'

Lirana sank down onto her bed. She seemed strangely relieved. To Ahren, it appeared as though the tormented woman was only too happy at not having to experience a second Night of Blood – especially, as she was still in the service of the Enemy, who would discover her treachery should she draw His attention to her. She was safe here within the Charm Circle – for now, at least.

'Let us go,' said Falk, his voice quaking. 'I want to be with the others.'

Ahren nodded once more to the black-garbed woman, gently pressed his hand on the shoulder of the dozing Sleeps-in-Treetop and then quickly followed the other Paladins through the passageways and down the stairwells of Highstone. Every now and then, he would glance anxiously at Lanlion, but the Bloodless seemed to have regained control of himself since the Bane Spell of the dark god had shrouded the castle in complete darkness.

'I have been cut off from the night,' murmured Lanlion, having noticed Ahren looking at him again. 'It is difficult to describe, but I cannot sense it through this enforced darkness.' The pale Paladin gazed sadly at Ahren. 'I shall be of far less value in this battle than I had hoped.'

Ahren pointed at his own neck before asking: 'Do you need…?'

Lanlion laughed. 'More than you could provide me with, and much, much more than it is wise for you to give.' The Bloodless stared down at the floor for a moment. 'I shall take up position in the Heart Hall. Haminul will remain by your side. He insists upon it – and it is my desire, too.'

Ahren knew what his friend meant. Their plan meant that badly wounded Paladins – and those unable to fight for other reasons – would serve as final bulwarks in the Heart Hall should the enemy manage to force their way into the most secure of all the chambers. The war, in any case, would well and truly be lost were this to happen.

'Are you sure?' asked Ahren in a low voice.

Lanlion nodded. 'It is as if I am deaf and blind.' He swallowed hard. 'And terrifyingly thirsty. Becoming wounded at the wrong moment could cause me to break my chains – if you understand my meaning.'

Ahren did – all too well. 'Go,' he murmured. 'Be our ultimate shield against the foe.'

Lanlion smiled, then quickly hurried along the corridor until he was out of sight.

'What was that all about?' asked Falk.

'Lanlion will fight in the Heart Hall,' said Ahren. 'The Bane Curse of the Adversary leaves him with no other option.'

Falk muttered under his breath: 'Then there are only ten of us?'

'*Ten?*' echoed Fisker, confused.

'Think about it, you fool,' snapped Quin-Wa irritably. 'Aluna is too exhausted to fight, and Trimm was never a friend of physical combat – even with his companion animal. And now that Eken is gone…'

A sullen silence descended on the group, and the only thing that they could now hear as they continued making their way to their friends was the incessant sound of scraping against stone.

Ahren prayed earnestly to the THREE that the unholy noises truly *were* an illusion.

'And about time!' growled the First as Ahren and the rest of his little group appeared in the doorway of the Shield Chamber which contained the entrance down to the Heart Hall.

Hurricane lamps hung from the walls, illuminating every inch of the square room, in whose middle stood the walled-in descent, looking for all the world like an unadorned mausoleum. The steel doors were closed, a ring of Dwarfish guards standing around it, their shields creating an impenetrable barrier, while the quartet of Dragon Bows, one in each corner of the room, stood at the ready.

All the Paladins – with the exception of Lanlion and Aluna – had gathered, and Ahren could almost taste the power. Here there was no charm to soften the gods' Blessing, no carefully arranged distancing. It felt to Ahren as if the Blessing within his chest wanted to burst through his ribs and join in a joyful roundelay with those of his brothers and sisters.

As he began to walk over to his fellow Paladins, who were mixing with all the companion animals that didn't have wings or scales, he was suddenly grabbed by the shoulder and spun around. Khara was facing him, her eyes blazing and her face suggesting that she was anything but happy.

'So – the world outside is in danger of falling completely apart and all you do is let me continue to *sleep?*'

Ahren didn't know what to say.

How about the truth? suggested Culhen, his tongue lolling. *That you forgot the love of your life – pure and simple.*

I didn't forget her, countered Ahren snootily. *I just had so many things to worry about that I…uh…*

'I'm sorry,' was all he managed to utter.

Khara looked at him critically before nodding curtly. Instinctively, she rubbed her bracelet, Ahren gently removing her hand from the sorcerous piece of jewellery.

'There is a reason why we haven't put it to use yet,' he reminded her in a soothing voice.

'I know,' she said irritably. 'But down here, without Charm Circles and with all these Paladins in the one spot, it feels as if there are a thousand ants scrabbling around inside my head. The bracelet *wants* to be used.'

Ahren nodded. 'Ever since we came in here, I have been suppressing a desire to shout out our battle cry to the world...' He stopped in his tracks as he noticed Trimm, standing silently behind the other Paladins, his eyes fixed on the solitary entrance to the chamber. Ahren pointed with his chin to the portly man, Khara then accompanying him as he made his way over to Trimm.

'Hello, Khara. Hello, Ahren.'

His words sounded hollow and completely lifeless. A shiver ran down Ahren's spine. Eyes, red from crying, seemed to look through him. The Forest Guardian thought he could make out something *insane* darting about within them – like the threatening shadow of a Carapace Whale just before it soars up and powerfully breaks through the ocean surface, intent on destroying a hopelessly exposed fishing boat.

'Trimm...' The expression of condolence that Ahren had formulated in his head now stuck in his throat. Instead, he tried to embrace Trimm, failing, however, on account of the barbs jutting out of the man's armour. Finally, Ahren abandoned his effort at sharing with the Paladin his feeling of sorrow, a look of relief then appearing for a heartbeat on Trimm's face.

There is a time for grieving and a time for fighting, said Culhen, underlining his point by transmitting an image of a pack of wolves struggling with a Dark One. Several of the family members lay dead on the ground, the others redoubling their efforts in their desire to save the den and the whelps that were hiding within it.

'You're staying?' asked Ahren instead, pointing at Trimm's armour and the two daggers that his normally so cowardly friend was clutching.

The opulent Paladin groaned helplessly. 'One of my worst fears has now been realised. It can no longer hold me in its grip.' Trimm looked up at the ceiling with a tortured expression, tears in his eyes. 'Does this make any sense to you?'

Ahren gently laid his hand on the cold Deep Steel armour of his friend, between the finger-length barbs that jutted above Trimm's heart. 'We are all with you. And we always will be.'

Trimm nodded, then turned away, Ahren leaving his distraught brother to his grieving.

I would so much like to share a few words of comfort with him via Sun Shimmer, said Culhen, whose concern seemed to Ahren like a deep, calm pool of water. *But Eken is not here to deliver my message. And you humans are so inept at expressing that which is really important.*

The general sense of disquiet only increased as soon as Likis and Falagarda entered the chamber.

'If I may, Chief Marshal, you really shouldn't be here,' said the First firmly. 'Our plan envisaged you co-ordinating the defence at the Ring.'

'The sorcery enveloping the castle caught me just as much by surprise as it did you,' countered the woman abruptly. 'As it happens, I was merely in Highstone to make some final preparations for tomorrow. Certain commands that I didn't want the wrong ears to pick up on.' She looked meaningfully at the others. 'I hope you *all* understand what I mean.'

'Can we not at least speak openly *here?*' asked Bergen irritably.

'You mean, now that we are so *safe*?' countered Sunju. 'Are you telling me that Karkas hasn't been presenting you with a picture of Deepstone, in whose middle a mass of pure blackness is lurking?'

The blonde Paladin fell silent, scowled and nodded.

'Nevertheless, you should still not be *here*,' insisted the First. 'In this chamber we are waiting for the most devious assassins that the Adversary has ever conjured up in His vindictiveness.'

The commander waved away the objection. 'I have fought against Dark Ones before, don't forget.'

'None like these ones,' countered Falk with such certainty that a look of doubt appeared in the tall woman's eyes. 'There is one reason why we ordered all the servants to leave the castle and why the special chamber beneath us was built with Dwarfish hands. The enemy that will hunt us down tonight has been created for one purpose and for one purpose only – namely, to kill *us* and *all* those whom we love.'

'I still don't understand how the attack that we are expecting tonight is in any way different to those that are taking place along the Ring,' countered Falagarda. Ahren heard a trace of stubbornness in the woman's words – although perhaps she was only trying to cover up her own uncertainty.

'The creatures that will shortly be assaulting us…' began Quin-Wa, breaking off for a heartbeat, however, before managing to continue: 'The Adversary is creating them at this very moment – while we are talking. Their bodies will not be designed to last longer than a night. They *will* die – one way or another. But before that, they desire to spill the blood of the new-born.'

Ahren swallowed hard. Was the Dark god really capable of transforming His High Fangs into such deviant entities? Bodies, which would self-destruct during an orgy of sheer, naked violence and bloodletting? Looking at his fellow Paladins, it took him no time to find out the answer.

'Go, Falagarda,' murmured Sunju. 'We will need your keen mind on the battlefield tomorrow. We must survive the Night of Blood on our own.'

Likis cleared his throat apologetically. 'Not *alone*,' he said in a low voice, Ahren immediately flying into a rage.

'You are *not* staying!'

Likis raised his hands in a calming gesture, grinned crookedly and said reassuringly: 'Of course, I'm not. I have only come here to give you some news. The Blue Cohorts and the Fox Guards are protecting all the entrances to the castle – as commanded.'

'Tell them they should always stay in groups,' said Hakanu, the concern of his apprentice for the welfare of the men and women under his command moving Ahren deeply. 'And that they…'

'They are all battle-hardened veterans, lad,' interjected Ahren. 'Their task tonight will be to tie up the enemy as much as possible. But it is *us* who will have to win this battle.'

'I wish the Blue Cohorts could fight by my side,' murmured Bergen, looking thoroughly miserable.

The First shook his head firmly. 'Look around you. There are so many of us here already that we are practically standing on each other's toes. Thirty-nine more swords would be more a hindrance than a help.'

'Tomorrow, you will be relieved to have spared your mercenary troop,' added the Father of the Mountain reassuringly.

'If there *is* a tomorrow,' murmured Trimm, the others all suddenly falling silent.

'This waiting is going to kill me,' complained Trogadon, the dwarf being one of the final defenders to have taken up position in the Shield Chamber. 'I could easily have spent more time with Jelninolan.'

Ahren loosened his cramped shoulders and sheathed his Wind Blade. The eighth false alarm had only now sounded, the scraping sounds along the castle walls having become noticeably wilder and louder. The Adversary was toying with them and was wearing out the Paladins and the other defenders in equal measure.

'How is she?' asked the Forest Guardian, 'and how is Uldini?' Anything to distract from the tension in the air.

Trogadon took off his helmet and scratched his head. 'You're asking *me?* The pair of them are just sitting there, brooding over their implements of sorcery. *Mirilan* is positively humming with power, while *Flamestar* is illuminating the entire chamber – it's as if Uldini has plucked the very sun from the sky and locked it in his crystal ball.' He scratched his forearm. 'I'm getting goosebumps just talking about it.'

Ahren missed the two Ancients terribly, but he was keenly aware that their greatest moment would have to wait until the decisive battle. If their magic didn't reach the intended target during the assault on the Obsidian Fortress, then…

If, if, if, grumbled Culhen, who was grooming Yoka between the ears and earning jealous looks from Muai. *Stay in the here and now, please. It's already frightening enough without having doubts about the future.*

'Do you feel that the Paladins have split into two camps, Master?' asked Hakanu, who was huddled in a little group containing Lyssin, Khara and Trogadon, as well as Ahren.

'Those who have already experienced the Night of Blood, and those who have yet to get to know its horrors,' said Lyssin, answering in the Forest Guardian's stead. 'Not much of a revelation, dunderhead.'

The young warrior was able to give as good as he got. 'But it still isn't *right*,' said Hakanu, jutting out his chin belligerently. 'We must stand together or fall alone.'

'Hakanu us right,' said Khara, turning to Ahren. 'The others are sinking deeper and deeper into their gloomy memories. We must do something to counteract that. Even the conversations among the dwarfs seem to revolve around their own imminent executions.'

Ahren knew that he, on his own, was powerless against the pervasive ill-humour of his older companions, but he had an idea of whose assistance he could call on to distract the veteran Paladins from the visions of the original Night of Blood now tormenting them, so fearful were they that the dreadful occurrence might soon be repeated. Once the idea had fully formed in his head, he transferred it to Culhen.

Not ten heartbeats later, Selsena began radiating waves of trust and hopefulness, causing a smile to appear on Ahren's lips and Falk to go over to his Titejunanwa and pat her lovingly on the nose. Cassobo clambered onto Fisker's shoulder and chattered cheerfully into his ear while Hanulf pushed his heavy body past the grinning Father of the Mountain only to heartily embrace the First in a gentle but firm bear hug. Haminul whinnied belligerently, the echo in the room causing the sound to penetrate even the most closed hearts, making them beat faster. Culhen and Yoka rubbed against each other like a pair of playful whelps, and even Muai found herself stealing the helmet off an infuriated dwarf before lying down and playing with it as if the big cat had found an extra-large ball of wool.

Kamaluq, on the other hand, whimpered as he pitter-pattered around the room, looking even more innocent and sweet than usual as he approached Trimm, wide-eyed.

'Is that such a good idea?' wondered Ahren when he saw the corpulent Paladin tensing up.

'I don't know,' said Hakanu. 'But according to Kamaluq, it was *your* idea that the companion animals should look after the fearful Paladins. My fox, at any rate, believes that Trimm deserves a little affection, no matter from whom.'

The cowardly Paladin turned abruptly away, but the fox simply ran between his legs and looked up at him again, all the while whimpering in a manner that would melt anyone's heart.

'Let go of me, you ugly bedside rug!' exclaimed the First, whose voice betrayed an unequal amount of anger and mirth. Hanulf grunted and simply knocked the age-old Paladin over. Then the bear nudged the veteran's helmet off the old man's head with his nose before licking the man's forehead. 'I don't *have* any honey for you,' guffawed the First, now totally overcome with mirth. 'And your tongue is terribly tickly.'

Selsena and Haminul took it in turns to distribute hope and courage in equal measure to all those present, while Muai, Yoka and Culhen were continuing to act quite idiotically so that even the most frustrated of hearts would lighten up with enjoyment.

Only Trimm remained silent and morose, his eyes fixed on little Kamaluq. Ahren was about to tell Hakanu to call off his companion animal when the little fox threw himself on his back, waved his legs in the air and whimpered up at Trimm.

First, one of the daggers that the corpulent Paladin was clasping clattered to the floor. Then the second one did. Trimm awkwardly pulled off his barbed, armoured gloves and slowly dropped to his knees, as though he was diving down through thick, murky waters in search of some invaluable treasures on the seabed. Ahren held his breath as Trimm's trembling fingers gently touched the fox's stomach fur, the Paladin sobbing as he pressed the little animal to his face. Kamaluq licked Trimm's nose and cheeks, wiping away the tears that the agonised and unhappy soul was now shedding.

'A beginning,' said Ahren slowly. 'Trimm's sorrow will stay with him forever. But at least Kamaluq has ensured that our grief-stricken friend will endure the night without risking his life through a mixture of rage and despair.'

Khara wiped her eyes, then glanced at her beloved from the side. 'Do you know something,' she said. 'I have an idea. To implement it, though, will require a certain amount of bravado – and we will need a few helping hands.'

'I don't need any bravado,' said Ahren dryly, nodding towards Hakanu. 'This is why I have *him.*'

'Very funny, Master.'

Ahren stared impassively at his protégé. 'Do you see me laughing?'

Khara poked her Paladin in the ribs. 'Enough of that now. Tell me if you're going to help. If we're going to act, then we're going to have to do so quickly – before the enemy stops making do with the *illusion* of death-bringing claws.'

Ahren looked around the room, which was echoing to the sound of laughter and good-natured banter. The companion animals were being patted and cuddled by an abundance of hands, and even the generally grim-looking dwarfs seemed to be in the best of spirits. Suddenly, it seemed to Ahren that their chances of surviving the night had increased dramatically.

'What *are* you plotting?' he asked Khara.

'Come with me.'

'Lucky that the First didn't spot us,' said Ahren as he, Khara and six volunteers from the Dwarfish watch arrived at the castle kitchen. 'I feel like a godsday pupil who has slunk away from a particularly tedious lesson.'

'It's a risk,' admitted Khara, quickly looking around the gloomy room, illuminated only by a couple of candles that were already burned down more than halfway, having undoubtedly been left behind by the kitchen staff, who had long since taken flight. The array of pots and pans looked like a slumbering army, only waiting to be roused and given their marching orders so that they might attend their own particular battlefield, which came in the form of three mighty ovens.

Is everything calm? he asked Culhen, the ever-present scraping of claws along the outer walls of the castle making him think of a particularly determined mole, which had gotten the scent of tasty rainworms in its nostrils.

It's just as calm as it was twenty heartbeats ago, countered Culhen. *Sun Shimmer and Karkas are circling high above Deepstone and will inform you all as soon as they notice any sign of an assault on Highstone.*

Ahren sensed that his friend was holding something back. *Spit it out, Culhen!*

An attack is taking place from the third gateway of the Obsidian Fortress. The goal of the Dark Ones are the catapults, which – now that the Adversary has released the sorcery of the outer walls – are now totally exposed on open ground.

This was only to be expected, said Ahren. *How are our troops coping?*

Quite well, was the less than convincing response. *But Cassobo believes that the attack is simply a foil so that a group of Dark Ones can secretly move in an arc around the defenders of the catapults before heading for Deepstone.*

Ahren cursed silently. *How certain is our clever little monkey?*

He says, he would do precisely that if he were in the Adversary's shoes. Culhen then transmitted an image of Fisker's black-furred little friend with a blood-red, pompous-looking crown on his head standing on the battlements of the Obsidian Fortress, chattering commands to wave after wave of Dark Ones.

Ahren couldn't suppress a chuckle. *Leave it,* he scolded his wolf. *You are supposed to lift the mood of the long-serving Paladins, not mine.*

We're long past that point, countered the wolf in a smug tone. *Now, they are caressing us and showering us with affection while singing songs from days of yore. Their hearts were in a dark place and thirsting for the light that you have presented them with.*

Ahren blinked, clearing the moisture from his eyes. *Thank you,* he said. *I knew I could rely on you.*

Oh, Ahren, announced Culhen with an air of pomposity. *You should know this by now – if you want anything done, just ask us companion animals.*

Khara gently shoved the Forest Guardian in the shoulder, distracting him from his mental conversation. 'First, you're all go, go, go – and then you simply stand around the place doing nothing to help.'

The Swordsmistress's arms were already laden down with thick sausages, while under one elbow she held half a round of cheese. She was now grabbing loaves of dark bread, piling them on top of one another while her beloved continued to dawdle. Then she started to walk carefully towards the Shield Chamber, her mountain of food balanced before her.

'The dwarfs have discovered a large cauldron of stew, which is still warm. It seems that the cooks in this castle were cunning enough to think of feeding an army of hungry mouths.' She nodded towards a little door. 'There are supposed to be jugs of watered-down wine inside,' she announced to Ahren and those of the dwarfs still capable of carrying more. 'Get as many of them as you can and then go back to the others. But don't overdo it. We don't want to serve up a banquet that will make everyone replete and lazy – we just want to lift the mood with our little supper.'

Ahren nodded assiduously, and within twenty heartbeats he was carefully making his way back to the Shield Chamber in the company of the snorting, muttering dwarfs who were carrying the enormous cauldron between them. Cheerful Paladins and dwarfs awaited them, all of them willingly distributing Khara's bounty amongst the others. The First was standing there, too, but he was fuming. The first cheers rose up as the stew and jugs of wine arrived. Ahren just managing to pass on the diluted liquid before the age-old veteran accosted him.

'What by the THREE do you think you are doing?!' snarled the First. Behind him, little wooden bowls were being dunked into the cauldron before being passed along. Sounds of laughter, smacking of lips and contented murmurings filled the room. 'We are on the verge of facing the most horrible thing that the Adversary could possibly dream up in His worst nightmare, and you are organising a damned *Autumn Festival!*'

Ahren smiled at the veteran, while taking a precautionary step backward as he did so. 'Firstly, it was Khara's idea – so you can thank her for what is happening here.' A flicker of doubt crossed the veteran's eyes. The special relationship between him and the Swordsmistress seemed to calm him down ever so slightly. 'Secondly, I would like you to have a good look around you – and don't rush it. What do you see? Camaraderie, genuine enjoyment and *hope* within these walls.' As if to underline Ahren's words, Fisker whipped a little wooden flute from his pocket and began to play a catchy, rhythmical little melody for the assembled defenders. 'Before the companion animals stepped in here, everyone present was gloomily pondering a dreadful death – thanks to the prognostications of you veterans – thereby, playing straight into the hands of the Adversary.' Ahren pointed at the wall to his right. 'You didn't hear these scratching noises during the original Night of Blood, did you?'

The First shook his head. 'We had no idea – until it was too late. We had never expected such an assault. The Adversary was thought to be powerless and surrounded.'

Ahren nodded gently. 'This is precisely what I mean. The Adversary is making use of your fears and memories. He wants you to believe that the Night of Blood will repeat itself. But this time the circumstances are different.'

Don't talk only to him, advised Culhen in a solemn tone. *Address them all.*

Ahren grasped the First by the shoulder and shook it in a friendly manner. Then he positioned himself at the entrance to the chamber, making sure that everyone could see him. 'I was not present at the Night of Blood,' he said in a loud voice, the laughter and idle chatter immediately dying away. 'I did not see what some of you had to see, experience, and suffer.'

Be careful, Ahren. You don't want to destroy the mood, warned Culhen, the wolf gazing at his master with his sparkling eyes.

The Forest Guardian took a deep breath before continuing. 'But my not having been there is of no relevance now,' he continued in a firm voice. 'I am *here*, with *you*, tonight – to prevent what could not be prevented then.' He clenched a fist and placed it before his heart. 'The

Adversary made you *believe* that he was *weak* – but this very night he really *is* so!'

This was greeted with the first murmurs of agreement – it was as if a giant, who had slumbered for aeons, was now awakening and preparing to enter battle.

'The Adversary surprised you all when you were asleep, when you were alone, when you were separated from your brothers and sisters. This time we stand armed and ready and *united!*'

The dwarfs rose to their feet as one, slamming their weapons against the broad shields with which they would protect the Paladins, the soul companions, and the new-born babies deep in the recesses of the Heart Hall.

'The Adversary believes that He can again break the Paladins – but *our* will is the will of the THREE! *They* have decided that HE, WHO FORCES has cast His long shadow over Jorath for long enough. The Dark god believes that this night will prove our end. And yet – His assault, doomed to failure, will give *us* the strength to force Him to His knees tomorrow!'

Now the rest of the Paladins were cheering at the top of their lungs.

'The Adversary —' began Ahren only to be cut off by Culhen, who had jumped to his feet, the other companion animals suddenly in a similar state of high alert.

The attackers have arrived, announced the wolf. *They must have been able to hide from Sun Shimmer using some sort of sorcery. She says that all the guards at Deepstone's northern wall are dead.* The wolf was clearly shocked. *There was no skirmish – nothing but a fleeting darkness that crept over the wall. According to Sun Shimmer, they were all dead within a few heartbeats.*

The sound of anxious murmuring arose from those Paladins that had been similarly informed by their companion animals.

'It is beginning, isn't it?' asked Trimm.

'Yes,' said Ahren, drawing his Wind Blade. He joined his brothers and sisters, all of them – together with the dwarfs – forming a circling around the entrance to the Heart Hall. 'The trap has been sprung!' he announced, his words echoing back from the walls and drowning out the scraping sounds from outside. 'Let the Adversary know that the battle tonight will be fought according to *our* terms!'

'At last,' whispered Khara beside him, the Blessing Band flaring up a heartbeat later, whose use had been deliberately avoided for so long as possible in the vicinity of the Dark god.

Ahren's smile transformed itself into a warlike grimace as he physically began to sense that this brothers and sisters to his left and right were standing, strong of will and ready to fight, to bury the Night of Blood in the past, where it belonged. The gods' Blessing was seething and surging within his chest.

Let the enemy come!

The first screams could be heard echoing down the castle corridors, coming from human throats as well as from creatures that only seemed able to utter tortured, multi-voiced screeches which hurt Ahren's ears. The possessors of these voices, thought Ahren, would despise every single heartbeat of their own existences, their terrible self-hatred causing them to desire the deaths of as many other lives as possible during their suicidal mission.

'They sound *different*. More *animalistic*,' gasped Falk hoarsely. 'And judging by the number of voices, there are many, many more of them than last time.'

'Very good,' said Ahren triumphantly. 'Just as we wanted.' He raised his blade above his head. 'The Adversary has over-extended Himself in His desire to deny us the grace of another dawn!' he yelled at the top of his voice. 'Let us show Him what a fatal mistake He has made!' He drew as much air into his lungs as he could manage, the Blessing Band alerting him to the fact that his brothers and sisters were well aware of his intention.

Eleven mouths opened wide.

'PALADINIM THEOS DURALAS!' echoed so loudly around the room that Ahren believed the very stones would shatter under the unified power of the Paladins.

The Blessing Band pulsated.

Their will was one.

The Paladins stood at the ready.

The first of the shadows flitted along the passageway towards the chamber, hastily dispatched bolts flying towards them.

The power of the Paladins flowed between the Champions of the gods. Their hope was unbroken.

The flickers of darkness moved with such speed and so erratically that Ahren couldn't believe his eyes. Not a single bolt hit its target. The first shadows flowed into the room, bringing a living blackness with them, which quickly enveloped the shooters like a protective shroud portending nothing but disaster.

Then the Blessing Band that united them vibrated, its ever-circling power now aiming towards the unborn baby in Quin-Wa's body, the fragile life reacting to the sheer might of the strengthening gods' Blessing. Behind Ahren, he heard a gentle splashing sound.

'Oh, ye gods, not *yet!*' screamed Quin-Wa, horrified. 'My child no longer wants to *wait!*'

Chapter 18

'Now?!' yelled Bergen. '*Now* of all times?!']

The dwarfs were storming valiantly forward, defying the mysterious attackers, the Paladins staring in shock down at Quin-Wa in their midst, who was leaning heavily against the Heart Hall doorway, standing in a puddle of amniotic fluid.

'The Blessing Band strengthens the gods' Blessing...' she gasped. 'Too much power...our babies react to it! They are either awakened or...or...called into this world! The Blessing Band must immediately stop working – I do not want to risk it causing problems during childbirth!'

Khara reacted to the plea immediately, the presence of the Paladins vanishing immediately from Ahren's mind, while to his horror his gods' Blessing too seemed to lose all force – like a wave that had smashed against a quay wall and was now merely splashing about uselessly.

The first of the Dwarfish defenders staggered back out of the darkness, cuts and stabs decorating any gaps in their armour.

'Quin-Wa must get through this door!' yelled Ahren. 'Hakanu – help her! The rest, do what we are here for – defend the Heart Hall!' Then he threw himself forward into the seething darkness.

It was like stepping out of a cosy hut into a bitterly cold winter's night. Life, love, warmth – they quickly faded away. He skilfully evaded the lightning-fast thrusts from pallid figures, all of which seemed to be holding broken swords in their hands, their faces resembling those of half-starved prisoners who had not seen the light of day in decades.

Otherwise, they seemed beneath their black robes to be all too human – just as Falk had remembered them from the Night of Blood – but only until Ahren scored his first gaping cut on an attacker, ripping its garment in two. Dozens of teeth were jutting outward through the entire torso of the High Fang, causing its cadaverous body to drip with blood!

Ahren paid for his moment of stunned surprise with a nasty stab that managed to slip between his ribbons just above his right elbow. Immediately, the Paladin began swiftly and nimbly moving through the ranks of the enemy, ensuring that the weak points in his armour would close in the blink of an eye. He thrust left and right in front of him, ramming his body into the terrifying High Fangs, kicking violently when the time was opportune and even head-butting several of the vile creatures. The murderous monsters were undoubtedly agile, and Ahren knew too well that they would become even more dangerous should they divide up within the chamber instead of getting in each other's way as they forced their way in through the entrance.

'Hakanu!' he bellowed, unable in the darkness to quite make out where he and his friends were situated within the Shield Chamber. 'Some light would be welcome!' Hastily, he turned his head as a High Fang attempted to stab his right eye with its jagged weapon. The blade scraped horribly along the cheek protector of Ahren's helmet, a mere inch away from the corner of his eye. Ahren skewered the High Fang with his weapon, then using its body as a shield so that he could stagger back several paces.

They are taking advantage of any weaknesses we might have without paying any attention to their own safety, he realised. *They are already as good as dead, anyway, so they fear nothing.*

There are too many of them, groaned Culhen. *Did the Adversary metamorphose all the High Fangs that he could find in His fortress?* Ahren could already sense two small wounds in his friend, where quick stabs had successfully penetrated between the plate armour of the wolf.

The more that attack us now, the fewer of them will be alive tomorrow to command the Low Fangs, explained Ahren, smashing his fist into the face of a High Fang, his blade being stuck in the torso of another one.

Culhen replied with an image of a wolf, who had bitten into too big a chunk of meat and who was now struggling to get it out of his mouth.

Ahren would have loved to have given his friend a few words of encouragement, but he had his hands full defending himself. 'Hakanu!' he yelled hoarsely.

'Close your eyes, everyone!' came the prompt reply, and hardly had Ahren followed the order when through his eyelids he could make out a sudden change in the surrounding brightness. He opened them again and smiled grimly. Kamaluq's flash of light had ripped through the darkness like a storm tearing an abandoned spider's web to shreds. Tatters of dissolving darkness hung everywhere in the chamber, the dozens and dozens of High Fangs now clearly visible. The fighting stopped for a few precious heartbeats as all involved struggled to deal with the effects of the lighting flash that the young fox had created.

'Damn!' cursed Falk, three paces ahead. 'I was too slow.'

A spear whizzed past the old man, immediately nailing three High Fangs together.

'Good work, Kamaluq!' cheered Hakanu, causing his weapon to return with a flick of his wrist. 'Brave fox!'

Kamaluq whimpered proudly as he disappeared into the stairwell, whose door was now ajar. Quin-Wa struggled down the steps, four dwarfs protecting her from being attacked.

'Shut the door!' yelled the First. 'Let's delay these bastards long enough for daylight to finish them off!'

As though the veteran's words had unleashed them, the creatures threw themselves forward at the Paladins and their allies in a wave of jagged steel, claws, wide open mouths and treacherous fangs. More and more of the monsters wafted into the Shield Chamber, the all-enveloping darkness returning with them.

'Stay resolute!' screamed Sunju. 'PALADINIM THEOS DURALAS!'

The gods' Blessing flared up in Ahren's chest once again, reinvigorating him, giving strength to his arms and legs as he filled his lungs with air.

A groan could be heard from the stairwell.

'*Not* helpful, my dear sister,' gasped Quin-Wa. Then the door slammed shut again and the entrance to the Heart Hall was secure for the moment.

Ahren and his friends were still fighting for their lives, even with their gods' Blessings. High Fang after High Fang appeared in the Shield Chamber, and for every creature that fell, two more wafted through the doorframe. More than two dozen dwarfs already lay dead on the floor of the large room, while the four Dragon Bows stood abandoned and useless in the corners of the internal battlefield. They were of no value against the lightning-fast opponents and hadn't been used once.

Step by step, Ahren and the other defenders were pushed backward, and the tighter the circle around the doors to the Heart Hall became, the easier it was for the High Fangs to surround them.

'Thirteenth!' bellowed a commander with so much blood running down his beard that Ahren couldn't tell whether it came from a High Fang or the officer himself. 'This hall is lost. Retreat to the Rune Chamber!'

'He is right!' roared the First as he meted out blows with his two-hander insofar as this was possible, given the sheer number of defenders squeezed in around him. 'If any more dwarfs fall, no-one will be able to give us support.'

Ahren quickly glanced left and right to orientate himself, using the senses of the wolf to help him.

Khara was a whirlwind of blades, the Swordsmistress well able to hold her own against High Fangs. Her right ear was bleeding, but she seemed otherwise uninjured.

Beside her, Falk and Sunju had created a bulwark with their two broad shields, behind which everyone who needed to, could take a precious breather.

Fisker and Trimm, too, fought side by side, each supporting the other with their nimble fighting when their partner was in need.

Hakanu's face exhibited his sheer love of combat while he sprang here and there behind the dwarfs, every throw of his spear boring through two or more High Fangs.

Lyssin and the Father of the Mountain, on the other hand, seemed to present an opposite way of fighting with their very calmness. *He*, with his spinning steel ball creating enough room for *her* to shoot arrow after arrow at the enemy.

Amongst all the Paladins, the companion animals waited for their opportunity to participate in the battle. If it was easy enough for Culhen, Muai, Hanulf and Yoka to attack the High Fangs, Selsena and Haminul had their own problems on account of the lack of space. The rest of the animals were inhibited by the smallness of their stature. Nonetheless, Ahren was grateful to each and every one of his animal friends for the effort they were putting in.

'Alright then!' he called out. 'Fall back!'

Immediately, Fisker withdrew from the battle, pressing his hand on the relevant stonework, and thereby causing the mechanism to go into operation, the steel doors swinging open.

'Companion animals first!' commanded Falk. 'Fisker will accompany them so that he can utter the password!'

But... muttered Culhen, who was about to complain.

It is the right decision, countered Ahren. *That means you can all arrange yourselves strategically downstairs and play to your strengths once the High Fangs have broken through up here and begin storming the Rune Chamber.*

Culhen acquiesced in silence, the loyal animals disappearing one by one down the stairwell as fast as they could. During this short period, three more Dwarfish guards lost their lives and the First suffered a stab to his right hip while the bodies of the furiously fighting High Fangs began to pile up, dozens more of these metamorphosed servants of the Adversary streaming into the chamber simultaneously.

'Is there no end to this?' groaned Ahren as the gloom accompanying the fresh enemy onslaught submerged the room in almost complete darkness despite the abundance of lanterns on the walls.

'Eyes closed!' yelled Hakanu, Ahren reacting this time with such speed that he was neither blinded nor had to spend too much time blinking as soon as Kamaluq's lightning had flashed. Following his farewell present, the fox had been the last companion animal to disappear down the stairwell, Ahren taking advantage of their opponents' disorientation by creating more room for manoeuvre for the other Paladins with several scythe-like swings of his sword.

'Trimm, Hakanu, Lyssin – down you go!' he bellowed, the two younger Paladins obeying immediately. Trimm, however, shook his head stubbornly.

'I will be the last to leave – with Sunju and Bergen,' he muttered grimly. His barbed armour was flecked with pieces of flesh and splatters of blood, and there was even a High Fang skewered and hanging from the back of the Paladin. Clearly, he was determined to avenge Eken's death mercilessly. For every single hair of his loyal tomcat, he would dispatch a Dark One.

'But...'

'Stop *arguing!*' yelled the First, filling a breach in the defensive ring created by the death of yet another dwarf by swinging his two-hander wildly. 'Ahren, Falk and I will go next. Then the others!'

Ahren was about to protest against the sequence, which seemed arbitrary to him, but already he could hear the gurgling death rattle of a dwarf to his right, and so he fell into line.

Quickly, he ran through the archway leading to the steps and he was about to begin his descent when a sudden shove to his back caused him to tumble downward. His right ear was tortured by the sound of hoarse screeching, and he was able to smell the foul breath of the High Fang that must have jumped on him as he'd begun his retreat, the pair of them now rolling down the steps. Razor-sharp claws searched for the weak points in Ahren's armour and two bony fingers of the High Fang found his lips and began to stab. Keeping his wits about him, Ahren opened his mouth as he rolled over his opponent and bit as hard as he could as soon as the High Fang had rammed its claws between his jaws. He tasted blood when the nails of the enemy stabbed into his tongue, and he continued to clench his teeth, preventing the fingers of the creature from penetrating any deeper.

Again and again, they rolled over each other, the High Fang punching Ahren repeatedly with its free hand. The Paladin, however, concentrated fully on throwing his full armoured weight on the monster every time he was on top of it, and once they arrived at the bottom of the steps, a welcoming committee of four drawn blades dispatched the High Fang, bringing its fury to an inglorious end. Ahren spat out the fingers of the creature and struggled to his feet in an effort to make room for the following Paladins.

'Sh…shanks,' he mumbled to Yantilla and the assembled Ice Wolves, blood spattering from his mouth.

Hakanu was beside him in a heartbeat. 'Master, are you wounded? You are spitting an awful lot of blood!' Under normal circumstances, Ahren would have found his protégé's concern touching, but there was no time for sentimentality now.

'Shounge,' he mumbled, opening his mouth wide.

Hakanu flinched in horror. Clearly, Ahren's injury wasn't a pleasant sight.

'Here, Master,' said the lad, handing the Forest Guardian his leather bottle with the sacred water.

Ahren was about to dismiss the offer, but instead of words, a fresh fountain of blood spurted out of his mouth. Grunting, he poured a little of the liquid into this mouth, gargling until he got the taste of musty leather and iron. Then he spat it out and tried to speak a comprehensible phrase. 'Damned Shatterlings,' he grunted.

That sounds much better, commented Culhen approvingly.

'Shatterlings?' asked Fisker quizzically.

Ahren shrugged his shoulders. 'The Adversary has shattered the bodies and minds of these poor souls. Even their swords are shattered. I must say, I find the name rather appropriate.' He turned to Falk, who had arrived at the bottom of the stairs. 'Although they don't seem at all like masterful assassins to me.'

The old Paladin's face darkened. 'Wait until the number drops and the will of the Adversary is guiding each and every one of them. *Then* you will understand what I told you.'

The First stormed into the chamber, immediately reducing his speed however and carefully stepping over the first of the many Charm Lines that decorated the floor of the quadrangular room, resembling a succession of border crossings between the ascending and descending stairwells.

'The dwarfs are buying us time,' he said gravely. 'They are going to close the door behind us.'

A moment later and as if in confirmation, a metallic clang echoed down the stairwell, the sound of fighting instantly reducing in volume.

Ahren swallowed hard at the sorrow that he was feeling. Dozens of Thousand Halls veterans had already met their end, and no more than a hundred heartbeats had passed.

'Were there…?' He struggled to control his breathing so that he wouldn't sound so shocked. 'Were there this many attackers the last time?'

The First shook his head, Trogadon – closely followed by Bergen, Sunju, and Trimm – now reaching the bottom of the stairs. When Trimm finally closed the door, the ensuing silence was funereal. Then the age-old Paladin continued: 'There were maybe a couple of dozen at most, that time. But their intention was not to fight with us but to slip into the nurseries…'

Ahren nodded. He had always imagined the Night of Blood to have been a desperate, rear-guard action but in fact it had materialised as focused assassinations, aimed at the weakest in the Paladins' communities. And because tonight, the enemy had been deprived of such an opportunity, the Adversary had resorted to considerably more violent methods. Methods that the Champions of the gods – with the help of their allies – would hopefully continue to defy, even if many defenders would sacrifice their lives for the sake of a free Jorath.

Only one night and one day, prayed the Paladin. *Then this madness will be over for once and for all.*

'What are you doing there?!' barked the First as he glared at Trogadon who was hurrying from one lantern to the next, quickly lifting their lids and throwing something onto their flames.

'Just a little surprise for our darkness-infatuated friends,' said the blacksmith innocently.

'Leave him,' said Bergen, who was down on his hunkers trying to catch his breath. 'Every little bit helps.'

Yantilla leaned into Ahren. 'How bad is it up there?' she murmured.

'Worse than it sounds.'

'Oh.'

'Exactly.' Ahren fixed his eyes on the commander of his honour guard. 'No acts of heroism,' he warned her. 'The Ice Wolves need their leader.'

Yantilla's features immediately hardened. 'The Ice Wolves follow only one person – and that is *you*. The Thirteenth Paladin. *I* am irrelevant.'

This was followed by a staring duel – not for the first time. 'No…acts…of…heroism,' he repeated, speaking slowly and firmly. 'If I go, then you and will go with me down these stairs. Swear!'

The gaunt woman turned away. Only when the upper steel doors of the Shield Chamber opened with a crash and the stairwell was filled with the screeching of High Fangs did she finally turn back and nod. 'I will be right behind you. I swear.'

Ahren stared at her again before nodding approvingly. Then he looked at Khara, who now had a little dressing on the tip of her right ear.

'It's still attached,' she said with strained cheerfulness. 'Although I am really looking forward to having a decent bath in the healing water of the Heart Hall.'

Ahren scowled. 'According to Quin-Wa, it has been contaminated already by too much Paladin blood for it to be truly effective.'

Khara attempted a smile but failed terribly. 'Then we are running out of healers,' she murmured. 'Akkad is trapped in his own Arcane Wall spell. Uldini and Jelninolan are preparing for tomorrow, Quin-Wa is in labour, and Sleeps-in-Treetop is on the point of unconsciousness, so focused is she on shielding Lirana from the Adversary.'

'The enemy is outside the lower door!' Yantilla's exclamation put a stop to the whispered conversations within the chamber. 'Ice Wolves! Form a semi-circle, three deep. The rest, position yourselves before the doors to the Blade Chamber. And beware of the magic runes when you are fighting. Let the enemy ignite them!'

Screeching, the Shatterlings began to hammer on the steel doors from the outside. The fists of the High Fangs were ineffective, but the darkness sliding in through the gaps around the door began to bend and buckle the metal – as though thanks to the Adversary's sheer willpower.

'What shall we Paladins do in your battle formation, esteemed Commander?' asked the First a little too politely to be credible.

'Look good and fill in the gaps when the first Ice Wolves fall,' countered Yantilla with such a matter-of-fact tone that the age-old veteran blinked in surprise.

'A cold-blooded response if ever I heard one,' he said. 'How refreshing.'

'I *was* a mercenary in my day – have you forgotten?' asked the gaunt woman with a smile so brittle that Ahren half expected it to shatter and fall to the floor. 'There was no room for sentimentality in my life before I got to wear this handsome tabard.'

I have a feeling that her jibes are aimed at you, commented Culhen. *She is still sore at you for having commanded her to retreat.*

I can live with that, murmured Ahren. *As long as she survives, too.*

The mind of the wolf suddenly seemed morose, almost impenetrable. *You do realise that many will die tomorrow, don't you? Perhaps even those who are very close to you.*

Ahren thought he could hear a hidden message in what the wolf was saying. Was Culhen talking about himself?

You...

He got no further. The doors that led to the steps from the Shield Chamber gave way, the Shatterlings flooding into the room in a tangle of claws and jagged blades. With them came the darkness, immediately washing over the first row of Ice Wolves. The unfortunate soldiers were dead within five heartbeats.

'Ye gods!' gasped Yantilla, retreating several paces with the rest of the Ice Wolves.

'At the ready!' bellowed the First, positioning himself in the now considerably larger and lighter semi-circle of defenders.

Ahren, too, got into position. To his left was Khara, while Trogadon was on his right.

'Everyone – retreat *one* step!' yelled Yantilla as the High Fangs lunged forward. 'Beware of the Charm Lines!'

As one, the Ice Wolves placed their right feet back a pace, admittedly an awkward looking move, but nonetheless effective. Clearly, Yantilla had drilled her soldiers well. Hardly had the Paladins, Trogadon and Khara imitated the manoeuvre when they were all rewarded with a spectacular sight. It took only one Shatterling to place its foot on the sorcerous line for an entire line of runes to ignite.

A wall of fire raced towards the doorway to the Shield Chamber, setting all the Dark Ones in its way alight. The flames blazed for no more than a blink of an eye, yet the sudden heat reminded Ahren immediately of the powerful volcano in the Cutlass Sea. The Dark Ones, now enveloped in the spell, were turned into a cloud of ash, leaving behind only their scorched and gleaming stunted swords.

'That's useful,' said Bergen as he felt a nasty swelling to his cheek which was already turning blue. He blew the swirling ash away. 'The good-for-nothing who did this to me is now floating off with his pals.'

Ahren counted the remaining Spell Charms on the floor. 'Four left,' he said.

'And they must be put to good use,' added Yantilla. 'The Shatterlings must be packed close together on the other side of the runes, which means we will have to delay them for as long as possible! Only then do we release the magic and….' She pointed at the swirling ash that was slowly sinking.

Ahren looked down at the charred remains of the dead Ice Wolves. 'And better that none of us ends up on the other side of the sorcerous lines.'

'*We* should have practised that step, too,' muttered Trogadon nervously. 'I mean, I *am* able to withstand most sorcery, but I *never* want to have to be tested by *this* charm.'

'The next group of Shatterlings are coming down the stairs,' interjected Trimm. The Paladin was still looking terribly strained, his voice a mixture of exhaustion and fury.

'Does anyone else think that these High Fangs are deliberately gathering together rather than storming into this chamber on their own?' asked Lyssin.

'I'm not sure. Falk said that they become more dangerous, the fewer of them there are for the Adversary to control,' countered Ahren grimly.

'Watch out!' roared the old Forest Guardian, raising his shield. Already the next group of Shatterlings were throwing themselves at Ice Wolves and Paladins alike.

For dozens of heartbeats the defenders fought an unequal battle against the slavering High Fangs, which were screaming out their frustrations and despair. Ahren was sweating with the effort of not putting a foot wrong and inadvertently activating the deadly runes, which were lurking on the floor with their promise of a quick death by fire.

Ice Wolves were falling all the time now, and even the companions were suffering significant injury. The Shatterlings cut with speed and stabbed with force during their waves of aggression. The light and almost playful manner in which they flicked their jagged weapons led to cut after cut being scored on the skin of the defenders. Ahren quickly calculated that although only every tenth Shatterling or so succeeded in slicing through the skin of his companions, it was abundantly clear to him that they would all bleed to death before the night was over – especially as all the companions had already paid more than enough in terms of blood spilt during the course of the day just past.

'Retreat!' bellowed Yantilla.

Ahren sought in vain for an escape strategy, for a High Fang was attacking him stubbornly, *Sun* already parrying furiously on account of another Shatterling's onslaught. Another wave of darkness enveloped the onrushing attackers, washing over Ahren and his friends.

Blind and exhausted, Ahren tried to remember where precisely he had been standing and how far the next Charm Line was from his feet. Claws, scraping at his armour, shoved him mercilessly backwards. He stumbled, almost losing his balance completely and nearly stepping on one of the runes when suddenly a hissing sound was heard coming from the four walls, the flames in the hurricane lamps flaring up so violently that the room was banished of all darkness.

Ahren and the other defenders seized their unexpected chance, retreating with considerable relief behind the next Charm Line before the Shatterlings had a chance to react. Yantilla stomped gleefully on the runes, a powerful fire again igniting before cleansing the area entirely of the enemy.

'Hm…those lights were supposed to have flared up much earlier,' grumbled Trogadon, shrugging his shoulders apologetically. 'Alas, this special powder takes an awful long time to get hot enough for it to ignite.'

'Forward!' yelled Yantilla, narrowing the semi-circle of swords and spears before the opposite stairwell again. 'Carry on as before!' she urged her men and women. 'Let them pay for every step with their own blood and lure them to the next Charm Line!'

Again, darkness enveloped the room, bringing violence and death with it. Ahren noticed that the eyes of the Shatterlings were becoming less and less animalistic, while their screeching was interrupted now by periods of concentrated silence. Their attacks were less chaotic – and more focused. The Ice Wolves and the other defenders found themselves having to retreat far more quickly than during the previous attacks if they were to avoid being overrun entirely. Not ten heartbeats after the latest assault had begun, the next wave of fire swept through the room leaving not dozens of dead Dark Ones in its wake but a grand total of only *eight*.

'They really *are* becoming awkward customers,' grunted Trogadon, wiping the blood from his face. 'And did you see how the ones to the rear fled from the Flame Charm back up the stairs?'

'The Shatterlings are metamorphosing from a wild horde to expertly employed marionettes,' explained Falk. 'The more of them we kill, the more powerfully the Adversary is holding them in His merciless grip. They are going to get even more devious, believe me.'

'Take a breather and re-form!' commanded Yantilla, the Ice Wolves taking up position behind the next Charm Line.

By now, there were no more bodyguards standing at the descent to the Blade Chamber. The attrition rate among the soldiers who had sworn personal fealty to Ahren was appalling. The Forest Guardian forced himself not to think of those who had died. There was too much at risk for the others still living. Every remaining sword and shield was needed at the vanguard.

The ashes of the Shatterlings filled the air or stuck like a thick patina to the floor. Ahren could literally taste the enemy every time he took a breath. If he could only spit, it would be a mercy, but his mouth and throat were painfully dry. Together with his friends and the Ice Wolves he stared into the darkness of the stairwell opposite, waiting anxiously for a new wave of Shatterlings to appear.

Ahren gripped his Wind Blade harder, noticing how his fingers were trembling. He and his companions had raised their weapons too many times since dawn had broken for them not to be exhausted by fighting, and even the gods' Blessings seemed unable to reinvigorate the Champions. Ahren slipped into Pelneng to ameliorate the effects on his weary body.

'A break would be nice,' whispered Khara beside him. His beloved understood exactly what he was going through.

'They are as quiet as mice,' murmured Bergen, cocking his head.

'The Shatterlings are creeping towards us,' said Khara. 'Muai can hear them. Prepare yourselves.'

Hardly had the Swordsmistress uttered the words when another wall of darkness invaded the room, accompanied by whooshing shadows that formed into a battleline, just far enough away for them to be only barely visible.

'That won't help you, you know!' exclaimed Hakanu, hurling his spear at the wall of blackness. Pallid bodies fell silently forward, skewered by the Paladin's weapon, the apprentice grunting contentedly before calling it back with a wave of his hand.

Lyssin shot arrows at the shadowy Shatterlings, but although both she and Hakanu slew another three of the Dark Ones, the enemy line stayed where it was. The gloom intensified directly above the Shatterlings until it resembled an impenetrable tidal wave reaching up to the ceiling.

'Hakanu,' said Ahren, fearing the worst. 'How is Kamaluq?'

'Exhausted,' replied the apprentice. 'Let him have a rest before the next lightning flash.'

'We don't have the time,' grunted the First. Then the Shatterlings stormed forward.

Blackness, claws and jagged blades searched ravenously for Ahren's soft flesh and that of the other defenders. Kamaluq's weak whimpering was little more than a whisper when he ignited his unique gift.

Hardly had Ahren opened his eyes after the lightning flash when he saw that the Shatterlings were fighting back with considerably less fury than he had expected. Devoid of their protective darkness, they seemed to be waiting for something.

Can you see anything, Culhen? he asked nervously as he tried both to keep the two Shatterlings opposite him at bay as well as peer into the stairwell from where the deep black darkness was forming.

No, said Culhen before sinking his teeth into a High Fang and ending its suffering.

'*There!*' screamed Fisker. 'Cassobo has spotted one of the Shatterlings *above* us!'

Out of the corner of his eye, Ahren could see no more than a spiderlike shadow scuttling across the ceiling, having already moved behind the line of Ice Wolves. Suddenly, the Shatterlings seemed totally possessed as they screeched and clawed and stabbed, sheer madness having seized control of whatever was left of their reason.

'The Charm Line!' screamed Sunju, panic-stricken. 'It is going to ignite the Charm Line behind us!'

Ahren spun around, one hand grasping for *Fisiniell,* but immediately two powerful claws grabbed him from behind and began pulling him towards the enemy line. He swung *Sun* wildly in all directions, desperately trying to stop himself from being dragged away into the darkness and could only see the Shatterling dropping from the ceiling, landing directly behind one of the Charm Lines.

We are all going to be cremated! thought the Forest Guardian.

The Shatterling raised its foot.

None of the Ice Wolves or Paladins were close enough to stop it. Hakanu cursed as he drew back his spear, Lyssin's hand reaching for the quiver only to find it empty.

The Shatterling's cunning was proving a terrible success.

Suddenly, Haminul whinnied, so shrilly and with such an undertone of sheer defiance that it seemed as though he was once more the Black Bodach of yore that had roamed the Forest of Ire and its environs. The call of the black Titejunanwa ricocheted with such force off the walls that it felt to Ahren as if daggers were piercing into his ears. With an agonised groan, he sank to his knees – as did all the others in the chamber that were not Elven chargers. The Shatterling at the Charm Line doubled over for a good three heartbeats before it began stretching its foot towards the sorcerous sign again.

This was more than enough time for Selsena to storm towards the High Fang. She whinnied with such a screech that Ahren was sure his eardrums had punctured, the Titejunanwa then sinking her horn into the Shatterling's back, lifting the creature up into the air before galloping away from the Charm Line, making sure not to touch the sensitive rune with her hooves.

'And who says that equines have no business being in enclosed areas?' groaned Falk as he struggled back to his feet.

Get up, everyone!' commanded the First, already upright himself and stabbing his blade into an onrushing Dark One. 'The next wave of attackers is on its way!'

'Retreat!' yelled Yantilla.

Ahren pulled a dazed bodyguard to his feet, before yanking both himself and his fighting companion to safety by leaping back over the magic rune. The High Fangs to the front tried their best to fall back, only to be prevented from doing so by their support to the rear.

'Burn!' exclaimed Yantilla, relishing the sound of the word as she stamped on the Charm line. A hissing sound permeated the room, and once again the air was stiflingly hot and filled with ash.

The Father of the Mountain coughed. 'It's getting harder and harder to breathe in here.'

Ahren was amazed at the calmness and gentleness in the dwarf-like Paladin's voice despite the appalling circumstances in which they found themselves. He found himself looking down on the numerous dead soldiers around him, all of them wearing the charred tabards that bore his crest. There were no more than ten Ice Wolves still capable of holding a sword and a shield. He and Yantilla exchanged sorrowful looks before nodding to each other in silence.

'We must vacate the Rune Chamber!' exclaimed the Forest Guardian, having forced himself to seize the initiative again. 'The next assault will cost us our final Charm Line!'

No-one protested, the steel doors behind them then opening while the surviving bodyguards stood to attention before Ahren and Yantilla, saluting the pair. 'It is an honour to serve you, Thirteenth,' said a young soldier, who could hardly be much older than Hakanu.

'Come with us,' said Ahren almost pleadingly as the companion animals began making their descent.

'Someone must close the doors behind you and buy you some time,' countered Yantilla. 'Please let me remain with them,' she pleaded. 'A commander must stay with their unit to the bitter end.'

Ahren felt sick to the stomach as he continued. 'No!' he snapped. 'I am not willing to lose you. As long as you live, so do the Ice Wolves!'

Ahren was tempted to grant the woman her wish only for the commander to be unceremoniously pushed towards the stairs by the shield of a female Ice Wolf.

'Save the commander,' said the young soldier as she righted her helmet and turned to face the Shatterlings. 'Save the Ice Wolves!'

That was enough for Ahren. He descended the stairwell, shoving the cursing Yantilla before him. Behind him, the steel doors closed with a percussive clang, the sound causing the former mercenary to sob. Ahren continued to force himself to descend, his conscience telling him that he should be up above, standing by the men and women who had protected him so loyally. The darkness at the bottom of the stairwell caused him to hesitate – until he remembered that the special gloom down here was designed to be of advantage to him and his fellows. Here, in the final chamber, the Night Soldiers would confront the Shatterlings, reminding the accursed creatures of that feeling of fear which had been driven out of them by the Dark god.

The doors closed behind them, Ahren recognising nothing but leaden darkness now.

'We shall lead you,' murmured Ro-kani into his ear, the same Night Soldier who had crossed paths with him so often before. With a hand firmly grasping his upper arm, Ahren was led swiftly through the labyrinth with its deadly traps set for all those who had not internalised perfectly its lethal geography.

'They will crawl up the walls and along the ceiling,' he whispered, breaking the ominous silence.

'All the better,' was the eager reply. 'Sharp protruding blades will be here to welcome them.'

A low, spitting sound permeated through the gaps around the steel doors behind them.

'The last Charm Line,' moaned Yantilla.

'You could never have led a better group of men and women,' said Ahren, but he knew that his words sounded hollow.

'We have arrived,' said Ro-kani. 'Your friends are here already.'

'Ahren?' murmured Khara, not two paces to his left.

'Here I am.'

'Good.'

'How *exactly* are *we* going to fight?' asked Bergen gruffly. 'I am *not* able to see in the dark and have little desire to find myself impaled in this labyrinth of traps.'

'Anyone who wants is welcome to retreat to the Heart Hall,' muttered the First.

Ahren listened closely but could hear no movement whatsoever. Then a tiny torch was ignited behind him, its weak light causing him to blink. The illumination extended no more than six paces across. The doors to the Heart Hall loomed to the rear of the assembled Paladins, the soul companions and new-born babies waiting within the chamber in the hope that the Paladins would keep the horror of the night from crossing the threshold.

'The brand is illuminating the area within which we can move,' said the First, placing the torch in a wall bracket directly beside the doors to the Heart Hall.

'That's not enough room for all of us,' complained Fisker.

'We will form two lines,' said Sunju. The warriors who need a lot of room, stay here. The companion animals – except for Kamaluq – are to go deeper into the Heart Hall. The ranged attackers and shield bearers like me will locate ourselves in the entrance area. Only retreat under cover of the fox's lightning flashes – if the worst comes to the worst.'

'Does anyone else have the feeling that we have dared, thrown the dice and lost?' asked Fisker. The trembling in the Paladin's voice sounded to Ahren like an alarm bell. 'We are now standing directly in front of the Heart Hall and the Shatterlings are still continuing their assault.'

'Do not let yourself be led astray,' said Trimm suddenly, responding to Fisker's complaint. 'Fear stabs deeper than any blade.'

This was met with a stunned silence.

'You have all heard your brother,' said the Father of the Mountain, the pride in his voice unmistakable. 'If Trimm is able to find his courage in the darkness, then so should we all.'

Ahren feared that it was something grimmer than courage that was driving the portly Paladin, but he kept that thought to himself. So long as Trimm's example put steel into the backs of the Champions of the gods, then he was truly grateful to the grieving grandee.

Another hissing sound – the sound of a Bane Charm that was louder than the Charm Line that had signalled the end of the Ice Wolves.

'The doors to the second protective chamber have fallen,' announced Khara.

Hopefully, the spells on them have transformed a few of those good-for-nothing s into soot and ash,' muttered Trogadon.

'Enough talk,' warned Falk. 'Everyone into position.'

I really don't like leaving you on your own, said Culhen, quickly licking a cut on Ahren's cheek. At some point during the battle, the Forest Guardian had lost his helmet – although he had no idea when.

I will be no more than thirty paces away from you, said Ahren, comforting his wolf. *Your task is to make sure that no Shatterlings get through to the new-born babies if we are forced into a retreat.*

'Culhen,' warned the Father of the Mountain in a gentle voice. 'It is time.'

Once the warriors had divided themselves up into their allotted groups, Ahren waited, along with Khara, Yantilla, the First, Trimm, Trogadon and Bergen before the double doors to the Heart Hall. The Forest Guardian wanted nothing more than for his one remaining bodyguard to be safe, but her look was no less grim and determined than that of Trimm. Both desired to see their enemies swim in rivers of their own blood.

Hakanu gave his master and Kamaluq, who was standing beside Ahren, one last, pained look before pulling the heavy doors closed behind him, every position outside the Heart Hall now being occupied in preparation for the final skirmish.

'I love you.' The three simple words whispered to him by Khara slammed into his stomach with all the force of an arrow. He tried not to imagine that she was bidding him farewell.

'I love you, too,' he said, trying to see into her eyes in the dim light cast by the torch, but already a shattering bang sounded from the steel doors opposite, followed by the noise of a Shatterling being skewered by a blade.

The enemy had arrived in the Blade Chamber.

Ahren's heart was beating so wildly, he was afraid it would burst out of his chest.

He and his companions were standing there with weapons drawn, condemned to doing absolutely nothing – and what seemed like for an eternity. The Shatterlings were fighting, killing and dying in total darkness. Every now and then, Ahren could hear the tell-tale smacking sound of flesh being torn asunder, and the fact that he couldn't *see* what was happening only made every noise all the more horrifying. It was only because snippets of the skirmishing were audible that he could sense what he already *knew* deep in his pounding heart – the Night Soldiers were fighting courageously, but also suffering heavy losses. The dreadful sounds of the bloody battle were getting ever closer.

'Four more paces,' murmured Trogadon, loosening his tense shoulder muscles. 'Five if we are lucky.'

'Silence,' said the First. 'We must not miss the moment now that…'

For the briefest of heartbeats, Ahren made out two pallid, blood-spattered High Fangs leaping into the weak light before an impenetrable darkness enveloped their contours.

With their jagged blades, the Shatterlings lunged at Ahren and Khara, the couple reacting with clean parries, however, Trogadon then smashing his hammer into the High Fangs, sending them back into the darkness that they had emerged from. The sound that followed indicated the unerring effectiveness of further hidden traps.

'If more of them succeed in getting through to us, we are going to need more light,' said Bergen. 'I can hardly see what I am supposed to hit.'

Another High Fang jumped into the torchlight, being immediately greeted by the blonde Paladin's axe.

'Seems to me you're doing alright,' commented the First dryly.

'Careful!' screamed Khara, successfully deflecting a blade that had been aimed directly at Ahren's head.

'Now I recognise the fighting methods of those devious murderers that ambushed us during the Night of Blood,' muttered Trimm grimly.

The First grunted. 'This is good. It means there cannot be many of them left. Yet, the will of the Adversary will ensure that they will be absolutely ruthless in their battle against us.'

'I wonder if Quin-Wa has managed to give birth successfully,' murmured Ahren.

'What makes you think of *that* now?' asked the First.

'Because it is high time for our call to arms,' whispered the Forest Guardian.

'One moment, please,' muttered Trogadon, reaching into his belt bag. Then he held a handful of powder over the little torch. 'Are you all ready?'

'Wait!' Khara's bracelet lit up and the Blessing Band came glowing to life. 'Let me listen first,' warned the Swordsmistress, Ahren and the other Paladins having already drawn breath.

A tiny tug along the invisible threads connecting all the Paladins was enough for Ahren to sense the exhaustion and relief on both Aluna's and Quin-Wa's part. Their children had been born! Now the little ones had to be protected at the very dawn of their existence from those horrific creatures whose task it was to assassinate them.

Ahren's unshakeable determination was like a second sword, forged by his oath to break for once and for all the curse of the Night of Blood.

He breathed in as much air as his lungs would take.

The Shatterlings were advancing towards them – a concentrated semi-circle of drawn, jagged weapons.

'PALADINIM THEOS DURALAS!'

The words echoed on both sides of the doors to the Heart Hall, the heavy metal sheets vibrating under the force of the call like a Keeper's bell, summoning the village to the godsday prayer. Trogadon drizzled the powder onto the little flame of the torch, the modest fire immediately flaring to glorious, blinding light.

Time seemed to stand still as Ahren, under the influence of the now re-united gods' Blessing following centuries of splintering, thwarted the seemingly sluggish assault on the part of the Shatterlings, *Sun* carving its way through their distorted, emaciated bodies. The entire room was delineated in the white glare of the glowing torch, revealing a battlefield the likes of which Ahren had never before seen. Black robed bodies, whether those of Shatterlings or Night Soldiers lay scattered around the place in a sight so dismal that the Forest Guardian had to avert his eyes.

Beside him, the other Paladins as well as Khara, Trogadon and Yantilla were fiercely fighting the High Fangs. A good three dozen of the pallid creatures were besieging his friends and forcing their way forward.

The light went out – and with it the power of the Blessing Band. Suddenly, Ahren felt completely alone in the darkness of the chamber. He shivered as he slashed his sword in the direction of the snorting Shatterlings while screaming in Khara's direction: 'What happened?!'

Sparks flew as Trogadon ignited another torch, which he threw unceremoniously onto the floor. It was a flickering bastion surrounded by an all-embracing darkness.

'Aluna…' muttered Khara a few heartbeats later, her voice reflecting her utter confusion. 'She…I think she…*absorbed* the Blessing!'

'What's that supposed to mean?' snarled the First, skewering two Shatterlings with his broadsword and suffering a cut below his pauldron in the process.

'How do *I* know?!' gasped Khara. 'It's not as if this is an everyday situation now, is it?'

'I must admit, I *would* quite like to have the Blessing Band back,' groaned Bergen. 'These old muscles really could do with a little help after all the fighting they have endured today.'

Ahren could see that the broad-shouldered Paladin kept feeling his stomach when he wasn't swinging his axe. A small, constant stream of blood was streaming from his body.

The darkness of the Shatterlings was driving the light of the torch further and further back. Already, the companions were almost on top of each other as they fought valiantly.

'Retreat,' gasped Ahren, his disappointment audible to all.

'Are your sure?' asked Trogadon. 'There are no more than twenty left.'

Khara stumbled backwards, a swelling having appeared over her right eye, which was growing bigger and bigger. 'But they are fighting with the fury of a hundred,' she gasped.

'It is repeating itself,' whispered Trimm, horrified. Deep as his desire for revenge was, it was being extinguished by a flood of rekindled memories.

Ahren slammed his fist against the steel door to his rear, his swordhand simultaneously deflecting the devious thrust of a jagged blade to his stomach.

'We need you!' he yelled over his shoulder, the movement of his head almost costing him his life but for Yantilla's intervention.

The sword of the High Fang sank deep into her shoulder.

'No!' gasped Ahren, dragging the wounded woman to safety as the double doors behind him swung open.

The darkness slid over and beyond Ahren like a ravenous Swarm Claw that at last had caught sight of its prey. Shatterlings, leaped, scrambled, crawled along the floor, the walls and the ceiling – past the Paladins, their eyes fixed greedily on the cradles situated at the far side of the hall.

Six, seven, then eight High Fangs fell victim to furiously swung weapons, but the Paladins, for all their valour, were hopelessly overrun and quite simply ignored as the darkness and the will of the Adversary whipped the Shatterlings forward so that they could fulfil His dark promise to the Champions of the gods.

Paladins and soul companions alike screamed in agony. The newborn babes cried helplessly in their cribs, their fathers, mothers and valiant she-dwarfs bending over the innocent ones like living shields.

Ahren stabbed and swung as he desperately tried to make his way deeper into the Heart Hall, but his progress was marginal on account of the chaos caused by the presence of so many panic-stricken bodies. Hakanu and Lyssin shot three Shatterlings down from the ceiling, but four more had already arrived high over their prey.

Ahren felt a shudder in his right arm, which was still holding the wounded Yantilla. He froze, realising that the gaunt woman had been bored through by a splintered sword, its jagged end protruding through the design of the leaping Ice Wolf on her blood-soaked tabard. The woman who for so long had been his bodyguard was being ripped from his hand and pulled into the darkness.

Ahren's mouth formed into a cry of rage and despair only for another's voice to scream out the word he had been about to utter.

'YANTILLA!'

A pallid figure rose up from the healing pool filled with Jelninolan's sacred water – and with the blood of over half a dozen Paladins. Lanlion's face was a mask of unutterable horror, his eyes were shining with the dying fire of a cold, moonless night. His fingers glided over the red water as he sucked up as much of the Paladin blood as he could manage. The scream of the pallid Champion of the gods had caused both friend and foe to stagger and fall. Then the Bloodless climbed out of the pool, now robed in his sorcerous blood-red charm for which there was no name in all Jorath.

At that very moment, four High Fangs dropped from the ceiling onto the floor beside the cradles, their jagged blades raised and ready to stab into the tenderest of flesh, only for a cry to be uttered, so powerful that the very walls creaked and trembled and gasped.

'YE BROKEN, SHATTERED HIGH FANGS WOULD LIKE TO BE MONSTERS OF THE NIGHT, WOULD YE?' The question of the Bloodless echoed back from the walls and within Ahren's mind.

'LET ME SHOW YE A REAL MONSTER!'

An extraordinary, dark redness seemed to swallow all around it – first the light, and then the darkness. Ahren heard a multitude of tearing sounds, of smacking noises, of agonised gurgling. Men, women and babies screamed out in fear. Something glided along his skin, something so cold that he was sure he would never feel the warmth of life ever again.

Then it was over.

The light returned – like a shy farmer's lad, remembering to do his humble tasks on a warm summer's day. Peace settled as tear-stained faces looked around in disbelief, blinking away their tears as well as the fears that had so horribly afflicted them.

The Shatterlings were lying like broken dolls, scattered around the chamber, their faces as white as fresh snow. Not one of their wounds was bleeding anymore.

Ahren looked at the entrance to the Heart Hall, and there he observed a lonely figure – it was Lanlion, and he was carrying something in his arms – the body of Yantilla.

'Be not afeard,' whispered the pallid Paladin in a voice of unbearable tenderness. 'Death shall not take custody of you.'

Ahren saw the Bloodless wrap his cloak over Yantilla's battered body before he melted into the darkness of the Blade Chamber.

Ahren felt a lump in his throat. Fighting back tears he looked around. All the Shatterlings were dead, but the children of the Paladins were alive.

'It is over,' he whispered, hardly able to believe his own words. 'This Night of Blood has come to an end. And ironically, it has been a Paladin who has dedicated his life to both night and blood that has brought this about.'

Khara stepped towards him and placed her arms around his neck.

'In the end,' she breathed into his ear, 'it is *always* love that gives us unimaginable power.'

Chapter 19

The Adversary sensed the last dying husks that had brought His darkness right into the ranks of the enemy.

It had required much energy on His part over the past few weeks and especially during this night – but it had been well worth it. The Paladins had returned empty-handed from Kelkor, some of their most powerful allies had fallen this night, and, thanks to all the chaos and death caused by His *Shatterlings* – as that fool, the Thirteenth had named them – his enemies had forgotten the most important point – this blind spot on their part would reward them with a final, *humiliating* defeat.

The Night of Blood had never been merely an attack from without – just as important was the fact that it was also an assault from *within*.

***

Following the restlessness within her heart, Khara turned east at the meeting point of the two corridors. The all-enveloping silence within the castle combined with the constantly burning torches on the walls still seemed somehow unreal, colliding as they did with her memories of the darkness-seeped night, her thoughts a wild riot in her head as a consequence.

'Where are you going?'

Ahren's voice was slurring with exhaustion. He had already turned to the west, where their room was situated. Unlike her, he hadn't had the chance for a short sleep following their arrival on Sun Shimmer in Highstone the previous evening.

Khara turned to him, gesturing to her beloved that he should retire to their bedroom. 'I just want to pay Sleeps-in-Treetop and Lirana a visit,' she said.

Ahren nodded, Khara rewarding him with a peck on his cheek. 'How is Quin-Wa?' he asked softly. The blade of a Shatterling had wounded the empress during the chaos, and it had been a serious injury that had remained unnoticed for the several heartbeats that Lanlion had been casting his spell.

Khara's mind flew to Muai. The tigress was lying before the healing pool, which now looked almost as dirty again as it had done before

Lanlion had absorbed the blood of the Paladins. Only Quin-Wa was left in the water, all the defenders of the Heart Hall having already bathed. Her face was pale, her hair like a black fan framing the face of the sleeping Cochan as she floated peacefully.

Her chest is rising and falling, said Muai, responding to Khara's mental question. *Quin-Wa is strong. She will wake up soon.*

The Swordsmistress blinked away the tears. Her emotions were running riot and there was nothing she could do about it. She, too, was in urgent need of sleep.

Ahren gently hugged her. 'The healing pool was only a few paces away. And Muai was very quick to drag her into the water as soon as we had gotten over the immediate shock of Lanlion's intervention.'

Khara enjoyed the warmth of his arms embracing her. He seemed to be silently reassuring her that nothing bad could happen to them as long as they stayed together. She allowed the illusion to fully take hold of her, only escaping from it once the restlessness within her could no longer be ignored. She released herself from Ahren and wiped her eyes.

'I will go to the council chamber and then retire to our bedroom immediately,' she murmured. 'I simply *must* reassure myself that everyone who didn't fight alongside us is fine and see if or how Likis and Lina found safety in the Heart Hall – otherwise, I will not be able to sleep.' The inner turmoil, which had been plaguing her more and more since the end of the battle, was luring her especially to Lirana – but for some mysterious reason, she had no desire to share this knowledge with Ahren.

Her beloved was struggling to suppress another yawn. 'It will not be long until morning, and soon the bugles will be announcing our assault on the Obsidian Fortress,' he warned her, his voice ever so gentle. 'Every moment of rest is priceless.'

Khara smiled. 'I will hurry. That's a promise.'

Ahren nodded and walked away towards their shared chamber. Khara could see how her beloved was almost staggering, he was that exhausted. The healing water had done them all good, but it had been unable to banish their weariness.

She quickly whooshed along the corridor, making her way to the council chamber.

***

The Adversary concentrated on His dispatched will, which was now hanging from the ceiling as a little shred of darkness in a remote part of the castle. It reminded Him of a fat, black spider, waiting hungrily for its prey.

The Paladins had retired to bed, exhausted but content following their victory over His broken playthings. The Dark god laughed mockingly in the all-embracing darkness of His fortress. As though He would even need these High Fangs once those fools began knocking at His door with their catapults, their flames and their swords. He was awake now and He, personally, would command His servant.

Until then, He would focus solely on springing the surprise that was waiting for its opportunity in the very heart of Deepstone...

***

Khara breathed in sharply when she saw the dead guards lying before the council chamber. Their wounds suggested the work of Shatterlings. Drawing her weapons, she peeked into the large room, both doors being slightly ajar.

A High Fang lay perfectly still on the floor, its head so twisted that there was no way it could still be alive. Sleeps-in-Treetop was slouched on her chair, her loud snoring suggesting that she was in a deep slumber.

Lirana, on the other hand, was looking at Khara expectantly. The smouldering fire behind the woman, cast her features in a glow that was a mixture of pallid red and almost impenetrable black.

'Is it over?' asked the soul companion of the deceased Thirteenth, her voice betraying her nervousness. 'I can sense the Charm Circles weakening around me. If the Dark god discovers my treachery, He will understand that the repetition of the Night of Blood was nothing but a trap...'

Khara raised her hand. 'The soul companions and their children are alive. So are the Paladins.' Khara swallowed hard as she remembered Cochan. 'Even if some of them only escaped death by a hair's breadth. All the Shatterlings have been slain,' she added. 'Clearly, also those who were *not* looking for the Heart Hall.'

'This one must have sensed me,' whispered Lirana, her eyes glittering with silent triumph at Khara's report. 'I assume it wanted to know what precisely was hidden behind the doors to this chamber.' She pointed her chin towards Sleeps-in-Treetop. 'It was she who defeated it before it had a chance to enter. She fell asleep immediately afterwards. The Charm Circles protecting me are demanding their tribute from her.'

Khara struggled to suppress a yawn. 'I will send new guards,' she said sleepily. It was as if an inner burden, a hypnotic urge had fallen away now that she was standing here, looking into Lirana's eyes.

'The guards can wait,' said the black-robed woman, rising from her bed. 'Come closer. There is something that you must know.'

Khara did as she was bidden. It almost seemed as though a part of her rational mind had already fallen asleep, and that Lirana's voice was leading her through a mysterious dream. 'I must go to bed,' she murmured.

'Oh, and that you shall,' said Lirana, her face taking on an almost triumphant look. 'Go to your peacefully slumbering Paladin…'

Whatever the Woman in Black then said, it was swallowed up by the weariness that had taken hold of Khara as Lirana's face came closer and closer to her own. It almost felt as though the woman's body was melting into her own.

Then Khara turned and walked slowly away, returning to her bedroom like a sleepwalker, where Ahren was waiting for her to lie down beside him.

***

A sound that had driven many a weak-willed spirit insane echoed through the Obsidian Fortress. It was the joyless cackling of the Adversary, stirred by a gentle tug that had its source in distant Castle Highstone. He sensed the route of the impulse, His cackling turning into triumphant laughter. He recognised a splendid opportunity, relayed to Him by his most capable spy.

Quickly, He reached His power out towards His extended will, the darkness then scuttling along the ceiling of a corridor at whose end lay the bedchamber of the Thirteenth Paladin.

***

Ahren emerged sleepily from the depths of his exhausted slumber as he sensed Khara slipping into bed beside him.

'Are Lirana and Sleeps-in-Treetop in good shape?' he mumbled.

'Yes.'

Good,' he whispered, dozing off again, his mind not having realised that the voice he had heard was not exactly that of his beloved.

***

It seemed to Khara that she was drowning in the depths of her own understanding. Lying pressed in against Ahren under the warm sheepskin blanket, she was neither asleep nor awake.

Here, Master, she heard. It was Lirana's voice in her head. Coldness was dripping from every syllable. *The lass has already been prepared by a Bane Spell on my part. If You gather Your power, You should be able to break her effortlessly.*

On hearing these words, Khara forced her eyes open, her eyeballs then darting erratically in their sockets. There was nothing else in her body that she was able to control. She could only lie there and see how a ball of darkness dropped on top of her from the ceiling before seeping through her pores and into her body. Waves of coldness washed through her muscles which refused to obey her will.

HOW FITTING.

The voice in Khara's head was too powerful for her understanding. She sensed how she was losing herself with every heartbeat that the Adversary was *within* her.

AND AGAIN, IT WILL BE THE THIRTEENTH WHO WILL FALL AT THE HAND OF THE PERSON HE LOVES.

Khara fought. Her understanding struggled violently in the stranglehold of the Dark god, unable, however, to free itself.

To her horror, she sensed herself very quietly – so as not to wake Ahren – drawing a kitchen knife from her jerkin. When had she taken possession of it?

I WILL REWARD YOU, LIRANA, purred the Adversary, now grazing on Khara's helplessness. ONCE THIS DEED HAS BEEN COMPLETED, YOU WILL BE RELIEVED OF YOUR LONG SERVICE TO ME.

Khara fought with all the power she possessed, resisted with every inch of her body the presence in her mind.

In vain.

With a featherlike movement, she placed the tip of the knife on Ahren's back, so that the blade would slip effortlessly between the ribs and into his heart.

Thank you, Master, said Lirana. *And now – gather all Your will. Let her thrust and thereby free me of my agony!*

FINALLY, murmured the Adversary, slowly licking His lips in joyful anticipation.

Her despair was driving her insane as she sensed the Dark god squeezing her once more with His urge that held her in its grip. Again, she was being forced into preparing for the darkest of deeds that would inevitably unfold. Khara felt her muscles tensing up as they prepared for the final push – the thrust that would mean the end of her happiness and her future, smashing Jorath's future to eternal smithereens.

ALL THE EFFORTS OF THE THREE – IN VAIN! rejoiced the Adversary in His moment of triumph.

Despite herself, Khara placed her second hand on the grip of the knife. The stab would be quick and deadly. Already, her hands were tightening, accompanied by the tears of the distraught Swordsmistress that were now flowing freely…

Now, Khara!

Lirana's voice was little more than an echo in the Swordsmistress's mind. For a heartbeat, she was back on the Hill of Five Waters, diving in its pool, surrounded by attacking Stone Morays. But the Wind Blades in her hands were made of sheer darkness. Instinctively, Khara understood that her will was once more her own, and so she slashed, turning elegantly in the water, she cut the bonds of evil enslavement here and the tentacles of the blackest magic there.

TREACHERY! The word thundered through her head.

The hand holding the knife trembled but did not thrust.

It is as you have said, Master! Lirana's voice was filled with hatred, with a desire for retribution, but also with an unbreakable, wild hope. *Once this final deed has been completed, I will be relieved of my long service!*

Khara sensed Lirana's willpower melting into her own. The unfathomable love and grief of the soul companion for her deceased

Paladin were like two beacons of strength within Khara, while the sorcery of the Woman in Black resembled a furious storm in her heart.

With her shimmering Wind Blades, Khara effortlessly sliced through the countless bonds connecting the two women to the will of the Adversary. Together they broke through the surface of the pool, filling their lungs with air and boundless euphoria.

The knife fell from Khara's opening fingers.

The Adversary wailed in fury as His will was broken and He was driven from her spirit.

A life for a life. Lirana's words echoed in Khara's mind. They were still no more than an echo, fading away to an almost inaudible whisper. *After all this time, I have at last been able to save the Thirteenth Paladin...*

Then she was gone. And Khara was free.

Quickly, she picked up the knife, tossing it onto the floor and away from their shared bed. Her hands were trembling.

Ahren shifted, disturbed by her movements. 'I love you,' he mumbled.

Khara wrapped herself around him, the tears running down her cheeks.

'And I love you, too,' she whispered. She believed that she had never uttered anything so beautiful and true in her entire life.

***

Ahren woke up with the first rays of the morning sun. Blinking and yawning, he tottered over to the window.

Hadn't the heavy wooden shutters been closed when he had fallen into bed? Cold air streamed into the room, causing him to shiver. The hinges of the shutters were loose – it was as if someone had pushed them violently open in an effort to flee the chamber.

Ahren glanced around the room but could see nothing that suggested the presence of an unwelcome visitor. He caught sight of a small, innocuous kitchen knife that was lying carelessly on the floor, beneath the table. Had they eaten breakfast in the room the previous morning? He couldn't remember.

He felt woolly-headed. He knew that he still hadn't gotten enough sleep, and soon he would be called once more to arms. He grunted and reached for the shutters. It would be good to close them so that they could enjoy a little more peace and warmth. He stopped in mid-action. He blinked and stared in surprise in the direction of the rising sun.

'Did Lirana escape the Charm Circles?' he asked aloud even before he realised that he had woken Khara with his question.

'Why?' mumbled his beloved sleepily.

Ahren closed the shutters and climbed back into bed. The sheepskin and Khara's body radiated a comforting warmth, causing his shivering to ease off. 'I could have sworn that I saw her riding on Camentumar towards the horizon and the rising sun. But then, a heartbeat later, it seemed as though she had been swallowed up...' He stopped and looked at his beloved. 'Are you crying?' he asked, his voice full of concern. 'Why?'

'I'll tell you later,' said Khara, wiping away her tears and smiling lovingly at the Paladin. 'Now – go back to sleep. Remember, there is still a god to be vanquished today.'

Chapter 20

An extended blast of a bugle roused Ahren from his slumber. His eyes sticky and his heart beating quickly, he sat up. He felt light- and heavy-headed at the same time.

This was the day.

The last day of the war against the Adversary – if all went well.

'I'd hoped we'd have had more time,' mumbled Khara, still half asleep, her words ending in an extended yawn.

Ahren smiled. 'Me too, my love. Did you get enough sleep?'

Khara looked at him accusingly, dark rings under her eyes. 'Don't tell me *you* did?'

Ahren shook his head. Even thinking about it was making him yawn. 'Let us hope that our plan has sufficiently weakened the Adversary, so that we can defeat Him.'

Khara smiled mysteriously. 'I am sure that He paid a high price for His activities last night.'

'What is it that you're not telling me?' Ahren's anxiety regarding what lay ahead was heightened by a vague, uneasy feeling. He peered at his beloved.

Khara leaned over to him and kissed him gently. 'What I have to relate is a story that is impossible to tell lightly in the morning, nor can one repeat it. Let us go to the council chamber, and I will reveal all there.'

Ahren gave the Swordsmistress a long, critical look before shrugging his shoulders. 'As if I needed another excuse to hurry.'

Despite his words, he and his beloved took their time getting ready. Every crease in their underwear was smoothed, every piece of their armour put on with care, while their bundles were carefully tied up, the contents having been reduced to the bare minimum.

As the couple came out of their bedroom, the bugle sounded a second time.

Together, they hurried to greet the day, whose fate was so inextricably bound up with the hopes of the THREE.

'I told you that it was a good idea to sound the second bugle early,' laughed Bergen as Ahren and Khara came running into the council chamber. 'At least, now we can begin without delay.'

The room with the round table was unrecognisable. Lirana's bed and the Charm Circle that had surrounded her had both vanished, and every inch of the large chamber sparkled with cleanliness. Honeyed candles illuminated those corners that the morning rays of sunshine had not yet reached, while on the table, the arrangement of the troops around the Ring had been updated to the latest positions.

A quick glance was enough to confirm why the mood among the Paladins, the Ancients and his other friends was so relaxed – judging by the map, the soldiers were ready for action. The only things missing were the Champions of the gods who would lead them to victory.

'Cochan isn't here,' murmured Khara anxiously, her eyes having scanned the familiar faces that had gathered around the table. 'But Aluna is – and she looks remarkably perky.'

The fresh-faced mother to twins was chatting to the First, and she looked more rested than all the other Paladins put together.

'It seems that her absorbing all our gods' Blessings did her good,' said Ahren, suddenly remembering what it had felt like to be fighting for his life before the Heart Hall without the power of the gods to assist him. 'I am delighted that she is in good condition.' He glanced around the room. 'Lanlion is missing too. But, apart from that, I see many more of our friends,' he added, nodding towards Jelninolan and Uldini, who were standing with Trogadon, Likis, Falagarda and the Father of the Mountain.

The Thirteenth did his best to disguise his concern at the absence of Lanlion and Quin-Wa. All the Paladins were to have gathered on hearing the second bugle call – and yet there were two missing.

'You are looking well, considering how hard you have had to fight for victory since yesterday morning,' said Likis in greeting, the slender man smiling at Ahren and Khara, who had arrived over at the group and were hugging the others heartily, with even Uldini allowing himself to be embraced.

'They were hard-fought victories, indeed,' added Ahren, glancing surreptitiously over at Trimm.

The portly Paladin in his barbed armour was standing at the window, his hands firmly clenched behind his back.

'My sincere condolences on the loss of your Ice Wolves,' said Falagarda, Ahren immediately flinching.

'Thank you,' he replied flatly. 'I have not had the time to mourn for them yet.' He suppressed his feeling of guilt as much as he could. Today, he would have to concentrate completely on the living. Tomorrow he would grieve for the dead – those who had already been claimed by the war, and those who were yet to lose their lives before nightfall – assuming there would *be* a tomorrow.

'Two of the Night Soldiers have survived at any rate – among them a woman by the name of Ro-kani, who I believe you know,' said Likis. 'An incredible achievement, considering the carnage that was meted out in the Blade Chamber.'

'Alas, I cannot report of any survivors among the honourable dwarfs in the Shield Chamber,' added the Father of the Mountain sadly.

'The rest of the Highstone sentries were for the most part unharmed,' said Falagarda. 'Only the ones guarding this room were found dead. There is no sign of Lirana whatsoever. We suspect that she was dragged away by the enemy.'

'Or saved by Him,' muttered Uldini coldly. His words sounded hoarse – as if the Arch Wizard had spent a week without speaking while surviving on an inadequate supply of water.

Khara shook her head vehemently. 'You are wrong – both of you. Lirana helped me – *us* – more than you can imagine.'

'Why don't you explain what you know to the council?' asked Jelninolan, whose eyes seemed a little too absent to disguise the fact that the Ancient was somehow bound up with the spells that she had been preparing for a considerable time now.

'As soon as we are all here,' insisted the Swordsmistress mysteriously.

'I have already sent for Lanlion,' interjected Likis. 'And Quin-Wa is being carried up to us as I speak.

Khara frowned, anxiety gripping her. 'How is she? Muai and the other companion animals are holding a meeting, making it impossible for me to contact her.'

Ahren immediately tested out his connection with Culhen's mind, but the invisible wall that he came up against suggested that the wolf, too, was listening to Sun Shimmer.

'She has survived the night well,' explained the Father of the Mountain. 'She is strong – only not so strong that her body can withstand both a difficult birth and a stabbed heart without suffering serious consequences.'

Ahren, too, was becoming increasingly nervous. 'And what does that mean for us?'

The Father of the Mountain shrugged his shoulders. 'When I left her to come here to the council of war, she seemed angry rather than frustrated regarding her health. I am absolutely convinced that she will find the best possible way of supporting us in the decisive battle.'

'And Lanlion?' asked Ahren.

Likis shifted uncomfortably from one foot to the other. 'He is taking care of Yantilla. Apparently, he knows of ways and means of keeping her blood thirst under control. I won't deny it – it makes me very nervous having a newly created Bloodless resting in the Blade Chamber. Lina and our child are sheltering with the soul companions for as long as the battles rage.'

Ahren's heart sank as he thought of the dark fate that awaited Yantilla. Lanlion had succeeded in countering the curse of his unnatural condition, by using his gods' Blessing as a pawn to ensure his own spiritual health. Yantilla, alas, did not have this luxury. The Forest Guardian feared that the commander of the Ice Wolves might be lost forever, replaced by a creature in the form of a ravenous Bloodless.

'Maybe we should talk to Lanlion about it,' said Khara. Her sad eyes revealed to Ahren that she shared his fear.

The Father of the Mountain shook his head gently. 'I have tried. But until Lanlion sees with his own eyes how Yantilla is losing her mind, he will not listen to the necessary advice from anyone. When our melancholic friend falls in love, he is completely smitten.'

Ahren spent another while mixing with the other Paladins so that he could have a few words with Aluna and reassure himself concerning the health of all the new-born babies in the Heart Hall. Suddenly, there was a commotion at the entrance to the council chamber as Quin-Wa appeared. She was carried in on a simple sedan shouldered by four Sun Legionnaires dressed in gleaming plate armour. Behind her was a grim-looking Justinian.

'What is the Sun Emperor doing here?' asked Uldini in amazement. His irritation on seeing the ruler was impossible to miss. 'He is supposed to be commanding the troops at the southern section of the Ring. Is no-one adhering to our plan?'

The Father of the Mountain placed a hand on his shoulder. 'He arrived at dawn. Once he had received news of Quin-Wa's injury and the birth of their child, there was no stopping him. According to the stable hands in the castle, he changed horses three times so that he could get here quickly.'

By now, Quin-Wa had been carried to one of the council chairs, which she shifted herself onto with an audible groan.

'Let us begin,' she said instead of greeting the others. Her voice trembled.

Ahren and Khara exchanged a look of concern.

'Lanlion is missing,' grunted the First once everyone had taken their place around the table. There were no scribes in the room, the meeting this morning consequently feeling smaller and more intimate, with only the Paladins and their closest allies being present.

'I *am* here,' announced the Bloodless, stepping out of the shadows from a corner of the room where the candles had burnt out.

Falk muttered a curse under his breath. 'Have you been blessed with the gifts of a Fog Cat now?' asked the old man irritably.

Lanlion shook his head. Once the man stepped into the daylight, Ahren saw that his eyes were extraordinary red – as though all their blood vessels had suddenly burst. 'A little spell,' said the gaunt Paladin, 'nothing more. I must use up the power flowing through my veins from time to time – otherwise, they will destroy me from within.'

'You mean the power of *our* blood,' concluded the First with a cold rationality.

Lanlion nodded. 'It did us good service last night and will do so again during today's battle.' The Bloodless hesitated before sitting down on his chair. 'I shall do my best to put your gift – even if given unwillingly – to its greatest and most practical use, even before we reach the Adversary. My gods' Blessing must be as…pure…as possible when we confront Him.'

'If Lanlion is in a position to create mighty magic with our blood, then I will happily put more of mine at his disposal.' Trimm's eyes showed no hint of emotion as he spoke. Clearly, the portly Paladin was, for the moment, not focussing on the grief that he was undoubtedly still harbouring. 'Better for Lanlion to get it rather than the countless Dark Ones standing between us and the Dark god.'

To Ahren's surprise, Lanlion shook his head vehemently. 'As with everything in life, a *measured* approach is necessary.' He pointed up at his red eyes. 'And I have exhausted my supply for today.'

'We are wasting time,' said Bergen. 'The sun is inexorably climbing the heavens. If it sets again and the Adversary is still living, then it will surely be our new-born children and all Jorath who will pay for our failure.'

'The special forces are not yet fully in position,' countered Falagarda. 'In line with the plan, they are holding back until the third call of the bugle.'

Fisker irritably brushed his blonde locks away from his anxious eyes. 'Are we sure that we are not simply walking straight into a trap? So far, every act of guile on our part has been responded to with a greater one by the Adversary which we never saw coming.'

The First shook his head. 'We have slain the last child of the Dark god. We have established and successfully defended a bridgehead in enemy territory. We have eliminated the Shatterlings completely, and we now find ourselves ready for action on the morning of the day when the the Adversary is at His weakest. Whatever intrigues He is now forging, we simply must be able to overcome them.'

Ahren slowly looked around the table at all his companions before speaking. 'The assault on the Obsidian Fortress will take place today.'

'Shouldn't we first talk about *this?*' asked Aluna icily, pointing at the spot that Ahren had already explained to her as being where Lirana had been trapped within the Charm Circle the previous day. The young mother seemed full of life and perfectly healthy. The delivery of her twins had been far from easy, marked as it had been by the smouldering remains of the guileful curse that had plagued her for weeks despite the antidote of healing magic. According to Aluna, it had been the gods' Blessing that had strengthened her in her moment of greatest need, which the Paladins within and in front of the Heart Hall had released in unison, enabling her to win her fight for life and overcome the agony that had been torturing her.

Ahren couldn't imagine the pain his sister must have suffered – it had taken the combined strength of her fellow Paladins for her to win the silent battle against the black magic of the Adversary and bring her two babies safely into the world.

'Has the enemy spy returned to the embrace of His dark arms?' asked Aluna in the icy voice that was so particular to her.

To Ahren's amazement, Khara got to her feet and shook her head energetically. 'We are all deeply indebted to Lirana.' She took a deep breath before continuing. 'Let me relate to you the latest malevolent plan of the Dark god, which a tortured soul managed to thwart by means of a long-planned subterfuge…'

A heavy silence hung over the chamber like a dark cloud unwilling to dissolve itself following a violent thunderstorm.

'What a crazy, reckless plan,' muttered Uldini, eventually. 'Is it clear to you all what Lirana has gone and *done?*'

Ahren was still stunned by the news of how close he had come to being killed – and without having been at all aware of the danger. If either Lirana or Khara had weakened, then…

'I will be more careful with kitchen knives in future,' he murmured.

'She saved Ahren and inflicted a heavy defeat on the Adversary. According to Khara's story, He expended an extraordinary amount of energy and yet still lost,' said Jelninolan, confused. 'What's the problem, then?'

Uldini waved his hand dismissively. 'Lirana did more than that – and quite deliberately. 'In the Green Sea she helped Khara stand up to the gods so that the Swordsmistress could stay by Ahren's side even though she *wasn't* a soul companion. And last night, Lirana used this "gap" in Khara's being to hide herself in so that she could fool the Adversary into believing that Khara had indeed been chosen by the THREE for Ahren after all. When the Dark god took control of Khara's will, He found Himself at the crucial moment dealing with not only the fierce tenacity of the Swordsmistress but also with the knowledge and power of a Blood Wizard. Lirana must have spent centuries preparing for this moment.' Uldini slammed the edge of one of his hands onto the palm of his other – like an axe slamming onto an executioner's block. 'When Khara sliced through the bonds with which He had anchored His will to her spirit, she sundered not only her own, but also those chains between Lirana and *her* enforced Master. Khara freed them both from His influence. This move had been carefully orchestrated by Lirana.'

'The result was the same,' murmured Lyssin, shrugging her shoulders. 'The Thirteenth is still alive, and the Adversary's ruse came to naught.'

'A ruse that we didn't see coming – yet again,' muttered Sunju. 'We thought that the Night of Blood would be different this time because *we* provoked it and prepared ourselves beforehand. And yet, the Dark god almost defeated us a second time by making *this* Night of Blood identical to the previous one with an attack on the sleeping Thirteenth Paladin – something that we never expected.'

Falk glared angrily. 'And the Thirteenth would have been slain by the hand of his beloved again,' he muttered morosely. 'Does anyone at this table doubt that such a deed would have robbed of us all our fighting spirit?'

His answer came in the form of complete silence as the eyes of all those present turned towards Ahren, who flinched mentally from the thought that he could so easily be stabbed to death in his sleep by Khara…

The young man cleared his throat. 'How likely is it that the Adversary has more surprises in store for us?'

'*Hate* has been destroyed,' said Jelninolan, using her fingers to list off her points. 'The outer walls of the Obsidian Fortress have fallen, the Adversary having used their magic for His failed assault on Highstone. Then there is the injury that Khara and Lirana have done to His willpower. According to Khara, the pair of them have cut deeply into His ability to force other creatures to do His bidding. Our troops will, for the moment, be safe from His malevolent whisperings, even *if* they come too near to Him.' The elf looked at the others meaningfully. 'We cannot get much closer to victory without coming face to face with the Dark god.'

'Which brings us to our last problem before we head into battle,' said the First. 'All thirteen Paladins must confront the eternal enemy together.' He looked over at Quin-Wa.

She snorted before responding. 'I am the Eternal Empress,' she said as coolly as her trembling voice would let her. 'Trust me – I have come up with a solution for my temporary indisposition.'

Jelninolan wrang her hands nervously. 'Healing Charms cannot help you now, Quin-Wa. What you need are two or three days of rest —'

'I know,' interjected the wounded woman gently. 'Which is why I will *not* be accompanying you all.'

Ahren's immediate dismay and frustration was reflected in the faces of the others present.

'Please let us in on your secret of how you expect things to proceed,' said the First.

The forced politeness of the veteran made a shiver run down Ahren's spine. The age-old Paladin resembled a volcano about to erupt.

'Careful!' muttered the Sun Emperor, glaring at the First. The fact that the ruler had been silent up to this point gave the implicit threat in the word additional weight. The atmosphere in the room had markedly changed, and Ahren was afraid that a fight would be inevitable.

Quin-Wa, however, remained calm. 'Please, gather around me, Champions of the gods,' she murmured mysteriously, pushing her chair back sufficiently from the table with the help of Justinian so that the Paladins were able to position themselves in a tight circle around the sitting woman. The gods' Blessing in Ahren's chest began to dance. The thirteen Paladins had never been so close together before. Ahren sensed that they were only one call away from uniting their combined strengths.

'It's nice and tight here,' joked Fisker, breaking the tension in the air. 'Anyone want to swap with me? I'm about to be skewered by Trimm's porcupine armour.'

'Please touch me with your fingers,' continued Quin-Wa, unperturbed. The Paladins turned so that each of them could place a hand on the body of the empress.

'Good,' said the Ancient. 'And now, Khara, activate the Blessing Band, please.'

The Swordsmistress closed her eyes for a moment, Ahren sensing the connection between him and his brothers and sisters swelling up like a crescendo until it was almost at its peak.

'No battle cry,' instructed Quin-Wa firmly, Falk's mouth already triumphantly wide open. 'What I need now is control, not chaos.'

Ahren bit his tongue, so urgently did he feel the age-old cry of the Paladins surging within him. he knew that the words were only a ritualised form of expressing the power within him, but it was as if they had taken on a life of their own, wanting to break forth so that they could be free at last…

'Don't take your hands away,' said Quin-Wa, the power then suddenly flowing out of Ahren, leaving him feeling himself to be nothing more than an empty shell as he nearly stumbled backwards, the force penetrating and filling Quin-Wa.

Through the Blessing Band, Ahren could sense how the eternal empress was trying to create the effect that had saved Aluna and the lives of her twins the previous night when she had struggled with the hidden remains of the Bane Curse while simultaneously giving birth.

'It doesn't want to work!' gasped Quin-Wa through gritted teeth, unable to hide her disappointment. 'You cannot strengthen me.'

'Why not?' asked Bergen, clearly shattered. 'What is different this time?'

'Quin-Wa's body has reached the end of its natural tether,' explained Jelninolan sadly from outside the circle of Paladins. 'Only time can give her back her old strength.'

Ahren sensed that Quin-Wa was still clinging onto the concentrated Blessing of the Paladins like a drowning woman.

'Then I must think of another plan,' she gasped, releasing the Blessing.

Releasing all the Blessings.

To his astonishment, Ahren felt his power flowing back into him as that of the other Paladins returned home to their possessors. Quin-Wa's Blessing was carried by this maelstrom of movement, running along the Blessing Band – until it arrived at its point of origin.

Khara stared down in disbelief at the brightly shimmering bracelet, beaming a pure, clear sheen – as though the light from the very first morning of Creation had been re-awakened for a few, precious heartbeats.

'What have you done?' growled the First, flabbergasted.

Quin-Wa smiled, even though her lips were now blue and her complexion pallid. 'I have ensured that my Blessing will accompany you. Khara is of my blood – even if too distant in my ancestral line to be a permanent Paladin.' Her eyes met those of the shocked Swordsmistress. 'But for the duration of a single day, she *can* – with the help of her bracelet – carry my Blessing within her, and without the power tearing her to pieces from within.'

'You might easily have left out the last part of the sentence,' scolded Sunju as she let go of Quin-Wa.

Ahren stepped quickly out of the circle of Paladins and approached his beloved. 'How are you feeling?' he asked. He couldn't hide the anxiety in his voice.

'Alright,' suggested Khara uncertainly. 'Not really any different to before – if one ignores the fact that there is one particular Elven sentence that I am dying to shout out into the world.'

'You'd best reserve that until we are on the battlefield,' said Falk, laying a comforting hand on her shoulder, 'little sister.'

Khara's eyes filled with tears, and she swallowed hard as the Champions of the gods huddled around her, silently welcoming the Swordsmistress into their ranks.

'That's that, then,' said Quin-Wa, her voice expressing both her satisfaction and a great weariness. 'The Thirteen Paladins are united and ready to go to war with the Adversary. Ride off and complete the task that should have been finished a long, long time ago.

'Stop staring at me the whole time,' muttered Khara with a frown as she walked out of the stables, leading her horse. The large stallion was dressed in heavy Deep Steel armour and stamping the ground belligerently with his hooves.

'I apologise,' said Ahren with a grin. 'But the fact that you are one of us today…I find it…well…*fitting.*'

Khara grunted impatiently. 'I could really do without carrying the burden of Jorath's future on my shoulders.'

Ahren chuckled and cocked his head. 'Don't worry – you'll get used to it…in two or three days.'

'Very funny.'

A loud clatter sounded behind them, and Ahren turned to look before whistling approvingly through his teeth. 'Wow – that's an impressive horse cart you have there,' he said.

Trimm, the Father of the Mountain and Trogadon were standing in a chariot a good four paces in length, drawn by six horses wearing armour equally impressive to that of the horse Khara was holding by the reins. The bright sheen of the vehicle's sides suggested that it was of Deep Steel, as were the sharp scythes attached to the spokes on the four wheels.

'Deliveries of ore from Murgamolosch were responsible for this beauty and for the horses' equipment,' said Trogadon proudly. 'As were parts of the Thrumthal'kor that the Golem revealed to us in Thousand Halls and which Kamkanzakur then had smelted.'

Ahren remembered the oversized Deep Steel platform drawn by diligent dwarfs and to what practical use it had been put to by the ruler of Thousand Halls. 'Speed and manoeuvrability will be of primary importance today,' said the Forest Guardian, nodding approvingly.

Tell that to those on their armoured nags, commented Culhen haughtily as he trotted beside Ahren before giving an exaggerated yawn. *At least you will be carried smoothly, safely and elegantly across the battlefield, borne by your loyal Ice Wolf.*

You do realise that the safety of all the Paladins is of vital importance, don't you? chuckled Ahren. *This is not a competition.*

Everything is a competition, countered Culhen casually. *But fear not – I shall win for us both. After all, I am always there when you need me.*

Ahren gazed into the wolf's yellow eyes. *What's the matter?* he asked. *You are behaving even more oddly than usual.*

Culhen whimpered before lowering his head and looking up at his master with sorrowful eyes. *The Adversary placed a knife to your back, and I was nowhere to be seen! I am the worst companion animal of all time.*

Ahren placed his arms around his friend and squeezed the wolf's white fur. *Only Lirana knew what the Adversary was planning. And she had us deliberately walk into the trap to escape Him.*

Culhen wasn't really listening, he was wallowing so much in guilt and regret. *It was said that we companion animals were to sleep in the Heart Hall until we were allowed to visit the Healing Pool, and I was so tired, and Yoka was just as exhausted as the rest of us, and then she cuddled up against me, and then...*

Culhen! It's fine, said Ahren firmly. *Muai hadn't any idea of the subterfuge either even though she is connected to Khara.*

The wolf immediately raised his head. *Of course – you're right!* he exclaimed joyfully. *The silly cat concentrated completely on Quin-Wa and failed in her duty.*

That's not what I said! interjected Ahren, but already Culhen was licking his master's face.

Thank you, said the wolf, thoroughly relieved. *You really are a good Paladin.*

Ahren wasn't so sure about that. Furthermore, the fact that the tigress beside Khara was now glaring at him suggested that Sun Shimmer had been listening in on their conversation and had relayed it verbatim to the feline.

'If the Adversary doesn't kill me, then a certain big cat surely will,' he muttered.

'What did you say?' asked Khara inquisitively.

'Nothing important.'

A bugle sounded long and hard from the western tower of the castle. Others blasted out their reply in the distance, the tones fading away over the large expanse, stretching as far as the snow-covered horizon, which gleamed a blinding white thanks to the sun that was breaking through a restless blanket of cloud.

'The Ring is awakening,' said the Father of the Mountain, pointing at the armies forming in the distance. 'We should be over there.'

Ahren nodded as he swung himself onto Culhen's back. Khara, having mounted her horse moved to his left, while the large chariot was to his right. 'Should we wait for the others?' he asked.

'They rode off long ago,' chuckled Trimm. 'We three are still here because it takes an eternity to prepare a chariot.' He looked challengingly at Khara and Ahren. 'And what is *your* excuse?'

Khara clicked her tongue in response, her horse beginning to trot, which immediately caused Culhen to move off at a slightly quicker rate, ensuring that he was a little in front of the equine.

Ahren scanned the scene as they rode through the inner, western gateway of Highstone. The road was lined with the citizens of Deepstone, all of them dressed in heavy winter clothing, but this time there was no jubilant cheering. Instead, Ahren could see pleading faces and wide eyes expressing a mixture of sadness and hope. The crowd knew that this day was going to be a special one, and that the past night had been a hard test for the Paladins. One by one, the men, women and children went down on one knee and placed a hand to their heart.

Ahren struggled to swallow a lump in his throat as he realised the significance of their ride. The Obsidian Castle would fall today and with it the Dark Lord who had created it. Ahren refused to think of the possible alternative as he blinked away his tears.

Slowly but surely, the outer city archway came into view, both gates opened wide. Guards stood to attention in honour of the approaching riders, and as Ahren reached the city wall, Likis joined him from a side street. He was dressed in dazzling armour and a ceremonial sword was hanging from his belt. His horse could hardly move, so weighed down was it with metal plates. The helmet was tilted at a ridiculous angle on his friend's head – it almost seemed as though Likis missed the simple merchant's hat that he had always loved to wear.

'And behold – here cometh the saddest knight of all the realms,' laughed Ahren as he stopped beside his friend.

'Not funny,' grunted Likis. 'If I don't want to be known as Likis the Cowardly for the rest of my life, then I have to ride into battle, and Lina was adamant that I wear everything that might ensure I come home in one piece.'

'Let this experienced coward give you a little advice,' said Trimm, a flicker of a smile appearing on his otherwise gloomy face. 'The bards rarely remain on the battlefield once the first assault has begun. Make sure that you are highly visible when the weapons are drawn the first time. Raise your sword now and again whenever there is a victory, and make sure that by midday you have disappeared into one of the many army supply tents – your name will still be praised throughout Jorath on account of your valour.'

Likis blinked at the corpulent man as though the latter had lost his mind. 'Are you serious?'

'Deadly serious,' interjected the Father of the Mountain with a good-natured smile. 'There is no-one more expert at avoiding battle than our portly brother here.'

Trimm nodded solemnly before clicking his fingers, which caused his glove to clank noisily. 'Oh – and if you are discovered in your little hideaway, just say that you discovered a spy and followed him to the tent. Then ask others to help you in the search – this little trick always works.'

'Not always,' countered the Father of the Mountain. 'When *you* used this excuse three times in a row, we all knew you were lying.'

Trimm shrugged his shoulders before pulling on the reins, causing the chariot to begin moving again. 'Should the esteemed governor pro tempore find himself in four battles today, one after another, then I am sure he will be able to come up with his own excuse if necessary.'

'Ahren,' groaned Trogadon, scowling exaggeratedly. 'Please get me out of this chariot of fools!'

The Forest Guardian grinned. He was delighted that Trimm had returned to his own self for a moment, even if the smile on the portly fellow's face had already faded. 'Was it Jelninolan who suggested that you should accompany the two of them?' he asked the blacksmith.

'Yes – why?'

Khara, who was beside Ahren, giggled. 'She must have thought, then, that you fitted in perfectly!' she shouted after the dwarf.

The Father of the Mountain and even Trimm guffawed – which was music to Ahren's ears.

The Forest Guardian shook Likis' hand, the pair looking into each other's eyes. For a brief, timeless moment, they were the carefree boys once again, who had imagined glorious futures for themselves as either a bailiff or a merchant when they weren't stealing firewood from the village bullies or making fools of themselves in front of the girls at the Autumn Festival. Ahren wallowed in these memories of simpler days, silently vowing to hold them forever in his heart.

Then the moment was past, leaving a Paladin and a local dignitary to seal their bond of friendship yet again with a silent nod. Their task now was to ensure that the next generation of girls and boys could follow *their* dreams and aspirations.

The time had come to depart, the battle with all its horrors waiting grimly for its participants. Culhen carried his master quickly towards the Ring, the Thirteenth's heart now pounding like a drum of war.

The men, women, elves and dwarfs looked like a mottled sea of metal flowers.

Armour and weapons sparkled wherever they were not covered by tabards, plumes of feathers on steel helmets or banners fluttering in the wind. Rays of sunshine danced on row after row of expectantly standing soldiers in those places where the golden orb of the sun peeked through the dark clouds that scudded across the sky as if performing a harried, feverish dance of death, while dropping tiny powdery flakes of snow onto the world. Already the first scars that had marked the snow-covered landscape during the previous day's skirmishes were disappearing beneath the fresh fall, while here and there, Ahren heard muttered curses regarding the ankle-deep snow that was not going to make today's marching any easier.

I love the snow, said Culhen. *But soon the countless boots are going to turn it to slush.*

Imagine how it will look with the specks of blood, added Ahren grimly as he anxiously scanned the scene from his friend's back. Uldini was floating towards them, flying close above Trimm's chariot, *Flamestar* hidden beneath a black cloth. Ahren wondered what the Arch Wizard had up his sleeve this time.

The rest of the Paladins and friends were waiting near Culhen. They were all looking expectantly towards the soaring Obsidian Fortress to the west, now missing the black maelstrom of the previous night that had accompanied the living darkness of the Shatterlings during their assault. The no-mans-land, previously contained between the Ring and enemy territory, stretched over five furlongs now that the outer walls of the fortress had disappeared, the Jorathian armies using this additional room as their deployment zone.

Dozens of catapults stood at the ready, all of them under the command of experienced Dwarfish officers supported on this fateful day by giants, who were able to effortlessly place the weighty payloads into the buckets. Ahren was sure that he recognised one of the Blue Moss-Stone warriors that they had met in Kelkor standing by a catapult, and indeed, the giant waved over at him cheerfully. He returned the greeting with a smile.

'Would a clear blue sky be too much to ask for during our assault?' asked Fisker, glancing upwards before pulling the hood of his woollen coat over his head. 'You can catch your death in weather like this.'

'Enough of your merriment,' scolded the First. Then he pointed skywards. 'Sun Shimmer can do with the cloud cover. The Swarm Claws of the fortress still have it in for her.'

'I should really be up there with her,' said Sunju longingly. She, too, was sitting on an armoured horse – as were all the Paladins who could not ride on their companion animals. 'She has to confront the superior forces on her own.'

The First's eyes flashed coldly from beneath his dragon helmet. 'Sun Shimmer is perfectly capable of carrying out her vital role without you sitting on her back. All she has to do is to distract the Swarm Claws so that they leave us in peace.'

'Without being torn to shreds in the process,' murmured Trimm absently.

'Not helpful!' snapped Aluna before suddenly flinching as she remembered Eken's fate. 'Oh...I'm so sorry,' she added apologetically.

'I am still convinced that a canal from the sea to here would have solved many of our problems,' said Bergen cheerfully. 'Fjolmungar would undoubtedly have had fun with the fortress Dark Ones.'

'Did I not say to cut out the witticisms?' growled the First furiously.

'I have a suggestion,' grunted Falk, turning to the age-old Paladin, having quickly winked at Ahren. '*You* relieve us of our mortal fear, and *we* will stop trying to numb it with gallows humour.'

The First merely snorted before shaking his head in silence.

Suddenly, a sound split the air – but this time it wasn't that of a bugle but an extended melodious tone that lifted every heart and made the awareness of every listener razor-sharp.

'It is beginning,' said Trogadon, his eyes sparkling. 'We must make our way to Jelninolan and Akkad.' With that, he nodded towards the softly shimmering cupola of light that was competing in the distance with the sun, and which had been tended by Akkad since the previous day. Both the kneeling Ancient and the upright elf, who was playing *Mirilan,* were easily recognisable.

The thirteen Paladins set off, accompanied by their most loyal friends. Whether on wolf, Titejunanwa, normal equine or war chariot, the Champions of the gods were ready as they rode into battle – hopefully, the final one.

The mass of soldiers divided before the martial party, allowing the heroes and heroines to make their way forward to confront the Dark god. From up close, Ahren could see the fear and exhaustion in the eyes of the soldiers. Most of them had marched for a day and two full nights to get into position for the decisive assault that was going to inevitably unfold this morning. True, there would be simultaneous attacks in the northern, southern and western parts of the Ring, but they were designed merely to engage as many Dark Ones as possible so that they wouldn't rush over to the east. The main assault would be launched from here, from the Deepstone direction – and this fact had immediately become clear to friend and foe with the arrival of the Paladins.

Every step that Culhen made towards Jelninolan and Akkad was accompanied by the invigorating music of the elf, whose melody penetrated Ahren's heart and flooded his mind. All around him, he could see weary shoulders lifting themselves up, aching backs straightening and gasping lungs expanding as they drew in the fresh air. The sorcery of Jelninolan Storm Weaver spoke to the troops, eased their exhaustion and promised them victory over the evil that had been tormenting Jorath longer than most of its realms had been in existence.

Finally, Ahren and his friends reached the musicking elf, who with closed eyes and her powerfully vibrating *Mirilan,* was enchanting tens of thousands of soldiers as she gave their hearts new hope. Akkad was kneeling beside her, grimacing and with his eyes firmly closed. Ahren wished that he could offer his friend the same slumber that Sleeps-in-Treetop was now enjoying, the Ancient having protected Lirana to the very end. But Akkad's task was about to begin in earnest.

'Time for a little noise,' said Trogadon with a grin before blasting the bugle that was now hanging from his neck.

The earth beneath Ahren's feet trembled as the entire assembly of catapults on the eastern front hurled their payloads westward over their heads – their target being the gleaming blackness of the third ring around the Obsidian Fortress, whose towers and gateway rose no more than five furlongs distant.

Rock after rock slammed against the enemy wall, the ensuing cloud of black dust rising into the air reminding Ahren of the skin of an enormous, fiendish monster, coming to destroy them all.

Akkad mumbled some words, his Arcane Wall gleaming like a fortification of sheer light. The dust was blowing westward and onto the ranks of Dark Ones positioned on the battlements, while cheers rose from the soldiers as they watched the first salvo of the catapults transforming the gateway, its flanking towers and a considerable section of wall into a heap of rubble.

Ahren commanded Jelninolan with a look alone, the priestess nodding in agreement. Suddenly, *Mirilan* was being *accompanied.* Those Wrath Elves that the Storm Weaver had given lessons to in the Forest of Ire now appeared from the ranks of soldiers, gathering around the elf, their voices, hearts and instruments creating an enchanting carpet of sound, the music giving the entire army a bountiful supply of power. Jelninolan's True Form was blazing now – as if the priestess wished to reassure the world that her light alone would ensure that the following day, sunshine would inevitably smile down on a new, better Jorath.

'Speak,' she said to Ahren in a powerful, booming voice. 'Speak and they shall listen.'

Ahren swallowed hard. A last address. A last entreaty before violence would win the upper hand.

The Forest Guardian steered Culhen onto a mound of Obsidian Fortress rubble, from where Ahren could look into the eyes of thousands of expectant faces belonging to elves, dwarfs and humans. The sun peered through a large gap in the clouds, bathing the armies in its golden sheen, the sight of whom was almost too overwhelming for the Thirteenth Paladin. They had achieved greatness already. And so much more lay ahead of them.

It's now or never, murmured Culhen, encouraging his master. *Give them courage.*

'Free nations of Jorath!' began Ahren – and it seemed to him as if his voice was everywhere and nowhere. It sounded from the clouds, it sprang from the earth, it danced on the wings of Elven Storm Weaving as it radiated through the air. 'Today is the day that we Champions of the gods will finally fulfil the promise that we have made! But no Paladin can stand alone!' proclaimed the Thirteenth, allowing himself to be carried along by his inner conviction.

Catapults continued to hurl their payloads through the air, already ripping a gaping hole in the fourth defensive wall of the enemy – and yet, every word that the Paladin uttered rang as clearly as a bell. 'United, we must look Evil in the eye, and united we must bring about *His* downfall.'

Another fortress wall crumbled, revealing the black barrier to its rear.

'But when I say *united*, I do not mean only the Thirteen who have been chosen to defy the Adversary!' yelled Ahren, his voice filled with passion. 'We are nothing more than the foam on the waves that crash against the rocky shore!'

Again, rocks flew. Again, walls shattered. Again, cries of jubilation rang out.

'All of you are the *sea!* Countless drops in an ocean of loyalty that will carry us forward and make our ultimate victory possible!' Ahren raised his Wind Blade high above him. 'Let us *roll over* this fortress! Let us *wash it off* the face of our beautiful Jorath! Grant us the strength that we need so that we can *smash* the Adversary with maximum force! LET US FREE JORATH FOR EVER FROM THE DARK FORCES THAT HAVE BEEN PLAGUING IT!!'

As one, the other Paladins raised their weapons towards the heavens, Khara, her face blazing with pride, a fully-fledged member of the sworn community.

'PALADINIM THEOS DURALAS! they cried in unison, the firmament echoing the words back down onto the battlefield.

Then the Champions of the gods turned to the Obsidian Fortress and stormed forward together, a wave of such power that Ahren was convinced no-one, or nothing could stop them.

Ahren's head felt light, his mind appearing to him as a flashing thunderbolt of focused willpower. Every individual Paladin was so manifestly tangible – as though his brothers and sisters were extensions of himself. If one of them sensed something, then they all did.

As had been already agreed, their closest allies clustered around them as they advanced. Today, the Paladins truly were not alone.

The Blue Cohorts protected their backs, the Fox Guards were a cocoon of steel around Hakanu. To the left and right of the Paladins, the black Wrath Elves, clad in dark leather, formed the vanguard of the army, equipped with blowguns and powerful short bows as they rode on armoured Tree Martens. The Animal Whisperers of the Eathinian elves followed behind their southern cousins, those riding the armoured bears and the Woolly Rhinos of the Icy Vasts.

By the time the Paladins and their mounts had paved their way through the rubble of the third Obsidian Fortress wall, the Tree Martens had long since raced onward and were now scurrying up the narrow steps to the battlements, intent along with their riders to assault the Low Fangs that had been positioned there.

The elves with the larger animals, on the other hand, carved a passage through the debris for the army behind them, the rest of the Animal Whisperers helping the Champions of the gods to fight off the masses of Glower Bears, Blood Wolves, Horde Bulls, Hook Bisons, Sickle Hoppers and all the other Dark Ones that the Adversary had gathered over the last several moons within His fortress.

The unusual cavalry was reinforced by the armoured riders of Senius Blueground's kingdom, who, under the command of their king, intervened in any skirmishes that threatened the spilling of Elven blood.

It wasn't long before the infantries of the Sunplains and the Eternal Empire streamed into this scene of bloody chaos under the watchful eye of the mounted archers of the Green Sea, whose accuracy ensured that nowhere on the battlefield was safe for the ranged fighters of the enemy.

Meanwhile, the allied giants pushed the specially reinforced Dwarfish catapults along to the rear of the Jorathian armed forces. Hardly was the gateway of one defensive wall destroyed, thereby enabling the army to proceed through, when the siege machinery was repositioned so that its payloads could be hurled at the next obsidian barrier.

Ahren's sense of time was now as vague as all his other thoughts not directly connected with pushing his way through the ranks of Dark Ones – he and his fellows now moving like a stream of steaming water through a snowdrift. Yet Ahren knew all too well that the inner fire of the Paladins would eventually be cooled down by the coldness surrounding them, should the Champions of the gods take too much time getting to the Adversary.

Onward they pushed, step by step, blow by blow, and wall by wall – all the while hoping that they would reach the heart of the Obsidian Fortress in time – before they ran out of energy. Whether Sickle Hopper, Blood Wolf, Fog Cat, Glower Bear or any other Dark One that confronted them, it was clear that the enemy was fighting with a death-defying tenacity that confirmed the Adversary's willingness to sacrifice His servants as long as they managed to delay and weaken the Paladins sufficiently. Ahren, however, stood his ground, making full use of his own iron will that had been forged through years of journeying and secured through the Blessing Band so that it neither weakened nor submitted, no matter how hard his foes attempted to hold up the Jorathian army's advance.

At some point, in the midst of the countless assaults, skirmishes and evasive manoeuvres, Ahren looked up at the sky and saw the sun on its glimmering course – it had already passed its zenith, proving that the afternoon was now well advanced.

'Faster!' he yelled to his comrades. 'We must progress at even greater speed!'

The First, who was further ahead, dropped back a little and grinned at the Forest Guardian. 'You want us to go even *faster?* You are beginning to sound like me! This is already *the* perfect assault on the fortress. We are achieving in a matter of heartbeats that which would normally take us days or even weeks.'

'Today, I have every reason to emulate you,' said Ahren, pointing up at the sun. 'All our preparations and all our allies will be of no use whatsoever once tonight's constellation will have dispersed again.'

The troops around the Paladins, having noticed that the Champions of the gods had now stopped their forward motion so that they could calculate the best strategy, swiftly formed a protective cordon around the men and women.

'Trogadon!' yelled Ahren. 'Can the catapults be moved more swiftly, or their payloads dispatched with greater speed?'

The dwarf shook his head. 'It is only thanks to the giants that we are able to follow our current tactics at all. If even more pressure is put on the wooden siege weaponry, we run the risk of the catapults snapping like a toy in the hands of an angry child.'

Khara took her canteen from her belt, drank a draught of water before giving some to her horse. 'Jelninolan's melody prevents us from feeling tired, hungry or thirsty,' she warned. 'The same applies to the animals. If we are not careful, they will collapse under us.'

Immediately, the Champions of the gods dismounted before watering themselves and their mounts. Ahren, Falk and Hakanu distributed healing herbs from their belt bags, applied blood-stilling creams and handed out reinvigorating leaves that their companions placed under their tongues.

'Sun, Bergen – what can Sun Shimmer and Karkas report? How is the battle behind us unfolding?' asked Falk, hoarsely. The blood splattered on his steel and leather was replicated on the clothing of the other Paladins and their fellow fighters.

Ahren knew, thanks to the Blessing Band, that none of the Paladins had been badly wounded. Their combined gods' Blessing made them faster and stronger, while Khara's bracelet warned them of the dangers surrounding them on the battlefield. No blow of their weapons missed, and no gap in their defence remained for longer than an instant. Ahren now understood why only the thirteen Paladins could put a final stop the Adversary. It seemed to him as if he and his brothers and sisters would be unbeatable for as long as they stood and fought as one.

'The losses on both sides are devastating,' said Bergen. 'Because we are driving into the Obsidian Fortress in a spear formation, it means that our flanks are exposed. However, we are better armed than the Low Fangs, and the sorcery of the Storm Weavers is having a miraculous impact on our morale and fighting spirit.'

'Sun Shimmer says that we have progressed a third of the way to the heart of the fortress,' announced Sunju. Her subsequent silence confirmed what Ahren already knew.

'We are too slow,' he muttered grimly. 'We must —'

A rumbling noise that seemed to come from all around him caused the Forest Guardian to break off. He was sure that he had heard such a sound once before – at the beginning of the Night of Blood.

Uldini, whom the Paladins had been protecting as much as possible and who had managed to float to safety during critical moments, gasped as he continued to clutch the black cloth that had been covering *Flamestar* since the commencement of the battle. 'I feared this would happen,' he muttered. 'The Adversary is releasing the fortress sorcery.'

The rumbling seemed to be coming from everywhere simultaneously. Ahren saw pitch-black clouds spiralling heavenward from the heart of the citadel before combining to become a veritable maelstrom of crimson darkness.

'This sorcery was already unnerving when we watched it from the security of the castle,' growled Trogadon. 'Having it directly above our heads while we are surrounded by Dark Ones is terrifying.'

Another rumble sounded, the broken wall directly behind the Paladins then transforming into smoke. Suddenly, from where he was standing Ahren could make out the Ring five furlongs behind them. They had come this far, and yet it was some distance to their destination. Defenders and Dark Ones alike stared up at the unnaturally darkened sky. The former, because they were fearful, the latter, on account of their fateful connection to their Dark Lord.

'Have faith,' said the Father of the Mountain from the mud-spattered chariot. 'By now, Akkad will have taken over the coordination of the Arcane Wall. He and the other Ancients know what must be done.'

'I'm not so sure,' countered Aluna. 'Now that the walls are gone, there is nowhere that we can seek cover. If the Adversary metamorphoses these sorcerous clouds into Bane Curses and lets them fall on us, we will be completely exposed.'

As if in confirmation of her words, the first crimson flashes streaked down from the whirling maelstroms in the heavens, striking into the fighting masses below, seemingly oblivious of distinguishing between friend and foe. Ahren saw how a Horde Bull, standing tall in a melee, was hit by a thunderbolt, immediately falling over on its side, its head now a smoking ruin of burnt flesh.

Ahren feverishly calculated what to do next. 'Trogadon – give the signal for another salvo from the catapults! They are to aim for the ninth gateway!'

'But they are not yet in position. They might easily fall short of the wall ahead of us and waste precious time and munitions.'

'Do it – please!' urged the Forest Guardian as the clouds above them began to divide into mini-tornados, dancing in the sky. Dozens of flashes streaked the heavens, promising death and destruction.

Immediately, Trogadon uttered a blast of his bugle. It took no more than a dozen heartbeats for the payloads to fly towards the black wall. Many overshot their target, some landed too short and burying numerous Dark Ones in the process, but five of the eight chunks of rock hit their target, crashing into the obsidian gateway and causing the door on the right to be yanked out of its anchoring.

When Ahren nodded his satisfaction to the blacksmith, Trogadon blew his bugle again, signalling that the catapults should stop shooting and re-position themselves.

'Forward!' screamed Ahren, pointing at the newly created gap. 'Let us move on to the breach! Seek shelter under the archway!'

The Paladins and their companions, the spearhead of the entire army, advanced fiercely, while from within the fortress, Dark Ones streamed forth in an effort to deny the Champions of the gods access to the life-saving cover. Clearly, the Adversary recognised the strategy of His archenemy and was doing all in His power to thwart it.

Crimson thunderbolts shot down from the clouds with ever-increasing rapidity, dancing to devastating effect like living fingers of the Dark god as they sent dozens into the greedily waiting arms of death.

'Karkas says that the clouds are coming towards us!' bellowed Bergen as he swung his axe left and right in an effort to keep the raging Low Fangs surrounding him at bay. 'He can hardly maintain position on account of the supernatural winds swirling up there.'

'You should ask Sun Shimmer how *she* is getting on!' gasped Sunju, who was skewering a Blood Wolf with Hakanu's assistance, the Dark One having tried to block the path of the Paladins. 'She is still being plagued by the Swarm Claws, which are positively sticking to her tail feathers!'

For the briefest of moments, Ahren found himself shielded from the enemy, and he used the opportunity to look up to the clouds, both sorcerous and natural, shreds of blue sky competing both with them and the unnatural flashes of unleashed sorcery for control of the heavens. The drama that presented itself to him resembled precisely how he had always imagined the downfall of Jorath to be.

A fleeting shadow was visible between the clouds for the blink of an eye, followed immediately by an enormous swarm of smaller outlines. Sun Shimmer was playing her almost invisible part, and Ahren fervently hoped that the song of the Storm Weavers was giving *her* strength, too. Then Culhen shot forward, eager to assist Lyssin, who seemed in some difficulty, his appearance bringing to an end the miniscule period of deceptive peace.

The flashes of lightning were coming closer and closer to the little group of Paladins, while the gateway was still a good one hundred paces further ahead.

'We must move faster, or the Bane Curse of the Adversary will be upon us!' yelled Ahren.

A rumbling sound, far in the distance, rolled in from all directions.

'What sort of subterfuge is bearing down on us!' screamed Falk, who was now using his lance instead of his shield and sword.

Uldini, still holding onto his black cloth with both hands, grinned. 'This is the sound of inrushing help,' he said. 'Akkad has managed to coordinate the Wizardly Domes into a unified force.'

The droning sound was approaching with extraordinary speed now – it was rolling from the Ring directly towards where the Paladins found themselves. Clouds seethed in the sky. They were grasped by an invisible force that formed them anew. The lightning flashes abated and stopped as the maelstroms that were feeding them gathered into a thick cover of cloud, which seemed to hang over the land like a burial shroud.

'There are no more thunderbolts forming!' shouted Bergen over the noise of the battle. 'But I still don't like the look of that sky one little bit!'

'Akkad has bought us time!' roared the First. 'But it is clear that he and the Ancients in the domes still haven't broken the sorcery of the enemy!'

'Let us take advantage of the opportunity offered to us,' said Lanlion. 'We can reach the archway before the Bane Curse of the Adversary forms again.'

Surrounded by the loyal troops who were fighting and dying by their side, the Champions of the gods moved on again towards the breach. Already the smoothed sky was beginning to churn up again under the will of the Adversary. The storm clouds that were seething anew were a mixture of black magic and natural tempests, spreading out over the entire battlefield and as far as the wall of the Ring. The first flashes of lighting raced to the ground, primeval forces of crimson threads, resembling a hurricane whipped up by dark powers.

'Out of the frying pan and into the fire!' yelled Falk, a bolt of lightning slamming into the earth not ten paces away from him.

Despite Jelninolan's sorcery, Ahren felt an uncomfortable tingle racing through his body, Culhen flinching as his muscles cramped up for a fraction of a heartbeat.

Further flashes of lightning hit the ground around the Paladins, and as they finally approached the safety of the gateway, a massive Glower Bear, covered in dented plates of armour, began pushing its way through the opening in their direction.

'This is one of *Hate's* mounts!' screamed the First.

'It was obvious that there would be several of these damned creatures, if you think of how our bloodthirsty friend liked to ride them to death,' remarked Fisker. His blonde locks were stuck to his blood-spattered face, the sight rather undermining his forced jocularity.

'Falk, Ahren – you come from the right, Sunju and I will attack it from the left,' commanded the First. 'Maybe we can push it back!'

A sudden draught of air beside Ahren's cheek caused the Forest Guardian to flinch, before he observed an arrow sticking into one eye of the Glower Bear, a spear having penetrated its forehead. The monster gurgled as it collapsed to the ground, never to move again.

'Got you!' shouted Hakanu with a laugh. He and Lyssin exchanged grins, so pleased were they with their booty.

'I am *so* proud of the pair of you!' snarled the First, clearly irritated. 'And how do you propose getting the corpse out of the archway? It's blocking the space so important to us, imbeciles!' That was why I wanted to push it *back!*'

Hakanu glanced over at Ahren. 'Oh.'

'Not to worry!' shouted Trogadon. 'Better we cuddle up to the dead Glower Bear than continue being target practice for thunderbolts!'

The friends quickly gathered in a semi-circle beneath the archway, their backs pressing into the immobile colossus. Darts of lighting struck the ground all around them, while the air hummed with the electrical discharges. Meanwhile, the armies of the Paladins were coming under increasing pressure as they pressed in on the companions from left and right, taking heavy losses as a result of the Adversary's sorcery.

A scream from Khara caused Ahren to spin around. A Blood Wolf had leapt out from within the fortress and onto the cadaver of the armoured Glower Bear, from where it was attacking the Swordsmistress with its slavering fangs. Khara's blades were, indeed, darting upwards, but she didn't have sufficient room to manoeuvre effectively and was only managing to keep the beast at bay with awkward feints. The Father of the Mountain allowed his steel ball to fly through the air, and a heartbeat later, the wall of death in the archway had another occupant on its summit.

'The longer we wait here, the more impassable the gateway will become,' scolded Aluna. 'And there is no doubt that the Adversary is coercing His servants into a killing spree, causing them to attack our wedge-shaped assault from both sides in an attempt to cut us off from the rest of our troops. If we continue to stay under the archway or if this Storm Spell isn't broken, we will be well and truly trapped!'

'While what is left of the Obsidian Fortress remains untouched!' added Bergen, his chest heaving with effort. 'Time is running out!'

Trogadon raised his bugle and looked questioningly at Ahren. The Paladin shook his head. There was a trump card that could help them, but the Forest Guardian knew that it would be needed later. The Thirteenth glanced over at Uldini. Should he ask the Arch Wizard for help before the planned time?

A thunderbolt hit the archway from above, small stones then raining down from the ceiling. This was followed by another discharge from the seething heavens, then a third. The first chunks of rock loosened from the wall and slammed onto the ground, Falk and Sunju quickly raising their shields above their heads to provide protection to those without a helmet.

'Uldini —' began Ahren as another droning sound began emanating from the Wizardly Domes. This one was even stronger and was accompanied by vibrations so powerful that the fighting temporarily stopped as both friend and foe struggled to remain upright. Again, an invisible force swept across the sky, but this time the supernatural forces were not simply smoothed and placated by the sorcery of the Ancients, but instead, the clouds were pushed into and above each other as though a giant noose was slowly tightening in the sky, forcing the Bane Curse of the Dark god into an ever more constricted space.

'Akkad – you cunning old fox!' shouted Uldini in exhilaration as he floated above the cadavers of the Dark Ones so that he could see through the opening in the archway.

'Would it trouble you greatly to explain to us what is happening?' muttered the First sarcastically. The battlefield continued to be afflicted by thunderbolts, which were growing in number and intensity as the unnatural thunderstorm thickened above them, causing devastating losses amongst the Jorathian troops and the Dark Ones. 'It seems to me that Akkad's attempt at helping us is doing more harm than good!'

'Patience, my friend,' murmured Uldini. 'Soon you will see what I mean.'

'Give me a hand here,' growled Trogadon as he leapt off the chariot. 'Seeing as we aren't being besieged by bloodthirsty Dark Ones for the moment because they are concentrating on escaping their Lord and Master's sorcery, we may as well shove these corpses out of the way.' With that, he began pushing with all his might against the combined bodies of the Glower Bear and the Blood Wolf.

Ahren swung himself off Culhen's back, and soon all the Champions of the gods, as well as their friends and companion animals were struggling against the bulwark of flesh. Shoving the Blood Wolf aside proved easy enough, but the Glower Bear remained stubbornly in situ.

Hakanu's face reddened so much that Ahren feared that his protégé would over-extend himself in his desire to compensate for his error.

'Careful,' said Ahren. 'Jelninolan's magic has caused us to forget our physical limits. It's not going to help anyone if you end up pulling a muscle while trying to shift a dead Glower Bear.'

'There!' shouted Trimm triumphantly. 'The fleabag has shifted at last!'

'This bear is causing us more trouble dead than alive,' grunted Bergen.

Hanulf growled and glared at the blonde Paladin.

'*Glower* Bear,' interjected the Father of the Mountain with a chuckle. 'Hanulf says, there's got to be time enough to say that, brother.'

'Less talk and more pushing,' scolded Sunju. 'The thunderbolts to our rear are becoming less frequent.'

'What?' asked Ahren, alarmed. 'Why so?'

'You can ask the Dark Ones that are going to attack us once they have overrun our soldiers!' countered the First angrily.

With a crunching sound, one of the plates of the dead Glower Bear's armour loosened from where it had been lodged in the rubble, the companions then managing with great effort to roll the corpse sufficiently away from the archway so that the horses and the chariot could proceed through the gap.

Ahren stumbled through the newly opened entrance and couldn't believe his eyes as he looked towards the heavens to the west which Uldini had already marvelled at.

Like a voracious giant, the Adversary's thunderstorm was towering above the Obsidian Fortress ahead of them. In the midst of the blue sky, the storm clouds soared up into the air, while with every heartbeat dozens of thunderbolts slammed into the earth below – all of them onto the Dark Ones situated on or behind the walls. The battlefield stretching before Ahren and his friends was strewn with dead Dark Ones that had been struck by lightning.

'Akkad has turned the sorcery of the Adversary against him,' laughed Uldini. 'Instead of spellbinding it, he tied it up over the Obsidian Fortress like an Autumn Festival present.'

The companions cheered, Sunju, however, not joining in as she stared up at the tempest, her face even paler than usual.

'What's wrong?' asked Ahren anxiously.

Sunju's lower lip trembled. 'There is one thing that Akkad did not take into consideration when planning this ruse. Sun Shimmer has also been caught up in the Adversary's Bane Curse.' She raised her hand nervously and pointed at the concentrated cloud of crimson darkness. 'My poor Roc is trapped in there and fighting for her life.'

All colour drained from the faces of the little group.

'Sunju…' murmured Trimm. 'I am so, so sorry.'

'Is there nothing we can do?' asked Khara, turning to look at Uldini, who was plucking nervously at the black cloth.

'I would do Sun Shimmer more harm than good.'

'Cannot Akkad release the storm again?' asked Aluna urgently.

'Look!' commanded Uldini, nodding towards the tempestuous sorcery, which was still sending deadly flashes down behind the enemy walls. 'With every heartbeat that this sorcery continues in its present form, it will destroy Dark Ones that cannot be used against us at a later stage of the battle.'

'But the risk of Sun Shimmer not surviving will increase at the same time,' muttered Ahren, shaking his head. 'We cannot allow this to happen!'

Uldini sighed, a tortured look on his face. 'You must understand – Akkad wants to force the Adversary into abandoning His Bane Curse of His own volition. Even the enemy cannot allow His own troops to continue dying.'

'We will not sacrifice Sun Shimmer in a battle of wills!' exclaimed Khara, everyone – with the exception of the First – nodding forcefully in agreement.

Sunju gasped, Ahren immediately fearing the worst.

'Is she...?'

The pale woman shook her head. 'Not yet,' she murmured hoarsely. 'But she says that we must not yield, and that it would be an honour for her to save so many lives by sacrificing her own.'

The First's shoulders began to tremble. 'That is what *she* said, too. Those were her exact words.'

Trimm silently placed a comforting hand on the age-old Paladin's back. He, Sunju and the First stood there, devastated by what was inevitably about to happen.

Sun Shimmer... Culhen's whimpering combined with that of Yoka, as well as with the whinnying of the Titejunanwas, the growling of Hanulf, the chattering of Cassobo and the melancholy cheeping of Kamaluq.

'What about Karkas?' whispered Ahren as he turned to Bergen. 'Is he caught in there, too?'

Bergen pointed at a solitary shadow in the bright blue sky. 'He was able to ascend to safety in time. It was Sun Shimmer who had been tackling the Swarm Claws in the dizzying heights.' The blonde man's response was little more than an apologetic whisper.

The concentrated tempest continued to rage. Flash after flash shot down onto the fortress, Dark Ones dying by the dozen. Then Sunju stiffened and gasped.

'She has been hit. Her wing…' The woman clenched her fists in silent pain.

'The Bane Curse,' muttered Uldini bitterly, pointing up at the rupturing clouds. 'Only now is it beginning to dissipate.'

'The Dark god waited until Sun Shimmer was hit before He yielded!' spat Falk as if the words he had spoken were poisonous.

The destruction within the citadel had ended, the crimson clouds now vanishing – as if their previous appearance had been nothing more than a mirage. The blue sky of a late afternoon in winter stretched out in all directions, the low sun shining directly into the Paladins' faces.

'There,' said Lyssin joylessly. 'I see her.'

Ahren followed the outstretched finger of his fellow Forest Guardian with his eyes, spotting the bird's large shadow as she beat one wing in desperation, spinning around in uncontrolled circles while rapidly losing height.

'She is trying to reach us,' sobbed Sunju. But she will not manage it. She is going to come down in enemy territory!'

Lanlion leapt onto Haminul's back. 'If she is not going to reach *us,*' he snarled, a deep red darkness enveloping the Bloodless like a second cape, 'then *we* shall go to *her!*' Even before the other Champions of the gods had a chance to say anything in response, Haminul galloped away, whinnying triumphantly. For a moment it looked as though Lanlion was going to declare war on the entire Obsidian Fortress single-handedly.

'I'll be damned if I'm going to let our pallid brother gain all the Bardic fame for himself!' exclaimed Falk, grinning wildly. 'Trogadon – blast your bugle if you please. There are eleven gateways yet to be conquered!'

Hope pulsated from the Blessing Band, shaking Sunju out of her state of shock and shaking her to life. 'Sun Shimmer!' screamed Ahren's pale sister. 'Stay strong! We are coming!'

And so the Paladins surged deeper into the Obsidian Fortress, their eyes fixed on the downward spiralling Roc – and without giving it a second thought, they were now leading a full-scale assault, the Jorathian troops hot on their heels and yelling triumphantly, the soldiers freed from the Adversary's Bane Curse and filled with fresh courage thanks to what they could see ahead of them – the gleaming example of the fearless Paladins thundering forward.

Chapter 21

The dust created by the impact of the catapulted rocks had not yet settled by the time the companions had raced through the next gateway. Their reckless charge had already created a considerable gap between them and the troops behind, which did nothing to stop them however, from continuing their advance through the ranks of Dark Ones.

Lanlion's sorcery was everywhere – tentacles of smoke rubbing against throats, touching eyes and filling lungs. Had Ahren concentrated on his friend's ability to extinguish the lives of all those that his haze was making contact with, he would have been horrified – but the Forest Guardian only had eyes for Sun Shimmer, who was continuing to tumble downward.

'Karkas says that she will hit the ground at *this* section of the fortress!' shouted Bergen, pointing at a spot three hundred paces north of their position.

'Lanlion!' yelled the First, indicating the same point to the Bloodless.

The latter nodded and changed his course, the Paladins in his deadly slipstream.

'You are all aware, I assume, that we are leaving our army in our wake,' muttered Uldini anxiously. 'It won't be long before we're up to our necks in slavering Dark Ones.'

'Why don't *you* stay behind and wait for the cavalry?' suggested Falk mockingly. '*We* have a Roc to save!'

The Ancient didn't even raise a sceptical eyebrow as he flew onwards with the Champions of the gods to the spot where Sun Shimmer was heading for, the large bird cawing and struggling to maintain her direction. It was clear to Ahren that the Roc's right wing had been badly scorched, and this was why she could not maintain her balance.

'Sun Shimmer is bringing unwelcome visitors with her,' said Khara grimly, pointing up at a multitude of smaller shadows on the horizon that were veering down on the large bird. 'It seems that the Swarm Claws have, for the most part, survived the sorcerous tempest.'

Ahren cursed as he used *Sun* to deflect a Low Fang that had been about to leap onto Sunju's back. Thanks to the Blessing Band, the Paladins had been able, with a succession of well-chosen parries, to protect the woman – who was single-mindedly focused on Sun Shimmer

– from the attacks of Dark Ones. But Ahren sensed that his sword arm was weakening and that his breathing was becoming laboured. It was true that Jelninolan's Storm Weaving had strengthened their hearts and multiplied their courage, but the Forest Guardian knew all too well that magic had its natural limits – no body in the world could simply rely on sorcery in the long term – Quin-Wa being living proof of this fact.

'We are going to need a break,' said Ahren to the others. 'Once Sun Shimmer has been saved, we will have to take a rest.'

'Ahren is right,' gasped Aluna. 'I have already seen the first of our soldiers collapsing, their hearts no longer able to cope with the power of Jelninolan's sorcerous urging.'

The First grimaced as he demonstratively looked around at masses of Dark Ones furiously attempting to break through Lanlion's protective sorcery and the almost clairvoyant power of the radiating Blessing Band. 'I really don't think that *this* is the place to have a picnic!' he snarled.

Uldini turned to Trogadon. 'Sound the signal for reinforcements. The Bane Curse of the Adversary has been broken. It is time for Akkad and the other Ancients to come up with something else. Let us take advantage of the present situation to gain the sorcerous upper hand.'

The dwarf raised his bugle. 'Three short, two long, right?!' he shouted above the noise of the battle.

'*Two* short and *three* long!' snapped the First. 'Unless you want the troops to fall in for a rollcall, now of all times!'

The blacksmith sounded the signal while the Paladins thrust and parried on their mounts as they continued to battle their way forward to the tumbling Roc. The scattered Swarm Claws, meanwhile, continued to approach from all directions.

'You all – maintain your positions on the ground!' commanded Lanlion, his voice echoing with the coldness of a tomb. 'I will take care of the aerial Dark Ones!'

With that, Sun Shimmer slammed onto the ground amid the enemy.

Immediately, she began slashing all around her, simultaneously using her enormous claws as weapons.

'Sun Shimmer!' screamed Sunju, panic-stricken, urging her horse into a crazy gallop so that she could break through the final few paces to her Roc, all the while thrusting wildly at Dark Ones. 'We are here!'

'Hakanu! Lyssin!' yelled Ahren, the pair immediately clearing the area around the Roc with a succession of arrows and judicious throws of the spear, their companions giving them the cover they needed. While Sun Shimmer struggled to her feet, Ahren unshouldered *Fisiniell* and dispatched five precious Deep Steel arrows, thereby preventing three Glower Bears from slashing the Roc's flanks or neck.

At last, the Paladins reached Sun Shimmer and formed a wide protective circle around the Roc.

'Hakanu – the healing water!' shouted Sunju, who was already by the large bird's injured wing, examining the wound.

Ahren's apprentice looked doubtfully at his master.

'Do as she says!' shouted the Forest Guardian. 'Imagine if Sun Shimmer was Kamaluq – you wouldn't give it a second thought!'

Immediately, the boy threw the canteen of precious liquid over to the waiting Sunju before turning his attention back to the attacking Dark Ones.

'Am I imagining things, or do I see more and more Low Fangs?' shouted Khara over the noise of the skirmishes.

'The thunderbolts hit the larger creatures first,' explained Bergen. 'There are plenty of charred Glower Bears and Blood Wolves lying around the place – not to mention Horde Bulls.'

'Lanlion!' shouted Sunju anxiously as she continued to carefully apply the sacred water to Sun Shimmer's wing. 'The Swarm Claws are here!'

Immediately, the Bloodless mounted the wooden carriage on Sun Shimmer's back, from where he sent out his sorcery in the form of grasping tentacles of fog, which now whipped around the Roc as extraordinarily long, thin threads, the slightest of touches sending the Swarm Claws tumbling and lifeless to the ground.

'Akkad is very welcome to hurry up,' said Lanlion, his voice sounding strangely absent despite the urgency of his magicking. 'My supplies of sorcery are running low.'

'Thank the THREE,' grumbled Bergen. 'This Lanlion who has had his fill of Paladin blood is just too *weird* for me,' he added before slaying three Low Fangs with a single swing of his axe.

'But he *is* damn useful,' countered Trimm. The daggers in his hand were no more than blurred outlines as they thrust and withdrew repeatedly and at speed, each forward action sending an attacker to its death.

'Make sure you have enough room to move,' warned the First. 'On no account should you retreat. 'If the Dark Ones deprive us of room to manoeuvre, we will all be lost!'

Ahren took the warning to heart, pushing a Low Fang backwards, the creature sliding, lifeless, off his blade. 'Use the bodies as a barricade. Build a ring around our position with them!'

'I will be *very* happy when I am no longer pondering mountains of Dark Ones,' mused the Father of the Mountain as he let his steel ball fly. 'How I wish I was in Thousand Halls.'

'We are fighting to maintain the existence of the Dwarfish kingdom!' shouted Hakanu. 'Remember this whenever your thoughts become gloomy!'

'I'll bet anyone ten gold pieces that it was Kamaluq who came up with this pearl of wisdom!' exclaimed Fisker with a grin as he skewered a Low Fang with his slender sword. 'Would anyone like to place a wager?!'

Ahren was about to reply with a joke of his own, but he was interrupted by the sound of Lanlion gasping behind him. Risking a glance over his shoulder, he saw that the Bloodless was weakening. The mist-like tentacles that were assaulting the screeching Swarm Claws were less powerful and frequent than they had been only a couple of dozen heartbeats earlier. 'Let us hope that Akkad has another good idea up his sleeve that he can quickly implement,' muttered the Forest Guardian.

Khara pointed one of her blades skyward before she instigated a whirlwind of stabs and thrusts, causing the barricade of corpses to rise a pace before her. 'We will find out soon enough!' she exclaimed with a chuckle.

When Ahren saw a ball of golden energy moving hesitantly in their direction, his heart skipped a beat with joy. The very sight of the charm filled him with hope – even if he had no idea what function it had.

'Stay strong!' he shouted. 'Help is on the way!'

At that very moment, the walls of the Obsidian Fortress before and behind the Paladins dissolved, sending the Dark Ones that had been standing on them tumbling to their deaths.

For a heartbeat, Ahren was about to cheer, so convinced was he that the slowly approaching ball of light had been responsible for this magical act. Immediately, however, he saw how the released sorcery of the

Obsidian Fortress manifested itself into a similar ball – except that this one was *black* – which now began hurtling straight for the one that the Ancients had dispatched. The two sorcerous orbs smashed into each other, immediately resulting in a dull bang, which was followed by the sudden absence of all magic in the sky. The Adversary had turned their hoped-for help to dust in the blink of an eye.

Being cut off from their army and caught within a seething ocean of foes, the walls of the Obsidian Fortress had worked *for* rather than *against* them up to now – because they had kept the Dark Ones contained within the individual rings. Now, however, the more monstrous servants of the Adversary who had survived the thunderbolts were swarming directly towards them through the masses of Low Fangs.

'Oh, no!' shouted Lyssin. 'This is *not* good!'

'Karkas has calculated that there are more than twenty Glower Bears, dozens of Blood Wolves and two Horde Bulls in the immediate vicinity,' said Bergen anxiously. 'And there are still hundreds of Swarm Claws above our heads.'

'Any ideas?' asked Falk, glancing at the others. 'We won't be able to withstand these superior forces for much longer – even *with* the Blessing Band.' Already, the first horses of the Paladins had fallen victim to the claws and fangs that were slashing at the besieged companions from all sides.

'Uldini?' asked Ahren, looking demonstratively at the black cloth that the Arch Wizard was clutching. 'Maybe the time has come?'

The eyes of the Ancient were full of scepticism. 'My sorcery is priceless. To waste it here…'

Ahren frowned and repelled another Low Fang. Uldini had been very vague during the planning for the assault and had merely muttered something about a superior spell that would take the Adversary by surprise. None of those present knew exactly what the cunning Arch Wizard had up his sleeve, only that he needed to be protected until he put his plan into effect.

'Can you help us or not?' asked Bergen gruffly.

Uldini shook his head and drew the cloth closer to his chest.

'Then let us hope that Akkad will come up with something,' muttered Trimm grimly. 'Our troops are too slow. They will not reach us before the large Dark Ones.' With that, he pointed his chin eastward, from where Ahren could make out the combined Jorathian armies fighting a good three furlongs away. The Dwarfish, Elven and human soldiers from all corners of the earth were making slow progress, and it was clear that they would be too late to be of any assistance to the Paladins.

'We should —' began Ahren, only to be interrupted by a screeching Swarm Claw that began hacking in the direction of his right eye. Culhen sealed the creature's fate with a snap of his fangs, but already more of the little flying monsters were within range of launching an attack on the Forest Guardian.

'Lanlion?' he heard the First call out. 'The Swarm Claws are breaking through!'

'I…can…no longer…persevere,' was the Bloodless's tortured reply.

'Trogadon – blow the bugle again!' exclaimed Bergen. 'Let the Ancients know that —'

Already, an unholy rumbling sound was filling the air as another wall of the Obsidian Fortress metamorphosed into swirling sorcery. Then another. And another.

'What's going on here?!' shouted Falk in alarm.

Ahren looked on in disbelief as the next wall of the enemy was transformed into another rising cloud, so that only the innermost five remained.

Besieged by Dark Ones, surrounded by Swarm Claws and cut off from all reinforcements, Ahren saw how the newly released sorcery of the Obsidian Fortress floated across the skies as crimson threads before spinning themselves into slim, dark arrows – that were flying directly towards the Wizardly Domes!

DO YOU REALLY BELIEVE THAT YOUR FRIENDS IN THEIR PATHETIC STONE CUPOLAS WILL BE ABLE TO HELP YOU?

The voice of the Adversary seemed to be falling upon them from heaven itself, every syllable a sharp weapon aimed straight for their hearts.

'*No!*' gasped Uldini.

Two heartbeats later, loud thunderclaps echoed across the land, while oily clouds of smoke rose skyward in the distance. Ahren guessed where the Adversary's Bane Curses had hit their targets.

'The Wizardly Domes! How could He have destroyed them so easily?' Now in a state of shock, Ahren nevertheless still managed to slice Swarm Claw after lunging Swarm Claw, all the while vaguely aware that the first of the Blood Wolves would soon reach their defensive ring. All the normal horses belonging to the Paladins had now been slain, while the circle that they had established around Sun Shimmer was becoming ever smaller as they found themselves increasingly having to yield ground to the raging horde.

'The Ancients were as exhausted as you all are,' sobbed Uldini. 'I don't dare to imagine how many of them haven't survived this assault.'

NOW YOU ARE ALONE, LITTLE ULDINI. WHAT DO YOU THINK? FOR HOW MUCH LONGER WILL YOUR PRECIOUS PALADINS BE ABLE TO HOLD OUT – NOW THAT THEY HAVE NO MORE SUPPORT?

'Why don't you speak to me *face to face?*' screamed the Arch Wizard as he glared at the Obsidian Fortress, still soaring in the distance, although now it was no more than an extended bulwark of five walls with a gloomy palace in its middle. 'You are too *cowardly* to hurl your sorcery at *me,* and you would do well to continue fearing the *First among the Ancients!'*

Out of the corner of his eye, Ahren could see how Uldini's hands were feverishly clawing at the black cloth that he was holding.

THE SUN IS FOLLOWING ITS INEVITABLE DOWNWARD COURSE AND IT WILL BE NIGHTTIME SOON, LITTLE PALADINS, mocked the Adversary in a milder, yet more provocative tone. WOULD IT NOT BE SIMPLER FOR YOU ALL TO SURRENDER? ALL THOSE DEATHS THAT ARE YET TO WEIGH ON YOUR CONSCIENCES – THOSE COULD SO EASILY BE SPARED!

'Don't listen to Him,' said the First. 'He spouts nothing but lies!'

'Although He is correct in one respect,' countered Fisker. 'The sun *is* now dangerously low, and we are stuck in a hole that we have dug for ourselves.'

Hakanu hurled his spear with a loud groan, the missile hitting a Blood Wolf in the head and sending it crashing to the ground. 'We must get away from here,' gasped the lad. 'If the Glower Bears reach us…'

With that, Lanlion collapsed with a gasp, the Swarm Claws immediately falling on the Paladins like a furious blanket woven from claws and beaks.

Ahren's sword seemed to be working of its own volition. By dint of sheer instinct, the Forest Guardian deflected the Dark Ones' attack from all sides, insofar as he was able.

May the THREE protect us and all Jorath, he prayed in silent desperation, not knowing what else he could do. They were all caught in a terrible trap.

There was a crescendo of beating wings, and the air was filled with Swarm Claws that were screeching, scratching and hacking. Weaknesses in the Blessing Band were sought for and found by the dozen. The first wounds were inflicted – both on the bodies of the Champions of the gods and to their confidence. Up until now they had progressed with little physical damage, but now the luck of the THREE seemed to have deserted them.

Ahren tried to catch Khara's eye – but the sheer number of bodies in the way prevented him from seeing her.

'*Uldini!*' he yelled. '*Do* something!'

'Too late!' came the tortured cry from the Arch Wizard over the noise and chaos. 'Oh, what a *fool* I am! I waited too long!'

Ahren would have liked to have taken his cantankerous friend to task, but whatever air was in his lungs was too precious to him, and death was too close for comfort. Again and again, the Swarm Claws inflicted minor injuries on the Paladins, all the while weakening the companions before the inevitable onslaught of the Glower Bears, which were at this moment shovelling away the wall of corpses in preparation for their final assault. The noise of the relentlessly beating wings of the Swarm Claws filled Ahren's mind, turning the pinions of the monsters into a nightmare of sound, which had come to darken the sun and to cast Jorath into an everlasting age of darkness.

Now a Glower Bear attacked. Its giant paws scraped along Ahren's Deep Steel armour, the pungent smoke emanating from the creature causing the Forest Guardian's breathing to become laboured. Ahren could retreat no further – Sun Shimmer's plumage was already sticking into his back.

The beast rose up on its hindlegs, preparing to launch its final attack that would tear Ahren into smithereens – only for the monster to be yanked skyward as it bellowed out its surprise and lashed out in all directions!

The Paladin blinked in shock, wondering perhaps if he had lost his reason in his moment of despair, only for another enormous, scaled creature to slam through the cloud of screeching Storm Claws, this one plucking another Glower Bear from the ground. Ahren caught a fleeting glimpse of a grinning, tattooed dwarf, strapped into the saddle of a flying dragon. The wildly whooping figure was wearing nothing more than a loincloth and a pair of flimsy woollen gloves, his lips blue from the cold. Then the giant saurian ascended high into the sky, futilely struggling Dark Ones in its claws.

Powerful blasts of incredibly hot air blew over the heads of the Paladins, sending scorched Swarm Claws plummeting by the dozens to the ground. Within a matter of a few heartbeats, there were no Glower Bears or murderous birds surrounding the astonished Paladins, all of whom had lowered their weapons – fourteen Southern Dragons, spewing out boiling hot air as they carried their delighted dwarfs into battle.

'Are they…from the Wild Clan?' asked the First, Ahren rarely having seen the age-old Paladin so non-plussed.

Look – it's Fire Falcon! exclaimed Culhen, whimpering delightedly. *And the dragon that he's riding on looks like Xandrolfor. His wing must have healed in the meantime!*

Ahren stood there, open-mouthed, in the midst of a chaos of dead Dark Ones and watched as the Wild Dwarfs methodically cleared the skies and the area around them of Dark Ones. Two of the dragons were wounded by leaping Blood Wolves in the process, the giant saurians' riders immediately bringing their mounts high into the air before retreating to safety. This was no surprise to Ahren, for he knew that the health of their animals was of paramount importance to the Wild Dwarfs.

While the remaining dragons then flew in low circles above the Paladins, protecting them from the enemy, one of the dwarfs landed his flying beast near Sun Shimmer before dismounting.

'Ahren!' shouted the stranger cheerfully. 'Or should I say, Thirteenth? Nice to see you again.'

Ahren looked the fellow up and down. He was bald, even his eyebrows having been shaven off. Instead of hair, his head was decorated with elaborate tattoos. They displayed an image of an incredibly long tunnel in Thousand Halls, as well as heavily armed horsemen, sending a young dwarf holding a chest towards a shaft…

'Corin?!' gasped Ahren, unable to believe his eyes.

'The very fellow!' laughed the Wild Dwarf. 'You accompanied me out of Thousand Halls that time so that I could see my Andramuna again.' He pointed at a she-dwarf, who was recklessly steering a snow-white dragon that looked even bigger than her conspecifics. 'You cannot imagine how amazed and enchanted I was when I arrived in Dragon Ridge to discover that she had already broken in Snow Wings.'

Ahren could only nod. Words failed him.

'It's not that we aren't delighted at your arrival,' gasped Falk, going down on his hunkers and supporting his arms on his sword and shield so that he could draw breath. 'But why are you here?'

'Ah,' said Corin, laughing. 'When elves and Wrath Elves are fighting in one and the same battle – and they are on the same side – then there is surely room for the Wild Clans to take their places among the boring types of Thousand Halls and Silver Cliff!'

'In other words, all we needed to do over the past few years was simply to ask, and the Wild Clans would have come to our aid?' asked Khara, blinking in disbelief.

Corin shook his head sheepishly. 'You can thank Fire Falcon and Moss Rose for us being here.' He cocked his head. 'And Daddy Four Claws as we call him now. The fact that you cured him from his sorrow without killing him impressed the Wild Clans no end. Enough to send the best dragon riders to support the Paladins.'

'Modest Corin, too!' roared the dwarf from above whom Ahren had gotten to know in the Ice Fields and with whose convoluted manner of speaking he was familiar. 'Corin years for spoke war favour Adversary against for. Named Paladins had he him helped I you our caves in treated Thirteenth better.'

Ahren waved amicably, completely taken aback by the turn of events.

'I have a selfish reason for being here, too,' admitted Corin in a low voice. 'Andramuna and I swore to set aside our old names only once we were able to assist those Paladins who had stood by us.' He shrugged his shoulders. 'We had intended to join up with your troops in a formal manner and were surprised to find you in the middle of what seemed like a very sudden offensive war,' he added.

The First cleared his throat. 'This is down to the fact that we must confront the Adversary when night falls.' He nodded towards the sun, now low on the horizon. 'Which will not be long now.'

Corin frowned. 'Why the hurry?'

'The Dark god will increase His power for centuries once a particular constellation has dissolved,' said Fisker, glancing nervously at the horizon. 'Much as it pains me to admit it, the First is right – I think we should put off the chatting for another time. I'll never hear the end of it from Wamakohane if she finds out that I have been standing idly by while the world as we know it goes to rack and ruin.'

Corin acknowledged the blonde Paladin with a sincere, loud chuckle. 'We will happily escort you all to the Dark god,' said the Wild Dwarf. He pointed at Sun Shimmer. 'You lot fly on her back, and we will set off on our dragons. No harm will befall you while we are with you.'

Sunju shook her head. 'My Roc's wing is only provisionally healed. Can we not travel with you?'

No dragon! protested Culhen immediately. *Riding in Sun Shimmer's wooden crate was bad enough, but I am not going to allow myself to be carried like a juicy cow in the claws of a dragon over a horde of Dark Ones!*

'Our dragons only tolerate dwarfs on their backs. The smell of other species makes them...well...*hungry*.'

The heads of the remaining Paladins spun around pleadingly to Sunju.

'Sun Shimmer says she can transport us,' she sighed. 'But only for a short time.'

Uldini pointed eastward, to what remained of the once expansive Obsidian Fortress. 'It is not far now. But if we can travel the distance on the wings of a Roc, the cold heart of the Adversary will burst with fear.'

'Then let us go,' said the Father of the Mountain with a hopeful smile on his lips. 'Let the final onslaught of the Paladins be of such a quality that the bards will sing of it to the end of time.'

Ahren's hands wouldn't stop trembling.

For one thing, the winter air was truly freezing up here, so high above the battlefield. For another, Ahren had a perfect view of the death and destruction meted out this day on the nations of Jorath. The smoking ruins of the Wizardly Domes formed a foreboding frame to the enormous battlefield, which stretched in all directions within the Ring. Like an enormous wedge, the Jorathian troops were eating through the masses of Dark Ones from an eastward direction, while the sheer number of corpses scattered around the battlefield was too much for Ahren to comprehend.

The Dragon Riders of the Wild Dwarfs flew on either side of the Paladins, the hot breath of their mounts incinerating any Swarm Claw that ventured to threaten the Roc and her precious cargo.

Ahren and the others breathed in deeply the cold air, their bodies welcoming the break from fighting that the flight brought with it. Muscles slowly relaxed, while their lungs expanded and contracted, not because they were gasping but in a perfectly normal manner.

You know, compared to the battlefield, Sun Shimmer's back isn't that bad at all, said Culhen. It was true that the wolf was still lying as flat on the floor as he could manage, but this time his head was raised so that the wind could blow into his nostrils, his slobbery tongue hanging out the side of his mouth.

The Roc was flying in a gentle curve. Her wing only having been provisionally healed, Sun Shimmer moved slowly and sedately, making use of every current of air that would make the flight easier. Hence, she wasn't taking a direct course towards the Obsidian Fortress, following a wide arc instead.

Ahren fixed his eyes on the destination of their short flight – the threatening-looking palace at the heart of the fortress, which looked like a travesty of a royal residence with its black-glass structure. Jagged and thorn-like barbs protruded from beside embrasure-like windows, its slender towers ending in razor-sharp points, its heavy gates made from steel of the deepest black. This was no property that a living creature would dare to call home. This was the seat of power belonging to a self-proclaimed god, whose intention was to develop the darkest of realms which would swallow up Creation in its entirety. If they should fail, Ahren was certain that he was looking down on the centre of the future capital of Jorath.

Suppressing a shiver, he turned to look at his friends. Thanks to the Blessing Band, he sensed that every one of them was calmly and determinedly preparing for the final battle, ready to fulfil the task for which they had all been selected.

Bergen was absently stroking the feathers of the dishevelled Karkas, the First was polishing his two-hander in a ritualised manner, Lyssin was gazing at the bow in her right hand while instinctively reaching back with her other one to count the arrows in her quiver.

Hakanu was cuddling Kamaluq, pressing the fox close to his chest. The young warrior looked so innocent at this moment that Ahren could only smile. If they were to be victorious, then perhaps the lad would be able to hold on to the childish part of his personality for ever.

Falk was staring into the middle distance, a hand placed on Selsena's mane, while Lanlion seemed to be dozing off as he lay in the rear of the of the carriage, completely exhausted. Aluna and Fisker were whispering to each other, giggling from time to time over a privately shared joke. The bad blood that had poisoned their relationship for so long seemed to have been washed clean on the battlefield.

Sunju, meanwhile, was down on her hunkers, humming merrily into Sun Shimmer's neck, delighted that her Roc had escaped death, the Paladin's positive energy now shining like a beacon in the pulsating bond of the Blessing Band.

Ahren's eyes scanned the rest of the companions on Sun Shimmer's back. The Father of the Mountain was telling Trimm something in a low voice, and whatever it was that he was relating to the opulent Paladin, it seemed to be reining in the fire of revenge that was burning strongly in the eyes of the grieving man. Uldini, on the other hand, was in a crouched position, constantly rubbing the top of the cloth, under which *Flamestar* was hidden.

A cry of jubilation rang out from beside Sun Shimmer. It was Trogadon, the dwarf sitting on one of the dragons behind the pilot, and it seemed that, despite the adverse circumstances they all found themselves in, the blacksmith was at one with himself and the world.

Finally, Ahren's eyes rested on Khara, who was snuggled in close to him, stroking the purring Muai as well as she could manage, considering the blood-spattered condition of the tigress's fur.

The Swordsmistress noticed his look and laid her head against his shoulder. 'There are surely better days to be a Paladin,' she murmured.

Ahren could sense that she was smiling. He leaned his head in, too, until it was touching hers. 'But none more important than this one.'

'Muai is *completely* with me,' said Khara in a low voice. 'Not only through my amulet, but also directly within my heart. I can hear her purring as if it is my own. This is the greatest gift of all.'

The tigress turned her head, her green eyes twinkling in the golden evening light. Then she licked Khara's forehead and hair – as if she wanted to wash her Paladin clean.

The formation of the dragons accompanying them changed. Ahren turned to look, watching as one of the large beasts separated from the flock, one of the two riders on its back waving cheerfully.

'Trogadon must be the first living dwarf ever to have flown on a Roc *and* a dragon,' said Ahren, watching his friend growing smaller and smaller.

Khara giggled. 'And he will never tire of reminding all Jorath of his achievement, I'm sure.'

Ahren suppressed his concern for the departing dwarf, for the last thing he wanted to do was to contaminate the Blessing Band, which was currently radiating total harmony amongst the Paladins. 'I know that he has to be by Jelninolan's side for the last act of our battleplan, but I must admit, I'm going to miss his hammer.'

'*Only* his hammer?' teased Khara, distracting him from his anxiety.

Ahren pretended to ponder the question. 'Maybe more than that. His crossbow is also not to be scoffed at.'

The young couple burst out laughing, and for one precious heartbeat, there was nothing more that they needed than the fresh winter wind, the presence of the other Paladins and – most of all – one another.

The moment passed – swept away by the indifferent river of time and the pressure of the imminent conflict. Very soon they would be flying over the remaining walls of the Obsidian Fortress. The battle with the Adversary was within touching distance.

A rumbling sounded from below them, but Ahren had heard it often enough by now to recognise it immediately. Sorcery rose skywards as one by one, *all* the obsidian walls metamorphosed into crimson blackness. The closer the Roc came to the fortress, the more the walls disappeared, no longer fit for purpose, thanks to the flight of the Paladins and therefore destroyed on the spot so that what was left of them could serve a new purpose.

It was a glimpse of a future world, which HE, WHO FORCES would create.

'What are you going to do, my enemy of old?' mumbled Uldini. The eyes of the Arch Wizard were looking down with feverish expectation at the newly created sorcerous clouds that were swirling around the Obsidian Palace. 'Are you going to attack, or hide – in the expectation that Father Time will do your dirty work for you?'

Ahren glanced over at the slowly setting sun, now no more than a hand above the horizon. The Forest Guardian knew what *he* would do if he were in the Dark god's shoes.

A shimmering veil settled around the palace, looking for all the world like a crimson, glimmering version of the Pall Cloud. Life itself seemed to be expiring with the pall of black magic, so great was the sense of death and destruction that pulsed forth from the swirling fog. A figure, enormous yet haggard, was visible for a moment on one of the Obsidian Palace balconies.

COME, LITTLE PALADINS, mocked the Dark god, retreating a step into the shadows of His citadel. COME IF YOU DARE.

Ahren glanced over at Uldini, who nodded with a wicked grin as he continued to rub the top of his cloth. 'His fear is greater than His scorn,' whispered the Ancient. 'Which is good. Very good.'

A bugle call sounded in the distance, from where the Jorathian troops were pushing their way through the sea of Dark Ones. Jelninolan and Trogadon were beginning their final task.

'Sun Shimmer is tiring!' shouted Sunju. 'She is going to have to land somewhere soon.'

Uldini nodded and looked over the side of the wooden carriage. 'I must see if there are any traces of the old landscape which the Bane Cloud and the Obsidian Fortress has now mutilated,' he murmured. Then he forcefully stabbed his finger downward. '*There!*' he exclaimed. 'She must head for *that* spot!'

'Well, now – I can only see a seething mass of Dark Ones that would be only too delighted to tear us all to shreds the moment we land amongst them,' said Falk.

'You don't see what *I* see,' countered Uldini. Then he closed his eyes and with a groan raised one of his hands – now formed like a claw – as if he had grasped something heavy that he was lifting. Within a heartbeat, Ahren saw a gap appearing where the Roc was to land, an enormous rock then pushing its way up steeply, upon whose summit Sun Shimmer would be able to settle safely.

'Keep the rock free from the enemy!' commanded Corin, the dragons fanning out to incinerate any Dark Ones foolish enough to attempt climbing up the newly created feature.

Sun Shimmer began her descent, and it wasn't long before her claws landed with a loud scrape on the raw rockface.

Falk shook Lanlion awake, the latter mumbling something about being able to fight, the Bloodless then drinking a sup of the Sacred Water from a canteen, which clarified his vision and stilled his dark hunger a little. Meanwhile, the other companions prepared to leave the flying carriage. Hardly had Sun Shimmer lowered her tail feathers to make disembarkation easier when Ahren hopped off the giant bird. He looked down at the seething, hissing, snarling hordes of Dark Ones surrounding the rock, which was now being protected by the low-circling dragons. Myriads of hate-filled eyes reflected the will of their Lord and Master not five furlongs away.

'What now?' asked Ahren, looking at the others.

'We wait,' countered the First laconically. 'As per our plan.'

'Is it still valid, though?' asked Hakanu. 'I must admit, I've lost track of things.'

Khara pointed at the bellowing dragons that were circling them. 'We have had to take diversions, yes, but now we are where we had intended on being.'

'Does anyone else think that any further delay would be a foolish idea – considering the position of the sun?' asked Fisker. The yellow orb was now completely hidden by the Obsidian Palace, and the light that it was casting had now taken on a reddish tinge. It would not be long before the first stars would be twinkling in the firmament, and once some of them moved into their fateful positions and then moved away from each other again…

'The armies of the world have placed their trust in us,' said the Father of the Mountain. 'Now it is time for us to place our trust in *them*, or our journey ends here.'

The dragons were still keeping individual Dark Ones at bay, but most of the grotesque bodies seemed perfectly content to simply lay siege to the Champions of the gods standing on the summit of the rock.

'Neither Trogadon nor Jelninolan were sure if their plan was going to work when we were discussing all this,' interjected Trimm nervously. 'What if they over-estimated their abilities?'

The First peered eastward. 'The Obsidian Fortress has as good as fallen – even if in a completely different manner than we originally imagined. The result is the same – our troops have a route as far as the threshold of the Adversary. Now, they only have to push their way through to us.'

'Except that *we* were supposed to be with *them*,' muttered Aluna as a reminder.

'A good plan always involves a considerable amount of improvisation,' said Falk soberly as he patted Selsena's flank. 'If you ask me, we've made a pretty good fist of things, all things considered.'

Bergen snorted. 'Not that difficult if one had a flock of flying dragons as allies. And yet, we are now well and truly stuck in the middle of a sea of Dark Ones, watching the sun go down.'

'Listen!' laughed Khara, nodding at Muai's pricked-up ears. 'They are coming!'

Everyone on the rock fell silent. Ahren and his fellow Paladins hardly dared to breathe. At first, only a low melody was audible – the sorcerous song that Jelninolan and her pupils had been weaving into the hearts of the soldiers since early morning. But then, another sound joined in.

More challenging, more rhythmical. Darker.

The stomping of boots.

The slamming of axes against shields.

The rumbling singing through thousands of Dwarfish throats.

Like a steel wyvern, the dwarfs of Jorath were carving a passage through Dark Ones, their bodies and minds firmly in the grip of their martial music, which was penetrated and strengthened with Elven Storm Weaving.

Enveloped in a white light, the musicking Jelninolan swayed in the midst of the Dwarfish army, surrounded by her Wrath Elf pupils and protected by hammers, axes, shields and steel. His eyes filling with tears, Ahren could nevertheless make out mighty blows sending Low Fangs flying through the air, Glower Bears being simply pushed aside with the impact of shields, and Blood Wolves in mid-leap being skewered by spears before crashing to the ground. If a dwarf lost their life, another singing one would take their place, the unfortunate victim being lifted up, their body being then passed back along the line while the warriors continued to sing, their rhythmical battle song growing all the while in volume, forging the will of thousands into one common purpose.

Armies of human ranged fighters followed the unstoppable, singing throng, peppering any attacking Dark Ones with arrows and bolts wherever the creatures dared to attack the flanks of the gigantic wedge that was pushing its way inexorably towards Ahren and the rest of the Paladins.

A race began between the setting sun on the one side, and the Jorathian armies on the other. Elves, dwarfs and humans fought their way through the hordes of Dark Ones as one – singing, musicking and dying.

When the light of the sun was little more than a weak, distant memory on the western horizon, the troops arrived at the tall rock, upon which the Champions of the gods were holding out, the army immediately beginning to secure the area. Trogadon, his helmet sitting askew on his head, and the blood on one half of his face telling a silent tale of deadly combat, cheerfully clambered up to the top of the rock and grinned broadly at Ahren.

'Here I am again,' he said. 'And I've brought a few friends.'

'Nice to see you.' Ahren hugged the blacksmith. the latter flinching, however.

'Not so tight,' whispered the dwarf. 'Because I wanted to talk to you, I didn't sing along with the others to avoid being caught up in the exhilaration of the battle song. Which means, alas, that I can feel every one of my battered and bruised ribs.' With that, the dwarf wriggled out of Ahren's embrace and turned to Uldini. 'Jelninolan will not be able to keep up the intensity of her sorcery for much longer, and even the hearts of these Dwarfish warriors have their limits. I hope your master stroke is going to work as promised.'

Uldini nodded. 'Everyone – off the promontory!' he commanded sharply. 'Those in possession of large wings must fly – and I mean now!'

Fisker looked at the circling dragons while the other Paladins did as they were told. 'Does it have to be so? I would very much like to watch the Dark god squirm as we launch an aerial attack on Him with a fleet of giant lizards!'

Ahren, meanwhile, waved at Corin, Fire Falcon and Andramuna, having already ordered them to steer their dragons away. Sun Shimmer, too, took off and was immediately surrounded by the giant saurians, who now acted as her escort.

'Wherever my girl goes, she has her entourage,' murmured Sunju with a chuckle.

Uldini was now standing alone on the summit of the rock, staring belligerently down at the Obsidian Palace.

'ADVERSARY!' he screamed, his voice resonating like a dozen bugles. 'BEHOLD THE PALADINS! BEHOLD YOUR DOWNFALL!'

'What's going on?' hissed Falk. 'There are no bards here to impress – and time is not on our side.'

Ahren pointed at the Arch Wizard. 'Look at Uldini's hands, and his cramped back. Our friend is afraid. He is trying to give *himself* courage.'

Both Forest Guardians exchanged worried looks. What *was* their friend plotting?

A movement within the crimson veil drew Ahren's attention. The outline of the Dark god was vaguely visible under an archway, high in the façade of the palace.

ULDINI, he replied mockingly, making the Arch Wizard's name sound as if it was hardly worth uttering. OF COURSE, YOU ARE PRESENT. NO MONUMENTAL FAILURE EVER TAKES PLACE WITHOUT YOU.

'TODAY, YOUR TIME ON THE FACE OF JORATH WILL COME TO AN END! Countered the Arch Wizard. His magically amplified voice droned so much that it seemed the heavens themselves were trembling.

WE SHALL SEE ABOUT THAT, growled the Adversary, spreading out His arms.

A darkness now covered the sun and enveloped the battlefield in an impenetrable gloom. Suddenly, Ahren found breathing difficult, and he heard countless throats, both of friends and foes, gasping for air. The Dark god would sacrifice every living creature on earth in His lust for total control of the world.

I can't breathe, complained Culhen.

Ahren's fingers trembled as they searched for his friend's fur. He wanted to give the wolf heart, but the darkness was paralysing his mind.

'At last, you understand, my enemy of old.' It was Uldini's hoarse voice that Ahren heard muttering, the words resembling a beacon in an ocean of black ink. 'And *finally,* I can beat you at your own game.'

A glimmer suddenly appeared in the all-enveloping darkness. It was *Flamestar*, its contours clearly visible even from beneath the protective cloth. The childlike figure's fingers were cramped – as though Uldini was suddenly experiencing great pain or was trying to break through an invisible barrier within himself. Then his arms suddenly went limp and hung there as if all life had drained from them.

The Arch Wizard's cloth flew heavenward, fluttered in the wind before being blown away, revealing *Flamestar*, its inner fire burning ever brighter as the orb continued to rise – into the black sorcery of the Adversary, higher and higher – until it sundered the evil spell!

A thunderclap echoed across the battlefield, the weak light of the setting sun suddenly appearing again, and with it the ability to breathe. Gasping and stumbling, thousands of living creatures inhaled the precious, life-preserving air.

VERY IMPRESSIVE, mocked the Dark god. YOUR GLITTERING CRYSTAL BALL IS GONE – AND ALL TO BANISH ONE OF MY SPELLS. HOW ARE YOU GOING TO STOP ME NOW, WHILE I DESTROY ALL THESE CREATURES THAT REFUSE TO BOW TO MY WILL? Again, He spread out His arms and the earth below Ahren's feet began to shake terrifyingly.

Unruffled, Uldini shook his head. The way that he was carrying himself suggested that a great weight had been lifted from his shoulders. 'Names have power,' he replied matter-of-factly, the sound of his voice resonating with evermore confidence. '*How* we name things has an influence on whether they fulfil their true potential.' He craned his neck and gazed up at the evening sky, smiling. His voice turned into a call: 'A CRYSTAL BALL MAY NOT SEEM DANGEROUS TO YOU…'

Ahren blinked as he spotted a tiny point of light in the firmament, which gradually became bigger and bigger. 'Is that…?' he whispered.

'BUT YOU CAN HARDLY IGNORE A *FLAMESTAR!*' thundered the Arch Wizard.

The sky was filled with a blinding light as the fiery ball came hurtling down, a comet spewing sparks and smoke behind it. Uldini spread out his fingers, a shield of shimmering air coming instantly to life, enclosing the Paladins and the ranks of troops that were closest to them.

'Down on the ground!' yelled Uldini, and as Ahren threw himself onto the whirling dust at the foot of the rock, *Flamestar* was already smashing onto the roof of the malevolent Obsidian Palace, destroying whole towers and smashing to smithereens the main section of its western wing.

Yet, the impact had sounded strangely dull – almost soundless.

The light of the star went out.

Lifting his head and blinking, Ahren wondered if Uldini's sorcery had failed – only for the Obsidian Palace to explode into a maelstrom of light and darkness.

Antagonistic spells spread forth and struggled against each other in a complex, dancing powerplay. The sight was far beyond any comprehension of sorcery that Ahren possessed, a blast wave now sweeping across the landscape as far as the Ring. The air was filled with dust as small pieces of rock and rubble rained onto helmets and pieces of armour. Then there was silence.

Ahren struggled to his feet as he blinked in amazement. The Obsidian Palace was gone. In its place was a gaping hole, a good hundred paces across and at least a dozen deep. A heavy cloud of smoke obscured his view, but Ahren was nonetheless able to make out the figure of the Adversary, prostrate in the centre of the newly created sinkhole. The Dark Ones of the self-proclaimed god had been swept away by the blast, a circle stretching two hundred paces beyond the crater was free from foes.

'Uldini,' said Ahren hesitantly, while the remaining Paladins and their allies got to their feet. '*Flamestar*...your magic?'

The Ancient shrugged his shoulders as he smiled painfully. '...will probably never be as it once was.' He pointed at the immobile Adversary. 'But by the THREE, it was worth it to see this, don't you agree? You all brought me to this place without me being able to help you. You all looked death in the eye while I clutched *Flamestar* close to me.' The eyes of the Arch Wizard lit up with an inner fire which even his beloved orb could hardly have competed with. 'I have defeated Him,' he said proudly in a satisfied voice. 'He hurled His sorcery at us, and for once, I defeated Him – in a magical duel.'

Khara walked over to them, her hands instinctively running along Ahren's body to check that he hadn't been hurt. 'Is the Adversary dead?' she asked. 'The Dark Ones are not moving, anyway.'

Ahren, overwhelmed by everything, now looked around and, yes – as far as the eye could see, the servants of the Adversary were standing paralysed on the battlefield.

As though the Dark god had heard the question, He raised a hand, and immediately a hint of life returned to His benumbed armies.

'The vast majority of His sorcery is gone,' said Uldini, his voice serious. 'Incinerated by a *Flamestar*.' He looked Ahren in the eye. 'At least until His power returns once the constellation has moved on.'

Nodding, Ahren drew his Wind Blade. 'The time of the Paladins has come,' he said.

'Then go,' countered Trogadon hoarsely, the dwarf supporting the dazed Jelninolan. The elf looked worn out, her fingers were bloodstained from so much musicking. 'I will ensure that no-one disturbs you.' Then he forced himself into bellowing: 'Companies! Position yourselves around the crater! Nothing must get in before the Paladins have fulfilled the task that the gods have chosen them for! Buy them the time that they need! FOR JORATH!'

'FOR JORATH!' roared thousands of voices as one, the troops then dividing themselves up around the crater, ready to greet the gradually recovering servants of the Adversary in the manner that they deserved.

'This is it, then,' said Falk as the Paladins gathered at the crater's edge. The Dark god was up on His feet again and staring silently up at them. 'Move by move, we have stalked each other, deceived each other, fought each other. And now – at last – we are here.'

Ahren swallowed hard. The Blessing Band was vibrating with the tension of the combined Champions of the gods. 'The journey has been long,' he said, looking first into the eyes of his erstwhile master, then into those of Khara and finally, into Culhen's. 'One battle left,' he added.

I am ready, announced the wolf.

Ahren shook his head. 'No,' he said firmly. 'Help Trogadon and the others. You companion animals have accompanied us this far and protected us from each other. Watch over us from the edge and help us in this way to fulfil our final mission.'

Culhen whimpered, the rest of the Paladins' animals also voicing their protest, but the Blessing Band, its connections quivering this way and that, left Ahren, together with his brothers and sisters, with no other choice but to recognise the simple truth. In the end it would be the Thirteen confronting the One. Throwing any other living creatures into the balance would only mean more losses, more deaths – or even the total failure of their mission.

I will wait here for you, said Culhen solemnly, licking Ahren's face one last time. *We all will.*

Ahren nodded and embraced his friend. Then he turned and, together with his fellow Paladins, descended the slope into the crater. With every step, the sound of battle between the warring parties above became fainter until it was drowned out by the thrilling hum of expectation flooding into Ahren from the Blessing Band.

I HAVE BEEN EXPECTING YOU, said the Adversary ominously, His frame slowly becoming visible in the clouds of dust, which had stubbornly remained in the deepest part of the crater. An arm that was too long, which ended in a claw-like hand, pointed up at the darkening heavens. YET I FEAR THAT YOU HAVE LEFT IT TOO LATE.

Chapter 22

Ahren looked up at the night sky.

The light of the torches that the Jorathian armies had ignited was diffuse and only faintly visible from where he and his fellow Paladins were standing in the crater – it seemed as if the veil of swirling dust from the destroyed fortress was intent on cutting them and the Adversary off from the outside world.

The starry constellation was now twinkling in the firmament, a clear sign to those in the know that the Dark god was on the point of regaining His power. The Archer stood directly over the Great Gelding – as if the former were riding the latter. Beneath them, the stars of the THREE were glittering, and Ahren earnestly hoped that the gods were now watching over the deeds of their Champions. Surrounding the three zodiacal signs were the eight shining points of the Maelstrom – like a wreath framing this strange drama. The stars were all in their predetermined positions, but as soon as one of them left the Maelstrom constellation…

'Do not allow yourselves to be deceived by His words – we still have time to vanquish Him,' said the First coolly, his eyes fixed on the Adversary. 'He lies whenever He opens His mouth. And the longer we hesitate, the more likely we will, indeed, fail in our mission.'

OH, HOW CLEVER. BUT WOULD YOU NOT LIKE TO KNOW IF—

An all too familiar stream of air tickled Ahren's cheek.

Hakanu's spear disturbed the dust surrounding the Dark god before the weapon slammed into the haggard figure with a satisfying crunch, spinning the Adversary around.

Ahren and the other Paladins looked at Hakanu in amazement.

'What?' asked the wide-eyed apprentice. 'I thought we *weren't* supposed to listen to Him.'

The Adversary uttered a cry of rage as He turned back to look at them. His scorn seemed to set the very air in motion, the dust around him spinning in all directions.

Ahren quickly protected his eyes with his hands, and when he lowered them again, he could clearly see the Adversary at last – face to face.

The Dark god looked almost the same as when He had haunted Ahren during his Naming, but this time, His appearance had no elements of immateriality, of incompleteness. Three paces tall, haggard beyond belief and completely garbed in long shreds of black material, the Paladins' greatest enemy stood before him. Loose ends fluttered around him in a silent breeze that no-one else could sense. Where the Adversary's eyes should have been, there were only two black holes of impenetrable darkness – biting, piercing, enervating. Eyes that would break the will of any normal human being with a glance.

GOOD THROW, said the self-proclaimed god. LET ME GIVE YOU BACK YOUR WEAPON.

With a movement that was almost too quick for Ahren's eyes to comprehend, one of the loosely flapping shreds of material wrapped itself around Hakanu's spear, yanked it out of the Adversary's body and hurled it full force back at the apprentice.

'*No!*' yelled Ahren, but already the clang of Deep Steel against Deep Steel had resounded.

With considerable presence of mind, Falk had raised his shield between the missile and Hakanu's face, no damage thus ensuing apart from a dent in the metal armour.

'We *never* attack on our own,' growled the old man as he glared at the apprentice. 'We must divide His attention – otherwise, He will slaughter us one by one.'

The First took a step toward the Adversary. 'Fan out. Encircle Him. That should work.'

'And feel the Blessing Band between you,' added Lanlion. '*Sense* what your brothers and sisters are thinking of doing.'

Ahren was relieved that the Bloodless felt re-energised enough to make a useful contribution.

Immediately, the Paladins spread out, the Adversary unfolding His shreds of material to their full length until there were eight, seemingly living extensions surrounding the Adversary, giving Him the appearance of a half-starved, upright spider.

THIRTEEN AGAINST ONE. The voice of the god dripped with sarcasm. HOW BRAVE! HMM…LET ME THINK. YES – I WILL ARM MYSELF APPROPRIATELY. LET'S SEE IF ANYTHING HAS SURVIVED THE DESTRUCTION OF MY FORTRESS.

While the Paladins completed their encircling of the foe, He lowered His hands, His eight ribbons of woven darkness reaching to the ground, hammers and axes then flying up from the compacted earth, attaching themselves to the ends of the expectant shreds or snuggling into the grasp of the over-long fingers of His hands.

THAT'S BETTER NOW, chuckled the Dark god as He spun the ten weapons cheerfully. NOT EVEN A *FLAMESTAR* CAN SMELT DEEP STEEL, IT SEEMS.

'Those are the abandoned weapons of our deceased brothers and sisters,' muttered the First grimly. 'He's been collecting them for centuries.'

AND THEY ARE STILL ACCUMULATING, interjected the Adversary with false sorrow. IT SEEMS THAT EVERY GENERATION OF PALADINS BECOMES MORE COWARDLY. AH, YES – I RECOGNISE MANY *OLD*, FAMILIAR FACES. The Dark god cocked His head. WHAT HAPPENED? ARE YOU HAVING PROBLEMS PRODUCING *OFFSPRING?*

He's goading us, thought Ahren, the older Paladins having already raised their weapons as they moved in on their age-old enemy.

Muttering a curse, the Forest Guardian joined in the attack, but a skilfully wielded old-fashioned axe was now dancing up and down in front of his face, easily parrying his blows, causing even Khara to enviously admire the artistry of the Adversary's fighting style.

The other Paladins were not doing much better, with only Lyssin managing to hit the target with one of her arrows, the uncharmed arrow not seeming to bother the haggard figure a whit, however.

'This tactic is useless,' said Ahren, leaping backwards. The others, thanks to their shared Blessing Band, did the same, the companions forming a perfect circle again around the enemy as, breathing heavily, they stared at the Dark god, who was still spinning His weapons with unerring accuracy.

TIRED ALREADY? teased the Adversary. IF YOU PREFER, WE CAN HAVE A FRIENDLY CHAT INSTEAD OF FIGHTING. He looked up at the stars. I HAVE ALL NIGHT, AFTER ALL.

Once more, Ahren examined the situation of the fateful constellation, a sense of hopelessness temporarily overwhelming him. All the zodiacal signs were still close together, but some of the stars in the constellation had already changed their positions slightly.

'The THREE,' he said nervously, pointing up at the slowly separating Maelstrom. 'The stars of the THREE are still in conjunction. But not for much longer.'

'Then let us try again,' said the First, the Paladins beginning a renewed assault.

'Lyssin, Hakanu – close combat fighting!' commanded Ahren as they moved closer. 'There are thirteen of us, but he only has ten weapons. Let us force him into deciding who he will ignore.'

YOUR NEW THIRTEENTH CAN COUNT, mocked the Adversary. QUITE AN IMPROVEMENT OVER HIS PREDECESSOR.

Ahren gritted his teeth and forced himself not to listen. He had known for a long time that words were weapons as far as the Adversary was concerned, devious tools with which He forced those around Him to obey His will.

As if possessed, Ahren launched himself at the creature, using every manoeuvre and every feint that he had learned over the years. In vain. The shreds of material swung easily this way and that, the weapons blocking each swing and thrust of the Paladin.

Ahren's frustration grew.

'He won't attack,' growled Bergen. 'Why won't He attack?'

'Because all He needs to do is wait!' shouted Sunju, the Dark god laughing gleefully as a result. 'He merely has to wait for the correct position of the THREE.'

PRECISELY, MY DARLINGS. ONLY ANOTHER FEW INCHES AND THE STARS WILL LEAVE THE MAELSTROM AGAIN. IT SEEMS THAT YOUR GODS HAVE GROWN IMPATIENT AND ARE TURNING THEIR BACKS ON YOU.

Using their Blessing Band, the Paladins repositioned themselves around the Adversary again and gasped for air.

'This is proving to be just as difficult as I feared,' said Fisker, blowing his golden locks from his sweat-drenched forehead. 'Maybe we should come back in thirteen hundred years' time…?

No-one else laughed at the Paladin's weak joke.

Aluna pointed her trident at the Adversary's weapons, which were now circling sedately. 'It is as if all His weapons have a unified will. We must imitate His method.'

Ahren saw the Dark god stiffening, the young man then filling his lungs with air.

'PALA —'

He got no further.

As if out of nowhere, the Adversary threw Himself at the young man, flailing at the Paladin with all His strips.

Ahren did a backward roll, deflecting an incoming spear as he did so, yet he only managed to survive thanks to Khara and Falk, who were fighting on either side and who had the presence of mind – and because the Blessing Band was throbbing intensively in each of the Paladins' head – to thrust their blades and spear into the path of the attacking Deep Steel.

'Ha!' shouted the First as Ahren continued to parry desperately for his life, the age-old warrior, meanwhile, thrusting his blade forward and into the torso of the Adversary. The haggard figure doubled over, His weapons darting back to their Lord and Master before spinning around Him like a steel cocoon.

'Good hit!' exclaimed Trimm, his eyes burning with a naked thirst for revenge.

'It's a start,' said the First matter-of-factly as he looked down at his blade. There was no sign of blood.

'Hold on a heartbeat,' muttered Lyssin as Ahren struggled to his feet and the Paladins took up their positions again. 'A thrust into His body doesn't *kill* Him?'

'He is a god,' said Sunju, using her spear to test out the still doubled-over Adversary's defensive reflexes, one of His swords easily deflecting her weapon, however.

'All thirteen Paladins are necessary for that,' said Falk. 'This is all we know.'

'In other words, each of us has to stab Him once?' asked Trimm, the frustration evident in his voice.

The First nodded. 'My Blessing stirred when I hit Him. Perhaps each of us must score a hit so that our Blessing can, as a unified force, extinguish Him at last.'

IMBECILES! thundered the Adversary as he got to His feet. YOU CANNOT KILL ME!

Not as long as He doesn't attack us, thought Ahren. He quickly exchanged looks with his brothers and sisters. They all seemed to be thinking the same thing.

'PALADINIM...' screamed Khara, the Adversary reacting immediately with a wild assault.

Ahren and Sunju supported the Swordsmistress with precise parries while the rest of the Paladins stabbed or hacked at the Adversary.

Ahren, meanwhile, had a brainwave. Instead of parrying the inrushing sword that was aiming for Khara, he would cut the ribbon holding it. *Sun* sliced easily through the black material, the blade clattering to the ground with the severed cloth.

Ahren's triumphant smile was only brief, however. Within a heartbeat the two sections had reunited, and the Adversary was swinging His weapon as though nothing had happened.

'Got you!' snarled Lyssin, stabbing the Dark god in the leg, Bergen closely following with a powerful thrust to the Adversary's back.

Ahren sensed the Blessing Band throbbing as the weapons made contact with the enemy. HE, WHO FORCES stumbled forward, and again a flashing cocoon of Deep Steel surrounded him.

'Let us take advantage of His weakness,' urged Trimm. 'He fears our battle cry, so let us call it out in unison.'

'Every attempt we have made has tempted Him out of the defensive,' agreed Aluna. 'It's certainly worth a try.'

Ahren looked up at the heavens. One of the Great Gelding stars was now approaching the edge of the Maelstrom, too. The Forest Guardian's anxiety spread to the others in no time, thanks to the Blessing Band, no words then being needed for the thirteen Paladins to come to a consensus. Even as the Adversary was struggling to His feet with a groan, the Champions of the gods had begun yelling.

'PALADINIM THEOS DURALAS!'

The battle cry echoed throughout the crater as if an enormous bell had just tolled. The Blessing Band became so concentrated that Ahren almost felt that he could read the minds of his brothers and sisters, and when they attacked the Dark god this time, it was as if they were *one* being, contending against the fallen Custodian of Creation.

The blows of the Adversary missed their target, so aware were the thirteen pairs of eyes – thanks to the Blessing Band – of the others' sight, for them not to react when one of their number was in danger. Where parries were necessary, they were kept to a minimum as they continued to aim at the ribbons. Even the heartbeat it took between cutting and re-connecting was used to bring a blade to its target.

Hit after hit was landed on the Adversary in a frenzied assault, the Dark god stumbling left and right while He screamed so furiously that the ears of the Paladins hurt terribly.

Finally, when only Ahren and Trimm were left to land their blows and finally prove the veracity of their theory, the Adversary roared particularly loudly and stamped His foot in rage. The ground trembled, scattering the Paladins while guileful swords, axes and spears raced into their defensive positions.

TROUBLESOME PALADINS! yelled the Adversary. YOUR MEASLY STINGS DO NOT EVEN ITCH!

Ahren could taste the Enemy's fear, and the Blessing Band throbbed with the joy of victory.

'Let us not become cocky,' warned the Forest Guardian as he did another backward roll to beyond the reach of the Adversary. As he got to his feet, he nimbly changed weapons, reached back for three Deep Steel arrows before shooting them simultaneously. He glanced over at Trimm, and thanks to the Blessing Band, the two brothers understood each other in the blink of an eye.

Trimm nodded to Ahren without a moment's hesitation, the Forest Guardian suddenly filled with pride for his fellow Paladin, who had previously been so cowardly. One of the three arrows then ricocheted off a swinging axe, the other two, however, boring deep into the Dark god's torso.

Trimm took his opportunity as HE, WHO FORCES was thrown forward, the corpulent Paladin plunging one of his daggers into the Adversary's stomach.

The Dark god shuddered before collapsing limply to the ground. The ribbons holding His weapons seemed suddenly lifeless, the Deep Steel of long dead heroes clattering onto the dusty surface of the crater.

Ahren stumbled, so overwhelmed was he by the Blessing Band, which was positively glowing thanks to the concentrated joy of the Paladins.

'Is He dead?' asked Trimm, grinning broadly. 'Have I *really* killed the Adversary?'

'You mean *we,* surely,' chuckled the Father of the Mountain, correcting his friend.

'The thirteen Paladins combined,' said the First, delightedly. 'I can hardly believe it was so easy to —'

With a humming and hissing, ten weapons rose from the dust and headed directly for the unprepared Paladins.

Ahren was still holding *Fisiniell* in his right arm as he raised it to protect his face. The axe slammed into the bow – easily slicing the unicorn-hair string.

The Forest Guardian gasped as his arm was immediately numbed by the impact of the axe, *Fisiniell* now slipping out of his limp fingers. Then he felt a terrible tugging in his head – a sure sign of pain among his fellow Paladins who had been even unluckier than him.

Trimm staggered backwards, his cheek newly cut. Falk, his breastplate dented, could hardly breathe, while Bergen, his right thigh wounded, collapsed – Lanlion, thankfully, having the presence of mind to drag him out of the danger zone.

The Paladins struggled to get beyond the range of the twirling weapons, the Adversary getting to His feet and guffawing.

SO MUCH POWER, AND YET YOU HAVE NO IDEA HOW TO USE IT. YOUR GODS SENT YOU OUT INTO THIS WORLD BLIND, DEAF AND VERY, VERY DUMB. GIVE ME YOUR BLESSING AND I WILL PUT IT TO GOOD USE. The Dark god enveloped Himself again in the spinning weaponry and looked up at the firmament. GIVE ME YOUR BLESSING! He commanded again, BEFORE I RIP IT FROM YOUR MISERABLE BODIES!

'Unified…we *will* defeat Him!' gasped the First. The veteran had a cut to his stomach, but through their Blessing Band, Ahren sensed that the age-old Paladin was still able to fight.

'Trimm and Bergen are temporarily incapacitated,' muttered Falk in frustration. 'There is no chance of us fighting Him in unison.'

IT IS BETTER THIS WAY, purred the Adversary. SURRENDER. BEND TO MY WILL, LITTLE PALADINS.

Khara staggered over to Ahren, Sunju all the while protecting Bergen and Trimm with her tower shield. 'I have an idea,' said the Swordsmistress, her eyes sparkling and holding up her wrist with the bracelet on it. 'Do you remember what Aluna did after the birth of her twins? Or what Quin-Wa attempted this morning?'

Ahren nodded anxiously, parrying a blow from a weapon that the Dark god was playfully jabbing at him. The Forest Guardian realised that the Adversary was doing His best to separate the Paladins. If He succeeded, more of them would be in trouble.

'*And?*' he asked urgently.

'Thirteen Paladins,' murmured Khara conspiratorially. '*Unified.*'

Ahren understood.

'Do it!' he whispered after looking up at the sky. By now the zodiacal sign of the THREE had come dangerously close to the edge of the Maelstrom. The constellation was in danger of dispersing.

'*Me?*'

'You're wearing the bracelet. You have the most control over its magic.'

Khara swallowed hard. Then she nodded.

A questioning tug manifested itself in the combined understanding of the Paladins. It was Khara, trying to collect the Blessings of the Champions of the gods so that she could unify them in her bracelet – just as Aluna had done in the Heart Hall or when Quin-Wa had lent her own Blessing to Khara. Khara could feel resistance and she broke off her attempt.

'What are you *doing?*' muttered the First, laboriously parrying blows from the Adversary. 'You will only make the rest of us weak and powerless.'

WEAK. The Dark god revelled in the word as He uttered it, strengthening His attacks on those who were still standing.

POWERLESS...YES.

'Trust us,' gasped Ahren as he continued to defend himself from the relentless attacks, manipulating *Sun* as best he could. His breathing was laboured, and his right arm was still numb. 'We have no other choice.'

'May the gods forgive me,' muttered the First as the resistance in the bracelet melted away.

Instantly, Khara seized the initiative. This time, it was no hesitant request but a confident inhalation of all the power that the combined Paladins had to offer. Khara's entire body was casting a powerful golden light, illuminating the crater as it pulsated from the Swordsmistress, transforming her movements into a dazzling dance, too fast for the naked eye to see. The Adversary screamed, His voice cascading with fury and dismay. Then began an exchange of blows, the likes of which Ahren had never before beheld.

Two blades of light against ten Deep Steel weapons controlled by a living darkness, straining to deliver the killer blow.

Khara vanished in the whirlwind of stabs and thrusts from the enemy, and yet her two blades were always in the right place at the right time. She seemed untouchable, yet she could not manage to move in on the Adversary by so much as an inch. A deadly stalemate was the result, which could only, ultimately, play into the hands of the Dark god.

A glance to the heavens was enough for Ahren to see that the first star of the THREE was now in line with the lowest stars of the Maelstrom. The breadth of a finger stood between the Enemy of Creation and His ultimate victory.

'*Ahren!*' screamed Khara, the Forest Guardian feeling through the Blessing Band the increasing agony that his beloved was suffering – like water seething in a pot hanging over a blazing fire. 'There's something *wrong!*'

'No being can master the power of the Paladins over an extended period!' shouted the Father of the Mountain. 'Which is why the THREE divided it up!'

Khara's and Ahren's eyes met. In a fraction of a heartbeat, he understood what she was planning.

'No,' he whispered, but already Khara was using the Blessing Band to fling the unified power of the Paladins to her beloved, screaming in pain and throwing herself to the side. Three of the darting weapons sliced through her Deep Steel robe and cut into her flesh.

'KHARA!' roared Ahren, lunging forward, his Wind Blade shining like the blazing orb after which it was named. Now, the Adversary was no longer his *enemy*, He was an *obstacle* that the Paladin had to sweep aside so that he could get to his beloved.

With attacking blows that were faster than he, himself, could comprehend, he drove the god back through the crater, away from Khara and the blood that was flowing freely from her body. Lanlion was now with her as Ahren and the Adversary exchanged blows a good thirty paces beyond the other Paladins. Ahren sensed that the flow of blood had been stanched, Lanlion using his knowledge of the priceless juices to great effect.

Fear for the life of his beloved gave way to an iron will. Ahren now concentrated his mind fully on his Wind Blade, stabbing, cutting, slicing at the body of the Adversary.

'Paladinim theos duralas,' he whispered, reaching not only for the gods' Blessing that his brothers and sisters had surrendered to him through the Blessing Bands but also for their *other* qualities, which he now so desperately needed:

Will-power.
Responsibility.
Memories.
Hope.

Ahren was One and yet he was *Thirteen.*

The weapons of the Adversary slid past him, scraped along his armour or ricocheted painfully but harmlessly off his artfully arranged Deep Steel plates, while *Sun* now slid forward in a simple, straight, stabbing movement – through the chest of the Adversary until the tip of the blade reappeared, gleaming as it protruded from the Dark god's back.

'*Die,*' murmured Ahren – and, as if his word was the law, HE, WHO FORCES shuddered and then collapsed in a cloud of swirling dust.

Ahren stared down at the lifeless bundle at his feet and exhaled.

It was over.

'The will of the THREE has been achieved,' said Ahren, turning to face his friends. 'May —'

'*Ahren!*'

Khara's cry caused him to spin around, but it was too late.

With a scrunch, an old-fashioned blade sank into his chest. Dust was trickling out of the wound that Ahren had inflicted on the Adversary, and the eight long ribbons hung completely lifelessly, yet HE, WHO FORCES still existed!

YOU CANNOT KILL ME, LITTLE PALADIN, said the Adversary, raising His blade, and with it the skewered Ahren.

Coldness radiated from the Forest Guardian's chest. He heard his own blood splattering onto the ground. *Sun* fell from his powerless fingers.

I STAND *OUTSIDE* CREATION. DEATH IS FOREIGN TO ME.

Ahren's senses began to weaken. He could barely hear the horrified gasps of his brothers and sisters.

The Adversary brought him closer to His mummified face and pointed upwards with His free hand. LOOK UP! He said gleefully. LET THE SIGN OF MY RE-AWAKENING POWER BE THE LAST THING THAT YOU EVER SEE!

Ahren coughed up blood. His vision became blurred, and now his life was rolling past him in bright, flashing images, too quick for him to be consciously aware of.

Here was Deepstone, the sleepy village with its local drunkard and his timid son.

Falk, standing in the village square with his improvised shield, looking for a lad to train as an apprentice.

Keeper Jegral's chapel, a place of learning every godsday...

An idea suddenly glimmered within Ahren. An idea so audacious that he, himself, flinched from it. Swirling snatches of words from the depths of his subconsciousness, learned so long ago in the godsday lessons, repeated by the good Keeper Jegral, and by Falk when he had journeyed with his master. Words that Ahren had never quite understood. Until now.

...*together*...

...*thirteen Blessings, their power equal to that of the Adversary*...

...*the means of restoring the harmony of Creation*...

He opened his eyes. This was going to be the most difficult thing that he would ever do. 'Our Blessing...' he wheezed.

The Dark god looked at him. YES? The look of utter triumph in the fallen Custodian's face was unmistakable.

Ahren coughed again – the pain was unbearable. The coldness had reached his arms and legs. He could hardly feel his limbs anymore. Through sheer willpower, he laid his pale hand on the chest of the Dark god. 'Our Blessing,' he said again. 'I will give it to you – willingly.'

'AHREN!' screamed Falk.

'Traitor!' cursed the First.

'*No!*' pleaded Khara.

The Blessing Band trembled at the protest of the Paladins, but already HE, WHO FORCES, was using His will, sucking the powerful force from Ahren and into Himself.

Ahren abandoned all resistance and let it happen. The Blessing of the thirteen Paladins flowed into the Adversary, the very gift that had been denied the fallen Custodian for so long – and now the Dark god was satiating Himself on it.

But Ahren had given the creature that was still skewering him with His sword more than sheer power. He had given him memories.

Of love.

Of grief.
Of pain.
Of hope.
Of life.

Centuries and centuries of life experience travelled from the assembled Paladins, flowed through Ahren, and streamed into the Custodian, who was now staggering, doubled over and *altering* as a result of the relentless images.

'Recognise what it is to *live,*' murmured Ahren weakly.

Every attack of a Dark One, every witnessed delinquency done towards Creation – the Adversary was experiencing them now, too. Just as He was enjoying those priceless moments of sheer joy that made existence so precious to every mortal. The birth of a child. The fathomless love between two people. The happiness at knowing that one was not alone as one travelled through the world.

In the blink of an eye, the Adversary experienced entire lifetimes. He learned what it was to be a part of Creation.

'Welcome,' whispered Ahren as the stream of memories and emotions began to fade, the gods' Blessing being nothing now but a dim and distant echo in each and every Paladin. 'Do you now wish to serve as the THREE desired?' he murmured weakly. 'Do you now acknowledge the beauty of Creation, to which you belong?'

For a heartbeat, the Adversary simply stood there – it was as if He had been paralysed by what He had just experienced. The shreds hung from His chest, the only thing that moved as He struggled for air. His eyes were now no longer holes filled with blackness – they were completely human – if one ignored the golden glimmer in their depths. The glimmer of the gods' Blessing.

'Do I wish to serve again?' said the Custodian, repeating Ahren's question. 'Now that I possess so much power?'

'And so much knowledge about life,' whispered Ahren, the young man slowly drifting away. Without the gods' Blessing, he was mortal through and through. His body began to shut down. 'Abandon your mission. Free yourself from your madness.'

Ahren's heart skipped a beat.

Full of sorrow, Ahren thought of what might have been. The perfection of life. The harmony that might have been attained. Then he summoned his last reserves of strength and pointed to the heavens with his right hand.

The Adversary tilted His head back and laughed. 'Die, little Paladin,' He said as He revelled in the dispersing constellation in the firmament. 'The stars are perfectly *mis*aligned for such an occurrence.'

Ahren wanted to smile, but he was no longer in control of his mouth. He could do nothing more than mumble as he reached with his left hand for the innocuous knife that he always had tied to his breastplate. A present from a cantankerous master to his eager pupil. A loyal companion to Ahren over the years.

Then he stabbed, deep into the heart of the Adversary.

'The stars cannot help you,' Ahren whispered. 'After all – you *are* a part of Creation now.'

The adversary dropped his sword – and therefore Ahren, as well – before staggering backwards, desperately grasping the simple blade in his chest. As the Forest Guardian fell to the ground with a groan, he could see the erstwhile god yanking the knife out of his body before staring in disbelief at the blood shooting from the newly created wound.

He stumbled and turned, stretching an arm out to Ahren in a gesture of pleading.

But he was alone.

And he died alone.

Ahren watched the life extinguishing in the eyeballs of the adversary, a life which only so recently had flamed for a moment.

Then his own vision became completely blurred.

He heard Culhen howling.

He heard Khara calling his name.

Then he heard nothing.

***

The rain drummed on the dark earth, as though it was insistently announcing to every Jorathian that today was a day of mourning.

Although Falk wanted to wipe the drops from his beard, he simply didn't have the energy for this basic action. He stared down into the grave, which would soon be filled with soil. Flowers had been strewn within it, whether brought from lands not in the grip of winter or grown magically, he neither knew nor cared. Either way, they seemed out of place, being so colourful and cheerful, decorating the white coffin that held one of the best to have borne the title of Paladin.

Falk was one of the few who still hadn't fled the downpour into the shelter of the castle. He didn't want to leave.

'Senseless,' he muttered under his breath.

Khara, garbed in black, began crying again. Falk wanted to squeeze her hand, but again his good intention was defeated by his lack of willpower.

'He experienced the end,' said the Father of the Mountain, who had officiated at the ceremony, here in the shadow of Highstone, the grave having been dug in a small, ornamental garden. 'Which is a small comfort, is it not?'

Falk tried, and failed, to supress a sob. He turned away and buried his head in Selsena's mane, the Titejunanwa sharing his sorrow.

'His death seems so unfair,' murmured Khara. The adversary was gone.' She struggled for breath as she pointed down plaintively at the grave. 'The THREE might have been merciful. Why did they have to take him with them?'

'He always knew this – after life, comes death. He never denied this fundamental truth,' said the Father of the Mountain gently. 'And I think that he accepted his own end gracefully.'

A distant thunderclap indicated that the winter rain would soon develop into a full-blown storm.

'Let us go into the castle,' suggested Quin-Wa, who had remained in the background until now. The Eternal Empress, too, was dressed in black, but she was hiding her grief well. Nonetheless, Falk could see the pain she was feeling in the deep shadows under her eyes.

Khara shook her head stubbornly. 'Not yet,' she said. 'I am not ready to leave him alone.'

Falk understood. He, too, could hardly put one foot in front of the other. Even standing was an effort.

Behind him, he heard the sound of paws scrunching on the gravel. Culhen moved over to the graveside, whimpering heartbreakingly. Soon, the sound had developed into a bone-shuddering howl. Both Falk and Khara began weeping again.

'None of us would be standing here if it weren't for him.' The voice came from behind Falk's stooped back. 'For which the nations of Jorath are eternally grateful.'

Falk nodded, now feeling a comforting hand on his shoulder. 'You are late,' he murmured haltingly.

This was met with by a sigh. 'Someone had to be present at the memorial service for all those who fell at the Ring. I thought it right that at least one Paladin attend.'

Falk reached for the hand on his shoulder and squeezed it. 'Good that you are here now, lad.'

Ahren stepped beside the old man and smiled sadly. 'Of course. The First is worthy of our mourning. His death marks the end of an era.'

'And the end of the adversary,' added the Father of the Mountain while Ahren placed a comforting arm around Khara. 'The will to live in the one expired as soon as the will in the other had been finally extinguished.'

'His heart was worn out,' murmured Ahren. 'It had beaten for so many centuries and with only one goal in mind. Once that had been reached…'

Falk saw how his former apprentice was struggling to control his emotions.

'Bergen said that the First was smiling when he left us. What more can we ask for?'

It took another while before they finally sought refuge in the castle. But when they did so, a comforting warmth awaited them, as well as the feeling that peace could finally reign over Jorath.

***

It was well into the night, the fire in the council chamber was burning low and Ahren's goblet of wine was almost empty when Trogadon, puffing on his pipe gazed through the smoke at the Forest Guardian, his bushy eyebrows raised quizzically.

'How did you know?' he asked in a low voice.

The murmured conversations in the room died down as all the companions who had survived the battles around the Obsidian Fortress looked at Ahren expectantly.

At first, the Forest Guardian wanted to do no more than shake his head wearily and answer vaguely by mumbling something about sheer luck or that the THREE had been responsible for his flash of inspiration, but his friends deserved more. He pushed himself against Culhen's fur as he leaned against the wolf's flank and stared down at the smouldering coals.

'When I was lying there, dying…' he began, only to stop as he tactfully waited for Khara's, Falk's, and Hakanu's sobs to abate while Culhen whimpered and licked him. Indeed, Ahren's face had rarely been dry over the past few days. 'There were so many images of my life swirling around in my head that I tried to hold onto anything that would make sense. Why was it impossible to kill the Adversary even though the Paladins were united? It was the Dark god Himself who provided me with the decisive clue – He said he was *outside* Creation, being its Custodian. Always standing to the side, just as Keeper Jegral had taught me from the ancient scripts that he was so fond of…'

Uldini snorted, thereby drawing everyone's attention to him. 'Ancient scripts – don't make me laugh. I have ordered investigations over the past few days to discover how far back the distorting of our history through the Dark god went.' The Arch Wizard was constantly moving his hands restlessly, as though feeling under his robe for something that he was missing – and that he would never find again. 'There are at least twenty-six local variations regarding the origin myths of the Paladins. In one version, it even states that the Paladins were sent to support the Adversary, which, looking back on it, is as accurate as it is ambiguous. It wouldn't surprise me at all if some of the more deceitful versions were planted amongst the people by High Fangs.'

'Jelninolan and I helped to piece together the stories,' said Akkad.

The two Ancients looked completely worn out. Not even countless reassurances that they would soon be better lessened Ahren's concern. He would only rest easy once Jelninolan's colour and Akkad's joie de vivre had returned.

'There *are* indications that a Keeper received inspiration from the gods during the time of the original Paladins,' explained Akkad. 'The first pilgrims were already on their way to his chapel when a horde of Dark Ones slaughtered them. The world never learned what the wise man had to say.'

Jelninolan leaned forward slowly – even the slightest of movements causing her difficulty. From what Ahren had been told, nothing less than an Unleashing had been necessary to retrieve him from death's door. Not only the crater, but also what had once been the Borderlands had been covered in a thin layer of ice by the time Jelninolan had completed her sorcery. Even now, one could still see with the naked eye an icy patch from the top of the castle.

'I, too, found similar, although considerably less concrete clues,' reported Jelninolan in a monotone. 'It seems that the sleeping gods tried repeatedly to make contact with us. But HE, WHO FORCES was cunning enough to destroy every piece of knowledge before it had the chance to become generally known.'

'We were so clueless,' sighed Lanlion.

The Bloodless was sitting in a corner of the room, far from the others. They all possessed no more than a faint echo of the gods' Blessing, and none of them knew if the madness common to all Bloodlesses would eventually take hold of their fellow Paladin, his anchor of humanity now replaced by nothing more than a thread.

'This is all well and good,' growled Trogadon, plunging a poker in the coals to stoke up the fire before putting the tip of the implement into a jug of wine. 'But my question remains unanswered.' The dwarf stood up, walked over to Jelninolan with the hot wine and pouring some out for her.

'Thank you, my heart,' she whispered. 'It will take days before I stop shivering.'

'I know,' he grunted, placing his arms around the sitting elf from behind. The happiness in the faces of the two warmed Ahren more than any goblet of wine could. 'How did you know that your Blessing really belonged to the Custodian?' pressed the dwarf.

The Forest Guardian shook his head. '*Know* is putting it too strongly. I had an *idea.*'

Falk guffawed. 'You and your ideas…'

The Father of the Mountain raised a hand to stop Falk in his tracks. 'Let him speak. Or do you *still* refuse to believe that the gods deliberately made the Thirteenth compassionate, intuitive and not a little bit foolhardy.'

Ahren looked at the dwarf-like Paladin in surprise. 'You mean my tendency to having weird ideas was the *intention* of the deities?'

The Father of the Mountain shrugged his shoulders. 'You tell me. If one keeps trying to convey information to a group of Paladins and one fails every time, wouldn't it make sense to ensure that at least *one* of them might come up with the right answers on their own?'

Ahren scratched his head. All these big questions were too much for him. Let the wise men and women dispute the answers themselves in the decades to come. 'I knew that our power was on a par with that of the Adversary,' he explained, trying to keep things as simple as possible. 'The Echo of Belsarius talked in the Sanctum about the balance of Creation. The Adversary stood with all his forces *outside,* whereas we gathered with ours *inside* Creation. He used his power *against* the will of the gods, while we used ours to *carry out* their will.' Ahren turned as he struggled to put what he was thinking into words, and was grateful to Khara for squeezing his hand, thereby giving him some inner peace. 'It struck me at that moment that our *Blessings* would change him, just as they had changed us when we received them. The Adversary was a jug filled with darkness. I poured in the light and bound him in this way to Creation and its rules.'

'And did you *really* believe that He would leave His path of forcing and controlling?' asked the Father of the Mountain.

Ahren nodded sadly. 'I hoped so. With all my heart. After all, He received all our memories and the experiences connected to them, which revealed what it is to be alive. How rich this world would be with a Custodian by its side who was kindly and aware of the precious nature of life! I wanted to give Him the opportunity to save Himself – for deep in my heart, I believe that the true mission of the Paladins was to…*save*…the Adversary. To remind Him of whom He ought to have been – a protector of life. Maybe that is why He hated us so much. We were doing what He had long since given up doing.'

'The Adversary is dead and my nearest and dearest are safe and sound,' said Bergen, getting to his feet with a groan. 'That's all that matters as far as I'm concerned. And on that note, I will go and join them now.'

As though the broad-shouldered Paladin's announcement were a secret code, everyone in the council chamber got up and prepared to leave the room to go in search of the peace and comfort of their beds.

Only Falk remained by the fire for a moment. Ahren gestured to Khara to bide her time, the two of them holding back for the old man.

'What is troubling you?'

Falk laughed – the tone of self-irony was unmissable. 'The adversary is dead. Our Blessings are gone – well, almost.' The Forest Guardian peered into his protégé's eyes. 'What is there left to do?'

Ahren took his mentor in his arms and hugged him. 'We will carry on with our lives and let the world continues as if it no longer needs us,' he said with a smile. 'Isn't this enough?'

Falk's eyes were moist when Ahren released him. 'And how,' whispered the old man. 'I can hardly wait to start.'

Epilogue

127 years later

Ahren was dozing under the canopy of leaves. The brook in front of him was babbling pleasantly, the cheerful melody of its flowing water making it all too easy for the Forest Guardian to continue daydreaming. His thoughts drifted back to the last Autumn Festival when Yandra, Darius and Nivia along with their children had been visiting. He chuckled sleepily. The hut had been bursting at the seams.

'Ahren!'

Khara's call echoed through the forest, rousing him from his drowsy state.

'Here!' he shouted, his voice hoarse through languor and age.

His beloved appeared between the trees, her greying hair tied up in an elegant knot. Her Deep Steel robe and the weapons hanging from her sash were as spotless as ever. Instinctively, Ahren straightened his green-brown tunic, to which at least a dozen leaves were sticking. He enjoyed not having to be battle-ready anymore. She enjoyed not having to turn her readiness into action.

'Are you fishing again?' she asked, her eyes sparkling as she nodded towards the fishing line sticking out over the stream. The line was floating on the water without a bait, the fishing bucket had been knocked over and plundered. 'And with the same success as usual.'

Grinning, Ahren pulled himself up at the trunk of the copper beech that was looming over him. 'There were two fish in it. But then So-ahn crept up and I didn't want to spoil her fun in her act of larceny. You know how much she loves it.'

Khara shook her head and laughed. Then she sat down beside him and rested her head against his chest, causing him to sigh contentedly.

'They are so sweet when they are whelps,' he said, already drifting off again.

Khara's giggling echoed in his mind like the new-fangled glockenspiel that Akkad had presented on King's Island two years earlier. There had been so many oohs and aahs, but Ahren had initially wondered why the Ancient had spent a full twenty years tinkering at the melodic plaything. Only when he and Khara had returned to their home in Eathinian, had the answer dawned on him – all of them, including the popular Ancient, were able now to follow their dreams.

'Since when have we become a shelter for ill-mannered young animals?' murmured Khara.

Ahren laughed. 'Since ninety years ago, I would imagine. When the joys of parenting began to wear off for our companion animals once they had produced a dozen litters and realised that they needed a break.'

'Clearly, the gods didn't think of *everything* when they blessed us,' said the Swordsmistress with a chuckle.

Ahren looked at his beloved from the side, but she had already closed her eyes. 'Or they knew exactly what they were doing,' he mused. 'The Ice Wolves of the north and the White Tigers from the Sunplains are legendary, and their numbers are growing, not least because of Muai, Yoka and Culhen. And don't forget that almost all the Paladrims who carry the call of the goddess within them find *their* companion animals among the offspring of *our* diligent, furry friends.'

Khara sighed. 'I *do* wish that we could have had more children. Three are too few for all these years of living.'

Ahren grinned. 'Our pupils have been keeping the house full of life since Nivia, our youngest, moved out into the world. And the gods are wise. We have three children and nine grandchildren, of whom four are also Paladrims. Otherwise, Jorath would be overflowing with ancient humans in a couple of centuries. And they would all begin bickering with each other on account of their varying talents.' He frowned. 'There are already rumours that some of them are striking off on their own.'

'You mean the Paths, don't you?' said Khara ruminatively. 'The Path of the Will, the Path of the Blade and the Path of the Animal.'

Ahren snorted. 'Pompous titles, nothing more than that.'

Every Paladin who had survived the war – with the exception of Lanlion – had been granted the joy of three offspring. Each child had received one of the three gifts that had at one time been granted to all the Champions of the gods – hence, each of these children was called a Paladrim – which meant 'little Paladin' in the Elven tongue.

Yandra, Ahren's and Khara's oldest child, had received the gift of the Keeper, for example. Her strong sense of will was only matched by her ambition – her greatest wish being to make a name for herself at the court of King Juskum, great-grandson of Likis the First, who had been crowned with great acclaim by the Hjalgarian populace.

Indeed, many Paladrims who followed the Path of the Will found themselves in positions of power in Jorath – some of them even on thrones. Darius, named after Ahren's erstwhile master, had followed the Path of the Animal and now had not one, but *two* companion animals, who were constantly testing his patience with their bickering.

Finally, there was Nivia. She had followed the Path of the Blade and become, like her mother, a celebrated and tireless Swordsmistress. She now lived in the Sunny Realm – the name given to the joint nations of the Sunplains and the Eternal Empire.

'Do you not want to know *why* I came looking for you?' teased Khara.

'I thought my company was reason enough,' grumbled the Forest Guardian.

Khara laughed and punched him playfully in the ribs. 'Of course. Nevertheless, letters have arrived. Quite a few, in fact.'

Ahren was all ears now. There was nothing he liked more than to get news from the four corners of Jorath, which was why those friends of his who were still living wrote him letters constantly, keeping him up to date with the goings on of the world.

'And who delivered them?'

Khara's grin broadened. 'Guess.'

Ahren stood up with a curse, thereby forcing Khara to follow suit. 'You could have told me sooner,' he grumbled. 'You know what he's like when he thinks I'm ignoring him.'

Khara chuckled. 'You mean, he's just as cantankerous as you have become in your dotage?'

Ahren hooked arms with his beloved, the couple following the babbling brook in a westerly direction through the eternally amicable sunshine of Eathinian. Ahren took a deep breath, enjoying both the forest air and the distant sounds of countless animals. He stopped for a moment when he noticed the track of a Blood Wolf, but then he shrugged his shoulders. The animal had just as much right to be here as those creatures who weren't a danger to Ahren and Khara. The Dark Ones had fled after the death of the Adversary, and those who were of animal origin had sought shelter in the unpopulated regions of Jorath – in thick forests, on high mountains and in deep caves. They were all a part of Creation, and as such were multiplying and hunting as all the normal predatory animals had been doing for aeons.

It was true that Jorath was more peaceful now, but in the wilderness, it was no safer than it had been before, which meant that Forest Guardianship was all the while gaining in recognition. In the end, the Dark god really *had* created life – it had merely required His own demise for life to flourish freely. For a moment, Ahren wondered if he should stop by Falk's grave, but then he decided against it, for he was intent on concentrating his attention on the living today.

The gods had been merciful enough to conjoin the life spans of the Paladins with those of their soul companions. Falk and Bergen had died a few years previously, together with the women they loved. Ahren's mentor had been the first to succumb to old age. Then Bergen had passed away, closing his eyes for the last time shortly after Falk's demise, having donated so much of his life force to his Blue Cohorts over the previous centuries. The rest of the Paladins and their soul companions were still alive. Uldini figured that the younger ones amongst them still had one or two centuries of living ahead of them.

Ahren? Culhen's voice announced itself grumpily in the Forest Guardian's head. *Well, you took your time, I must say.*

The Paladin stepped onto the neatly maintained gravel footpath which started at the dark red fence, which was decorated with the insignia of the Sun Empire. Culhen was waiting solemnly at the entrance to the house made from wood and rice paper, which – according to Khara – was an exact replica of the residence on the Hill of Five Waters. There was even an examination pool, filled by the water from the stream, the current then flowing below ground towards the west coast of Jorath, not three stones' throw away, where there was a little bay, protected by trees, and in which Khara could go swimming all the year round, thanks to the Eathinian weather.

A couple of dozen paces behind the couple's house was a long, rustic-looking hut, where their pupils lived when they weren't attending the countless lessons in the depths of the forest or sweating it out on the horseshoe beach, learning how to master their Wind Blades. Ahren and Khara had an average of six pupils a year, the boys and girls always eager to learn. In one of Uldini's latest missives, Ahren had been informed that their homestead was commonly known as the *refuge of cosy learning,* an appellation that the Forest Guardian was secretly quite proud of.

'Nice to see you,' said Ahren as he stood before his loyal wolf, who visited him several times a year. He hugged the animal before looking him up and down. 'Is that a grey hair I see on your nose?'

Culhen gained his revenge by imparting a slobbery kiss on his friend's face. *It's silver, I'll have you know,* he retorted snootily. *And Yoka says it makes me look dignified.*

'Where *is* your better half?' asked the Forest Guardian while Khara pushed her way past the two of them and took the letters out of a leather satchel, which the Ice Wolf was carrying. Companion animals had become such reliable messengers that any carrying such mail satchels enjoyed a particularly high status in Jorath.

Yoka has gone on ahead with the little ones, said Culhen. *I promised her that I would follow them once I had seen you two.*

'Oh,' said Ahren sadly.

Again, Culhen's tongue darted forward and slobbered his face.

I'll come again next moon, I promise. The wolf was already mentally rejoicing at the prospect. *Then you will have your new batch of pupils, and I can impress them all with my genius.*

'Is there any important news?' asked Ahren, ignoring his friend's natural boastfulness and nodding towards the letters. Culhen always insisted on learning their contents off by heart before setting off to deliver them in case they got lost. He took his responsibility surprisingly seriously.

Nothing that the whelps cannot sort out. This was what the wolves called all those Paladrims and companion animals who had been born after the assault on the Obsidian Fortress – even though some of them had more than a century under their belts.

'Thank you,' said Ahren, taking one of the letters. He recognised Uldini's neat handwriting.

Culhen stood up restlessly. *I really better get going. Yoka can get terribly grumpy if she is kept waiting.*

Ahren guffawed. *Unlike you, then.*

That's completely different, complained the wolf. Then he pushed affectionately against his Paladin and disappeared into the forest.

Ahren distracted himself from the pain of bidding farewell to his friend by sitting down beside Khara at the training pool, which was ringed with white stones from Thousand Halls. He had hardly finished reading the first three lines when he grunted in surprise.

Khara peered at him with one eyebrow raised. 'Spit it out,' she chuckled. 'I know how much you love it when we exchange the latest news.' She waved the parchment that she was holding. 'Cochan has interesting things to relate, too.'

Ahren looked over the lines again to make sure that he hadn't misread anything. 'Jelninolan is pregnant.'

Khara let out a whoop of joy. 'How *lovely!*' she exclaimed. 'And they tried *everything* to become parents.'

'Apparently, Uldini was able to give them some sort of potion that he managed to concoct after much experimentation.'

'The elf-maiden and her dwarf are going to have a family,' said Khara with a grin, playing on the title of a certain heroic ballad that had done the rounds after the assault on the Obsidian Fortress. The song described Jelninolan as a shimmering figure, glowing and floating as she gave the armies the courage that they needed to attack the enemy, while her true dwarf valiantly kept her safe from harm.

The Dwarfish clans and the elves of Eathinian had buckled faster than a stalk of wheat during a summer downpour when the question of the couple entering the Bond was discussed. Now the priestess and her blacksmith were living on Murgamolosch and had turned the island into a centre of reconciliation and diplomacy, where the dwarfs lived under Trogadon's command on top of and within the mountain, the elves, meanwhile, studying Storm Weaving with Jelninolan on the slopes and in the forests. The fishing families went to sea under the protection of Aluna's independent western fleet. During the crises of the previous century, the island had served as neutral territory where just solutions to political problems were often discussed and agreed.

Khara scanned the missive that she was holding. 'Once again, there is a dispute concerning the Bountiful Land. Hjalgar and the Knight Marshes are squabbling over a small valley. Sometimes, I really *do* wish that Aimenata hadn't used her sorcery to extend the Green Sea all the way to the Borderlands.'

'She did so at the request of the surrounding nations,' said Ahren. 'And the Bountiful Land *was* fairly divided. But the temptation to surreptitiously obtain this or that acre from one's neighbours seems to be an ever-present problem.' The Paladin didn't like thinking about his former soul companion. Three times he had tried to apologise to her for his companions mistakenly believing that they had recognised traces of

Lirana in her. And three times she had dismissed him with a laugh – even though Ahren's explanations had been sincere. After all, the Thirteenth's soul companion had never died, and Sings-in-Saddle had therefore remained an entirely independent person. Furthermore, the reputation of the Woman in Black – as she was now called by the population at large – which had been so maligned over the years had now been fully restored. Indeed, the former servant of the Adversary had often been seen on a black Hanta when people found themselves in difficulty and was considered a protective spirit for the desperate.

Ahren, however, had never seen the Woman in Black again. The only ones of his friends who had ever caught a glimpse of her recently had been Lanlion and Yantilla, both of whom were busy imparting knowledge in the Hall of Powerless Arts to those who were denied traditional magic. Thrice already, courageous Paladrims had been forced to protect this unusual place of learning from superstitious and cynical gangs, who considered the teachings of the two Bloodlesses to be a danger to society. The sleeping gods remained as stubbornly silent on this topic as they did on so many others.

Ahren roused himself out of his daydreaming and looked down at the parchment again. 'The Father of the Mountain has found a worthy dwarf and is training him to be his successor.' The Forest Guardian chuckled. 'He is confident that his protégé will be able to take over the reins in three hundred years.'

Khara cocked her head. 'Has it occurred to you how many of us are now teaching? You and I were the first. But now there is Uldini, who is rebuilding the Council of Ancients, Jelninolan and Trogadon on Murgamolosch, Lanlion and Yantilla in the Hall of Powerless Arts, Quin-Wa, who in her role as the Eternal Consul has been advising every successor to the jade-coloured Sun Throne, and last but certainly not least, the Father of the Mountain.'

Ahren nodded. 'Perhaps we are all trying to help create a *new*, post-Adversary Jorath – without even thinking about it. After all, this world was *supposed* to have a Custodian. It *was* not and *is* not perfect because it doesn't have a protector. And the sleep of the gods is deeper than ever, so they either cannot or will not tell their priests and priestesses how things should go on with Creation.' He looked impishly at Khara. 'The mighty of this world are quite content for us to stick to teaching, at any rate. Think of those of us who have *not* had enough of participating in the hurly-burly of life.' He began counting the Paladins with his fingers. 'There's Trimm, for starters. He has led Cape Verstaad to independence, and under *his* control – against the protestations of both Uldini and Quin-Wa.'

Khara nodded. 'That was after Justinian abdicated, so that his daughter, a Paladrim, could ascend to the throne – isn't that so?'

Ahren had to think for a moment before nodding. So much had happened over the past decades. 'And *then* Trimm allied himself with Fisker and Aluna, both in command of a fleet, having amicably divided the seas between themselves into east and west so that they could…*secure*…the shipping routes, so to speak. For a hefty *fee*, of course.'

Khara laughed. 'As a result of which there are no pirates anymore.'

Ahren scowled. 'Ask all the merchants being fleeced by the smiling Trimm, Aluna and Fisker for the dubious pleasure of being *protected* at sea.'

'You're exaggerating.'

'A little,' he admitted. 'But if you add to that the chaos that Hakanu and his seven daredevil foxes leave in their wake whenever they get the urge for acting heroically, then you must surely understand what I mean. As teachers, we are welcome – but as actors in the world's events, we are forces of nature that need to be tamed. Jorath has changed and can manage very well without us.'

Khara giggled. 'Wherever does your apprentice manage to get these madcap men and women from to follow him? No matter how many of them are wiped out, he always finds more in no time at all.'

'There will always be willing fools to be duped,' grumbled Ahren.

'Ah, now – don't be such a sourpuss. Think of Sunju, who looks after the Rocs of Thousand Halls. There are so many of them that they have been spotted in other mountain ranges. Or what about Lyssin, who as speaker of the Ice Fields takes care of the interests of the native Wild Dwarfs as well as those of Four Claws? *Their* names are revered everywhere now.'

Ahren shrugged his shoulders. 'I simply think that Jorath has seen more than enough of us. It is now up to the Paladrims to lead the countries on the right path —' He stopped in his tracks, staring down at Uldini's letter in amazement. 'An adventurous Roc pilot, who was flying east from Murgamolosch is certain that he spotted land beyond the

Ravenous Maw.' He looked at Khara, wide-eyed. 'Apparently, the coastline was completely unknown to him.'

Khara seemed surprisingly happy. 'But this is *good* news,' she said. 'More land means fewer squabbles over borders among the nations.'

'*And* new dangers,' murmured Ahren.

'Ah, now, stop!' scolded Khara. 'First, you want to leave Jorath to the next generation, and then you worry about Creation developing without us. You need to make up your mind regarding what you want.'

Ahren laid down the parchment and took Khara in his arms. He snuggled into her, enjoying the sun on his face, the rustling of the leaves in the breeze and the gentle lapping of the pool.

'The age of the Paladins is over,' he said contentedly. 'Let new heroes and heroines give their name to the new era. We gave Jorath the most precious gift imaginable – and that should suffice.'

'What do you mean?'

Images of the long and dangerous journey that they had travelled on for so long suddenly flashed through his mind.

'The alliance of the nations is holding. The deep wounds inflicted during the Dark Days are slowly healing, and the inhabitants of the realms are looking to the future. There are many adventures but little evil to experience on the face of Jorath.'

He winked cheekily at Khara before gazing lovingly into her eyes.

'It's a start.'

And so, the saga of the Thirteenth Paladin and his companions has come to an end. I would like to thank all of you who have supported me. Your names would fill another volume.

If you have enjoyed Ahren's epic adventure, then please leave a short (spoiler-free) review – in volume one, AHREN, if you like.

Where one story ends, a very different one begins. If you would like to learn more about my next project, keep your eyes peeled for "The Stormfell Academy"

Printed in Great Britain
by Amazon